THE SHADOW OF THE LION

BAEN BOOKS by MERCEDES LACKEY

BARDIC VOICES
The Lark & the Wren
The Robin & the Kestrel
The Eagle & the Nightingales
The Free Bards
Four & Twenty Blackbirds
Bardic Choices: A Cast of Corbies
(with Josepha Sherman)

The Fire Rose
Fiddler Fair
Werehunter
Lammas Night
(edited by Josepha Sherman)
The Ship Who Searched
(with Anne McCaffrey)
*Wing Commander:
Freedom Flight*
(with Ellen Guon)

URBAN FANTASIES
Bedlam's Bard (omnibus with Ellen Guon)
Beyond World's End (with Rosemary Edghill)
Spirits White as Lightning
(with Rosemary Edghill)

The SERRAted Edge:
Chrome Circle
(with Larry Dixon)
The Chrome Borne
(omnibus with Larry Dixon)
The Otherworld
(omnibus with Mark Shepherd & Holly Lisle)

THE BARD'S TALE NOVELS
Castle of Deception
(with Josepha Sherman)
Fortress of Frost & Fire
(with Ru Emerson)
Prison of Souls
(with Mark Shepherd)

BAEN BOOKS by ERIC FLINT

The Philosophical Strangler
Forward the Mage (with Richard Roach)

The Belisarius series, with David Drake:
An Oblique Approach
In the Heart of Darkness
Destiny's Shield
Fortune's Stroke
The Tide of Victory

The Tyrant (with David Drake)
(forthcoming)
1632
Mother of Demons

BAEN BOOKS by DAVE FREER

The Forlorn
Rats, Bats, and Vats (with Eric Flint)
Pyramid Scheme (with Eric Flint)

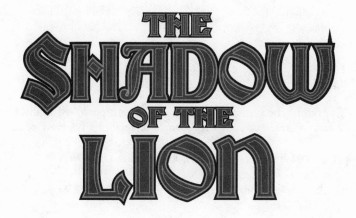

THE SHADOW OF THE LION

Mercedes Lackey, Eric Flint & Dave Freer

BAEN

THE SHADOW OF THE LION

This is a work of fiction. All the characters and events portrayed in this book are fictional, and any resemblance to real people or incidents is purely coincidental.

A Baen Books Original

Baen Publishing Enterprises
P.O. Box 1403
Riverdale, NY 10471
www.baen.com

ISBN: 0-7434-3523-0

Cover art by Larry Dixon

First printing, March 2002

Library of Congress Cataloging-in-Publication Data

Lackey, Mercedes.
  The shadow of the lion / Mercedes Lackey, Eric Flint & Dave Freer.
    p. cm.
  ISBN 0-7434-3523-0
  1. Venice (Italy)—History—1508–1797—Fiction. 2. Brothers—Fiction.
  3. Monsters—Fiction. I. Flint, Eric. II. Freer, Dave. III. Title.

PS3562.A246 S53 2002
813'.54—dc21   2001056466

Distributed by Simon & Schuster
1230 Avenue of the Americas
New York, NY 10020

Production by Windhaven Press, Auburn, NH
Printed in the United States of America

10 9 8 7 6 5 4 3 2 1

To the world's firefighters;
and, especially:
to the hundreds of those in the
Fire Department of New York
who died in the line of duty on
September 11, 2001.

The Great Powers Of Europe

Muscovy

Mongol Khanates

Territories Controlled by the Knights of the Holy Trinity

The Grand Duchy of **Poland and Lithuania**

Norseland

Vilna

Kiev

Black Sea

Baltic Sea

Warsaw

Hungary

Budapest

The Balkans

North Sea

Berlin

Vienna

Prague

Holy Roman Empire

Adriatic Sea

Mainz

Milan

Genoa

Rome

London

Paris

Aquitaine

Orleans

League of Armagh

Mediterranean Sea

Atlantic Ocean

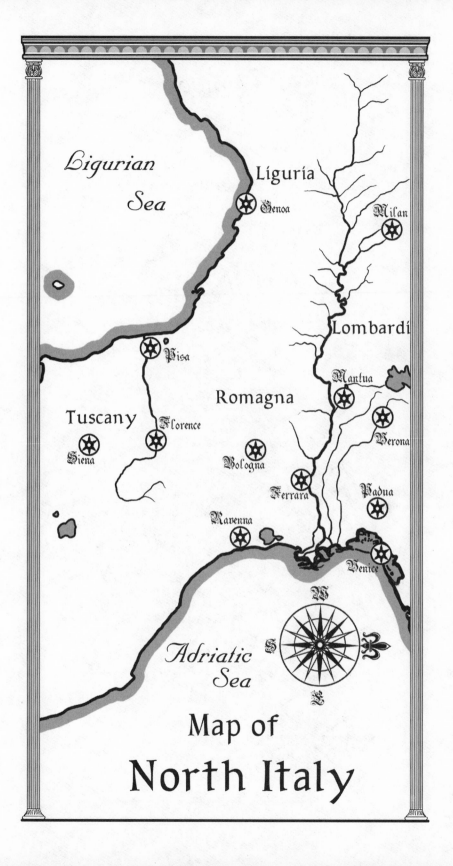

Map of

North Italy

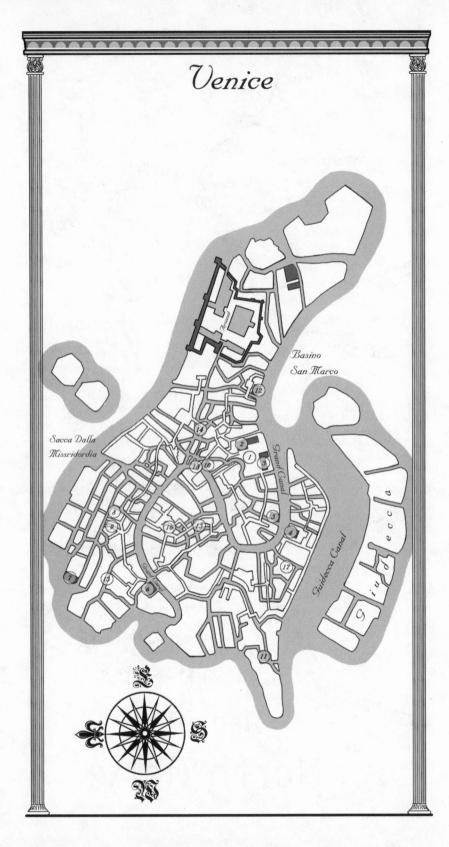

Key to Venice

1 Piazza San Marco
2 Doge's palace
3 Marciana Library
4 Accademia
5 Imperial Embassy
6 Casa Dandelo
7 Casa Montescue
8 Marco and Benito's appartment in Cannaregio
9 Calle Faranese
10 German Hotel
11 San Nicolò del Mendicoli
12 Casa Dorma
13 Canal di Canareggio
14 Barduccis
15 Caesare and Maria's home.
16 San Zan Degola
17 San Trovaso
18 Rialto Bridge

Also shown:
Giudecca
Grand Canal
Sacca della misericordia
Basino San Marco
Arsenal

Family Trees

Dell'este of Ferrara

Dell'este, Enrico (1474–)
Duke of Ferrara, Modena, Este, and Reggio Nell' Emilia
M
Elena di Catania (d)

Stephano (d)   Valeria (d)   Rosabella (d)   Lorendana (1501–1534)
                                                M   L
                                Fabio Valdosta (1494–1522)   Carlo Sforza
                                                              (1495–)
                                │   │
                                Marco Valdosta (1521–)   Benito
                                M   Valdosta
                                Angelina Dorma (1519–)   (1523–)

Casa Montescue

Lodovico Montescue (1472–)
M
Serena Contarini (d)
│
Nicolò (1493–)
M
Rosa da Capello (1495–1533)

Alfredo (1514–1533)   Katerina (1521–)
M
Alessandra Brunelli (1517–)
│
baby Lodovico (1533–1533)

House Hohenstauffen

Conrad II
(1471–1523)

Charles Fredrik   Magaret of Weimar   Isolde of Swabia   Stephen (d)
(1483–)   (1487–)   (1492–)
M   M   M
Clothilde of   Prince Bernard of   Prince Hanno of Brittany
Saxony (d)   Bohemia (1478–)   (1486–)
│   │   │
Charles III (d)   Conrad (heir) (1510–)   Manfred (2nd in line)
                   Bertha   (1520–)
                   Wilfreda

THE SHADOW OF THE LION

Prologue
April, 1537 A.D.

MAINZ

The yellow lantern-lights of Mainz's dockside inns reached out across the dark Rhine. Standing on the prow of the riverboat, Erik Hakkonsen stared at them, thinking of little more than food and a bed. He'd left his home in Iceland three weeks earlier, to answer the Emperor's summons. They'd had a stormy crossing. Then the late spring thaw had ensured that the roads of the Holy Roman Empire were fetlock deep in glutinous mud. And, finally, the river had been full and the rain steady. Tomorrow he would have to go to the Imperial palace, and find out how to seek an interview with Emperor Charles Fredrik.

But tonight he could sleep.

The riverboat nudged into the quay. A wet figure stepped out from under the eaves of the inn. "Is there one Erik Hakkonsen on this vessel?" he demanded, half-angrily. The rain hadn't been kind to the skinny courtier's bright cloak. The satin clung to him, and he was shivering.

Erik pushed back his oilskin-hood. "I'm Hakkonsen."

"Thank God for that! I'm soaked to the skin. I've been here for hours," complained the man. "Come. I've got horses in the stable. The Emperor awaits you."

Erik made no move. "Who are you?"

The fellow shivered. "Baron Trolliger. The Emperor's privy secretary." He held out his hand to show a heavy signet. It was incised with the Roman Eagle.

That was not a seal anyone would dare to forge. Erik nodded. "I'll get my kit."

The shivering baron shook his head. "Leave it." He pointed to the sailor who had paused in his mooring to stare. "You. Watch over this man's gear. Someone will be sent for it."

As much as anything else, the alacrity with which the sailor obeyed the order drove home the truth to Erik. He was in the heart of the Holy Roman Empire, for a certainty. In his native Iceland—or Vinland, or anywhere else in the League of Armagh—that peremptory order would have been ignored, if not met with outright profanity.

"Come," the baron repeated. "The Emperor is waiting."

2

❋   ❋   ❋

Passing from the narrow dark streets and sharp-angled tall houses into the brightness of the imperial palace, Erik had little time to marvel and gawk at the heavy gothic splendor of it all. Instead, Baron Trolliger rushed him through—still trailing mud—into a large austere room. As soon as Erik entered, the baron closed the door behind him, not entering himself.

In the center of the room, staring at Erik, stood the most powerful man in all of Europe. He was a large man, though now a bit stooped from age. His eyebrows seemed as thick and heavy as the purple cloak he was wearing; his eyes, a shade of blue so dark they almost matched the cloak.

Charles Fredrik. The latest in a long line of Hohenstauffens.

Guardian of the Church, Bulwark of the Faith. Lord of lands from northern Italy to the pagan marches in the Baltic. Ruler over millions of people throughout central Europe.

The Holy Roman Emperor, himself. In direct line of descent from the great Fredrick Barbarossa.

All of that mattered little to Erik. His tie to the Emperor was a clan tie, not a dynastic one. He was there to become the Emperor's servant, not his subject. So, Erik simply bowed to the old man, rather than kneeling, and spoke no words of fealty. Simply the old oath: *"Linn gu linn."*

The words were Gaelic, but the oath that bound him came from the cold *fjells* of pagan Norway. An oath that went back generations, to the time when a Hohenstauffen prince had rescued a pagan clan from demons set loose by their own foolishness.

Charles Fredrik spoke like an old man—despite being no older than Erik's father. But he voiced the ritual words strongly. "From generation to generation."

He held out the dagger that Erik had heard described with infinite care all his life. The dagger was iron. Old iron. Sky iron. Hammered with stone in the pagan Northlands, from a fallen thunderbolt. The hilt was shaped into a dragon head—the detail lost in the blurring of hundreds of years of use.

It still drew blood for the blood-oath like new steel did. "Blood for blood. Clan for clan." Erik renewed the oath calmly.

After binding their wounds himself, Charles Fredrik took Erik by the elbow and led him across to a window. The window was a mere arrow-slit, testimony to the palace's ancient origins. Against modern cannon, such fortifications were almost useless. But . . . there was a certain undeniable, massive dignity to the huge edifice.

There they stood, silent for some time, looking out at the scattered shawl of lights which was the great sleeping city of Mainz. Erik was quite sure that those lights represented more people than lived in all Iceland. Their lives, and those of many more, rested in the hands of the old man standing next to him.

The Emperor seemed to have read his thoughts. "It is a great load, at times," he said softly.

His heavy jaws tightened. The next words were spoken almost harshly. "I have called for the Clann Harald because my heirs have need. My son is . . . very sickly. And I do not expect my only surviving brother to outlive me. Not with his wounds. So I must take special care to watch over my two nephews, for it is quite likely that one of them will succeed to the throne after I am gone."

The Emperor sighed. "Your older brother Olaf watched over my nephew Conrad for his bond-time, as your father Hakkon watched over me." A slight smile came to his face. "To my surprise, I find I miss him. He used to beat me, you know."

"He has told me about it, *Godar* of the Hohenstauffen." Erik did not add: *Often.*

Charles Fredrik's smile broadened. "According to your brother Olaf—'often.'" He chuckled. "It did me the world of good, I eventually came to realize. Nobody had dared punish me before that. Do you know that your family are the only people in the world who don't call me 'Emperor,' or 'Your Imperial Highness?' I think it is why we trust you."

"Our loyalty is to the *Godar* of the Hohenstauffen. Not to the Empire." That too his father had said. Often.

"You must sit and tell me the news of them once I have given you your task. I warn you, it will be a more onerous chore than Olaf's. Manfred, my younger nephew, reminds me of myself at that age. You will have to—as your father did with me—serve as confrere in the monastic order of the Knights of the Holy Trinity. Of course—as then—your identity and purpose must remain secret. Manfred's also."

Erik nodded. "My father has told me about the Knights."

The Emperor's eyes narrowed. "Yes. But things have changed, Hakkonsen. It is one of the things that worries me. The Knights have always been—nominally, at least—independent of the Empire. Servants of God, not of any earthly power. In practice they have served as the Empire's bulwarks to the North and East. In your father's day the nobility from all the corners of the Holy Roman Empire came to serve as the Knights of Christ, in the pious war against the pagan. And *many* brave souls came from the League of Armagh, not just the handful of Icelanders sworn by clan loyalty to the service of the Emperor."

Erik nodded again. "My grandfather says that in his day, Aquitaines made up as many as a quarter of the order's ranks."

The Emperor clenched his fist, slowly. "Exactly. Today, no knight from that realm would dream of wearing the famous tabard of the Knights of the Holy Trinity. Once the brotherhood Knights were truly the binding threads in the cloak of Christianity. Today . . . the Knights of the Holy Trinity come almost entirely from the Holy Roman Empire. Not even that. Only from some of its provinces. They're Prussians and Saxons, in the main, with a small sprinkling of Swabians. A few others."

He paused. Then he looked Erik in the eyes. "They're beginning to take an interest in politics. Far too much for my liking. And they're also—I like this even less—getting too close to the Servants of the Holy Trinity. Damn bunch of religious fanatics, that lot of monks."

Charles Fredrik snorted. "All of it, mind you, supposedly in my interests. Some of them probably even believe it. But I have no desire to get embroiled in the endless squabbling of Italian city-states, much less a feud with the Petrine branch of the church. The Grand Duke of Lithuania and King Emeric of Hungary give me quite enough to worry about, leaving aside the outright pagans of Norseland and Russia."

Again, he sighed. "And they're not a binding force any more. Today, the common people call the church's arm militant 'The Knots,' more often than not. And, what's worse, the Knights themselves seem to relish the term."

"The Clann Harald do not mix in Empire politics," stated Erik firmly. His father had warned him that this might happen.

The Emperor gave a wry smile. "So your father always said. Just as I'm sure he warned you before you left Iceland. But, Erik Hakkonsen, because you guard Manfred . . . do not think you will be able to avoid it. Any more than your father could."

The old man turned and faced Erik squarely. "Politics will mix with you, lad, whether you like it or not. You can be as sure of that as the sunrise. Especially in Venice."

Erik's eyes widened. The Emperor chuckled.

"Oh, yes. I forgot to mention that, didn't I?"

He took Erik by the arm again and began to lead him toward the door. "But we can discuss Venice tomorrow. Venice, and the expedition of the Knights to that city, which you will be joining. An expedition which I find rather . . . peculiar."

They were at the door. By some unknown means, a servant appeared to open it for them. "But that's for tomorrow," said the Emperor. "What's left for tonight, before you get some well-deserved rest, is to meet the cross you must bear. I suspect the thought of Venice will be less burdensome thereafter."

About halfway down the long corridor leading to the great staircase at the center of the palace, he added: "*Anything* will seem less burdensome, after Manfred."

It took the Emperor, and quite a few servants, some time to track down Manfred. Eventually the royal scion was discovered. In the servants' quarters, half-drunk and half-naked, sprawled on a grimy bed. Judging from the half-sob and half-laugh coming from under the bed, Manfred and the servant girl had been interrupted in a pastime which boded ill for the prince's hope of attaining heaven without spending some time in purgatory.

Erik studied the young royal, now sitting up on the edge of the bed. Manfred was so big he was almost a giant, despite being only eighteen years old. Erik was pleased by the breadth of shoulders, and the thick muscle so obvious on the half-clad body. He was not pleased with the roll of fat around the waist. The hands were very good also. Thick and immensely strong, clearly enough, but Erik did not miss the suggestion of nimbleness as the embarrassed royal scion hastily buttoned on a cotte.

He was pleased, also, by the evident humor in the prince's eyes. Bleary from drink, true, but . . . they had a sparkle to them. And Erik decided the square, block-toothed grin had promise also. Whatever else Prince Manfred might be, he was clearly not a sullen boy.

It remained to be seen how intelligent he was. There, Erik's hopes were much lower.

The Emperor, standing in the doorway of the servant's little room, cleared his throat. "This is your Clann Harald guardian, you young lout. You'll have to mind your manners from now on."

The prince's huge shoulders seemed to ripple a bit, as if he were suppressing a laugh.

"This—willow? Uncle! The way you always described these Icelandic sheep farmers, I got the impression—"

Manfred gasped, clutching his belly. Erik's boot had left a nice muddy imprint. The prince choked, struggling for breath.

"You stinking—" he hissed. A moment later the prince was hurling himself off the bed, great arms stretched wide. Erik was pleased by the rapid recovery. Just as he had been when his driving foot hit the thick muscle beneath the belly fat.

Manfred's charge would have driven down an ogre. Unfortunately, ogres don't know how to wrestle. Erik had learned the art from an old Huron thrall on the Hakkonsen steading, and polished it during his three years in Vinland—much of which time he had spent among his family's Iroquois relatives.

Manfred flattened nicely against the stone wall, like a griddle cake. The palace almost seemed to shake. The prince himself was certainly shaking, when he staggered back from the impact.

Not for long. Erik's hip roll brought him to the floor with a crash, flat on his back. The knee drop in the gut half-paralyzed the prince; the Algonquian war hatchet held against the royal nose *did* paralyze him. Manfred was almost cross-eyed, staring at the cruel razor-sharp blade two inches from his eyes.

"You'll learn," grunted the Emperor. "Give him a scar. He's overdue."

Erik's pale blue eyes met Manfred's brown ones. He lifted an eyebrow.

"Which cheek, Prince?" he asked.

Manfred raised a thick finger. "One moment, please," he gasped. "I need some advice."

The prince rolled his head on the floor, peering under the bed. "You'd better decide, sweetling. Right or left?"

A moment later, a girlish voice issued from under the bed. "Left."

The prince rolled his head back. "The left, then."

Erik grinned; the hatchet blurred; blood gushed from an inch-long gash. He was still grinning when he arose and began wiping off the blade.

"I think the prince and I will get along fine, Emperor."

The most powerful man in Europe nodded heavily. "Thank God for that." He began to turn away. "Tomorrow, we will speak about Venice."

"No politics," insisted Erik.

There was no response except a harsh laugh, and the sight of a broad purple back receding into the darkness.

ROME

"Come, brothers," said the slightly-built priest who limped into the small chapel where his two companions awaited him. "The Grand Metropolitan has made his decision."

One of the other priests cocked his head quizzically. "Is it the Holy Land, then, as we hoped?"

"No. Not yet, at least. He has asked us—me, I should say—to go to Venice."

The third priest sighed. "I begin to wonder if we will *ever* make our pilgrimage, Eneko." The Italian words were slurred, as always, with Pierre's heavy Savoyard accent.

The small priest shrugged. "As I said, the Grand Metropolitan only requires *me* to go to Venice. You—you and Diego both—are free to carry out the pilgrimage we planned."

"Don't be a typical Basque fool," growled Pierre. "Of course we will accompany you."

"What would you do without us?" demanded Diego cheerfully. Again, he cocked his head. "Yes, yes—granted you are superb in the use of holy magic. But if it's Venice, I assume that's because of the Grand Metropolitan's scryers."

"Do those men *ever* have good news to report?" snorted Pierre.

The Basque priest named Eneko smiled thinly. "Not often. Not since Jagiellon took the throne in Vilna, that's certain."

Pierre scowled. "Why else would we be going to that miserable city?"

Eneko gazed at him mildly. "I wasn't aware you had visited the place."

Pierre's scowl deepened. "Not likely! A pit of corruption and intrigue—the worst in Italy, which is bad enough as it is."

The Basque shrugged. "I dislike the city myself—and, unlike you,

I've been there. But I don't know that it's any more corrupt than anywhere else." Then, smiling: "More *complicated*, yes."

Diego's head was still cocked to one side. The mannerism was characteristic of the Castilian. "Eneko, why—*exactly*—are we going there? It can't be simply because of the scryers. Those gloomy fellows detect Lithuanian and Hungarian schemes everywhere. I'm sure they'd find Chernobog rooting in the ashes of my mother's kitchen fire, if they looked long enough."

"True enough," agreed Eneko, smiling. "But in this instance, the matter is more specific. Apparently rumors have begun to surface that the Strega Grand Master was not murdered after all. He may still be alive. The Grand Metropolitan wants me to investigate."

The last sentence caused both Diego and Pierre to frown. The first, with puzzlement; the second, with disapproval.

"Why is it our business what happens to a pagan mage?" demanded Pierre.

Again, Eneko bestowed that mild gaze upon the Savoyard. "The Church does not consider the Strega to be 'pagans,' I would remind you. Outside our faith, yes. Pagans, no. The distinction was implicit already in the writings of Saint Hypatia—I refer you especially to her second debate with Theophilus—although the Church's final ruling did not come until—"

"I know that!" grumbled Pierre. "Still . . ."

Diego laughed. "Leave off trying to teach this stubborn Savoyard the fine points of theology, Eneko. He knows what he knows, and there's an end to it."

Eneko chuckled; and so, after a moment, did Pierre himself. "I suppose I still retain the prejudices of my little village in the Alps," he said grudgingly. "But I still don't understand why the Holy Father is making such an issue out of it."

"Pierre," sighed Diego, "we are *not* talking about some obscure witch-doctor. *Dottore* Marina was considered by every theologian in the world, Christian or not—especially those versed in the use of magic—to be the most knowledgeable Strega scholar in centuries. He was not simply a Magus, you know. He was a Grimas, a master of all three of the *stregheria* canons: Fanarra, Janarra and Tanarra. The first Grimas since Vitold, in fact."

"And we all know how that Lithuanian swine wound up," growled Pierre. His Savoyard accent was even heavier than usual.

Eneko's eyebrows, a solid bar across his forehead, lowered.

"Pierre! I remind you—*again*—that the Church does not extend its condemnation of the Grand Dukes of Lithuania onto their subjects."

The Savoyard priest looked away. Then, nodded acknowledgement of the justice of the reproof.

"Besides," continued the Basque, "the criticism is unfair in any event. Vitold's fate derived from his boldness, not from sin. Rashness, if you prefer. But I remind you—"

Eneko's stern gaze swept back and forth between his two companions. "I remind you, brothers, that we have set ourselves the same purpose as that of doomed Vitold—to stand firmly against Chernobog and all manner of evil."

For a moment, his eyes roamed the austere interior of the chapel. Finding comfort there, perhaps, but not forgetting how long it had taken them to find such a chapel in Rome.

"To *challenge* it on the field of holy battle," he continued softly, "instead of lolling in comfort while our Pauline brethren wage the struggle alone."

Hearing the Paulines referred to as "brethren" brought a momentary tightness to Pierre's lips, but the Savoyard did not challenge the term. As often as Eneko Lopez's odd views grated on the Savoyard's upbringing and attitudes, he had long since made the decision to follow the man anywhere he chose to lead them.

As had Diego. "Well enough, Eneko. Venice it is. And we should send for Francis in Toulouse as well. He would be invaluable in Venice, dealing with Strega."

Lopez shook his head. "No," he said firmly. "I want Francis to go to Mainz and try to get an audience, if he can, with the Emperor. I'm not certain yet, but I think he will be far more useful there than he would be in Venice with us."

The Basque priest's words caused his two companions to stiffen. Again, Diego made that cocked-head quizzical gesture. "Am I to take it that the Grand Metropolitan is looking more favorably on our proposal?"

Lopez shrugged. "He keeps his own counsel. And he is a cautious man, as you know. But . . . yes, I think so. I suspect he views this expedition to Venice as something in the way of a test. So do I, brothers. And if I'm right as to what we will find there, we will need a private conduit with Charles Fredrik."

Those words cheered Pierre immediately. "Well, then! By all means, let's to Venice!"

The next morning, as they led their mules through the streets of Rome, the Savoyard finally unbent enough to ask the question again. This time, seeking an answer rather than registering a protest.

He did it a bit pugnaciously, of course.

"I still don't understand why we're looking for a Strega scholar."

"We are not," came Eneko's firm reply. "We are soldiers of God, Pierre, not students. Battle is looming, with Venice as the cockpit— on that every holy scryer in the Vatican is agreed. We are not looking for what the scholar can explain, we are looking for what the mage can summon. Perhaps."

Pierre's eyes widened. Even as a boy in a small village in the Alps, he had heard *that* legend.

"You're joking!" he protested.

Eneko gazed at him mildly, and said nothing. It was left to Diego to state the obvious.

"He most certainly is not."

VILNA

Not for the first time, the shaman thought longingly of the relative safety of the lakes and forests of Karelen from which he had come. It required all his self-control to keep from trembling. That would be disastrous. His master tolerated fear; he did not tolerate a display of it.

As always in his private chambers, Jagiellon was not wearing the mask which the Grand Duke wore in his public appearances. Jagiellon was officially blind—due to the injuries he had suffered in his desperate attempt to save his father from the assassins who murdered him. Such, at least, was Jagiellon's claim. The shaman doubted if very many people in Lithuania believed that tale; none at all, in the capital city of Vilna. Most of the populace of the Grand Duchy of Lithuania and Poland were quite certain that Jagiellon had organized his father's murder in order to usurp the throne.

Few of them cared, in truth. Succession in Lithuania was often a bloody affair, to begin with, and in the four years since he ascended to the throne Jagiellon had made it quite clear that he was even more ruthless than his father had been.

But, if they doubted his other claim, few Lithuanians doubted Jagiellon's claim of blindness. Indeed, they took a certain grim satisfaction in the knowledge. Jagiellon was more savage than his father, true—but at least the father had managed to blind the son before succumbing to the usurpation. Not surprising, really. Jagiellon's father had been as famous with a blade as Jagiellon himself.

The shaman suffered from no such delusion. In the time since he entered the grand duke's service, the shaman had realized the truth. Jagiellon had made his way to the throne by delving into magic even blacker than his father had been willing to meddle with. And . . .

Had delved too deeply. The demon Jagiellon had thought to shackle to his service had been too powerful for the rash and ambitious young prince. And so, while Jagiellon had indeed lost his eyes, that loss had been the least of it.

Eyes were still there, after all. Easily seen—naked and visible—with the mask removed. But they were no longer Jagiellon's eyes, for all that they rested in Jagiellon's face.

The eyes were black, covered with eyelids so fat and heavy they turned the orbs into mere slits. But the shaman could see them well enough. Far too well. Those eyes had neither pupils nor irises, nor any trace of white eyeball. Ebony-colored and opaque; uniform throughout; appearing, at first, like two agates—until, deep within, the emptiness could be sensed. As if stones were really passageways into some place darker than any night.

"*Do it,*" commanded Grand Duke Jagiellon, and his huge hand swept across the floor, re-opening the passage.

Stifling a whimper of protest, the shaman underwent the shape-change again. As always, the transition was accompanied by agony—and even more so the passage through which his master sent him. But those agonies were familiar things. The source of the shaman's terror lay elsewhere.

Nor did the terror stem from the lagoon itself, as much as the shaman despised the stink of the waters—in his new form even more than he would have in his human one. His fishlike body swam through the murky shallows, nosing the scents drifting through the mud swirls and reeds.

He detected the mage soon enough, as familiar as he now was with that scent. Again, as before, the odor was very faint. The mage remained near water at all times, but rarely ventured into it. To do otherwise would have been dangerous.

More dangerous to leave the water's vicinity than to enter it, in truth. The shaman's jaws gaped wide, displaying teeth that could rend human flesh easily. But the display was more for the purpose of driving away the shaman's own fear than any prospect of savaging the mage. The mage had protectors in these waters. The shaman was not the only thing swimming there which possessed sharp teeth.

And there were worse perils than teeth, anyway. Much worse. It was to detect the greatest of those perils that Jagiellon had sent the shaman back—again and again—to scour the waters of Venice and the Jesolo.

Keeping a wary eye out for undines, the shaman swam for two hours before turning away from the marshes. He made no attempt to cut short his investigation. Jagiellon would be watching him. The grand duke could see through that magic passageway as well as send the shaman through it—or return the shaman to the palace in Vilna, in the event of disobedience. Once given to Jagiellon's service, escape was impossible for the servant.

For the same reason, the shaman did not stint in his ensuing search through the canals of the city. That search also lasted a full two hours, despite the fact that the shaman hated the canals even more than the marsh waters. True, the canals were not as dangerous. Undines rarely ventured into the city. But the stench of human effluvia sickened the shaman. He was, in the end, a creature born and bred in the wilderness of Finland. Civilization nauseated him.

Enough. Even for Jagiellon—even for the thing which Jagiellon truly was—this was enough. The shaman swam back into the open sea and waited for his master's summons.

The summons came soon enough, and the shaman underwent the agony. Almost gaily, now that he knew he had escaped once again from the peril which lurked in Venice. The Lion still slumbered.

❀ ❀ ❀

Fear returned quickly, however. Great fear, once the grand duke explained his new plan.

"You would do better to use the broken god," the shaman said softly, trying his best to keep the whine out of his voice. Simply a counselor, offering sage advice.

In the end, his master took the advice. But not before flaying the shaman. Jagiellon's conclusion rested on the frailty of shamans as compared to simple monsters. He accepted the fact; punished the frailty.

The next day, the new shaman was summoned to an audience in the grand duke's private quarters. The shaman, just arrived in Vilna, was also from the lakes and forests of Karelen. The grand duke was partial to that breed of Finns, especially for water work.

"Sit," commanded Jagiellon, pointing a huge finger at the heavy table in the center of the kitchen.

The shaman stared. Whatever else he had expected, the shaman had never thought to see the ruler of Lithuania cooking his own meal over a stove. The sight was incongruous. Erect, in his heavy robes of office, Grand Duke Jagiellon seemed as enormous as a bear. The ease and agility with which those great thick hands stirred food frying in a pan was equally incongruous.

Despite his astonishment, the shaman obeyed instantly. Jagiellon was . . . famous.

Grunting softly, the grand duke removed the pan from the stove and shoveled a portion of its contents onto a wooden platter. Then, as if he were a servant himself, laid the plate before the shaman.

"Eat. All of it. If your predecessor poisoned himself, I will need to discard the rest. Which would be a pity. It's one of my favorites dishes."

The shaman recognized the . . . food. Fortunately, he managed not to gag. More fortunately still, he managed to choke it all down. As he ate, he was aware of Jagiellon moving to the door and opening it, but did not dare to watch. Jagiellon was . . . famous.

When the shaman was done with the meal, Jagiellon's huge form loomed beside him again. "Take the platter with you to your quarters," commanded the grand duke, his heavy voice sliding out the words like ingots from a mold. "Do not clean it. Display it prominently. It will help you to remember the consequences of failure."

The shaman bobbed his head in nervous obedience.

"My project in Venice will require subtlety, shaman, lest the spirit that guards the city be roused from its slumber. That is why I summoned you here. My last shaman was subtle enough, but he lacked sufficient courage. See to it that you have both."

The shaman was confused. He had heard of Venice, but knew nothing about the city. Somewhere in Italy, he thought.

"I will explain later. Go now. You may take this with you also. It will remind you of the consequences of success."

As he rose from the table, clutching the platter, the shaman beheld a woman standing next to the grand duke. She was very beautiful.

"You will not have the use of it for long," warned the grand duke. "Soon enough, the thing must be sent off to Venice."

The shaman bobbed his head again; more with eagerness, now, than anxiety. The shaman was not given to lingering over such pleasures, in any event. In that, too, he was a creature of the wilderness.

By the time he reached his chambers, the woman following obediently in his wake, the shaman had come to realize that she was no woman at all. Simply the form of one, which his master had long since turned into his vessel.

The shaman did not care in the least. A vessel would serve his purpose well enough; and did so. But the time came, his lust satisfied, when the shaman rolled over in his bed and found himself staring into an empty platter instead of empty eyes. And he wondered whether he had made such a wise decision, answering the summons of the Grand Duke of Lithuania.

Not that he had had much choice, of course. Jagiellon was . . . famous.

FERRARA

Each hammer blow was a neat, precise exercise of applied force. Enrico Dell'este loved this process, this shaping of raw metal into the folded and refolded blade-steel. His mind and spirit found surcease from trouble in the labor. At the moment, as for the past several years, he needed that surcease. Needed it badly.

Besides, a duke who worked steel was intensely popular among his steelworking commons. Duke Dell'este, Lord of Ferrara, Modena, Este, and Reggio nell'Emilia, needed that also. Ferrara stood between too many enemies in the shifting morass of Italian politics in the year of our Lord 1537. Ferrara had no natural defenses like Venice, and no great allies. All it had was the Duke Enrico Dell'este—the Old Fox, as his populace called him—and the support of that populace.

A page entered the forge-room. Shouted above the steady hammering. "Milord. Signor Bartelozzi is here to see you. He awaits you in the sword salon."

The duke nodded, without stopping or even looking up from his work. "Antimo will wait a few moments. Steel won't." He forced himself to remain calm, to finish the task properly. If Antimo Bartelozzi had bad news he would have sent a messenger, or simply sent a letter. The fact that he needed to *talk* to the duke . . .

That could only mean good news about his grandchildren. Or news which was at least hopeful.

Dell'este lifted the bar of hammered metal with the tongs and lowered it into the quenching tank. He nodded at the blacksmith standing nearby, who stepped forward to continue the work. The duke hung his tools neatly and took the towel from the waiting factotum. "The Old Fox," he murmured, as he dried the sweat. "Tonight I just feel old."

The room the duke entered was spartan. Stone-flagged, cool. Its only furnishings a wooden table which leaned more to sturdiness and functionality than elegance; and a single chair, simple and not upholstered. Hardly what one would expect the lair of the Lord of the cities of Ferrara, Este, Modena, and Reggio nell' Emilia to look like. On the wall above the fireplace was a solitary piece of adornment. And that was absolutely typical of Dell'este. It was a sword, hung with crimson tassels. The pommel showed faint signs of generations of careful polishing. The wall opposite the fireplace contained an entire rack of such weapons.

The Old Fox sat at the table and looked at the colorless man standing quietly in the corner. Antimo Bartelozzi had the gift of being the last person in a crowd of two that you'd ever notice.

He was also utterly loyal, as the duke well knew. Bartelozzi had had ample opportunity to betray the Dell'este in times past.

The duke used other spies and agents for various other tasks. Antimo Bartelozzi was for family affairs. To the duke that was the only thing more precious than good sword-steel.

"Greetings, Antimo. Tell me the worst."

The lean gray-haired man smiled. "Always the same. The worst first. The 'worst' is that I did not find them, milord. Either one. Nor do I have knowledge of their whereabouts."

The Old Fox shuddered, trying to control the relief which poured through him. "My grandsons are alive."

Bartelozzi paused. "It's . . . not certain. To be honest, milord, all I've established is that Marco Valdosta was last seen the night your daughter Lorendana was killed. And I had established that much two years ago. But I did find this."

The duke's agent reached into a small pouch. He handed over a small, sheathed knife, whose pommel was chased and set with an onyx. "This dagger is a signed Ferrara blade that turned up in the thieves market at Mestre. The seller was . . . questioned. He admitted to having bought it from one of the Jesolo marsh-bandits."

The duke hissed between his teeth. He took the blade and unscrewed the pommel. Looked at the tiny marks on the tang. "This was Marco Valdosta's blade." He looked at the wall. At the empty space next to one of the hereditary blades on its rack. The space for a small dagger given to a boy, next to the sword—still in its place—destined for the man. His grandson Marco's blades.

"And you don't take this as another bad sign? Perhaps whoever stole the dagger from him killed the boy." The Old Fox eyed Bartelozzi under lowered eyebrows. "You found one of the bandits. Questioned him."

Antimo nodded. "They robbed the boy, yes. Beat him badly. Badly enough that the bandits assumed he would not survive. But . . . there are rumors."

"The Jesolo is full of rumors," snorted Dell'este. "Still, it's something."

He moved toward the blade-rack. "Tell me that I can return it to its place, Antimo. You know the tradition."

Behind him, he heard a little noise. As if Bartelozzi was choking down a sarcastic reply. The duke smiled grimly.

" 'No Ferrara blade, once given to a Dell'este scion, may be returned until it is blooded.' You may hang it in the rack, milord. That blade is well and truly blooded. I slid the bandit into the water myself. The thief-vendor also. There was barely enough blood left in them to draw the fish."

Dell'este hung the dagger and turned back. "And the younger boy? Sforza's bastard?"

Antimo Bartelozzi looked decidedly uncomfortable. "Milord. We don't *know* that the condottiere was his father."

"Spare me," growled the duke. "My younger grandson was the spitting image of Sforza by the time he was ten. You knew my slut daughter, as well as I did. She was enamored of all things Milanese, and Sforza was already then the greatest captain in Visconti's service."

Antimo studied Dell'este for a moment, as if gauging the limits of his master's forbearance. It was a brief study. For Bartelozzi, the Old Fox's limits were . . . almost nonexistent.

"That is a disservice to her memory, milord, and you know it perfectly well. To begin with, her devotion was to the Montagnard cause, not to Milan. Your daughter was a fanatic, yes; a traitor . . . not really."

The duke's jaws tightened, but he did not argue the point. Bartelozzi continued:

"Nor was she a slut. Somewhat promiscuous, yes; a slut, no. She rebuffed Duke Visconti himself, you know, shortly after she arrived in Milan. Quite firmly, by all accounts—even derisively. A bold thing for a woman to do, who had cast herself into Milan's coils. That may well have been the final factor which led Visconti to have her murdered, once she had fallen out of favor with her lover Sforza. Not even Visconti would have been bold enough to risk his chief military captain's anger."

Dell'este restrained his own anger. It was directed at the daughter, anyway, not the agent. Besides, it was an old thing, now. A dull ember, not a hot flame. And . . . that core of honesty which had always lain at the center of the Old Fox's legendary wiliness accepted the truth of Bartelozzi's words. The duke's daughter Lorendana had been headstrong, willful, given to wild enthusiasms, reckless—yes, all those. In which, the duke admitted privately, she was not really so different from the duke himself at an early age. Except that Enrico Dell'este had possessed, even as a stripling prince, more than his share of acumen. And . . . he had been lucky.

Bartelozzi was continuing. "All we *know* about the younger boy is what we learned two years ago. He was thrown out of Theodoro Mantesta's care once the true story of Lorendana's death leaked out. Mantesta, not surprisingly, was terrified of Milanese assassins himself. Your youngest grandson seems to have then joined the canal-brats."

"Damn Mantesta, anyway—I would have seen to his safety." For a moment, he glowered, remembering a night when he had slipped into Venice incognito. The Duke of Ferrara was no mean bladesman himself. Theodoro Mantesta had been almost as terrified of him as he had been of Milanese assassins. Almost, but . . . not quite. And for good reason. In the end, Dell'este had let him live.

The Old Fox waved his hand irritably. "I know all this, Antimo! Shortly thereafter, you discovered that a child very like him, from the poor description we had, was killed about three weeks later. And while it wasn't certain—hundreds of poor children live under the bridges and pilings of Venice—it seemed logical enough that the victim was my youngest grandson. So tell me what you have learned *since*, if you please."

Antimo smiled. "What I have learned *since*, milord, is that the boy whose throat was slit had actually died of disease the day before."

The duke's eyes widened. "Who would be that cunning? Not my grandson! He was only twelve at the time."

"Two ladies by the name of Claudia and Valentina would be that cunning, milord." Bartelozzi shook his head. "You would not know them. But in their own circles they are quite famous. Notorious, it might be better to say. Tavern musicians, officially—excellent ones, by all account—but also thieves. Excellent thieves, by reputation. And according to rumor, shortly thereafter the two women gained an accomplice. A young boy, about twelve. I've not laid eyes on him myself, mind you—neither have any of my agents. The boy seems to have been well trained in stealth. But I have gotten a description, quite a good one. In fact, the description came from a former mercenary in Sforza's service. 'Could be one of the Wolf's by-blows,' as he put it. 'Lord knows he's scattered them across Italy.' "

The Duke of Ferrara closed his eyes, allowing the relief to wash over him again. It made sense, yes—*it all made sense.* His youngest grandson had been a wily boy—quite unlike the older. As if all of the legendary cunning of Dell'este had been concentrated in the one, at the expense of the other. Combined, alas, with the amorality of the father Sforza. Even when the boy had been a toddler, the duke had found his youngest grandson . . . troubling.

His musings were interrupted by Bartelozzi. Antimo's next words brought the duke's eyes wide open again.

"The two women who may have succored your grandson are also reputed to be Strega. *Genuine* Strega, too, not peddlers and hucksters. The reputation seems well founded, from what I could determine."

"Strega? Why would they care what happened to the bloodline of Valdosta and Dell'este?"

Bartelozzi stared at him. After a moment, Dell'este looked away. Away, and down. "Because Venice is the best refuge of the Strega," he answered his own question. "Has been for centuries. If Venice falls . . ."

A brief shudder went through his slender but still muscular body. "I have been . . . not myself, Antimo. These past two years. All my offspring dead . . . it was too much."

His most trusted agent's nod was one of understanding. But pitiless for all that.

"You have other offspring, milord. Of position if not of blood. All of Ferrara depends upon you. Venice too, I suspect, in the end. There is no leadership in that city that can compare to yours. *If* you begin leading again, like a duke and not a grieving old man."

Dell'este tightened his lips, but accepted the reproof. It was a just one, after all.

"True," he said curtly. Then, after a moment, his lips began to curve into a smile. Hearing Bartelozzi's sigh of relief, he allowed his smile to broaden.

"You think it is time the Old Fox returned, eh?"

"Past time," murmured Bartelozzi. "The storm clouds are gathering, milord. Have been for some time, as you well know. If Venice is destroyed, Ferrara will go down with it."

The Duke of Ferrara began pacing about. For all his age, there was a spryness to his steps. "Venice first, I think. That will be the cockpit."

He did not even bother to glance at Bartelozzi to see his agent's nod of agreement. So much was obvious to them both. "Which means we must find an anchor of support in the city. A great house which can serve to rally the populace of Venice. The current quality of Venetian leadership is dismal, but the population will respond well—as they have for a thousand years—if a firm hand takes control." He sighed regretfully. "Doge Foscari was capable once, and still has his moments. But—he is too old, now."

"If either of your grandsons is alive . . ."

The Old Fox shook his head firmly. "Not yet, Antimo. Let our enemies think the ancient house of Valdosta is well and truly destroyed. That will be our secret weapon, when the time comes. For the moment—assuming they are still alive—my grandsons are far safer hidden amongst the poor and outcast of Venice."

"We could bring them here, milord."

The duke hesitated, his head warring with his heart. But only for an instant, before the head began shaking firmly. Not for nothing did that head—that triangular, sharp-jawed face—resemble the animal he had been named after.

"No," he said firmly. "As you said yourself, Antimo, I have a responsibility to *all* of my offspring. Those of position as well as those of blood." For a moment, he paused in his pacing; stood very erect. "Dell'este honor has always been as famous as its cunning. Without the one, the other is meaningless."

Bartelozzi nodded. In obeisance as much as in agreement. He shared, in full measure, that loyalty for which the retainers of Dell'este were also famous.

"Valdosta cannot serve, for the moment." The Old Fox resumed his pacing. "Of the others . . . Brunelli is foul, as you well know, however cleverly that house has managed to disguise it. Dorma has potential, but the head of the house is still too young, unsure of himself."

"Petro Dorma may surprise you, milord."

The duke glanced at him. "You know something I don't?"

Bartelozzi shrugged. "Simply an estimate, nothing more."

Dell'este stared out the window which opened on to the little city of Ferrara. Looked past the city itself to the lush countryside beyond. "Perhaps, Antimo. I'm not sure I agree. Petro Dorma is a judicious man, true enough. And, I think, quite an honorable one. But that's not enough. A sword must have an edge also."

The duke sighed. "If only Montescue . . . *There's* the man with the right edge. And, for all his age, the tested blade to hold it."

Hearing Bartelozzi's little choke, the duke smiled wryly. "Don't tell me. He's still trying to have my grandsons assassinated."

"It seems so, milord. Apparently the same rumors have reached him as well."

The Old Fox turned his head and gazed squarely upon his most trusted agent and adviser. "Instruct me, Antimo. In this matter, I do not entirely trust myself."

Bartelozzi hesitated. Then: "Do nothing, milord. *Casa* Montescue has fallen on such bad times that old Lodovico Montescue will not be able to afford better than middling murderers. And"—again, he hesitated—"we may as well discover now, at the beginning of the contest, how sharp a blade your grandsons will make."

The Duke of Ferrara pondered the advice, for a moment. Then, nodded. "Spoken like a Dell'este. See to it then, Antimo. Pass the word in Venice—very quietly—that if either of my grandsons come to the surface, we will pay well for whoever takes them under his wing. Until then . . . they will have to survive on their own. Blades, as you say, must be tempered."

His lips tightened, became a thin line. Those of a craftsman, gauging his material. "No doubt iron would scream also, if it could feel the pain of the forge and the hammer and the quenching tank. No matter. So is steel made."

PART I
June, 1537 A.D.

Chapter 1

The silhouette of the Basilica of St. Mark was black against the paling predawn sky. The pillar and the winged lion in the Piazza San Marco could just be made out.

In the bow of the gondola Benito shifted uneasily, looking at it. "*Figlio di una puttana*, woman," he said, trying to sound older than fourteen. "Can't you get a move on? It'll be sunup before I'm home." He wished his voice would stop cracking like that. Marco said it was just part of growing up. He wished that that would stop too. Being bigger was no advantage for climbing or running. And if he stopped growing, he might stop being so hungry all of the time.

Up on the stern the hooded oarsman ignored him, moving slowly and steadily.

"You want me to row this thing for you?" he demanded.

"Shut up," she hissed. "You want to attract attention? At this time of the morning, only people in trouble are rushing."

Benito had to acknowledge that it was true enough. Even now there were three other vessels moving on the Grand Canal. All of them slowly. He sighed. "I just need to get back home. I'm supposed to see my brother."

She snorted. "If you hadn't held us up, we'd be the other side of Campo San Polo by now. And you can't be in any more of a hurry to get back to whatever rat-hole you sleep in, than I am to see the back of you. I should never have agreed to take you."

Benito huddled down in the bow. This woman's tongue was even sharper-edged than Maria Garavelli's. The wind between the ornately facaded buildings was cold. He was cold and, as usual, he was hungry. It had been a fruitless night. Mercutio had let him down. Again.

He liked working jobs with Mercutio. His ideas were exciting, daring and, well, crazy. You always knew with any job he organized it was going to be nip-and-tuck. Skin of your teeth stuff and needing lots of luck. But somehow Mercutio always seemed to have that luck.

Benito sighed. Mercutio also had the habit of not turning up for a job. Benito had sat waiting for four cold hours for him tonight, and not a copper's profit to show for it. He could have used some more coin. All he had in the attic was a half crock of elderly *fagioli stufata*. It was definitely past its best. The beans were producing gas before they even hit his stomach.

His eye was caught by the body. It bobbed in the dark water under the pilings as the tiny fish plucked at it. That was a fine cloak. . . . A few knife slashes could be dealt with. His jaw dropped. The rich soft swollen white hand still had rings on it.

He turned to speak.

"Don't even look," she hissed between clenched teeth.

"But . . ." he started to point.

She hit his hand with the oar. "*Shut it!*" There was such intensity in that quiet command that Benito didn't even dare to glance at the corpse again.

They poled on in silence, the bow of the shabby gondola cutting the oily, still water, here where it was sheltered from the predawn breeze. Most of Venice was still sleeping.

When she spoke, they were a good hundred yards past the corpse. "Despini." Her voice shook slightly. She was plainly shocked.

Benito looked warily at her. "What?" A stray strand of long, wavy, copper-colored hair had found its way out from under her hooded cloak. She pushed it back. Whatever this girl moved must be valuable. That was a well-fed wrist.

"Gino Despini. He was one of my customers. He had a booth down on the Calle Farnese. Sold love philters, charms and amulets of protection against the French Pox."

Benito nodded sagely. That was the sort of cargo she moved. The frauds, hedge magicians, tricksters and petty Strega around the Campo Ghetto didn't always want to declare their imports to the state or the church. Dangerous, tricky cargoes. But valuable. "So why didn't you want to stop? Get those rings, or take him to his family..."

She raised her eyes to heaven. "You're a fool. Whoever killed him could have sunk him if they just wanted him dead. They didn't even rob him. What does that mean?" she demanded.

Benito knew he was out of his league here. He was a good enough sneak thief. But this... "He was wounded but escaped, died and fell in the canal," he ventured warily.

She shook her head. "You don't know anything, do you, boy? If they left his body to float, they're not scared of the Schiopettieri."

Benito swallowed hard. The Schiopettieri were professional soldiers under the official command of Venice's *Signori di Notte*... The Lords of the Nightwatch, answerable to the Senate of the Great Republic. In effect, they were the city's police force. You didn't mess with them.

"That spells someone with influence and power," she continued. "Whoever killed him obviously doesn't need money." She pursed her lips. "There was a rumor about that he was more than what he seemed. A Strega Mage proper, not a charlatan. He was left to float either as message, or more likely, as bait."

Bait. "Who did it?" he asked, huskily. This was deep, dark water.

The woman shrugged. "Maybe the Servants of the Holy Trinity. They've been pretty active lately. So have the agents of the Council of Ten. Maybe other Strega. But I don't think so. They favor magic or poison. He'd been stabbed."

"Bait..."

"They'll take whoever comes to go on with their questioning. If it's the Servants, you know how they question people. With knives. And fire. And prayers for your soul." She raised an eyebrow and said sardonically, "You were thinking of sneaking back there, weren't you?"

"I didn't understand." The boy answered humbly. "But Katerina..."

"Who told you my name?" she demanded fiercely.

"Captain Della Tomasso... Look!"

While they'd been talking, a flotilla of rowing boats had appeared and were coming along the Grand Canal. Rowing steadily in measured strokes. The leading ones were definitely Schiopettieri oarships.

"*Merda!*" Katerina spat. "It must be a sweep. We've got to get out of here." She began to scull frantically, pushing the gondola towards the mouth of a narrow canal.

Benito got up hastily. He was getting off the unfamiliar water and onto the buildings. Quickly. "They'll have blocked off the side canals, Kat."

"Right." She pushed the boat into a group of tied up gondolas and small craft moored to poles at the water-door of the marble-faced mansion. She dropped a loop over the bollard. "Lie down . . . little brother. We're poor boatkids who've lost our parents and have to sleep on the water."

Benito looked askance at her. But he lay down on the gondola ribs next to her. She pulled a grubby piece of sailcloth over them. She also tied a piece of cord to a knobbly yellow oilcloth parcel from the bow. She dropped the parcel gently over the side, down into the still water. Hastily she tied it off.

Benito wondered what the hell cadging a ride across from Guidecca had gotten him into. He liked a bit of excitement, but messing with people who knew people who were being killed by the Servants was too much.

It was too much, thought Katerina, lying on the ribs of the gondola. Here she was with a cargo that could get her burned at the stake. Even if they never picked it up . . . well, if it came to hard questioning they might get her name. Under that sort of questioning, especially if they used magic, they could find out everything. Unless, like Despini, you had defenses that would kill first. Holy Mother. She must *not* be caught. The dishonor to the family if she were! It would kill the old man. Every time she'd gone out she'd known it was a risk. But they could simply not afford to lose another cargo. And who else could they trust? Somehow the *Casa* Montescue, secure for all these years, had been infiltrated. There was no other explanation.

She looked up. They were tied up beside the Imperial embassy. Across the canal was the pretentious *Casa* Brunelli. Pah. Nouveau riche. *Curti*. They had glass windows instead of the varnished silk that real *Longi Case Vecchie* used. The kind of neighborhood that the Schiopettieri would not take kindly to finding loiterers in, even if they didn't pick up the parcel dangling from the bow.

She looked across, not without a certain envy, at the ornate marble-faced building. She was startled to realize there was someone on the third-floor balcony of the *Casa* Brunelli.

"Lie still," Kat said between clenched teeth to the wrigglesome urchin next to her. "There is someone on the balcony up there."

To give him credit, the boy didn't peer. He froze. "Who?"

"How would I know? You . . . you canal-brat. It's hard to make out anything in this light. A man, by the way he stands."

"He must have seen us come in," whispered the boy. Kat could feel him tense next to her. Getting ready to run.

"Stay still!" She hissed.

Benito's dark eyes flickered nervously. Then she felt him tense again. "They're stopping. They're coming here!"

Kat reached for the slipknot on the cord. "How do you know?"

The boy's eyes darted. "You can see the reflection in the window," he mumbled.

It was true enough. The two Schiopettieri oarships were slowing. Backing water. The vessels behind them . . . weren't Venice-built. She'd swear to that. Whoever made them needed lessons in shipbuilding. Tubs. But tubs bright with steel. So much so that it was a miracle they didn't tip over. That would've emptied all the armored men, in bright triple-cross-enameled breastplates and their gilt-trimmed helmets, into the canal.

Benito and Katerina gaped, forgetting the watcher on the balcony. The Teutonic Knights of the Holy Trinity. The fabled Arm Militant of the Pauline Orders. The soldiers of God who beat back the Huns, the Norse, and the various Slavic and Magyar pagans and heretics on the northern and eastern frontiers of Christendom. The borders of Emperor Charles Fredrik's Holy Roman Empire rested squarely on their steel shoulders. Those breastplates were unmistakable, a legend across the Christian world. And they were half feared, as well as admired and respected, by the southern and Mediterranean folk who generally followed the Petrine currents in the Church.

"What the hell are they doing here?" Benito got it out seconds before Kat. His voice had more admiration in it than Katerina Montescue would have voiced.

"Going to the Imperial embassy, by the looks of it," said Katerina with relief.

Benito too sounded more relaxed. "I always wanted to be a knight."

Katerina shook her head. "Fighting trolls and hellspawn in the frozen northlands? Dealing with pagan Russian and Tatar princes and their demons? And—even worse—the heretic Grand Duchy of Lithuania and the Kingdom of Hungary and *their* sorcerers and shamans? Ha! It's dark half the year up there. And they look silly in that armor. It's no good anyway. One of the new pistols from Spain will put a ball right through it. Besides, they take the sons of the nobility of the Empire, not canal-brats."

The boy looked militant. "I'm more than just a 'canal-brat.' My father . . ."

"Was the Holy Grand Metropolitan of Rome himself," snapped Katerina. "And your mother was the Duchess of Milan, and just a canal-side *puttana* in her spare time. Now shut up. They still wouldn't be pleased to find us here. The Schiopettieri would run us in and beat us up just for being in this part of town."

The boy bit his lip. His dark eyes fumed at her. But he lay still. Katerina turned her attention back to the pageant reflected in the windows of the *Casa* Brunelli. With shock she recognized the file of gray-cassocked and hooded men filing out of the embassy onto the stone-faced landing. Even in the poor light there was no mistaking the white triple crosses on the backs of those cassocks. The monastic Servants of the Holy Trinity did not inspire the same awe as their sibling Paulines, the Knights, did. They simply inspired fear and distrust. Especially for Katerina Montescue. And they weren't an unfamiliar sight in Venice. Their war on the Jews and the Strega was not officially sanctioned by the Doge. On the other hand, Doge Giorgio Foscari was turning a very blind eye. Well, at his age your thoughts started turning more to Heaven than earth anyway. And the Servants claimed to be the custodians of the keys to Heaven. Kat suppressed a chuckle. That had gotten Metropolitan Michael very steamed up in the pulpit last Mass. Rome and the Holy Grand Metropolitan did *not* approve of the strident claims of the Paulines.

A querulous, elderly whiny voice sounded across the canal. It rose above the soft sonorous sound of the plainsong that the Servants of the Holy Trinity were beginning to chant. "My best cassock. I wanted to wear it for this occasion . . ." Someone hastily hushed the old monk as the boatloads of knights drew up to the quay.

A trumpet sounded, sharp and bright. Steel-clad figures

disembarked from the boat and came up the steps. They were in military array, formed up around a palanquinlike structure which was borne by several of the hefty knights. It was plainly heavy, but too small to hold a person.

"What are they carrying?" whispered Benito.

"How in the names of all the Saints do you expect me to know?" Katerina hissed savagely. "Do you want me to go over and ask them?"

Benito sniffed. "There's no need to bite my head off. It's just that it looked like a chest. There were big locks. Maybe it is treasure."

There was a thoughtfulness in that young voice that made Katerina catch her breath and shake her head. This boy was going to die young. "Are you crazy? Don't even think of stealing from them. Don't even think of it."

Two figures now left the tail of the procession. One was a gray-cassocked and stooped monk. The other was a woman. True, she wore a nun's habit. But she walked like a duchess. Her head held up with an arrogant tilt that revealed a silhouetted prow of an aristocratic nose.

"Sister Humility," whispered the incorrigible canal-brat next to her.

Katerina had to bite back a snort of laughter. Then, when she realized what the reflected-in-glass figures were doing, it made her forget all about laughing. They were getting into a small gondola with a single arquebus-armed Schiopettieri. A knight carried a small brazier over to the vessel. Another brought a box from their ship. Katerina knew enough of magical practice to guess that they were about to conduct a rite of enclosure. They could hardly fail to pass her gondola. Heaven alone knew what was inside the parcel from Ascalon that she was supposed to deliver. But having it inside a magical circle of enclosure was *not* a good idea. She pulled the cord, and the slipknotted parcel went down to the mud.

Benito had plainly also seen what was happening. "Over the side. Quick!"

Katerina shook her head. "I can't swim."

"You don't have to," Benito snapped impatiently. "You can hold on to the boat. Come *on*. Be quick and quiet about it. They'll be here any minute." He slipped over the side and into the water between the boats like an oiled rat.

Nervously, hastily, Katerina followed. Icy cold canal water slid up her legs, soaking into her petticoats. Her heavy twilled bombazine dress was more resistant to water. It bulged up around her like some clumsy bubble. She clung to the gunwale.

"Here," he whispered hoarsely, pulling her hand. "Take the bow-rope."

She had to give up her precious hold on the gondola and flounder. Her head went under but she managed to grab the rope. The bow came forward, cracking into her head, nearly stunning her.

"Quiet!"

They waited in the water. Through the narrow gap between the canalboats she could see the windows of the *Casa* Brunelli. They still provided a mirror-view. The two watchers in the water could see the gondola with the monk, nun and a slowly rowing Schiopettieri come down the side canal. The nun was chanting prayers, waving the censer. The monk had a pole with something on the end which he ran along the wall. If it made a line, it didn't show up in reflections.

Benito pressed his mouth against her ear. "When they get to the edge of the boats, you take a deep breath and hold it. I'll take you under. Start breathing deeply now."

When he did pull her under it was all she could do not to struggle frantically for the surface. And they seemed to stay down forever. Then she felt Benito tug—upwards. She bumped her head against the gondola again.

"What was that sound?" The voice was male, but high and cool. The diction was faintly stilted, as if this was a second language.

"Perhaps a fish, Monsignor Sachs. They shelter among the boats." The voice of the Schiopettieri was frightened, respectful. Katerina, trying to breathe quietly, was not surprised. The Servants of Holy Trinity were terrifying enough without magic.

"Who do those boats belong to? Why are they here?" the man asked. The nun continued her low melodious chanting as if the man had not spoken.

Katerina could imagine the soldier's shrug even if she could not see it. This was Venice. There were gondolas and skiffs everywhere. "They are for the staff of the embassy, Monsignor."

The foreign monk was plainly unimpressed. "They will no longer be able to use this door. The embassy can only be entered by the portal. Have them moved," he commanded. "And I am Abbot Sachs.

I will be addressed as such. Not by southern titles." It didn't sound as if he approved of those either. But at least their voices were getting farther away.

"I will see to it, Abbot," said the Schiopettieri.

"*Merda*," whispered Benito. "We have to get out of here." He started to pull on the gondola.

Katerina shook her head. "Wait," she said quietly. "Give it another minute. They're not far enough away yet." So they waited in the water. It seemed an eternity before they decided it was safe. Benito took a deep breath and ducked under the water; then, thrust up and hauled himself over the gunwale. Katerina tried to pull herself in. Her petticoats, dress and sodden hooded cloak all impeded her. Even Benito's hauling was not sufficient. He let go and she fell back. Little *bastardo*! Then she realized he'd let go in order to take the oar and push the gondola closer to the water-door. He was quick-thinking, if inexpert with an oar. There were slimy steps under the water. Dripping, Katerina was able to get back into her boat and flip the bow-rope free. She seized the oar from the inept Benito and sent them out into the canal. He could swim but not handle a boat.

As she turned the vessel with quick, skilled movements of her feet and oar, a movement caught the periphery of her vision. Someone up there . . . She'd forgotten about the watcher on the balcony of the *Casa* Brunelli.

He was watching, impassive. It was much lighter now, and she could see him as clearly as he could doubtless see her dripping self. The man was slight. Reddish haired, with dark eyebrows that met to form a forbidding line. A gaze like an eagle. It was not a face that you could forget. And it looked . . . implacable.

She sculled hard. It was not something which could be done too hastily, without ending up in the water. She nearly did that again.

"Why didn't he call out?" asked the wet Benito, once again huddled in the bow.

"One of life's little mysteries," snapped Katerina, trying to keep her teeth from chattering. Sculling was an exercise which could leave you pretty warm, but she still hadn't recovered from either the cold water or the fear. However, by the expression on the man's face, she was sure that the only reason he hadn't called out was that he didn't want to be seen himself.

The largest of San Marco's bells began to peal the dawn. When it was still, the Arsenal's *Marangona* bell began to sound. It would ring for some time, calling the shipwrights, carpenters, and caulkers to work. Venice was stirring. And Kat was a long way from home. She could hardly help being seen, wet. Well, at least she *could* get dry, and she had other clothes. She was probably better off than the boy. But her cargo was somewhere in the canal mud outside the Imperial embassy.

Bad.

She couldn't come back that evening, or the next. The Solstice Feast with its celebrations, ridottos, and balls would go on for two more days. She would just have to pray that the heavy parcel would not wash with the tide, and that the boy would keep his mouth shut.

Worse.

And because she had never learned to swim, she'd have to ask this shivering canal-brat to get it back for her.

Worst. Damnation!

Chapter 2

It was a *racasse*. A scorpion-fish. The only catch of the day, and it *had* to be a Godforsaken *racasse*.

Marco Valdosta stared at the reed-woven fish trap. It was the best and newest one he owned. He stared at the contents, which flopped around getting its long, poisonous spines nicely wedged, then cursed a curse which was long, literate, and alliterative.

The words did not match the speaker. Benito's older brother was a painfully thin, ragged sixteen-year-old, dressed only in tattered breeches, balanced on his haunches on a scrap of raft cobbled together from waterlogged flotsam. A marsh-dweller—one of the mixture of destitutes, refugees, and criminals who scratched out a living among the islands, and the mosquito-singing Jesolo marshes to the northeast. The coastal lagoon that sheltered Venice was pleasant enough around the city but closer to the mainland, away from the cleansing ebb and flow, the marshes that fringed the lagoon were an ooze of thick stinking muds and stagnant, brackish waters. The townsfolk of Venice called the people who lived there "loco."

Marco looked it. His dark hair was nearly waist length, indifferently clean, and held back in a tail with a twist of marsh-grass; his lean tanned face was smudged with mud above the almond eyes and along the cheekbones. This was not the sort of creature from which one expected anything intelligible, much less intelligent.

Marco was flat out of patience, with the day (which was hot and stank), with his luck (which smelled almost as bad as the day),

35

and with the world (which smelled worse than his luck). For anyone else on this muddy lagoon, for anyone else fishing between the quays of this sinking, stinking city, a *racasse* would be cause for rejoicing. They were fine eating. And you could sell the spines. There was always a market for poison. All you needed was a 'priest' to club the fish with, and some care. And—if it was stuck in a fish trap—a good long harpoon.

But Marco didn't *have* a harpoon. There was no way to kill the fish in that trap, short of clubbing the painstakingly woven structure to reed-splinters. He had a knife . . . of sorts. But it was no more than a splinter of stolen Murano glass, with one end dipped in a caulker's tar-bucket, and wrapped with string.

All he could do was to stare at the three-times-damned thing wedging itself more and more tightly in the depths of his fish trap and try not to cry. The only catch of the whole day, useless, and he hadn't eaten since yesterday morning. Damn the Saints and damn the trap. His only hope was the chance that the fish might relax when it died, enough to let him slide it out. Or if he could find a fisherman with a harpoon. He would lose half the value of his catch, but he might get something.

He poled the raft toward the wharves in hopes of finding a fisherman; there was just the barest possibility there would be someone there with a bit of a coin or something edible to trade— he'd willingly swap fish, trap and all for a little bread. He hadn't had any real bread in months.

Real bread—the smell of bread baking—used to drive him nearly out of his head. Mama would laugh at him—tell him he'd never be a fighter, he wasn't carnivore enough. Marco wanted to be a healer, not a fighter.

Mama *had* been a fighter; but meaner people had killed her.

He almost missed the shadow under the wharf pilings that moved wrong. Almost. But living with the marsh-folk gave you paranoia, if nothing else, and when the shadow lunged down from its perch on a crossbeam he already had in hand the only thing on the raft that could count in a fight.

The trap that was full of scorpion-fish.

The trap wasn't much more substantial than a marsh-dweller's promise; it shattered as it hit the man (all dressed in dark colors he was; real clothes and not rags, and his face covered). The man got a spine in one eye and the rest in the hand that came up to fend it off. The dagger in his other hand flew into the water.

He was already insane with pain when he hit the raft; which promptly capsized, but Marco had been ready for that. He dove with the push of the raft behind him, took off into deep water and shoved off the mucky bottom; then, came up with a rush that got him halfway back onto the raft before his attacker finished his death agony. The man floated, a dark bundle that twitched and rolled, being slowly pulled back under the wharf by the current. No more danger from *him*, for sure.

Marco got himself back onto his raft—and started to shake.

A man—waiting there, like he knew it was part of Marco's regular circuit. Man dressed all dark, with his face covered, and a knife in his hand. Man that came down on him like he *knew* exactly what he was doing, who he was going for. *Assassin*. Had to be!

They were hunting him—after two years, *They* were hunting him! Now, They'd found him again and They'd get him like They'd got Mama . . . Oh, God.

Marco poled back towards the Jesolo marshes in a fog of panic, hunger forgotten, casting glances back at the wharf to see if anyone had found the body, if there were any more of Them after him. But all he could see was the normal working small craft and a few of the other marsh-dwellers out bobbing on the lagoon—most of them too busy fishing or dozing in the sun to take any notice, the rest not wanting to notice trouble lest it fall on them, too.

Got to hide. That was all he knew, his pulse pounding in his ears and his knees wobbling with weariness. He pushed the scrap of the raft into the marsh, where the high, yellow reeds made a maze you could easily get lost in. He brought it in up against a particular reed-islet—which he and Chiano knew wasn't an islet at all. He looked around again; then crouched and listened.

Nothing out of the ordinary. Sea birds mewling, reeds whispering, nothing else. He jumped off the raft—water was just a bit more than waist deep here, though the bottom sucked at his feet—and picked up an edge of the islet. It was a kind of basket made to look like a hummock with reeds sticking out of it, resting on a much larger raft. Marco heaved his little raft atop the big one, climbed onto them, and lowered the basket down to cover himself and his "home" again.

There was just enough room under the "roof" to sit hunched over, with his chin on his knees—but it was safer than anywhere else in the swamp, especially with Them out after him. Only he, and old Sophia and Chiano, had these hideaways that he knew of. Chiano taught the two of them how to make the hideouts. The half-crazy old man swore they were called "blinds" in the Camarque and that you used them to shoot birds from. Marco's hide was the reason he was still alive; he'd waited out many a loco-gang hunt in his, and no end of searches by Big Gianni.

But would it hold against Them?

Whoever They were. Mama had had plenty of safeguards, but none of them had helped *her* . . .

Ends of reeds tickled his back and arms as he pushed the thought of discovery resolutely away. No. He wouldn't think about it, he needed to think about something else. But songs weren't any good—the only ones he could remember right now were all grim. *Think. Get calm. Keep your mind occupied, or you'll panic.*

He began breathing deeply and quietly, willing his pulse to slow, making himself a bit calmer, telling himself he had nothing to worry about. The raft bobbed a little; if anyone came by Marco would know it by the disturbance of the water. There was no way anyone could get near him without him knowing.

As usual when he wanted to relax and calm down, Marco relied on mathematics. He loved figures and calculations. *Now—if you started with a load of salted fish; say forty barrels, say two hundred thirty-seven fish to a barrel, and you transported up the Po, with your costs going up but the worth of those fish going up, the farther you went . . .*

The heat under the basket, the bobbing of the raft, the close air and exhaustion, all conspired to put him to sleep.

It began again.

Benito tugged at his elbow. "*Si?*" Marco responded absently; he was doing Mama's accounts, and there'd been a lot of business today.

"Mama said I should stay with Theodoro overnight—Marco, can he be on the ship up to Milan? Please?"

Dream-skip again; stumbling around in water and mud up to his waist, lost in the dark and crying—that was how the marsh-dwellers had found him. And beat him up, and robbed him of everything but his breeches and the paper he kept clutched in one hand. He lay in shallow mud and water; freezing, dazed, hurting and crying. . . .

He woke crying—but silently, silently. He'd learned since then never to make a noise. He wiped the tears from his face with the tail of his hair, and listened. Nothing. And it was getting on towards sunset, judging by the red that filtered through the basket and the go-to-bed sounds the marshbirds were making.

Oh, God—he was supposed to meet his younger brother Benito at dawn. He had to warn him that *They* were on the hunt again. Benito could be in as much danger as Marco. But first he had to find Chiano and Sophia.

They would probably be out on their usual squat—the bit of dry sand bar off the end of the Lido. It had formed during the last really big storm, and likely the next one would take it away again, but for now it provided a good spot for clams and drift-wood.

Old Sophia and Chiano. As unlikely a couple as ever decorated the face of the lagoon—Sophia maybe forty and looking four hundred, Chiano ten years older and looking thirty. She had been a bargee's wife, until a fifteen-hundred-ton *roccaforte* with a fol-lowing wind behind it ran down their small barge and sent her man and kids to the bottom. Chiano claimed to be everything from a stranded Sicilian seaman to the Prince of Damascus.

She was the closest thing to a chirurgeon and healer the marshes boasted, and so was inviolate from most of the may-hem that raged among the marsh-dwellers. He proclaimed himself to be the One True Prophet of the Great Mother herself. He was treated with superstitious care, although Marco was sure that if Chiano hadn't lived with Sophia the marsh-dwellers would have burned him out.

The two of them had found Marco, in pain and half delirious—and for some reason known only to themselves picked him up and carted him back to Sophia's hovel, and nursed him back to a sem-blance of health. They'd taught him how to survive, during that vague six-month period during which shock had kept him pliant enough to adapt. He'd paid them back for their care by sharing the scroungings that Benito gave him and writing down Chiano's "prophecies." Chiano induced visions with fly agaric and was obviously then in no condition to record his prophecies himself. Why he wasn't dead twenty times over—well . . .

It was a mystery, like where Chiano came from in the first place, or got the paper, or what he did with the pages after Marco filled them with the "holy words" in his careful, clear hand. Chiano kept him safe too. Chiano wasn't big, but the fear that he really might be a witch helped Chiano keep the swamp-dwellers, who wanted a boy, at bay. The swamp gangs wanted runaway boys as their slaves; Big Gianni wanted them for—other things. All of them were crazy, mostly from chewing blue lotos, and no telling what they would do to someone who got between them and what they wanted. But Chiano stood by him until Marco was big enough to fight back and canny enough to hide from what he could not fight.

Chiano and Sophia were where he expected to find them. They had lit a small fire of driftwood and were grilling fish spitted on reeds over it. They looked like images out of hell; red lit, weather-and-age-twisted faces, avidly watching their cooking dinner.

Marco didn't make much noise, but they heard him anyway. "That you boy?" Chiano called into the dark.

"*Si*. Chiano, I got trouble."

"Boy, the *world* got trouble," replied Chiano easily. "Never-youmind. What's the matter this time? Big Gianni? One of the gangs?"

"Wish it was just that! Somebody jumped me, out at the wharf—a man dressed all in dark clothes, with his face covered, and waiting like he knew I was coming. He had a knife. I think *They*'ve found me."

"Damn! That be trouble and more'n ye need!" Sophia coughed. "You got any notion who They be?"

"No more than I ever did. Could be anybody: slave-takers, Schiopettieri, even . . ."

"Milanese," Chiano growled.

"Damn it all, *no*! Not Milanese; *never* Milanese. Milanese would be trying to help me, not kill me!"

"I'll believe that when I believe . . ." Sophia hushed Chiano before he could say any more.

"Fine," Marco said, "But whose mama was a Montagnard agent, huh? Who saw Duke Visconti's agents coming and going? So who should know?" It was an old argument.

"And whose mama was probably killed by the order of the Duke Visconti she served, hmm? Marco, leave it, boy. I know more politics than you do. Still, I notice you may have thought Strega. But you didn't say it. You off to give Benito a warning?"

"Got to. He's in danger too."

"Boy—" This was another old argument.

Sophia chimed in forcefully. "No buts! Ye're young; this ain't no life for th' young. We'll be all right."

"She's got the right of it, boy." There was a suspicion of mist in Chiano's slightly crazed eyes. "The Words of the Goddess are complete now, thanks to you. You go—"

Chiano claimed the Words were complete about once a month.

"Look, I'll be back, same as always. Benito won't have any safe place for me, and I won't put danger on those as is keeping him."

For the first time in this weekly litany Chiano looked unaccountably solemn. "Somehow—I don't think so—not this time. Well, time's wasting, boy, be off—or They might find Benito before you do."

Sophia's face twisted comically then, as she glanced between Marco and their dinner; she plainly felt obliged to offer him some, and just as plainly didn't really want to have to share the little they had.

"You eaten?" she asked reluctantly.

Marco's stomach churned. The fear and its aftermath made the very thought of food revolting.

"*Grazie*; but no. I'm fine."

She smiled, relieved. "Off wi'ye, then, ye'd best hurry."

Marco went, finding the way back to his raft, and poling it out into the black, open water of the lagoon. In the distance were the lights of Venice. But the tide was out. He would have to pole the channels. At least coming back he would be able to run with the turn of the tide at dawn.

Lots of lights in the city tonight—lots of noise. Marco blessed it all, for it covered his approach. Then remembered—and shame on himself for not remembering before—that it was Solstice Feast. What night of the Feast it was, he couldn't remember; his only calendars were the moon and stars these days, and the seasons. By the noise, probably well into the festival. But that meant Benito would be delayed by the crowds on the bridges and walkways. That might prove a blessing; it gave him a chance to check all around their meeting place under the wharf for more of *Them*.

He poled all over beneath the wharf, between the maze of pilings, keeping all his senses alert for anything out of the norm. There wasn't anyone lying in ambush that he could find, not by eye nor ear nor scent, so he made the raft fast and climbed up into their meeting place among the crossbeams out near the end of the wharf.

The first time they'd met here—after Marco had slipped into the town with his heart pounding like an overworked drum, and passed Theodoro a note to give to Benito—they hadn't said much. Benito had just wrapped his arms around his brother like he'd never let go, and cried his eyes sore and his voice hoarse. Marco had wanted to cry too—but hadn't dared; Benito would have been shattered. That was the way the first few meetings had gone.

But boys are resilient creatures. Before too long, Benito was begging for Marco's stories again, and the tears only came at parting—and then not at all. But now the stories included another set—how they would find the agents of Duke Visconti; get Mama's message to them. The original paper was long gone, but the contents resided intact in Marco's head—and what Marco memorized was there for good and all. That was why Mama had taken him everywhere with her—when she'd ask later, he'd recite what had been said and done. And just as a precaution, Marco had made plenty of copies of that paper over the last two years. He made a new one as soon as the previous copy began deteriorating, and kept it with him at all times, mostly hidden on his raft. One day, they'd get that message back to Milan—and the Visconti would rescue them, take them home to Milan, and train them to be noblemen. Benito hadn't liked that story as much as the tales about the steelworks in Ferrara, and the doings of their grandfather the famous Old Fox, but it had comforted Marco.

When had Benito started scrounging for him? Marco wrinkled his brow in thought, and picked at the splintery beams under him, staring at the stars reflected in the wavelets in the harbor. Must have been that winter—that was it; when he'd showed up, as usual, in nothing but his trousers, shivering, and pretending he wasn't cold. Benito had looked at him sharply, then cuddled up real close, and not just for his own comfort; he'd put his little body between Marco and the wind. Next meeting, Benito'd brought a woolen cloak—old, faded, snagged, and torn, but better than anything

Marco could get in the Jesolo. After that he'd never come to a meeting empty-handed, though Marco refused to ask him for anything.

Lord knew he needed those meetings himself; needed the comfort, needed to hold someone, to talk to somebody sane. Chiano and Sophia were only sane sometimes. He'd needed company even more than the material comforts Benito brought, and he needed those desperately.

He waited. And waited. But before the largest bell at San Marco pealed, he had to leave to cross the lagoon. The uncertainty and fear it brought gnawed at him.

As he always did at times like this, he thought about magic. Chiano was a magician—a master of his craft, if one believed the stories he told when he was around Marco and felt no need to be cautious, or the cheap rotgut he brewed went to his head. Perhaps no one but Marco and Sophia did, though, because he never used magic much anymore. "Too dangerous," he said, and it went without saying that he was probably right. Someone had certainly tried to kill Chiano, leaving him wandering senseless in the marshes, and his magic hadn't protected him any. Of course, if the people who'd beaten him had been wearing steel armor, his magic wouldn't have been much use against them.

Chiano claimed that people—other magicians—could tell when magicians were casting a spell, what kind it was, where the magician was, and even who was doing the casting. That was why it was too dangerous for him to use magic unless there was no other choice. But then, there was Marco.

Marco could be a magician; that's what Chiano said. He was perfectly willing to teach Marco everything he knew. There was just one little problem with that: Chiano was Strega, and Marco was Christian—and not just any Christian, but one who had been indoctrinated by his mother in the Pauline creed. It was a sin for any Pauline who was not an ordained priest to dabble in magic, for only a priest was sufficiently armored in holiness to withstand the blandishments of the Evil One, who was always on the watch for magicians to tempt them into using their powers for selfish purposes. It was, according to everything Marco had been taught, a short step from selfishness into real, black sin. And it was doubly, triply, impossible for a true Christian to even think of using Strega magic. Marco was already deep enough in sin as it was, associating with the pagans.

But life would have been so much easier with the help of a little magic . . . a little magic to tease the fish into his traps, a little magic to keep him warm in the winter, a little magic to protect him—

No, he told himself. That was temptation, and behind temptation was the Evil One. Surely God was watching him—well, maybe not God, but an angel, anyway—watching and waiting to see if he fell; and if he fell, washing His hands of Marco, who was not strong enough to resist so minor a temptation.

But oh, it was hard, hard to resist at times like these.

The sounds of Solstice Feast drifted over the water; over there, people thronged the waterways, the streets, the plazas, everyone wearing some sort of mask, even if they couldn't afford a costume. People who had saved all year for this time were stuffing themselves with fatty sausages, bread, rich bean soup, Salame, Mortadella, Cotechino, still-steaming loaves of ciabatta, thick fragrant zuppa di fagioli—

Don't think of food!

With Lent on the horizon, they were throwing themselves into pleasure.

Pleasure leads to temptation, and temptation to sin, he reminded himself. But even Mama's stern Dell'este family had enjoyed Solstice Feast. And when Mama had come here to Venice, she had made certain that at Solstice Feast there had been masks and costumes for all three of them, and that at least once during the three days of the festival they had all gone out together, to see the stilt-walkers, the jugglers, the musicians, even a puppet-show or a play. She always seemed to know what great house was giving away food after a feast, too—wonderful food, bread as white as could be, soaked with the juice of the meat the great folks had eaten, piecrust heavy with gravy with bits of mushroom and venison clinging to it, the broken sweetmeats of marchpane and sweet cake—

Don't think of food!!

Faintly the sound of singing floated over the marsh, and Marco bit his lip, overwhelmed for a moment by loneliness. *Don't think of Mama either.*

There were thousands of people over there, across the lagoon, and somewhere among them was Benito, probably enjoying himself as only Benito could, with or without money.

With never a thought for the death that might be, even now, stalking his path.

Chapter 3

"You are afraid, old man."

The undine called Etheria stared at Chiano with her flat golden eyes, and challenged him to deny his fear. He couldn't. He could only hang his head and nod.

"I am afraid," he admitted. It was always better to admit the truth to the elemental creatures, at least the ones that he had regular congress with. Some of them were damnably good at ferreting out lies. He stared at his dirty, bare feet, at the grasses and reeds of the hummock on which he perched, and heard the undine sigh.

"You should *be afraid,"* she said, grudgingly, and he looked up. She settled her arms and upper back against the hummock across from him, looking like some odd and exotic courtesan relaxing upon the divan in her salon. Her hair was just beginning to dry along her hairline, and it frizzed out in little filamentous green kinked strands.

"Tell me, please?" he asked, humbly. Humility; it was a new emotion to him, or rather, new to the person he had begun to reassemble from the bits and pieces of his past. He remembered the confidence, bordering on arrogance. *What do the Christians say? Pride goeth before a fall.*

Etheria didn't show emotions in the way that a human would, for the undine's face was less mobile, more fishlike—but she was clearly as afraid as he was. *"First—there are* things, *evil things that can change their shape, in the lagoon, snooping about the Jesolo, and in the canals. There have always been such things, but more often*

46

now; and much, much more evil. At first, we think, they looked for you, but you worked little magic, very little, and they may believe you are no more. Now they prowl more freely—when we do not find them first." She bared her sharklike teeth. *"They are no match for us. But we think that one day, perhaps soon, something stronger will come."*

Chiano shuddered. "Why?"

The undine studied him. *"There is more blood in the water, of late. More bodies. There is more fear on the water; we can taste it, hear it in the voices of the fishermen, the boatmen. The world of you humans is fragmenting, and we do not know why."* She licked her lips, but not in anticipation. *"When you mortals are at war, we suffer too, for your world affects ours. As below, so above."*

"As above, so below," Chiano sighed. He knew. Whatever happened in the spirit world was reflected in the material world, and vice versa. If there was trouble here below, there would be trouble in *their* world as well. If something evil came to prey upon humans, evil that preyed upon those who were not human would be attracted. Unnatural death brought unnatural destruction.

"The Silvani—can they tell me anything more?" he asked at last, when it was clear that Etheria had nothing more to give him.

"Perhaps. I know of one who will come if I do call her. And you might be wise not to call one yourself." At last the undine's expression softened. *"It is little enough for all that you have done for me and mine."*

He reached for the taloned hand she offered. "There will be no talk of debts between us, sister-of-the-waters. Perhaps—"

"When you have found yourself again," the undine said firmly. *"You must find yourself again."*

She took her cool hand from his, patted him on the head as if he was a child, and slipped beneath the water. Left to await the Silvani, Chiano shook like a reed in the wind. *Again. Again that call to "find myself."* His memories were still clouded; there were still key fragments missing, things that might protect him so that he could work magics safely again. He had known so much—and now it was all in pieces, shattered, and somehow he had to put the pieces together again. *Someone* had feared him enough to want him dead, and the self-confident and—yes, arrogant—person he remembered being was the sort who could attract such enemies. He who was Grimas of *stregheria,* the master of the three magics of stars, moon and earth—yes, evil would come looking for him, and he was bound to combat it. But he was a warrior whose sword lay shattered, his shield broken in two, and his courage beaten to the ground.

But he could pray; he could still pray.

Carmina, Agenoria, help me find my skills again! Fortuna, guard me! Nortia, give me back my memories! Fana and Fanus, Tana and Tanus, Jana and Janus, restore what I once had, and oh Aradia, help me protect this place again!

He hugged his knees to his chest and rocked back and forth in an agony of fear and longing—the longing to be himself again, and the fear of what must surely follow if he ever regained what he had lost. He didn't notice the Silvani until she brushed against his hair and blew into his face to attract his attention.

Then he looked up. If he had not had such an affinity with water-creatures, the Silvani surely would have been his favorites; they appeared as lovely girls, not more than two feet tall, dressed all in red and winged. This one hovered just barely above the water, wings blurring to keep her there, and regarded him with wide eyes.

"What would you, old man?" she whispered. "I think I know you."

"I wish that I remembered," he replied sadly. "Just—of your courtesy, what do you know of the evil our friend tells me is abroad in the city?"

"More than I wish to," she replied in a breath. "Something terrible has come, bound in a strong box of iron and guarded by men in steel, hedged about with spell and sword. *We* dare draw no nearer to it than the island on which it dwells."

For once, he felt a stirring of hope. There were enough Christian mages in the city, surely there was no need for one broken old man! "If it is hedged about—" he began.

"The hedges are ... peculiar," the Silvani said, frowning severely. "And among the guardians at least one is unclean. Perhaps more." The Silvani looked so human it was easy to read their expressions, and this one assumed an air of pleading. "Let me speak for those of the air, the Silvani, the Laura, the Folletti and Folletto—you *must* come again into your powers! The path of the future is shrouded, and the one who veils it from us is—" She shivered, and clearly was not willing to say more.

Well, he could hardly blame her. He suspected he knew the name she would not speak, even though he could not remember it himself. Did not, indeed, *want* to remember it. But he had a momentary image of something huge and monstrous, squatting in a dark forest littered with rotting tree stumps and shattered bones, devouring . . .

The image fled. Or, perhaps, he fled from it.

"Thank you," he said, his spirits sinking. There was no choice then; it would be more of the rue and the fennel and the fly agaric; more of the visions to sort through looking for what was memory and what was hallucination . . .

The Silvani took his thanks as a farewell, and vanished, leaving him once more alone.

Chiano remained on the hummock for some time thereafter, thinking through his course of action. By sunset, he had come to one definite conclusion.

He would have to take steps to protect Marco. He could sense that the boy would not remain in the Jesolo for much longer. In the marshes, Chiano had been able to shield the boy as well as shelter him. The marsh locos were afraid of Chiano—Chiano, and his undine friends. The undines would not voluntarily leave the water, true. And so what? No dweller in the Jesolo could avoid approaching the water, within easy reach of a lurking undine. Not even crazed and vicious Big Gianni was willing to risk *their* anger.

But if Marco returned to the city, the undines would be of no use. The elemental creatures rarely even entered the canals, for they found the city's waters very unpleasant. And they would not be able to protect the boy, anyway, from the perils he would encounter there.

Not now, for a certainty. Venice would have been dangerous for Marco under any circumstances. But now, with a new assassination attempt having been launched against him, the city was ten times more dangerous than ever. Chiano's memory was still too fragmented to understand the exact nature of that danger. But, in truth, that hardly mattered. Chiano had long ago understood Marco's true identity. For *that* boy, with *that* lineage, deadly threats could come from any direction.

No, the undines would no longer make suitable guardians. City assassins were not marsh locos. They did not have to perch by the water every day for their sustenance.

And . . . Chiano was not ready yet—if he would ever be—to return himself.

So. Practical steps. If necessary, bloody steps. And he had the perfect instrument for the task, right here at hand in the marshes. In that, too, he understood, the Goddess was giving him a sign. And a gentle warning: *no more softness.*

He even understood, to a degree, the Goddess's insistent and unusual hardness. Marco *had* to be protected. Not so much for his own sake, but for that of Venice. Chiano wasn't sure exactly why—yet—but he knew it was so. From the very first moment he had laid eyes on Marco, he had seen the great shadow which the slender boy cast in the spirit world. Venice would need that shadow, some day, of that he was certain. And he was certain of it because Chiano himself cast a similar shadow—or had once, at least. But never as wide, never as broad, never as deep.

Chiano sighed. He knew what to do, and how to do it. Even though that doing was . . . distasteful. Even, in the end, perhaps wicked.

No more softness, old man!

Oh yes, and he'd gotten his little tail well scorched, had the former Swiss mercenary turned fanatic assassin. Fortunato Bespi had been dying when the undines had fished him out and brought him to Chiano. It would have made a pretty wager, whether shock or drowning would have gotten him first.

Neither did. Chiano and Sophia had patched him up and kept him dosed against fever. He had been bleeding from blade wounds, and burned all over. From what Chiano and Sophia had been able to piece together from the man's semi-incoherent ravings, he had fought off his assailants until they set fire to the house he had barricaded himself in. Even then, apparently, the man had been able to escape and try to find shelter in the marshes, which were the traditional refuge for Venice's outcasts and outlaws.

Eventually, Chiano had been able to glean his identity from the ravings. And, when he did, had come very close to killing the man himself.

Fortunato Bespi! Of all men! If Sophia hadn't restrained him, Chiano would probably have rolled the man back into the waters. This time, with his throat slit and a weight around his ankles.

Fortunato Bespi! Even with his broken memory, Chiano had recognized the name immediately.

Bespi was notorious. Perhaps the best—certainly the most

ruthless—Montagnard assassin in all of northern Italy. A fanatic, by all accounts. A true believer, not simply a sellsword. A man so dangerous that, apparently, the Montagnards themselves had decided to kill him. Such, at least, was the explanation Chiano had eventually deduced from the words Bespi muttered in the days of his slow healing.

But . . . Sophia had been firm. So she and Chiano had hidden the badly injured man on one of the firmer reed-islands, under a basket made to look like a reed-hummock. Sophia, with her own eccentric "theology," had insisted that the spirits had brought Bespi to them for a purpose. And, over time, Chiano had come to half-believe it himself.

And was glad he had, for it was now clear that Sophia had been right all along. Who better to guard Marco from assassins than Fortunato Bespi?

It remained only to . . . begin the transformation. And he needed to begin immediately, because the transformation would take many weeks to complete.

Chiano found Bespi where he expected to find him—squatting on his little island in the reeds, staring at an insect. Bespi did very little else, since he'd finally begun recovering from his injuries. He stared at everything; studied the most insignificant things for hours on end. A man betrayed by the cause he had devoted his life to was trying, Chiano understood, to find meaning in *something*. Even if it was only the reason that an insect climbed a stalk of grass.

Chiano made no attempt to approach silently. It would have been pointless, anyway. Whatever else Bespi had lost, he had certainly not lost his assassin's reflexes and senses. By the time Chiano appeared in the little clearing where Bespi squatted, the former assassin was awaiting his arrival. Staring at him with the same intentness he stared at everything.

Bespi wanted *reasons*. Chiano would give them to him.

He held out his hand. "You must begin to eat these also now. With the other food we bring you."

Bespi's burn-scarred face held no expression. He simply stared at the fly agaric and belladonna in Chiano's outstretched palm. He said nothing.

"You are not who you think you are," continued Chiano softly.

"I have discovered your true name and your true purpose, in my visions. Now you must discover them also. These will help."

He said nothing further. Simply allowed Bespi the time to examine the possibility of *reasons*.

Eventually, as Chiano had known he would, Bespi reached out and took the substances. He did not ingest them, simply held them in a loose fist. But Chiano knew that Bespi would begin eating them with his next meal.

There was no expression on the assassin's face. Chiano had not expected to see one. Bespi was an empty man; Chiano would fill him.

He felt some qualms in so doing, but not many. It was, after all, mostly a change in orientation, not in nature. *This*, without a doubt, was what the Goddess had intended when She'd caused Bespi to be stranded out here. Chiano was sure of it. He rose, and began to turn away. He would return later that night, once Bespi was well into the trance, and begin the transformation.

Bespi's first and only words that day stopped him. "What is my true name, then?" he asked, in a whisper. "They told me it was Fortunato Bespi."

Chiano hesitated. Then, squared his shoulders and turned back to meet the hollow eyes. "They lied. Your true name is Harrow."

"A hard name," murmured Bespi. His lips seemed to tighten. But not with distaste so much as—anticipation.

Chapter 4

Kat closed the door of the Church of St. Hypatia di Hagia Sophia behind her. It shut off the riot of the Feast quite as effectively as one of her old tutor *Dottore* Marina's silence-spells would have done. The thought, as always, brought melancholy. She missed the *dottore* terribly. Still, after all these years.

This was a church designed to be full of light and space; the floor was of cream-colored stone, the timbers and woodwork of light ash. Even the wall frescos were painted so that the background colors recalled the white buildings and brilliant blue skies of ancient Alexandria, and the windows held clear, not colored, glass. There was discreet gilding everywhere so that the light of sun or candles was multiplied. The moment she entered the place, her spirits lifted.

With her footsteps echoing on the pale marble of the floor, she walked slowly around the walls until she came to the choir stalls. The whole church was empty except for herself and a few of the members of the Hypatian Order. By their white linen robes, they were all full siblings, sworn to chastity and celibacy, and very probably magicians. Somehow that made her feel safer than she had felt in days, as if, no matter what horrible magics were running loose along the canals and the back streets, nothing could come in here.

She eased into the choir stalls and knelt with her hands clasped before her on the rail, the familiar frescos of the life of Saint Hypatia glowing on the wall opposite her. They weren't the most beautiful frescos in Venice; they'd been painted by a mere pupil of Bellini, not the master himself. They had heart, though; that

was what Kat loved about them. Lucia Astolanza must have felt
a special kinship for Saint Hypatia of Alexandria to have infused
so much life into them.

In a procession around the walls were the important events of
Hypatia's life. Nearest the door at the back of the church, in the
first panel, she lectured on Neoplatonic philosophy to her pupils.
Not yet a Christian, Hypatia was shown garbed in Grecian robes
with a laurel wreath crowning her close-braided hair to represent
her great learning. Her pupils at her feet. Unlike many painters,
Lucia had given this part of Hypatia's life as much importance as
the incidents after her conversion.

Next, of course, the Unknown Shepherd Boy appeared for one
of her lectures, debating her in front of her amazed pupils, and
ultimately convincing her and all of her pupils as well that Christianity was a logical extension of her own beliefs. Lucia had, inter-
estingly enough, portrayed the Unknown Shepherd with a faint
beard, the halo of Sanctity, and the Dove of the Holy Spirit above
his head, hinting that the Shepherd was actually a visitation of
Christ. Very daring; rather an interpretation that Kat herself favored.

The next panel was more complicated, showing, on the right
side, Hypatia lecturing to her pupils on the melding of Christianity
with Neoplatonism into a new and inspiring philosophy. On the
left, their faces scowling, were the Archbishop of Alexandria and
his followers. Lucia had painted them in colors and shadows that
suggested prejudice, close-mindedness, and treachery as they plotted
Hypatia's murder. Their bitterness at her pulling more and more
of their own congregation into her new flock and undermining
their views was masterfully portrayed.

The next panel, the last on that wall, showed the Miracle.
Hypatia being surrounded on the steps of the Great Library of
which she was the Librarian by the followers of the Archbishop.
They carried razor-sharp shards of clam and oyster shells in their
hands, which they intended to use to slice her to ribbons. Hypatia
stood facing them calmly, lips parted, presumably in prayer. She
was not praying for herself; she prayed for *them.* She prayed that
they should receive Hagia Sophia, Holy Wisdom—the Truth, as
only a Neoplatonist would mean it.

The first panel on the altar wall showed the moment of the
Miracle itself, the moment when Hypatia's prayer was answered,
and God (shown in the form of hundreds of rays of painstakingly

applied gold leaf emanating from a cloud above Hypatia's head) touched the minds of the would-be murderers. They saw the Truth, only too surely; *all* the Truth, about everything in the world, all at once, shoved into their narrow little minds until their skulls practically cracked with it. Lucia showed this with the shards of shell falling from their hands, the bulging eyes, the slackened mouths, the knees bent in a way that suggested they were losing physical as well as mental balance. Hypatia was in the same pose still as in the panel before, but the Dove of the Holy Spirit hovered over her, now. Kat had more than once thought that Lucia had painted just the faintest of smiles on her lips, and a knowing glint in her eyes.

Kat wondered, as she had before, how much of the scene depicted was truly accurate. From things which she remembered *Dottore* Marina telling her, she suspected that the defeat of Hypatia's enemies had probably been a lot messier and more complicated than the artist's portrayal of it. And involved more in the way of intrigue and maneuver—perhaps even violence—than the purely spiritual portrayal of the victory which was depicted on the wall of the church.

Farther down the wall, behind Kat, were the John Chrysostom panels. The first showed Hypatia in her study, writing to her fellow Christian philosopher. The two had formed an alliance, a meeting of minds that would steer the course of the Christian Church from that moment.

Again, Kat suspected that the portrayals were . . . sanctified quite a bit, with all the rough edges smoothed away. She knew, for one thing—her former teacher had told her once—that Chrysostom's bigotry against Jews had been the cause of frequent clashes between him and Hypatia. The famous alliance between the two theologians had not been as harmonious and trouble-free as the frescoes made it seem. The fact that the figure of the prophet Muhammad was included in the panel alongside the Jews and pagans made it obvious to Kat that the artist had given scant heed to picayune historical accuracy. Muhammad had not even been born until a century after Hypatia's death.

She smiled, for a moment. She thought that most historical accounts were probably like that: "cleaned up," as it were.

She leaned back and studied the ceiling. In the fresco above, Lucia showed Hypatia, silver-haired but still beautiful, being welcomed into Heaven by the Dove, surrounded by the ancient Prophets, Christ and the Madonna—and Muhammad, again!—along with a host of angels, peris, and figures that bore more than a passing resemblance to Plato, Socrates, and other pagan philosophers. She held in her hands the Library that she had guarded all her life, the Library that would have been burned to the ground if not for the Miracle, presenting it to God as representative of her life's work. If the Library *had* burned, all of the knowledge of the workings of magic that brought people from all over the world to study in Alexandria would have been lost forever. There would be no shining Order of Hypatia and the Siblings who studied magic and used it to defeat the powers of darkness.

Given the current situation, Kat found herself wondering if that would have been so bad, after all . . . for if there was no Order of Hypatia, there would also be no Servants of the Holy Trinity.

Don't be an idiot. If that knowledge had been lost, we'd all be worshipping Chernobog right this very minute.

Without the knowledge of the Library, the evil magicians of the barbaric North and East would have had it all their own way, and their warriors, disorganized as they were, would still have conquered everything now ruled by Emperor Charles Fredrik. They'd probably be storming the gates of Venice at this moment.

Still, Hypatia and Chrysostom hadn't prevailed, not completely. They weren't as ruthless as their foes within the Church, the followers of Saint Paul. If they had been, there wouldn't be the fanatical Order of Saint Paul, nor its offshoots, the Servants of the Holy Trinity and the Knights of the Holy Trinity, with their Inquisitions and their purgings.

What were you thinking? Kat asked the image of Hypatia silently. *Why did you have to be so—so diplomatic and conciliatory? They wouldn't have been if they'd gotten the upper hand! You and Chrysostom would have been walled up in hermit's cells in the desert "for the good of your souls"! And why were you so compromising with Augustine? Without him, there never would have been a Pauline creed at all.*

Hypatia's painted image didn't answer, and Kat sighed. She was no theologian, and this was getting her nowhere. She needed to talk to someone older and wiser. If she could have turned the clock back, her first choice would have been *Dottore* Marina. For all that he'd only come twice a week, in the evenings, *Dottore* Marina had been the one among her her tutors who had always seemed to understand. She still remembered the fight between her mother and her grandfather about his teaching her at all.

Her grandfather had insisted. For all that it was many years ago, she could still remember what he'd bellowed. "He is one of the Doge's own librarians! Yes, he is Magister Magi, and a Strega to boot. Saint Hypatia, woman! The child needs a bit of broadness in her education. And no one in all Venice has more broadness than *Dottore* Marina! Even Metropolitan Michael says he is a great scholar of Christian philosophy."

At first she'd been a little afraid of this "pagan" her mother had muttered about. But he'd been a good tutor, kindly and patient. He stuck out from all the rest like a beacon. He *listened*, for one thing. And, for another, she could use—today, in a way she hadn't needed then—the *dottore*'s understanding of the dangerous complexities of Venetian politics.

But . . . he was gone; had been for several years. So one of the Hypatian counselors would have to do. At least she knew she could trust *them* to keep what she said under the Seal of Counsel. That was more than could be said of the counselors of some of the other orders.

Especially the Servants of the Holy Trinity.

She got up and left the choir stalls, returning to the rear of the church to the line of three enclosed closets where someone in need of counsel could speak with one of the siblings anonymously. She dropped the curtain across the doorway and sat down on the thin cushion over the bench inside, waiting for someone to speak to her on the other side of the scrim-covered window. Compared to the brightness outside in the church it was dim in here. Dim and cool.

She didn't have to wait for very long. A male voice, one she didn't recognize, the intonation slightly foreign, coughed, then said: "Peace be with you, my child. How may I counsel you?"

A very good question, that. "I'm not sure how to start, Brother," she said, in frustration. "It's all gone so horribly wrong!"

"You might start with *what* has gone wrong," the voice replied helpfully. "Although from the sound of your voice, I fear that you are going to tell me that it is everything."

"It very nearly is." She tried to keep the bitterness out of her voice, but it was still there. "But most of it is nothing I had any control over—and it's the situation *now* that I need advice with."

"If it has any bearing on the present, I should like to hear it anyway." The voice sounded patient, but Kat wondered about her own patience level. *I'll sound self-pitying and whiny, I know I will.* Despite that a sibling wasn't supposed to let such things color his counsel, she couldn't help feeling that it would make her look— well, unpleasantly petty.

But the counselor had asked, and you weren't supposed to hold back. Kat took a deep breath and started. She did her level best to keep the nasal complaint out of her own voice that she heard so often in her sister-in-law's.

She tried keeping things as brief as possible, but the voice interrupted gently from time to time, asking more questions about her father, her grandfather, and her own studies as a girl with a private tutor, dwelling on *Dottore* Marina for reasons she couldn't fathom.

Still, that segued very nicely into the current situation. "That was why—I remembered *Dottore* Marina seeming so *good* you see— that when we needed money, we began delivering things for the Strega, and not just the Jewish community. My . . . family has always brought in some cargo that the Doge's *Capi di Contrada* never saw. You know, Counselor: every trader in Venetia does a little. At first it was just because of the duties I think. Then, when the Sots— I mean, the Servants of the Trinity—began to have more influence on the Doge it was to avoid possible persecution. Then *Dottore* Marina just vanished. . . ." She paused.

"Then?" prompted her counselor, gently.

Kat took a deep breath. "Then the Strega I knew became very frightened and needed me to get things for them more than ever. We made more money from them. And we became more reliant on it."

"Did they ever ask you to obtain things of a"—the voice paused delicately—"dubious nature?"

"No, I don't think so. I don't know, of course, what some of the things were . . . still, even the best of things can be put to evil use, Counselor. But I always wear the Saint Hypatia medallion that my father gave me—it's supposed to warn me when there's evil magic around—or that's what the sibling who bespelled it for him told him—"

She paused; was that too superstitious for this counselor? What if the medal was bogus?

But— "Quite right," the voice replied. "If there had been evil in what you handled, you would have felt the medallion grow warm, even hot, depending upon the strength of it. You should be certain to continue to wear it at all times."

Kat bit her lip; should she tell him about the warning it *had* given her when the Knots and the Sots brought that shrouded box into the embassy? It had been so hot even when she'd gone under water that she'd been surprised the water hadn't boiled, and equally surprised that there wasn't a burn on her chest.

"So, the Strega have not asked you to convey anything for an evil purpose?"

"No. Well, I don't think so. It's because of the persecution. The preaching outside their houses and shops. But—we don't dare take their commissions any more and I don't know what to do!" she cried. "If they aren't asking *me* to help them in dark magics, then why are the Servants saying that dark magic is all they do? And if the Servants are wrong, why is the Doge going along with what they tell him to do? The next package I carry might get me arrested. If that happens grandfather will go mad, and the House will be ruined. W*hy* is everyone letting the Servants do what they want, anyway? They aren't Venetian, they aren't even Petrine! Why are they doing this to Venice? Why has everyone gone crazy? How am I going to keep my family from getting destroyed by all of this insanity?"

The last came out in a wail, and she clapped her hands over her mouth, only belatedly realizing that she had blurted out far more than she should have.

But the voice only asked, curiously, "Before *Dottore* Marina disappeared . . . Had he said anything to you that makes you think now that he was warning you he was intending to leave?"

The Counselor seemed entirely fixated on *Dottore* Marina— which caused Kat to reply in a flash of irritation: "No. If he did, it was years ago when I was only fourteen and I don't remember. And even if I did, what has that to do with *my* difficulties *today*? You remember—the ones you're counseling me with?"

There was a faint sound from the other side of the scrim; something like a muffled snort of amusement, and it didn't sound male, it sounded female.

Well, maybe this counselor was new to the task, and was being overseen by an Elder Sister. If that was the case—Kat felt some of her annoyance fade. He must have gotten distracted. Maybe he even knew *Dottore* Marina and was trying to find out what had happened to him.

"I beg your pardon, my child," said the voice apologetically.

"All *anyone* knows is that *Dottore* Marina just disappeared one night," she told him earnestly. "I know; I've asked all over in the years that have gone by since, and no one knows what happened to him. He wasn't even—" she gulped "—found—floating."

"Ah." Just that one syllable, but it held a world of disappointment.

"But what am *I* supposed to do?" she continued stubbornly. "My House depends on me; how am I going to help them when I can't even tell from moment to moment what next piece of insanity is going to threaten us?"

Silence. "If I told you to trust in God, I suspect you would be tempted to throttle me through the scrim," the voice said dryly, which surprised a tense and strangled giggle out of her. "Nevertheless, that is all you *can* do for now. But child, believe me when I tell you that God and his angels are *not* far from us, that they move to protect us at those moments when we have given the last of ourselves and have no more to give. I know. I have seen it."

There was something in his tone that sobered her; she couldn't doubt him, not for a second. He *had* seen such interventions.

Not that the Archangel Raphael is likely to drop out of the clouds bearing one of our lost ships in his hands . . .

"You and yours are in the exceedingly uncomfortable position of being sardines in a sea in which great sharks are maneuvering," the voice went on. "I cannot at this moment give you any counsel that will make you any safer."

Her heart sank into her shoes, but the counselor wasn't done, yet.

"I *can* advise you that regular counseling—here—will not only be of aid to your soul, but might also be of benefit to your secular self. While I may not have any advice other than what I have given you today, there is no saying whether something the order learns might not be of benefit to you on the morrow, or next week." He uttered a dry little laugh. "After all, our blessed Hypatia herself was no mean politician; it will certainly be in the tradition of the order."

Her spirits lifted a little. At least this brother—whoever he was—had a firm grasp not only on sacred matters, but on secular, and he wasn't afraid to give advice on both sides of life. "All right, Brother," she said, feeling as if she was making some kind of a bargain. "I'll make a point of being—more regular in my devotions."

"Go in peace, my child," came the standard response, signaling the end of a session.

Once the sound of the girl's footsteps on the marble had ended with the opening and closing of the door, the priest emerged, moving with a pronounced limp. Sister Evangelina followed, her lips compressed over the laugh that threatened to burst through them.

"I don't know that I've ever seen anyone put you so firmly in your place, Eneko," she finally said, eyes twinkling merrily.

"I'm overjoyed that you found it all so amusing, Gina," he said dryly. "If I have brought a little humor into your humdrum existence, my life has not been lived in vain."

He stared at the heavy doors through which the girl had left the church, his face tight with calculation. After a moment, the sister at his side cleared her throat.

"She spoke under the anonymity of counseling, Eneko." The woman's tone was half-admonitory, half . . . almost fearful.

The priest twitched his shoulders irritably. "I am well aware of that."

Apparently, the answer did not satisfy Evangelina. "You may not—"

He waved her silent with an abrupt motion. "Please! I have no intention of violating the sanctity of counseling. I just wish I knew who she was. If we could find out *anything* about what happened to *Dottore* Marina . . ."

For a moment, Evangelina seemed to shrink away from his intent gaze. The priest recognized the expression which lurked half-hidden in her face. He had seen that same expression many times now, in the years since he received what he thought of as his "calling." Respect for his well-known learning and piety, combined with uneasiness—almost fear—at the intensity of his convictions.

He suppressed a sigh. Then, managed a smile. Whatever else he was, Eneko Lopez de Onez y Guipúzcoa was also a superb politician. He needed to maintain good relations with the Petrine clergy in Venice, whatever his misgivings concerning the laxity of their faith.

"Please relax, Gina. I assure you—again—that I have no intention of violating the sanctity of counseling. I neither asked the girl's name nor did I make any attempt to see her face. I have no idea who she is—I wouldn't even recognize her on the street if she walked past me."

Evangelina's lips quirked. "You'd recognize her voice readily enough, if you heard it again. Don't deny it, Eneko!" A soft laugh emerged from her throat. "Your acuity is already a byword in Venice, even in the short time since the Grand Metropolitan sent you here."

Lopez returned her words with a rueful little smile of his own. "True enough," he admitted. "It's odd, really. As a young man, before that cannonball ruined my leg, I was rather notorious for being hard of hearing. But since I gave up a soldier's life—"

He broke off, twitching his shoulders with exasperation. "I'm hardly likely to encounter her again in casual conversation, Gina! So I think you may set your fears to rest. I am simply, as always, frustrated by the lack of clarity which seems to surround everything in this city. I can't tell you how much I wish the Grand Metropolitan had allowed me to go on pilgrimage to the Holy Land, instead of sending me here."

He stared at the door through which the girl—whoever she was—had left the church, his lips pursing. "And that young lady was quite right. The things her family transports may not in themselves be evil. Tomb-dust is not evil. But it *can* be put to evil use, and I do not share her naïve belief that all Strega are simply harmless healers. It is good that she has her medallion, but—as you well know—magic can be shielded from detection by other magic."

He rubbed his crippled leg, in an old and absentminded manner. "I just wish it were all less . . . murk and shadows."

The sister laughed, a bit ruefully. "It *is* a foggy city, after all, as often as not."

Eneko shared in the laughter and then produced still more laughter by recounting several amusing anecdotes concerning the ways in which a rural Basque priest had often found the metropolis of Venice a most confusing place. By the end, whatever doubts Sister Evangelina might have had concerning his own intentions seemed dispelled.

She departed, thereafter, leaving Eneko alone. He drifted over to the wall where the frescoes depicted John Chrysostom, the Golden Preacher, and stared up at the panels. A few minutes later, he heard the footsteps of two other men coming into the church.

He did not turn around. Eneko Lopez knew those footsteps as well as he knew the arhythmic sound which his own limp produced.

He gestured with his chin toward the frescoes above him. "He was a false man, you know, in many ways. Intemperate, harsh, often arrogant, full of error and wrong-headedness. Still, they made him a saint. And do you know why?"

He swiveled his head to bring his companions under his gaze. Diego and Pierre said nothing. After a moment, Eneko looked away.

"They made him a saint," Eneko said harshly, "because whatever his faults the Golden Preacher understood one thing clearly. There is such a thing in this world as *evil*. Not simply—"

The next words came out almost like a curse: "—error and misunderstanding."

Brother Pierre spoke, in his heavy Savoyard accent. "True enough. And what is your point, Eneko?"

The Basque priest's lips twisted wryly. Then, he turned his head again and looked at the other priest.

"Brother Diego, I need you to begin an investigation. I have been led to believe that the Strega Grand Master was once the tutor for a girl in this city. Fourteen years old, she was, when he disappeared. Find out who that girl is. It should not be too difficult. Only a very wealthy and prominent family could have afforded his services as a private tutor—and would have dared employ him, for that matter."

Brother Diego nodded. "What was the source of your information? That might help me in my search."

"I have no doubt that it would. I also have no doubt that you don't wish to know."

Diego looked at the counseling booths. Sighed. "Can you offer me any other clues?"

"And how do we know she is not a witch herself?" asked Pierre.

Eneko smiled faintly. "Oh, I think not. Whatever that girl might be, I rather doubt you will find a witch."

"You never know," countered Diego. "We are surrounded by evil here."

The Basque nodded, his eyes returning to the frescoes. "No, you don't; and yes, we are. Still—"

The hawk eyes of John Chrysostom gazed down upon him. He did not seem to find the weight of them hard to bear. Not in the least. "Still, I doubt you will find a witch there."

Casa Montescue looked—from the outside—as if it belonged to one of the wealthiest families in all Venice. It was only once you got inside, thought Katerina bleakly, that you realized what a hollow front that was. She walked the long corridor moodily. It was a case of too much grandeur . . . and too little upkeep. Show was very important in Venice, but more than one *Case Vecchie* family had found that keeping up appearances could be ruinous. This place needed an army of servants just to keep it clean. Without them it deteriorated fast. There had been six upstairs maids when she was a child. Her father had once told her there'd been ten when he was young.

Her musing was cut by the sound of her grandfather's voice.

"—nothing to do with us! It was Fortunato Bespi who killed her. He was a Montagnard assassin. She must have fallen out with her masters."

Another voice, higher pitched. "Nonetheless you spent a great deal of money pursuing her sons, Milord Montescue. Money long outstanding with our house."

The first voice, again: "And now we discover that you just recently hired yet another assassin! Such men do not come cheaply, even incompetents like the ones you apparently employ." There came a snort of derision. "The man's body was found just this morning, you know. Imagine—a blade man *poisoned* by his target. What kind of assassin—"

Kat winced. Grandpapa's obsession with taking his revenge on the Valdosta family disturbed her deeply. More for its unhealthy effects on the old man's state of mind than the Montescue purse. But she hadn't realized he'd started hiring assassins again. And, wincing again, she could just imagine what kind of fumble-fingered dimwits the old man could find with the few coins he had available.

The second voice continued: "We were promised a payment within this month, and that is very nearly at an end. We really don't want to inconvenience such old and valued clients, milord, but the truth is you're far behind."

"We've had a delay," growled Lodovico Montescue. "Not a reverse— a *delay*." He said the words with a confidence which was far from what his granddaughter was feeling about the matter. Grandpapa was talking about the money they'd get from the parcel she'd had to drop into the water outside the Imperial embassy. What if that urchin Benito had stolen it? What if water ruined the contents? What if they couldn't find it?

"Milord. We can't give you endless time . . ." said the unfamiliar voice.

"Damn your eyes, man!" snapped Lodovico. "We've always paid at least the interest. We should have a tranche of cash in the next three days."

"I really hope so, milord. We'd hate to even think of foreclosure."

Katerina turned away. If she went in now she'd tear that moneylender's head off. He was being polite—which, she'd gathered, wasn't normally the case. The trade they were in did make some powerful people beholden to them, people she was sure had protected them in the past. Things must be dire now.

She came back some time later, intent on at least trying to cool her grandfather down. He was sitting at his desk, staring at a piece of paper. Not looking angry, just morose. His craggy face seemed more lined than Kat could ever remember it; his hair, thinner and whiter. Even his dark eyes—almost coal black, normally—seemed muddy-colored.

"What sort of mess are we in, Katerina?" he said grimly. "First that damned moneylender. Now this. They want their 'supplies'— but they're too scared to even sign their names." He waved the letter. "Your great-grandfather always told me 'stay out of politics and stay out of religion. Make money.' But *he* got involved in politics, because he had no choice. And we are involved, against our will, in religion. Still, I think my father's backing of Rome was the start of the rot. He granted the first mortgages."

Kat groped for his meaning. She understood the general point. The principalities of Italy were a maze of shifting alliances. But there were always two poles. Rome—and Milan. The Milanese under the Visconti were, officially at least, Montagnards—believers in one united Christian realm, under the aegis of the Holy Roman Emperor. Not without reason, their neighbors viewed this lofty and always-distant goal as little more than an excuse for the Visconti dynasty's insatiable lust for immediate conquests of territory in northern Italy.

Rome's priorities—which was to say, the priorities of the Grand Metropolitan of Rome—were more nebulous, beyond opposition to having northern Italy absorbed into the Empire. But those priorities had more than once involved taking occasional territory; always for the good of the people, of course. Grandpapa had said before that his father's politics—the Montescues were tradition- ally allied with the "Metropolitans," as the anti-Montagnard fac- tion was called—had gotten *Casa* Montescue into trouble. But she hadn't realized the trouble had extended to their relations with the family's financial supporters.

"It can't be that bad, surely, Grandpapa?"

He sighed. "I'm afraid it can, dearest Kat. Floriano's—and we've borrowed money from Floriano's since I was a boy—have actu- ally started talking about foreclosure."

Kat put an arm around him. The feel of her grandfather's still- broad but bony shoulders brought sadness. She could remember, as a girl, thinking that her grandfather must be the strongest man in the world. "Can't we sell off the farm? Or this place, for that matter? We can't keep it up, anyway."

He shook his head, sadly. "No. The truth to tell, we dare not sell anything. We haven't just borrowed from Floriano's. Much of what we have is double mortgaged. If we show any signs of failing . . . the gull-gropers will be onto the flesh of Montescue and rip it to shreds. There will literally be nothing left. We've been in difficulties for twenty years. . . ."

He leaned back from the desk, pushing himself away with arms that had once been heavy with muscle. Only the size of his hands reflected any longer the strength which had once been a legend in Venice. One of those hands reached around Kat's waist, draw- ing her close.

"The worst of it, of course, has only been in the last three years, since your father left. Vanished at sea. He borrowed heavily for that venture."

She felt the hand squeezing her. The slight tremble in the fingers was heartbreaking. "I don't know what I would do without you, Kat," the old man said softly. "You have been the mainstay of this family since your father . . ." Sadly, and for the first time, he whispered the word: "Died."

Kat didn't know what to say. Her thoughts were fixed entirely on a parcel at the bottom of a canal. Hoping desperately that it was still there; and hoping, just as desperately, that a street urchin named Benito could be relied upon to save the fortune of one of Venice's four oldest and—once—wealthiest and most powerful families.

Chapter 5

When Marco returned, there was no Benito at the dock—just a scrap of dirty paper wedged beneath it. *Got a job. Come tamarra.* Which left Marco to go back to his hide again, wondering if the "job" was a real task, or something Benito made up so he could enjoy another night of the festival.

Or . . . a ruse to lure Benito into the clutches of Them. Surely not. Surely They wouldn't go to all that trouble. Surely Benito would smell a rat if they tried.

By this time, Marco felt faint with hunger, and on his way back to shelter spotted a lone marsh-mallow just at the edge of what he knew to be dangerous mire. He took a chance, and worked his way out to it—but he had to stop just out of reach, when the hungry mud beneath the water sucked at his foot and nearly pulled him down. He stared at it in despair. He hadn't eaten in two days now. . . .

There was no way to reach it.

Choking on tears of frustration, he turned his back on the tantalizing plant, and headed for the hide again.

He crawled inside, too cold to shiver, wrapped a scrap of blanket around himself, and waited for the sun to warm the hide a little. There was just enough room under the lumpy dome for him and a few precious belongings. Sunlight filtered through the mass of enmeshed weeds at the entrance as he got feeling back into his toes and feet. Finally, for lack of anything else to do, he picked through his packets of herbs and oddments to see if he might have left a scrap of food in there.

Nothing. Except a single fishhook and a bit of line, left from the times he had something to bait the hook with.

He paused, with his hand over the packet.

It wouldn't be much of a sin. Maybe not any sin. Even in Milan—

Even in Pauline-dominated Milan, fishermen got blessings on their nets to increase their catch.

But he wasn't a priest, to give such a blessing.

On the other hand, if he passed out from hunger, he wouldn't be able to warn Benito.

Saint Peter—you were a fisherman! Blessed Saint Peter, send me a sign!

There was an angry squawk and a commotion just outside and above his hide—a thump, a splash—

He shoved his head and arm outside, just in time to wave frantically at the gull about to recapture its dinner from the water at his door—lost in a fight with the other two gulls circling overhead. He snatched the hand-sized gray mullet out of the water and withdrew back into his protection as the gull stabbed at him with its beak.

Thank you, Saint Peter!

He took his knife and worried slivers of flesh from the bony fish, eating them raw, and thankful that once again he had been saved from committing a sin.

He spent a terrible, anxious, miserable day in the hide, not even prepared to go and share his fear with Chiano and Sophia. With the dusk he was off to wait again.

This time he was rewarded. There was a pad of bare feet overhead—then tiny sounds that marked someone who knew what he was doing and where he was going, climbing down among the crossbeams.

"Hi, brother?" Benito's whisper.

"Right here."

"Be right with you." A bit of scratching, a rasp of wood on cloth and skin, and someone slipped in beside him with a quick hug, and then pulled away.

"Riot out there tonight. Sorry about yesterday. I couldn't get here in time. I tried but I got held up."

"Benito—I've got to go under cover again. One of *Them* nearly got me yesterday. Assassin. He was waiting for me, Benito. He knew who I was and where I was going. It has to be Them."

Swift intake of breath. "God—no! Not after all this time! How'd you get away?"

"I just—outran him." *Don't let him know what really happened. He'll think he has to share the danger.* Marco had been careful never to let his brother even guess that he'd had to kill—and more than once.

"All right." The voice in the dark took on a new firmness. "That's it. You're not gonna run any more, big brother. Running don't cut it. You need a protector, somebody with weight."

"Get serious!" Marco answered bitterly. "Where am I going to find somebody willing to stand up for me?"

Benito chuckled. "Been thinking about that. New man in town—got contacts, got weight—everywhere, seems like. Been watching him."

"Big fat deal—what reason is he going to have to help me?"

"Name's Aldanto. Caesare Aldanto. Familiar?"

Marco sucked in his breath. "Lord and Saints . . ."

"Thought I 'membered," Benito replied with satisfaction.

Marco did indeed remember that name—it went all the way back to their being exiled to Venice, an exile that Grandfather Dell'este thought would take them out of the reach of Mama's pro-Milanese friends and of her lover. Caesare Aldanto had been one of the Milanese agents in Ferrara—a friend of Mama's lover Carlo Sforza. Carlo was (presumably) Benito's father—that was probably why the name 'Aldanto' had stuck so fortuitously in Benito's memory.

"You can never forget anything, brother. What's the Aldanto you saw look like?"

Marco closed his eyes and rocked back and forth a little, letting his mind drift back—Lord and Saints, he'd been a seven, maybe, eight-year-old boy—

"Blond. *Pretty* guy. Moved like a cat, or a dancer. Blue eyes—tall, dressed really well."

"Dunno about the eyes, but the rest is him. It's the same man. Appears to me he'd have reason to help us. Appears to me you'd want to get Mama's message to him, no?"

"Lord—" Marco said, not quite believing this turn of events. "It's—"

"Like that story you used to tell me? Yeah, well, maybe. I'm more interested in seeing you safe, and I think this Caesare Aldanto can do that. Right then, we'll go find him. Now. Tonight."

Marco started to scramble up, but Benito forestalled him. "No *way* you're going to pass in the town, brother. Not dressed like that."

"Oh. Yes."

"You wait here—I won't be long."

Benito thought he'd managed that rather cleverly; he thought he'd remembered Caesare Aldanto's name when he'd first heard it, and he had just been biding his time, waiting for the opportunity to get Marco to take the bait he was going to offer. The marshes were no place for Marco—sooner or later someone or something would get him. Venice was safer, by far. Besides, since he'd been thrown out from Theodoro's family, Benito had been getting lonelier and lonelier. He had friends—Lola, for instance. Well, she was sort of a friend. Mercutio, he was fun, and he looked out for Benito. But it wasn't the same as having Marco around. He wanted his big brother back!

Well, now—first things first; a set of clothing that wouldn't stand out in the Solstice crowds. Benito took to the rooftops and thought while he climbed. Nearest secondhand clothing store was close to the Palazzo Mastelli. That was the area he was hanging out in at present—no go. Off limits. He could hear Valentina now, cracking him over the ear for even thinking about it. "Never soil your own nest, boy. Rule one."

The air up here was fresher, the breeze carrying away a lot of the stink. Benito slipped around chimneypots and skylights as easily as if he'd been on a level walkway. So: the next closest was over toward the Ca' d'Oro. Old man Mirko was a stingy *bastardo*, too cheap to put good shutters in his windows. And the Dalmatian wouldn't miss the loss. Mirko's place it was.

He crossed the bridges on the support beams below, keeping a sharp eye out for watchers, finally getting himself up on the supports of the high-level bridge that crossed the Rio Malpaga. Mirko had a second-story window just below and to one side of it. Benito unwound the light rope and grapnel from his waist, spied a sturdy cornice, and made his cast.

Solid. He pulled three times. ("*Always* three times, no matter how rushed you are," came Claudia's voice from memory.) Then he swung himself over, in the shadows all the way.

Within a few minutes Mirko's shop was lighter by a pair of breeches, a shirt, and a cotte, all sized for someone thin and not over-tall, along with some other small items. And Benito was most of the way back to the wharf, dancing across the rooftops and bridge-beams like a half-grown cat.

"Huh-*uh*," Benito said, keeping his grip tight on the bundle he carried and handing something small to Marco instead. It shone white in the starlight. "I sto—found some soap, too. Down, brother; in the harbor. Get clean first, or they'll know you, by the smell, for marsh scum."

Marco flushed with embarrassment—living in the swamp was changing him, and in ways he didn't like. He used to be so fastidious. . . .

He grabbed the proffered soap and dropped straight down into the water next to the wharf—trying not to remember the twitching thing that had so lately floated there. He was so used to being chilled that the cold water wasn't much of a shock to his system. He soaped and rinsed and scrubbed until he thought his skin would peel off, then washed his hair three times for good measure. Benito had shinnied down to his raft and handed him back up onto it with a sniff that held approval. "Better. You smell better than a lot of canal-dwellers now. Here—"

A piece of sacking to use for a towel, and a comb. Getting the tangles out of his hair was a job—Marco had to be content with just getting most of the major knots out, and smoothing down the rest, tying it back with the piece of ribbon (Lord—*ribbon!*) Benito handed him. Then into the clothing—oh, heaven, clean, and warm, and not ripped in a dozen places—and even the right size. The precious Message went into his shirt pocket.

Marco stood up straight with one hand steadying himself on the piling, and felt like a human being again for the first time in years.

Benito grinned at him, teeth flashing white in his shadowed face. "Know what, brother? You clean up really pretty. I can think of a couple of girls just might like to share a blanket with you."

Marco blushed hotly, and was glad the dark hid it.

"Thought I'd warn you—because that's who we're going to go see first."

They took to the rooftops, much to Marco's bewilderment; oh, he still remembered how to climb, he was fast and agile enough to keep up—but why not take the walkways openly? And—where had Benito gotten this kind of expertise in roof-scrambling?

It was more of a maze in Venice-above than it was in Venice-below. If there was a level space up here on the roofs that was more than three feet square, it was a rarity. "Up here" was a work of towers, cupolas, skylights, and spires. Benito danced along the spines of peaked roofs and jumped from structure to structure as if he were half cat. Marco followed as best he could. He was just lucky that "above" also sported rain gutters and collection pipes on every surface, for without these aids he'd never have been able to emulate Benito. From time to time Benito would half-start toward something Marco *knew* was unclimbable—then glance back as if suddenly remembering his brother's presence and choose some easier path. Marco couldn't help but wonder what he'd have done if Marco hadn't been there.

Benito paused on the roof edge overlooking the bridge across the Rio della Misericordia. Balancing carefully, he scrutinized the bridge and its attendant walkways.

"Looks good," he said finally, in a whisper. "If anybody followed, they've lost us. Come on." And he shinnied down a drainpipe to the walk below them. Marco followed suit. Shielded torches on the bridge danced and smoked; they were placed so far apart they did more harm than good. There seemed to be no one about in this area, and their bare feet made no sound on the bridge, which contributed to the gloomy atmosphere.

"From here we go to Rio Del Servi, then down by the Maddalena— just in case we get separated," Benito said in an undertone, moving uncomfortably fast for Marco, who was accustomed to poling a raft rather than walking. "The ladies I want to talk to should be in a tavern called Barducci's on the Rio di San Marina—it's down on the water. There'll be a lot of canalers tied up at it. Got that?"

Marco nodded, saving his breath.

"Good, because once we get to the Maddalena, we'll be going up again."

They didn't get separated, but Marco was weary and aching by the time they stood at the tavern door. And confused, and lost. Only rarely had they crossed bridges by the normal paths—more often they'd scrambled underneath on the cross beams, or worse, inched along the support cables overhead. It made good sense in a way—for surely no one would ever have been able to follow them—but Marco was thoroughly exhausted by the time they reached their goal.

They descended to the walkway, cold and wet under their bare feet, and walked decorously enough to the wooden porch that marked Barducci's front entrance. There were boats tied up here, and lanterns everywhere; light and noise and confusion that dazzled Marco's eyes and made him more than a little nervous. The water of the canal looked very black and cold compared with all that light and warmth, and Marco found himself hoping they weren't going to find out just how cold it was.

There was a food-smell; waves of garlic from the *bruschetta* toasting over the charcoal, grilling *Sarde*, and the heady bouquet of young red wine. There was smoke, little wisps of it, from the lanterns. There was more smoke from the charcoal grill. There was sound—people laughing, talking, arguing, and singing. Most of all, singing. Just as they got to the wooden porch a great roar of a chorus bounced out of the open door and off the brick of the wall opposite.

"Hoo—they're rabble-rousing tonight, for sure!" Benito grinned. "They best hope there ain't no Schiopettieri around!" Somewhat to Marco's surprise, he was talking just like the canalers, chameleon-like acquiring the coloration of his surroundings.

Marco began to make out some of the lyrics. Benito had the right of it. The song skirted just the high side of treason—but oddly enough, he couldn't identify what faction the song was in favor of.

"Valentina and Claudia and they ain't on anybody's side." Benito elbowed his way in through front door, with Marco trailing warily behind. "They just like to rile people up, I guess."

The tavern room was hot and redolent with the bouquet of food, drink and humanity; crammed full, every table and chair occupied and people jammed in against the walls. The objects of their attention were perched on the bar, grinning insolently and singing for all they were worth. Their voices were amazingly strong and clear; Marco could hear them long before he could see them.

Benito finally wormed a place for them in beside the bar, and Marco managed to get a good view under someone's elbow. They were something to stare at, were Valentina and Claudia, though which was which he couldn't guess. One was playing a lute, her hands moving on the strings so fast Marco could hardly credit his eyes. She seemed the older of the two by five, maybe ten years. The other was setting up a complicated pattern on a couple of hand drums, but Marco could see a mandola leaning up against the bar next to her. Both had dark, nearly black, straight hair, tied around with red scarves. The older one wore hers long, past her shoulders, the younger, shorter than Benito's. Both had sharp features and ironic grins. Both were wearing flounced red-patterned skirts. Both had pale, pale skin—as if they didn't see the sun much.

And both of them were wearing at least three knives that Marco could see.

"Hope they get the crowd calmed down before they finish up," Benito muttered, "or with this lot, half-drunk as they are, no tellin' what they might do."

To Marco's relief they did just that, finishing up at last with something melancholy enough that one or two of the more sodden customers began sniffling into their wine. Then, ignoring demands for more, they picked up their instruments and hopped off the bar. Benito waved at them. The older one spotted him and motioned him over. Seeing that he'd been summoned by one of their darlings, the crowd parted politely so that the two boys could make their way to the singers' tiny table, crowded into a cramped nook to one side of the bar itself. There was barely room for both women, the boys and the instruments.

The older one reached over the table and tweaked Benito's nose. "Where've y' been, cull? Y' haven't been here since the Feast started—we was beginnin' t' think y' didn't love us no more."

"Out an' about, earnin' a wedge or two. You tryin' t' get yourselves invited down to the Doge's torture chambers? What'f there'd been Schiopettieri around?"

"Huh, Schiopettieri are all dead drunk by now. Besides there's a crow on the door. That's the latest ballad out of Syracuse."

"With additions by you, Valentina, I got no doubt," Benito snorted. "The Servants don't hold with Moorish music, y'know, and they say the Doge is favoring 'em these days. God rot th' senile old fool. Ye're gonna find yourself at nubbing cheat, an' not because of what y' do outside the walls."

"Listen to the kitten, telling the old cats how to prowl!" the younger woman crowed. "Who taught you, hmm? Ins and outs, ups and downs—"

Benito cleared his throat with a sideways glance toward Marco— and only then did the women seem to see him.

"Well! Who's *this*? Can't be related to you, kid—he's too pretty." Marco felt his ears burning.

"This, Valentina, is my brother . . . Marco. *You* know."

"Oh-ho. Brought him out of hiding, hmm? And y' need something, I don't doubt. Make him someone's cousin?" Claudia—the older woman—caught Marco's chin in one long, sharp-nailed hand, and turned his face from side to side, examining it closely. "Just feeding him'd do. I'd think a little flesh on him, and no one'd tumble to 'im."

Benito shook his head. "No go. He needs more; needs protection, needs somebody with weight backing 'im. So I'm askin'— you seen that pretty blond—the one that ain't from these parts—in here lately?"

Claudia shook her head, letting go of Marco's chin. "Not me. Valentina-love?"

She too shook her head. "No. Know who would, though—that canal-rat that used't work for Antonio. Maria Garavelli. She's living with him, people say."

"*Oh, no*—" It was Benito's turn to shake his head. "Ain't messin' with that one. That Maria keeps an eye on 'im; push him, she'll know—I damn sure don't want her knowin' I'm trying to touch her man. She's got a nasty way with folks as bothers 'im."

"Point," Valentina agreed. "All right. Best I can say is try that runner-girl of yours, Lola. She's been doin' runs down along where he mostly seems t' hang out—'specially lately."

A fistfight broke out across the room, interrupting them. For a few seconds it remained confined to the original two combatants—but a foot in the wrong place tripped one up and sent him into a table and its occupants—and things began to spread from there.

Valentina and Claudia exchanged glances filled with unholy glee. "Shall we?"

"Let's—"

With reverent care, they handed their instruments to the bartender, who placed them safely behind the wooden bulwark. They divested themselves of knives—this was a fistfight, after all—then charged into the fray with joyful and total abandon.

"Women," Benito said, shaking his head ruefully. "Well, at least they'll come out of that with full pockets. Back way, brother." Marco followed him outside with no regret.

Benito led the way again, back over the rooftops, climbing towers and balconies, inching over drainpipes and across the support beams of bridges until Marco was well and truly lost yet again. Fatigue was beginning to haze everything, and he hadn't the least notion where in Venice he could be—except that by the general run of the buildings, they were still in the lower-class section of town. When Benito finally stopped and peered over a roof edge, Marco just sat, closing his eyes and breathing slowly, trying to get his wind back, with a gutter biting into his bony haunches.

"Hi!" he heard Benito call softly, "Lola!"

There was the sound of feet padding over to stand beneath where Benito leaned over the edge. "Benito?" answered a young female voice. "You in trouble?"

"No. Just need to find someone."

By now Marco had recovered enough to join Benito in peering over the roof edge. On the walkway just below him was a child—certainly younger than Benito, pretty in the way that an alley-kitten is pretty.

"I'm waiting," she said, and "Oh!" when she saw Marco.

Benito shook his head at the question in her glance. "Not now. Later, promise. Gotta find that blond you're droolin' after."

She looked incensed. "I *ain't* drooling after him! I just think he's—nice."

"Yeah, and Valentina just sings cute little ballads. You know where he is?"

She sniffed. "I shouldn't tell you. . . ."

"Oh c'mon! Look—I promise I'll give you that blue scarf of mine—just tell."

"Well, all right. He's in Antonio's over on the Rio della Frescada. I just run a message over there and I saw him. I think he's going to be there awhile."

"Hot damn!" Benito jumped to his feet, and skipped a little along the edge of the coppo tiles while Marco held his breath, expecting him to fall. "Bright-eyes, you just made my day!"

※   ※   ※

Benito had traded on the fact that he was a known runner in order to get into Antonio's. It wasn't a place Marco would have walked into by choice. The few faces he could see looked full of secrets, and unfriendly. They approached the table that Aldanto had taken, off in the darkest corner of the room, Benito with all the aplomb of someone who had every right to be there, even if he was only fourteen years old. Marco just trailed along behind, invisible for all the attention anyone paid him. The place was as dark as Barducci's had been well lit; talk was murmurous, and there was no one entertaining. Marco was not at all sure he wanted to be here.

"Milord—" Benito had reached Aldanto's table, and the man looked up when he spoke. Marco had no difficulty in recognizing the Caesare Aldanto from Ferrara. Older, harder—but the same man. "Milord, I got a message for you—but—it ain't public."

Aldanto looked at him. Startled at first, then appraisingly. He signaled a waiter, and spoke softly into the man's ear; the man murmured something in reply, picked up the dishes that had been on Aldanto's table, and motioned them to follow.

The waiter led them all to a tiny room, with barely room for more than a table and a few chairs in it—but it had a door and the door shut softly behind them. Aldanto seated himself at the table and put down his wine glass. The way he positioned himself, the boys had to stand with him seated between them and the door. The lantern that lit the room was on the wall behind Aldanto's head and made a sunblaze out of his hair.

"I'm waiting," was all he said.

"Milord, my brother's got information that you might be able to use—it might be you and him know the same people. We want to sell it."

He poked Marco with his elbow. Marco shook himself into awareness.

"Information?" Aldanto did not look amused. "What on earth could you two have that would be of any use to me?"

"Milord, somebody thinks it's important. My brother has been having to hide out in the marshes because somebody thought it was important enough to kill my mother, but she passed it on to Marco here. See, we know who you are. We know where you're from. We reckoned you would be the right man to know what he's got. And we figured you'd be the best man to pay our price—and that's to keep him safe after he's told you."

The blond man began to look angry. "If this is some kind of a scam—"

"Brother," Marco said clearly and distinctly, "the viper strikes." It was the password of those in the service of the Milanese Duke Visconti.

Aldanto, who had just taken a mouthful of wine, coughed and practically choked.

Marco took the most recent of his precious copies of The Message from his shirt pocket and handed it to him.

Hazed with fatigue, Marco was blind to Aldanto's reactions—but Benito wasn't.

Within a few moments, Benito had figured Aldanto was not pleased with their recognition of him as a Milanese agent. Moments after that he knew by the worried look that Aldanto wasn't working for Duke Visconti anymore.

This required recalculation.

Then Aldanto's mouth began to twitch as he read the paper Marco had given him.

"Where did you come by this?"

"I told you," Benito said, stalling for time. "Our mama was something with the Milanese—passed their messages and whatall. Except somebody figured that out an' came for her, and Marco ran for the marshes to hide out with the last thing she got. Figured things were fine until he got jumped out there a day or so ago, and it weren't just any nightbird, it was an assassin. We are Valdosta; you might know the name—you might know people Mama knew—Ventuccio. You going help us out?"

"Valdosta. Well . . . well . . ." Aldanto pointed at the paper. "Nothing here for me," he said. His mouth was amused but his eyes were hard. "What you've got is an out-of-date infiltration schedule. Useless. And worthless."

Marco's mind went blank. All the hope—the plans—all in ruins; and the man Aldanto didn't seem the least bit interested in helping, much less being the shining rescuer Marco had prayed for.

"But—somebody must think I know something," he said desperately, "or why try to kill me? And why send an assassin? They could have hired one of the marsh-gangs, easy." Now all he wanted was to be able to think of something useful to Aldanto; something worth the cost of protecting both himself and Benito. It was far too late now to go back to the Jesolo marsh. "Maybe—maybe I know something someone doesn't want out—like a name, or a face—can't you use that?"

"Absolutely—Marco never forgets anything," Benito chimed in. "That's why Mama took him everywhere with her. He knows all kinds of things—things maybe still worth knowing."

"Like I remember you, milord. You were with Mama's man, Carlo Sforza—it was—around the beginning of October, I think, about nine years ago. You were wearing brown velvet, and you and Carlo talked about the bribes your father'd been paying . . ." Marco trailed off at the grim set of Aldanto's mouth.

"Besides—damned Milanese are out after us along with you," Benito interrupted, stepping hard on Marco's foot. "Mama would have sold us to slavers if they'd told her to. Duke Visconti never got us anything but trouble, and I bet it's him as sent the assassin. You need something, well, I can get it, or I know who can; I can get things done, too—get people disappeared—get you disappeared too, only less permanent. We've got connections you can't get from the *Case Vecchie* or the boatpeople. You *need* us, milord—about as much as we need you."

"Interesting. Valdosta . . ." Aldanto said, then said nothing more, obviously thinking hard. Marco turned on Benito, and tugged him into a corner of the little room.

"What the hell—"

"Truth, damn it!" Benito whispered harshly. "It's all true and you know it! Mama *used* you—why do you think she never paid me any attention? Theodoro's folks knew what was going on; told me too. Told me it was probably Duke Visconti's people that got Mama."

"Uh—"

"That's why they turned me out, couple of years ago. They were afraid, and I don't blame 'em. Lucky I ran into Claudia and Valentina."

"They're thieves! I know thieves cant when I hear it!"

"'Course they're thieves! How d'you think I came by all that stuff for you? Where'd you think it came from? The Moon? I've been living in bloody attics for two years now! Look, brother—I've mostly given up thieving—the odds aren't in it. I'm a messenger now. But I couldn't get stuff for you, and feed me, on what

I make running, and I wouldn't leave you without. So I stole. And I still steal. And I'll keep doin' it. 'Cause you're worth it—like Mama wasn't. Tell you what else. This Aldanto may have been Montagnard before, but he damn sure ain't now! Or didn't you notice him have a fit when you hit him with the password? Our best bet is to figure something he needs bad."

The fog began to clear from Marco's head, as Benito's words and his memory started to come together. Certain things were becoming a lot clearer than they'd ever been before.

Item: Chiano and Sophia had been trying to tell him—in gentler terms—exactly what Benito was telling him now. If three so very different people—one of them his own flesh and blood—were saying the same things about Duke Visconti and the Montagnard cause, and Mama's involvement with it, well it followed that he had probably been dead wrong and dreaming all these years.

Item: stripped of the fairy-tale glamour Mama had decked them in, Montagnards were not in the least attractive. Take the rhetoric of united Christian Empire away, and they became little more than highly trained, professional killers.

Item: they were now alone with this unhappy professional assassin, who was probably thinking that no one would miss them.

Marco looked over Benito's shoulder at Aldanto, who was contemplating them with a face of stone. Marco's blood ran colder than the spring-melt water that the Brenta carried down from the Alps.

Item: they were a liability. And Aldanto was looking at them like someone who couldn't afford liabilities.

Benito suddenly broke off, seeing Marco's face turn pale and still. "Brother—you all right?" he whispered, unable to fathom why Marco should suddenly look as if the great Lion of San Marco had come to life and confronted him. He knew that some of what he'd said was bound to come as a shock to Marco, but he hadn't thought any of it was enough to turn him white to the ears!

He shook Marco a little, beginning to feel worried. The way Marco was staring at Aldanto, sort of glassy-eyed—it wasn't like him. Marco was always the quick one, the alert one—except—

Benito went cold all over. Except when Marco had been sick . . .

❧　　　❧　　　❧

Marco was watching Aldanto's eyes, the only things in his face that were showing any change. They were growing harder; and Marco's blood acquired ice crystals.

Item: they were quite likely to be dead very soon. Benito, with the panache of a fourteen-year-old unable to believe in his own mortality, had led them into dangerous and unfriendly hands—and with no way to escape. Aldanto was between them and the door, in a room barely big enough to hold all of them and the table and chairs.

Looking at those calculating eyes, Marco *knew* exactly what their fate was going to be. They had, at most, a few more minutes.

He forced himself to smile at his brother; he couldn't protect him from what was coming. "Nothing—just—you're right. About all of it. I've been plain stupid."

Benito shrugged. "No big deal. Everybody makes mistakes, and hell, I probably wouldn't believe anything bad anybody said about you, either."

"And I never told you how much I missed you, half." The old nickname made Benito grin. "That was even stupider. We're the team, right? So, from now on it's going be you and me—aye? All the way."

Benito dropped his pretense of adulthood and threw both arms around his brother in an affection-starved hug. Marco tightened his own arms around Benito's shoulder and stared at Aldanto, trying to beg with his eyes, and figuring that it was a lost cause before he started.

But to Marco's surprise, Caesare suddenly cleared his throat. A little sound, but the older boy started as violently as if a gun had gone off in his ear.

"You say your mother had connections with Ventuccio?"

Marco stared, unable to get his mouth to work. It was too much to comprehend—he'd expected the knife, and he'd only hoped Aldanto was good enough to make it fast and relatively painless. And then—this—

His ears roared, and little black spots danced in the air between his eyes and Aldanto's face.

"Ventuccio?" he heard himself say stupidly, as his knees suddenly liquefied on him.

❀　　　❀　　　❀

Benito felt Marco start to collapse, and held him up by main force. *Oh, God, please—no!*

The last time Marco had done this, he'd missed the meetings for the next month; and when he finally showed up, he was pounds thinner, with eyes gone all hollow, and a rasping cough that lasted for weeks. *Please, God*—he begged, struggling to keep Marco on his feet long enough to pull a chair under him, *don't let it be fever, he might not make it this time—and we're almost home free—*

"Milord, just let me get him sat—milord, he's all right!" Marco heard Benito over the roaring in his ears, over the scrape of a chair on the floor "You don't—milord, you don't need—"

Something shoved up against the back of his legs; hands were under his armpits letting him down easy, the same strong hands then pushing his head down between his legs.

"Stay that way for a bit—" Aldanto's voice. And the roaring went away, his eyes cleared. When his head stopped spinning he looked up. Aldanto sat on his heels beside him, Benito looking frantic, trying to get between them without touching the man. "Better?"

"I—" Marco managed. "I—"

Aldanto took his chin in one hand, tilted his eyes into the light, scrutinizing them closely.

"I'm sorry, milord, I'm all right," Marco whispered, thinking, *Daren't, daren't show weakness in front of this man!* "Honest, I'm all right."

"You're not—but you will be."

Ignoring Benito's worried protests (*Great*, thought Marco dizzily, *now he realizes we could be in trouble*), Aldanto went to the table and brought his glass of wine to Marco, who took it with hands that shook so hard the wine slopped. Poison? No—not likely. Not when he'd had the chance to kill them easily and hadn't. An assassin as physically capable as Aldanto so obviously was, wouldn't bother with anything other than a blade. Not, at least, dealing with two poor boys in a place like this.

"Get yourself on the outside of that."

Marco sipped, the alcoholic warmth spreading from his stomach to the rest of his body. His hands stopped shaking, slowly.

"When did you last eat?"

"Eat?" Marco was taken totally by surprise by the question and the funny half smile on Aldanto's face. "Uh—I don't remember."

"Then it's been too long. Small wonder you're falling at my feet. They're reserved for women, you know."

As Marco tried to adjust to the fact that Aldanto had just made a joke, the blond man turned to Benito. He held out a piece of silver. "Go out there and get some bread and *risi e bisi.*"

Benito scampered, and returned with a steaming bowl moments later. Some customer was going to have to wait a little longer for his dinner. The thick green rice-and-pea soup was set down, and Benito scampered off to fetch bread and a bowl of shaved Parmesan. Aldanto held out the spoon to Marco.

Marco stared at it as though it was alive, not taking it.

"Go on, eat." Aldanto pried one of Marco's hands off the glass and pressed the spoon into it. "Marco—"

God and Saints, they were saved. Marco's head spun—this time with relief.

"About the Ventuccio—"

Marco took the bread which Benito had now brought. He dipped it into the soup and took a tiny bite. He swallowed around a lump in his throat, and began.

When Marco had finished telling Aldanto all he knew and most of what he guessed, and when his knees could hold him upright again, Aldanto considered them both carefully for several long moments. Marco took advantage of his preoccupation to finish every drop of soup and every crumb of bread.

"Something must be done with you two," Aldanto said at last. "The safest you can be is in plain sight. And Ventuccio can do that better than anyone."

Marco didn't argue with him—after all, he'd just proved how poor his own judgment was. Aldanto pondered something silently for a very long time, while a young riot of shouting youths passed by outside and moved on.

"I think it's not too late to get speech of Ventuccio," Aldanto said abruptly. "It's Solstice, after all. Come along."

Before Marco could protest, before Benito could do anything more than look stunned, Aldanto had chivvied them out of the door and onto the walkway. Benito, for once, looked appropriately apprehensive, but that could easily have been because he'd run errands for Ventuccio and reckoned on being recognized there.

Aldanto had not been speaking rhetorically, for a brisk walk brought them straight to *Casa* Ventuccio proper.

At least he didn't take them to the main door of the great house. Instead, he led them down to a water-door, where he tapped out a sequence of knocks, and was answered.

The man who opened the door frowned ferociously when he saw who it was, but at least he listened to Aldanto's whispered words and, after a moment, nodded.

"I'll see about it," the man growled, and allowed them, grudgingly, past the door to stand waiting in the damp entry while he went away somewhere. Presently, he came back, still looking displeased, but jerked his head as a sign that they should follow. He led them down long, unlit halls of wood and stone, and finally into a room piled with ledgers that was so brightly lit Marco was blinking tears back.

Now they fronted a man Aldanto called by name, and that man was coldly angry. "You have a lot of balls, coming here, Caesare," the man spat. "And for calling me away from my guests on a night of the Feast—"

"Granted," Aldanto said coldly. "However, I think you happen to take your honor and your pledged word fairly seriously, and I have just learned that you happen to have an unpaid debt and a broken promise you might want to discharge. These boys are Valdosta. Marco and Benito Valdosta."

Marco had rarely seen words act so powerfully on someone. The man's anger faded into guilt.

"I've brought them here," Aldanto continued deliberately, "so that we can even some scales. You made a promise to Duke Dell'este, and didn't keep it. I—lost you some people. Both these kids are useful."

Now the man looked skeptical, as if he doubted Aldanto's ability to judge much of anything.

"Milord," Benito piped up, "you've used me, I know. Ask your people. I'm a messenger—a good one. I don't take bribes, I'm fast—"

"You could take him on as a staff runner and train him for bargework as he grows into it. And the older boy clerks," Aldanto continued.

"You don't expect me to take that on faith!"

Marco took a deep breath and interrupted. "Set me a problem, milord. Nothing easy. You'll see."

The man sniffed derisively, then rattled off something fast; a complicated calculation involving glass bottles—cost, expected breakage, transportation and storage, ending with the question of how much to ask for each in order to receive a twenty-percent profit margin.

Marco closed his eyes, went into his calculating-trance, and presented the answer quickly enough to leave the man with a look of surprise on his face.

"Well!" said the man. "For once . . . I don't suppose he can write, too?"

Aldanto had a funny little smile. "Give him something to write with." He seemed to be enjoying the man's discomfiture.

Marco was presented with a quill pen and an old bill of lading. He appropriated a ledger to press on, and promptly copied the front onto the back, and in a much neater hand.

"You win," the man said with resignation. "Why don't you tell me exactly what's been going on—and how you managed to resurrect these two?"

Aldanto just smiled.

The man took Aldanto off somewhere, returning after a bit with a troubled look and a bundle, which he handed to Benito.

"You, boy—I want you here at opening time sharp, and in this uniform. And you're not Valdosta anymore, forget that name. You're Oro; you're close enough to the look of that family. Got that?"

Benito took the bundle soberly. "Yes. Milord."

"As for you—" Marco tried not to sway with fatigue, but the man saw it anyway, "—you're out on your feet. No good to anyone until you get some rest. Besides, two new kids in one day—hard to explain. You get fed and clean, real clean. We've got a reputation to maintain. And get that hair taken care of. I want you here in two days. 'Oro' is no good for you. Make it—uh—Felluci. I don't suppose you'd rather be sent back to your family?"

"No, milord," Marco replied adamantly. "I won't put danger on them. Bad enough that it's on me."

The man shook his head. "Saints preserve—you're a fool, boy, but a brave one. Dell'este honor, is it? Well, Dell'este can usually deal with most things, too. Anyway . . . Right enough—now get out of here. Before I remember that I'm *not* a fool. Ventuccio honor's real enough, but it isn't that hammered steel version the Old Fox insists on."

Aldanto escorted them to the door, stopping them just inside it.

"This wasn't free—" he told Marco quietly.

"Milord. I know that, milord."

"Just so we both know, I'm going to be calling in this debt—calling in all those things you promised me. I may call it in so often that you'd wish you'd never thought of coming to me."

"Milord Aldanto," Marco replied, looking him full in the eyes, "I *owe* you. And I can't ever pay it all."

"Well . . ." Aldanto seemed slightly embarrassed. "They say the one who wins is the one who is left standing, so by all counts you came out of this a winner. Be grateful—and remember to keep your mouth shut."

Marco figured that that was the best advice he'd had in a long time.

Benito hauled Marco back to Valentina and Claudia before taking him "home." The Marco that came from their hands was much shorter of hair by a foot or two; and a bit darker of complexion—not to mention a lot cleaner and with a good hot breakfast in his stomach. It wasn't quite dawn when he and his brother climbed up to the garret where Benito had made his home. Benito gave him a pair of blankets to roll up in, and he was sleeping the sleep of the exhausted before Benito had gotten into his store clothes. Benito smiled to himself, a smile warm and content with the world, and set to one last task before heading back to Ventuccio.

He pried up a particular board in the attic, felt around until he located the little bag he had hung there, and pulled it out. Caesare's woman Maria Garavelli was bound to hear of this—and he reckoned he'd better have a peace offering. And there was that scarf he'd taken off that duelist to prove to Claudia that he was able.

After the Ventuccio let him go for the day, he waited under the Ponto di Rialto knowing she'd be by. When he spotted her, he swung down to hang from the support by his knees.

He whistled. She looked up.

"Maria—" he called. "Peace, huh? Truce? Okay? Here's something for sorrys." He'd knotted a pebble into one corner of the scarf—and it was a nice one; silk, bright red. He dropped it neatly at her feet, and scrambled back up before she could get over her surprise. With Maria Garavelli it was a good idea to get out of the line-of-sight and find out about reactions later.

Besides—he warmed to the thought—he had to get back home. His family was waiting. And once they'd eaten there was a bit of swimming he'd promised to do for that smuggler-girl.

Chapter 6

What was that *about?* wondered Maria. She stared after Benito's rapidly receding form, pausing for a moment in her rowing of the gondola.

"Peace?" "Truce?" I didn't know there was a fight between me and Benito in the first place. If there is . . . we'll see whether there's a truce or not!

Maria Garavelli looked at the bright rectangle of silk lying on her duckboards and bent down and rescued the precious scrap before it got wet. It was the expensive color that dyers called *golden flame* or *oriflamme*. It was just the color of the evening sun-trail on the water of the lagoon. She shook her head clear of these impractical thoughts. Honestly! Sometimes she behaved as she was some *Case Vecchie* lady, instead of a canal-girl.

That bridge-brat Benito . . . He hung about with young Mercutio Laivetti. Mercutio was Trouble if she'd ever met trouble, and you didn't get to be sixteen as an orphaned girl on the canals of Venice without being good at spotting it. She'd fended for herself for three years since Mama died, leaving her nothing but the gondola. Cousin Antonio had offered to let her move in with them, but heaven knew there were enough mouths to feed there. Saint Hypatia! And his wife was the worst shrew and gossip in all Venice. Maria pulled a wry face and tucked the silk scarf into the top of her blouse. She went back to sculling.

Some of that gossip was about her in the last few months, she was sure. The cousins didn't approve of Caesare. They really, really didn't approve of her living with him. It wasn't just that they weren't

89

married. A fair number of Caulker-guild brides, those of the Garavelli cousins among them, had tried for the reputation of having been the most pregnant at the altar. Cousin Rosina had looked as if she might just have to get the priest to help with the delivery! But Caesare came from above the salt. The Garavelli were artisans. Mostly caulkers, cladding Venice's great ships. They had a pride in working with their hands and not much liking or trust for a man who didn't.

She worked the oar just a bit faster. The only reason that bridge-brat Benito could have been giving her a silk scarf—a stolen silk scarf, she'd bet—was something to do with her Caesare. She set her mouth in a grim line. Scarf or no scarf, she'd sort that Benito out if he'd brought trouble onto her!

All the same . . . it was a gorgeous red, that scarf. It would set off her thick dark hair beautifully. She craved for lovely things like that—not for themselves but because they'd make her look a little less like a canal-girl. Caesare was so fine. Everything about him said *Case Vecchie*, from the smooth, curved golden hair that looked as if it were cast in bronze, to the long white hands. Her hands were work-hardened and brown. She'd *kill* young Benito if he'd brought trouble.

Without even realizing it, her fists were clenched tightly on the oars. Maria Garavelli was not one to back away from a fight. She'd been fighting for most of her young life; she could say it had even begun before she was born, when her mama's own people had thrown her out for getting pregnant without the benefit of a husband. Like *she'd* have starved, except that she had a small boat, inherited from her grandfather, and a regular list of customers she made deliveries for, gotten on her own initiative. So Mama had worked right up through the first labor pains (so she'd said) and then headed for the canalside midwife she'd already made arrangements with, and the next day she was up and working again with Maria wrapped up in swaddling in a cradle made of half a cask.

Maria had grown up, like every other canal-brat, knowing that it was only fight and hard work that kept you that bare nail-paring away from starvation and disaster. She'd worked at Mama's side from the time she could stand, and when Mama took the fever and died, she kept right on working.

And fighting. She had to fight with the toughs who saw her as an easy mark and tried to take her cargo or her pay. She had to fight with the other canal-boat owners who tried to steal her customers with implications that a "little girl on her own" couldn't do what she'd pledged. She even had to fight Mama's family who wanted her to come work at some miserable pittance of a dead-end job for them. She had to fight the boys—relatives and canalers and toughs—who figured since her mama had been "loose," the daughter's skirts were there for lifting. *They* finally let her be when one of their number had to join a *castrati* choir when she'd finished with him.

So it was no wonder that she'd never exchanged so much as a single solitary flirtatious glance with a boy, much less had anything like a romance. Oh, she'd certainly *thought* enough about it. She wasn't made of wood, after all. When a good-looking tough sauntered by, flaunting himself for the admiration of the *puttanas*, or she'd see a wedding coming out of a church with the bride beaming—when she'd hear a snatch of song and see some love-sick student balanced precariously in a gondola, serenading a window she couldn't help thinking . . . Even, on the rare occasions that she went to Mass at Saint Lucia's and spent the entire time contemplating, not God, but the pale and beautiful face of Father Raphael—how could she not think about the ways of man-with-maid?

But she'd had no illusions, either. She knew she was hard and rough, not smooth and silky. She knew only too well that her skin was brown and weathered, not soft and pink like rose petals.

She'd had no illusions about her looks, but still—she'd had dreams she never told anyone, just cherished to herself, and played over in the theater in her head when she was halfway between waking and sleeping. Someday, some handsome fellow would drop into her life—she'd rescue him from a flood, or from footpads, or he'd hire her boat to visit some worthless, heartless bitch who would throw him over. He'd look at her, and see something in her that no one else ever had—he'd take off her cap, pull all her hair down around her face, and say, "Maria—you're *beautiful!*" in tones of moonstruck surprise. And he'd love her forever, and it would turn out that he was the long-lost heir to one of the Old Houses—

Oh, stupid dreams, and she would never, ever have admitted to anyone that she had them. She would never, ever have believed them, either.

Except that . . . one night they came true.

She'd been tied up for the night under a bridge to get out of the rain, when she heard the sounds that no Venetian—boater, canalside dweller, or high-and-mighty—ever wanted to hear. A scuffle. The sounds of a blow. Then the sound of two men carrying something heavy up to the top of the bridge.

It was a dark night on top of the miserable rain, what with the moon hidden by the clouds, but she knew she didn't dare move or make a sound. She huddled under the roof of what she grandly called the "cabin" of her little boat, and hoped that the men up there wouldn't notice that she was tied up in the shadows underneath. She might be able to fight off one or even two, but from the sounds there had been more than that.

A grunt, and a heave, and something dark and heavy drooped over the edge of the bridge. It hung up on the railing for a moment, and before it dropped, there were footsteps running away. Then, as she strained her eyes against the dark and the rain in horrified fascination, the thing tore loose from the coping and tumbled down.

Into her boat.

It had been a fairly low bridge; getting hung up had slowed the object's fall. Otherwise it probably would have overset the boat, or even driven a hole right through it. When it—the body, for that was clear what it was—had landed, it had done so on its feet, crumpling, or else it would have bashed in its skull (if it wasn't already bashed) or broken its neck (if it wasn't already broken). Probably the stone tied to its ankles had helped out there.

And all she could think of was—*get it off my boat!*

She'd scrambled out of the cabin, and Fate or God or something had undone all of her good sense and intentions.

For just as she reached the body, it gave out a groan and turned face-up. And just as it did so, the clouds parted for a moment, and a ray of moonlight shone down on what must have been the most beautiful man she had ever seen apart from Father Raphael, who was in any case a full priest and out of the running so far as romance went.

And *that* was how Caesare-the-handsome, Caesare-the-dangerous, Caesare-the-all-too-persuasive-damn-him ended up in her shack, in her blankets, and in her care.

And it was just like one of her daydreams, from start to finish. She moved Caesare into her little shack near the canals, where there would be no spying eyes and ears. She nursed him and kept him warm and fed him from a spoon for days—and then, suddenly, one day he looked up at her with sense in his eyes, and said "Who are you? Where am I?" and she answered him. And *then*, like he'd been watching the same dreams, he reached up, and pulled off her cap and her hair came tumbling down and he said, "My God, you saved my life, and you're beautiful!"

Well, what was any girl to do when a handsome man said that to her, in her own bed, in her own house, on a moonlit night when the lagoon was bright and glassy-smooth?

He didn't tell her a lot about himself, afterwards. Except that he was a danger to her, and he had to leave her—which she expected, really. But what he said then she didn't expect.

"How can I leave you? I love you!"

—and she, fierce as a lion with a cub, swore she could help him, keep him safe from those enemies—she'd known they were enemies all along, no footpad ever bothered tying a rock to someone to sink him. But then he told her who those enemies were—the Milanese— and that he'd been working for them right up until the moment that they betrayed him. Almost, almost she took it all back, almost told him to leave. Almost.

But she hadn't. And she'd hidden him until she was able to get him to someone who could offer him, for a price, a precarious bit of protection. Then a little more. And him, with his sneak's ways and his angel's face, clawed and fought his way up to being very valuable—alive—to enough people that it was no longer more profitable for him to be dead. For now, at least.

And that was why Maria Garavelli found herself rowing her boat along a back-canal in the dead of night, roused by a messenger; going, once again, to pick up her lover from wherever-he-was now; short on sleep, short on temper, and wondering if *this* time, despite passwords and safeguards, it wasn't him, but an ambush. And lovesick idiot that she was, she'd have been sculling through canals of fire if she had to, to get to him.

The ache in her fists suddenly registered on her brain, and she eased up her grip on the oar. For some reason, that reminded her of Benito and his peculiar "peace offering."

For a moment, Maria's natural combativeness caused her to frown. But, within seconds, the frown cleared away and she uttered a soft little laugh.

That scamp!

Truth be told, she thought she was probably fond of Benito. Maybe.

And it *was* a lovely red, that scarf.

Chapter 7

Steel. Heavy steel. Angular and Gothic. The spike-shouldered breastplate had curlicues and inlays on the points, for heaven's sake. Not for the first time, Erik Hakkonsen stared in irritation at the heavy plate armor, as he stood sharpening the blade of his Algonquian war hatchet. He was waiting, not with any eagerness, for his squire-orderly to help him into it. He'd drawn the guard-stint for this State banquet. He looked balefully at the closed-pot helmet he'd be sweating in one hour from now. No good German *Ritter* would consider wearing anything else but full armor.

Only . . . Erik was not a German *Ritter*. An Icelander wasn't as stupid and hidebound as these continentals. Any Icelander, much less one who had skirmished on the Vinland frontiers, would turn up his nose at elaborate plate armor. A crossbow bolt would punch through it and a ball from an arquebus or a good pistol would shatter the steel. For that matter, at close quarters Erik could find the joints and cut them apart with his blade-and-pick tomahawk, as easily as shucking clams.

And carrying all those pounds of useless steel without a horse to help . . .

He heard the creak of the door. "What kept you, Pellmann?" he snapped, putting the whetstone down. "I've been waiting half an hour. . . . Oh."

The visitor had flopped onto the caryatid-pillared bed. The accommodation was a far cry from the cells in the bleak monastery at Greifswald. It wasn't his churlish Pomeranian squire-orderly admiring the caryatides. The bed protested as the large human negligently sprawled on it rolled closer to inspect the finely carved detail. Manfred whistled appreciatively.

His reaction to the carving was predictable. Perhaps even justified, Erik was willing to admit. Erik himself had blushed when he realized that the carved nymph was perfect in every anatomical detail. The bed's reaction was also quite predictable—and justified. Young Manfred was designed by nature to wear armor. To wear armor without noticing it.

It never failed to irritate Erik. The steel would chafe his lean, angular, sinewy body raw. Manfred was better shaped and padded for this sort of thing.

The solid, blocklike Manfred grinned, revealing slightly skew solid blocklike teeth in a jaw whose musculature matched the rest of him. Erik suspected Manfred could crunch clams without even bothering to open them.

"Well, you'll just have to go on waiting." The young knight-squire drew a bottle from under his cotte, and tossed it to Erik. "Here. Try some of this."

Erik drew the cork without thinking, and took a deep pull. He spluttered. "What is it? Armor polish?" Then he remembered himself, and his duty. He was sworn to the order and God for another two years. He rammed the cork home and tossed it back to the laughing knight-squire. "In heaven's name, Manfred! If Abbot Sachs catches you with that stuff, he'll have you pushing guard duties until you turn gray."

"He's with Sister Ursula again. Doing abbotly duties, no doubt," said the worldly-wise scion of the imperial court at Mainz.

Erik felt his face redden. "Jesu! Manfred, don't say things like that! He's a man of God."

In reply the young knight-squire drew the cork from the dull green bottle with his teeth. He took a deep pull. He did not splutter. He set the bottle down on the stone-flagged floor. With beer-brown innocent eyes he looked mournfully at the Icelander. Then, sighed heavily.

"Erik, alas, I am a man of the flesh. And this is Venice! It's supposed to have the best courtesans and the best bordellos in all Europe. We've been here for nearly two days and I haven't sampled them. You're supposed to look after me! What say you we cut this banquet tonight and go whoring? These local girls will go wild over that blond head and that chiseled chin of yours."

Erik felt himself blush, again. He couldn't help liking his young charge. And he couldn't help wishing that Manfred had been placed under someone else's eye. He understood why he'd been singled out for this. It was, he supposed, a great symbol of trust, and a great honor. It was also a great headache.

He tried an appeal to piety and reason. "Manfred. You're a Knight of the Holy Trinity, even if only a confrere. A moral example to these soft, corrupt southerners. Not a mercenary out for the customary three nights of sacking."

The young knight-squire grinned. "That's why I was planning to pay my way. Not being a ladies' delight like you . . ."

"I've got guard duty, tonight," interrupted Erik, hastily. "And so have you, come to think of it."

Manfred yawned. "I'll swap out. Come on, Erik. I'll go without you, otherwise."

This was a dire threat. It had worked when Manfred had wanted to sample the taverns of Innsbruck. But it was a vain threat this time.

"Abbot Sachs himself put up the list," said Erik, grimly. "And besides, my Breton friend, your court Frankish isn't going to get you anywhere. Without a grasp of the local dialect you couldn't ask your way to the nearest church, never mind anything else."

"That's why I need a linguist like you, Erik," grinned Manfred. "And I sure couldn't get back without my sober, respectable mentor to guide me. Come on, Erik . . ."

"Not a chance." Erik glanced at the light from the high enchased window. "Now you'd better leg it back to get suited up. I'd better yell for that useless Pellmann."

"You'd do well to shove his surly face up his hinder-end instead," said Manfred, rising and stretching.

Erik had yet to get used to the way these continentals treated their servants. Thralls back home were more like part of the family, and as likely to yell at you as you were at them. But Pellmann's insolent attitude toward serving anyone but a North German *Ritter* was beginning to rub even the egalitarian Icelander raw. "I think I will, if I don't find him in two minutes," he said grimly.

Pellmann bustled in abruptly. The nasty piece of work had plainly been listening outside.

Manfred snorted. "Ah, well. I'll see you at the banquet. Maybe there'll be some pretty women there." He left, leaving Erik to Pellmann's mercies. The Pomeranian knew by now that the worst

Erik would do when a buckle pinched him was curse under his breath. Erik would swear the Pomeranian used this opportunity to make the foreign confrere knight's life a misery.

Pellmann's knuckles dug into his rib cage, harder than was necessary. Erik clenched his jaws, restraining a fierce impulse to use his own knuckles on the surly underling's pudgy face. Instead, he satisfied himself with glaring at the walls of the embassy. Even in this modest suite, the walls were covered with wood paneling, ornately carved in the imperial manner.

The sight of those paneled walls darkened his mood further. The very fact that this ceremony was being held here, in the embassy of the Holy Roman Empire, was a sign of the rot. By rights, it should have been held in the Knights' own hospital. And if the one in Venice was too small for the purpose, a suitably neutral site could have been easily found in a city as large as this one. Holding it here simply reinforced the common perception that the Knights had become nothing more than an extension of the imperial power, pure and simple.

Erik sighed, remembering his father's words as he bade his younger son farewell. *Remember, lad, stay out of politics! Church or state, it matters not. Your duty is that of the clan, to the Emperor alone. Nothing less, mind—but also nothing more. Nothing else.*

But between the Pomeranian squire and the Prussian knight-commander it was hard. The Prussian, Von Stublau, was irritating him even more than Pellmann.

"Prussian son of a bitch," muttered Manfred, as he marched into the banqueting hall. He said it quietly, though. He'd been hoping for duty carrying the Woden-casket from the chapel nave to the banqueting hall. Instead he'd drawn the delightful duty of being one of the door-wardens. To stand for the entire length of the banquet and watch while the church delegations and the imperials wined and dined the oligarchy of Venice.

Not for the first time he wished he could pack this up and go home to Bretagne. Or even back to Mainz. However, his mother and his uncle had made it painfully clear that he was going to do service as confrere knight in a monastic order . . . or else. And Uncle Charles was quite grimly capable of making the "or else" a long stay in the imperial dungeons. On the whole being a confrere was a better option. Just.

If he had to be strictly honest about it, and he usually was with himself, Manfred had brought it on himself. Going to the Gothic grandeur of Mainz from the impoverishment of Bretagne had been a shock, when he had been sent to the imperial court as a twelve-year-old page. When he went back home to Bretagne, he'd run a little wild.

His mother had hoped the pious, monastic knights would rid him of his taste for low companions and teach him piety, and allow him to mix with people of his own order. Mother was Swabian to the core and regarded her husband's court, and the chiefs and duniwasals of Bretagne, as little more than barbarians.

So far it had made him dislike most Saxons and positively detest most Prussians.

He tried to find solace in what he could. The one advantage of the closed pot, after all, was he could ogle pretty girls at will. Of course he couldn't actually speak to them. As a penance he could watch the chased silver platters of delicacies being carried in. On the plus side he got to watch Abbot Sachs flinch from an array of whole crispy fried baby squid. To make up for it the sound of the rebecs seemed to be trapped in the helmet. . . .

The Venetian musicians were stilled. The great doors at the far side of the chamber were flung open and the party bearing the captured Woden-casket advanced. And there was Erik. Carrying one side of the spear bier the casket was transported on.

Manfred almost laughed. All you could see of the Icelander were those chilly blue eyes. Impossible for most people to read anything in that gaze. But Manfred knew him well enough to sense the Icelander's irritation with the man leading the little party.

Prussian son of a bitch.

Von Stublau had the opposite end of the spear that Erik had been assigned to. He was even taller than Erik, which was unusual among the Knights. Needless to say, he had the shaft end of the spear. "Pick it up higher, *auslander*," grumbled the burly German knight-proctor, as they clanked down the passage toward the hubbub of the embassy's banquet hall.

Erik lifted his side slightly. Von Stublau was right. The thing should be borne on a level. The four knights advanced in step, bearing the crucifix made from four lashed spears. Strapped to the crucifix with bands of steel was the Wodenite casket. To Erik, the weight of souls in that casket was far more than the mere heavy oak, black iron studs and rune-etched bands. Even if each soul it had devoured was lighter than swansdown.

True, the capture of a Svear heathen god—even that of a small tribe of Smålanders—was a triumph for the forces of Christ. Its public display and the enactment of the Rite of Forbidding greatly enhanced the Knights' prestige. But Erik knew that the creature of darkness had been taken from a temple of bells and bones. The bones of infant sacrifices . . . The bells made from the skulls.

Like most people from the League of Armagh, even those of Norse descent, Erik was a follower of the Gaelic creed within the Church. That tradition—the more so in Vinland—was not given to theological stringency. Until arriving in the continent, he had paid little attention to the endless doctrinal disputes between the Petrine and Pauline trends within the main body of the Church.

He had known that the Pauline creed was dominant in the Holy Roman Empire; and that the Knights were specifically devoted to it. But the knowledge had been abstract, until he joined the militant order. Since then, the Icelander had come to find some of the practices of the Pauline orders—especially those of the Servants— a bit frightening. His private opinion was that it would be far better to destroy the Woden-godling than to display it.

The banquet hall of the embassy nearly took Erik's breath away. Part of the impact was the smell. Beeswax and alchemistic silver-cleansers clogged the nostrils, even over the smell of perfumes. Part of it was the heat produced by thousands of candles in silver sconces. He was becoming almost inured to the wasteful opulence of the Holy Roman Empire. Still . . . the banquet hall took that opulence to extremes he had not witnessed even in Mainz. He wasn't as bad as the Orkney islanders who made such a virtue of their unavoidable frugality, but the sheer ostentation still bothered him. The high walls were slit with lancet windows, the inter-vening spaces hung with tapestry. Underfoot was soft with Turkish carpets, imported from the great realm of the Mongol Ilkhan.

The crowded room was silenced by the entry of the marching Knights. As they moved slowly into the chamber, Eric studied the crowd through the narrow slits of his helmet.

At least in one small way, the Venetian notables packed into the banquet hall reminded Erik of the Icelandic Althing-gatherings and Vinlander volk-meets. Far more, in truth, than the people attending the court functions he'd been to in the cities of the Holy Roman Empire, as the triumphant party of Knights displayed their captured trophy in their progression down to Italy.

Those crowds had been composed almost entirely of the nobility. Whereas some—many, Erik suspected—of the grandees of Venice were plainly just wealthy tradesmen. Something about their posture said it.

Erik examined Giorgio Foscari. The Doge of Venice was an elderly man—an octogenarian, in fact—who looked as if he'd be more at home counting coins on his estate than leading Venice's Signori in the Senate and Grand Council. And the "condottiere" General Aldo Frescata, on the Doge's right, looked as though he'd be more at home leading a fashion parade than a march. The Castillian consul sitting next to him, engaged in quiet conversation with the elderly Father Maggiore, head of the local chapter of the Servants of the Holy Trinity, looked far more like a soldier.

The Venetians, on the whole, were dressed to display the fact that this was still probably the richest independent city in Christendom. A city which was itself the owner of a small empire. Still, there was an underlying hardness—a sort of marine tang—that appealed to Erik.

The Servants of the Holy Trinity, spiritual and magical guardians of the casket, came forward from where they had been seated. Their leaders, both of the local chapter and of the delegation from the monastery at Hochstublau, left the high table and joined them.

"*Sanctus. Sanctus in mirabile dictu . . .*"

The low chant began, as, with swaying censer, blessed salt and the sprinkling of holy water, the monks began their ninefold circle. Sister Ursula began preparing for the evocation of the guardians. Erik was not well versed in magic, other than some of the practices of shamans in Vinland, but he knew it was going to be a long ceremony. The weight of the casket seemed to press down still further.

Out of the corner of his eye Erik caught sight of Manfred, one of the armored door-wardens, as he ripped a browned piece of the whole roasted chamois that had just been carried in by the liveried servants. The supposed door-warden cracked his visor and popped it into his face.

Erik sighed. In the private interview he'd had with the Emperor upon his arrival in Mainz, Charles Fredrik had said that his young nephew Manfred's piety compared well to a Vinlander's city polish. Being more or less half Vinlander, Erik understood the metaphor too well. In another two years he'd have finished his stint as a confrere knight with the Order, and he could go back. Already he'd more or less made up his mind. Vinland. It was such a wide, open place, even compared to Iceland. . . .

"*Conserva me!*"

Erik's idle thoughts were interrupted by that sudden loud cry. His eyes, half-closed behind the heavy armored visor, opened wide. He wasn't certain, but he didn't think that shout was part of the ceremony. . . .

The chanting stuttered to a halt. Father Maggiore, the local chapter head of the Servants of the Holy Trinity, had turned and was now staggering blindly into the orderly procession.

Eric frowned. He had half-suspected that the elderly, whiny-voiced prelate was beginning to lose his wits during his hour-long rambling sermon that morning. Now it looked as if he were having a minor fit. The wispy white-haired monk flailed out wildly, knocking to the floor one of the brothers who had tried to approach him.

Monks scattered like sprats as the elderly man began to shriek. His voice quavered upwards above the panicky babble beginning to break out among the grandees of Venice.

Abbot Sachs put down his censer and stepped forward. His open hand was raised, and he plainly intended to slap the old man. Before he could do so, before he could even touch the man, the abbot was flung away, as if by a giant unseen hand. He landed on his backside, legs flailing above his head.

Then the old man stopped. His voice, as whiny as ever, seemed almost normal as he said, "*Conserva me, domin . . .*"

Then he shrieked terribly, briefly. And then, as the flesh on his face itself began to bubble, melt and flow, laughter, black, deep and evil, erupted from lips pulled into a parody of a grin.

Manfred, armor and all, vaulted the table, sending ornate Venetian glassware, wine and silverware flying. He raised his broadsword . . . and reversed it. Taking it by the guard to form a cross, he advanced on the monk who was tearing aside his robes with frantic bloody fingers.

"Back!" yelled Abbot Sachs, scrambling to his feet. "Back, you fool! Knights! Seal the doorways." Already the nobles and notables of Venice were heading for the great doors in panic-stricken streams.

Knights positioned at intervals around the walls rushed for doors, broadswords at the ready. For a moment it looked as if they would be mobbed down. But steel armor and the fearsome swords quelled the rush, after a part of the crowd had managed to flee the chamber.

Young Manfred, meanwhile, continued to advance on the tortured and still obscenely laughing monk—slowly, as if through thick mud. Sparks leapt from his spiky armor.

"Put this damned thing down," snarled Erik. He had to help the young fool. It was his duty to God and Emperor Charles Fredrik, despite the fact that the hair on the nape of his neck was rising. He had seen combat in Iceland and the magic of pagan shamans on the Vinland frontiers, but nothing like this.

"Stand!" snapped Sister Ursula, advancing with rapid strides on Abbot Sachs, who was pushing his way toward Manfred. The abbot looked as if he was struggling through quicksand.

"Von Stublau!" The nun's eyes singled out the burly Altmark knight. "Protect the casket at all costs. Do not allow it to be set down. This is but a distraction." Then she snatched a basin of holy water from one of the horrified watching monks, and strode—as if it was the easiest thing in the world!—to link arms with Abbot Sachs. Together they held the basin. Together they dipped fingers into it and flicked the water onto Manfred's armor.

The effect was cacophonic. With a discordant jangle like the cracking of bells, Manfred was flung backwards. He landed in a broken-doll sprawl against one of the spindly legged chairs. The delicate piece of furniture splintered under his great weight, fragments flying everywhere.

The nun and the gray-cassocked abbot advanced on the writhing remains of Father Maggiore. Little flames were beginning to dance above the bubbling flesh. The two clerics reached their hands into the basin and . . .

The silver basin cracked in two as if it were a brittle stick. The two clerics retreated hastily, not quite running. Erik was relieved to see Manfred sitting up, feeling for his broadsword among the smashed splinters of the chair.

"A circle!" commanded the abbot. "Servants of the Trinity, form a circle! Knights—put a ring of steel around that casket. The forces of pagan darkness seek to free the Woden."

Hastily, the monks and knights moved to comply.

But it was too late for the former Venetian chapter-head of the Servants of the Holy Trinity. The old monk would never give another whiny-voiced rambling sermon, or come around demanding to know whether anyone had seen his missing cassock. The naked figure was shriveling and blackening even as the monks chanted.

By the time the monks had closed in on the body and sprinkled holy water, there was little more than ashes left.

Father Sachs stilled the monks. Then he marched up to the high table where he had been seated with Doge Giorgio Foscari. He turned on the Signori of Venice. With a gesture he stilled the rising babble from the crowd.

"Hear now my words, people of Venice!" he shouted into the silence, his voice full of righteous anger. "Is it not written: You shall not suffer a witch to live? Evil flourishes here within the see of Venice. *Evil I say!* Evil flourishes and you are too lax to tear it out, root and branch. The accursed Strega, Jews, and Mussulmen ply their sinful trades in the open. Mammon and Belial have misled you from the holy path given to us by the apostle Paul. I tell you, he who falters from the Gospel is a heretic and damned to eternal hellfire with torments of white-hot scorpions. Your laxity has meant that the evil servants of the Antichrist dared to attack, even here, in the presence of the Master of your city. What hospitality is this that your own guests can be so abused? What has become of the sanctity of guests?"

Erik raised his eyes to the bacchanalian string-courses near the ceiling in irritation at the waste of precious time. Every moment now was vital. The miscreants must be among the "guests." But some had fled. It was essential that they be pursued. There was little doubt that honest steel would destroy the magic of pagans.

Instead he stood and ground his teeth as Abbot Sachs continued to harangue the Venetians.

Chapter 8

"Party lookin' for you," said Lola, green-eyed suspicion in her voice. The runner-girl wore the scarf he'd given her for telling them where to find Caesare. And a fine silver pin she'd got from someone else. That was Lola for you. *You* had to be loyal to *her*. . . .

Benito winked at her from his rooftop. He had to get back to Marco, but it paid to stay on top of the canal-talk. And Lola knew most of it before it even got out. "Who'd that be, Bright-eyes?"

Lola raised a dark eyebrow. "That girl we call 'the Spook.' You never see her in daylight. Always wears a hood. Got connections on the Rio del Ghetto."

Benito started guiltily. *Kat!* He'd forgotten he was supposed to meet her tonight. Getting Marco to move out of the swamp had driven the whole thing from his mind.

"Where is she?"

Lola sniffed. "You find her."

"Come on, Lola," pleaded Benito. When she was in this sort of mood, which was most of the time, Lola could be very capricious.

Lola just sniffed and shrugged.

Benito tried reason. "C'mon, Lola. It's a job."

The runner shook her head. "With that one you're safer chasing her body than getting into her line of work." And she was off. Benito knew it was useless to chase after her. Even if he could catch up, which was no certainty, because Lola was fast and knew every alley and shortcut in Venice, she wouldn't talk. And pressing her was a bad idea, anyway. Lola had several large and unpleasant friends.

He tried the arranged rendezvous. But Katerina wasn't there.

Seeing as it was close to the noise of Barducci's, he slipped in. It was early still and the sailors weren't there in numbers yet. On the spits they were cooking rows of toresani. The juniper and rosemary scented squabs gave Benito's stomach an abrupt, pointed reminder that he hadn't eaten yet. He hastened past to the bar where Valentina was plucking a complex melody. Claudia was counterpointing it, softly, with a treble flute. The audience was still a small one. Which was just as well. This was crying in your wine music. . . .

He waited. When the tune was finished, Claudia tipped him a wink. "Someone casting dabblers about for you. That 'Spook.' I've seen her on the water, but never in here. Wants to meet you at the Campo San Felice about ten. You'd better take care, Benito. Those are bad people you're mixing with."

Coming from Claudia, that was scary. Still. All Katerina wanted him to do was to recover that parcel. She'd offered an entire ducat for the job, too. She'd been pretty pointed in her comments about what would happen to him if the stuff turned up on the market. *If you're lucky, the Servants of the Trinity will get you before my . . . associates do.* Yeah. He'd fish that parcel out and leave her well and truly alone. He had responsibilities now. He might even have turned away from that ducat if he hadn't been feeling guilty about not getting to the rendezvous. In the shadowy side of Venice, you were a man of your word or you didn't survive.

Katerina Montescue was feeling guilty. Being late had been unavoidable. But you had to be careful here in the gray canal and dockside world. It had its own rules. You could kill someone. No problem, so long as you sank them quietly and didn't get the Doge's Schiopettieri stirred up. You could steal from them. Lie to them. But a deal was a deal. God help you if you broke it. Word got around. Only the marshes would offer refuge then. She, it was true, could go back to the *Casa*, her identity unknown. But *Casa* Montescue was in such straits that it could die. It was *likely* to die, if this cargo was lost.

She moved the gondola quietly along to the Campo San Felice. And the boy detached himself from the shadows and dropped into the boat, almost without rocking it. He moved as lightly as the thief he undoubtedly was. She shuddered. This was a scary world that she was forced to move in.

They did a magnificent duet.

"I'm sorry I was late. Problems."

"*You* were late . . . ?"

"You were late . . . ?"

"Why are you repeating everything I say?" snapped Katerina.

"I'm not. I was late. . . ." Benito burst out laughing. "So, we were both late, huh?"

"I was delayed," said Katerina, sourly. "Unavoidably."

Benito grinned. "Me too. So, let's get to it."

Tight-lipped, Katerina poled away. The shabby gondola prow cut a silent notch through the still water. After a while, though, she found herself almost smiling. For all his ragamuffin ways, there was undoubtedly something a little charming about young Benito.

From the high windows of the Imperial embassy, streamers of light spilled whitely onto the thin mist-shroud clinging to the dark canal-water. Inside the building all might be warmth, light, music, and occasional trills of laughter. Here, in the shadowy darkness of the side canal, it was cold. Katerina shivered. At least she didn't have to get into it.

"So what are you waiting for?" she hissed. "Get on with it and we can get out of here."

The boy did not look eager. The way he was taking off his jacket spelled reluctance. She could understand that. She wouldn't want to get into the smelly cold dark water either. She gritted her teeth. If necessary she *would*.

Benito looked doubtfully at the canal water as he dropped his jacket into the boat. It wasn't so much the swimming part, as the getting into the water that he hated. It was all right when you had the sun on your back, or when things were dire, but just to do it in cold blood on a misty night . . . The worst part was when the water got to your upper thighs. "Do you want to do it instead?" he asked, crossly. "I'm just wary. It's early in the evening for no one to be around."

Katerina shook her head, irritably. "The Schiopettieri did a clear-out here earlier. They're doing regular patrols. We've got a bit of time before the next one comes through. Get a move on."

He shrugged. No sense in asking her where she got such precise information. She wouldn't tell him, and he wasn't sure he wanted to know. He stripped off, down to his breeches. No sense in getting all his clothes wet.

He slipped into the water. It was cold, even at this time of the year. A couple of deep breaths and he duck-dived under the water. Swimming down for the bottom he forced himself to open his eyes. He might as well have kept them closed. Well, up was dimly lighter. His hands touched ooze. He felt around and realized this was not going to be an easy job after all. The water-door was plainly where the embassy threw out its garbage. He went up, breaking water with relief.

Katerina was a dark figure against the lights. "Did you find it?" she hissed anxiously.

Benito shook his head. "No."

He heard her sharp intake of breath. "It must be there. *It must.*" There was more than a hint of desperation in her voice.

"Yeah, maybe," he agreed hastily. "But look, there is lots of rubbish on the bottom. You got something heavy I can use to keep myself down there?"

She had the rock in a rope bag that did the poor-man's duty for an anchor. It gave him something to pull down on, and a point to feel around. That was a broken pot. That was . . . *eughh.* He pulled his hand back from something rotten enough to crumble. It took willpower to feel again. And then he screamed. Underwater. Which is never a good idea. Something slimy and snakelike had slithered up his arm. By the time his conscious mind had worked that out, he was already spluttering and pulling himself up into the boat. He nearly had the gondola over in his haste. "*Saint Marco, Saint Theresa . . .*"

"Hush!" snapped Katerina, looking around. "What's wrong?"

"There is something dead down there! And it is full of eels." The Venice lagoon was famous for its eels. You didn't want to think too much about what they ate. Benito didn't even want to say that what he'd touched felt like . . . cloth.

Katerina could see that the encounter with eels had scared this canal-wise urchin nearly witless. Still, they only had a short time left to find the parcel. Inquiries—discreet inquiries, but nonetheless alarming inquiries—had begun to come in about when the consignment would be delivered. They'd had to take money in advance for some of this lot. The inquiries had been . . . polite. Among that fraternity word had gone around that the Montescue were to be treated with respect. But they'd been insistent, nonetheless.

She shook Benito. Gently, though. "It was only eels. They'll have gone by now."

Benito shuddered. It was all Katerina could do to suppress her own shiver of sympathy. She knew only too well just what eels liked to eat. But for the Family, it must be done. "You gave your word."

"Eels . . ." Benito whispered.

Katerina shook him hard this time. "Come *on*! We've only got a little time."

The boy looked at her with big eyes. And took a deep breath. "One last try. Try and work out exactly where you put it in."

Katerina gritted her teeth. She'd been frightened as hell, and lying down too. How would she know? She looked about, trying to gauge things. "A bit further out, I reckon. And maybe a bit more toward the Grand Canal. It's difficult to judge without the other boats here." The noise from the embassy hushed. They both tensed. Then from inside came the familiar sound of voices uplifted in the Latin of a plainsong chant.

"Go," said Katerina roughly, pushing him, hiding her own shrieking nervousness in abrasiveness. As Benito slipped off into the water she decided that she'd try on the other side of the gondola with the boathook she'd brought as a last resort. He wasn't going to find it. The hook might damage the parcel. But even damaged was better than lost completely.

He wasn't going to find it. He knew he wasn't going to find it. He was only making this last effort for honor's sake. The bottom had been stirred up by his precipitous flight from the . . . corpse. Now it was so black down here that only the direction his body wanted to rise told him where up might be. It was claustrophobic, crushingly so, down here. He felt around. Very, very tentatively. And his fingers encountered fiber. He almost repeated his rapid ascent before he worked out it was twine. Coarse, thick twine, the kind merchants use for baling. He was almost out of air, but he couldn't risk losing it. He swam, following the cord. It was a fairly long swim. His hands encountered fabric . . . oilcloth. He had Katerina's precious parcel. Gripping it with both hands he turned and kicked for the surface.

Something hauled at it. Trying to pull it away from him.

❀   ❀   ❀

Katerina was beginning to realize the boy hadn't lied. Her attempts with the boathook had so far dredged up some scrap metal. It looked like an old bird-cage. And a piece of . . . cord. Baling-cord. She dropped the boathook in her haste to grab it. And it was plucked neatly out of her grasp. Swearing, forgetting the need for silence she snatched at it, nearly upsetting the gondola. She missed. Her sleeve wet to the shoulder, she hauled the boathook she'd dropped out of the water. Fortunately the cork handle—intended for idiots who drop boathooks—had kept it afloat. Shaking the bird-cage remains clear, she hooked furiously.

"That's me! *Stop it! You madwoman!*"

To Katerina's horror she saw she'd hooked the something all right. Benito's breeches. He was clinging to the pole with one hand and her oilskin-wrapped parcel with the other. Benito jerked angrily at the boathook pole, and Katerina lost her balance. She landed in the water beside Benito with a shriek and a splash. Benito swam away as she came up.

"I can't swim!" she yelled, spluttering. Fortunately there was quite a lot of air trapped in the thick serge of her dress.

Benito backed off to the stairs at the water-door. "You tried to murder me!" he accused, also forgetting to keep his voice down.

Katerina shook her head. She was getting lower in the water. "You were on the other side of the boat. Now get me out!"

"Oh. Yes. Like I was supposed to stay where I went down." Benito clutched the parcel to his chest, and retreated.

Katerina managed to grab the edge of her gondola and, having learned from last time, hauled herself hand over hand along the boat to the mooring post and thence to the steps.

Benito held the precious parcel in front of himself like a shield. "You come any closer and I'll throw it back into the water."

Katerina found herself trapped between fury and embarrassment. "Look. It was an accident. I told you."

"Accident, my foot!"

By the tone, Katerina knew she was in trouble. She couldn't offer him more money. A ducat was stretching things as it was. "Look. I can offer you more work. . . ."

"*Va'funcula!*" spat Benito. "Are you crazy? Claudia warned me—"

A terrible shriek, a sound not intended to issue from a human throat, came from the embassy behind them.

It silenced both of them. Briefly.

Benito snapped out of it first. "Holy Saint Mark! What . . ."

A terrible inhuman laugher erupted. Katerina felt the hair on the nape of her neck rise. She knew she had little magical skill, but she was sensitive to it. This was magic. Something dark. The medallion on her chest felt very hot.

"Never mind what!" Katerina scrambled into the gondola. "Come! Let's get out of here."

Benito looked doubtful, his face white in the reflected light of the unshuttered windows. Then there came more sounds from the windows, as if tables were being overturned and glass breaking.

A man's voice, shouting: *"Back! Back, you fool! Knights! Seal the doorways!"* Followed immediately by a swelling chorus of many voices screaming in panic.

"Come *on!*" Katerina barked. "Get in. You can hold the parcel. Just get in! We've got to get away from here!"

The boy jumped into the boat and cast loose hastily.

Katerina pushed off. With skill, she turned the gondola and sent it gliding away from the embassy.

Breathing a prayer she looked back. And nearly dropped the oar. It was hardly surprising really, with all the noise they'd made and the goings-on over at the embassy. But at the *Casa* Brunelli, the doors leading onto the upper-floor balcony were thrust open, flooding the balcony with light. She saw him clearly. The same slight red-haired man. The same single forbidding line of dark eyebrows. He was staring at them. Katerina would swear the expression on his face was one of triumph.

She shivered. And the shiver had nothing at all to do with her wet clothes.

Benito felt for his dry jacket. He was shivering. It was partly the cold and partly the fright. The boathook, bobbing in the canal behind them, had barely scratched his thigh. Hell. He loved thrills. It was the best part of being a roof-climber. But this was deep dark water. She could have her parcel. Then he'd be off. He wanted no part of this woman and her business. Fortunately, they'd part ways in a few hundred yards and he would never have to see her again. She'd never be any part of his world. He could look after himself, but he didn't want Marco involved with someone like this girl.

Chapter 9

The monster was dragged away from its feeding by a shrill of command from its master. The master's servant, rather, through which Chernobog usually spoke and gave commands.

Emerging from the darkness of its feed—snarling, reluctant— the monster's world began to take on a semblance of color. Insofar, at least, as various shades of gray could be called "color." After a time, red streaks began to appear in the mist. Those were not real, however—simply reflections of the monster's own rage.

The sight of those scarlet flashes brought courage. Again the monster snarled, and this time with bellowing fury rather than frustration. The clump of gray that was the form of the master's servant seemed to waver, as if she were cowering in terror.

The monster's moment of pleasure was fleeting. In an instant, the master himself billowed through the mist, an eddy of gray so dark it was almost ebon.

Silence, beast! Do not challenge me.

Again, red streaks came into the mist. But these were like blazing bolts of lightning, overwhelming the monster's own fury as easily as a flooding river flushes aside a child's pond. For just a fleeting instant, the monster thought to catch sight of Chernobog behind the shadows and the mist. The master was terrifying—huge, and tusked, and horned, and taloned. Scaled like a dragon, bestriding a broken earth like a behemoth.

One of the scarlet flashes curled through the mist like a snake, and struck the monster's flank. Agony speared through it. The monster whimpered. Broken words pleading forgiveness tried to

112

issue from lips that had once, long ago, had the semblance of human ones.

But that semblance was too ancient, now, too far gone. The words would not come any longer. Not over lips that were no more than a gash; not shaped by an ox-thick tongue writhing in a mouth that was more like an eel's gullet than a man's palate and throat.

Again, the spearing agony. The monster wailed. Wailing, it could manage—as could any beast.

Some part of the monster retained enough intelligence to think, if not speak, a protest. *I was a god once!*

"Only the shadow of one," came the sneering voice of Chernobog's servant—as if she were anything but a shadow herself. "And he isn't much of a god anyway, which is why he crouches at Great Chernobog's side. Wearing his master's leash."

The servant drifted forward, now fearless. For a moment, the monster sensed a vaguely female form coalescing, stooping. It felt another flash of rage—but a quickly suppressed one. She dared to inspect its feed!

"Not much left," she purred, jeering. "But then, I imagine the old monk's soul was mostly gristle anyway."

The form straightened and moved back into the mist. The gray of the shadow servant merged at the edges into the gray mist that surrounded the monster everywhere. Only a vague fluttering was left to indicate her shape.

The monster recognized the pattern. Chernobog would now speak himself, using the servant's voice.

"You have done well, beast."

The monster's momentary relief was immediately shredded by another scarlet lash coming through the mist, ripping into its flank like an axe. Gray-black blood spurted from a wound that was insubstantial—healing almost in the instant it was formed—but agonizing for all that. The monster wailed again, and again, crouching in terror.

"Which is why I punish you so lightly for your insolence."

The servant's vague form was replaced by another of those horrifying forward surges in the surrounding mist. The ebony billow that was Chernobog himself, threatening to take full and visible shape.

Do not forget your place, beast. I allow you to be powerful, at my convenience. I could as easily make you a worm, for my dining pleasure.

For a moment, the monster caught another glimpse of Chernobog on that broken landscape. Hunching, this time, over a mound of squirming souls. Much like worms, they looked; especially as they disappeared into the maw that devoured them, a few spilling out of the gigantic jaws onto the charred-black soil.

Another image flashed through the monster's mind. Itself—himself, then—held down by Chernobog's enormous limbs while the master tore out his manhood with that same maw and left the monster a bleeding, neutered ruin. Less than a eunuch, who had once been a god.

The monster was now completely cowed. Its heavy brow was lowered, the muzzle that had once been like a man's pressed into its chest. Oddly enough, perhaps, the chest itself was still hairless—quite unlike the shaggy limbs and the heavy spine that protruded like a ridge, covered with a long and stringy mane of hair.

At another time, the memory of what that hairless chest had once signified might have brought anguish. Now, the monster had no thoughts beyond submission.

"Good." The monster felt relief at hearing the servant's voice instead of Chernobog's own. As much as the monster hated and resented taking orders from one who was even less than it was . . .

Nothing was a terrifying as Chernobog, unshadowed.

"Good," its master repeated. "Your recent task also. It was well done, beast. The priest burned very nicely. Though I believe you wavered once, before this shadow restored your courage."

The monster whined. *The master was unfair!* A holy symbol held by such as *that* one—encased in steel—was a thing of great power. The master *knew* that. Such a fearsome one should never have been allowed—!

Silence.

The monster's thoughts fled. After a moment, the master spoke again. Thankfully, through his shadow voice.

"No matter. As elsewhere, this servant has her uses. And now the way is cleared for the creature Sachs."

The gray mist swirled and billowed. From experience, the monster knew that Chernobog was retreating into his own counsel. It managed to restrain any overt sign of relief. The master would know its thoughts, of course, since Chernobog had taken its soul.

But . . . so long as the monster maintained all visible signs of docility, it would not be punished.

Not much, at least.

How long it was before the master spoke again, the monster knew not. In that mist-shrouded place where it was kept—caged, for all intents and purposes—time had little meaning.

The servant's voice rippled with the master's own amusement. It was an odd sound—as if a torrent in a cavern were being heard through an echoing chamber far distant. Raw and unrestrained male power, channeled through the pleasant modulations of a female throat.

"And now I will reward you, beast. Tonight I will allow you to hunt."

In an instant, the monster's fear and submissiveness vanished, replaced by ravening eagerness.

Hungry!

The servant's voice echoed, faintly, the master's own humor. Not glee so much as simple satisfaction. There was very little left, in the monster, of what had once been a god's mind. But it understood, vaguely, that Chernobog's pleasure was more that of a game master than the monster's own much cruder urges. At another time, had its lust not been so overwhelming, the monster might have felt some grief. It had played games once itself, it remembered, and played them extremely well. Even giants—even gods!—had trembled with fear at that gamesmanship.

"Indeed," chuckled the servant's voice. "And a better soul than the one you just fed upon, I imagine. Younger, at the very least."

The image of a man came to the monster's mind, put there by the master. The man, and his raiment, and the fine house where he lived; and all the byways of the city by which he could be reached. Late at night, in the darkness.

The servant gave him a garment. Something once worn by the victim-to-be. It was full of man-scent, full of tiny fragments of skin. The monster snuffled and mouthed it. He had the scent, the taste of the intended victim. "I constrain you. On this occasion you will abjure from feeding on any other. Or you will face the master's wrath."

Hungry! Hungry!

"Do not feed too quickly," commanded the servant's voice. "The thing must be done in blood and ruin—*not quickly.*"

The monster would have sneered if it still had lips that could do so. As if it would hurry such a feast!

The time that came after seemed endless, though the monster had no way of gauging it. But eventually, it came.

"Go now," commanded the servant's voice, and the monster sensed the grayness vanishing.

Soon enough, the gray mist was gone altogether. Replaced by the dark—but sharp—shadows of Venice's narrow alleys and streets.

The monster scorned the streets, however. The great tail it had acquired, as if to substitute for its lost manhood, drove it through the waters of the city's canals as quickly and silently as a crocodile. Though no crocodile had such a blunt snout, or had a ridged spine protruding from the water, or a spine that trailed such long and scraggly hair.

It was spotted only once, along the way, by a street urchin searching the canal late at night for useful refuse. But the monster had no difficulty disposing of that nuisance, beyond the fierce struggle to restrain itself from consuming the child's soul. Once they had sacrificed children to him. Their souls had a distinctive taste.

A quick turn in the water, a powerful thrust of the tail; the boy was seized before he could flee and dragged into the dark waters. The rest, once the monster overcame the urge to feed, was quick. By the time sunrise came, the blood would have vanished and the fish would see to all but the largest pieces. And those, once spotted, would be useless to any investigator.

The monster was not concerned with investigation, in any event. In what was left of a once-divine brain, it understood enough to know that its master would be pleased by the deed. The small murder, added to the greater one still to come this night, would increase the city's fear. Among the canalers, at least, even if Venice's mighty never learned of an urchin's disappearance.

The only thing the master cared about was that the monster itself not be seen by any survivor. And so, as the monster drove quietly through the canals, the one eye that remained to it never ceased scanning the banks. Still blue, that eye, and still as piercing as ever—even if the mind behind it was only a remnant of what it had once been. But none of the few people walking alongside the canals ever spotted it.

❀   ❀   ❀

The shaman trailed behind, staying as far back as he could without losing sight of the monster completely. Which—in the murky waters of the Venetian canals—meant following much closer than he liked. He had to force down, time and again, the urge to follow using scent alone. The struggle was fierce, because the temptation was so great. In his fishform, in the water, the shaman's sense of smell—taste, really—was much better than the monster's, for anything except the scent the monster was tracking.

But . . . in the end, the shaman was more terrified of his master than he was of the monster. His master had made clear that he wanted a full report, and had demonstrated the depth of his desire by feeding the shaman the cooked skin of a retainer who had failed to satisfy him. Spiced with substances which had almost gagged the shaman at the time, and still made him shudder.

So, the shaman stayed within eyesight of the monster, however terrified it was of the creature. If the monster spotted him . . . it would interpret its master's command to "leave no trace" in the most rigorous manner. The shaman might be able to evade the monster—here in the water, he in his fishform and the monster in the shape it possessed. But he had no doubt at all that if the monster caught him, he would be destroyed—just as easily and quickly as the monster had destroyed the street urchin. A creature it might be today, but . . . the monster had once been a god, after all.

No longer, however. That once-god had been broken by a greater one. So, however reluctantly, the shaman stayed within eyesight.

Just barely.

The final destination loomed into sight, just as the master had planted the image in the monster's brain. One of Venice's great houses, its walls rising sheer from the Grand Canal.

Once it entered the Grand Canal, the monster submerged completely and continued swimming several feet below the surface—much too deep in those murky waters, even in daylight, to be spotted by anyone in a boat. The Grand Canal, at any hour of the day or night, bore a certain amount of traffic. The monster could hold its breath long enough to swim through the great waterway and enter the side canal that flanked the house.

It did so, emerging slowly and carefully to the surface. Unlike a crocodile, the monster could not simply lift its eye above the water. Half the misshapen head had to surface before it could see enough.

Then, for several minutes, it did nothing but study the situation; maintaining its position by slow sweeps of the tail and breathing as silently as it could.

It dismissed the side door without a thought. There was no way to enter through that portal without alerting the house, and the monster was not certain it could slaughter all the inhabitants before someone fled beyond its reach. Not in such a great house, which would be full of servants as well as family members. The one imperative was that it not be seen by anyone who could tell the tale afterward.

Carefully, it studied the wall itself. Then, satisfied, it sculled to the side and, with a great heave, hoisted itself onto the wall. The ugly octopuslike suckers on what had once been a deity's well-formed hands and feet had no difficulty adhering to the rough surface. Moving up the wall like some great half-lizard/half-ape, it worked its way quickly to the balcony three floors above.

Had the shaman still been in human form, he would have heaved a great sigh of relief when he saw the shape of the monster lift out of the canal. His task was done, for the moment. In his fishform, he could not follow the monster except in the waters. Not even his master expected that much.

The relief was short-lived, however. The greatest danger would come when the monster re-entered the canal. No longer preoccupied with its prey, the monster would be more alert. And in the meantime . . .

Hidden in the shadows of the pilings across the canal, the shaman studied his surroundings warily. Then, began to relax. There would be no danger from undines here, he realized. Not now, at any rate; not after the monster's passage. Undines were not very intelligent, true. But they were quite intelligent enough to understand they were no match for the monster, even if they didn't understand what it was. If there had been any undines in any of the canals through which the monster had passed, they were long gone by now.

❀   ❀   ❀

Just before reaching the balcony, the monster paused and scanned the surrounding area. There was no one watching. Another great heave, and it slithered its still-wet bulk onto the balcony.

Again, it paused. Still, no one had spotted it—except a cat, hissing in a corner of the balcony. The monster could move with astonishing speed for such a large and clumsy-looking creature. The hiss was cut short by a yowl, and the yowl cut short even quicker.

The monster had no difficulty restraining itself from devouring the cat. It did not like cats; never had.

Then, it spent five minutes studying the large double-door that opened onto the balcony from the room inside. It was not studying the door itself, so much as it was pondering a problem. The monster could remember—vaguely—a time when it had been superb at pondering problems, and felt a slight anguish at the memory. Today—

It was not good at problems. But, eventually, it decided the risk was too great to simply break through the door and sweep inside with a murderous rush. The master had not told it whether the intended victim rested in whatever room lay immediately beyond. A mere servant might be sleeping there. Granted, the murder of a servant would satisfy the master—in part. Not enough, however, to forestall a certain measure of punishment.

No matter. The monster's ugly and bizarre-looking hands were capable of delicate work as well as other, more congenial tasks. It was the work of less than two minutes, using one of its claws, to open the impressive-looking but crude lock.

One half of the double-door was pulled open; quietly, slowly. The room beyond was a short hallway. Empty, and unlit except for a single taper at the far end. There were two doors at that end of the hallway, one on each side. From their well-made construction and ornate decoration, they were clearly not the doors leading to servants' quarters. The monster was certain that in the rooms beyond the master of the house and his wife were sleeping.

But which one, behind which door?

There was no way to know without looking. Moving slowly, as silently as it could, the monster slouched down the hallway until it reached the end. Then, for no reason other than whimsy, it reached up and tested the latch on the door to its right.

The latch came up easily and silently. The door was unlocked.

Slowly, gently, the monster eased open the door and peered through it.

Darkness. The faint sound of breathing. The sounds of sleep. The monster pushed the door open far enough to allow itself to enter—which meant pushing it almost completely aside. It remained on all fours as it crept toward the side of the bed. Then, slowly, raised its head to study the bed's inhabitant. It sniffed softly.

It was the wife.

For a moment, a furious rush of lust almost overcame the monster, driving it to feed. It was an odd sort of lust, with nothing of the sensuality the monster could vaguely remember from its former existence. But if concupiscence had been replaced by something uglier, the lust was—if anything—more powerful still. It could barely restrain itself. Even now, after all that had passed, the monster still preferred female victims.

But—

The master had made his wishes clear. Remembering the nature of Chernobog's discipline . . . the monster shrank back, almost whimpering.

It turned and slouched away, back to the door. Then, once in the hallway, closed the door behind it. Softly, gently.

Almost, now. The monster could feel the craving rise, and no longer made any attempt to control it. When it opened *this* door, it made no attempt to remain silent. Just quiet enough not to awaken the woman in the other room. The monster cared not in the least whether the sound of its entrance roused the man in the room from his sleep.

It strode across the room in great steps, almost as erect as it had been in a former life. By the time it reached the side of the bed, the man in it had barely begun to open his eyes.

One great smashing thrust of the monster's left hand closed those eyes forever. Two talons pierced the eyes; the clawed thumb, hooking beneath, kept the jaw from opening; the suckers smothered the face. There was no sound beyond the blow itself and the sudden thrashing of limbs tangled in bed-sheets.

The man's strength was pitiful. Any man's strength would have been, much less that of a middle-aged and corpulent one. The only real difficulty the monster had, in what followed, was keeping its gurgling delight from turning into a howl of triumph.

The thrashing ended quickly. The monster began by breaking

and dislocating the major joints. Its huge right hand moved from knees to ankles to elbows, wrenching and tearing and crushing. That done, pausing just an instant to savor the moment, it drove its talons into the man's abdomen and began disemboweling him.

By the time it was done, the man had long since gone into shock. The monster cared not at all. The soul could not hide from it behind the veil of unconsciousness. As much pleasure as the monster took from the physical torment it inflicted on its prey, that was nothing compared to the ecstasy of destroying a soul.

Much like a cat might knead a dying mouse, the monster began slowly shredding its victim's body while it turned its real attention elsewhere. It paid little attention to the work of its hand; just enough to make sure it did not kill the man too quickly.

Mist, again, began to surround the monster, blurring its vision. Not the gray mist of its master's cage, but the savage and exciting colors of its spiritual hunting ground. Dark colors; purplish-reds so thick they shaded quickly into black, as the monster plunged deeper into the hunt. It followed the fleeing soul through that mist, tracking it as surely as a hound tracks a hare. Then, cornering its prey in a place which could not be described outside of a nightmare, it proceeded to feed and feed; until there was nothing left but scraps of pinkish violet, fading away into the billows.

Under other circumstances, the monster would have saved a small portion of the prey's soul, to gnaw on afterward as a dog gnaws a bone. But carrying even a scrap of soul back to its cage ran the risk of alerting some cleric who might by chance be encountered during its return. If that cleric possessed magic ability . . .

The master wanted no complications. Not yet, at least. So, reluctant but obedient, the monster devoured the soul entire.

Its vision began returning. Under its hands, it could feel the lifelessness of the corpse even before its eye could once again see its surroundings.

The surroundings returned, eventually. The same dark room; darker, now that the bedding was no longer remotely white. The monster had no idea how much time had elapsed, exactly. Not much. Surprisingly little, in fact. What the monster thought of as "feeding time" always seemed much longer than it really was to the world at large.

It straightened and stepped back slowly from the carnage on the bed, all of its senses alert once again.

Nothing. Not a sight, not a sound. Just the quiet and darkness of a great house in sleep.

The monster was not surprised. For all the havoc it wreaked while feeding, the process was actually almost silent. Had it still been capable of the pride that had once been a cherished vice, it would have felt pride at its skill.

But that ancient god was gone. Only animal satisfaction remained.

Before leaving the room, the monster took the time to lick itself carefully and thoroughly. Not because of any fastidiousness, but simply because the master's instructions had been clear. *Leave no trace of your passage.*

The thick purple tongue removed the blood and gore quickly and expertly. Then, like an animal moving away to sleep after feeding, the monster returned to all fours and slouched its way out of the bedroom; down the hallway and out onto the balcony; taking care to close the doors behind. *Leave no trace.*

On the balcony, it paused long enough to lick away any large puddles of canal water left by its entry. What remained would evaporate with the sunrise. A lurch and a slither and it was creeping back down the wall, scanning carefully to make sure there was no one to see.

It slid into the water with hardly a sound. The tail began to move again, and the monster glided through the canals.

The master would be pleased. Remembering Chernobog's discipline, the monster felt relief sliding alongside satiation.

Although, somewhere inside the mind that had once been divine, a small rage burned and burned. There had been a time . . . when the monster had disciplined others; and smiled coldly, seeing relief on the faces of those he spared.

It might have wailed then, with despair. But the master's instructions had been clear. *Leave no trace. Make no sound.*

During the return, the shaman barely managed to obey his master's instructions—and then, only by the sketchiest interpretation. Several times he lost sight of the monster swimming ahead of him through the canals.

But . . . he had no trouble following the creature. The monster might have cleaned itself well enough to fool human investigators, with their dim and dull senses. But the shaman—even in his human form, much less this one—was not fooled for an instant. The monster left a trail of havoc and horror that reeked worse than anything the shaman had ever encountered.

Except . . . in the presence of his master.

PART II
September, 1537 A.D.

Chapter 10

Dell'este tapped the sheet of paper. "Well, Antimo? How do you assess this?"

Bartelozzi said nothing. Just looked, unblinking, at the duke. A lesser master might have taken it for insolence. The Old Fox knew better. Antimo Bartelozzi always considered his answers very carefully; that was just his manner.

The duke waited.

Bartelozzi tugged his ear. "Caesare Aldanto overstates his importance in caring for the boys. But basically he is being accurate."

The old duke sighed. "Grandchildren are for spoiling and dandling on your knee, Antimo." For a moment he paused, allowing—once again, as he had time after time since Antimo brought him the news—joy and relief to wash through him.

But the pause was brief. The grandfather was disciplined by the duke. "These two are not grandchildren," he said harshly. "They are Dell'este bloodline. If they survive."

"You could bring them home, my lord," said the agent, quietly. "As I suggested once before."

Duke Dell'este shook his head grimly. "For a first thing, they may well be safer hidden in Venice. For a second, the Dell'este bloodline is like steel. Steel needs to be tempered to both harden it and make it flexible. It must be heated, hammered and quenched." He took a deep breath. "Some steel becomes the stuff of great swords. But if the alloy is not a good one, if it is not tempered between the furnace and ice, then you must throw it away because it is worthless."

Bartelozzi looked at the report on the desk. "By the part about the Jesolo marshes, written in Marco's hand, he's been through the fire. Young Benito has I think also been tested, perhaps not so hard. They're only fourteen and sixteen years old."

The duke shrugged. "Different alloys take heat differently; age has nothing to do with it. And I'm worried more about the younger than the older, anyway. Marco's father was a Valdosta. Benito is Carlo Sforza's son. They don't call Sforza the 'Wolf of the North' for nothing, Antimo. Between that savage blood and his mother's . . . recklessness, it remains to be seen how Benito will turn out."

The duke's eyes wandered to the sword-rack on the wall, coming to rest on the blades set aside for his youngest grandson. "But . . . hopefully, Caesare Aldanto will deal with him. Benito will get himself into the furnace, I have no doubt of that. Aldanto must just deal with the quenching."

Antimo Bartelozzi was silent for a time. "And is this Aldanto the right person to handle the quenching, my lord?" he asked at last.

"He is not a good man," said the duke heavily. "But he's a survivor, a great swordsman, and something of a tactician. I would struggle to find a tutor quite as skilled at all those things. Part of the quenching process is for those boys to learn their moral judgment. When they realize Aldanto's nature—and if they still choose to follow after him . . . then they're not fit to be part of Dell'este bloodline. If they choose honor instead, I will know I have good steel, flexible, ductile, yet sharp and true." He sighed. "They fell into Aldanto's lap by accident, but he was among those you hired to search for them. He is being well paid to care for them, to watch over them. While that income continues and while I am alive they are safe. But if I die, Antimo, Caesare Aldanto is to be killed within the day. He is not to be trusted."

Bartelozzi nodded. "I have arranged it already, my lord. And I will see it is done. Myself."

The Old Fox smiled. He could ask for no better guarantee. But, as usual, he accompanied the smile with a tease. "You *always* insist on doing my business in Venice personally, Antimo. I suspect you of keeping a woman."

For the first time in the interview, Bartelozzi allowed himself a smile. "We are all subject to weaknesses of the flesh, my lord. In my case, however, it's the food. Venetian courtesans are far too intelligent for my taste. Dangerous, that."

Chapter 11

Midday at the House of the Red Cat, and the house was as silent as a church. There wasn't one of the whores who rose earlier than Francesca, and most didn't ever see daylight. Lazy sluts. They'd never be more than they were now, and most would begin a slow decline to canalside the moment their looks began to fade.

Withered old Fernando poked his head inside Francesca's door. *Is it that he never learned to knock, or is it that he's under orders not to?*

"You asked me to make sure you were awake, Francesca," he said speciously. She hadn't done anything of the sort, of course. She was always awake and dressed this time of day. Evidently the Madame was checking on her.

"I'm going out," she said, with an ingenuous smile. She didn't say where; she had no intention of saying where. And although Fernando lingered long past the moment of polite withdrawal, she didn't add that information; which was, in all events, neither Fernando's nor their employer's business.

She picked up her cloak and tossed it over her shoulders, then headed purposefully for the door. Fernando prudently withdrew, and when she shut the door behind her, she saw him retreating down the stairs ahead of her. By the time she reached the ground-floor salon—silent, and tawdry with its shabby, rubbed velvet and flaking gilt—he was no longer in sight.

Well, if he intended to follow her, he was going to get a sad disappointment, and he was going to wear out his legs. Francesca always went out for exercise at this hour of the day—if there was one sure way to end up a dockside *puttana* prematurely it was to get fat—but today she was going to go a bit farther than usual. All the way to the Molo in fact, and entirely on foot. Not only was it good exercise, but Francesca had no intention of spending so much as a single clipped coin on a gondola if she didn't have to. Besides, it was a lovely day: the sun was shining, the sky blue. Even the most fearful of citizens had come out to do a bit of shopping, shaking off their fear of the rumored monsters prowling by night.

Francesca didn't bother with a mask, although even in daylight a great many people did, in or out of Solstice season. She wanted men to look at her and wonder, though she gave no sign of noticing their attention. That wasn't the game. Let them wonder if she was respectable—or *other*. There was nothing about her dress or her manner to mark her as belonging to either class. If they wondered enough, they might be on the lookout for her, and find out for themselves. A long chase always made the quarry more desirable.

It was a long walk. Francesca allowed the crowd to carry her along for the most part. No point in hurrying, but no point in dawdling either. She was paying close attention to the scraps of conversation she heard, though, and the general mood of people, and she didn't like what she heard. Death prowled the waterways in the shape of something other than fever and footpads; the rumors of a bloodthirsty monster had gained in strength and detail since the last time she went out.

There were other rumors too, of those foreign Servants of the Trinity—*Sots*, people called them, with sniggers—who came storming into churches, surrounded by armored and armed Knots, making accusations of heresy and witchcraft and dragging perfectly ordinary people off their knees and out of the church. No one had actually seen any of this, of course, but everyone knew someone who knew someone who had. Still, the rumor probably had some foundation, and if you couldn't go to your church to light a candle without facing the possibility of finding yourself up on a charge of heresy, where *could* you be safe?

There was a great deal of fear in the telling of these tales, but plenty of anger, too. How *dared* these foreigners come in and start dictating to Venetian citizens how to conduct themselves? How *dare* a lot of Pauline fanatics lay down religious law to devout Petrines in their own city?

Very, very interesting, if bad for business—at least the business of someone in the mid-level, like Francesca. The courtesans, in whose number Francesca was not as yet included, were immune from the persecutions and difficulties of the working poor and lower half of the middle class. In good times or bad, unless one's fortune was lost entirely, the rich were never troubled in their pleasures by sacred or secular dictates.

All the more reason to make the jump and make it soon.

Francesca did not spend a single *lira* on dresses, cosmetics, perfumes, sweets, or any of the other indulgences that the other girls at the Red Cat squandered their earnings on. Granted, she didn't need to; her looks and inventive imagination were more than enough to keep the customers coming. She ate lightly, but well; her teeth were her own, her breath always sweet, her skin kept soft as velvet with some very inexpensive unguents purchased from a little Strega herb-seller named Donatella, whose advice she was scrupulous in following. The same herb-seller provided her with some very efficacious little sponges she kept steeping in herbs-and-vinegar when they weren't—well—inside *her*. It was from this same Strega that Francesca had gotten a name and an appointment. If Francesca was right, the girl she was going to meet might provide her with what she needed—possibly with *everything* she needed.

Midway between Sext and None, at Fiorella's food-stall, on the Molo.

Francesca knew Fiorella's. They had a pastry made with Asiago cheese and artichoke hearts that qualified as a mortal sin. She could eat it while strolling along the Molo, along with a piece of bruschetta.

I shall have to do something about my breath, after, though, she thought ruefully. *Too much garlic . . .*

Knowing she was going to the Molo, she had not lunched and had only eaten lightly of breakfast. That, and the brisk walk to and from the Red Cat should make up for the richness of Fiorella's pastry. Her Strega herbalist had strong ideas about diet that Francesca did not altogether agree with—moderation in all things had been good enough for the ancient Greeks.

She crossed the Piazza San Marco, crowded at this hour just before the close of business with everyone who wished last-minute bargains. Except for her looks, no one would have given her more than a passing glance, so completely did her clothing blend in with that of the others who thronged the plaza. Every possible level of wealth and status passed through here during the day. The poorest of the poor crouched in odd corners and chanted their beggars' cries, while the most wealthy of the *Case Vecchie* set paraded by in their silks and jewels. Housewives bargained sharply over food-stuffs, and women who might be courtesans, or might be the daughters of the rich, fingered silks and laces.

The stalls continued down on to the Molo, the wide promenade that faced the lagoon. Francesca walked slowly towards the food-stall, eyeing the other customers, looking for someone who fit the description of the girl she was to meet.

Aha. There she is. Looking restless, a young woman paced back and forth before the stall, her head lowered, casting occasional glances at a gondola tied up directly opposite. Her face was almost completely obscured by a hood. Only someone who stood close and looked carefully would be able to discern her features. Beneath her skirt—plain but of good quality—Francesca caught a glimpse of trews. With the Sots on the rampage, liable to take offense at practically anything, such an odd combination of cloth-ing was a prudent move for a woman who might have to tie her skirts up above the knee in order to better handle a boat or cargo.

Francesca's hopes rose. The extreme care the girl was taking in keeping herself from being recognized fit the tentative assessment Francesca had made from the herb-seller's rather vague descrip-tion of her—deliberately vague, she was convinced. This was a girl from Venice's upper crust, working the "gray trade" in disguise. Possibly for her own profit, but more likely because the family was in dire straits. She might even be from one of the *Case Vecchie* families, which would be ideal.

Francesca walked directly toward the young woman, making certain to catch and hold her eye the next time the girl's surrep-titious glance swept searchingly over the crowd. Relief suffused the woman's shadowed features, and she stepped forward to meet Francesca halfway.

"I'm Kat. Are you Donatella's friend?"

"Yes I am. I'm Francesca." She paused for a moment. "I'm tem-porarily at the House of the Red Cat. . . ."

She waited to see what Kat's reaction would be, but there was none—or at least, there wasn't one visible, which was all that mattered. Again, that fit Francesca's assessment that the girl or her family was in narrow financial straits. Presumably money was needed badly enough that the source didn't matter. Which also, of course, explained why the girl would be running cargo for the Strega—who were hardly in good odor with the authorities, especially these days.

"I haven't eaten yet—" Francesca began. She wasn't really *that* hungry, but the girl was so obviously tense that Francesca thought it would be wise to allow her time to settle down. And retreat to a less visible location.

Sure enough: "I have, so why don't you go get something and meet me at my boat? We can talk there while you eat." Kat softened this slightly brusque response with a smile. "I'd . . . rather not stay out in the open. And your time is probably short anyway."

Francesca nodded and made her way to the stall to purchase the pastry while the girl retreated to her boat.

When Francesca was seated in the gondola, Kat waited politely while she took the edge from her hunger. "I understand there are some things you need?" Kat asked. Hurriedly: "But I have to tell you in advance that I only handle high-priced items. High-priced and low volume. I'm sorry if that's not what you're looking for— Donatella was not clear about it—but that's all I can handle. I need—"

She fell silent, apparently unwilling to elaborate. In her own mind, Francesca filled in the rest: *I need to generate a lot of money quickly, with only my own labor and this little gondola.* Francesca had to force herself not to show any signs of glee. Perfect! The girl *was* from the Venetian elite. Probably, in fact, nothing less than *Case Vecchie.*

"I'm not really looking to buy, Kat," she said easily. "Although there are some items I could use. Mainly, I want to set up a conduit through which I can sell information—"

She hurried on, seeing the frown already gathering on Kat's face. "—*not for cash*, but for . . . ah, some assistance in a delicate matter of my own advancement."

The fact that Francesca wasn't asking for cash—which Kat was obviously in desperate shortage of herself—caused a momentary fading of the frown. But, soon enough, it returned.

"What kind of information? And I'm not sure how I might be able to help your 'advancement.'" A bit mulishly: "I don't have any cash to spend."

Francesca understood that she had to edge away from triggering the girl's uneasiness on the subject of her own identity. The easiest way to do that, of course, was to focus Kat's attention on Francesca's. So, bluntly and briefly, Francesca explained the exact nature of her profession—and, most important, her plans for professional advancement.

When she was done, she waited for Kat's reaction. Driving both her fears and her hopes under, and sternly. The girl would do whatever she would do. Whatever else Francesca had learned in her life, a stoic outlook was central to all of it.

For a time, Kat was silent. Her hooded eyes left Francesca and simply stared out over the waters of the canal. Then, to Francesca's relief, the girl's shoulders moved in a little shrugging gesture and she turned back to face her. Francesca was a bit surprised to see that the expression on Kat's face was one of disguised interest— almost fascination—rather than disguised revulsion. For the first time, she felt herself start warming to the girl. Whatever great house she belonged to, it was clear enough that Kat did not possess the typical noblewoman's haughtiness toward her social inferiors. Most girls from Venice's elite—especially from the *Case Vecchie*, which Francesca was now almost certain was true of Kat—would have been sneering at her. Indeed, would already be ordering her to depart their presence.

"I'd like to help, Francesca. But I'm really not sure the kind of information you could provide me would be enough of a help for me to spend the time at it. It depends, I guess, on what you want in return."

Francesca smiled. "I think you'll be surprised at how useful the information I'll be providing you will be. *After* I'm situated in Casa Louise, of course. The information I could provide you right now wouldn't be all that useful, I admit. Except . . ." She gave Kat a level gaze. "Even now, I could provide you with quite extensive information on the movements of the Schiopettieri. Several of their captains are regular customers of mine."

For a moment, Kat's face froze. Then, suddenly, the girl choked out a little laugh. "That'd be something! Ha!" She smiled. "All right. That's enough for me to gamble a little. Whether it goes any further . . . we'll see. You mentioned a few 'items' you could use. What are they?"

"A gown, perhaps more than one, a cloak, and accessories," replied Francesca. "Something—impressive, but not showy. Not the sort of thing that I would be able to purchase for myself, as I am now."

Kat nodded. "I think I know what you mean. *Case Vecchie* impressive. Would you object to something old, but newly remade?"

Francesca and Kat exchanged the conspiratorial smiles universal to every pair of Women Discussing Wardrobe. Something about this girl was striking a chord with her, and she could sense that Kat felt the same way. "You have anticipated exactly what I was going to ask for. As I explained, I am about to undertake a change in status, and for that . . ."

The two of them discussed gowns and undergowns, fabrics and colors for nearly half an hour. Kat, it seemed, knew both a seamstress and someone who was close in size to Francesca—and with the latest mode in laced gowns, a perfect fit was easy to attain provided the size was close.

When they were done, Kat hesitated, her face tightening a bit. Understanding the awkwardness, Francesca immediately said: "I'm quite willing to pay for these items, Kat. In cash."

It was Francesca's turn to hesitate. The kind of clothing she needed was extremely expensive; more than she could possibly afford to buy new. To make the right impression she *had* to obtain the finest quality silk clothing. That kind of silk cost between two and ten ducats an ell, and it would take roughly ten ells to make a single gown. Even used, she doubted she could find anything for less than twenty ducats—and that, in all likelihood, would be a hand-me-down for poor relations with all of the trimmings, beads, embroidery, and buttons removed. Which would be useless to her. Whatever else, Francesca could not afford to look like a "hand-me-down" of any kind. A courtesan had to seem, in every respect, as if she belonged to the elite herself and was not a street whore with delusions of grandeur. Few of her prospective patrons would really be fooled by the illusion, but the illusion was nevertheless essential—in order for them to maintain face.

And, there was this also . . . Now that Francesca had made this initial contact with Kat, she realized that maintaining the liaison could of great value to her in the future. Francesca was sure that

Kat came from an upper-crust family—*curti* at the very least. An elite house which had fallen on hard times, but still retained its social glamour. That was the reason, obviously, Kat was so careful to remain incognito. In Venice's complex and sometimes deadly social dance, losing face was as dangerous to such a family as losing money—more so, in many ways.

Which meant, in turn . . . Francesca managed not to wince openly. What it meant was that Kat's surreptitious "gray labor" required significant financial returns, or it simply wasn't worth the doing. There was no way the girl would agree to help unless Francesca was willing to part with—

This time, she was unable to completely prevent the wince from showing. *Everything I've saved up—that's what it'll cost me.*

But it was Kat, this time, who bridged the awkwardness. Smiling: "What can you afford, Francesca? As long as it's enough not to, ah, embarrass me . . ." She chuckled a bit nastily. "The truth is my greedy sister-in-law would eventually grab everything from my mother's wardrobe anyway. I'd just as soon you get some of those items instead of *her.*"

Kat named a price, a better one than Francesca expected. Better enough, in fact, that she could afford a few extras. There was a little bargaining, and the arrangement was concluded. The transaction would still take practically every ducat Francesca had managed to save up, but it was well worth it. With *that* wardrobe, she could saunter confidently into any salon in Venice, including a soiree at the Doge's palace.

The remaining arrangements were settled quickly. The first gown—the one she would need for her interview with the Madame of Casa Louise—would be ready within a day, and the rest within three. If Casa Louise accepted her, Francesca would have the remaining gowns sent there, to await her arrival. That was fast work, but if this seamstress was as expert as Kat claimed, it would be no great task for her to remake gowns in an older mode— perhaps a matter of new trim, adding the side-lacings, re-dyeing. As earnest, Francesca handed over half the agreed-upon price, and Kat generously offered to pole her to the Red Cat—or near it, anyway.

By the time they reached the Red Cat, Francesca sensed that the younger woman wanted to be friends, not simply business associates. That astonished her even as it warmed her heart. The knowledge was a bit of a treasure, even leaving aside the obvious advantage it would provide Francesca at a later time.

"When we need to meet again, where can I send word?" she asked, as she got gracefully out of the gondola without assistance, which was no mean feat.

Kat hesitated a moment. "Donatella can always find me," she said at last.

Not quite willing to trust me yet. Or else she's afraid her family will find out what she's been doing. If she was the sole support of an Old Family, they would not necessarily want to *know* what turns she was making to keep them solvent. *Having a summons come from a house of whores would certainly change that situation.*

"Excellent. And thank you," Francesca replied. "I will be waiting eagerly to see the results of our bargain."

"By Wednesday afternoon," Kat promised, and pushed off. Francesca turned and walked sinuously back to the door of the Red Cat.

There. That went much better than I'd even hoped, she thought, blithely greeting Fernando on her way to her own room. *Next, the interview with the Madame at Casa Louise.*

But before that, a full night at the Red Cat. She licked her lips and tasted garlic.

I had better go rinse out my mouth.

Chapter 12

A piece of plaster bounced off Marco's nose, accompanied by a series of rhythmic *thuds* from overhead. By that sure token he knew, despite the utter darkness of his "bedroom," that dawn was just beginning.

He reached over his head and knocked twice on the wall. He was answered by a muffled curse and the pounding of Benito's answer. He grinned to himself, and began groping after his clothing.

Thudathudathudathuda—pause—(Marco braced himself)—*thud*. A series of plaster flakes rained down. A professional dance-troupe had the studio above their "apartment" from dawn to the noon bells. From noon till dusk it was given over to classes—noisier, but less inclined to great leaps that brought the ceiling down. From dark to midnight the thuds were less frequent. The groans muffled.

Nobody around the Campo dell'Anconeta talked about what went on then, and nobody watched to see who went in and out. Marco knew, though; at least what they looked like. Thanks to Benito's irrepressible curiosity, they'd both done some balcony climbing and window-peering one night. A dozen or so hard-faced men and women had been there; and it wasn't dancing they were doing. It was some kind of battle training, and all of them were very, very good. Who they were, why they were there, why they were practicing in secret, was still a mystery. Marco smelled "fanatic" on them, of whatever ilk, and kept clear of them.

Then, from the midnight bell until dawn, Claudia's old acting troupe had the run of the place. That meant less ceiling-thumping—but a lot of shouting. ("Elena *deary*, do you think you *might* pay *less* attention to Kristo's *legs* and a *little* more to your lines? *All* right children, *one* more time, from the *top*...")

Marco had learned to sleep through it all, though noise generally made him nervous. It was friendly shouting, for all the mock-hysterics.

Being directly below the studio was one reason why this place, technically a three-room apartment—a room and two closets, more like—was cheap enough for two kids to afford. Now Marco hurried to pull on his pants and shirt in the black of his cubbyhole bedroom, wanting to be out of it before the other reason evidenced itself. Because the other reason was due to start up any minute now—

Right on time, a hideous clanking and banging shook the far wall. Marco pulled open his door and crossed the "living room," the worn boards soft and warm under his bare feet. He stood blinking for a moment in the light from their lamp; after pitchy dark it was painfully bright even turned down to almost nothing. He reached and turned the wick key, and the odor of cheap last-press olive oil assaulted his nose until it flared up. Then he unlocked the outer door and slipped down the hall to the big ewers and garderobe shared by most of the apartments on this level. That incredible ruckus was the Rio San Marcoula boatyard. It started about dawn, and kept it up till the late afternoon, and sometimes later. There was another apartment between them and the repair shop, but it didn't provide much in the way of sound-baffling. Fortunately for him, the tenant of *that* place was deaf.

Benito still hadn't turned out by the time Marco got back, so he pulled open the door to the other "bedroom" (just big enough for a wall-hung bunk and a couple of hooks for clothes, identical to Marco's) and hauled him out by the foot. There was a brief, laughing tussle, which Marco won by virtue of his age and size, and Benito betook himself off to get clean.

There weren't any windows in their home, so there was always the oil lamp burning up on the wall. The lamp was a curious blend of cast-off and makeshift; the brass container had once been good, and still could be polished to a soft golden gleam. The multiple round wicks were scrounged. The lamp came with the place. So did the cast-iron grate in the fireplace. The fireplace smoked, but provided some heat in winter—when they could find fuel—and something to cook on. The "main" room was small, but it was still bigger than both the "bedrooms" put together. All of it was bare wooden-floored and sooty-walled, but warm and without drafts; and it was too many floors beneath the roof to get leaks when it rained. On the wall opposite the oil lamp and next to the stove was a tiny fired-clay basin and an ewer of safe water from the rainwater cisterns. Everything else was theirs, and compared to the little Marco had owned in the swamp or what Benito had had in the attic he'd been hiding in, it was paradisiacal.

They now boasted a couple of cushions to sit on, a vermin-proof cupboard for food—and even a second cupboard for storage, which currently held two tin plates, two mugs, two spoons, a skillet and a battered saucepan, and assorted odds and ends. They also owned their bedding and three changes of clothing each, as well as a precious box of half a dozen or so battered, dirty, and mostly coverless books. The last were Marco's property. Some he had bought at secondhand stores, like the precious anatomy book, much in demand with medical students. Some were gifts from Claudia, a few from Benito. He knew the ones that Benito gave him had been stolen, and he suspected the same of Claudia's. But a book was a book, and he wasn't going to argue about its source.

All that hadn't come out of nowhere. Word had gone quietly upriver with a Ventuccio barge that Marco and Benito still lived— and a special verbal message had gone to Duke Dell'este from Marco as to why they weren't coming home again. Back down again, just as quietly, had come a bit of real coin—not so much as to call attention to the recipient, but enough to set them up comfortably.

With the coin had come another verbal message to Marco from his grandfather. "You salvage our Honor," was all it had said—and Marco nearly cried.

Grandfather had clearly felt that his mother Lorendana had befouled the Family honor by her activities with the Milanese. He had said as much when he sent them into exile. There was honor, and there was Dell'este and Valdosta honor, which had been something special for many hundreds of years. Dell'este honor was famous throughout Italy. And the Valdosta were not just *Case Vecchie*. They were *Case Vecchie Longi*. One of the old families; one of the *oldest* families. One that claimed to have already been living here in the marshes when Holy Saint Mark was greeted by an angel in the form of the winged lion. All Venice knew how dearly the Valdosta *Casa* held their honor.

That upright stiff old man of Marco's earliest memories had sent those few words and that parcel of coin. To do even that, he must have felt Marco had redeemed what Lorendana had besmirched—at least as far as the Dell'este were concerned.

That . . . *that* had been worth more to Marco than all the money.

Marco hoped that the rest of what he was doing was worthy of that Honor—although he was fairly certain in his own mind that it would be. Honor required that debts be paid, and he owed a mighty debt to Caesare Aldanto. So hidden under the books was his secret, beneath a false bottom in the box. Pen, ink, and paper; and the current "chapter" of Mama's doings, back in the Milanese days. When he had five or six pages, they went off to Caesare Aldanto, usually via Maria. He had written up to when he'd turned ten, now. How much of what he remembered was useful, he had no idea, but surely there was something in all that stuff that Aldanto could turn to a purpose. Something to even up the scales of debt between them.

Marco watered some wine, and got breakfast out—bread and cold grilled *sarde*, bought on the way home last night. Benito bounced back in the door, fighting his way into a too-tight liveried shirt.

No one would ever have guessed, to see them side by side, that they were brothers. Marco clearly showed his Ferrarese-Dell'este ancestry, taking after his mother, Lorendana. Straight black hair, sun-browned skin fading now into ivory, and almond-shaped eyes in a thin, angular face; making him look both older and younger than his sixteen years. Had he been back in Ferrara, nobody would have had any trouble identifying which family *he* belonged to, for Lorendana had been a softened, feminized image of the old duke. Whereas Benito, round-faced and round-eyed, with an olive complexion and wavy brown hair, looked like a getting-to-be-handsome version of the Venice "type"—and not a minute older than his true age of fourteen.

"Need to get our clothes washed tonight," Benito said, gingerly reaching for his watered wine. "Or tomorrow."

"Spares clean?" Marco asked around a mouthful of bread, inwardly marveling at the fate that had brought him full circle to the point where he and Benito actually had spare clothing. Of course things had been a great deal better back in Ferrara—but no point in harkening back to that. To go back home would put the entire Dell'este house in danger, and with the worst kind of enemy—the Visconti. They were like the vipers of their crest. Deadly, unforgiving, and prone to use poison. There was no way Marco was ever going to take that grudge home.

"Yes. I'm wearing 'em, dummy."

"So'm I. Tomorrow then. That's my day off; besides, I got to see Caesare tonight." Washing clothes meant getting the washroom after everyone else had gone to work; clearing it with the land-lord and paying the extra three pennies for a tub full of hot water besides what they were allowed as tenants. There was an incentive to Marco to volunteer for laundry duty. Benito was still kid enough to tend to avoid unnecessary baths, but Marco used laundry day as an excuse to soak in hot, soppy, soapy water when the clothing was done until all the heat was gone from it before rinsing the clean clothing (and himself) out in cold. After two years of alternately freezing and broiling in the mud of the swamp, a hot bath was a luxury that came very close to being a religious experience for Marco. Hence, Marco usually did the laundry.

Benito sighed. "All right. I'll clean the damn fireplace."

"*And* the lamp."

"Slaver. *And* the lamp. What are you seeing Caesare about?"

"Dunno. Got a note from him at work yesterday. Just asked me to meet him at Giaccomo's, because he was calling in favors and had something for me to do."

"Hey, can I come along?" Benito never missed the opportunity to go to Giaccomo's or Barducci's if he could manage it. Unlike Marco, he loved crowds and noise.

Marco thought about it; then, shrugged. "Don't see why not. Caesare didn't say 'alone,' and he usually does if that's the way he wants it. Why?"

"Gotta keep you safe from Maria, don't I?"

Marco blushed hotly. He'd had a brief crush on Maria Garavelli; *very* brief. It hadn't lasted past her dumping him headfirst in the canal. Benito still wasn't letting him live it down.

The memory of that embarrassing episode led Marco to thoughts of his current "romantic predicament." He rose abruptly, turning away from Benito enough to hide the deepening flush on his cheeks.

He hoped profoundly that Benito never found out about

Angelina—he'd rather *die* than have Benito rib him about her. He much preferred to worship her quietly, from afar—without having half the urchins Benito ran with knowing about it, too. He still didn't know too much about his idol—the only reason he even knew her name was because he had overheard one of her companions using it.

Oh, Angelina . . .

Enough of daydreaming. "Get a move on, we're going to be late," he replied, while Benito was still chuckling evilly.

There had been plenty of gossip among the other clerks today, and because of it Marco made a detour down to the Calle del Vin on the way home—to the *Casa* Dorma. He felt drawn there as if by some overwhelming force. What was really at work was the powerful, almost frantic, "romantic urges" that come suddenly upon any sixteen-year-old boy—which they are incapable of analyzing clearly. And Marco's years in the marsh had made him even less capable of understanding himself, at least in this respect, than almost any other boy his age. There had been no girls his age in the marsh with whom to gain any experience at all.

So there he was at Dorma's gatehouse, facing the ancient doorkeeper through its grate. Half of him feeling he was in a state of sublime bliss; the other half feeling like a complete idiot. He was glad it was nearly dusk; glad his dark cotte and breeches were so anonymous, glad beyond telling that the shortsighted doorkeeper of House of Dorma couldn't see his face. It took all his courage to pretend to be a runner with a message to be left "for Milady Angelina." He moved off as fast as was prudent, eager to get himself deep into the shadows, once the folded and sealed paper was in the doorman's hands. His heart was pounding with combined anxiety, embarrassment, and excitement. Maybe—well, probably—Angelina would get it, if only when the head of the household demanded to know "what this is all about."

And—Jesu!—they'd want to know what it was about, all right. Because it was a love poem. The first love poem Marco had ever written.

Anonymous, of course, so Angelina would be able to protest honestly that she had no idea where it had come from, and why. And Marco's identity was safe. He'd written and erased it twenty or thirty times before it seemed right. Then with a carefully new-cut quill and some of the fine ink from Master Ambrosino Ventuccio's desk, he had copied it out on the best vellum. And the only reason he'd found the courage to deliver it was because today he'd finally found out *who* she was.

Milady Angelina of Dorma. *The* daughter of the house. Not above Marco Valdosta, even though she was at least two years older than he—but *definitely* above the touch of Marco Felluci. If *Casa* Dorma discovered some ragamuffin like Felluci had dared to send a love poem to Milady Angelina...

The best he could hope for was a beating at the hands of Dorma retainers. If young noblemen of the family got involved, "Marco Felluci" might very well find himself run through by a rapier— and these great old families usually had a baker's dozen of brawling young cousins lounging around, all of them ready at an instant to defend their family's honor.

Marco sighed. He had buried Marco Valdosta quite thoroughly, and not even for the sweet eyes of Angelina Dorma was he going to resurrect the name he'd been born to. "Marco Felluci" he was, and Marco Felluci he would remain—even though it meant abandoning all hope of ever winning the girl he was quite certain was the love of his life. But even if he couldn't touch, he could dream— and, perversely, even if she were never to learn who her unknown admirer was, he wanted her to know how he felt. So he'd spent three hours struggling over that poem.

Just two weeks ago it was, that he'd first seen her. At Giaccomo's, with a couple of companions. Until then his daydreams had been confined to something just as impossible, but hardly romantic.

The Accademia! Lord and Saints, what he wouldn't give to get in there to study medicine! But—he had no money, and no sponsor, and the wrong political history. Not that he gave a fat damn about the Montagnards anymore, and their fanatical determination to bring northern Italy into the Holy Roman Empire. But there was no way he was ever going to pass for one of the young nobles of Venice or even a son of one of the *Casa curti*.

Still... Marco was young enough that sometimes, sometimes when the day had really gone well, it almost seemed possible. Because a long-buried dream had surfaced with this new life.

Marco wanted to be a healer. A doctor.

He'd had that ambition as far back as he could remember. Mama had owned a drug-shop for a while, which she'd set up with what money she had after her family cut her off. Marco had been just old enough to help her with it, and he'd found the work fascinating. The patrons of the shop had teased him about it—but right along with the teasing, they'd asked his advice, and had taken it too. That perfect memory of his, again. He remembered symptoms, treatments, alternatives, everything. He'd helped old Sophia out in the marshes, later, with her herbs and "weeds," dispensing what passed for medicine among the marsh-folk and locos.

Of course, since seeing Angelina for the first time, she'd crowded out that particular daydream more often than not. But it was still there, rooted so deeply he knew it would never go away.

And so, as he made his way from *Casa* Dorma, Marco's thoughts were brooding and melancholy. Two heartbreaks at the same time seemed a bit much, at the age of sixteen! He consoled himself by beginning to compose, in his mind, another love poem. A brooding and melancholy one, of course.

His feet were chilled as he padded along the damp wooden walkways. He couldn't get used to shoes again after two years without them in the marshes, so he generally went as bare of foot as a bargee. The temperature was dropping; fog was coming off the water. The lines of the railings near him blurred; farther on, they were reduced to silhouettes. Farther than that, across the canal, there was nothing to see but vague, hulking shapes. Without the clatter of boot soles or clogs, he moved as silently in the fog as a spirit—silent out of habit. If the marsh-gangs didn't hear you, they couldn't harass you. Breathing the fog was like breathing wet, smoky wool; it was tainted with any number of strange smells. It held them all: fishy smell of canal, smell of rotting wood, woodsmoke, stink of nameless somethings poured into the dark, cold waters below him. He hardly noticed. His thoughts were elsewhere—back with the inspiration for his poem.

Oh, Angelina . . .

He wondered if he'd see her tonight at Giaccomo's. Half-hoping; half-dreading. She tended to show up at Giaccomo's pretty frequently. Marco was under no illusions as to why. Caesare Aldanto, of course—the most handsome and glamorous man there. Hell, Caesare even had Claudia and Valentina exchanging jokes and comments about him. Marco wondered hopelessly if *he'd* ever have—whatever it was that Caesare had. Probably not.

❀ ❀ ❀

His feet had taken him all unaware down the cobbled walkways and the long, black *sotoportego* through to his own alleyway, to his very own door, almost before he realized it. He started to use his key, but Benito had beaten him home, and must have heard the rattle in the lock.

"About time!" he caroled in Marco's face, pulling the door open while Marco stood there stupidly, key still held out. "You fall in the canal?"

"They kept us late," Marco said, trying not to feel irritated that his daydream had been cut short. "There any supper? It *was* your turn."

"There will be. Got eggs, and a bit of pancetta. Frittata do?" He returned to the fireside, and the long-handled blackened, battered pan. He began frying garlic, a chopped onion, a handful of parsley—stolen, no doubt, from someone's rooftop garden—and the cubes of pancetta. Marco sniffed appreciatively. Benito was a fairly appalling cook, but always got the best of ingredients. And, as long as he didn't burn it, there wasn't much he could do wrong with frittata.

Benito tossed the fried mixture into the beaten egg in the cracked copper bowl. Then, after giving it a swirl, and putting in a lump of lard, he tossed the whole mixture back in the pan and back on the heat. "They gave me tomorrow off too, like you—something about a merchant ship all the way from the Black Sea. You got anything you want to do? After chores, I mean."

"Not really," Marco replied absently, going straight over to the wall and trying to get a good look at himself in the little bit of cracked mirror that hung there. Benito noticed, cocking a quizzical eye at him as he brought over an elderly wooden platter holding Marco's half of the omelet and a slice of bread.

"Something doing?"

"I just don't see any reason to show up at Giaccomo's looking like a drowned rat," Marco replied waspishly, accepting the plate and beginning to eat.

"Huh." Benito took the hint and combed his hair with his fingers, then inhaled his own dinner.

"Hey, big brother—y'know somethin' funny?" Benito actually sounded thoughtful, and Marco swiveled to look at him with surprise. "Since you started eating regular, you're getting to look a lot like Mama. And that ain't bad—she may'a been crazy, but she was a looker."

Marco was touched by the implied compliment. "Not so funny," he returned, "I gotta look like somebody. You know, the older *you* get, the more you look like Carlo Sforza. In the right light, nobody'd ever have to guess who your daddy was."

Benito started preening at that—he was just old enough to remember that the great condottiere had been a fair match for Caesare Aldanto at attracting the ladies.

Then Marco grinned wickedly and deflated him. "It's just too bad you inherited Mama's lunatic tendencies also."

"Hey!"

"Now don't start something you can't finish—" Marco warned, as his brother dropped his empty plate, seized a pillow and advanced on him.

Benito gave a disgusted snort, remembering how things had turned out only that morning, and threw the pillow, back into its corner. "No fair."

"Life's like that," Marco replied. "So let's get going, huh?"

Giaccomo's was full, but subdued. No clogging, not tonight; no music, even. Nobody seemed much in the mood for it. The main room was hot and smoky; not just from Giaccomo's lanterns, either. There was smoke and fog drifting in every time somebody opened a door, which wasn't often, as it was getting cold outside.

Lamps tonight were few, and wicks in them were fewer. Customers bent over their tables, their talk hardly more than muttering. Dark heads under darker caps, or bare of covering; no one here tonight but boatmen and bargees. Marco looked around for the only blond head in the room, but had a fair notion of where to find him. When he had a choice, Aldanto preferred to sit where he could keep an eye on everything going on.

Pretty paranoid—but normal, if you were an ex-Montagnard. Especially an ex-Montagnard from Milan. Even by the standards of Italy, intrigue in Milan was complex and deadly. Milan was the stronghold of the Montagnard cause, to which the Duke of Milan paid faithful homage. But Filippo Visconti had his own axes to grind and his own double-dealings with respect to the Montagnards. The "imperial cause" was a marvelous thing for the ruler of Milan— so long as it did not actually *triumph*. If it did . . . the essentially independent realm of Milan would become just another province within the Holy Roman Empire. And Duke Visconti was not the man to take kindly to the thought of being a mere satrap—any more than his condottiere Carlo Sforza's bastard son Benito took kindly to his older brother Marco's attempts to rein in his less-than-legal activities.

Politics in Milan, in short, was like a nest of vipers. Marco's own mother had been destroyed by that nest—and Caesare Aldanto, who hadn't, made sure he always sat where no one could get behind him.

Marco had been known to choose his seats that way too. Whether he liked it or not, and despite the fact that he no longer cared about such things, his heritage had entwined him hopelessly in the coils of Italian politics.

There he was—black cotte, dark cap, golden blond hair that curled the way the carved angel's hair curled. As Marco had expected, Caesare was ensconced in his usual corner table. But as Marco and Benito wormed their way closer, Marco could see that he was looking—not quite hungover, but not terribly good. Limp-looking, like it was an effort to keep his head up and his attention on the room and the people in it. Minor mental alarms began jangling.

Still, if the man wanted to binge once in a while, who could blame him? Ventuccio had plenty to say about him, not much of it good. Marco picked up a lot by just keeping his mouth shut and his ears open, doing the accounts they set him and staying invisible. What he heard didn't seem to match the Caesare Aldanto who had given two dumb kids a way out of trouble. Especially when it was more logical for him to have knifed them both and dumped them in the canal. He had a feeling that someday he'd like to hear Caesare's side of things. He also had a feeling that if that day ever came, it *would* be when Aldanto was on a binge. If he ever lowered his guard enough.

Aldanto's table had a candle over it, not a lamp—candlelight was even dimmer than lamplight. The two boys moved up to the side of the table like two thin shadows. Marco had brought his week's worth of recollections, neatly folded into a packet. Maybe it was the dim light—but they stood by the side of the table for nearly a minute before Aldanto noticed them. Marco bit his lip, wondering if he'd offended Aldanto in some way, and the man was paying back in arrogance—but, no; it was almost as if he was having such trouble focusing that he could only attend to one thing at a time. As if he *really* wasn't seeing them, until he could get his attention around to the piece of floor they were standing on.

When Aldanto finally saw them, and invited them to sit with a weary wave of his head, Marco pushed the sealed packet across the table towards his hand. Aldanto accepted it silently, put into a pocket, then stared off into space, like he'd forgotten they were there.

Marco sat there long enough to start feeling like a fool, then ventured to get his attention: "Milord—"

Now Aldanto finally looked at them again, his eyes slowly focusing. He did *not* look hungover after all; he looked tired to death and ready to drop. "You asked *me* to come here, remember? There is something you want us to do?"

"I—" Aldanto rubbed one temple, slowly, as if his head was hurting him; his eyes were swollen and bruised looking, and there were little lines of pain between his eyebrows. "There was—I know there was a reason—"

This was nothing like the canny Caesare Aldanto that Marco was used to dealing with! Alarmed now, Marco took a really hard look at him, eyes alert for things Sophia had taught him to take note of.

He didn't like what he saw. A thin film of sweat stood out on Caesare's forehead; his blue eyes were dull and dark-circled. Aldanto was fair, but he'd never been *this* white before. His hair was damp and lank; and not from the fog, Marco would bet on it. And his shoulders were shivering a little as if from cold—yet Giaccomo's was so warm with closely crowded bodies that Marco was regretting he'd worn his thick cotte. And now Marco was remembering something from this morning and the gossip among the other clerks at Ventuccio—a rumor of plague in the town. Maybe brought in on that Black Sea ship. Maybe not. Marco's bones said that whatever was wrong with Caesare had its roots *here*—because Marco's bones had once shaken with a chill that he'd bet Caesare was feeling now.

"Milord, are you feeling all right?" he whispered, under cover of a burst of loud conversation from three tables over.

Aldanto smiled thinly. "To tell you the truth, boy—no. Afraid

I've got a bit of a cold, or something. Felt like death two days ago and now it seems to be coming back. A bit worse if anything."

He broke into a fit of coughing, and his shoulders shook again; and although he was plainly trying, not all of his iron will could keep the tremor invisible. Marco made up his mind on the instant.

Marco turned to his brother. "Benito—go find Maria. Get!"

Benito got. Aldanto looked at Marco with a kind of dazed puzzlement. "She's probably on her way. What—"

"You're drunk—act like it!" Marco whispered harshly. "Unless you want Giaccomo to throw you in the canal for bringing plague in here! I don't much imagine he'd be real happy about that."

He rose, shoved his chair back, and seized Aldanto's arm to haul him to his feet before the other could protest or react. And that was another bad sign; Aldanto had the reactions of any trained assassin, quick and deadly. Only tonight those reactions didn't seem to be working.

Marco had always been a lot stronger than he looked—with a month of regular meals he was more than a match for the fevered Caesare Aldanto.

"Now, Milord Caesare," he said aloud—not too loudly, he hoped, but loud enough. "I think a breath of air would be a proper notion, no? I'm afraid Milord Giaccomo's drink is a bit *too* good tonight."

There were mild chuckles at that, and no one looked at them twice as Marco half-carried, half-manhandled Aldanto towards the door. Which was fortunate, for they both discovered when Aldanto tried to pull away that his legs were not up to holding him.

They staggered between the tables, weaving back and forth, Marco sagging under the nearly deadweight Aldanto had become. Out of the double doors they wove, narrowly avoiding a collision with an incoming customer, and down onto the lantern-lit front porch. Down a set of stairs were the tie-ups for small boats, only half of them taken tonight. And pulling up to those tie-ups was a gondola sculled by a dusky girl in a dark cap. Maria Garavelli and no mistaking her.

Marco eyed her uncertainly, not sure whether he was actually relieved that Benito had found her. . . .

Maria was notorious along the canals. Her mother, kin to half of the families in the Caulkers' guild, had done the unthinkable— she'd gotten pregnant by some unknown father, refused to name him, refused to marry in haste some scraped-up suitor, and had been summarily thrown out on her ear by her enraged father. The woman had outfaced them all, bearing her child openly, raising her openly, and taking the gondola her grandfather had left her and making a place and a reputation for hard honest work right up until the day she died.

Maria had continued that reputation, though she had been only just big and strong enough to pole the boat over difficult passages when her mother went to the angels (or the Devil, depending on who was doing the telling). With her skirts tied up between her legs for ease in movement, that dark cap pulled over her ears and all of her hair tucked up into it, she was as androgynous a creature as any *castrati*. Working a boat from the time she could walk had given her wide, strong shoulders and well-muscled arms. Her pointed chin and high cheekbones looked female, but the square jaw hinges and deep-set brown eyes, usually narrowed with suspicion, would have been more at home in a man's face. There wasn't anything about their expression that looked soft or female, nor was there in the thin lips, generally frowning. She hadn't a woman's complexion, that was for sure; she was as brown as any bargeman. If there were breasts under that shapeless shirt, it wouldn't be easy to tell. But there was more than a hint of womanly shape in the curve of her hips—and her legs were the best on the canal.

Of course, if you dared to tell her so, she'd probably punch you in the jaw so hard it would be three days before you woke up.

They were just in time to see Benito catching the line Maria was throwing him. Light from Giaccomo's porch lantern caught her eyes as she stared at them. There was something of a mixture of surprise and shock—yes, and a touch of fear—in the look she gave them.

"I think we need to get this fellow home," Marco said loudly, praying Maria would keep her wits about her. She might not know him well, but she knew that Aldanto had trusted them to spy for him, and guard his back, more than once. He just prayed she'd trust him too, and follow his lead.

She did; playing along with him except for one startled glance. "Fool's been celebratin'?" She snorted, legs braced against the roll of her boat, hands on hips, looking theatrically disgusted. She pushed her cap back on her hair with a flamboyant and exaggerated shove. "Ought to let him walk home, that I should. Ah, hell, hand him over."

Aldanto was in no shape, now, to protest the hash they were making of his reputation. He was shaking like a reed in a winter storm. His skin was tight and hot to the touch, as Maria evidently learned when she reached up to help him down the ladder onto her halfdeck. "Look—you—" was all he managed before another coughing fit took him and Maria got him safely planted. She gave no real outward sign that she was alarmed, though—just a slight tightening of her lips and a frightened widening of her eyes.

"Think we'd better come along, Maria," Marco continued, in what he hoped was a bantering tone of voice—for though they seemed to be alone, there was no telling who had eyes and ears in the shadows or above the canal. "Afraid milord is likely to be a handful. Won't like being told what to do." That last was for Aldanto's benefit. While he talked, he stared hard into Maria's eyes, hoping she'd read the message there.

Go along with this, he tried fiercely to project. *I can help.*

"You think so?" The tone was equally bantering, but the expression seemed to say that she understood that silent message. "Well, guess it can't hurt—"

"Right enough, then. Benito, give Maria a hand with that line." Marco climbed gingerly down into the boat where Aldanto sat huddled in misery, as Benito slid aboard, the bowline in his hand.

"What the hell—" Maria hissed, as soon as they were out of earshot of the bank.

"He's got fever. Looking at him, I think it is just the marsh-fever, what they call 'mal-aria,' not the plague. You got something to keep him warm?"

Without the need to guard her expression, Marco could read her nearly as well as one of his books. First there was relief—*Thank God, it could have been worse, he could have been hurt*—and that was quickly followed by anger and resentment. He couldn't guess at the reasons for those emotions, but that expression was chased almost immediately by stark, naked fear. Then she shuttered her face down again, and became as opaque as canal water. At her mute nod toward the bulkhead, Marco ducked under it, and out again, and wrapped the blanket he'd found around Aldanto's shaking shoulders.

Aldanto looked up, eyes full of bleary resentment. "I—" cough "—can take care of—" cough "—myself, thanks."

Marco ignored him. "First thing, we got to get him back home and in bed. But we gotta make out like's he's drunk, not sick."

Maria nodded slowly; Marco was grateful for her quick grasp of the situation. "Because if the people figure he's sick—they figure he's an easy target. Damn!"

"Will you two leave me *alone*?" muttered the sick man.

This time Marco looked him right in the eyes.

"No," he said simply.

Aldanto stared and stared, like one of the piers had up and answered him back; then groaned, sagged his head onto his knees, and buried his face in his hands.

"Right." Marco turned back to Maria, swiveling to follow her movements as she rowed the gondola into the sparse traffic on the Grand Canal. She wasn't sparing herself—Marco could tell that much from what he'd learned from poling his raft. Which meant she was trying to make time. Which meant she was worried, too.

"Second thing is, we need money. I got some, but not too much. How about you? Or him?"

"Some. What for?" Suspicion shadowed the glance she gave him as she shoved the pole home against the bottom, suspicion and more of that smoldering anger and fear. *Touchy about money, are we, Maria?*

"Medicine," he said quickly. "Some we send Benito for; people are always sending runners after medicine, especially in fever season. Nothing to connect Caesare with that." Marco fell silent for a moment.

"You said, 'some.'"

"I'll decide the rest after we get him back," Marco said slowly, "and I know how bad it is."

Campo San Polo at last. Up the stairs at water level they went, stairs that led almost directly to Aldanto's door. Aldanto tried to push them off, to get them to leave him at that door. But when his hands shook so that he couldn't even get his key in the lock, Marco and Maria exchanged a *look*—and Maria took the key deftly away from him.

Caesare complained, bitterly but weakly, all through the process of getting him into his apartment and into the bed in the downstairs bedroom. Not even with three of them were they going to try and manhandle him up the stairs to the room he usually used.

Ominously, though—at least as far as Marco was concerned— Aldanto stopped complaining as soon as he was installed in bed;

just closed his eyes against the light, and huddled in his blanket, shivering and coughing. Marco sent Benito out with orders for willow bark and corn-poppy flowers, also for red and white clover blossoms for the cough, not that he expected any of them to do any good. This wasn't *that* kind of fever. He knew it now; knew it beyond any doubting.

"I hope you can afford to lose a night's trade, Maria," he said, pulling her out of the bedroom by main force. "Maybe more. I'll tell you the truth of it: Caesare's in bad shape, and it could get worse."

"It's just a cold or somethin', ain't it?" Her look said she knew damned well that it was worse than that, but was hoping for better news than she feared.

"Not for him, it isn't," Marco replied, figuring she'd better know the worst. "Same thing happened to me, when I had to hide in the swamp. I caught every damn thing you could think of." Marco shook his head. "Well, he needs something besides what we can get at the drug-shops."

"The Calle Farnese . . ." she said doubtfully.

Marco shook his head firmly. "More than quack-magic, either."

He took a deep breath. "Now listen: I'm going to write down exactly what I need you to do with those herbs when Benito gets back."

"I can't read," she whispered.

Marco swallowed. With Maria's pride, you tended to forget she was just a woman from a large, poor caulker family. Even the menfolk could probably barely manage to cipher their names. "Never mind. Benito will read it for you. It should help him to stop coughing enough to sleep. The coughing is not serious. The fever is the part that is worrying. It should break soon and just leave him weak and tired. Then it'll start up again. Right now he needs sleep more than anything else. You stay with him; don't leave him. That might be enough—he'll feel like he wants to die, but he's not exactly in any danger, so long as he stays warm. But—" Marco paused to think. "All right, worst case. If he gets worse before I get back—if his fever comes again or his temperature goes up more—"

That was an ugly notion, and hit far too close to home. He steadied his nerves with a long breath of air and thought out everything he was going to have to do and say. What he was going to order her to do wasn't going to go down easy. Maria Garavelli didn't like being ordered at the best of times, and this was *definitely* going to stick in her throat.

"I know maybe more about our friend than you think I do. I'm telling you the best—hell, the *only* option. If he starts having trouble breathing or hallucinating, you send Benito with a note to Ricardo Brunelli. You tell him if he wants his pet assassin alive, he'd better send his own physician. And fast."

Maria's eyes blazed, and she opened her mouth to protest. Marco cut her short.

"Look, you think *I* want my brother going up there? You think we're in any better shape than Caesare is in this town? I don't know what you know about us, Maria, but we got as much or more to lose by this. I don't know if Caesare's let on about us, but—"

God, God, the chance! But they owed Caesare more than they could pay.

"Look at me—*believe* me, Maria. If Brunelli—any of 'em—ever found out about me and Benito, we'd—we'd wish we were dead, that's all. We know things too, and we got nobody but Caesare keeping us from getting gobbled up like sardines. Caesare they got reasons to keep alive—us—well, you can figure out how much anybody'd miss two kids. So trust me, the risk's a lot more on our side; if he gets worse, it's the only way to save him."

"Damn it, Marco—" she started; then sagged, defeated by his earnestness and her own fear and worry. "All right. Yeah, I pretty much know about your situation. Hell, though—what you've been doing—I dunno why we'd need a real doctor. You're as good a doctor as I ever seen—"

"Like bloody hell I am!" he snapped, more harshly than he intended. He saw Maria wince away, her expression chilling, and hastily tried to mend the breach.

"Look—I'm sorry, I didn't mean that the way it sounded. Maria, I'm scared too—for all of us." He managed half a smile, when he saw the hard line of her lips soften. "And you just—stepped on a sore toe, that's all. See, I'd give my arm to be able to go to the Accademia, to learn to be a doctor. And I've got about as much chance of that as your gondola has of flying." He sighed. "That's the problem with having things get better, I guess. When I didn't have anything, I didn't want things, because I knew I'd never get 'em. But now I got a little, seems like I want more. Things I've got no chance for."

He hadn't really expected Maria to understand. But to his surprise, she gave a little wistful glance back toward the bedroom, sighed, and nodded. "I reckon we both got a notion how that feels," she agreed. "But—I dunno, Brunelli—he's a shark—that doctor could just as easy poison Caesare as cure him."

"So I just gave you what to do in the worst case, hey? Worry about that when the time comes. Caesare's luck with skinning through, he'll be all right. But if not—I'll tell you now—you might just as well chance poison, 'cause if you want Caesare alive, you get him a *real* doctor as soon as he starts getting worse—*if* he does, before I make it back."

"Back? From where?" She only now seemed to realize that he wasn't planning on staying.

"I told you, I know this fever. I had it once, too. And Caesare needs more'n what we can get from the drug-shop. So I'm going to get the medicine he needs—the one place here I know I can—where I got what saved *me*. The place I spent the last two years. The marsh." He smiled crookedly at her stunned expression.

"How are you going get there?" She stammered. "I—"

"I said you had to stay here, didn't I? And keep Benito here to help when he gets back. I'll get in the same way I did the last time. Walk. Or swim. The tide is out and I know the channels. I should do. I lived there for long enough."

Chapter 13

"You're not going out *again!*"

Not for the first time, or even the thousandth time, Katerina Montescue wondered what had possessed her brother Alfredo to marry Alessandra. And why he had to die and leave Kat to cope with the silly shrewish bitch, who never thought beyond her clothes or belladona-widened eyes. Except for finding new ways to snipe at everyone and boast about her high-born family connections.

Kat took a deep breath. "Yes." She volunteered not one word more.

Alessandra looked at the dowdy rough-spun woolen hooded cloak Katerina put on over her plain gray twill. She sniffed disapprovingly. "I'm surprised your lover will let you wear things like that! It's not even clean."

It was! And this from an idle cow who never did a damn thing in a house that had ten servants too few to maintain it. Who pestered money they could ill afford out of Grandpapa to buy more frippery clothes to add to the cupboards-full she already owned.

Kat was too angry to keep her tongue. "Unlike you, I don't *have* to chase everything that wears breeches, Sandi." Alessandra hated having her name shortened. "I've got better things to do."

Battle was now fairly joined. "I hope so," said Alessandra loftily. "The way you are ruining your hands with that rough oar! It's commoners' work and you'll never get a man." Then, forgetting that she'd just said there was no chance of Kat getting a man, she went on. "Maybe he *is* a commoner. But even you couldn't sink that low, surely?"

157

Kat ground her teeth. "What I'm doing has nothing to do with men. Or with you either. I wish you'd stay out of my room. I never invited you in."

"I'm your sister-in-law," Alessandra said righteously. "As the married woman of the house I have a duty and responsibility to see to your welfare. I don't think I should let you go out to tryst with your lover, as if you were some common whore. What if news of this got back to the Brunellis?"

"Try stopping me, *sister*. Just try. I've got Grandpapa's permission." She walked purposefully towards the water-door.

"He's senile. You'll bring the plague back with you. It's rife out there."

Kat stopped. "He's *not* senile! He's just old . . . and, and hurt. Alfredo's death, Mariana's death, the baby and Papa . . . not coming back. And Mama and then Grandmama, too. It's just been a bit too much for him." Even thinking about it left her with a catch in her voice. And guilt. Alessandra's baby son had died too, after all.

But Alessandra dealt with the guilt with her next silly statement. "So you've got his permission to turn yourself into a courtesan, because of *that*?"

Kat looked at herself in the mottled full-length mirror. Like many things in the *Casa* Montescue it was past its prime. The reflection that looked back at her was, at best, merely pretty. She had too wide a mouth and too pert a nose. Carroty-colored slightly curly hair, that Alessandra was always at her to bleach a bit, so that she'd look— at least from behind—more like the glamorous Lucrezia Brunelli. Unlike Alessandra, Katerina didn't claim cousinship and intimate knowledge of the doings of Venice's most famous beauty. And after Alessandra's endless stories, she didn't want to.

She looked away from the mirror, knowing that its mottled surface was not disguising the truth. *Her* face, unlike Lucrezia's, would certainly never garner her any love poems. Neither would a nonexistent dowry. And she'd never have Alessandra's statuesque figure, either; or Alessandra's perfect rosebud mouth with the tiny mole accentuating it; or her white skin and raven-black hair.

She sighed. "Sandi, be reasonable. I'm not a beauty, never will be, and that's all there is to it. Now, excuse me. I've got things to do." She pushed past, heading for the water-door up the passage.

As often happened, Alessandra's mood underwent an abrupt change. "Oh, Katerina!" she cried, clutching at Kat's cloak. "Take me with you! I'm *dying* cooped up in here in this mausoleum. We could go to Barducci's. I hear it's all the rage to go . . . slumming there. A lot of the younger crowd are going."

Kat snorted, and shook off the soft slim white hand. "Saints, Sandi! One minute I'm going to my lover, the next I'm bringing plague. And the next *you* want to go off looking for thrills with the commoners you despise. Well, sorry. I've got other things to deal with. Practical things. Anyway, you go out more often than I do. You go over to Murano at least once a week."

Curiosity—a source for gossip, a vital feature of Alessandra's shallow life—took over. "Tell me what things?"

"Can't." Somewhere, Montescue was leaking secrets. Telling Alessandra anything that the spying cat didn't already know would add another leak.

"Mean, horrible, little *bitch*!" The water-door slammed behind her, leaving Katerina to get into the shabby gondola tied to the post.

Out on the water, in the darkness, Katerina felt her temper begin to subside. By the way the wind was blowing off the lagoon, there would be a storm soon.

Great. All she needed was to get wet again!

Still, that would be better than when the previous cargo had come in. The one she'd nearly lost. Rain, even a thunderstorm, took a while to wet you to the skin. Jumping or falling into the canal didn't. She sculled a little faster. This delivery was to the far side of the Grand Canal, too, not that that meant anything. She never delivered anything to Calle Farnese anymore. It was just too risky. There were more prowling agents of the *Signori di Notte* and those creepy Servants around there than there were Strega nowadays.

She sighed. Never mind the way that it was weighing on her grandfather, this pressure was making her snappy and shrewish. After all the difficulty of getting the last parcel from Ascalon, she'd hoped their fortunes would revive. Alas, it had only just staved off the creditors. So they'd gambled on going into a *Colleganza* on a cargo of silver on the galley fleet bound for the Black Sea. After all, there was so little risk in a galley cargo that they didn't even need to insure it.

And then . . . the galley had been one of three lost in a storm. Snapped in half by the waves, if the few survivors could be believed.

The ill-fortune that plagued *Casa* Montescue seemed endless. Now they were bankrupt—almost, anyway. Reduced to the desperate business of organizing high-risk cargos to and from Beyond-the-sea.

Kat tried to find solace somewhere. At least her grandfather couldn't blame *this* disaster on *Casa* Valdosta. That ancient house was completely destroyed, all of the family members dead except for—according to rumors gathered by Grandpapa's agents—one or two boys. Who, even if the rumors of their survival were accurate, could hardly pose a threat to Montescue.

Again, she sighed. Not that her grandfather cared about threats. For reasons which had never been very clear to Kat—and she'd been afraid to ask—the old man blamed *Casa* Valdosta for the misfortunes of the Montescues. He was consumed with a desire for vengeance on anything Valdosta—even boys who could not possibly be held responsible by any rational person. That was what worried Kat the most—her grandfather's obsession with revenge was not . . . entirely sane. It was dark, and cruel, and evil—for all that Grandpapa was not a cruel and evil man in any other respect.

And it was *expensive,* too! Spies did not come cheap, and assassins even less so. The old man would still be hiring assassins, if there was anything left to hire them with. Kat didn't doubt that he would do so again, if her efforts brought in some significant money. What a waste!

Kat tied the gondola up beside the shabby water-door. Lightning rippled across the eastern sky, showing a waterworn step and an odd, gargoyle-faced doorknocker. The iron eyes seemed almost alive in the sudden sharp light. It gave her something of a shiver, and it took quite some willpower to lift the ring that the gargoyle was devouring and rap out the coded knock. Thunder rumbled in the distance.

The door opened with an oiled silence that belied its decrepit look. A dark, hooded figure loomed behind the candle. She went in. Little was said on these rendezvous. These days, buyers—who used to greet her by name—were trying to pretend they didn't know her, and that she'd never even met them. These were dangerous times.

The hooded man led her to a desk, at which yet another hooded figure sat. Silently Kat handed over the little oilcloth parcel, putting it on the table. The hooded figure reached eagerly for it, a little silver and steel knife appearing suddenly in the long, shapely feminine fingers. The knife hilt, Kat noticed, was fashioned like a dragon's head with little chips of clear red stone for eyes. Eyes seemed everywhere tonight. She hoped none of them had followed her here.

The packet was slit, and the hooded woman gave a little crow of unpleasant glee . . . before hastily sweeping the vials back into the packet. Not for the first time Kat wondered what they were doing in this business. It had started with letters to and from the Jewish community. After all, her great-grandfather had been a Jew, even if he'd married out of the faith and the family were good Petrine Christians now. Somehow needs had driven things to this. When she'd been a child she'd often gone to meet the Strega with Grandpapa. She suspected that Grandpapa had been halfway to being a convert. But they'd been a different community then. Gentler.

The woman motioned her henchman forward. He reached inside his cloak and produced . . . money. That was always a relief. Kat knew she could get killed instead. Silently, he counted out ducats.

Kat slipped them into a washleather pouch, and slipped the pouch between her breasts.

Obviously, her pleasure in receiving the cargo had loosed the woman's tongue. "You deliver to many?"

Kat shook her head. "I really don't think I should say."

"Understood. But I will make it worth a great deal, a very great deal indeed, to know of one man. Ten times your fee, if you tell me where I can find him. His name is Marina. *Dottore* Luciano Marina. This is how he looks."

The woman flicked a handful of powder into the air and an image appeared therein. The man had an arrogant tilt to his head, but a kindly face. There was a wiry youthfulness about the face, which didn't match the eyes. The eyes looked as if they'd seen a lot.

Kat remembered it well. He had been a great figure of learning at the Accademia before he disappeared, Grandpapa had said. And her favorite tutor, as a girl.

Kat shook her head. "He hasn't been around since I was about fourteen."

"He is still around." The woman spoke very firmly, more to herself than Kat. "I can *feel* him. I just can't pin him to a place."

Kat shrugged, and looked at the desk. She must have lost a strand of hair there—not something you wanted to leave with the Strega. She twitched it off the table and into a pocket while the hooded woman's attention was still distracted.

"Haven't seen him for years," she repeated.

The woman appeared to notice her again. "You may leave," she said imperiously.

Outside, with the wind from the storm ripping and yowling between the buildings and the first heavy drops beginning to splat onto the water, Kat shook herself. The money would help. But the hole that the *Casa* Montescue was in meant that they'd have to continue with this. She flicked the bowline loose and began sculling.

As she came out onto the Grand Canal, she realized that she should have left earlier. Ahead the rain was coming down like a solid dark wall, obliterating all light. The water in the Grand Canal was already chopped into endless dancing myriad-peaked waves. Water slopped over the gunwales as Kat struggled to turn back into the relative shelter of the smaller canal she'd emerged from. There was no going home until this was over. She might as well find somewhere to try to keep dry. Even here angry gusts were rattling and shaking at hastily slammed shutters. This was no time to be outside, never mind in a boat. The nearby church of San Zan Degola was small and poor, but it would be open.

She moored the gondola to a post, hitched up her skirts, and ran for the shelter. The storm wouldn't last.

Chapter 14

Rain. The watcher in the reed bank noticed it without caring too much about it. His name was Harrow, and he was, by nature, a predator. When intent on a target he was not distracted by discomfort. The slim, willowy figure out there in the lightning-torn darkness wasn't his prey, but Harrow stalked him anyway from long habit. This marshland was not Harrow's environment, and the only way he'd learn it was to practice, to hone his inborn skills.

Besides, if it wasn't prey, it could possibly be someone hunting Harrow. Or Fortunato Bespi, as they would still think of him. They had tried to kill Harrow. Burn him, drown him. Somehow news could have leaked out of the swamp that he wasn't dead. Bespi had given his all to the Visconti, for the Montagnard cause. He'd always found peace in obeying orders, pleasure in hunting down his human prey. In repayment, Francesco Aleri had done this to him, and Harrow did not doubt for a moment that the orders had come from the Duke of Milan himself.

Hatred, forge-hot, seared at his gut for a moment. With an effort that was difficult because it came newly to him, Harrow tried to drive it under.

No. That was not the way. The marsh-wizard who had saved him and taught him his true name claimed he should turn his hatred to good cause instead. Harrow, who had cut down lives with no more compunction than most people had killed mosquitoes, had listened to his talk with intense concentration. And had listened to the visions with an even greater one.

Strangely so, perhaps, given his history. But . . . Harrow *believed* in reasons. He believed that he had a purpose in life; believed it with a fanatical intensity. As Bespi he'd always assumed that purpose was to serve the Montagnard cause, yet they had been the ones to order his death. And what disturbed Harrow the most was that there had been no *reason* for it. None good enough, at any rate.

Harrow, as much as Fortunato Bespi, wanted *reasons*. And so, as lightning lit the sky with white tracery, he watched as the trudging figure came closer. Not much more than a boy he was, Harrow could see now. He could warn him easily that there was a prowling loco on the trail ahead—a bad one, by the pitiful local standards. But Harrow was a hunter and hunted man himself, as well as a man who believed in reasons. So he simply waited, silent and invisible in the recesses of the marsh, as the boy passed by him in the storm. Then, followed. Stalking from habit, partly; and, partly, hoping he might find some logic in a reasonless world.

Marco could hardly feel his feet, they were so numb and cold. Still, it wasn't winter. Then he'd have had to worry about losing his toes, instead of just *feeling* like he'd lost them.

He was halfway out to Chiano's territory, and he was already regretting the decision he'd made, with the kind of remote regret of one who didn't have any real choice. The pack on his back was large, and heavy; the goods he had to trade with old Sophia for her herbs were bulky. Blankets didn't compact well, no more did clothing.

The cold was climbing up his legs, and his breeches were misery to wear: wet and clinging and clammy, and liberally beslimed with mud and unidentifiable swamp-muck. He'd forgotten how much the marsh mud stank; it was far worse than the canals. The reeds rustled, but otherwise there wasn't much sound but for the wind whistling and the water lapping against what few bits of solid stuff poked above the surface of the lagoon.

The wind was bitter, and ate through his clothing. Also there was a storm brewing, which meant that he'd be soaked before the night was out, even if things went well.

He was half-soaked already. Just because it was possible to walk into the swamp, that didn't mean it was easy. He was just grateful that his memory of the "trail" was clear; so clear he could find his way back in pitch dark—so clear he was only mud caked to his thighs instead of to his waist.

Overhead the clouds blocked out the stars and thunder rumbled, cloud-shadows taking the last of the light. But now the swamp itself flickered with an eerie phosphorescence, making it almost like dusk. There seemed to be more of a glow than there had been before—and a kind of odd, sulfurous, bitter smell he didn't remember as being part of the normal odors. The thunder came again, accompanied by flashes of lightning, and the wind off the sea began to pick up, bending the reeds parallel with the water.

Marco had just enough time for his nose to warn him, and then the rain came.

The first fat drops plopped on the back of his neck and trickled icily down his back, adding to his misery. This morning he'd been sure that there was no way he could begin to even up the debt between himself and Aldanto. At this point he was beginning to think that the scale might just be tipping the other way.

"Hee *hee* he-he-he! Well, lookee what th' storm washet ep—"

The voice that brayed out of the dark and the rain was one Marco had hoped never to hear again.

"I heerd ye gone townie on us, Marco—boy." The speaker was little more than a black blot against the phosphorescent water— a *large* blot. "I heerd ye niver come back t' see yer old friends. I heerd ye figger yer better'n us now."

It was Big Gianni, and he had the next segment of the trail completely blocked. To either side was deep water and dangerous mud—some of it bottomless, sucking mire-pits.

"C'mon, Marco—boy—ain't ye gonna run from Big Gianni? Ain't ye gonna give 'im a race?" Lightening flickered once, twice. The blot shifted restlessly.

Marco fought panic. "Get out of my way, Big Gianni," he shouted over the thunder. "Leave me alone. I never hurt you."

"Ye hurt Big Gianni's feelin's, Marco—boy," the hoarse voice came back. "Ye wouldn't play with Big Gianni. Ye sent that Chiano t' warn Gianni off, ye did. But Chiano, he ain't here now. Now it's jest me an' you."

Marco could run. He could shed that heavy pack and run back along the safe path until he came to one of the branches. Then he could get into an area he knew better than Gianni did, where he could outdistance him and get safely back to town.

But—without what he'd come for. And it was just possible that without Sophia's spell-woven medicine, Caesare Aldanto would die, fighting for breath, choking—literally drowning as his lungs filled. The way that Marco had almost died.

His knife was in his hand without his really thinking about it, and he slipped the straps of the pack off his shoulders, dropping it to the reed hummock he was standing on. With the feel of the hilt in his hand, his breathing steadied. He wasn't fifteen any more—nor was he armed with nothing but a scrap of glass. He had most of his adult growth now, and a good steel blade in his hand.

Watching from his hiding place in the reeds, Harrow was impressed. Not by the way the boy held the knife—pitiful, that was—but the mere fact he would do so. And stand his ground, in face of such a threat. Harrow had observed the one called Gianni before. The creature was not dangerous to Harrow himself, of course. But he was a fearsome monster for the marsh-dwellers. Very large, strong, half-crazed, and driven by savage and perverted reasons.

Harrow wondered at the boy's reasons. Powerful they must be, to cause him to stand his ground. Harrow had little doubt the boy could elude Gianni in the marsh if he wished to do so. The one called Gianni was strong, yes; but also clumsy and slow afoot.

Yet . . . the boy clearly intended to fight. *Very* powerful reasons he must have. And thus, Harrow suspected, reasons which were also true and clean.

So, a man covered with slime waited silently and invisible in the marshes. Just watching, to see if the reasons he so craved himself might emerge in such an unlikely place.

Marco had to swallow before he could speak. Then:

"I'm warning you, Gianni—get out of my way."

"Ye gonna make me?"

"If I have to," Marco replied unsteadily. Big Gianni had sloshed a step or two closer, and now his knife seemed all too small. Gianni stood as tall as Marco—and Marco was still standing on a hummock that rose several inches above the underwater surface of the trail.

And Gianni had a knife, too; Marco could see the lightning flickering on the shiny surface of the steel. It was ribbon-thin, honed almost to invisibility, but Marco would bet it could leave bleeding wounds on the wind.

Gianni cackled again, and there was no sanity in that sound. "Ye try, Marco—boy, ye g'won 'n try! Big Gianni don't care. He c'n play wi' ye live—or he c'n play wi' ye dead."

Marco's nerve almost broke—so before it could give out altogether, he attacked. Before Gianni had a chance to react, he threw himself at the bigger man with an hysterical and suicidal leap. Marco had no chance at all except one which was so desperate that not even a lunatic like Gianni would think to counter it.

He drove the open palm of his left hand frantically down on Gianni's knife—aiming at the blade, not the knife-hand—hoping to impale his hand on that blade and render it useless.

His dive off the hummock had caught the loco marsh-dweller by surprise. Marco had always run before. Gianni's twisted mind wasn't ready for him to attack.

So Marco's half-sketched plan worked better than he hoped.

Harrow rose from his crouch, his soul ringing like a cymbal. He understood at once the boy's maneuver—it was a theoretical gambit all assassins had considered—but had never once in his violence-filled life seen anyone actually *do* it. Such *reasons* the boy must have!

The point of Gianni's knife sliced into Marco's palm as he rammed his hand right up to the hilt. The pain split his arm like the lightning that was splitting the sky. Marco screamed and closed his fist around the crossguard anyway, wresting it out of the bigger man's hand. Gianni's grip was loose, he was so stunned by Marco's unexpected action. Then, as Marco's feet skidded in the mud, he fell forward, throwing all of his weight awkwardly behind an impromptu lunge with his own knife.

Gianni's screams were a hoarse echo of his own as the knife sank up to the hilt in his gut. He beat at Marco's head with both hands; Marco slipped and slid some more, and fell to his knees, but held onto the knife hilt, ripping upward with it.

Gianni howled and tried to pull himself off the blade, pushing at Marco. But Marco slipped more, falling underneath the bigger man. Gianni lost his balance on the slimy rock of the trail, falling forward farther onto the knife blade. As thunder crashed, the big man collapsed on top of Marco, screams cut off, pinning Marco under the muddy water

All the air was driven from his lungs as the crazy man fell atop him. Marco tried to fight free but the slimy mud was as slick as ice under his knees. Then he lost what little purchase he had, and the knee-deep water closed over his head.

The surface was just inches away from his face—but he couldn't reach it!

He clawed at the twitching thing that held him there; tried to shove it off, but could get no leverage. Raw panic took over. He thrashed and struggled, his lungs screaming for air, his chest and throat afire with the need for a breath. He was caught like an otter in a drown-snare. He was going to die, trapped under the body of his enemy.

The mud conspired to hold him down, now sliding under him, sucking at his limbs. Sparks danced before his eyes, and he wriggled and squirmed and struggled for the air that his hands could reach, but not his head. He had a strange crystal-clear vision of himself floating lifelessly beside the trail, touched by the morning sun—

Suddenly, the weight of the corpse on top of him was removed. With a last frantic writhe, Marco freed himself, slipping off the trail into the deep water on the right. His head broke the surface, and he gulped the air, great sobbing heaves of his chest.

A powerful hand seized him by the scruff of the neck and half-hurled him toward firmer ground. Marco reached for and caught a clump of reeds, and pulled himself to the trail. He hauled himself back onto the hummock where he'd left his pack, crying with pain and fear, and gasping for breath, while lightning flashed above him and thunder followed it, almost deafening him. He clung there with only his right hand, for Gianni's knife was still transfixed in his left. His frantic eyes flitted across the landscape, looking for whoever had lifted Gianni off him and dragged him to safety. Marco's rescuer could also be a threat.

But he saw nothing. His rescuer had vanished.

Why did he do that? Marco wondered. *For what reason?*

"My *God*, boy—" Chiano's eyes glared out at Marco from the shelter of his basketlike hidey. He and Sophia had anchored their rafts and their hides, side-by-side, on a bit of old wood Chiano had driven into the muck of the bottom to use as a safe tie-up.

"Lemme in, Chiano," Marco said, dully. His hand felt afire. He was shivering so hard that it was only because he was holding his jaw clenched that his teeth weren't rattling. He swayed back and forth, drunk with exhaustion and pain. He could hardly use his arm, much less his wounded hand—it felt like a log of wood. He'd tied up his hand as best he could, but he hadn't been able to do more than stop the bleeding. He knew he was probably falling into shock, but didn't care any more.

"Wait a moment." Chiano propped up the edge of the basket with a stick, reached out and shook Sophia's hide. "Wake up, you old witch—it's Marco and he's hurt."

"What? What?" The edge of Sophia's basket came up and she peered out at Marco. For some reason the sight of her struck him as funny and he began to laugh hysterically—and couldn't stop.

He was still laughing when they propped the baskets together, like two halves of a shell, and helped him up onto their combined rafts. Then, unaccountably, the laughter turned to sobs, and he cried himself nearly sick on Sophia's shoulder.

Sophia held him, wrapping her tattered old shawl about his shoulders and keeping him warm against her. Rain pattered on the baskets and, for the moment, there was no place Marco would rather have been.

In the corner of his eye, he saw a strange expression come into Chiano's face. The kind of expression a man gets when he suddenly, unexpectedly, remembers something long forgotten. Puzzled, despite the pain and weariness, Marco turned his head in time to see Chiano straighten his back and spread his arms wide.

"*Luminescence spareze. A Mercurio!*"

There was a commanding tone to Chiano's voice; seeming to be as forceful, for the brief time it took to utter those peculiar words, as the storm itself. Maybe it was the pain, or the shock, but in the sudden flare of witchlight the lean, sinewy man seemed somehow taller, his weathered face outlined in stark, sharp shadows.

Marco, his Pauline training coming to the fore, flinched from the sight. An old half-suspicion was now confirmed. Chiano really was a Strega man-witch. His reputation, carefully cultivated in the marshes, was a double front. He really *was* a pagan—and a magician to boot.

Marco . . . wasn't at all sure how he felt about that. Still, Sophia's wrinkled face and Chiano's weathered one were a heavenly sight. He decided not to worry about it, for the moment.

"Drink this, boy." When the sobs diminished, and the shivering started again, Chiano thrust a bottle into his good hand. "Let the old girl see to your hand."

He drank, not much caring what it was. It was harsh raw alcohol, and it burned his throat and brought more tears to his eyes. He put the bottle down, gasping; then gasped again as Sophia took it from him and poured its contents liberally over the wound. The clouds were clearing now, and the moon emerged; you could see it from under the edge of the basket. Sophia propped up one side of the basket and held his hand in its light, examining it critically.

He had occasion to stifle a cry and seize the bottle back from Chiano, more than once, before she was through with her probing.

"Should be stitched—but the grappa will stop the flesh-rot. I've a poultice against the swelling. You tied it off right well. I don' reckon ye lost too much blood. What happened?"

"Gianni," Marco coughed. His throat was still raw from screaming and crying. "He must've seen me; followed me in. Ambushed me." Sophia was smearing something onto the wound that first burned, and then numbed the pain. Then she reached back into the darkness behind her, locating rags by feel, and bound his hand tightly.

"I settle that one tomorrow." Chiano's eyes narrowed. "For good 'n ever, this time."

Marco shook his head weakly. "You won't have to."

Once the meaning of the words penetrated, Sophia looked up into his face with stunned awe. Gianni was a legend among the marsh-dwellers for his crazy viciousness. That *Marco* should have taken him out . . .

"There was someone else, too," Marco added, half-gasping the sentences. "Never saw him. Helped me at the end. I would have drowned otherwise. Never saw him, not once."

The alcohol had shaken Marco out of his shock and he was beginning to take account of his surroundings again. He noticed Chiano and Sophia exchange a glance.

"Well," Chiano said. Just that one word, but it held a world of approval. In some obscure way, Marco understood the approval encompassed more than just he himself.

"Boy, you needn't hide again? Ye didn't come crawlin' out here in th' dark an' th' rain fer the fun a' it." Sophia came right to the point.

That woke him fully—reminded him of his purpose.

"N-no. I'm fine in town—but Sophia, I need something from you, one of your 'cures.' I got a sick friend in town. He's got a fever—the one with the chills and the sweats every two days. Getting worse. He hardly knows where he is."

"I know it." Sophia nodded, her face becoming even more wrinkled with thought. "Only it don't gen'rally get that bad."

"Except my friend's not from Venice."

"Then that's bad, boy, that's *real* bad. He'll die, like as not, 'less ye can get 'im t' take my herbs."

"Look, I brought stuff to trade you—here—" He shrugged out of his pack and passed it to her. "Whatever you want. I got two blankets, a couple of good woolen cloaks, fish hooks, a knife—"

"Haw, boy, haw! Ye got enough there t' trade me fer every last dose I got!"

"Then give it all to me, Sophia, I got more friends. This fever is startin' to go through town like a fire—more of 'em may get sick. Strega came into town at Solstice claiming there wouldn't be any plague this year"—Marco noticed Chiano stiffening at that—"but I guess they were wrong. You can get more, can't you?"

Sophia nodded. "Aye, aye; stuff's just wild weeds—know where there's a good bit of it, still good enough t' pick. Ain't no cure though—ye know that—"

"Herbs with Artemis' blessing," said Chiano quietly.

Marco smiled wryly, remembering the nausea and the delirium. "I know; it just keeps you from dying—but makes you feel like you want to! Remember? I got it first winter I was out here."

"An' ye can get it agin—"

"So I'll keep some for myself. Deal, Sophia?"

"*Si*—oh *si si*, boy, 'tis a deal." She grinned, a twisted half-toothless grin, as one hand caressed one of the damp blankets. "This stuff'll make livin' right comfy out here, come winter. Tell ye what—I'll pick all I kin find, dry it up nice. Ye figger ye need for more, why just come on out here—by *daylight* this time, boy!—an' ye bring old Sophia more things to trade."

"You got yourself a bargain." Marco smiled inwardly, at peace with an old debt. Sophia would somehow not keep many, if any, of the "luxuries." They'd all end up with marsh-folk, keeping other people alive. Sophia was the one person in the reed-fringed Jesolo marshes who slept deeply. She could. Not even the most loco would put a hand to her. Her reputation as a healer was more potent even than Chiano's reputation as a worker of magics.

"You've got to go back t'night?" Chiano interrupted.

Marco looked at the swamp and shivered, but nodded reluctantly. "Got no choice, Chiano. My friend's bad sick, and you heard Sophia."

"No, no—not soaked through like that, and it getting up chilly. Sophia, pack your herbs in the boy's sack. This old man knows the harbor day *or* night. I got a dry blanket here. You wrap up in't. I'll pole you back to the wharf. Say some words over those damned weeds for you too, I will."

Marco accepted the shred of blanket, speechless with gratitude. And, witnessing the witchlight and certain hitherto unexplained mysteries of his time in the swamp, maybe those words held more power than he'd realized previously. Ecclesiastical magic could heal. Perhaps Strega magics were not the fraud the Petrine church claimed they were, nor the unadulterated evil which the Paulines labeled them.

Chapter 15

The church door had been slightly ajar. The rain and wind had
sent more than just Kat scurrying for shelter. Two bridge-brats,
a boy and a girl, had decided it would be warmer than huddling
under a bridge. They were engaged in bridge-brat mischief, down
at the altar, playing with one of the candles that burned there.
Doubtless a sacristan would emerge in a minute or two and give
them both a thick ear. In the meanwhile they were having fun.

Kat shivered slightly. She pulled out a dry scarf and covered her
hair. She was cold and wet. If she'd been close to a tavern she might
have broken her own rules and slipped into the warmth. Instead
she took a seat on a pew at the back. The brats hadn't even noticed
her.

They noticed the next incursion, however. Kat was so startled
she almost leapt from the pew.

The door swung open forcefully, slamming noise through the
church. Kat spun her head in time to see a party of knights and
monks pushing into the church. They'd obviously been to some
function, or off on some official business, because the knights were
in full armor, sheened and dripping with rain. Seeing the triple
red crosses of the famous twin orders of the Pauline creed, Kat
felt a sharp rush of fear.

In times past, the Servants and Knights of the Holy Trinity had
not held much sway in Venice, since the city was traditionally a
stronghold of the Petrine creed. The more so since the Servants
and Knights were closely associated with the Holy Roman Empire—
as was, in a different way, the Montagnard faction in Italian politics.

The Montagnards had their adherents in Venice, of course. But Venice was traditionally a neutral in the bitter Montagnard-Metropolitan conflict. If anything, the city's populace was inclined to the Metropolitans. So the Servants and the Knights were double-damned in the eyes of most Venetians—by religious and political creed alike.

But . . . since the current Doge began favoring the two orders, they had begun throwing their weight around—and the Servants, especially, were notorious for their heavy hand.

Katerina's mouth dried up. Surely they couldn't be looking for *her*?

They couldn't be. Anyway, she reminded herself, the cargo had been delivered. All she had now was the money. Quite a lot of it, true, but still just money. Probably they'd just come to get out of the rain.

This was confirmed by one knight's comment. "Off that God-forsaken water!" he snarled. "I thought we'd drown there, when that tub started to take water. Abbot Sachs, when do we leave this cursed city? A knight should *ride*. This boatwork is not for nobles."

The abbot was the same stooped man that Kat had seen perform the rite of enclosure on the Imperial embassy. "We leave this place of sin when God's work is done!" he snapped in reply.

The abbot's eyes left the knight and quickly ranged through the church. He did not spot Kat, sitting all the way in the back, since his gaze became fixed almost instantly on the two bridge-brats at the altar.

"And look!" he cried triumphantly, pointing an accusing finger at the children. "God has guided us to his work! The Devil cannot triumph against the workings of the Lord!"

Katerina was astonished to see the abbot striding down to the altar, for all the world as if he were marching on the forces of the Antichrist at Armageddon. *Was he insane?* The two terrified children who were the subject of his wrath stared at him, guilt written all over their small, hungry faces.

The abbot grabbed one of the children successfully. The other, the girl, ran screaming for the door. One of the knights slammed the door closed. He tried to catch the girl. The child squirmed clear, to find herself in the steel gauntlets of another knight.

In the meantime Sachs, the struggling little boy held in one hand, was peering at the candle. "See!" he shouted triumphantly. "See the Devil's work! They make waxen mammets from this consecrated candle to work their evil. Here, within the very nave of the Church. Venice, the corrupt and rotten! They will burn for this! You shall not suffer a witch to live!"

Several things happened with all the outcry. First the sacristan, bleary eyed and none too steady on his feet, appeared through a side door with a branch of candles, demanding querulously to know what all the noise in the house of God was about. The second was that two of the knights finally spotted Katerina, before she could decide whether to slide under the pew or run for the door.

Moving much faster than she would have imagined an armored man could do, one of the knights grabbed her shoulders with rough steel hands. The same one who had complained about the weather. Then, even more roughly, dragged her out to face the abbot.

"Got another one, Abbot Sachs!"

"Hold her there!" commanded Sachs. Almost violently, he thrust the boy into the hands of a monk who had come to join him. Then, stalked back up the aisle to stand before Kat.

The abbot gripped her jaw and lifted her chin, examining her as he might a vial of poison. With his left hand, roughly, he pulled off her scarf.

"The witch mistress," he pronounced solemnly. "Overseeing her children and their demonic work. We have made a fine haul tonight! Truly, the hand of God must have guided that storm."

Panic surged through Kat. "I'm not a witch! I'm not! I just came to get out of the rai—"

The abbot slapped her, hard and with obvious satisfaction. "Silence, witch! You will be put to the question and you will answer when we tell you."

Kat's cheek burned. The blow had been savage enough to leave her dazed, for a moment. Her mouth tasted of blood, and her head was cloudy with fear and fury. The moment was so—*insane*—that she couldn't seem to bring her mind into focus. The only clear thought she had was: *Why hadn't she stayed outside and gotten wet?*

A new voice spoke. One of the knights, Kat dimly realized. A very cold voice.

"Abbot—"

The abbot turned on him. "Go and ready our boat, Erik. We must take these prisoners back and put them to the question."

The knight shook his head. The gesture was abbreviated, quick; and very firm. "No, My Lord Abbot. We cannot do that."

"Why?" demanded Sachs angrily. "The weather is not so bad! Not for *pious* men."

The implied slur did no more than cause the knight to square his already very square shoulders. And harden a face that, to Kat, already looked as hard as an axe-blade. She was almost shocked to see that the knight was not much older than she was.

"Because we cannot remove these people from the sanctuary of the Church," said the knight. Calmly, even though Kat could sense the effort the knight was making to keep his teeth from clenching. "It is my solemnly sworn oath," he continued, almost grinding out the words, "as a Knight of the Holy Trinity, to defend the Sanctuary of the Holy Church. I will not break my oath."

Sanctuary! For a moment, Kat simply gawped at the young knight. Of all the scary-looking armed and armored men who surrounded her, he was the scariest. The last one she would have expected to come to her assistance!

Thunder pealed, and she could hear a fresh squall of rain sheeting down outside in the sudden silence. Even the two terrified children seemed to realize their survival hung on this rigid man with the harshly Nordic appearance.

The young knight seemed made entirely of sharp angles and icy ridges—as if his body and face had been shaped by the same glaciers that created the Norse landscape from which he so obviously came. His hair, long enough to peek below the rim of his helmet, was so blond it was almost white. His eyes were a shade of blue so pale they were almost gray. His chin was a shield, his nose a sword—even his lips looked as if they had been shaped by a chisel. And . . .

Scariest of all: lurking beneath that superficial calm, she could sense an eruption building. Kat had been told once, by her tutor Marina, that Iceland had been forged in the earth's furnace. Not knowing why, she was suddenly certain that this man was an Icelander himself—a land as famous for its clan feuds as its volcanoes. And that he possessed the full measure of the berserk fury that slept—fretfully—just beneath an outwardly still and chilly surface.

She noticed, finally, the peculiar weapon attached to his belt.

A hatchet of some kind, an oddly plain thing compared to the aristocratic sword hanging from his baldric.

Then her wits finally returned, and Kat seized the opening as a drowning man might an entire haystack.

"I claim sanctuary, in the name of—"

The knight holding her clamped a gauntleted hand across her mouth. Kat tasted blood inside her lips.

"Remove your hand, Pappenheim!"

The blond knight's command was not a shout so much as a curse—or a sneer, driven into words. A challenge so cold, so full of contempt, that an angel facing hellspawn would have envied it.

Except Kat could imagine no angel looking as purely murderous as this man. The young knight was on his toes now, as light on his feet as if he were wearing nightclothes instead of armor. He seemed to prance, almost, his whole body as springy and coiled as a lion about to pounce. And his thin lips were peeled back in a smile that was no smile at all. Teeth showing like fangs.

His hand flashed to his belt, so quick she could not follow the movement. The next she saw, the hatchet was held in his fist, in a loose and easy grasp that even Kat—no expert on such matters—could recognize as that of an expert. And she realized now that this was not really a hatchet at all. No utilitarian woodsman's tool, this—it was a cruel and savage weapon, from a cruel and savage forest. What was sometimes called a *tomahawk*, she remembered.

"Remove your hand, Pappenheim," the knight repeated, as coldly if not as forcefully. "As well as the hand on her shoulder."

His hand flickered, the war hatchet blurring back and forth. The lion lashing his tail. *"Or I will remove them for you."*

The sheer, sudden violence of the young knight's words and actions—all the more violent for that they had not yet erupted in the blood and mayhem they promised—had momentarily paralyzed everyone else in the church. Now, finally, the other knights began to react.

Kat felt the knight holding her flinch, his fingers almost trembling. She understood then that her own impression of the blond Norseman was no figment of her imagination. The knight, too, found him just as frightening. And presumably, in his case, from past experience.

The other knights shifted their feet, their hands fumbling uncertainly at their own weapons. It was clear as day that they had no idea how to handle the situation.

Suddenly, one of the knights who had been standing in the background moved forward. A very large knight, this one, built so squarely he resembled a block of granite on thick legs. Very young, also. Kat thought he was perhaps her own age.

"For God's sake, Erik!" he exclaimed. "Why are you—?"

The blond knight held out his other hand, staying the youngster with a commanding gesture.

"Be silent, Manfred. Do you think the world is nothing but a toy for your pleasure? You are nothing but an oaf. A spoiled child. *Begone!* This is a man's business."

The words caused the young knight's face to flush a sudden bright pink. Then, grow pale with rage. Then—

Grow paler still; and paler still. Shock, now, Kat realized. The young knight's jaw sagged loose. He stared at the one named Erik as if he were seeing him for the first time.

Then, as suddenly as everything else was happening, his face seemed to snap shut. He shouted something Kat did not understand—words in Gaelic, she thought—and strode forward to the knight holding her.

An instant later, Manfred's huge hands closed upon her captor's own shoulders and wrenched him loose as easily as a man wrestles a boy. Suddenly released, Kat staggered on her feet for a moment. By the time she regained her balance, the knight who had seized her was crashing down onto one of the pews, turning the cheaply made wooden bench into so much kindling. She found herself marveling at the strength that could send an armored knight flying through the air like a toy; almost giggling at the sheer absurdity of the sight.

But she had no real difficulty suppressing the giggle. The situation was now on the brink of utter carnage, almost a dozen knights ready to hack each other into pieces—with herself right in the middle of them.

The young knight named Manfred whipped out his own great sword and brandished it. *"Dia a coir!"* he shouted. Then, took two steps toward the abbot and commanded him: *"Unhand the child, Sachs!"*

The abbot, through all this, had been paralyzed. Kat realized, now, that he was a man whose authority had always come from his position—not respect gained from his subordinates in action. It was obvious that Sachs had absolutely no idea what to do, now that he was faced with open rebellion.

Neither did any of the other knights, for that matter. But it was also obvious, even to Kat, that they were about to react the way fighting men will when faced with such a naked challenge. These men were cut from the same cloth as the bravos of any great house of Venice—but were far better trained, and more deadly. In open combat, at least, if not in the subtler skill of the assassin.

The hands on swords were clenched now, not loose. And two or three of those swords were beginning to come out of their scabbards. Frightened they might be, at Erik's savagery and Manfred's incredible strength—but they were not going to crumple under it. Not men like these.

Suddenly, one of the other knights thrust out his hands, his arms spread wide in a gesture commanding peace. A somewhat older knight, this one. Most of them were men in their early twenties. His face, though not creased with middle age, was that of a man in his thirties. A man accustomed to command.

"Enough!" he shouted. "Enough! No weapons!"

His voice seemed to calm the situation instantly. Kat thought he must be the knight in command of the party. The hands on sword hilts loosened; some were removed entirely. Even Erik and Manfred seemed to settle back a little.

"Erik is right," the older knight said forcefully. "Quite right! And every *true* Knight here knows it!"

He turned to Sachs and glared at him. "You have completely exceeded your authority here, Abbot. Abused it grossly, in fact."

The abbot gaped at him. "But—*Von Gherens* . . ."

"Shut up," growled the older knight. "You disgust me, Sachs." Seeing the abbot's hand still on the child's shoulder, the knight reached out his own hand and flicked it off as he might flick off an insect.

"My family has held the frontier in Livonia for six generations. Unlike *you*, Sachs, I have faced real demons—not figments of your fevered imagination."

Stolidly, the knight examined the still-trembling boy. "Had you ever seen a child's body on a pagan altar, *Abbot*"—the term was a pure sneer—"you would understand the difference."

Von Gherens. Erik. Manfred. As always, Kat found northern names harsh and peculiar. But for the first time in her life, she began to understand them better also. Harsh, yes; rigid and intolerant, yes. Yet . . . sometimes, at least, names which rang clear. Clearer, perhaps, than any of the soft names in fog-shrouded Venice.

Oddly, for a moment her mind flitted to old lessons of her tutor Marina. Lessons in theology she had not understood at the time. *There was a reason, child, that Hypatia compromised with Augustine, if not Theophilus. And treasured Chrysostom, for all his rigidity and intolerance. There is such a thing as evil in the world, which cannot be persuaded, but only defeated. And for that—harshness is needed in the ranks of Christ also. Neither Shaitan nor his monsters will listen to mere words.* She remembered his lips crinkling. *Even a* Strega, *you know, does not doubt the existence of either Christ or the Dark One.*

The gray-cassocked abbot looked as if he was about to have a stroke—or faint. Even in the candlelight Kat could see his face was suffused, simultaneously, with rage and—fear. His lips trembled as he groped for words; words which, apparently, he was unable to find.

Yet another knight had no such difficulty. With a slight clashing noise, he thrust his sword firmly back in the scabbard and removed his hand from the weapon.

"Von Gherens is right—Hakkonsen and Manfred also. We cannot take them out of here, by Church law. The law which, as Knights of the Holy Trinity, we are sworn to uphold."

The knight's eyes glanced at Kat, then at the children. His lips peeled back in a half-snarl. "And my name is Falkenberg—*also* a name of the frontier. And *also* one who can tell the difference between brats and devils."

Now there were nods and murmurs of agreement all around the circle of Knights. The tension was draining out of the scene as rapidly as water through a broken dam. All danger of physical violence was past. Whatever might be left would only take the form of words.

Words which Sachs was still quite incapable of uttering, it seemed. Only one of the two monks who accompanied him seemed disposed to argue the matter any further.

"We cannot let witches go free," he protested, almost squeakily. "God has guided us to this evil. We must root it out!"

"Didn' do no evil," whimpered one child. "Just came to get outa the rain."

Finally, Abbot Sachs tried to salvage something from the situation. He cleared his throat noisily.

"If we cannot take them away, we will put them to the question here." He essayed a sneer of his own; a feeble one. "Or do you deny my ecclesiastical authority for that also, *Ritters* Hakkonsen and Von Gherens?"

The blond knight's cold eyes did not waver for an instant. "Yes, Abbot Sachs, I *do* deny you the authority."

Von Gherens's words rolled right after: "The right to afford sanctuary, without arrest or violence, is inviolate. And by Church law, they may only be expelled by the priest of the parish."

Flushing furiously, Sachs turned on the terrified-looking old sacristan. "Fetch me your priest, then! I'll *have* these hell-spawn. So help me God—I will *have* them."

The sacristan left with as near to a run as the old man could muster, and never mind the rain.

Sachs turned on Von Gherens. "As for you—I'm going to make an example of you!"

Von Gherens barked a laugh. "For obeying the oath of the Order? I think not!"

"And who will enforce your 'example,' Abbot?" asked the blond knight. The question was posed quietly, but grimly. The war hatchet was back in the scabbard, but his hand was still perched on it.

"Yes—who?" demanded the big one called Manfred. Quite a bit more loudly, if not as grimly. The tone was almost mocking.

Kat saw the Knights clustering together a bit more closely. One order closing ranks against another, she realized—and realized, as well, that the identity she had always assumed existed between the Knights and the Servants of the Holy Trinity was not as solid as she'd thought. Which, she remembered vaguely, was something else *Dottore* Marina had once told her.

Silence followed, for some time, while they waited for the sacristan to return with the priest.

The silence was so thick with hostility between the knights and the monks that it could almost have been cut with a knife. The only movement during that time was the slow and painful return of Pappenheim to consciousness, stumbling back onto his feet from the splintered pew where Manfred had sent him. He seemed too dazed to really comprehend what was happening; simply collapsed on another pew, leaning over with his head in his hands. His helmet had apparently come loose in the force of the impact. Kat was a bit amazed that he had no broken bones. Manfred's strength was genuinely incredible. He had not so much tossed the knight into the pew as he had hurled him down upon it.

Finally, the sacristan returned, the priest close on his heels. The priest was a young man; who, like the two bridge-brats, looked as if he could have used a few more meals himself. It was a small church.

He looked in puzzlement at the scene, and then bowed to the abbot. "I am Father Ugo, and this is my parish. Why have I been called here?"

"We have called you to throw these evil miscreants out. They were defiling your church with satanic practices."

The little priest blinked, taking in the steel, and the "miscreants."

With a start, Kat realized she knew the little man. Of course, he'd been smaller and plumper then.

"*Ugo Boldoni?*" she said, incredulously.

The priest peered shortsightedly at her; then, gasped. There *were* some advantages to her distinctive carroty-colored hair, even if it was not fashionable.

"Kat—Milady Katerina! What are you doing here?"

Kat shrugged. "I was caught in the rain and came in to take shelter."

"She was practicing satanic rites!" shouted one the monks, waving a threatening finger at her.

"I was sitting on a pew!" she snapped back at him. "Quietly sitting, getting some shelter from the rain—when you came in—like demons yourselves!—and grabbed those children who were playing up there. They were fooling around with one of the candles. I assumed the sacristan would come out and give them both a clout. Instead this—"

She glared at Sachs. "This foul man who *calls* himself an abbot came in and behaved as if they were having a black mass, instead of just fiddling with the candle wax."

The priest looked puzzled. "But . . . but where *was* old Giovanni?"

"They bewitched me into sleep!" said the old man hastily.

"Demonspawn they are. I'm allus chasing them out of the church. Allus up to mischief."

The big young knight named Manfred snorted. "Smell his breath! Unless the children magicked him a bottle of wine—and if they could do that, they'd have magicked themselves some food. They don't need questioning. They need a square meal and a place in a household."

The priest nodded. "Alas, sir knight. This is a poor parish. There are many such souls."

Sachs, glaring back at Kat, attempted a commanding sneer. The expression failed of its purpose; seemed more childish than anything else.

"These are mere lies! And the poor you have with you always. It is their souls, not their bodies we must deal with. Now, as your senior in the church I order you to put them out of here, Father—ah—"

The priest's name had obviously escaped him. "Priest. I will have a word with Bishop Pietro Capuletti, and see you are moved to a more worthy station. We'll have the truth out of them. The Servants of the Trinity have ways of dealing with the most hardened servants of Satan."

A look of pleasure came into the abbot's hooded eyes. The kind of pleasure that comes to a man when he finds himself back on his own ground after stumbling into a marsh.

Kat shivered. The knights, she suspected, would obey the abbot—however reluctantly—if the priest who had actual authority here denied sanctuary to her and the children. And how could once-fat, timid little Ugo Boldoni stand up to this?

"Yes, servants of Satan have no place demanding sanctuary," put in one of the two monks unctuously. "Such rights should be denied the likes of them. And the abbot is your superior!"

That was apparently the wrong thing to say to Ugo Boldoni. His spine straightened. "You attempted to remove them from the sanctuary of the Church? *You?* You had no right!" He glared at the abbot. "Nor is *he* my 'superior.' In this see, that is the Metropolitan Michael—no other! In this church *I* am the final arbiter."

The little priest's anger was peppery hot. "Get out of this church! Get out right now. *Go.*"

And that was enough—more than enough—to end the whole affair. The knights were entirely in support of the priest, not the abbot. Within a minute, all of them were gone, the abbot and the two monks scurrying ahead of the knights as if afraid that if they didn't move fast enough they would be manhandled out. Which, Kat suspected, was not far from the truth. On the way out, Manfred seized the still-groaning Pappenheim by the scruff of the neck and, using only one hand, dragged him out of the church as easily as he might drag a sack of onions.

When they'd gone, Father Ugo turned to Katerina. "Just what *are* you doing here, milady? The *Casa* Montescue is a long way from here, and it is late."

Kat shrugged. Boldoni's father had been a sailing master. A good one too, apparently. And it showed in the son's manner, she reflected. "About my father's business," she said quietly. She knew that he'd know that Carlo Montescue was long overdue back from sea. Missing; presumed, by nearly all, dead.

Ugo nodded. He knew perfectly well that the Montescue might be *Case Vecchie*, but they were in financial trouble. All of Venice knew quickly enough whenever one of the famous old houses fell into difficult times. And knew as well, that there were some tasks only family could be relied upon to do.

"You swear that there is no truth in what that abbot said? Your soul is clean?"

"I swear by all the Saints and upon the holy cross that it was a complete lie." Her conscience twinged slightly. "These two children are naughty, but were not practicing any kind of witchcraft."

She took a deep breath and turned around, so that Ugo could not see. She reached into the pouch and took out one of the ducats. The *Casa* Montescue was in a desperate state, but not that desperate. Not compared to those two children, still wide-eyed and frightened. She returned the bag to its warm nest and turned around.

"Here." She held out the coin.

Father Ugo's eyes bulged slightly. Ducats didn't come his way often. But he was of iron principle. "You cannot pay me to free you of sin, Katerina," he said, sounding extremely doubtful.

"It's not for you. It is for those two children. A small thank you to God for sparing me from the Servants of the Holy Trinity."

His voice was troubled. "They do God's work, Katerina Montescue."

"That one young blond knight did God's work. Had it not been for him, that abbot . . ." She shuddered. "Anyway, forget it. I'm grateful. So is Montescue. So take this for those two children you also saved."

He took the warm ducat. "I'll buy a candle."

Kat shook her head. "Food. They'd only play with the candle!"

It was the ragged little girl's turn to shake her head. So fiercely that it looked as if it would come off her skinny shoulders. "Never play with no candles no more." She looked earnestly up at the priest. "Promise!"

A smile lit Father Ugo's countenance. He patted the children's heads gently. "Do you both promise?"

They both nodded, eyes still wide with fright.

"Good! When the rain is over I will go and check that the Servants have really left. Now, I think we will go to the altar and I will lead you all in some prayers. Tomorrow I will go to speak with Monsignor about this. Be easy, Katerina. He is Venetian, you know."

As the party of knights and monks trudged through the rain, Erik and Manfred bringing up the rear, Von Gherens paused to allow them to catch up with him. Then, walking alongside, spoke softly.

"I am forever in your debt, Hakkonsen." His square, solemn face was creased with worry. "I fear I have allowed myself . . ." The next words were almost hissed. "Damn the Servants and their witch-hunts, anyway! They're twisting my mind. Sachs sees a witch under every cobblestone in Venice."

Manfred snorted. "Witch-hunts! *What* witches? So far all we've 'uncovered' are a few quacks selling charms as magical as a brick."

Von Gherens nodded. "Who then took the holy test of faith before Venice's Metropolitan without fear." He sighed heavily. "I miss Father Maggiore. He was often a bit obnoxious, true, but— far better than Sachs. And he was familiar with Venice. He had knowledge of the city, spies who knew something instead of Sachs's absurd gaggle of informers. Since his horrible death, the Servants have blundered about like hogs in a salon."

Erik's words were clipped. "We're doing nothing more than spreading fear and mayhem, *Ritter*—and for no purpose. If Sachs were *trying* to, he couldn't damage the reputation of the Knights worse than he has. This is the most gossipy and intrigue-filled place I've ever seen. Everything we do is spread all over the city within a day."

For the first time since they'd entered the church, Von Gherens smiled. "True. But I daresay what you did tonight will spread just as fast—and go a long way to repairing the damage."

"What *we* did," insisted Erik quietly.

Von Gherens shook his head. Then, placed a thick hand on Erik's shoulder and gave it a little squeeze. "No, Erik. What *you* did. Had it not been for you, the rest of us would have allowed Sachs to drag us further into the pit. I will not forget it."

The knight raised his eyes and glared at the dim figure of Sachs in the rain ahead. "I will not forget," he repeated. "Von Gherens is a proud name. Respected by all. Feared by none save demon-ridden pagans. My family is in your debt as much as I am."

He said nothing further and, a short time later, quickened his steps in order to resume his rightful place beside the abbot.

Manfred watched him go. "Odd, really. He's also Prussian—yet so unlike Von Stublau."

Erik said nothing. Manfred sighed. "And me too, Erik. I will not forget either."

Finally, a touch of humor came to Erik's face. "Really? No more carousing? No more—"

"Not that!" choked Manfred. "I meant the other stuff." His great hands groped in the fog and the rain, trying to shape the distinction—and failing quite miserably.

It was only later, sculling home, playing over the events of the night that it occurred to Kat that whoever her mysterious customer was . . . she wasn't Strega. Her knife had been steel and silver— both metals the Strega would avoid like the plague.

But Kat was too tired to think too much about it. Getting free had cost her one ducat—and her scarf, which the wretched abbot had apparently kept—but the rest would soon be sitting safe in her grandfather's near-empty strongbox.

When she got home, Katerina collapsed into bed and slept the sleep of the infinitely relieved. The gold was safe enough. Good pure unpunched Venetian ducats. The coin valued beyond all others in the world.

It was well into bright morning when she awoke. There was someone in her room, looking through her clothes from the night before. They'd just been dumped in a soggy heap when she came home. Reaction had set in and she'd been just too exhausted.

Her first half-lucid thought was that someone was going to steal the bag of ducats. She sat up and yelled before her groggy mind recalled that she'd taken the gold to the old man the night before.

It was only Alessandra, snooping as usual. "There's no need to shout the house down! Just because you've spent the whole night with your lover and are too lazy get up," she added tartly.

"Oh, go away!" snapped Kat, rubbing her tired eyes. It was certainly bright out there. "Leave me to sleep. There's no lover—as you know perfectly well."

Alessandra cocked her head on one side; raised a perfect eyebrow. "Oh. What's this hair then? I'm going to look for men with honey-auburn hair with just that touch of red. I mean, I know you've got no dowry, but I didn't really think..."

"What *are* you talking about?"

"This hair from your pocket." She held up something, golden-red in the sunlight.

Kat blinked. *Hair?*

Oh, yes. She remembered now. One of hers she'd not wanted to leave with that Strega... actually non-Strega she thought, remembering that knife. "It's one of mine."

"Ha! The day you have hair that color—"

She snatched it from Alessandra's hand. True. In daylight, Katerina could see it was thicker and more curled and it certainly didn't match hers.

So—she must have picked up a hair from the woman herself, not one of her own. In the poor light she hadn't realized.

She shrugged. "I was snuggling up to Lucrezia Brunelli last night. In my sleep. Now go away before I throw this ewer at you."

Alessandra turned. "I'm going to tell Grandpapa if you don't tell me," she threatened.

Kat reached for the ewer. Alessandra showed a remarkable turn of speed leaving the room, quite out of keeping with her normal languid progress.

Kat lay back again. But like Alessandra, sleep had left the room.

There was a greater risk of being recognized, but she was going to have to start doing more deliveries in daytime.

Chapter 16

Marco was out on his feet by the time he got to Caesare Aldanto's apartment near the Campo San Polo. Even if he could have found a gondolier at this hour, he had nothing to pay with—all his money and Maria's had gone into trade goods for Sophia. He had stopped at his apartment long enough to drink some watered wine and get into dry if dirty clothing; figuring that a half-hour more or less would make little difference in Aldanto's condition. Once dry and warm, he slipped on a waterproof cloak—the rain had begun again—cast a longing look at his bed, and went out again into the night.

He was ready to drop and staggering like a drunk by the time he got to Aldanto's door. It was a process that was not aided by the fact that he had had to walk a few miles through the winding dark alleys, because he didn't have a single lira for the canal traghetto. He'd had to go the long way over bridges walking, then wet footed along the tile rail to the water-door, before actually reaching it. But there was no other choice for him to make; he was *not* up to an argument with the guard on the gated street doorway. The stair seemed to go on forever, and the door looked like the portal to Heaven when he finally reached it. He leaned wearily against the lintel and let his fist fall on it.

The door opened the barest crack. "Who's out there?" said a muffled voice.

"'S me, Maria, Marco. Lemme in before I fall down."

The door opened so quickly he almost did fall in. "Ye get th' stuff?"

"Uh huh. How is he?"

"Sleepin'. Don't *seem* no worse, but I had to pour a helluva lotta brandy in him t' get 'im t' sleep. Got him upstairs."

Marco slogged the few steps into the sitting room, let his pack fall to the floor, peeled his cloak over his head and dropped it beside the pack. "Where's Benito?"

"Sleeping too, upstairs. I figured if I needed him I could wake him up. And it's not a bad idea having him bedded down across the door up there, no? The least, somebody forces it, he c'n scream his lungs out. May kill a boarding party by scarin' 'em to death!"

Marco made his way lead-footed to Aldanto's bedside—you *don't* try to walk silently around an ex-assassin!—and stood in the dark listening to the sound of his breathing. A little wheezy, a little hot, but not bad. He'd gotten back well in time. There would be no need for a "real" doctor.

Satisfied, he dragged himself back out. "Boil me some water, would you, Maria? I got to get this stuff measured right—"

As she trotted back to the kitchen, he sat down on the soft warm carpet beside the pack and began taking out parcels of herbs wrapped in rags, identifying them by smell, eye, and sometimes taste. Sophia had literally given him her entire stock. The artemisia could be tricky to use—too much and you got even more horrible side effects.

"Maria," he called softly, "think you can find me a couple of big jars or bowls or something? I need something to put this stuff in besides a rag."

"Lemme look." She clattered down the stairs and returned a moment later. "These do?" She brought him a pair of canisters, the kind spices came in, with vermin-proof lids.

"Perfect."

Sophia had gone by "handful" measurement—but it was a very precise handful. Although it was a little awkward to work one-handed, Marco weighed the herbs in his palm, adding or subtracting a few leaves at a time until he was satisfied; then, carefully crushed what he'd selected into the tin, trying to get it as fine as possible.

He crushed the resulting canisterful yet again, until he had a mixture as fine as possible, then crushed a second bunch of artemisia into the second canister.

"Maria, that water ready?"

"Aye." She must have seen how tired he was, and brought the pan of hot water and spoon and cup to him. "Show me—"

"I intend to—you're going to have to do this from now on. Look, exactly two flat spoonfuls of this for every cup of water—you can put it in the cup or the pan, don't matter which." He measured two spoonfuls into the cup and poured the still-bubbling water on it. "Right, so I'm taking another flat spoonful of this stuff from the other canister and adding it. You want to keep him alive, you do the same. Now you let it steep for as long as it takes to count to a hundred."

He concentrated on the dull throbbing of his hand while the mixture seeped. He noticed with a tired little chuckle Maria's lips moving silently as she marked the time. She could count if not read. He resolved, quietly, to teach her at least to cipher her own name. His own good fortune demanded that he pass it on.

"It ready now?"

"It's ready. We strain off the leaves. If you leave them, it'll get stronger and can kill a man." He suited action to his words. "Here—" He handed the cup to her while he got himself slowly and painfully to his feet. "Let's wake him up."

Maria brought a candle with her, and lit the oil lamp beside the door across from Aldanto's bed. *Some* of his instincts, at least, were still holding. Caesare was awake and wary as soon as the light touched his eyes.

"Got som'thin' for ye, layabout," Maria said cheerfully—real cheer. Marco was touched at her implied trust. "Marco here says it'll fix ye right up."

"Oh—" Aldanto blinked, but before he could continue, he began shaking, great tremors that shook his entire body.

"Caesare—" Marco had never used Aldanto's first name to his face before, but it slipped out. "I mean, Milord Aldanto—"

"Caesare is fine," Aldanto said wearily, when the coughing fit was over.

"Caesare Aldanto, I've had what you've got—honest, this will help. And if you *don't* drink it, you could get a lot sicker. Believe me—I almost died. You don't come from Venice. Kids here get it when they're small. Lot of them die. But if they live, then they will live when they get it again. But you could die. Now, this medicine is going to make you feel even sicker, but I swear to you, it'll help. On my family's honor, I swear. But it is going feel like death."

Aldanto gave him a long, appraising look—then wordlessly took the cup from Maria and drank it down in two gulps.

"*Feh*—that—is—*vile!*" he choked, face twisted in distaste. "That better work fast, because if it doesn't, I'm not drinking more!"

"That's more words in a row than you've managed yet tonight," Marco pointed out. "We'll sugar it next time." Without being asked, Maria brought the brandy and looked inquiringly at Marco.

"Good notion." He approved, thinking that a bit more brandy wouldn't hurt and might help keep Aldanto in bed. "Caesare—I hate to ask—but is there anything around here I can use as a bandage? I love old Sophia, but I hate to think where her rags have been."

"Spare room," said Aldanto around the brandy.

"I'll get it," said Maria.

Aldanto sagged back against his pillows, eyes going unfocused again. Marco carefully unwrapped his hand. The poultice of colts-foot and lance-leaf plantain and Heaven knew what else was working quite well—and Sophia had included more bundles of the herbs in his pack to allow him to put fresh dressings on the wound.

Despite the herbal poultice the wound looked bad, red and swollen. But it was sealing shut, and Marco thought by the look of it that it wasn't infected. He was just beginning to realize how lucky he was. His hand ached, but so far as he could tell all the fingers were still working. He could have easily gotten some ten-dons sliced and wound up with a crippled hand.

"That's a knife wound." Aldanto was staring at the wounded hand, surprised and shocked alert.

"It is, Caesare. I know you think I'm a kid, and you're right sometimes—but you're not right this time. I had to go into the Jesolo for that stuff. Sophia was the only place short of a real doctor where I was going to find what you needed. A man tried to stop me."

Now Aldanto was looking wary, even perhaps a bit alarmed. Marco could have kicked himself for not thinking. Of course, Aldanto would suspect those enemies of his of trying to follow Marco—

"No, no," he hastened to assure him. "Nothing to do with you, he was a marsh-loco. I had to fight him to get through. That's where I got this, and lost my own knife."

"Was?"

"Was. And don't you ever tell Benito I killed a man. He wasn't the first—but I don't want Benito to know about that."

"You have a reason?" Aldanto was staying focused, which rather surprised Marco, given the amount of brandy and the artemisia he had in him, not to mention the fever.

"Because—" Marco looked up from his hand, and he knew his eyes and mouth were bitter. "He'll think he has to be like me. Next thing you know, he'll go out looking. He'll either get himself killed—or he'll kill somebody, and for all the wrong reasons. And that would be worse than getting himself killed. I remember more than just you from home. I remember what some of the younger Montagnards were like when they were my age and Benito's. They started like that—first each one trying to out-risk the other—then it got worse. I don't think he'd ever turn out like them, but I'm not taking any chances on it."

Aldanto nodded slowly, relaxing and letting himself give way to the drugs and the alcohol. "I think maybe I've been underestimating you."

"Only sometimes. You getting sleepy yet?"

Aldanto shivered hard again, then got it under control. "Getting there—and feeling a great deal less like death would be welcome."

"That's the whole idea, Caesare." An idea occurred to him, and he decided he wanted to broach it while Aldanto was in a generous—and intoxicated—mood. "Could you do me a favor? When you feel more like talking?"

"Maybe," Aldanto replied wearily, obviously wishing Marco would leave him alone. "What's the favor?"

Maria came in with clean bandages, salve, and a cheap broach. Marco felt his face flame with embarrassment. He hated to ask in front of Maria, but this might be his only chance. "Could you— could you tell me some time—how to—how to get a girl—to— to like you?" *And what do you do with her after that*, he thought, but didn't say.

"Oh mercy—" Aldanto shut his eyes and leaned his head back on his pillow, his mouth twitching. Marco had the uncomfortable suspicion that he was trying to keep from laughing. Behind him, he heard Maria choking a little, as if she hadn't quite managed to suppress her own humor.

"If you'd rather not—"

"Later, Marco. We'll see about it later." Aldanto opened his eyes and gave him a not-unsympathetic wink, shivered again, harder this time, and lost his amusement as a shudder of chill shook him. "Surely it can wait?"

"Sure—sure—" Marco hastily backed out of the bedroom, taking the bandages from Maria as he passed her. By the time she joined him, he was sitting on the couch, trying to rebandage his wound one-handed.

"Here, you fool, let me do that." She took the things away from him and undid his clumsy work. He leaned back into the soft upholstery and allowed her to do what she wanted. "How much of this stuff of yours he gonna need?"

"Just what's in the canister."

She looked suspiciously at him. "I looked in your pack. You brung back a lot more'n that—"

He shrugged. "I know. I could catch it again, or Benito, or you. There's likely to be a use for it before a cold snap kills the fever. Sophia says I can come trade her for more, anyway. And I brought other herbs."

Maria looked thoughtful. "You know—this *could* be worth something. You say this is the same fever that kills the little ones."

"The thought crossed my mind. But I was mostly doing it for Caesare."

"I owe you one, Marco," she said softly, earnestly.

He relaxed and shut his eyes, feeling his tired and bruised muscles go slack. "Don't go talking debts at me, I owed him."

"Damnfool *Case Vecchie* honor," she jeered back. There was respect in that jeer, however. The *scoulo* families like hers might be poor, but their honor was as deep and as precious. She worked slowly, gently and precisely, first cleaning the wound with some more of Aldanto's brandy. He could tell it wasn't the first knife wound she'd dealt with.

"Just one of Ventuccio's clerks." Fatigue made irrelevant thoughts swim past and one of them caught what little was left of his attention. A thought and a memory of a couple of days ago.

What the hell, he'd risk her temper. "Maria—it's 'aren't' when you're talking about you or more than one person, and 'isn't' all the rest of the time. Except when you're talking about yourself, then it's 'am not.' Got it? Think that'll help?"

He cracked an eyelid open to see her staring open-mouthed at him.

"How did you—?"

"Noticed you fishing for it the other day. Figured nobody'd ever given you the rule. Hard to figure things out if nobody tells you the rules. Claudia could help you better than I could. She was an actress for a while and she knows all the tricks." He yawned. "She could make Brunelli sound like a bargee, or a bargee sound like"—yawn—"Brunelli." His lids sagged and he battled to stay awake.

"Ain't nobody put it quite like that before," she said thoughtfully. "Huh. Damn, this is a bad 'un. Looks like it hurts like hell. What'd you do here, ram your hand down on the point?"

"Had to. He outweighed me by about twice. It was the only way I could think to get the knife away from him." He ran his right hand up to check the lumps on the back of his head and encountered his not-too-nice hair. And remembered.

"*Oh hell!*"

Maria looked up, startled. "What's the matter? I hurt you?"

"There's no food in the house, I need a bath worse than I ever did in my life, all the clothes are filthy and *have* to be washed and I don't have a copper for any of it! I spent every last coin I had for trade goods for Sophia! Oh *hell!*" He squeezed his eyes shut to stop their burning, but a few shameful tears born of exhaustion and frustration escaped to embarrass him. To have gone through this whole night only to have to run against *this*—

"Oh, don't get upset." Maria still had his hand and he managed to get enough control of himself to open his eyes to look at her. She was smiling broadly and pointedly not looking at his tears. "I reckon Caesare owes you a good bit. We got food here, we have a tub and a fireplace. And good soap. You want, I can row you back to Cannaregio when Benito wakes up, get your things, bring it all back here. Given this hand, I reckon I could help you with the clothes even. You just be damn sure not to waste nothing. That suit you?"

Relief turned his muscles to slush and he sagged back. "More than suits—"

"You've got that thinking look again."

"You get most of your work at night, right?"

She looked more than a little uncomfortable, but nodded.

"We work days. So—if you wanted, we could stay here just long enough for him to get better. Or—hell, half the town's sick. You could take a note to Ventuccio's saying *we* are, and we could even spell you in the daytime that way. Saints! The way I feel right now it wouldn't even be a lie! I figure Caesare should be getting better in four, five days; a week, tops. We watch for trouble while you're out, whenever. We can feed him too, make sure he takes the medicine. Keep him from going out when he isn't ready to."

The last two sentences came out a little uncertainly. Keeping Caesare from doing whatever he felt like doing was an improbable scenario—sick or not.

"And you get?" asked Maria.

"Food and a hot bath. I know damn sure Caesare can afford to eat better than we can." He grinned wearily, his bruised facial muscles aching. "You'll have to talk him into covering the pay we'll lose, though. Hell, Maria, you know we can't afford to lose pay any more than you can."

"I know he trusts you." She looked back at the hand she was holding and finished pinning the new bandage with the broach. "I expect after tonight ye've proved it out. We got weapons enough here, between the two of us. And if I don't show up for too long, it's gonna look funny. We don't dare let anybody guess he ain't well enough to fight. All right; you do that." She sniffed, her mouth quirking a little contemptuously. "Hell, the way he throws his money around, he'll cover you if I say so."

"We'll cook and clean up after ourselves."

"You'd damn sure better, 'cause I ain't gonna—" She looked up to see he'd fallen asleep, wedged into the corner of the couch. His head was sagging against the couch cushion and he'd gone as limp as a loaf of water-soaked bread. She chuckled and went to find him a blanket.

Chapter 17

Francesca waited on the walkway outside the Red Cat for Kat to arrive with the last package. Madame was not going to object if any of her girls chose to take a little sun on the walkway while she waited for a delivery; it served as good advertisement. And when that girl was Francesca . . . it guaranteed a full house.

The Sots, though they might harass women they suspected of being whores in and around their own stronghold or inside churches, had not yet become brave enough to go after the Scarlet Women at their own doorsteps. For that much, Francesca was grateful. From Kat's own lips she'd heard the story of the incident with the Sots at the church two weeks before. It had sent chills down her spine. It wasn't so much that they'd dared—a fanatic would dare anything, any time, any place—as it was that their leader had so *instantly* seen heresy and witchcraft where there was none.

Small wonder the Strega she knew were digging holes in the water to hide in. She wanted her talisman, and she wanted it badly.

As if the mere thought of Kat had conjured the girl, the next gondola to make the turn and negotiate its way into the Rio dei Mendicanti was hers. Francesca waved cheerfully to her; with both hands on her pole, Kat could hardly wave back, but she nodded.

There was no need to hide anything. Kat's usual costume, with the hood that covered her distinctive hair, disguised her well enough from anyone except people who knew her well. Which meant, Francesca was now certain, anyone from the *Case Vecchie* circles. As a young woman of the *Case Vecchie*, Kat would not be

196

known to anyone in Venice's lower classes except the few people with whom the girl had set up commercial arrangements—which, for their reasons as well as her own, would be kept highly secret. So there was no danger of Kat being recognized here, so long as she kept her face shadowed and her hair covered by a hood—not in the vicinity of *this* bordello. The House of the Red Cat did not have a low-class custom, true, but it was still several cuts below the kind of establishment that the city's elite would frequent.

Nor did Francesca have any reason to hide the transaction from the watchful eyes of the Madame of the Red Cat. Prostitutes received frequent parcels from boat girls; not even a suspicious brothel keeper would wonder about *this* parcel. In fact, the very openness of the delivery was the surest protection. Besides, Francesca was too impatient for the pose of the languid lady. She caught the rope that Kat tossed to her and tied up the boat with her own hands. Kat threw her the package she had been waiting for, then balanced up and over the deck and onto the walkway, jumping across the water to land beside Francesca.

"Do you want to check it and make sure it's all right?" Kat asked.

The gown within the outer wrapping—a very special gown—had been an extra, ordered after the successful interview with the Madame of Casa Louise. Madame wanted her to make an entrance and a stir when she first arrived (officially) at the House. Kat had promised she could come up with something spectacular. Tonight, or tomorrow, depending on what Fate presented in the way of opportunity, saucy and inventive Francesca of the Red Cat would vanish, and Francesca de Chevreuse, gracious and educated courtesan from Aquitaine, would appear at Casa Louise—with no way of connecting the two. Certainly her potential customers would never guess. The social strata that patronized Casa Louise wouldn't even glance down the Rio dei Mendicanti as they passed by on their way to some important social or business function.

All the rest of the new gowns, including the interview gown, were in her new apartment at Casa Louise, conveyed there by the ever-resourceful Katerina. Francesca was taking no chances on the Madame of the Red Cat sniffing out her imminent defection. A bruised and broken-boned courtesan was not an object of desire, and the doorman had heavy fists.

Kat had cleverly managed to squeeze everything into a rather small package that looked *exactly* like a parcel from a food-stall.

"I don't suppose you'd care to come in, would you?" Francesca asked doubtfully. She was surprised by the answer.

"I would love to. I'd like—to ask your advice."

On what, I wonder? Kat knew Donatella, the same Strega herbalist who provided Francesca with the means of preventing pregnancy, so it couldn't be that, could it? Unless Kat wasn't aware that there were such things—

Ridiculous. She couldn't be making deliveries on these waters without finding out within a fortnight.

"Then by all means, please come in." Francesca gestured that Kat should follow her.

It was too early for the doorman to be on duty, and plenty of the other girls had female friends or relatives from outside the House, so Fernando paid no attention to Kat whatsoever. They reached Francesca's room in short order, and Francesca dropped the latch into place when Kat was inside.

"I hope you'll forgive me, but there's really no place to sit but the bed," Francesca said apologetically. Kat shrugged, and took a seat at the foot, looking around with curiosity.

"Ease my mind and have a look through there. I think you'll like what I found, and I want to make sure that the goldsmith gave me the right *thing.*"

Thing. That would be the talisman. Francesca smiled; she wouldn't wonder that Kat was suspicious—it didn't look like something a goldsmith should have held in his keeping. She cut the string holding the parcel together and unfolded the dark, tabby-weave cloth.

Ah, the cloak. Kat had used the cloak she'd asked for as the wrapping, lining-side out. Inside were the dress, the undergown, the shifts, the hose, with one of the undergowns wrapped around another bundle.

"These are perfect," Francesca assured the girl. "Especially the choice of colors. Every other courtesan is going to be in blue or red; not only are these good colors for me, but they'll make me stand out immediately." She untied the shift and shook out the ornaments. "These are even better, if that's possible," she pronounced. "Whoever taught you about jewelry was a wise woman. *Never* choose fake anything, when for the same price you can have something genuine." She held up the sparkling strands of Murano glass beads that she would weave through her hair, then the three-tiered necklace with carved amber pendants and the matching earrings. "Can you see how much richer and substantial these look than gilt chains and faux pearls?"

"I didn't like the look of the other things I was offered," replied Kat. "I can't explain it, and no one taught me."

"Then you have very good instincts," Francesca told her, taking out the last piece, her precious amulet. It had been her mother's, and had come all the way from Aquitaine with Francesca. It was very crude—a wooden heart encased in a plain silver cage. It was also very old, and would probably get her burned on sight if one of the Sots ever got wind of it. It held a luck-spirit: not a terribly powerful one, but powerful enough to keep Francesca safe so long as she didn't do anything monumentally stupid . . . and *quite* powerful enough to keep her safe from prowling canal monsters by making her invisible to the eyes of evil creatures and black spirits.

It was also indisputably pagan. Which was why Francesca had chosen her Jewish goldsmith to hold it for her while she was in the Red Cat.

"Instincts good enough for me to do what *you're* doing?" came the bitter question.

Francesca clutched the amulet to her breast quite unconsciously and stared at the girl. "You can't possibly be saying you want to become a whore!" she blurted.

Kat flushed, but persisted. "You seem to be doing well enough. And if . . . my grandfather dies, I may have no choice."

Francesca had known from the first day she met Kat that the girl's family was in dire straits. She was fairly certain she even knew, from the rumors that swirled through Venice along with the tides, which of the old houses it was—Montescue—even though she had never made any attempt to find out. But this . . .

She sat down on the head of the bed, put her talisman aside, and seized Kat's hands in both of hers. "I am the *exception* to the general fate of women in this profession," she said bluntly. "Or, at least, I intend to be. I've had to fight and scheme my way with every step I took since I came to Venice, and if I had not had the training from early childhood, *and* exceptional looks, I would not be going where I am." She was not going to speak the name of Casa Louise aloud, not here. Until the moment she went out of the door in this dress, there was still danger.

"Listen to me—I'm not going to give you my life's story, but I'm going to tell you enough. *My* family was the equivalent of *Case Vecchie*—elsewhere. My father was ruined by another old house when I was fifteen; then excommunicated and executed for supposed 'treason.' My older brother was murdered within a month. My mother fled with me and a single mule-load of her belongings. She set herself up as a courtesan in another city by appearing at a very exclusive House in one of her fine gowns and letting the Madame know that she—and her daughter—were available. The Madame tested her—and myself as well. A courtesan is not a whore; if she were, no man of wealth and taste would bother with what he could have cheaper, elsewhere. Simple rutting, however luxurious the setting, is not sufficient for the price that a man pays for a *cortegiana*."

Kat's face flamed, but Francesca was going to give the girl the whole truth as brutally as possible. "My mother prospered until she did something unbelievably stupid. She had the opportunity to strike back at the man who had destroyed her husband and son, and she took it. She was condemned and hung as a murderess. By then however, I was—in the business. I took my accomplishments and what I could carry and the Madame kindly assisted my flight to Venice. The Madame and my mother saw to it—as the next generation in their profession—that I had every accomplishment. I read and write in four languages, I speak six. I play the lute and sing. I dance. I can converse with a learned *dottore* of letters on the works of the Greeks and Romans, or on the works of the poets and philosophers of our own age. I even write poetry myself—it's *bad* poetry, but I can write it. I know as much about politics within Italy and the wider world as most of the gentlemen of the *Case Vecchie*. Quite a bit more, in fact. And as for the games of the bed—well, let me just assure you that I am a notable athlete. *That* is what is required to be a courtesan."

She paused thoughtfully. "You may believe the rewards are great, and . . . they are. Or can be, at least. I will, in the course of a year, earn as much as a good ship's captain, and that is *my* share—the Madame will earn as much from my labors as I do. But to get to this point, I have had to strip my soul down to the bones, and be more ruthlessly honest with myself than anyone other than a priest should ever be forced to be. I must look in the mirror every day, and rather than admire my own beauty, search ruthlessly for any

flaw. I must keep my body in a state of perfection. I must lie gracefully and believably to my customers—I must be able to read them
so well that I seem to read their thoughts. Every day I face the
possibility that a customer will injure or even kill me, and if he does,
no punishment will come to him. Lately there is also the threat that
the star of the Servants of the Trinity will be so on the ascendant
that they will dictate Venetian morality—they will be looking for
women to make into examples, and they will take the ones who
stand out. Now—consider what I am, what my accomplishments
are, and ask yourself—*are* you my match? *Can* you do what I do
every day? If not—you'll find yourself here, in a House like this one.
The risks are greater, here; the likelihood of a customer committing some outrage higher. The Schoppies are frequent visitors, and
demand pleasure as the price of leaving us alone. The servants are
spies, and the Madame herself can order her girls beaten as punishment for some infraction, real or imagined. Unless extreme care
is taken, the risk of disease as well as injury is *very* high."

"Oh," Kat said, and gulped.

"I quite understand that from the outside—although my life is
ridden with sin—all this looks moderately attractive," Francesca
said more gently. "I am also aware that the life of a courtesan
looks . . . well, quite glamorous, in a tarnished sort of fashion. And
it is quite possible, for a clever and careful woman, to find herself wedded to the man of her choice. You've heard the whispered
gossip, no doubt, perhaps you even know of such a woman. But
let me tell you now, that although I fully intend *precisely* that sort
of fate for myself, it will require all the resources I can muster,
all my energy, thought, and time, the planning of a great general,
and, frankly, a certain amount of luck."

"Ah," said Kat; she looked both disappointed and relieved, and
Francesca patted her hands and let them go.

"Such luck as *you* have been for me," Francesca continued. "A
courtesan remembers her friends, Kat. I think you'll soon find that
the information I can provide you once I move will be of considerable help in mending your fortunes, as you have done the
things that helped me to repair mine."

She smiled. "If worse comes to worst, a Grand House like the
one I'm moving to often requires discreet boatmen to ferry messages, as well as clients who need a certain privacy. And, what
would be even better . . ."

Francesca hesitated, not wanting to bruise Kat's already damaged pride any further. But—

"Kat," she said firmly, "within a much shorter time than you might expect, I will be . . . well, not exactly awash in wealth, but certainly rich enough to afford—even require—my own gondolier. Having one who was herself a pretty girl—or, better still, a pretty girl cleverly disguised as a *very* pretty boy—would give the thing a certain *cachet*. Which a courtesan requires more than anything else. So if your fortunes come tumbling down, and you find yourself destitute and alone—*please* come to me *first*. Before you think of taking any, ah, desperate measures. All right?"

As she had made her suggestions, the color had faded from Kat's face. But it returned, soon enough. And her expression had become almost hopeful when Francesca came to the part about the private gondola. That gave Francesca a feeling of great relief—Kat did *not* have the makings of a courtesan, and she didn't want to see the girl in the situation that most of the Red Cat women were in. Kat, she knew, would not survive that life for more than a handful of years.

"Now, I know you must have deliveries, and I have an evening of work ahead of me—" She fished for the pouch of coins she owed Kat, and pressed them into her hand.

"I do," Kat said, springing up from her seat on the bed. She paused at the door, and turned around. "Francesca—thank you. For everything."

"You are most welcome, dear." Francesca gave her a knowing wink that made Kat blush all over again before she whisked out the door and was gone.

Chapter 18

The monster waited until the vessel was completely engrossed. As always, Chernobog's shadow voice aroused the pathetic creature to a frenzy of uncontrolled emotion. Every emotion—anger and fury as well as lust. The vessel was careless. And so, as he combined fury with lust, satiating himself on the servant's body while he imagined an insolent young witch in her place, he gave not a moment's thought to the effect his emotions would have on the monster's shackles.

The monster could sense the coming moment, when the vaporous cage that restrained it would soften, grow tattered. It could escape then, without either the vessel or the servant noticing its passage into the outer world.

The monster's own lust grew rapidly, as the gray mist that surrounded it began to take shape and color. Some small part of its mind urged caution—*the master will be angry!*—but the monster ignored it. Why should Chernobog care if the monster devoured another soul? And it could always claim that it had been commanded by the master's own servant. Had she not aroused the vessel? Had not the vessel's own fury and lust sent the monster on its way—even selected the prey?

Somewhere in what was left of what had once been a keen mind, the monster knew that Chernobog would see through the deception. But—

It no longer cared. Let the pain come, later. For the moment, the monster could think of nothing beyond the immediate prospect of feeding.

And such a magnificent feed! The monster could barely restrain itself from clawing at the cage.

Too soon, too soon. Wait until . . .

The gray mist faded and faded. Finally—it was enough.

The monster glided through and found itself, once again, in the outer world. The small room was dark; more of a crypt than a room, with the casket at the center. Once it had been a small chapel, but no longer. It was devoted to a different creed now— as the bones and infant skulls and arcane symbols on the walls attested.

The monster ignored its surroundings. It was not really part of any faith, and found the trappings meaningless. Instead, moving slowly, it opened the door that led to the room beyond. The door was neither locked nor bolted. There was no reason for it to be, since the larger room beyond was given over to the privacy of Chernobog's servant. It was a spare and austere room, lit only by a single candle.

The monster crept through the room toward another door on the opposite side. Behind that door was the bedchamber where the master's voice slept. Slept, and, every night, aroused the vessel.

The door to the bedchamber was not only unlocked, it was ajar. The room beyond was dark. Before entering, the monster listened for the sounds it was hoping to hear. *Yes.* The vessel was grunting his lust atop the master's voice, in the bed against the far wall; the monster could hear the voice responding with soft cries of faked passion.

The sounds meant nothing to the monster. It had a different lust to satisfy.

Silently, stealthily, so as not to disturb the rutters, the monster crept on all fours through the bedchamber. Another austere room, it was, well designed to disguise the servant's true nature. The monster's thin lips peeled back in jeering scorn, seeing the crucifix attached to one of the walls. Normally it would avoid such a holy symbol, but this one was meaningless. The servant had long ago, as she had with all the paraphernalia of her supposed faith, defiled the crucifix in such as way as to make it harmless. Still, the monster did not come any closer than necessary to the holy symbol as it glided toward the pile of discarded clothing on the floor.

The item it sought was there, just as it had sensed it was. Still tucked away, forgotten, in a pocket of the vessel's tunic. Carefully, slowly, the monster teased it out with its long, thick tongue. Savoring the taste, absorbing the scent...

It was enough. It could find the prey, now. Easily.

The monster sidled away, backing toward the crypt where its cage was kept. Again, being careful not to disturb the rutters on the bed; and, again, staying as far away as possible from the crucifix on the wall.

Once back in the crypt, the monster re-entered the cage with an eagerness it did not usually feel for that act. But that was because the cage was a cage no longer. Not with the vessel's mindless lust shredding the vaporous bars. The cage was now...a portal.

As soon as the monster felt the waters of the canal, and was finally able to see the outer world again, it flinched. It had not realized the time of day. The vessel and the voice usually rutted at night, but night had not yet arrived. It was only sunset.

With a quick thrust of its tail, the monster drove beneath the surface and hid amidst some pilings shoring the side of the canal. Cursing silently at the frustration, but unable to do otherwise. It would risk Chernobog's anger at an unauthorized feeding, but it would not risk the master's rage if it were seen. On *that* matter, Chernobog's instructions had been far too clear for the monster to claim an unfortunate misunderstanding.

So it waited, for the sun to disappear and the darkness to come. And, as it waited, felt its frustration mounting to the point of sheer fury.

Especially when it saw the prey herself passing by! Not forty feet distant!

The monster's eye, peeking above the surface of the water in the shadows amidst the pilings, watched the prey row her gondola past. Its eel-throat gaped wide; thick tongue writhing in the water like a giant worm, tasting her scent.

The prey was so—*splendid*. Fresh, young, innocent. The monster knew that her soul would taste as fine as her hair, shining like copper in the sunset. So much tastier a soul than the wretched things the master had been feeding it.

It would be so easy. . . . The monster could capsize the gondola in an instant. Then, seize the prey once she was in the water and drag her to a hidden feeding ground.

So easy . . . *Now! Now!*

But . . . not even the monster, not even when it was burning with lust, was crazy enough to do it. Not while it was daylight. Not with people in other boats on the water, and walking alongside the canal. No matter how fast it moved, someone would witness the act. Might even catch a glimpse of the monster itself.

Chernobog's rage would not stop at mere punishment, then. Chernobog would feed on the monster itself, and not be satisfied with simply a portion.

Remembering the one time the master had fed upon it, the monster almost whimpered. Its lust receded, replaced by terror. Enough, at least, to enable the monster to bring itself back under control.

Wait. Night is coming, and I can find her anywhere. The scent will be easy to follow.

The monster was so intent on its own desires that it never noticed the priest standing on the opposite side. Never noticed that the priest was also watching the prey, as she receded down the canal—and with as much concentrated attention as the monster itself.

Nor did it notice the moment when the priest suddenly started and cast a gaze across the canal. Then, scrutinized everything in the area, as if a hunter had suddenly heard a noise in the forest and was trying to detect its source.

Nor did it notice when the priest spun on his heels and began striding hurriedly away.

The shaman, however, did notice. Naturally enough, since the shaman had been sent on this incredibly dangerous expedition for that very purpose. The monster thought it had "escaped." In reality, Chernobog had foreseen this eventuality and had decided to use the monster's lust to test his opponents. The shaman's master did not understand either the purpose of these peculiar priests in Venice, nor their power.

Chernobog also, the shaman understood, wanted to test the depths of the Lion's slumber. Once before the shaman's master had misgauged the Lion, when he tried to murder the Strega Grand Master with

too open a hand. That attempt had roused the Lion from his sleep.
The ancient spirit had not only slain the assassins before they could
finish the work, but had carried the still-living Marina himself into
the Jesolo.

Three years ago, that had been. The time had come, Chernobog
decided, to see if the Lion had returned to his slumber. The shaman
understood the logic—even agreed with it, abstractly. But it was he,
not Chernobog, who was forced to lurk in the shadows of the canal
and watch, while a monster roamed loose. A monster which would
not hesitate for an instant to devour the shaman as readily as it would
devour its intended prey.

The time finally came. It was dark enough, now, if the monster moved carefully. It eased out of the pilings and began driving up the canal with slow and powerful strokes of its tail. Keeping
a wary eye for boats and passersby, and diving below the surface
whenever necessary.

The scent was strong. As easy to follow as blood spoor, but far
more delicious.

When Pierre came into the room, his face was as pale as a sheet.
His eyes, open and strained; he looked for an enemy, but not one
of this world.

"Something . . . is out there. . . ."

Eneko Lopez rose from the table where he had been writing a
letter, his head cocked. "Yes?"

The Savoyard priest shook his head violently, and shuddered at
the same time. "I don't know. I was watching the girl, the one you
wanted to find out more about. Then—suddenly—I felt something.
Something horrible. Evil more concentrated than anything I can
remember in my life."

The Basque at the table turned his head and stared out the
window. "Was it she herself, perhaps?"

Pierre shook his head again. Less violently, this time. "I . . . don't
think so, Eneko. It was connected with her somehow, I felt. But
I had the sense that it was something watching her, rather than
she herself."

Reluctantly, as a priest will speak of such things. "It seemed
very . . . lustful. A horrible sort of lust, and not the sort of thing
that anyone would draw willingly unto themselves. And I am not

so sure, now, that it wasn't actually hunting her, and not just watching her."

Lopez limped out through the open door near the table and onto the balcony beyond; then, peered down at the canal below. The waters were already dark with the evening. He raised his eyes and studied the massive edifice across the canal that housed the Imperial embassy.

Something watching—perhaps hunting. Something evil. A true innocent might, *might* be safe from such a thing, but how many people were true innocents, once out of leading-strings?

"Too late . . ." he murmured. "For anything except prayer."

He turned back, sharply and decisively. "Join me, Pierre. Here. Now. Whatever it was—let us test the thing. If it is what I think it is . . . Chernobog has made a serious error."

Pierre hesitated. The Basque priest's solid bar of eyebrow lowered. "It is not forbidden, Pierre!" he snapped. "And what is the alternative? To allow a girl who may be guilty of nothing more than venial sins to be devoured by Chernobog?"

The Savoyard's uncertainty vanished. A moment later, he joined Eneko on his knees, crucifix in hand.

"Protections?" Pierre asked. Eneko shook his head.

"No time, but *we* are not the ones it is hunting—" Eneko cleared his mind of the distracting worry that this might be a trap for him and his own people. "Saint Mark—"

"Ah!" Pierre caught his meaning. "I found a prayer in the Accademia library that might be what we need."

The Savoyard bent his head over his clasped hands and began murmuring the words; Eneko concentrated on them, and on special, sacred magic of a Hypatian priest-mage, that of directed, aimed prayer, with power behind it.

Blessed Saint Mark . . . patron and protector . . .

The power flowed, outward and upward, as Eneko concentrated; he felt another power join to his—Pierre's—and their souls sought for that place where prayers were answered.

But *then*, what he had not dared hope for.

He felt something stir; sensed sleepy eyes opening, somewhere, in that place that was outside space and a time beyond time, in that *other* where spirits dwelt. Something ancient.

What—

He did not have the means to answer that question; *It* could

not hear him, he lacked a voice It would respond to. But he didn't
have to answer it; he sensed It was now ... *looking*. For just an
instant, Eneko thought he saw a pair of great eyes, opening.

The monster was at the water-door. Not because it sought entry
by that means—too risky—but simply because it wanted to be
certain. It required only a moment of soft snuffling, licking the
door with its tongue.

Yes. So strong! So delicious!

It moved slowly down the canal, searching the walls. A very great
house, this was. Still massively impressive, despite the little signs
of disrepair.

That disrepair would be of good use to the monster. There was
a route up the walls—as easy to climb as a chimney to an experienced mountaineer. The monster almost chortled with glee.

Then ... restrained itself again. It was still too early. Night had
fallen, yes; but the house would not be asleep. The monster could
not risk Chernobog's anger that much.

Wait. Wait.

Something else awoke, stirred from long slumber by prayers.
Opened golden eyes, and then ... understanding the meaning of
the prayers ...

Great muscles rippled down a tawny back. Huge wings began
to unfold.

In my city? You grow too bold, Chernobog!

There was some fury in the thought. Not much. Mostly, the
thought was just ... amused. *Christian priests, no less! They're not
usually that smart.*

*From his hiding place in the pilings nearby, the shaman watched.
He was awash in fear. The shaman understood what the monster
was doing, and he knew that the slightest motion on his part would
draw its attention. Should that happen, the shaman was far too close
now to even hope to escape. In open water, with enough of a lead,
the shaman in his fishform could outswim the monster. But here,
in the narrow canals—the shaman had seen how quickly the monster could move in a lunge—*

*The shaman prayed to his pagan deities. Prayed desperately, hoping
that time itself would move faster in its course.*

❀   ❀   ❀

It was time!

Still almost silent, for all its eagerness, the monster heaved out of the water and began climbing up the wall. It made swift progress, even stopping from time to time to scan the area in order to be certain there were no observers. The heavy wall's disrepair made climbing easy.

The shaman, still almost shuddering with relief after seeing the monster's form lift out of the water, froze with new terror. Something new was stirring! He could sense it! Something . . . immensely powerful.

He turned and began swimming away. But an iron thought came from his master.

STOP, SLAVE. I MUST SEE THIS. YOUR LIFE IS OF NO CONSEQUENCE.

There was no balcony providing ingress to the house. But the monster had seen the roof garden, and it served the purpose just as well.

A quick slither, and the monster was into the garden. Being careful, still, not to crush or disarray the vegetation. *Leave no trace.* Silently, on all fours, it crept through the lush vegetation. Too lush, really—the garden also showed signs of poor maintenance.

Eneko thought he heard a thunder of wings, and felt a shadow pass over him, before he and Pierre fell back into their heavy, mortal selves.

"It is done," he whispered. "Let us pray it will be in time."

A little shudder passed through Pierre's shoulders. "I wouldn't worry about *that*, Eneko. If the legends are even half true—" He gave his Basque companion a look that was almost baleful. "What *have* you gotten us into?"

When the monster reached the glass-paned double doors that opened onto the garden, it thrust its misshapen head cautiously between two large potted plants. The curtains on the doors were not closed, and the monster could see into the room beyond. Could see everything quite clearly, despite the overcast and the absence of a candle in the room itself. The monster was a creature of

darkness, after all. It could see as well at night as in daytime—
better, in truth, since the sun was painful to it.

Its great body grew taut as a drum, almost stunned by its good
fortune. It had expected a difficult time, creeping through the house
in order to find the prey.

Instead—

She was there! Sleeping in the bed!

It made sense, of course. Even the dim mind of the monster
could understand that much. A girl with such coppery hair—such
a coppery, splendid soul—

Hungry!

—would want to wake to the sunrise. Feel the coppery rays
bathing her in a new day.

A new day which would never come again. Soft laughter began
to gurgle up in the monster's thick throat. But it forced the sound
under. Just a moment more of silence, and it would—*feed.*

A claw reached up for the latch. The monster knew, for a certainty, that the door would be unlocked. Such an innocent
soul . . . it gathered its haunches.

Hungry!

The vise that clamped down on its head struck like a god's
hammer. It vaguely remembered such a hammer. . . .

But there was no time to think of ancient weapons. The monster writhed like a lizard, caught by a hawk, its limbs thrashing
and flailing.

Thrashing and flailing in—nothing. Talons smote thin air; a
tail lashed in emptiness. Everything was dark, a darkness not
even the monster's eye could penetrate. Dimly, stunned, it
realized that its head was in a giant maw. Realized—dimly,
stunned—that it was being carried through the air. Like a lizard,
caught by a hawk.

The monster's thrashing grew frenzied. Something smote its back.
Almost—not quite—breaking the spine. But the blow was enough
to paralyze the monster.

*Not even his fear of Chernobog could have kept the shaman from
fleeing in terror, now. The spirit that had passed over him had seemed
like a golden avalanche of fury and destruction.*

As it happened, the shaman was quite safe. He was beneath the

Lion's contempt. Nor did he have to fear Chernobog's wrath. His master was far too busy—far too frantically busy—forging his own defenses to worry about the doings of a pitiful slave.

Some time later—how much, the monster was too dazed to know—it was tumbled to the ground, its head spit out of a maw like a bad seed.

Wildly, scrabbling to get back to its feet, the monster looked around.

It was back in the cage. Except . . . even as it watched, the tatters in the vapors closed in, barring any exit.

No, not *closed* in . . . were *driven* in, by the flapping of great wings. Seeing the size of those wings, the monster flinched.

Then, flinched again, as it finally looked at its assailant. Flinched, and sidled away. Whining in its throat.

There are rules, creature. The voice hammered into the monster's brain. *This is no longer our time—neither yours, nor mine. But there are still rules!*

The monster howled as a great paw slammed into its flank, ripping gouges in the flesh. The blow was terrifying in its power. For all its own strength, the monster knew it was no more than a mouse at the mercy of a cat.

A very large and angry cat.

Another blow, which broke the arm the monster raised to fend it off. Another blow, which shredded its snout. Fangs like swords clamped on its haunches. The monster was jerked off its feet, shaken like a mouse in the maw of a cat.

This time, the monster's spine did break. So did its shoulder, when it was hurled to the ground. So did its rib cage, under yet another hammerblow of a paw the size of an anvil.

The monster was shrieking pure terror, now. Another blow shattered its jaw, bringing silence.

That's better. You'll live, of course. Here in this . . . foul cage. Heal, soon enough. Those too are the rules.

The growling voice turned into a rumbling laugh. *But I dare say you'll not try that again.*

A giant paw was raised, in question. Frantically, the monster gargled agreement through a broken jaw.

Remember, beast. This is my city—no one else's. Tell that to Chernobog, when you see him next. He may attempt to destroy

*it, if he can. But he may not do as he pleases. THERE ARE
RULES!*

Another blow came, crushing the monster's skull.

Diego found his two companions in Eneko's room, looking wan
and exhausted.

"Did you see a ghost?" he asked cheerfully.

They glared at him. "Near enough," muttered Pierre. He pointed
a weary finger at the Basque. "He summoned the Lion. I think."

Diego's eyes widened. Eneko chuckled. "It was Pierre's prayer,
you know. How odd that he didn't mention that. . . ."

The Basque priest lurched to his feet and walked out onto the
balcony. He leaned on the balcony and studied the Imperial
embassy across the canal. The huge edifice was now somber with
nightfall. Only a few lights could be seen, tapers and lamps flickering behind curtained windows. Behind him, Eneko could hear
Pierre's murmured words, as he explained to their Castillian com-
rade what had transpired.

His companions joined him on the balcony a short while later.

"Are you certain it was not she herself?" asked Diego quietly.
"We must be certain about this, Eneko."

The Basque shrugged. "I'm not *certain* of anything. But . . . no.
I am now almost sure the girl is an innocent. The more so, since
you discovered her identity."

"The name 'Montescue' is an old one, Eneko," said Diego uncertainly. "Evil enough, in that family, over the centuries."

Again, the Basque shrugged. "And of what old family can that
not be said?" With a little laugh: "Certainly not mine! Did I ever
tell you about my great-grandfather—"

"Several times," growled Pierre. "Just as Diego has bored me
endlessly with tales of his own wicked Castillian ancestors. My own
progenitors, on the other hand," he added cheerfully, "were virtuous peasants."

His companions bestowed skeptical looks upon him. "Each and
every one!" he insisted.

The moment of levity was brief. Diego returned to the subject
like a dog chewing a bone. "Still, Eneko. We *must* be certain."

The Basque was back to his study of the Imperial embassy. His
gaze was intent, as if he could penetrate the heavy stone walls and
see what transpired within.

"It doesn't make sense, Diego. I've discovered, as you know, that *Casa* Montescue is in dire financial straits. And the girl Katerina is the only member of the family young enough—and trusted enough—to be working at the 'gray trade.' Her grandfather is too old, her sister-in-law . . ." His lips tightened with distaste. "Untrustworthy, by all accounts. That's enough—more than enough—to explain her mysterious habits."

Diego began to say something, but Eneko drove over it. "Besides, consider the logic of what just happened." He gestured with his head toward the Savoyard. "Pierre is wrong, incidentally. I'm sure of it. We did not *summon* the Lion, we simply . . . woke it up for a time. To actually *summon* the thing requires knowledge I do not possess, and—if the legends are to be believed—the participation of one of the four ancient families of Venice. Which are: Terrio, Lacosto—both families long vanished; Valdosta—destroyed, presumably by the Montagnards. And—" He paused, giving the next word added emphasis. "Montescue."

Diego stared down the dark canal, in the direction of *Casa* Montescue. "You think the Evil One was trying . . ."

"The same legends also specify a *son* of the families, Eneko," objected Pierre. But his demurral was not spoken with any great force.

Eneko smiled grimly. "Yes, I know. But does *Chernobog*?"

He sighed. The next words came iron hard, for all the softness of the tone. "Enough, I say. I'm satisfied that the Montescue girl is innocent. We've got few enough resources as it is—just the three of us. We've learned all we can—and need—for the moment, concerning Katerina Montescue. Time to concentrate on two more important matters."

"What really happened to the Strega Grand Master," mused Diego. "That's one. What's the other?"

Eneko's little chuckle was quite absent of humor. "What do you think? What *really* happened to the children of Lorendana Valdosta? Two *sons,* I remind you."

"*Casa* Valdosta was destroyed," protested Pierre. "Everyone says so."

Eneko stared into the darkness. "This is the murkiest city in the world, brothers. We cannot assume *anything.*"

❀   ❀   ❀

Agony led the way, dragging the monster back into consciousness. In the cage, true enough, its bones and flesh would knit and heal. But—not without pain. Immense pain, in this instance.

Worse than the pain, however, was the terror; once the monster's returning mind understood that Chernobog himself was here.

Here . . . and in a rage.

Another blow destroyed most of the healing. A second broke the monster's spine anew.

You imbecile! You had your orders!

The monster tried to babble its excuse. But it was impossible, with a still-mangled snout.

It would have done no good, in any event. Chernobog was not to be misled, and the monster—now that its mind was no longer clouded with lust—knew how foolish that thought had been.

You awakened the Lion!

Another blow sent gouts of blood flying, along with gobbets of flesh.

Thankfully, it felt Chernobog receding. The fury in the master's voice ebbed, slightly, replaced by a colder and more thoughtful anger.

Nothing for it. I cannot punish the servant, for there is nothing left to punish. Nor the vessel either, for the moment, since I still have use for it. But you . . .

The broken-bodied, half-paralyzed monster whined, begging forgiveness.

On you I will feed.

The monster howled for some time thereafter, as Chernobog held it down and tore out its innards. Not gobbling the intestines so much as chewing on them, slowly and with apparent relish.

When Chernobog was done, there was not much left of the monster. But, in the recesses of what had once been a mind, the monster knew that there was still . . . enough.

It would survive. Barely.

The healing would be painful. Agonizing.

I trust you will obey me, henceforth.

The monster tried to whine its abject obedience; but failed, quite miserably. The only sound it made was that of spilling blood. Chernobog had also devoured its tongue.

Chapter 19

Caesare Aldanto leaned back in the dark corner of the tavern where he had taken a table. For a moment, he closed his eyes, scowling inwardly as he felt the continuing effects of the disease he'd contracted. It had been almost two weeks now since Marco had begun medicating him. And while that medication had certainly helped enormously—quite possibly saved his life, in fact—Caesare was still feeling some lingering weakness.

Damn Venice and its miserable swamps anyway!

He sighed. He couldn't afford any weakness. Not at any time in his life, much less now. In Venice, less so than in any city in the world except possibly his home town of Milan itself.

In truth, he detested Venice. Still . . . it was an excellent place for a man like him to make his fortune. So, suppressing all else, Caesare reopened his eyes and gave the gloomy interior of the tavern another careful examination.

This was not Caesare's usual haunt, but it suited his purpose today. The tavern was dark, the food and wine were inferior enough that it wasn't very popular, and he wasn't known here.

Sensing movement at the door, his eyes flicked in that direction. Caesare had taken a table in the rear, as he had specified to the contact. So when Sachs's man entered, he didn't have to stand in the doorway peering around, which would have made him suspicious and uncomfortable.

As the new arrival made his way past the tables, Caesare realized that *this* man would have had no difficulty recognizing him anyway. They were old acquaintances, after all.

Relishing the shock he'd give the fellow, Caesare leaned forward, taking his face out of the shadows. "Good evening, Francesco," he said genially.

Francesco Aleri was good; Caesare had to give him that. Except for a momentary start, Aleri's astonishment was quickly covered. Not surprising, of course, for the man who was Duke Visconti's chief agent in Venice—which meant, in practice if not in theory, also the head of the Montagnard faction in the city.

Caesare, by sheer willpower, forced any trace of the weakness produced by the disease from his face. The grin that creased that face was purely savage. He could not afford to let Aleri suspect he might be ill.

And, besides . . . Caesare was genuinely enjoying himself. This must be a dreadful moment for Francesco, who had thought until now—and with good reason—that Caesare was safely dead. After all, Aleri had been the one responsible for cracking him over the back of the head and dumping him in the Rio dei Mendicanti.

That would have been the end of the matter for Caesare, if Francesco hadn't chosen to dump him off a bridge rather than rolling him over the side of the canal. But as it happened, there had been a small boat tied up under that bridge, and in the boat had been a young girl, alone, and . . . very susceptible to a handsome young man in obvious danger. Especially one who was as consummate an actor as Caesare Aldanto.

"You look prosperous, Caesare," Aleri said pleasantly, taking a seat across from him. The motion was easy, casual, relaxed—but Francesco's back, needless to say, was prudently to the wall.

Caesare smiled. "I do well enough," he said, in tones as smooth and bland as unflavored cream. "Despite the ungentle fashion in which I was discharged from my previous, ah, position."

"You seem to have landed on your feet," Francesco said, shrugging.

Aleri said nothing else, although Caesare had expected a retort, at least. From Aleri, who had been the one who had discovered that Caesare had been selling his information outside of Montagnard circles. Aleri, who had denounced him as a traitor.

Aleri, who had volunteered as executioner. As he always did, at such times. Aleri prized his position of being Duke Visconti's "enforcer" among the Montagnards. It had been Aleri, also, who saw to the disposal of Bespi. Although, in Bespi's case, the cause had been an excess of enthusiasm rather than cynical peculation. Like many true believers, Bespi had eventually found the contradictions between Montagnard ideals and Milanese realities . . . too difficult to handle. And had then been stupid enough to send a protest to Duke Visconti.

Caesare toyed with his wineglass. It was only there to give him an excuse for being here; he didn't intend to *drink* the vile stuff, not on top of lingering illness. He actually *had* landed on his feet; if he'd gone headfirst into Maria's boat, he probably would have died anyway of a broken neck. As it was, he'd been limp enough to collect nothing worse than a few more bruises. He'd feigned worse, naturally, when he realized where he was. He'd have been a fool not to; he had no money, no resources, and a Montagnard death sentence on his head. Maria had realized as much the moment he landed next to her, and had kept him safely hidden, becoming more and more infatuated with him with every day that passed. For his part, he had seen to it that the infatuation was fed until it spread through her veins like a fever and overcame the tiniest vestige of her common sense. Love was the surest hold a man could have over an inexperienced girl like Maria.

He also made certain that she remained ever-conscious of the difference between their ranks. It made her unsure of her ability to keep him with her, without making her jealous. Jealousy might break the spell he had over her; self-doubt and the uncertainty of being worthy of him kept her eager to please.

"I believe you requested a meeting," Caesare said lazily. "As I informed your contact."

"Not a meeting with *you*," Aleri snarled softly. "I was supposed to meet—" The Milanese agent broke off abruptly, muttering something under his breath. Caesare wasn't certain, but he thought the phrase had been: *that idiot monk!*

Assuming he was correct, Caesare pretended to sip from his wine and then added: "What can you do, Francesco? And the German cretins call *us* 'auslanders.' As if they could find their own assholes here in Venice. But, like it or not, I *am* the 'idiot monk's' chosen man for the job. Whatever the job might be."

He set the glass of wine down on the table. "So why don't you tell me about it, and save us both the useless recriminations. *I* don't have any hard feelings, after all, despite being the injured party in the affair."

Aleri's features were not distorted. The only sign of the rage that Caesare had no doubt was filling the Montagnard was the coldness of his gaze. "Your services were always for sale, Caesare." There was ice in Aleri's voice, too. "Just like every other *putta* in this filthy city."

Caesare did not rise to the bait; he'd been expecting it. Aleri was a true believer himself—which was odd, really, for a Milanese so close to Visconti—and that was his Achilles heel. He would do anything for faith; Caesare would do anything for money. They were two of a kind, and the joke was that Francesco didn't even see it. "The job," he prompted gently. "And my pay."

Aleri, Caesare thought, was very near to throwing his own wineglass in his face. But . . . the memory of how good a duelist Caesare was prevented him. As good as Francesco was with a blade, Caesare was better—and they both knew it.

Instead, after a moment's tense struggle with himself—for a moment, his face looked like a winter storm—Aleri reached into his cloak and brought out a leather purse. He slapped it down on the tabletop.

"I'd have hired a dog first, myself. But this incident you're to organize and carry out is a fool's business anyway. If the German cretin wants to hire a traitor for it, why not? It matters not to me."

Caesare took the purse and made a little show of pouring the coins into his hand and counting them. Aleri scowled slightly. "Stop being a fool. You always were too clever for your own good. It'll get you killed soon enough, and good riddance."

Caesare didn't rise to the bait. "Tell me about it," he murmured. "The *job*, Francesco. Save the speeches for your faithful followers."

By the time Aleri finished, Caesare was waging a fierce battle to keep from scowling himself.

That idiot monk! Typical German. Head as thick as a hog's.

His mind raced. That the plan would work, on its own terms, Caesare had no reason to doubt. But . . .

What is the point of it? And the trouble it might stir up! Does that clerical cretin have any *idea how—?*

He broke off the thought. It was none of his business, after all. For whatever reason, Caesare's new employer and protector had given his approval to the abbot's silly schemes. Though why

Brunelli, whose fortunes were tied to the Metropolitans, should have done so was a mystery to Caesare. Not for the first time, Caesare wondered if *Casa* Brunelli always operated with a single mind.

Interesting thought. But he had neither the time nor the inclination to pursue it. Soon enough, Caesare had little doubt, he would have to look for another employer anyway. And, for the moment, the one he had paid well and—

He smiled across the table at Aleri. *And keeps this one, and his cohorts, from peeling the hide off my back.*

Aleri's chair scraped slightly on the floor as he pushed back from the table and rose to his feet. "You'd better keep one eye open from now on when you sleep," he growled. "Because the moment that your new *patron* finds you too expensive to support, is the moment when I finish the job I bungled."

Caesare continued to smile. "In that case, I needn't worry," he mocked. "You'll have a long, gray beard before that day comes."

Aleri stared down at him. "And did you tell your new woman your real history, Caesare?"

Caesare must have shown something in his face; he cursed himself silently as Aleri continued: "*Of course* there's a new woman. There always is, with beautiful golden Caesare. You betray everyone, women even quicker than men. Whoever the girl is—and I'll find out, soon enough—I pity her. But my pity won't keep me from killing her also. An example must be set for what happens to traitors and their whores."

The Milanese turned and stalked out.

Caesare continued to play with his wine, and wait for young Benito to saunter in as a signal that it was safe to leave the place. As he did so, his thoughts drifted over his new . . . associates.

Maria was invaluable for the moment, leaving aside the pleasure her fiercely enthusiastic lovemaking provided. Very unskilled enthusiasm, to be sure, and Caesare was beginning to get bored with it. But that problem was easy to solve, after all. Caesare gave it no further thought, beyond an idle moment of curiosity as to which of several *Case Vecchie* girls would be the first to climb into his bed and provide him with more expert entertainment. Alessandra, for one. He was quite certain the Montescue woman was eager to rekindle their old affair.

The boys, on the other hand—Benito in particular—were proving far more useful than he would have guessed. No one ever looked twice at a child, particularly not a canal-brat like Benito. Aleri and his ilk would be looking for a woman. That they'd discover Maria soon enough, Caesare didn't doubt for a moment. Any more than he doubted what would happen to the canal-girl once . . . the situation changed. But the Montagnards would never suspect Caesare of employing the boys as his aides. Particularly not *those* boys— given how their mother had died, and by whose hand.

But that, after all, was part of the dance, wasn't it? Caesare flexed his right hand, for a moment, remembering the feel of Lorendana's throat as Bespi slid the knife between her ribs. She had been quite shocked when she died, he remembered. Not so much with the knife as with the hand that kept her from crying out. She had always understood the risk of assassination, moving in the circles she did. What she hadn't expected was that her own lover would set up the killing—and time it for the moment she was most defenseless. Naked, in her own bed, right after they finished making love.

A stupid woman, in the end, for all her quick wits. She should have known that once she lost the favor of Carlo Sforza she was sure to receive the delayed vengeance of Filippo Visconti. Yet she'd been careless enough to accept a Milanese adventurer as a new bedmate.

Stupid. As stupid as Bespi, with his idiot ideals. Caesare's lips twisted in a little smile, remembering the look on Bespi's face as he killed Lorendana. The assassin's eyes had been on Caesare, not his victim. Eyes cold with loathing and disgust. Caesare had never been sure, but he suspected that killing had been the one which finally tipped Fortunato Bespi over the edge.

No matter. Caesare was *not* stupid. And he enjoyed the irony of having Lorendana's orphans as his new underlings. It was the best proof imaginable that his own view of the world corresponded to reality.

Caesare considered the wine, and sat back into the shadows. The wine was execrable; the shadows—ideal.

Chapter 20

Erik shifted his feet in the antechamber before Abbot Sachs's door. He took a deep breath. Then, reluctantly, knocked on the thick oak.

He waited. He'd just knock again, and go. He could try later. He raised his hand. . . .

"Enter," said a voice from within.

Erik walked in. The room was sybaritically appointed. His eyes were still drawn first to the deep-set glowering stare of the abbot, rather than the furnishings fit for a prince of the blood. Sachs sat behind one of these, an escritoire of dark wood inlaid with ivory.

"You wished to see me, Abbot?" asked Erik evenly. The air in the room was overly warm and full of an acerbic incense. And maybe just a hint of . . . perfume? Erik found himself wondering if Manfred's frequent witticisms about the relationship between Sachs and Sister Ursula might not have a basis of truth.

Whatever the scent's nature, it was making his nose itch and his eyes water.

The abbot's sour countenance twitched. Then, to Erik's amazement, his face did something the confrere knight had never seen it do before—the thin lips dragged themselves into a smile. "Ah. Hakkonsen. Yes. I have a task for you."

Erik wondered whether it was too late to bolt for the door. It was either bolt—or sneeze soon. If there were two things Erik was certain of, the first was that Abbot Sachs disliked him violently; the second was that this incense was driving him mad. But as a confrere Knight he was, by order of Bishop-Commander Von

Schielbar, under the authority of the leader of the Servants of the Holy Trinity in Venice.

That remained true even if Erik had forcefully reminded the abbot, less than a fortnight ago, of the limits of his authority. The months they'd spent here in Venice had made their dislike mutual; the incident in the church over sanctuary had brought it into the open. In the two weeks that had gone by since, the abbot had spoken not a single word to Erik, prior to now.

The only official notice of the clash had been a summons to the quarters of Von Stublau, where the knight-commander began a stern lecture on the proper conduct of knights when dealing with abbots. It had been as brief as it was stern, because Erik had turned on his heel and left before Von Stublau finished his third sentence.

The Prussian had been outraged, no doubt. But not even Von Stublau was prepared to press the matter any further. Erik's conduct in the church had given him a reputation among all the other knights as a man to be dealt with very, very gingerly. The more so when the reaction of official Venice to the incident in the church made it as clear as crystal that Erik's behavior had been the *only* thing that had saved the Knights from what might very well have been a political disaster.

As Sachs had discovered two days later, not even the usually sympathetic Doge wanted to hear the abbot's side of the story. *Canal-brats are canal-brats, you idiot, not "servants of Satan."* Such had been the entirety of Foscari's opinion, before Sachs had been summarily dismissed.

And the Doge's reaction had been mild compared to that of Metropolitan Michael, who, by all accounts, had been livid when Father Ugo's story reached him. The prestige of the Pauline orders, always low with the Petrine patriarch, was now as low as it could possibly get. Rumor had it that the patriarch had only been dissuaded with difficulty from demanding the forcible eviction of the Servants and the Knights from Venice. And dissuaded, by his advisers, solely because they reminded the patriarch of his policy of trying to avoid clashes with Foscari.

Nor was there any doubt that if the Pauline orders lost the favor of the Doge, they *could* be expelled from the city—by force, if necessary. There were only a few hundred Knights in Venice. Leaving aside the actual military forces at the disposal of the Doge,

which were much larger, the sixteen thousand workers in the
Arsenal where Venice's great fleet was built were famous—or
notorious—for their willingness to take up arms readily. They were
also famous for their solidly Petrine allegiance in religious matters and for being a hotbed of Metropolitanism. Not even the
Servants of the Holy Trinity were rash enough, or arrogant enough,
to try to enforce their attitudes in the vicinity of the Arsenal or
the quarters of the city where its workers lived.

Being shown to be utterly wrong hadn't, needless to say, made
Abbot Sachs any fonder of the Icelandic knight. He had said
nothing to Erik in the two weeks afterward. But Erik had not failed
to notice that, each and every day since, he had been given nothing
but arduous and menial duties.

To Erik's surprise, however, the incident had also caused a
number of the knights—especially the younger ones and the
confreres—to view him with much greater warmth than they had
done previously. Some, bolder than most, had even whispered quick
congratulations into his ear when no one was watching. It was clear
enough that Sachs's arrogance grated on many others besides
himself.

Still—the abbot *was* his lawfully appointed superior. So long as
Sachs made no further attempt to transgress law and honor, Erik's
own stiff sense of honor obligated him to obey the man, and pay
him at least the outward signs of respect. Even if the wretched
creature did use the vilest incense Erik had ever encountered.

So all he said was: "I am yours to command, Abbot."

The abbot blinked. He looked as though he hadn't expected it
to be so simple. For a moment, Sachs seem to fumble for words.
Then:

"Well, the mission we have for you is not simple or easy. This
city is full of corruption and evil. We need to root it out. I,
personally, would like to put half of these ungodly ones to the
question."

I'll bet you would, thought Erik wearily. *Personally. And by the
time you'd finished with them they'd confess to anything you
pleased.*

But he held his tongue, and simply concentrated on not sneezing.

Sachs plainly expected a reply or a comment. "Well?"

"I am yours to command, Abbot," repeated Erik woodenly.

The abbot looked intently at him. Then, laced his fingers. "Very well. I shall command you. Tonight, just before midnight, you will proceed to the Calle Largo di Lorenzo. You will be unarmored, and without your sword, but wearing your surcoat showing yourself to be one of the Knights of the Holy Trinity. Get one of the boatmen to take you, as you'll never find it on your own. You will have wine on your breath, and you will be seen to be unsteady on your feet. Do you have that clearly? You will be *seen* to be unsteady. You will turn into the third alleyway and proceed down it. Perhaps you should sing. You will go to the last house on the left-hand side and demand entry."

Erik swallowed. Was this some kind of trap? Why in the seven hells was the abbot sending him to visit one of Venice's most notorious brothels? He didn't need a boatman to show him the way. He knew perfectly well where it was, down to which door. He'd hauled Manfred out of there not two nights ago. The Madame was *not* going to be pleased to see him again.

"Why?" he rasped.

At last, Sachs looked genuinely pleased. "Because I have commanded you."

"Yes, Abbot." And then Erik could contain it no longer. He sneezed. Then he sneezed again.

Sachs had obviously not expected this answer, because he did explain. "It is an ambush. One of our agents has brought us information that a large group of the ungodly pagans will be conducting their evil rites there. When you have gained entry, you will create a disturbance. You will continue to do so for as long as possible, while the Knights force entry at the water-door."

"*Haaachoo!* Yes, Abbot. Ndow will you excuse me? By dose is streaming."

The bed groaned as Manfred did his customary flop onto it. As usual, he gave his attention to the bedpost caryatides before turning to Erik. "What's up? Why are you pacing about, rubbing a thoughtful hand on that pious, sharpcut chin of yours?"

Erik took a deep breath. "I've got to go brothel-creeping!"

Manfred leapt to his feet in a single movement, like a crossbow snapping straight. It was at moments like this that the big knight revealed his true strength and agility. He rubbed his hands gleefully and grinned, revealing those blocky teeth.

"Oh, me too. Me too! But this time just to watch! What's

suddenly come over you, my pure Icelandic friend? Besides the need for female company, that is?"

Erik scowled. "I've got orders from Abbot Sachs to go to the House of the Red Cat. *You* will be staying here. Even if I have to lock you up, you will be staying here. And it's not funny," he snarled, seeing the young knight-squire's expression.

Manfred put his hand in front of his grin, trying to hide it. His shoulders began to shake. Then he gave up. He laughed. He guffawed. Eventually he collapsed onto the bed again, still fighting off paroxysms of chuckles while Erik stared at him in icy irritation.

Eventually he stopped long enough for Erik to start speaking. "It's a direct order!"

This provoked a snort of derision from Manfred. "I'll bet. Tell me another one. Unless Sachs is learning more from Sister Ursula than we realize."

"I'm supposed to be a decoy for a raid, you young fathead! I should take you out into the practice yard and teach you some decorum," snapped Erik.

Manfred sat back and raised his big hands in a pacific gesture. "I'm all decorum, I swear. I haven't forgotten the last time! Neither have my ribs. Has Sachs got wind of *your* last little visit and the friendly little chat you had with the Madame and her bouncers?"

"Jesu. I hope to God not." Erik crossed himself. "Let me tell you about what he wants me to do."

By the time he'd finished, Manfred wasn't laughing. He wasn't even grinning. "I suppose they'll be waiting by the water-door for the ruckus. This smells to the heavens, Erik! That idiot Sachs will get you killed—and I wouldn't doubt that's really what he wants. Why in the hell no sword and no armor?"

Erik pulled a wry face. "I suppose they don't want the bouncers too alarmed and deciding *not* to interfere. I'm supposed to create a disturbance."

Manfred had the grace to look shamefaced. "I think they're going to be a little alarmed just to see your face."

"Thanks to you, yes," replied Erik grimly.

Manfred stood up slowly. "True enough. Are you going anywhere in the next while?"

Erik shook his head. "Not until I leave smelling of wine, shortly after Compline."

Manfred pursed his lips. "That gives us plenty of time." The knight-squire headed for the door. "Wait here. That Pellmann is nowhere about, is he?"

Erik raised his eyes to heaven and shook his head. "When he doesn't have to be? Not likely."

Manfred nodded, and walked out and away up the passage. He could walk fast and quietly for such a big man.

A short while later he was back, with a bag and an oilcloth roll. He closed the door and bolted it before tossing the bag onto the bed. It clinked. Erik raised an eyebrow.

Manfred unrolled his oilcloth onto to the table and revealed a set of tools that would have done any torturer from Damascus to Vinland proud. "Get out of those clothes. If you've got a close-fitting quilted shirt, put it on. If you don't, we'll have to get you one. We'll need to fit this thing. It's too small for me these days, but likely it'll be still too big for you."

Erik looked doubtful. "What is it?"

Manfred stepped over to the bag on the bed. He hauled out a shirt of tiny chain links. They gleamed with an odd black pearly sheen. "Koboldwerk. My uncle had me wear it at court. Somebody must have washed it because it's shrunk."

Erik snorted. "Particularly across the belly."

It was an unfair observation. Manfred was as square as a foundation block, but he was also solid muscle. He'd been a great deal softer before Erik had started on him. He trained with Manfred from an hour before dawn until Lauds every single day. Then they'd put in at least an hour on the pells. Then they'd join the knights for morning drill.

To give the Breton squire his due, nowadays Manfred gave the training his heart and soul. At first, Erik used to have to haul him out of bed. But lately it was getting to be the other way around, despite the fact that Manfred had managed to explore the wilder aspects of Venice's nights quite successfully. Also, he'd noticed how the squire had put on inches, particularly across the shoulders, in the months they'd been together. The boy was finishing his growing, and it certainly wasn't around the waistline.

Erik suspected that Manfred had been genuinely shocked to discover how much more capable his Icelandic "keeper" was than he, when it came to any kind of extended fighting. Manfred's incredible strength and athletic ability had not been matched by endurance—leaving aside the fact that he had little of Erik's actual combat experience and the brutal skills the Icelander had learned in the island's savage clan feuds as well as frontier skirmishes in Vinland.

One thing Erik had come to realize about his charge. For all of Manfred's roustabout ways, the young scion of the imperial family was quite capable of learning something when he put his mind to it. And, if it accomplished nothing else, the incident in the church seemed to have finally brought a certain amount of seriousness to Manfred's outlook on things. The big young man had brooded for days afterward, obviously ashamed of his initial reaction to Erik's defiance of Sachs.

Erik suppressed a snort. Not that Manfred's new-found solemnity went all *that* deep. If Abbot Sachs kept the Knights here much longer, he didn't doubt that Manfred would even learn to speak the local dialect. Well enough, at least, to ask directions to any location in Venice. He'd already learned how to find the taverns and brothels.

Manfred slapped his stomach. "It's the wine," he said mournfully. "I need more."

Erik shook his head, and smiled ruefully. "That is the one thing you don't need."

"This is a matter of opinion. Now get out of that cotte and put on a quilted shirt."

Erik did as he was told. The chain-links were heavy and cold, despite the shirt. And while it was loose around the waist and a little tight around the chest, it fit across the shoulders.

Manfred grunted in satisfaction. "Too big I can fix. Too small would have been a problem. Stand still."

He reached for the tools, displaying a familiarity that surprised Erik. The Icelander watched in some amazement. "I thought you were a prince, not a blacksmith."

Manfred twitched a lockring loose with an evil-looking set of long-nosed pliers. "According to my father, the Breton chiefs were once both—blacksmiths as well as princes. This was his idea. I got to run tame in the castle smithy back in Carnac. Beat spending time with the tutors mother inflicted on me, that's for sure."

His thick fingers moved with expert skill. "That's the difference between Mainz and Carnac," he continued. "Too bookish in Mainz. The aristocracy either reads or fights. In Carnac, according to our old seneschal, my father used to do the winter slaughtering before mother got there and 'civilized' him. Now stand still. Old Sachs didn't say anything about that hatchet of yours, did he?"

"The subject never came up," said Erik, standing still as he had been told. Books were a treasure up in Iceland. Especially in winter. But he could see where sitting still with a tutor might aggravate a boy like Manfred.

Erik sighed. He was supposed to watch over him; guard him; teach him. But it seemed to Erik that Manfred's supreme skill was slipping off to have a good time. Taking his watchdog with him, if that was the only choice, but without him if he could manage it. It had been from one of those expeditions that Erik had retrieved him from the House of the Red Cat.

Manfred whistled tunelessly between his teeth. "Stretch your arms out." Erik complied. "Bring them round in front of your chest. Can you move easily?"

Erik nodded. "It's not very comfortable. But I can move."

Manfred snorted. "It's never comfortable. And be grateful. I even had to sleep in it."

Erik looked grimly at Manfred. Sooner or later the boy had to accept the fact that he was in close line of succession to the throne of the Holy Roman Empire, the largest and most powerful realm in Christendom.

"Your uncle wanted to make sure you stayed alive. And that is why I'm supposed to watch over you. No one but the High Abbot at Wurtemburg knows who you are. And that is your best defense. But somebody may just possibly recognize you. Even with that moustache."

Manfred's responding grimace was so like that of a boy denied a day's play that Erik almost laughed. He could sympathize with Manfred's plight, inwardly if not openly. By Manfred's description, life in rather ramshackle, relaxed Celtic Carnac had been a far cry from the stilted imperial court at Mainz. But there was no point in letting his charge see that sympathy. Manfred would only try to take advantage of it.

Chapter 21

Maria waited for them in the kitchen of the apartment. It was . . . homelike having them living here. The boys tried to keep quiet, but they were, in the manner of boys, not much good at it. Maria found the noises comforting. She hadn't been aware of Caesare's catlike quietness until she'd had the contrast. The occasional clatter and slip from whisper into a laugh or hastily stifled yell was pleasant, almost comforting. Maria had never had a real family, the way most people did. It had been just her and her mother, as she was growing up. Since then, her huge pack of cousins had offered to provide her with a home—well, until she took up with Caesare—but Maria had always declined the offers. She valued her independence too much. But the boys didn't really impinge on that independence. They just made her home . . . warmer.

Of course, she'd never tell them that. They obviously found the apartment pleasing too. They hadn't moved out although Caesare was getting up for part of each day now. There was not much wrong with him any more that Maria could see, except he tired quickly. She wanted a word with Marco about that. And she'd better sort Benito out before he got into real trouble. She felt a little awkward at the thought of trying to discipline Benito. He wasn't more than two years younger than she was, after all. But somebody had to do it. And Marco, for all that he was a good soul and gentle as a dove, wasn't up to dealing with his little brother.

She grabbed him by the ear when he came in. "Benito. You listen to me."

"Ow! Leggooo! How do I listen when you're pulling my ear off?"

Maria snorted. "You listen with the other one, and if I pull this one off maybe things won't just go straight in one ear and out of the other."

"I'm listening. I'm listening. Just let go," said Benito on tiptoes.

She did. "Now if this doesn't go in, next time I *will* pull it off. I hear from Giaccomo you're still hanging out with that Laivetti boy. Mercutio."

"Yeah," said Benito, defensively. "He's a friend of mine, see." His tone was surly.

Maria didn't like that tone. "He's trouble!" she snapped. "If you're going to stay with Caesare and me—you keep your nose clean. Caesare doesn't need extra troubles."

Benito was silent for a few moments. He bit his lip. "It's not as simple as all that, Maria," he said quietly.

"And why not?"

Benito shrugged. "You know, when you're living on the canals . . . um . . . some of the bigger boys they use the little 'uns like girls. Some of them are real fond of little boys."

Maria's eyes narrowed. "This Mercutio . . ."

"No! Mercutio, he's a ladies' man. But he looked out for me. Kind of let it be known that he'd deal with anyone who tried anything. Helped me out with food and—and a bit of coin a time or two. Showed me a few things that Claudia and Valentina left me to find out the hard way. And—he made me laugh when I needed a few laughs." Stubbornly: "I can't just turn my back on him. I *can't*, Maria."

Maria nodded. She understood this level of loyalty. It made her think better of Benito, actually.

"*Si*. I can see that, 'Nito. But there's a difference between being a friend, maybe sitting at Giaccomo's, talking, and doing the kind of crazy thievery and stunts that he likes to pull. You'll get killed. So will he."

Benito shrugged again. "That's what Claudia always says. But Mercutio—he's lucky."

Maria shook her head. She hadn't really gotten through to him. "Luck runs out. You stay away from his stunts, Benito."

Some of the grimness in that must have gotten to Benito. "He's out of town anyway, Maria. From what I can work out, no one's seen him since two-three days after Caesare took sick."

Maria smiled. "I know he's your friend, but I hope he stays away."

Benito's brother walked in, looking preoccupied. "Morning, Marco. You been to see the patient? Hope you not lookin' like that 'cause he's going downhill."

Marco smiled. "Sorry. I was just . . . thinking about something. *Si*, I've been to see Caesare. He's fine, Maria. It'll take him a little while to get his strength back. His endurance, rather—his strength's pretty much back to normal. If he rests, well, another few weeks and he'll be like this never happened."

Maria snorted. "I can't make him rest—he'll be out and about again today. He just won't accept it that he can't run around for very long. That's a nasty sickness."

Marco looked embarrassed. "Um. That's the treatment, not the disease. If you live through the disease without the herbs, you're better in a week or so."

Maria gawped at him. "What?"

Marco held up his hands. "Without the herbs, a lot of people just die. But the herbs are poison too. You can kill someone with them if they have too much. Old Sophia reckons the herbs make the body too poisonous for the sickness to live. It takes the body a while to rid it itself of the toxin. It won't do Caesare any harm to be up and about. He'll get tired quick, that's all."

"Well, that's good to know," said Maria with relief. "Although I wouldn't tell him you poisoned him!" The relief went away. Quietly, anxiously: "He's organizing something. I can tell by the way his eyes go thoughtful."

Out on the water carrying a cargo of copper nails to the Arsenal, Maria had time to think about what Marco had said. She just hoped the poison didn't make Caesare slower. He kept most of what he was involved in from her. He always said what she didn't know couldn't be tortured out of her. But on at least one occasion it had been a duel, which was strictly illegal. The young nobleman Caesare had pushed into it had been a thorn in the side of Ricardo Brunelli.

"Hey, Maria."

She looked up. It was Antonio, plying his usual load of fresh crabs for the fishmarket. It was a good line, that. Housewives wanted their crabs still alive. And they paid extra for it. But it meant Antonio was often ferrying a load in before Lauds. "*Ciao*, 'Tonio. How's trade?"

"Bit slow. Always is at this time. Look, I know you work nights a bit. I'm just passing a warning out. They found what was left of one of those young Ponto di Reggio brats dead in the water, stuck in some piles."

Maria thought of Benito. Maybe he owed his friend Mercutio more than he realized. "What killed him?"

Tonio shrugged. "Somethin' bad. *Real* bad. The body was pretty much missing, and what there was the eels and fish had eaten most of it. But the head, they say, was bitten in half. What kinda fish can bite right through a skull, eh? No natural one, that's sure and certain. Like nothin' anyone ever saw. They reckon it must be some of this witchery that's going on. The kid disappeared months ago, and they say it was the same night that rich banker got torn apart in his own bed. Does that sound like happenstance to you?"

He glanced around, searching the water, uneasy even in broad daylight. "Just thought I'd tell you to keep a weather eye out."

Maria clutched at the amulets she wore. Two were from the Calle Farnese, supposedly protection against demons of the night. The other, side-by-side with pagan charms, was a little leather bag containing—well, supposed to contain—a fragment of St. Ursula's skull. She hoped they'd protect her because she didn't have a whole lot of choice about working nights, moving stuff for Giaccomo sometimes.

Marco felt very uneasy here. This was the last place, the very last place, where a Pauline belonged. This was, if not the head-quarters of the enemy, at least a bastion—a chapel of Saint Raphaella, one of Saint Hypatia's fervent followers, martyred, not by fire, sword, or persecution, but by accident. Saint Raphaella had allegedly stood firm in the face of a tide of dreadful injuries all over Alexandria in the wake of the terrible earthquake of 735, had used herb and skill and yes, magic, to hold off the scythe of grim death from thousands who were dying. She cured them of injury or illness or both, and perished only when an aftershock toppled a broken column down on her as she was trying to help more who were trapped in the rubble and still alive. And even then, she did not cease her work, apparently; for all those who prayed to her recovered, and there were many who dreamed of her laying gentle hands on them in the night and woke healed. In the wake of so many miracles, it would have taken a stronger man than the then-Grand Metropolitan to deny the voices on all sides who called for sanctification.

Marco remembered his mother denouncing the saint, once, when he was a small boy. He only remembered because of his phenomenal memory. Lorendana Valdosta had denounced a lot of things.

She was headstrong, disobedient, not modest and self-effacing as Saint Paul told women to be. She defied her own priest, even, when he ordered her to stay out of the city. Told him to take his orders to the Devil!

If she hadn't, how many would have died? Marco could remember himself wondering that, after his mother finished her little peroration. And today, much older, he could look back on the episode and realize how absurd it was for his mother—the notorious Montagnard agent Lorendana Valdosta—to be denouncing other women for being headstrong and disobedient. As if she herself had not been! And for a far less worthy a cause than Saint Raphaella.

Still . . . Marco was unsettled. Whatever doubts he might have begun developing about all the tenets of the Pauline creed, it was the one he had been raised in, after all. And this was a tiny, dark little place, squeezed in between two warehouses, on a waterway so narrow a boy could jump across it. The reason Marco had come was that Brother Mascoli, who presided here, had sent a message that he wanted to speak to Marco about his herbs.

At least he's Hypatian. Horrible thought, that. Had they heard it spoken aloud—and had they enough authority—the Servants of the Holy Trinity would probably drag Marco up in front of a tribunal and in less time that it took to say "knife," have him declared a heretic.

The last light of day couldn't penetrate these man-made canyons, and although the sky had just begun to show the colors of sunset, down here it was twilight. Marco pushed open the door to the chapel and eased inside.

There wasn't much in the way of light here, just the few candles that burned in front of the statues of Hypatia and Raphaella, and the Presence-Light on the altar. Someone knelt in front of the altar, someone in a light-colored robe and not ordinary clothing, who got to his feet and turned around as the door creaked closed. Marco cleared his throat awkwardly.

The man who approached him was not terribly prepossessing; balding, with little more than a gray fringe over each ear. Thin, yet round-faced, he blinked mild blue eyes at the newcomer. "Peace be with you, my child," he said in a reedy voice. "How may I help you?"

"I'm looking for Brother Mascoli," Marco replied. "He asked to see me...."

The little man's face lit up with a smile that transformed it. "Then you must be Marco! Please, will you come back to my quarters? I'd like to ask you a few questions, about those herbs you have been giving some of my flock."

Marco would rather not have gone with him, but there didn't seem to be much choice. Reluctantly, he followed the sibling through a door behind the statue of Saint Raphaella and into a tiny closet of a cell that didn't hold anything but a pallet on a wooden platform, a stool and desk, a crucifix on the wall, and a lamp. "Please sit down, Marco," the Sibling said, taking the stool, leaving the only place for Marco to sit being the bed. He sat very gingerly on the edge as Brother Mascoli took out pen, ink, and a roughly bound book, opening it to a blank page.

"Now, if you would be so kind—I wonder if you could tell me—" the words were gentle, the interrogation ruthless. Brother Mascoli extracted every particle of information Marco had about Sophia and Chiano's herbs, even going so far as to take out an enormous herbal from beneath the bed and leaf through all the pages until he had identified the exact plants to his satisfaction. The herbal, Marco noted, was handwritten, the drawings quite accurate, and the script identical to Brother Mascoli's. Had the sibling actually ventured out into the marshes to collect samples of all of those plants himself? If so—his estimation of the rabbitty little man went up several notches.

"Now, what incantation did you use?" Brother Mascoli asked, briskly.

Marco froze. The sibling raised an eyebrow at his silence. "Well?" he prompted.

"None," he said stiffly.

"None?" The other eyebrow rose. "Surely not."

"*None,*" he repeated, his voice cracking with strain.

Brother Mascoli carefully blew on the page to dry it, and closed the book. He regarded Marco for a very long time with a deceptively mild gaze. Marco couldn't move.

"Marco," the sibling said quietly, "Why are you so afraid of your magic?"

Marco began to sweat. "What magic?" he squeaked.

He can tell! How can he tell? How does he know?

Chiano knew. . . .

Brother Mascoli's gaze ceased being mild. After another very long time, he sighed. "Marco—I am one single man, serving people who are the poorest of the poor. I have no help, and very little money, and although I am something of a mage, I am absolutely *the least powerful* of any in this city. And yet the people I serve number in the thousands and they are the most likely to become ill, to be seriously injured. Now, I continue to serve them because God saw fit to grant me a gift, and it would be a sin—*a sin*—not to use it to help as best I am able. And not a venial sin, either, but a mortal sin, the sin of pride."

"P-p-pride?" Marco stuttered in confusion.

Brother Mascoli nodded. "Pride. The pride of a man who would believe that he knows better than God. God has seen fit to give me this gift, and gifts are meant to be used for the good of all. To be shared. To refuse to do so is to refuse God's blessings, and to do so out of selfishness. And that," he added, examining his fingertips for a moment, "would be yet another sin. Sloth, perhaps—that one was too lazy to exert oneself? Avarice, that one wished to keep one's energies all for oneself? I suppose that it all would depend on the motive behind the selfishness."

Marco wasn't going to cave in that easily to this facile Petrine. "Use of magic should remain in the hands of anointed priests, who won't be tempted by such power."

"What in heaven's name makes you think that priests can resist the temptations of power?" the Sibling retorted.

"All the more reason then—"

"Marco," Mascoli said sharply. "Give over for a moment! Allow someone who has actually *studied* magic to speak, will you?"

Marco snapped his mouth shut, flushing.

"Magic, as even the most rigorous Pauline practices it, is *prayer.* Nothing less, but certainly nothing more. We hedge it round with ritual, we beg angels to attend us and fence our work off from the outside world and the interference of the Evil One, but when it all comes down to cases, it is nothing but intensely focused prayer. God allows us to use our own strengths to accomplish some tasks, and grants us His strength or that of his angels to accomplish those that are beyond our strength, but we never force, we only ask, for these graces." Mascoli's rabbity face took on a distinctly mulish look. "Now if you can find me, *anywhere* in Scripture or Holy Writ, a place where the faithful are told that only anointed priests may pray to God, I beg you to show it to me. That will certainly be a revelation to every Christian alive or dead."

Marco had only thought he was flushing before. Now a painful heat crept up his neck and over his face, until it felt sunburned. He couldn't counter the sibling, and he knew it. And Brother Mascoli knew that he had won the point.

At least he was gracious enough not to gloat about it. "Just think about what I've said, will you?" he asked. "You don't have to make any decisions right now, just think about it. And while you're at it, think about all those poor creatures up and down the canals that I can't help because I haven't the strength."

"All right," Marco mumbled, and when he got to his feet and shuffled out the door, Mascoli didn't stop him.

He had already told Benito and Maria that he was going to be late, so he didn't go straight back; instead he wandered the walkways and bridges trying to poke holes in Brother Mascoli's argument. If you took him at his word that all of the ritual and incantation of magic (at least as a good Christian would practice it, leaving out all the invocations of heathen spirits and elves and whatnot) was nothing but prayer, then what *he* had been taught was dead wrong.

Now, Mascoli could have lied, of course. He had every reason to lie; he served the poor, he needed help, and here was Marco who could give that help if he chose to. But Mascoli was, if not a full priest, certainly an avowed and oath-bound Sibling of Hypatia. If *he* lied—which was, after all, a sin—it was a worse thing than if Marco lied. And more especially if he lied about something like magic, tempting Marco into deep, black sin.

Marco twisted and turned the problem every which way, and still came up with the same unpalatable answer, that what he'd been taught was wrong.

Finally, having worn out quite enough shoe leather, he turned his steps back to Caesare's apartment, and walked into yet another mess.

At least this time it was none of *his* doing.

When he opened the door, Maria all but ran into him, only to choke off a muffled curse and half a sob when she saw that it was *him* in the doorway.

"What's the matter?" he asked, alarmed.

"He's gone!" she said, and fled up to the room she shared with Caesare. Fortunately, Benito had been right behind her and filled in the rest.

"Caesare decided he was well enough t' get up, an' off he went," Benito said grimly. "Right after Maria got back. She couldn' stop him, no more could I. An' he wouldn' tell us where he was goin', when he was gonna get back, nor what he was gonna do. He just went. It was right after he got some message, just after dark, and he took it with him, so we don't know what it said."

Marco realized immediately their concern. For a man in Caesare's condition to leave the apartment was no source of worry, in itself. Not so long as he was going to a tavern, or taking a walk, or—

Anything *except* . . . "Caesare's business."

Marco cleared his throat. "Ah. Ah, was he carrying—"

"Yeah, he took his sword," said Benito instantly, answering the unfinished question.

"Oh hell," Marco said weakly. Caesare normally didn't carry any weapon but a poignard. "If I'd been here—"

"Oh, you couldn' have done nothing with him, neither," Benito asserted. "He was that set. Said that things was gone to hell with him laid up, an' that if something or other went wrong 'cause he wasn't there, he'd be in deep. An' off he went."

Think!

"Was he shaky? Did he stagger? Lose his balance?" he asked desperately.

"Actually—" Benito put in a moment of thought. "Actually he looked pretty good. Kinda pale, maybe, but he moved all right."

We fed him good. He just might get through this, as long as he don't do something stupid. More to the point, something stupid that takes him too long to finish. His strength's okay, it's just—he doesn't really understand, I don't think, that he's got little stamina left.

He took a deep breath; then, sighed. "I'll go talk to Maria," he said, and went resolutely up the stairs to the room where he heard cursing and sobs—

—which might possibly be one of the bravest things he'd ever done in his life.

Chapter 22

Here, away from the occasional smoky oil-brands, in deep shadows where the moonlight did not penetrate, it was pitch dark. Erik wished he had the eyes of the cat he'd almost stumbled over. The only light was the red lantern at the end of the alleyway.

Obedient to his orders, Erik did his best to sing. That would tell the waiting knights he was coming. According to the family *skald* back home, his singing was good . . . for frightening seagulls. Well, with any luck the waiting knights were tone-deaf as well as accustomed to repetition. Erik only knew one line of the song he'd heard Manfred caterwauling one evening. It still made him red-faced, even here alone in the darkness.

Making as much raucous noise as he could, within the limits of his straight-laced temperament, Erik staggered to the door. He felt like a complete idiot, certain that his playacting would fool no one who was not another complete idiot.

It was almost with relief that he reached the door of the Red Cat and started pounding upon it. The worst that could happen to him now was an ambush. Which was something he *knew* how to handle.

The door swung open. Erik saw the back of the man who opened it receding into the darkness of the gloomy salon beyond, and thought he recognized one of the brothel's bouncers. Fortunately, the man didn't seem to have recognized him.

He stepped through the door hastily and closed it behind him, relieved that his ridiculous behavior was no longer subject to public scrutiny. Then he began following the bouncer toward the corridor on the other side of the salon. After taking not more than two or three steps, however, Erik suddenly realized that the red-velvet-and-brocaded salon was *much* darker than the last time.

He just had time to understand that an ambush was in fact awaiting him—and a far more ferocious one than Sachs had implied—when someone stepped through a side door and flung an entire jug of coarse brandy over him. Momentarily blinded by the harsh liquor, Erik sprang toward the far corner of the salon, avoiding whatever blow might be coming along next. He heard the heavy door to the brothel being bolted, and knew that at least one more man had come into the room.

His eyes cleared. Crouching in the corner—his hatchet was already in hand—he quickly scanned the room. There were four of them, and Erik was not surprised at all to discover that he recognized not a one. These men were not the brothel bouncers with whom he had clashed on his last visit—although he could see the figure of the one bouncer who had let him in the door, huddling in the far hallway. Almost cowering, it seemed.

No, these men were killers, not bouncers. Professional criminals, he suspected, hired for the purpose. They consisted of three swarthy, stevedore-built men, lightly jowled but not exactly fat, and an athletic-looking pale-faced blond. And unlike last time, when a cudgel had been the worst he'd had to deal with, this time three of the four had daggers. The fourth, the blond man, had a sword. Just by the way he held the weapon, Erik knew he was skilled in its use.

The blond swordsman spoke. "Make him scream, boys."

The biggest of the low-browed solid bruisers moved in. Feinted, in the way that an experienced street brawler does, before striking his main blow. He was obviously a bit disconcerted by Erik's left-handedness.

The contest of knife against hatchet was entirely one-sided. Erik ignored the feint entirely and slashed the hatchet across the thug's empty hand, which the man had carelessly extended. A forefinger and half a thumb flipped through the air, streaking blood.

The thug began to howl with pain. The howl turned into a gasp of shock when the hatchet swung back and caught the knife-hand at the wrist. A thick fist still holding a dagger flew through the air and slapped wetly against the wall. The man's gasp of shock, an instant later, gurgled into a death rattle. Erik's hatchet, now held at the base of the blade, had chopped straight through his throat—a short punch, with a razor-edged fist.

Erik seized the dying thug with his free hand, turned and flung him across the room with a hip roll. The man crashed into his two companions and brought all three of them down to the floor.

Erik kept moving—fast—heading for the blond swordsman. He knew full well that was the truly dangerous one, and hoped he'd gained enough time to deal with him before the two surviving bravos could jump him from behind. If not . . . he had time for a quick prayer that Manfred's mailshirt was as good as the Breton prince claimed. He might well need it to guard his back.

The blond swordsman was caught by surprise, both by the speed with which Erik had killed the first thug and his instant attack on him. Still, he was a cool one. He ducked under the first whistling hatchet blow, and lunged.

Erik managed to parry with the hatchet's wirebound shaft. The swordsman made an excellent recovery, before Erik could riposte. Once again he pressed the attack. This was no amateur swordsman. The blond didn't seem in the least confused by the fact that Erik fought left-handed. His sword skittered on the hatchet handle as he beat back the young knight. With the greater reach afforded by the sword and the blond's obvious level of skill, Erik knew that he was in severe trouble, even if the other two did not intervene. There was certainly no chance he could finish the blond assailant before the other two were back in action. In fact . . .

He wondered why they *weren't* back in action.

He risked a quick glance. And immediately saw the reason.

Manfred! You idiot!

Grinning cheerfully, Manfred had both of the remaining thugs in his fists, practically holding them up off the ground. Then, he began slamming them together, like a gleeful boy might pound cymbals. If he was carrying a weapon, Manfred showed no inclination to use it.

Cursing bitterly, Erik parried another sword thrust. The curse was aimed as much at Manfred's recklessness as it was at the damnable expertise of his opponent.

He should have guessed. *Of course* the young Breton knight-squire had made no mention of his intention of being here! If necessary, Erik would have taken him to Abbot Sachs to prevent it.

Manfred knew that. He also had a habit of getting his own way.

Erik snatched at a curtain—ripping it off its rail. If he could get that wrapped around his left hand . . .

The blond swordsman chose that moment to close. Erik dropped the curtain and grabbed his opponent's arm, staggering him. The bare arm was . . . hot. As the man twisted away, Erik's hatchet slashed across fine linen. First blood spilled, but it was anything but over. The swordsman still had the advantage. A feint and a fleche and Erik was on the defensive.

He caught his foot in the carpet as he dodged away. The sword-point hit his side. The Koboldwerk links didn't give; but Erik lost his footing, falling backwards over the body of the first thug.

The blond man rushed forward for the *coup de grace*. As he did so, Erik saw Manfred lift one thug and, with a huge grunt, fling him at the swordsman. The blond ducked, but was still knocked sideways by a flailing foot. Then was forced to duck again, to avoid the other thug whom Manfred heaved at him. Erik was impressed with the man's agility—the more so since, judging from that one touch, he was suffering from illness.

I'd hate to see what he's like when he's well!

And then there was an outburst of shouts and whistles, and the sound of rattles from outside.

"*Schiopettieri!*" bellowed someone. "Open up in the name of the *Signori di Notte* and the Doge of Venice!"

The assault on the heavy door showed they weren't waiting for it to be opened. By the shouting and female shrieks they'd already made entry by the water-door. The blond man stooped quickly, hefted the two thugs onto their feet, and darted down the short hallway toward the door at the other end. With much less agility, almost stumbling, they began to follow him. Then one of them stopped and stared back, his heavy face creased with emotion.

"Alberto!" he cried. "We've got to—"

Erik heard the snarling voice of the blond swordsman roll down the hallway. "He's dead, you fool! Come on!" A moment later all three men were gone. The door slammed shut behind them.

Manfred hauled Erik to his feet.

Erik shook his head. "I should have guessed you'd come here. How am I going to explain your presence here to Abbot Sachs?"

Manfred smiled grimly. "You won't have to. Those are Schiopettieri, not Knights. Since when do Knights sound rattles?"

Erik's eyes narrowed. "Do you know any other way out of here?" He looked at the side door from which one of thugs had emerged to toss the liquor over him, but saw at once that it led only to a closet.

Manfred shook his head. "Get thrown out or leave after paying your shot. Either here or by the water-door."

Erik grimaced. "Let's get out of this room, anyway. The Schiopettieri might want us to explain why we're sharing this salon with a dead body."

"That way." Manfred pointed to the door at the end of the hallway the ambushers had used for their escape. "Leads upstairs. Maybe we can find a balcony or something to jump from."

The staircase began just behind the door, to the left. They began running up it three steps at a time, Erik in the lead. He still had the hatchet in his hand, his eyes scanning ahead to watch for another ambush. He didn't expect one, though, since he was almost certain the blond swordsman and his two surviving companions had no further purpose beyond making their own escape.

They had just made the second landing in the winding staircase when they heard the street door burst open. Erik grabbed Manfred's arm and stopped him, gesturing for silence.

From below came a voice of authority. "—wearing a white surcoat with three red crosses on it. He must be taken. Kill him if you must."

Manfred pulled a wry face. "Some goddamned ambush!" he muttered. "It looks like *you* were the target."

"He went up the stairs!" cried another voice from below.

"Must be the bouncer," whispered Erik.

Manfred shook his head. "I put the bastard to sleep first. Come on. Give me a hand with this couch."

The couch was a venerable piece of furniture. Either it had been intended for some unusual antics in a higher bedroom, before its carriers had been defeated either by its weight or the angle of the stairs, or it was for elderly patrons who needed to lie down before going on to visit the delights on higher floors. It was solid and heavy, and made of some exotic black wood that Erik did not recognize. This was Venice. Strange things found their way here, even wood. The couch was about six cubits long and must have weighed at least four hundredweight.

Even with Manfred's oxlike strength, lifting it was not easy. They struggled to raise it above the banisters. On the other hand, the bunch of arquebus-armed men who came running up the stairs were unable to resist it as it came hurtling down at them. Neither was the wooden staircase up to this sort of treatment. It splintered. Amid the thunder of gunfire, the shouting—and screaming—of men, and the partial collapse of the staircase, Erik and Manfred fled upwards again.

"There are other stairs," panted Manfred. "Stone ones. They'll cut us off up those."

Erik pointed. "Take that next passage, any room and a window. If need be we'll break our way into the next house."

"Corner room. Give us two sides."

They legged it down the passage. Ripped open the door. And Erik suddenly remembered just where he was: in a notorious Venetian brothel.

The woman on the bed languorously raised herself up. Her very voluptuous self. She tilted her head and twitched full, red, red lips into an easy, provocative smile. "Two of you?" She had an ornately arranged head of auburn-red hair, and pale olive skin. She wore a string of gold-netted millefiori beads. That was all she wore, so the skin was very obvious.

Despite the circumstances, Erik found himself staring at the almond-skin color of the broad areolar rings around her nipples, like a snake-hypnotized rabbit. His eyes were drawn down instinctively until he wrenched them upward and away with a tremendous force of will.

She, in turn, stared thoughtfully at the three red crosses on his surcoat.

Manfred shut the door hastily behind them. He had no trouble looking at her.

"Your friend seems a little shy." There was amusement in her rich contralto voice.

Manfred snorted. "Don't mind him, demoiselle. In fact, don't mind us. We're just passing through."

"Demoiselle!" She chuckled. "Most of my visitors are just 'passing through,' darling." Her accent was a little strange to Erik, despite his skill with languages. Not that he was interested right now in worrying about where she came from.

"Well, we mean really passing through your room," said Manfred, heading for the window. "If you'd oblige us by not screaming about it, I'll come back for a longer and more generous visit when the fuss has died down. Oh."

The "oh" was aimed at the close-set steel bars in the window.

The woman laughed. Her laughter was low and cool, much like her chuckle. "Madame Claudia doesn't like customers leaving— or coming in—without having to pass through her cash box."

In the background they could hear the distant sounds of the pursuit. Getting closer. "We'd better get out there, Manfred," said Erik grimly, heading for the door. "We'll have to try and fight our way out."

"Wait," commanded the woman. "There is another way out. You'll just have to wait until the passage is empty." She had inserted herself between Erik and the door, as effectively—in his case—as a port-cullis.

"They're likely to search," said Manfred. Unlike Erik he had no problems looking at her. Or at picking her up and moving her . . .

Her means of thwarting *him* was to blow a kiss at him. "I think I can hide you for few minutes. For a . . ." she broke off, as if she'd reached a sudden decision. "Never mind." She looked appraisingly at Erik, and then turned to Manfred.

"You, and especially your shy friend, present me with something of a challenge." She laughed wickedly. "Come on, big boys. Both of you. Get those clothes off. There must be twenty of them out there."

"I'll go," said Erik hastily. "They're only looking for me."

Manfred grabbed him. "Don't be a fool, Erik. The demoiselle is right. If there are two of us—ah, occupied with her—they're likely to look elsewhere. Come on, Erik. Get them off. Especially that surcoat."

The woman began expertly removing the horrified Erik's trousers. "I have some wigs. Some of my clients like a little masquerade. And you'd better call me Francesca. As charming as 'demoiselle' is, my clients *do* know my name."

Looking up at Manfred's hairy thighs standing over him was, Erik decided, the best view from a moral standpoint. Even if it was not attractive in any other sense. He couldn't just close his eyes when a murderous bunch might burst in on him at any moment—

Not with him trapped in *this* position. With Francesca's silky

thighs straddled over him—muscular thighs, for all the soft
smoothness of her skin—if he looked forward his view was of large
naked breasts. Better to look at Manfred, even if large hairy . . .

The situation was grotesque! Especially because Manfred and
Francesca didn't share any of his own sense of modesty.

He couldn't *quite* see just what Francesca was doing with
Manfred, but the noise didn't leave much to the imagination. And
she didn't have to roll her hips on him like that! It wasn't as if
he *could* do anything.

When the Schiopettieri captain wrenched open the door moments
later, he was greeted with the sight of three naked people on the
bed, indulging in what his wife would have called "unnatural acts"
that he himself would fantasize about for weeks thereafter. The slim-
mer dark-haired fellow who was being straddled was plainly putting in a tremendous effort, to judge by his bright red face.

Francesca removed part of her oxlike client's anatomy from her
mouth. "We're busy, Luigi. You'll have to come back later," she said
lazily.

The Schiopettieri captain shut the door hastily.

"Give it a minute and I think you can leave. Unless you'd like
to finish off also," she added coquettishly, tickling the hastily
dressing and red-faced Erik in the ribs.

"Nothing Erik'd like more," said Manfred, smothering a guffaw.
"But I'm afraid we've got to go. Just how do we get out of here?"

She took a key from the drawer. "I was in a house that caught
fire once. Since then I have always made sure I had a way out.
There is a door at the end of the passage with a hoist-beam for
bringing furniture up from the Canal."

"Ah. Going to be a splashy, wet landing. You don't want to drink
this canal water if you can help it, Erik," said Manfred.

Francesca smiled lazily at him. "You'd make an even bigger splash
than I would. Wait a moment. I have some rope."

Manfred nodded. "Sounds good. Beats jumping."

Erik wondered why there would be rope in such a room. Then,
seeing the paraphernalia in the closet from which Francesca withdrew the rope, found himself blushing more fiercely. He had never
seen such things, although he had heard of them.

But by now Erik had finished dressing, and the relief of being no longer unclothed brought back his usual calm. He turned to the still-naked Francesca, carefully looking only at her face. "Will you be all right? Should we take you with us?"

Francesca shuddered. "Three stories? When the building's not burning? No thank you! I'm not planning on staying in this establishment much longer anyway. But when I do leave, I will use more conventional means. I am certainly not built for the climbing of ropes."

Her smile widened to a grin. "*My* strength is in my legs. I shall use them to walk out of the front door. Quite soon, in fact. This house does not have sufficient *cachet* for someone of my . . . talents, shall we say. I have no intention of remaining a mere brothel *puttana*, although it has taken me a while to gather resources. Now, I shall move to the Casa Louise."

She chucked his chin. "Just remember that you owe me a favor. And now, get out of here before Luigi comes back."

They slid down into the darkness. It was just as well they hadn't jumped, thought Erik. When he dropped lightly off the end of the rope, he found not water but the deck of a vessel. The boatman who had been waiting for the Schiopettieri didn't expect the "prisoner" to land on his boat. Not, at least, when that prisoner was armed and unescorted except for an even larger friend. But with Erik's Algonquian war hatchet at his throat, he wasn't going to argue about taking them away from there.

They left him tied up in his own boat, on the edge of the Grand Canal, a hundred yards away from the Imperial embassy.

Manfred looked back with regret. "You know, that Francesca had a certain something."

Erik shuddered. "She had a great deal of everything. But still. I owe her a debt."

"*I* owe her," said Manfred, shaking his head. "That sort of thing doesn't come for free. That's a mercenary profession if there ever was one."

"Even ladies of that stamp must have kindly impulses," said Erik stiffly.

Manfred pulled a wry face. Despite being five years younger than Erik he knew a great deal more about whores. He remembered the look on Francesca's face when she'd first seen Erik's surcoat. It had been . . . calculating. The Knights were all at least minor aristocracy. Many were confreres, merely serving a three-year novitiate. He would certainly not put it past that worldly-wise woman to know that. He'd already prepared himself for a hasty argument on price when she'd suggested hiding them, until she suddenly changed her mind or thought of something else. A few moments of Erik's reactions to a naked woman would have convinced the stupidest harlot that this one was a pure young knight. Francesca'd been very speculative, very suddenly. Manfred gave a low chuckle. He could see that perhaps he'd have to protect Erik against predatory female wiles. Well. It might not be unpleasant. "Yep. Maybe she did," was all he said.

"I will have to reward her," said Erik slowly. "Mary Magdalen too . . ."

"Oh, I think she'll be happy enough with a few ducats," said Manfred calmly, with an ease he didn't feel.

In the moonlight Erik looked doubtful. "Do you really think so? I mean it was an act of great v–v–virtue," he stammered.

Manfred swallowed his amusement. Only Erik could describe a harlot performing fellatio on one man while straddling another as "virtue." And believe it too. For all the Icelander's ferocious skill in combat, he was an innocent country boy in so many other ways.

"I'm sure," he agreed cheerfully. "And I think Abbot Sachs will be surprised to see you back. Unharmed."

Erik shrugged. "Maybe it was just some kind of mix-up."

"That'll be his story," growled Manfred, with court-honed wisdom far beyond his years.

Chapter 23

Well, that was certainly interesting.

Francesca pulled on an open-fronted robe, in case someone came back, tied it around her waist with a tasseled cord, and shook out her hair. Then she turned to the ewer and basin on the top of the table across the room where it wouldn't be knocked over in a moment of passion. She rinsed her mouth with herb-scented water and spat it into the basin.

And why did I do that, anyway?

It was not an idle question. Francesca had reacted to the situation based on reflex, because there had been no time to think things through carefully. But her reflexes had been honed by a perilous life, and she had come to trust them. Now that it was over and she *did* have a chance to think, she probed her memory to discover what twisted chain of logic had led her, almost without conscious thought, to behave in a way that she would normally have not.

Most certainly not! If men wanted her favors, they could damn well *pay* for them. She was no silly maiden to rescue a handsome man from danger without good reason—much less two of them, neither of whom was really that handsome anyway.

A pair of Knots, ambushed by the Schoppies. And not just any pair of Knots, either. Whoever arranged this particular episode either had no idea what kind of a mess he would create—or intended to. I wonder which?

She picked up the wooden comb from beside the basin and ran it through her hair, walking back to the bed as she did so. Francesca had not come from the streets. Before her family's ruination, they had been skilled players in the subtle and deadly intrigue which was the principal sport of Aquitaine's aristocracy. Her father had trained her in the political and diplomatic arts as thoroughly as her mother had trained her in other ways. So, a mind far better educated than anyone would have expected to find in that brothel worked at the problem, while she sat on the edge of the bed and combed her hair.

She had known, of course, from the moment she saw the two men, that they were what her mother—as chauvinistic as any Aquitaine—would have called, disdainfully, *étrangers.* The embarrassed blond was too fair to be Prussian or Austrian; and his companion had called him "Erik." He could only be a Norse of some kind. And that was odd, because there were very few Norse in the Knots. The Christian Norse who belonged to the Holy Roman Empire were Danes; and the Danes were rivals of the Knights of the Holy Trinity in the Baltic. The other Christian branch of Scandinavia were the Icelanders and their various offshoots—but they gave their allegiance to the League of Armagh, not the Holy Roman Emperor.

Except—

Her eyes widened. Like a flash, her mind focused on the other of the two men—the very large and square one. *Very* large, she remembered with some amusement, and in all respects; but he hadn't been rough at all, so she didn't hold it against him. *He* had spoken with a pronounced Breton accent—unmistakable, to one born and bred as Francesca had been in the Aquitaine.

And *his* name was "Manfred." His companion Erik had used it once.

Her eyes widened still further. *Manfred of Brittany? The Manfred of Brittany? Is it possible?*

Hair-brushing was too sedate. Francesca set down the comb, got to her feet and began pacing slowly about. Her quick mind raced, tracing the connections.

Nephew of the Emperor . . . probably second in line to the throne . . . third in line, for a certainty . . . still a just a youth, he'd be . . . bit of a rakehell, supposedly . . . what would Charles Fredrik do with such an imperial scion?

Of course! It's practically a tradition now with the Hohenstauffens!

Back and forth, back and forth. Her bare feet made no sound

on the floor. That, too, her mother had taught her. *Noise is something you make to please a man, when it suits your purpose. Otherwise—move silently.*

Yes, it all made sense. Charles Fredrik would have reached beyond the Empire altogether, called in that ancient clan favor. Brought in someone who could be trusted in such a matter, have no ties or links to the complex web of imperial politics, and also be quite capable of—

She winced, slightly, remembering the noise that had erupted earlier from the entry salon downstairs. *Those fools! They might as well have tried trapping a tiger with a fishnet.*

She was sure of it, now. The two men she had rescued were an imperial prince—Manfred of Brittany—and his Icelandic bodyguard.

Then, remembering Kat's description of her frightening encounter with the Knights in the church two weeks earlier, Francesca began laughing softly. Kat had not mentioned the name of either of the knights who had come to her defense, on that occasion, but she *had* described them. Her description, of course, had borne precious little resemblance to the two men Francesca had just finished . . . entertaining in her room. Granted, Manfred was very big; but he was not a giant. Nor—here Francesca's laugh almost gurgled—had the shy and red-faced Erik seemed quite the Nordic werewolf that Kat depicted.

Still . . . thinking about it, Francesca could well believe that those two young men—especially Erik—could be utterly terrifying under different circumstances. Judging from the sounds she had heard coming from below earlier that evening, a number of would-be ambushers had certainly found them so.

She had not, however. And, now that she was certain of their identity, Francesca found herself strangely delighted by the entire episode. She had chosen to rescue the two men out of half-conscious calculation, true. But . . .

Kat's a friend of mine. So I suppose I owed those two boys a favor anyway. Not—again the little gurgling laugh—*that Erik seemed to enjoy it much, even if Manfred certainly did.*

The laugh died away. Favors were favors, true, but self-interest remained. Where was the benefit to *her* in this thing?

This called for more leisurely reasoning. Once again, Francesca resumed her seat on the bed and went back to combing her hair.

She began by examining the ambush. She hadn't seen it, of course, but she didn't need to. She *had* seen the key piece of evidence—Erik's naked body, completely unmarked by any wound. Whoever set that trap had no idea what kind of ferocious "prey" would be walking into it. Which meant they were quite unaware of the true identity of Erik and Manfred. Whatever had been the purpose of the ambush, it had been aimed at two—or perhaps only one—junior members of the militant order. Not an imperial prince and his special companion.

That ruled out any of the Venetian factions immediately. Neither the Metropolitans nor the Montagnards would have any reason to ambush ordinary knights. Not in such an elaborate manner, at any rate, in a well-known brothel where there was bound to be a risk of capture by the Schiopettieri. If either of the factions had a quarrel to settle with a common knight, they would have stabbed him in the streets. A quick thrust from a doorway, followed by easy escape through crooked alleys in the dark.

Then . . . *why* had the Schiopettieri shown up so quickly? That was completely atypical. To have gotten here so quickly, the Schiopettieri had to have been forewarned—suborned, in fact. And whoever could wield that much influence would hardly have done it for the petty purpose of killing or injuring a simple knight.

Nor, again, was it something either the Montagnards or the Metropolitans would have done anyway. Not for their own purposes, at any rate. It was conceivable one of them might have done so as a favor to an ally, or for pay.

What ally, or paymaster? Not any of the powers within official Venice, for a certainty. The *last* thing official Venice wanted was any cause for quarrel with the Holy Roman Emperor. Charles Fredrik was a grim and dangerous man to have ruling the most powerful realm in Europe, especially one which was almost a neighbor of the island Republic. *But*—unlike some emperors of the past, Charles Fredrik was not given to grandiose ambitions. He was not a conqueror by temperament. Despite occasional frictions, Venice had gotten along quite well with the Empire since Charles Fredrik came to the throne, all things considered. It would be sheer insanity for the Venetian oligarchy to attack the Emperor's nephew.

All of which led Francesca to one inescapable conclusion. She set down the comb, folded her hands in her lap, and stared sightlessly at the far wall of her room.

Whoever was behind that ambush, and whatever the reason, it was someone whose motives were imperial. Or aimed at the Empire. This—whatever it is—goes far beyond petty Venetian squabbling.

She made no attempt to pursue that train of thought any further. She lacked sufficient information. Instead, she considered another question:

So. Was it a blunder, a piece of idiocy, or a calculated attempt to throw a tremendously big boulder into the already roiling pool of Venetian politics at present? For purposes which go quite beyond Venice itself?

After a minute or so, she set that question aside also. Again, she simply lacked the necessary information to make any kind of intelligent assessment. That left her with the final and most important question:

So. What do I do? Pursue this any further, or leave it be?

The answer to that question came almost as fast as the question itself. If she'd had any intention of *not* pursuing it, her well-trained reflexes wouldn't have led her to assist the two men in the first place. And, as always, Francesca trusted her reflexes.

For a rare moment, Francesca allowed herself a sheer grin. Not a seductive smile, but a true baring of the teeth with unrestrained glee.

What a grand game this would be!

The grin faded quickly enough. She was neither rash by temperament nor, certainly, by training. Patience had been drilled into her as a small girl. For the time being . . .

Meddling with this immediately or directly would make me a dangerous woman. I think I would rather not be dangerous at the moment, when I have my own pot to stir.

There was still a lot of noise and to-do going on in the rest of the house. Good. She'd intended to leave very soon anyway, now that Katerina had provided her with the last things she needed. Francesca had planned to wait a day or two more, but . . .

No. Tonight would be ideal. Once everything was sorted out and the appropriate bribes paid—this time, *to* the Madame of the Red Cat for a wonder, and not *from* her—things would be very quiet. The other girls would be upset, especially the young and not-so-experienced ones, the servants would be nursing bruised bodies and ill-tempers, and since by now the word had spread all up and down the Grand Canal that the Red Cat had been descended upon by the Schoppies in force, customers would be thin on the ground tonight. Tomorrow, of course, they'd be thick as fleas on a feral cat, wanting to know what happened, but not tonight. Tonight, in a hour or so, she could envelope herself in a cloak and walk out without anyone noticing.

Fernando, the aged servant who usually saw to the needs of the girls on this floor, stuck his head into the room without knocking—as usual. "Francesca—are you all right?" he asked.

She pouted. "I am, but my customers weren't happy. I only finished one off, and I suspect they sneaked out without paying. There were two—a big Circassian and a little Moor." *There. Now if anyone thinks to connect me with Manfred and his keeper, they'll be disabused of the notion. I doubt the captain was paying attention to complexions and hair colors, other than mine.*

Fernando frowned fiercely. "Half the house sneaked out without paying. I hope Madame soaks those Schoppies good!" He withdrew and shut the door. Francesca laughed softly to herself.

She waited, still as a statue, her hands folded in her lap, while the house settled.

Eventually, except for the murmur of distant talking and the hysterical sobbing of some girl too overset to be comforted, it did. Francesca bound her hair into a net to keep it in order until she could put it up properly, and got out the package that Kat had brought her early this afternoon, putting the latch on the door just in case. If anyone tried it, let them think she was having a case of the vapors herself.

Just as well that she was already naked under the robe, because she was about to go up several steps in the world, sartorially speaking, and the transformation would have to be from the skin outward, staring with perfumed oil. None of this had been cheap, but it was all necessary. Just as the Red Cat would turn away a mere *putta* who came calling at the door, so Casa Louise would turn away a whore from the Red Cat.

Silk hose; silk *knitted* hose, which clung to the leg as mere cut-and-sewn hose couldn't. Silk shifts, three of them, as fine as cobweb, and trimmed with lace. Undergown, of silk-satin, once white but re-dyed in ochre—not new, but no one would ever know that unless they got their noses within an inch of the seams. Overgown, also not new, but very, very cleverly put together from two "donor" gowns, one of which was the source of the embroidery, the other of the foundation fabric—silk-and-linen twill in a rich re-dyed brown.

Now, how am I going to use this little entertainment? It's too soon to throw any nets—and too dangerous—but a bit of bait...

Young Manfred was very much attracted to her, of that she was quite certain. But would he remember where she had told him she was going? Probably not. He did not strike her as the kind of young man who would remember such things. So—how to remind him?

It was as she was tying the embroidered girdle just under her breasts that it came to her, and she laughed. Of course! She would send him a short length of perfumed *rope*, with a card saying only *Casa Louise.* She would pay a messenger to see that it went only into Manfred's hands. He must go outside of the chapter house and the Imperial embassy sometime.

The sobbing had stopped, the buzz of conversation increased. Good. Time to go.

She gathered all that she wanted to take with her in a very small bag. She hadn't wasted any of her earnings—until now—on cosmetics or clothing as the other girls did. But her savings—except for enough to take her to her new home—weren't here. They were on deposit with a goldsmith. So the cosmetics and hair ornaments and jewelry all fitted into a very small bag. She left her robe lying on the floor with her two dresses; some other girl could have it and welcome. She flung over her splendid gown the cloak that had come wrapped around the dress and the rest—the plain side, a dark tabby-weave linen that no one here would look twice at. She drew the hood over her head, and slipped out the door.

The doorman was gone—nursing a bruised and possibly broken skull, she suspected. There had been no one in the Madame's room, either. Luck smiled upon her tonight.

She did have to walk a little, and this was the most hazardous part of the undertaking—footpads, toughs; she was fair game for anyone who saw her—but they, too, had been frightened out of the area along with the gondoliers. When she finally found one free and flagged him to the side of the canal, she was far enough away from the Red Cat that no one was likely to connect her to the place.

"Casa Louise. Don't hurry," she ordered the gondolier. She drew the curtains around the tiny "cabin," but did not blow out the lamp, for she was going to need it—and every moment it would take to get to Casa Louise.

By the time the boat nosed into the mooring at this most prestigious of Houses, Francesca had completed her transformation. Her hair was now arranged as elegantly as that of any merchant princess, twined with strings of lustrous glass and semi-precious beads, held in place with bejeweled pins. The careful use of cosmetics turned handsome features into something dramatic. And the cloak, now turned right-way around, showed its true face of ochre velvet and gold cording. When she drew back the curtains and the gondolier stooped to offer his hand to help her up, his eyes widened in admiration.

He aided her onto the walkway, and when he withdrew his hand, there was a coin of sufficient worth in it to assure his satisfaction and silence.

Casa Louise, unlike the Red Cat, boasted a landing lit by lanterns, with more lanterns on either side of the door, and two footmen beneath each one. The place was a well-lit stage, for very few of those who arrived here were reluctant to be seen.

Francesca glided up to the footmen with practiced grace and studied aplomb. "Francesca de Chevreuse," she told the right-hand man, taking up her new identity and name for the first time with immense satisfaction. She did not have to add *I am expected*, because he would already have been informed.

"*Madonna*," the footman murmured, and opened the door to the next stage of her life.

Chapter 24

As Marco carefully dressed and bandaged the long slash on Caesare's shoulder, he inspected their host. Caesare Aldanto should still be abed. He was definitely still pale, and it wasn't just loss of blood from that cut. Still, this wasn't the right time to ask how the man was feeling. By the grim set of Caesare's jaw, whatever had been going on when he acquired the wound hadn't gone well.

As Caesare's memory-man and scribe, Marco was still only privy to a small amount of Caesare's doings. The former Montagnard agent played things very close to his chest. One of the things Marco had realized quite fast in their relationship with Caesare Aldanto was that it was never wise to pry. The man had an uncertain temper.

"*Cornutto!*" Caesare swore. "Watch what you're doing!"

Marco handed him the waiting glass of grappa. "Sorry, Caesare. But this is going to hurt. You've got some dirt in there that needs to come out."

Caesare tossed the brandy off. "Make it quick then."

As Marco was working, Maria came in through the front door. As she turned to close it, two heavy-shouldered men bundled their way in behind her. Maria bit at the big hand that was clapped over her mouth and struggled vainly to reach for her knife. Her assailant clouted her, hard. "We want to talk to him, see. Now stop biting and you won't get hurt."

"I told you never to come here." Caesare's voice was icy. There was no sign of fear in it.

Marco felt in the bag for the comforting handle of the small, sharp knife that Caesare kept in with the dressings. He knew full well who these two were. You didn't mess around with the Matteonis. They were enforcers, debt collectors and rent-a-beating boys. He remembered how the crowd had parted around the three of them in Barducci's. He'd asked Valentina about them. Valentina had turned quietly to him, pulling a wry face. "Matteoni. Alberto, Stephano, and Luciano. Descended from a long proud line of barroom thugs and back-alley stabbers."

Claudia had snorted. "And this generation has sunk even lower."

Stephano Matteoni stalked forward. "Alberto's dead, Aldanto, you *mincha!*"

Marco smiled wryly to himself. Well, of course. Alberto *would* be dead if he'd attacked Caesare.

"Yeah," Luciano snarled. "You promised us the knight'd be unarmed and unarmored."

Marco swallowed. This wasn't quite what he had envisaged. He was well aware that the former Montagnard agent dealt sometimes in deaths as well as in information. But so far they'd had nothing to do with that part of Caesare's trade.

"You fools," snapped Caesare. "He is a *knight*. I told you he'd be dangerous."

Stephano had a big, clumsy, badly made hand-cannon in his hand. Calling it an "arquebus" would be stretching the point. "You said you'd deal with any real trouble. And . . ."

Caesare shook his head. "There were two of them—not one, like I was told. And the first one had that damned hand-axe, instead of being unarmed like he was supposed to be. *And* he was wearing some kind of armor." He blew out his breath. "Then the Schiopettieri arrived—"

"You promised we'd be out of there before that!" interrupted Luciano furiously.

"Things go wrong." Caesar shrugged. Then, winced as the movement pulled at the cut. "Now get the hell out of here before you're seen."

"We're not going until we've been paid," said Stephano sullenly.

Marco felt his mouth fall open. He'd thought they'd come for revenge because their brother was dead. They hadn't. They'd come for money.

Caesare stood up. His eyes narrowed. "For what? The man was supposed to be maimed in a brothel-fight and apparently drunk when the Schiopettieri arrived. You failed, and the Schiopettieri failed, too. I don't pay for failure," he added dangerously.

Stephano backed off a step. Then he remembered the hand-cannon. He steadied it, aiming straight at Caesare's chest. Of course it might not go off. This was one of the cheap fire-spell scroll ones. They were notoriously unreliable. But it might just work. At this range he could hardly miss. "Alberto's dead," he repeated grimly. "You owe us . . ."

"I owe you nothing, *orrichioni*," said Caesare dismissively. "The job's not done. That means *I* don't get paid and *you* don't either."

"And if you don't stop pointing that thing at Caesare," said Benito from the stair-landing, "I'm going to have to blow you *bastardos* in half." He had Caesare's arquebus resting on the hand-rail, pointed straight at Stephano's swelling belly. The slowmatch, far more reliable than a spell scroll, smoked and fizzed. "I'm giving you to the count of five. One." His voice cracked. But the muzzle of the arquebus was rock steady.

Luciano's grip on Maria must have slackened with the sudden intrusion of firepower. Maria bit savagely and broke away. She didn't go far. Just far enough to pull her knife and hiss like an angry cat at Luciano.

"And if you pull that trigger, Stephano," said Marco, producing the knife, "your surviving brother might have to explain to Brunelli just what you were doing. I think the Schiopettieri would be glad to hang him this time." Luciano looked uneasy at the mention of the *Casa* Brunelli. Distinctly uneasy.

Stephano sized the situation up. "All right. We're going. But we want money, Aldanto. We want money or we'll go straight to . . . Aleri."

Aleri. Marco pricked his ears. He knew that name well from his mother's Montagnard days. Francesco Aleri. The Milanese controller. Duke Visconti's spymaster in Venice.

Caesare laughed easily, unpleasantly. "You do that. He won't pay you either. Now get out. Keep out of trouble and there *may* be work for you again. Open those mouths of yours and you can join Alberto. Now go. *Get*. Don't ever come back here. I don't know you."

They backed out like whipped curs.

Marco felt the tension drain out of his shoulders.

"You can put that knife away," said Caesare.

Startled, Marco dropped it back into the bag. "Sorry." Then he realized that Caesare had actually been addressing Maria.

Looking at her stormy face, Marco realized that maybe he'd been too hasty about relaxing. The Matteonis had been a minor danger, comparatively. "How could you, Caesare? *Matteoni? Figlio di una puttana!* They're filth! Slavers. They sell . . . and make *castrati* to the east. And they broke my cousin Tonio's fingers! You know how a caulker with broken fingers finds work?"

"Put the knife away, Maria. I work with what I have to work with."

Her response was to put the knife down on the table, snatch a platter off it and fling it at his head. It shattered against the wall behind him. "*Testa di cazzo!* If my cousins hear you work with the Matteoni, they don't never work for you again!"

Caesare picked a pottery fragment out of his hair. His eyes blazed angrily in his pale face. He snapped right back at her. "They'll damn well do what they're told and you'll keep your damned mouth shut to everyone about it, bitch!"

"Damn you to hell, Aldanto!" she snarled. "I'll talk to who I want to talk to, when I damn well want to!"

Benito, up on the landing, put the arquebus down carefully. He'd already snuffed the slowmatch. He gestured to Marco with his eyes and head. Marco nodded, wide-eyed, and ducked as the next piece of crockery hit the wall. With a quiet that was quite unnecessary above the shouting, he headed to join Benito moving for the door. Even the risk of lurking Matteonis seemed less dangerous than staying.

In the relative quiet of Barducci's, Marco turned to Benito. "Does that sort of thing happen often?"

"What? The fights?"

"Yes."

Benito shrugged. "It's happened a couple of times that I know of. Maria's pretty quick to flare up. They always patch it up, after. Caesare needs her and she's crazy about him."

Marco looked across the room. Angelina Dorma and her *Case Vecchie* friends hadn't come in this evening. Barducci's was only one of the taverns they frequented. Quite frankly that crowd of hers worried him.

"I thought Caesare was too independent to feel like that about Maria."

Benito snorted into his wine. "He plays the field. But carefully. He needs Maria's cousins is rather what I meant."

"Oh." Marco let his curiosity get the better of him. He thought of Maria's extended family of "cousins." Even if she had no parents she had enough of those cousins to start a tribe. A poor tribe, though, and not . . . well . . . the sort of people you'd think would be of any value to Caesare in his shadowy world. Most of them were just caulkers, not even thugs like the Matteoni brothers. It was the poorest guild, putting the outer planking and caulking on Venice's ships. Not for the life of him could he see why someone like Caesare—with contacts like Ricardo Brunelli—would need to have anything to do with them. "Why?"

Benito looked around the tavern. "Come on, big brother. Finish up. I'm tired. That girl you've been mooning over isn't in tonight. If we take the long way back we should get back after the kissing and making up, and with any luck after the sweeping up, too."

Marco drained his goblet. He hadn't realized that Benito was aware of his fascination with Angelina Dorma. He felt a little embarrassed about it. On the other hand, he felt he'd better find out what Benito was talking about with Maria's cousins. He owed Caesare. It was only right to take care of his business for him. And he couldn't do that unless he knew what it was. Obviously his eternally curious brother had found out something. Equally obviously he wasn't going to tell Marco here.

He stood up and stretched. "Very well, it must be well the other side of midnight anyway."

They followed Benito's habitual "upper route." Even after all these weeks in town, and his frequent clambers after his brother, Marco would never possess half of Benito's catlike surefootedness across the pan-tiles. He would never have Benito's love for high places, either.

They stopped up against a chimney stack. While Marco caught his breath, Benito explained. "It's a great scam. A couple of Maria's cousins do the outer cladding at the Arsenal. They've been hollowing out a section from the actual keel timber of the galleys. Then it is fitted with a cunningly made cover, that you have to know exactly where to release. The Doge's customs and excise officers will never find it. You can only get to it from underwater."

"Oh." Well, that was relatively innocuous. Everyone tried to evade the Doge's customs to a greater or lesser extent.

Benito yawned. "Come on. Let's get back."

They both approached Caesare's apartment rather nervously. But all was quiet. And someone had swept up most of the broken crockery.

Chapter 25

The next day Caesare and Maria were being very careful around each other. But at least the worst of their fight seemed to be over. One of Maria's cheeks was distinctly bruised, but otherwise there was no obvious damage except a shortage of breakfast crockery that no one mentioned.

"I've an errand for you, Marco," said Caesare, carefully slicing a piece of frittata and placing it inside a flap of bread. "This evening before moonrise. You'd better go with him, Benito. Along that 'upper highway' you boast about, because I want this scroll delivered without anyone knowing. But Marco will go inside alone."

It was a sign of increasing trust, Marco knew. Up to now he'd only taken messages to Captain Della Tomasso—Benito's fence and a coast trader who added confidential message carrying to his quiver of expensive services. This was a step up. But he would have preferred it if Benito weren't involved.

The rooftops were slippery, curled with mist. The only light was that reflected up from windows and the occasional torches in the street below. Marco wished like hell he was down there. Roof climbing was difficult enough when you could see, although it didn't seem to make much difference to Benito. But for all the inconvenience, Marco understood why they were going along the rooftops. He understood at once, the moment Caesare had told him exactly where he was going: The *Casa* Brunelli.

Ricardo Brunelli was Caesare's "protector" among Venice's upper crust. He was a power in those elite ranks. Brunelli saw himself as the Doge-in-waiting, and there was no doubt that the information Caesare had been able to furnish him about the Montagnards and their adherents in Venice had been valuable. From a comment that Maria had made, Marco was sure that Caesare performed other services for the head of *Casa* Brunelli. The whispered knowledge that Caesare lay under the mantle of Brunelli protection was a shield the former Montagnard agent needed. Brunelli was a power in the Metropolitan faction in Venice, even if he kept a public distance from it. And although the Metropolitans did not have *quite* as savage a reputation as the Montagnards, they had one savage enough—and theirs was the stronger of the two factions in neutral Venice. So long as Caesare enjoyed Brunelli's favor, the Montagnards would steer clear of him. Revenge was not worth the risk of Metropolitan retaliation. Brunelli shielded Caesare just as Caesare's own mantle protected Marco.

It was a precarious way to survive. No wonder that Caesare didn't want to go himself to *Casa* Brunelli with a scroll destined for someone other than Ricardo. To be kept secret from Ricardo, in fact.

For a guest at the *Casa* . . .

"Well, there it is." Benito pointed down at the glass windows of the *Casa* Brunelli. Across the canal, Marco could see the massive edifice which served the Holy Roman Empire as its embassy in Venice.

"You stay up here," said Marco sternly. "Don't try and peek. I'll be out presently."

Benito shrugged. "Huh. Can't see anything on the south side anyway. Unless I climb up the Imperial embassy, and I hear they've got some of the Knights of the Holy Trinity on watch on the roof."

"Just stay here," repeated Marco, as he dropped off the guttering to a narrow, rickety wooden outside loft-stair. It was only when he was close to the cobbled street that it occurred to him that Benito knew more than was comfortable about watching the *Casa* Brunelli.

With a boldness he didn't feel, he went up to the arched doorway and raised the heavy knocker. Before the hollow boom of it had even died away, the door opened. The liveried door warden looked disdainfully at Marco. "Yes?" he asked frostily.

"I have a message—" began Marco.

The door-warden snorted. "Messages for those in the *Casa*

Brunelli are carried by the house messengers. Not by scruffy urchins."
The door began to swing closed.

"For Senor Eneko Lopez—your master's Castilian guest," said
Marco, hastily putting a foot in the way and hoping that the heavy
iron-scrolled door would not simply crush it.

The heavy door stopped. "He's Basque, not Castilian!" For some
reason, the point seemed important to the door warden. From his
slight accent, Marco suspected he was originally from Spain. But
Marco found Italian politics confusing enough, without wanting
to know the quirks of the Iberian variety.

"I will have it taken to him," the door warden added, grudgingly.

Marco shook his head. "No. My master said I must give it into
his very hands, and carry his reply."

The doorman snorted again. But he plainly did not want to
anger his master's guest. Reluctantly, he opened the door and
allowed Marco to enter. Watching Marco as if he expected this
cockroach-in-human-form to instantly begin laying eggs or stealing
the silver, he tinkled a small bell. A footman appeared hastily,
wiping his mouth with the back of his hand. The door warden
sniffed. "Louis. Take this . . . messenger up to Senor Lopez. He says
he is to wait for a reply."

The tone said: *and watch him like a hawk.*

The footman led Marco to the back stairs. Not for the likes of
him the front steps. They walked up four flights of ill-lit stairs . . .
And then were nearly knocked down them again by an extremely
angry woman, who was so busy looking back up that she failed
to see them. Even in poor light she was a truly beautiful lady, clad
in a low-cut azure Damask-silk gown, trimmed with a jabot of
finest Venetian lace. Her hair was on the red side of auburn; her
skin, except for flaming patches on her cheeks, a perfect unblem-
ished cream.

The footman nearly flung himself up the wall to get out of her
way, with a hasty terrified *"scusi."*

Marco pressed himself against the wall too. She didn't say
anything to either of them, but her angry look promised retribution
later. Marco was glad he wasn't the footman, and that he'd never
have to encounter her again. He had a feeling that despite her
legendary beauty, Lucrezia Brunelli (and this could only be her)
would enjoy making someone else's life a misery. And she looked

mad enough about something to be looking for a victim, shortly. But even angry, she was beautiful.

Marco shook himself guiltily. How could he think this of anyone but Angelina?

They walked on to the upper floor. The footman knocked.

"I am at my devotions, Lucrezia," said the voice from within. The accent was distinctly foreign. But the tone had a suggestion of tried patience.

The footman cleared his throat. He gave Marco a quelling look. "Senor Lopez. It is I, Louis. I have brought a messenger to see you."

"My apologies. Bring him in, Louis."

Marco found himself bowed into the presence of a short, slightly built man, who was carefully placing a marker in a book. He too had reddish hair. For a moment Marco found himself wondering why the woman who was considered to be the reigning beauty of Venice should interest herself in this man. Then Eneko Lopez turned and limped toward him and Marco realized what attracted Lucrezia Brunelli to this foreigner.

Power. There were the eyes of an eagle under that solid, heavy single line of dark brow. Even without a word spoken between them, Marco knew this to be a man in whom the fires of spirit burned high. And, by his calm assurance, someone to whom command was almost inborn. "Thank you, Louis. That will be all." The footman bowed respectfully and left.

"You have come from Mainz, or from the Grand Metropolitan?" The Basque held out his hand to take the scroll.

Marco swallowed, and passed over the scroll. "Neither, sir. My master is here in Venice. He said I must wait and take a reply."

Lopez sighed. "I had hoped . . . Never mind. All things will come to pass eventually. Sit."

So Marco sat down. The guest of Brunelli's occupied a room that filled him with envy. It was full of books, leather-bound volumes on volumes. Marco gazed hungrily at them. In the meantime, Lopez had taken his own seat at a small desk nearby. He cracked the seal and scanned the contents of the scroll.

When he finally spoke his voice was cold. "You may tell your master that I am neither prey for blackmail nor interested in treachery. He misinterprets my work here on the Rio del Ghetto, as he does my messages to Rome."

Marco rose hastily. Rio del Ghetto. Where the "magicians" sold their charms and wares. Where the Jews were supposed to remain, although in tolerant Venice that practice was widely ignored. Very close to where he and Benito had shared lodgings. Rome . . . well, the Grand Metropolitan was not overly enamored with Venice's religious health, if Father Del Igilo was to be believed.

But this was no time for debate. "Yes, Signor," was all he said.

As Marco turned to leave, the Basque rose from the desk and said grimly: "Stop. Since you chose to come here, I will have a few words with you as well."

Marco froze. "I d-didn't 'choose' anything, sir. My master—"

"How old are you?" demanded Lopez.

"S-sixteen."

"Old enough not to think like a boy any longer. What is your name?"

The man's force of personality was too great to resist. "Marco, sir. Uh, Marco—ah—Felluci."

The Basque snorted. " 'Felluci'? I doubt it. But if you chose a false surname—*chose*, young Marco—then you need to give a thought to all your choices. At sixteen, you can no longer use the excuse of being a 'boy.' You are a man, now. And a man chooses his own masters."

Marco said nothing. Lopez sighed. "Not a man yet, it seems. Very well." He resumed his seat and turned his face away, studying a document on the desk. "When you do decide to become a man, Marco-who-says-he-is-Felluci, I advise you to find another master. This one walks a path to ruin. If you continue to follow him, you will share his fate."

The footman was lurking outside the door. He saw Marco off the premises, with no comments but a tight set to his face. Well, thought Marco, at least he was being shown out and didn't have to deal with Lucrezia Brunelli in a foul mood.

Benito was loitering in the street. "I thought you were going to stay on the roof," said Marco when Benito joined him.

"Came down to meet you."

"How did you know . . . ?" Marco sighed. "Never mind. You've been peering in windows again, haven't you? You'd do this side of Caesare's business much better than I can."

Benito shuddered. "Believe me, brother. This was one time I was really glad it was you. That's a scary guy. I've seen him before, that time when . . . never mind. Now come on. Let's climb up there and get moving if you still want to drop in at Barducci's tonight."

Marco thought of Angelina. The thought was enough to get him
moving up to the slippery coppo tiles. Benito was already walking up the rickety stairs that had given them such an easy descent.
The roof was an easy jump and haul from there. Marco sighed.
It wasn't the roof walking as much as the looking down that
worried him.

Benito peered over the roof edge. They'd have to descend here
again. Then he put out a hand to stop Marco. There were two
people coming out of a *sotoportego* into the broad Calle dei Fabbri
below. To discourage cutpurses and cutthroats, there were oil lamps
burning in niches there. You could see the two men clearly, just
for a moment.

They were both tall, and one of them very large. The large one
was dark-haired; the other blond. The dark-haired man moved with
a sort of solid determination, the blond with catlike grace.

"Knights of the Holy Trinity. Even if they're not in uniform,"
whispered Benito. "I saw both of them . . ." His voice trailed off.

An errant night-breeze stirred the mist and brought a snatch
of conversation up from below.

" . . . shouldn't have come. This is my affair, Manfred."

A snort. "I think I owe her more for 'services' than you do, Erik."

The two stopped outside a building with long Moorish-style
arched windows, and knocked.

Benito gave a low whistle. "Well, well, well. Who would have
thought it?" He chuckled. "So much for their holiness."

Marco looked. It seemed a fairly innocuous if moderately well-
to-do three-story building. "What is it?"

Benito looked startled. "Sorry. I forget that you lived in the
marshes for so long. That's the Casa Louise. It's . . . um, a place
where wealthy merchants and some of the *Case Vecchie* maintain
their mistresses. I guess you could call it a bordello, but it's as high-
class as it gets."

Benito studied the two knights below, squinting a bit. "It's funny,
though. I wouldna thought knights—not that young, anyway—
could've afforded the women in *this* place."

Marco shook his head. His brother's knowledge of vice worried
him. He supposed that, having lived in town for all these years, the
boy would have more knowledge of things like that than he did.

Chapter 26

"Oh, my—" Kat stood in the doorway wide-eyed at the sight of Francesca's new suite of rooms. Francesca smiled wryly.

"Don't be too impressed, my dear," she said. "Remember how this is all paid for. My five current patrons are all over fifty, two are fat, one is bald and has a nose the size of a melon, and the last, poor man, needs—" She considered for a moment how to phrase what she wanted to say delicately. "—a great deal of encouragement to achieve his desires."

Kat blushed a charming color of pink.

Francesca's smile widened. "However, things may be on the verge of improvement. In one respect, at least. Do you recall that very large knight who was one of your rescuers at the church?" Seeing Kat's nod, Francesca cheerfully related the incident where she had provided Manfred and Erik with a means of escape from an ambush—sparing no details at all.

Kat blushed a charming color of scarlet.

Francesca laughed. "Don't be so innocent! That young knight certainly isn't—the large, young one, I mean. In fact, he and his blond friend visited just yesterday evening. To tender their thanks, they said. Which I have no doubt is all the blond one intended, but not large young Manfred." Her smile was now almost seraphic. "So I do believe I shall be acquiring a new patron, and very soon. He'll tire me out more, of course, but it'll still be a nice change of pace."

Kat's blush was beginning to fade; all the faster, as her face was creased by a frown of puzzlement. "I wouldn't have thought that

269

a young knight could *afford* you in the first place, even if—" She stumbled over the next words, trying to avoid offense.

"—even if his morals were scandalous for someone supposedly devoted to holy orders?" finished Francesca, grinning. "Such an innocent! Kat, one of my *existing* patrons is quite high-ranked in the Church—and no temporary confrere knight, either."

The grin faded, and Francesca looked away. "As for the other . . . I'd just as soon not talk about it. Better for you also if I don't, girl, trust me. Just remember that confrere knights, whatever their current state, are often young men from the elite of the Empire. So a large purse is not really that surprising. Large enough, at least"—waving her hand about—"for these purposes."

She shook her head. "But enough of that! I am really *so* glad that you accepted my invitation," Francesca continued merrily. "My afternoon is entirely free today, as it happens. I made certain of it." She gestured at the sofa, chaise, and chairs, inviting Kat to take her choice among them.

Kat gingerly took a seat on the sofa, which betrayed her with its softness as it was intended to do, drawing her into a cushioned embrace. Kat resisted for a moment, then, wearing a sheepish smile, allowed the sofa to have its way with her.

Francesca reclined on the chaise, which bore more than a passing resemblance to an ancient Roman dining-couch. Not only was it an attractive pose, it was supremely comfortable. "Help yourself to the fruit next to you, by the way," she offered. "If you don't, it will only spoil—one of my admirers sends it every day, far more than I can eat. Evidently his last inamorata had the appetite of an elephant." As Kat reached for a grape, she continued. "I've already taken some measures to protect you if . . . your personal situation becomes worse. I spoke to the Madame about having a house gondola. Although she doesn't believe we need one *yet*—" Francesca emphasized the *yet* "—she agrees that we could use a very discreet courier for various errands, which could include patrons who for one reason or another would rather not make use of public boats or their own. And she also agrees that I will soon need a private gondolier of my own, in any event. It wouldn't pay a great deal, but . . ."

Kat let out a sigh. "It would enable me to survive, whatever else." She tried to look on the bright side. "If nothing else, it'd be safer than what I'm doing now. No one's going to pester *Case Vecchie* in a gondola, or a courtesan going to visit one discreetly."

"That was my thought also, although"—another grin—"I saw no reason to mention your current activities to the Madame. You'd probably want to wear a mask, of course, since I imagine you'd want to keep your identity secret. From other *Case Vecchie* most of all, since yours is one of the four oldest houses."

She paused for a moment, allowing Kat to absorb the fact that Francesca had learned she was Montescue. But Kat was neither surprised nor worried. She'd realized very soon after meeting Francesca that the courtesan was far too intelligent for Kat to be able to keep her family identity a secret from the woman for very long. And, perhaps oddly given Francesca's self-admitted (say better, self-proclaimed) mercenary nature, Kat was not worried about betrayal. For reasons she could not pinpoint, but didn't doubt at all, she knew Francesca could be trusted completely. In this matter, at least, if no other.

So, she simply returned Francesca's gaze with a level one of her own. And then, slowly, smiled.

Francesca's face softened. Her eyes even seemed to acquire—just for an instant—a slight film of moisture. "Thank you for that, Kat," she said, very softly. "Friendship does not come often, to a courtesan. We treasure it all the more for its rarity."

But her gaiety returned immediately. "And now—enough of all this gloomy business. Let's look to a brighter future. Information I promised you, information I have. That's really why I asked you to come here. So. Let's trade gossip!"

"*Gossip?*" Kat asked incredulously.

Francesca laughed. "When women talk, it's called gossip; when men do it, it's called information. In either case, it's an exchange that could profit one or both of the parties. That was our arrangement, wasn't it?"

"I suppose—" Kat looked dubious now, and Francesca shook her head. "Believe me, dear, men are far worse at holding their tongues in the presence of a woman than a woman is in the presence of *anyone*. I may know something that you can turn to profit that *I* can reveal without breaking confidences. But let's start with you. What's the current news down on the water?"

When they were done, perhaps two hours later, Francesca was no longer smiling.

"None of this is good, Kat. Although I'm glad you'll be able to turn some of my tidbits of information to profitable use. But something's deeply wrong. Something . . ." She hesitated, groping for words.

"Good times and bad times," shrugged Kat. "The world is like that. Certainly Venice."

Francesca shook her head, quite forcefully. "This is more than simply 'bad times.' Something—someone—is deliberately making things as bad as possible."

Kat frowned. "Why do you think that? And why would anyone want to do it?" Before Francesca could answer, Kat made a little waving motion with her hand, forestalling objections. "Oh, sure— Duke Visconti wishes Venice all the ill in the world. But even he has nothing to gain by creating turmoil in the city. No matter how desperate Venetians ever got, the last thing they'd accept is Milanese intervention in our affairs."

The courtesan sitting across from her lifted herself up from the chaise and began pacing about slowly. Kat was struck by how silently she moved.

"'Intervention,' no. But what if the purpose wasn't intervention? What if it was simply—destruction?"

"And what would be the point of *that*?" cried Kat. "If Milan tried to destroy Venice—which they couldn't do anyway—we're an island and our fleet is far more powerful than anything they could muster—" Her words were coming in a rush.

It was Francesca's turn to wave down an objection. "Not *Milan*, Kat. Not, at least, as anything but a tool. I was thinking of Lithuania."

Kat's face went completely blank. She stared at Francesca, for a moment, as if she had suddenly found herself confronted by a raving lunatic.

Seeing the expression, Francesca chuckled. "I'm quite sane, I assure you. Yes, Kat, the Grand Duchy of Lithuania and Poland is very far from Venice. And has no common border with it. No apparent source for mutual conflict." She shrugged. "Not even the commercial rivalry which periodically agitates the Hungarians and the Genoese and the Greeks in Constantinople."

"Exactly. So why in the world—"

"Who *is* the great rival of Lithuania, Kat?" interrupted Francesca.

"The Holy Roman Empire, of course."

"Precisely. And what will happen if Venice is destroyed? Who will fill the sudden power vacuum in northern Italy and the Adriatic? Not Milan!"

Kat stared at her. Then, slowly, remembering things her father—and even more, her grandfather—had told her in times past . . . things *Dottore* Marina had told her also, now that she thought upon it . . . her face began to pale.

Francesca made a most unfeminine grunt. "Precisely. Grand Duke Jagiellon's reputation for insensate brutality is well-earned, girl. But don't be fooled by it. He is also a consummate manipulator. A man who prefers to let others bleed themselves to death, if at all possible."

Kat spoke in a whisper. "If Venice . . . is destroyed, the Holy Roman Emperor will have no choice. If he doesn't come in, the Hungarians surely will. And—and—"

"And Charles Fredrik, with Lithuania and the borderlands to deal with already, *cannot* also afford to see a more powerful Kingdom of Hungary—especially not one with a toehold in Italy. *Especially* not with a man on the throne like Emeric, who doesn't *quite* have Jagiellon's reputation—outside of Hungary, that is—but comes in a very close second."

"There'd be war between the Empire and Hungary!"

Francesca nodded. "For a certainty. With—for a certainty—Milan and Rome sucked into the vortex as well. Genoa also, be sure of it—soon enough, the Greeks as well." She resumed her slow, silent pacing. "Ever since he took the throne, one of Charles Fredrik's policies has been to stay out of Italian affairs. He's resisted—harshly, at times—every attempt of the Montagnards to drag him into this morass of endless bickering. 'The Po pisshole,' he's been known to call it."

Despite her own mild reflex of Italian chauvinism, Kat couldn't help but laugh a little at the crude expression. And admit, privately at least, that there was some justice to the barb. It was a fact that Italians—northern Italians, especially—were prone to endless and ultimately futile feuds and vendettas. Had not her own beloved Grandpapa, an otherwise sane and even kindly man, been obsessed for years with his feud against the Valdostas? A house which no longer even *existed*, except in vague rumors and her grandfather's heated imagination.

"What can we do, Francesca?"

Francesca shrugged. "Us? Nothing. You must tend to the affairs of *Casa* Montescue. I can think of few things which would be better for Venice than to have that house back on its feet again. Me?" She chuckled. "I'm just a very fancy whore, girl." She spread her arms wide, in a gesture of helplessness. "Do I look like the Emperor of the Holy Roman Empire?"

Kat sighed. "No." Then, giggled a little. "I've never met him, but . . . I don't think he's got your cleavage."

The Emperor's "cleavage," at that moment, was quite invisible. Covered as it was not only by the thick velvet of his imperial robes of office but by his own thick hands, clasped and folded across his chest as he listened to his adviser.

Baron Trolliger came to the last item on the agenda. "Oh, yes," he sighed, "that obnoxious Father Francis is still pestering you for another audience. I assume you'll want to me brush him off again. He's seen you once already. That's more than enough for the demands of courtesy. Irritating man! I'll tell him—"

"Send him in," interrupted the Emperor.

Trolliger stared at him. "He's just a priest, Your Majesty. Not even, from what I can tell, one in the good graces of Rome. He's certainly not an official emissary from the Grand Metropolitan."

Charles Fredrik's lips twisted into a wry smile. "I should think not, given his purpose here. I rather imagine the Grand Metropolitan has been tempted more than once to strangle him—even more so, the Father Lopez from whom Father Francis takes his directions."

The look of surprise vanished from Trolliger's face, replaced by impassivity. For all that the baron was one of the Emperor's closest advisers and agents, he knew full well that there were matters which Charles Fredrik chose not to discuss with him. This mysterious business of giving an obscure and apparently unimportant priest another private audience was obviously one of them.

"As you command, Majesty." Trolliger rose from his chair and began making for the door.

The Emperor stopped him. "I'd just as soon you were here for this audience, Hans. Have a servant bring the man."

The baron cocked an eye at the Emperor. Then, sighed. "I suppose this means I'll be traveling soon."

Charles Fredrik smiled and spread his hands in a gesture which expressed, in part, uncertainty. But which, mostly, expressed irony at the complicated world of political intrigue. "Most likely."

Trolliger managed, more or less, not to scowl.

An hour later, after Father Francis had come and gone, the baron was making no effort at all to keep his scowl hidden. "It's insane, Your Majesty. What these lunatics propose amounts to creating a Petrine version of the Servants of the Holy Trinity. As if the Servants aren't enough grief already. And then—then!—they want your permission to operate freely in imperial territory. I don't even want to *think* about the mess that would create."

Charles Fredrik studied his adviser under lowered brows, his heavy hands clasped over his purple robes of office. "I've *already* got a mess on my hands, Hans. Or are you so naïve as to think that the mission which the Servants sent to Venice was as innocent an affair as they claimed?"

Trolliger's lips grew pinched. The Emperor chuckled. A suggestion of "naïveté" was perhaps the ultimate insult in the baron's lexicon.

"No, I didn't think so," murmured Charles Fredrik. He rose to his feet and moved toward the narrow window nearby. "Then tell me, Hans—what *are* the Servants doing in Venice? Not to mention all those Knights they've assembled there." Now at the window, he cocked his head and gazed at his adviser.

Trolliger shrugged. "I don't know, Your Majesty. My spies tell me—"

"Nothing," interrupted the Emperor curtly. "Nothing worth knowing." He slapped the stone wall. "They're up to no good, Hans. I can feel it in my bones. And I've felt for some time anyway that the Empire was relying on them too much. At this point, I don't have a single magician worthy of the name who isn't a damned Sot. Where does that leave me—especially if Jagiellon is undertaking a campaign against me? Which I am now certain is what's ultimately at the bottom of these mysterious doings in Venice."

Not even Trolliger could keep a look of surprise from his face. "*Jagiellon?*" For a moment, he fumbled for words. "But—he's the archdemon in the Servants' pantheon of evil. Has been ever since he came to the throne four years ago."

"So?" shrugged Charles Fredrik. "It wouldn't be the first time in history that people got too close to their enemy, would it?" He scowled through the narrow window. "Which is what I suspect happened to Jagiellon himself. Until he seized the throne from his father, there had been no indication that Jagiellon was anything more than another ambitious and bullying Lithuanian prince. Since then . . ."

"There's something dark about the man," admitted the baron. "Even by the standards of the Lithuanian nobility."

"'Dark'?" snorted the Emperor. "Say better: 'black as night.'" He rubbed his heavy jaw thoughtfully. "Why does he wear that mask at all times, for instance? Simply to disguise the scars he claims to have received when he tried to fend off his father's assassins?"

Charles Fredrik turned away from the window and resumed his seat behind the heavy desk he used for working audiences. "I think not. I don't believe for an instant that Grand Duke Jagiellon is truly blind. Nor more than you. I think he keeps his eyes covered so no one can see the monster shining through them."

Trolliger took a deep breath and let it out slowly. "That is," he admitted, "my deepest fear also."

"Exactly," said the Emperor, nodding. "Which means that *if* Lithuania is behind the situation unfolding in Venice, we face something far worse than simple political intrigue. And if *that's* true, then I think I'd be a fool to keep relying on the Servants of the Holy Trinity."

"The Empire is Pauline, Your Majesty. The populace and the dynasty both. To allow—"

"Bah!" The Emperor's thick hand slammed down on the desk. "Do I care about the quarrels of theologians? I have an Empire to maintain, Hans. Be damned to all that!"

Again, the baron took a deep breath; again, let it out slowly. Then abruptly nodded his head. "True. And, as always, I am at your command." He pushed back his chair, beginning to rise.

"Venice it is, then. God in Heaven, I detest that city."

The Emperor waved him back down again. "It's not quite *that* bad. I think we can rely on Father Francis to pass on my message to his Father Lopez in Venice. No reason for you to go there. Instead—"

Trolliger didn't so much resume his seat as fall into it. The baron was quite familiar with the intricacies of northern Italian politics. He could see immediately the logic of the Emperor's train of thought.

"Oh, no," he groaned.

Charles Fredrik grinned. "Ferrara's not so bad. A very pretty little city, in fact, as I recall."

The baron's scowl would have frightened ogres. "Who cares about the city? Have you ever—*personally*—negotiated with Enrico Dell'este? You think they call him 'the Old Fox' for nothing?"

The Emperor's grin didn't so much as waver. "That's why I have advisers and trusted agents."

Chapter 27

Maria had observed that hooded look in Caesare's eyes for the last few days. He was planning something again. That always worried her. He seemed quite back to his strength now, and that new wound had nearly healed entirely. But still—it always worried her.

She often wished she'd fallen for a man who had some kind of ordinary, safe, boring job. But . . . he was so fine.

"Right," said Caesare that evening, after they'd eaten. "I've got some documents coming down from Milan. Stuff from a contact back in the old days. The worst of it is one of my informers tells me half the town also knows about it. My old *friend* Aleri will have his watchers out for sure. I hear that someone, probably that Montagnard *bastardo* Aleri, has tipped off the Council of Ten. I've got stuff in that parcel for Ricardo Brunelli, stuff which will bring a nice sum in Rome, and some things I want none of them to see. This is worth a good bit of money, and we're short. So I'm going to use people they're hopefully not watching. I haven't used you, Maria, for much of the serious stuff. And I'm pretty sure you boys aren't marked at all."

He paused, pulling a wry face. "The parcel is being dropped off at old Grazzi's factory on Murano. That's close to your regular Wednesday run anyway, Maria. Marco goes across under that tarp and jumps out under the Ponto San Donato. Marco, you wait a bit and when no one's around, you can go and pick the stuff up. I'll give you a ring to show the old man. Then you come and meet up with Maria. Then, coming back, Marco can slip off under the Ponto at the Calle del Erbe, go across and into Ricci's for a brioche

278

and glass of wine, as if he was just on his way to work at the booth on the piazza. One of the barmen, the Greek, is one of mine. I have him absolutely by the balls and I'm damned certain nobody knows it yet. He'll come up to you and say 'I'm Nicothedes.' You give it to him. Then you go to work at Ventuccio's as usual."

"I'm much better at sneaking than Marco!" protested Benito. "Let me do it. I'll be out of Maria's gondola like a greased rat and into old man Grazzi's so quietly—"

Caesare looked coldly at him. "If you'll just wait a moment, boy. Your job is the tougher one. The way this works is the other side doesn't know exactly when it's coming into town. They'll be watching me. They'll be watching my associates. They'll be looking for any break in the pattern. So you're going to be both yourself and your brother. He normally leaves here a good bit before you."

Benito punched Marco's arm. "He likes to dawdle along the way."

Caesare smiled wryly. "Fortunately. You—in his clothes—will go as far as Ricci's. That hat he's been wearing to show off to the girls is quite distinctive. Then you cut out and come back here over the rooftops. Then, in that green cotte of yours, you go out again and to work. Marco can't do the rooftops. It's a pity you're shorter than he is, but ten to one it'll be foggy tomorrow morning and at that time of day the light's bad. You'll also have to get Marco out of here and into the bottom of the gondola, maybe two hours before Lauds. Maria's gone long before then, but they'll be watching that water-door. She must leave alone."

Maria looked at the boys. Marco looked nervous. Benito . . . well, Benito looked delighted.

Marco had found it a grim morning so far. Firstly, Benito—whom he normally had to roust out of bed—had woken him in the pitch-black; then made him dress in the dark and climb out of a tiny window next to the kitchen-chimney. It wasn't meant for someone his age and size.

Benito had led him across what seemed a mile of coppo tiles to eventually bring him back to Maria's gondola. He lay cold, and decidedly uncomfortable, on the duckboards under the tarp. The tarp smelled of old spilled wine—probably from the barrels she sometimes transported. The wait seemed interminable.

He tried thinking about Angelina. But the thoughts were just frustrating. He still hadn't got up the courage to speak to her, and doubted he ever would. Angelina Dorma. *Case Vecchie.* Miles above his touch now.

But . . . oh, so beautiful.

The water-door banged. Moments later, the gondola rocked as someone stepped aboard. It had to be Maria. No one else whistled quite like that. She didn't say a word to him as she cast off and began to scull. They were out in the open water, judging by the rising and falling of the deck beneath him, before she said: "You can probably stick your face out, if you want a breath of air."

Marco did. The air was indeed wreathed with fog. Well, that much Caesare had predicted right. Hopefully, the rest would go well also. "Where are we?" he asked.

"On our way across to Murano. We should be there soon after the Marangona starts to ring. This fog'll hold a while yet. You should be able to get off nicely hidden by it. By the time we get back it'll have burned off though." Maria grinned sardonically down at him. "Then you'll have to run instead of lying flat on your back while I work."

In the distance the Marangona bell began to ring, calling the Arsenalotti to work. Two minutes later, Marco was clinging to the rotting bricks on the damp underside of the bridge. Nervously, he waited. Then, without anyone seeing him, he climbed out and made his way to the glassware factory.

The old proprietor was waiting for him—obviously as keen to get rid of this parcel of potential trouble as Marco was eager to get back to meet Maria, and get his part in this over with.

He waited. And waited. It was getting brighter next to the bridge. More and more people were about.

When she did finally arrive, Maria wore a scowl that would have frightened cream into unchurning itself back into butter. "Don't get on," she said. "We got trouble."

Marco looked around, warily.

"Tch." Maria clicked her tongue in annoyance. "Not here. Think I'd be stupid 'nough to bring trouble? Back in Venice. The Schiopettieri and the *Capi di Contrada* are searching all the small craft coming across from the east. Someone must have tipped them off."

"What do we do?"

Maria shrugged. "I go back to town. I've organized a lift across to the mainland for you. There's a pirogue heading for Mestre. You remember Tonio's cousin Alberto? His boat. He's down the glass warehouse at the end of the Fondamenta Serendella. You go there and slip onto his boat. Then in Mestre you cadge or buy a ride over to the west-side quays. You'll miss some time at work but Caesare has leverage with Ventuccio. I wouldn't come home with the parcel. See if you can get to Ricci's and deliver it to that Greek of Caesare's—Nicothedes. Now, I'm running behind schedule. I'd better get along or it'll look suspicious, and they might start wondering where I've been. They're probably going to search and harass me anyway. It'll keep 'em busy."

And with a flick of the oar she was gone to face the waiting Schiopettieri.

Marco got himself along to Alberto's scruffy pirogue. Two hours later he was near emptying his meager purse to get across the west quays. He was going to be very, very late for work. He was also very, very nervous.

Benito, hurrying along to Ricci's, literally ducking in one door and out the other, had his plans go awry too.

He slipped the new hat that was Marco's pride and joy off his head as he got inside the door. This time of morning there shouldn't be many people around. The Marangona bell had only just started to ring over at the Arsenal.

Except . . . the pasticceria was full.

Full of Schiopettieri.

Benito, hearing the door close behind him, felt sick right to the pit of his stomach. Then just before he bolted, he realized that his only "crime" was wearing his brother's hat. Personally, Benito had always felt the hat was ugly, but wearing it was still not a crime. Hat or no hat, the Schiopettieri weren't interested in him.

In fact they were discussing something he'd love to have stayed to listen to. Venice was buzzing with rumors about "magical murders" and "demon killings." If he heard the horrified talk aright, there'd just been another. And this time it sounded as if someone had actually caught sight of whoever—or whatever—had committed the deed. No wonder the Schiopettieri were in having a drink so early.

As Benito wormed his way across to the side door that would give him access to an alley with some easy-to-climb beams, he picked up snatches of the conversation.

"—suckers like an octopus—"

"—blood everywhere—"

"—poor priest was shaking so much he could hardly speak—"

And then he was out, heading upwards to the rooftops. Later he walked along to work as usual. Which was fine until one of the older Ventuccio came and asked him if he knew why Marco wasn't coming in.

After that, it was torture. Waiting in worry and uncertainty always is. *Where the hell was Marco?*

Marco alighted from a barge-load of chickens at the Fondamenta Zattere ai Gesuati. To his relief, there were no watching Schiopettieri. Now it was just a short cut across the Accademia, take a traghetto across the Grand Canal, and off to Ricci's. He was already trying to think of a good excuse to use at Ventuccio when he realized he was being followed. Or thought he was, anyway, he wasn't sure. Someone big, in a black cloak.

This was even more frightening than Schiopettieri. Marco paused and looked back surreptitiously. He couldn't see the big man in the black cloak any more. Maybe it had all been a figment of his imagination.

Then again—maybe not. If he *was* being followed by an agent of the Montagnards, it would be someone good enough not to be easily spotted. The Montagnard and Metropolitan factions had plenty of skilled spies—and assassins. His mother had been a Montagnard spy herself, far more skilled than Marco at maneuvering in these murky waters. But that hadn't prevented them from killing *her,* had it? Had she, too, once been followed like this?

His panic was rising rapidly. A Montagnard agent. One of his mother's killers, now following *him.*

Marco rounded the corner into Calle Pompea and started running. The street was crowded at this time of day. Dodging between the pedestrians and the porters, the students heading for classes, and the barrows of vegetables, Marco made fearful time around the corner, doubling back toward the docks, and down into an alley.

He looked back. And he ran smack into someone who was coming the other way. He dropped the precious parcel. The other person dropped a variety of things including a folding easel and at least a dozen brushes. As they both bent to retrieve their possessions they looked at each other . . . with mutual recognition.

Rafael de Tomaso!

He and Marco had struck a kindred note in each other from the first words they'd exchanged. Marco still remembered de Tomaso coming in to Mama's place, the first time, looking for plants for pigments. Rafael had been grinding and preparing his own paints already then. They'd struck up a conversation with the ease of two boys—unaware of the difference in politics or background. They'd met up again later, one evening at Barducci's and it was . . . once again an immediate encounter with a kindred spirit. It was as if the intervening years hadn't passed.

"Marco!" Rafael smiled.

"Rafael . . . can you hide me? Someone is after me. At least—I think so. Maybe."

Rafael didn't hesitate. "Licia's—my lodging—it's only a door away. Will that do?"

Marco looked around nervously and nodded. In a few moments he was upstairs in a dingy room long on artist's supplies and short on space or comfort. "What are they after you for?" asked Rafael curiously.

Now that Marco felt relatively secure, his fears were ebbing. In fact, he was starting to feel embarrassed. There were a lot of big men in Venice, after all, plenty of them wearing black cloaks. He was beginning to think he'd just imagined the whole thing.

"Well . . . I might have been wrong. Maybe there wasn't anybody. But if there was—" He held up the package clutched in his hand. "They'd want this parcel. I'm supposed to deliver it to Ricci's."

Rafael smiled. "Better safe than sorry, what I say. I'm on my way across to Castello to paint a portrait. It's not much of a commission but every bit of money helps. I'll toss it in my paint-bag and deliver it for you. You can stay here in the meanwhile."

Marco felt his muscles go slack with relief. "That would be fantastic."

The relief on Benito and Maria's faces when they saw him was almost worth missing a day's pay for. And Caesare was pleased with his parcel too. Benito and Maria did quite a lot of yelling at him, of course.

Chapter 28

Petro Dorma studied the body lying on the kitchen table. The two chirurgeons were still working on the pitifully mangled thing, but it was obvious to Dorma that the shopkeeper was as good as a corpse. The amount of blood spilling over the table onto the stone-flagged floor was enough in itself to doom him—leaving aside the ghastly trail of blood that led from the shop where the merchant had been attacked.

Blood, and . . . other things. Horrid pieces of a half-dismembered human body. Whatever had done this had been as insensate in its violence as in the previous murders. This was now the fourth victim Dorma had examined—assuming that the street urchin killed the first night had been one of them, an assumption which Petro had made long since. All of them displayed the same characteristics. Bodies ripped apart, as if by some kind of huge animal, not simply stabbed or bludgeoned in the manner of a human murderer.

He turned away and walked out of the kitchen, taking care not to ruin his expensive shoes by stepping in the blood. Once in the room beyond, he paused and examined the area once again. He had done so already, but Dorma was meticulous by nature. That was one of the reasons his fellow senators had elected him to the *Signori di Notte*. The Lords of the Nightwatch who controlled the city's Schiopettieri were too powerful a group to be given into the hands of careless men. The more so if one of them, like Petro Dorma, was also a member of the Council of Ten—the shadowy semi-official body of the Senate which had almost unrestricted powers to investigate and suppress whatever they saw as threats to the security of the city.

Petro Dorma had the reputation for being judicious as well as intelligent, and not given to factionalism or fanaticism of any kind—exactly the qualities which the oligarchy that controlled the Venetian Republic looked for in its most powerful officials. The Republic had now lasted for a millennium, maintaining its prosperity and independence in the face of many challenges, by being cautious and methodical. Venetian diplomats were famous the world over—notorious, perhaps—for being the most skilled at their trade. The challenges which had faced the city over that thousand years had been internal as well as external. Venice's secret police were every bit as expert as the city's diplomats.

Petro Dorma never thought of himself as a "secret policeman," much less as the effective chief of the secret police. In truth, he never really thought of his status at all. He simply took it for granted. The male head of one of Venice's most prominent houses, a wealthy and highly respected merchant, very prominent in the Senate. And, also, the dominant member of the Lords of the Nightwatch and perhaps the most influential within the Council of Ten.

So it was. Petro Dorma's position in Venetian society was as much a matter of fluid custom and tradition as it was of any official title. He did not care much about titles; did not even think of them very often. He was Petro Dorma, and . . . so it was.

The room was plain, unadorned. The narrow and cramped shop of a simple dealer in linens, nothing more. As with most small merchants in Venice, the shop was simply the front room of a residence. The kitchen adjoined directly; the bedrooms and living quarters were upstairs, accessible only by a narrow staircase leading from the back of the kitchen.

Absolutely typical—and completely different from the locale of the previous murders. The first victim had been a very wealthy financier, slaughtered in his own bedroom on the upper floor of one of the city's premier mansions. The presumed second victim a street urchin, killed by the canalside. The third a poor prostitute, butchered in an alleyway where she plied her trade.

That fact alone was enough to tell Dorma that he was dealing with no typical fiend. In his experience—considerable experience—

homicidal maniacs were obsessive in the way they selected their victims. As obsessive as they were in the manner with which they murdered.

This fiend, however, seemed not to care. Not, at least, with respect to the nature of his—or *its*—victims. And if the grotesquely brutal manner in which it killed the prey seemed obsessive, Dorma suspected that it was not. He suspected, more and more, that the fiend killed in this manner simply because it came naturally. Is a shark "obsessive" because it rends bodies into shreds with huge teeth? Or a lion with talons and fangs?

Petro did not believe, any longer, that he was dealing with a human murderer. As skeptical as he normally was whenever he dealt with charges of "witchcraft"—charges with which he had as much experience as he did with mundane crimes—Dorma had become convinced, in this case, that he really *was* facing something supernatural.

And *that* being true . . .

His thoughts wandered, for a moment, to the still-unsolved mystery of what had happened to Father Maggiore, the Servant of the Holy Trinity who had been burned alive months earlier at the ceremony in the Imperial embassy. As it happened, Dorma had been present himself on that occasion, and had personally witnessed the horrifying death of the monk. There had not been the slightest resemblance between the manner of that death and the ones which came after. But—

Who can say what form true demon-work can take? This might all be part of the same thing—whatever that "thing" might be.

He turned to the Schiopettieri captain standing respectfully nearby. A quick check of his excellent memory brought up the man's name.

"Ernesto, have there been any cases reported of people being burned to death? Say, over the past six months. Not murder cases—I would have heard of those—but things which simply seem like accidents?"

The captain frowned. "A few, Lord Dorma. But nothing which seemed more than misfortune."

Dorma pursed his lips. "Do me a service, if you would. Discreetly—discreetly, mind you—double-check all of those reports and tell me if anything strikes you amiss. For instance, a death with no eyewitnesses. Or a death whose cause seems unexplained.

And while you're at it, now that I think upon the matter, check to see if there have been *any* kind of mysterious deaths. Whether by burning or—" His eyes glanced for a moment at the door to the kitchen. "Or by any means."

The captain nodded. Dorma was satisfied that the man would do a thorough job. Petro was a polite man by nature; but that innate temperament had been reinforced by experience. He had learned long ago that treating his subordinates with courtesy produced far better results than arrogance and browbeating.

That done, Dorma sighed. Nothing for it but to deal with the family, now. That was the aspect of his work he truly detested. The grisly parts of investigation he could handle with reasonable aplomb, controlling his squeamishness easily enough. But talking with grief-stricken relatives . . .

Then, he remembered. And felt a little flush of guilt at the relief that flooded him.

"The poor man was a widower, no?"

"*Si*, Lord Dorma. His wife died two years ago."

"No children?"

"No, sir. Well—not here, not alive. Two children once, apparently. But one seems to have died long ago, of the plague. And the other took ship and has not been seen for several years. A son, lives now somewhere in Constantinople, I've been told. Estranged from his father, according to rumor."

Petro nodded; and, again, felt some guilt. He really should *not* feel relief at the misfortunes of a poor family, simply because it removed an unpleasant task from his shoulders. For a moment, he wondered at the life of that family. One child dead of disease, another estranged and long gone. The mother dead, and now the father horribly murdered.

It was a melancholy thought. He could only hope that the couple had gotten along well enough in the years they had spent together at the end, childless and alone. But there was nothing he could do about it now. Or could have, at any time. Once again, Petro Dorma reminded himself of the sharp limits to his power, for all its outward trappings. And in so doing, although he never once considered the manner, reconfirmed the wisdom of Venice's Senate in selecting him for his post.

One of the chirurgeons emerged from the kitchen, wiping his hands on a rag. Seeing Dorma, he simply shrugged, very wearily.

As expected. Dorma nodded, a nod deep enough to convey to the chirurgeon his respect for the man's efforts. Then, started for the doorway leading to the street outside.

"Take me to the priest now, Ernesto. If you would be so kind."

The priest was in the nave of his little church, located not much more than a block away. The elderly cleric was hunched on one of the pews, his head bowed, clutching a cross in his hands and trembling like a leaf. Clearly enough, reaction to the horrifying event which had transpired not long past was now setting in.

Dorma did not begrudge the man his uncontrolled shivering. From what he could determine, at the moment of crisis the priest had done all he could—and done so with a courage which would not have shamed any of the Church's great martyrs. The fact that, afterward, a humble parish priest had fallen into quiet hysteria was quite understandable. He was not, after all, a great condottiere like Carlo Sforza, accustomed to scenes of horrendous carnage and brutality.

Dorma stepped up to the priest, stooped, and laid a gentle hand on his shoulder. "Please, Father, can you tell me what happened?"

The priest raised his head and stared at Petro. His brown eyes were blurry with moisture.

"It's very difficult, Lord Dorma," he whispered shakily.

The fact that the priest knew the identity of his questioner did not surprise Dorma. Even though, to the best of his knowledge, he had never met the priest. In fact, he did not even think about it. Everybody in Venice knew who Petro Dorma was—his appearance and official position, at least, if not the full range of his powers and his membership on the Council of Ten.

"I'm sure it is, Father, and I apologize for disturbing you at such a moment. But I really must learn as much as I can about what happened."

The priest's nod was as shaky as his whispering voice. "Yes, yes, of course. It's just—I can't remember much. It was dark and—very confusing. And . . . and I was very frightened. Confused myself."

Dorma gave the shoulder a reassuring squeeze. "You handled yourself as well as any man could have, under the circumstances. Just tell me what you can, Father."

Visibly trying to bring himself under control, the priest took several deep and slow breaths. Then:

"It was very late at night. Near dawn, in fact. I had been spend-ing the night with Luigi—the linen merchant—sitting up with him and . . . talking, mostly. I was worried about him. Since the death of his wife, he has been very unhappy. I've been concerned that he might even be starting to think of suicide."

The priest paused for another deep breath. "We heard a noise. Downstairs, in the shop. Nothing loud. In fact, I didn't hear it at all. But Luigi had a shopkeeper's sensitivity to such things, of course. So he excused himself and went down the stairs, carry-ing a candle."

Again, the priest paused. For much longer, this time. Clearly, now that his tale was approaching the moment of horror, he was reluctant to continue.

Petro made no effort to hurry him along. He took advantage of the delay to review in his mind everything he had seen in the shop. And was struck again—as he had been at the scene of the financier's murder—at yet another contradictory fact. The same creature that slew in such an incredibly excessive manner was also quite capable of delicate work. The financier's mansion had been entered in so sure and subtle a manner that the Schiopettieri were still uncertain as to the murderer's exact route of entry. And if the entry to the linen seller's shop was obvious, the lock on the front door had been skillfully picked, not broken. Dorma suspected that the only reason the shopkeeper had heard anything was because he had been wide awake and, as often happened with elderly merchants, had become extraordinarily sensitive to the risk of burglary.

The priest was ready to continue. "Then I heard a scream," he rushed on. "Luigi's voice. I raced down the stairs. Through the kitchen. By the time I got to the front room . . ." He gasped, a moment. "It was *horrible*. Luigi was being held by—*something*. I couldn't see it clearly. He must have dropped the candle, so there was no light in the shop. Only what little light came through the open door from outside. Not much, because sunrise was—only still coming. Everything was dark, dark. Horrible."

"Was it a man?"

"I don't think so, Lord Dorma. If it was, it was a huge and mis-shapen one. But—no! It couldn't have been a man! I saw a tail—I swear! I remember that! And—then, when it must have heard me entering—I was probably shouting myself, I don't remember clearly—but I know I was holding up my cross and calling on the Virgin—"

The priest's voice was starting to rise hysterically. Dorma calmed him with gentle pressure on the shoulders, kneading the old cleric's thin bones and flesh with his hands. After a moment, the priest continued, his voice now dull and leaden.

"It flung poor Luigi at me and fled from the shop. I saw—something like suckers on its arm. Like an octopus, except it was more like a man's arm—huge one—than a tentacle. Then it was gone, racing out the door. I saw the tip of a tail. Like a reptile's, of some kind. No more." He shuddered. "Please, Lord Dorma. No more."

Dorma nodded, gave the priest's shoulders a last little reassuring squeeze, and straightened up. "Enough, Father. Get some rest."

On the way out of the church, he had a few words with the Schiopettieri captain. "See to it that a guard is maintained here at night, for the next few weeks. I don't expect there'll be any . . . trouble. The fiend doesn't seem to have returned to any of its other crimes. But—"

Ernesto nodded. "The priest is the only eyewitness. And the only one who interrupted the—whatever it is—before it finished. I'll see to it, Lord Dorma."

Later that day, after hearing Lord Dorma's report, the Metropolitan of Venice summoned the special envoy from the Grand Metropolitan of Rome to a private audience, in a secluded room in the cathedral.

Metropolitan Michael was becoming more than a little impatient with the envoy, so he did not preface his first words with the usual phrases of polite greeting.

"How much longer?" he demanded. "By the Saints, man, you should at least meet with Petro Dorma. He could be of great assistance to you."

The envoy shook his head firmly. Metropolitan Michael almost hissed with displeasure. The Grand Metropolitan's envoy did *everything* firmly, it seemed. He even managed to *limp* firmly, somehow.

"And why not?"

The envoy frowned. Firmly, of course. "I still do not know the identity of the evil, Your Eminence. The *source* of it, yes. It comes from Lithuania, like most of the world's demonry. But I still haven't determined the channels, or the conduits—not all of them, at least—nor, most important of all, its ultimate purpose. For all I know, Petro Dorma himself is entwined in these plots."

The Metropolitan threw up his hands with exasperation. "That's absurd! You might as well consider me a suspect!"

The Grand Metropolitan's envoy studied the Metropolitan calmly, saying nothing in response. As if he were examining him. After a moment, realizing the man was immovable, Michael sighed.

Even the man's eyebrows annoyed him. They, too, were firm. It, rather. Like a solid bar of rusty iron above implacable eyes.

Chapter 29

Eventually, the punishment ceased. The monster lay on its side, its flanks heaving, still trying to beg for mercy. The effort was pointless, since Chernobog had crushed its throat. But the monster knew from experience that so long as it was in the strange, gray-mist casket-world, its wounds would heal quickly. Any wounds, even mortal ones—and it wanted to be pleading for forgiveness as soon as any word at all could issue from its throat. Else Chernobog might renew the chastisement.

In the end, the monster's fears proved groundless. By the time the first croaking words issued from its healing throat—quavering with pain, those words, since healing was almost as painful as punishment—the master's rage had subsided. Chernobog was deep into cold contemplation. The monster could sense his dark form in the surrounding mist, hunched with thought.

Be silent, beast. Lest I return you to the place from which you came.

The thought brought a fierce yearning to the monster. To roam free again—!

But the urge was fleeting. Chernobog possessed the monster's soul, still. The monster had no illusions that the master would return it—nor that it would be cast back into its homeland uninjured. Chernobog would surely rend the monster before he set it free. And, outside of the casket-world, mortal wounds were genuinely mortal. The monster would simply bleed to death, disemboweled in a forest, leaving its soul to be chewed by Chernobog for eternity.

Besides . . .

The pain was receding now, as it always did. And the monster was able to remember the pleasures as well as the agonies of serving Chernobog. It would feed again, soon enough. That knowledge brought relief—relief from frustration, this time, not pain. The monster had not been able to devour the prey's soul because of that cursed priest. It was *hungry.*

Eventually, Chernobog ceased his ruminations. The monster could sense the dark form shifting somewhere in the surrounding grayness. As if some huge beast, roused from torpor, were stirring again.

It will have to be the burning again. At least for a time. I cannot risk another premature encounter. Especially not now, with the Shadow stirring in slumber.

The monster had to struggle not to cry out a protest. It was, in the end, a creature of the forest and the lakes and the mountains, who much preferred the corporeal rending of flesh in its beast-form to less fleshly methods. But the struggle was brief, very brief. There was a certain pleasure in burning also. More ethereal perhaps, but not without its own rewards.

Yes. The burning again. And soon. The monster sensed Chernobog's form seething with anger, but knew the anger was directed elsewhere.

Lest my enemies think a mere priest, with a common holy symbol, can bring them surcease. Their growing terror must be fanned, like flames in a forest, until all of the city burns.

Yes. The burning, again.

The monster's wounds were almost completely healed by now. Enough, certainly, to enable it to utter words of obeisance and submission. And if the tone of those words contained a trace of regret, there was not enough to reawaken the master's displeasure.

Again, the monster sensed the great form swirling, a darkness in the mist, as if an enormous arm was moving in a gesture of command. In an instant, its body began to shrivel and shrink. Soon enough, the beast-body with its talons and teeth and clawing suckers had vanished, replaced by something which bore a vague resemblance to a salamander.

As always, the monster's regrets vanished with the change of form. There was no room in that salamanderlike body for anything but salamander thoughts.

Burning soon. Hungry!

PART III
December, 1537 A.D.

Chapter 30

The Old Fox smiled. "Angelina Dorma. Well, well, well! How serious do you think it is, Antimo?"

The Duke of Ferrara's agent considered this silently. Finally he said, "Angelina Dorma is a young woman of some beauty and absolutely no common sense. Your grandson Marco is besotted with her—to the point of foolishness. Angelina has bragged about her 'secret admirer' to several *confidantes* both inside and outside the *Casa*. It was easy enough for my spies in the household to get wind of it, to see young Marco and to track him. This was done as part of our ongoing research into *Casa* Dorma, milord, not with our agent being aware of whom he was tracking."

The Old Fox raised an eyebrow. "We were all young and foolish about women once, weren't we?"

Antimo Bartelozzi didn't respond with a smile. "Foolishness gets people killed, milord. And Dorma is very protective about his family."

The duke pulled a wry face. "His *weakness* is his family, Antimo. His mother and sister can be used against him. It's been a factor which has held me back in my approaches to him, despite his many impressive qualities. And as for the foolishness, those it doesn't kill—learn. So, I want Dorma watched closely. I see possible alliances here as well as possible dangers. And it is conceivable my foolish grandson may have found a way to remove one loose cannon from the *Casa* Dorma, and tie it down."

Antimo nodded.

The duke put a hand to his chin and looked speculative. "Given

297

the current positions of the major factions in Venice—how do you assess Petro Dorma's strength?" He waited patiently for the reply he knew Antimo would eventually formulate. Privately he regarded Antimo Bartelozzi as his personal version of the mills of God. The agent ground slowly—but he ground very, very fine.

"Well—superficially his faction is the smallest, the weakest, and the most diverse and divided. Petro is very able, but he is not charismatic. He lacks the flamboyance and panache of Ricardo Brunelli, for instance."

The Old Fox looked at him through half-lidded eyes. The languor might have fooled a lesser man. "Ah. But you think there are other factors to be considered?"

"Yes." The agent smiled wryly. "Should circumstances prompt either the Metropolitan or Montagnard factions to lose support in Venice . . . that support may easily go to Dorma. He has long been seen as the firmest advocate of a centrist, neutral stance. His party's weakness is its diversity. But, as a broad church, it offers space to former adherents of both the other parties—the softer ones, if not the fanatics. And Venice's people—though they might lean Montagnard or Metropolitan with the blowing of the factional winds—have a strong tradition of independence. Like a heavy keel to a ship. That is Dorma's central creed. If either Rome or the Empire truly threaten Venice, I think its populace—and most of its senators—will remember that heritage. While Dorma has the smallest support base, and is not flamboyant like Brunelli, he *is* respected. You can find very few people who dislike him. And he has a reputation for hard, meticulous, scrupulously fair work—as you know."

The Old Fox gave a smile that, had he really been his four-footed namesake, would have sent every peasant farmer who saw it off to sleep—uneasily, with their boarspear and their dog—*inside* their henhouse.

"That's all shaping up nicely, then. And now that Baron Trolliger has arrived . . ."

Antimo's smile almost matched that of his master. "It's *such* a pleasure to have a capable Emperor sitting on the throne in Mainz."

"Is it not?" agreed the duke cheerfully. "Hohenstauffens of the past, more often than not, would have already been planting their great clumsy boots on the Brenner Pass. But Charles Fredrik is almost an Italian, the way he thinks. I assume he's offering us money, not soldiers?"

"Baron Trolliger hasn't been specific yet. He only arrived yesterday, after all. I doubt he will be, milord, until you meet with him personally. But those are the signs, yes. The Emperor, clearly enough, wants a proxy army here in northern Italy—just in case the situation in Venice proves to be as dangerous as he and we both think it is. And he's more than smart enough to see that Ferrara—little, innocuous Ferrara—is the logical choice."

Antimo's smile grew very wry. "Baron Trolliger's praise for the honor of Dell'este—as well as the cunning of the 'Old Fox'—has been most, ah, fulsome."

"As it should be!" chuckled the duke. "I've spent a lifetime developing that reputation, after all. Send the man in for a private audience, then, as soon as he's ready. Is he *still* cleaning his boots?"

"Probably," replied Antimo. "There's a man who genuinely hates to travel. His curses on that subject were almost as fulsome as his praise for Dell'este. And, I'm sure, quite a bit more heartfelt."

"There's no rush. Negotiations will be lengthy, in any event. I intend to squeeze as much money as I possibly can from the Empire. Charles Fredrik can certainly afford it."

Antimo nodded. "And what about Marco? Do you wish me to take any steps?"

The Old Fox raised an eyebrow. "No. Let him alone. Perhaps practice will improve his poetry."

Chapter 31

Lies.

That was what his whole life had become, over the last few weeks. Lies and evasions and dirty little twistings of what scraps of truth he *had* told—

Marco's gut ached like someone had punched it, hard. It had ached like that for days. His throat was so choked most of the time he could hardly swallow. And his heart—if it wasn't broken, it was doing a damn good imitation of *being* broken.

Marco Valdosta, he who called himself Marco "Felluci" these days, had good reason not to own to the *Case Vecchie* family he'd been born into. His Ferrarese mother had made sure of that with her fanatical Montagnard beliefs, and the long-buried secrets that went with what she had done to further the cause.

Still . . . this wasn't why he felt as if he must be one of the most pitiable sixteen-year-olds in all of Venice. He was looking miserable enough for Benito's friend Claudia to comment on it. Claudia had told him to his face that he was drooping like a four-day-old leftover bunch of *finocchio* leaves, and had wanted to know the reason. He hadn't dared tell her. He hadn't dared tell anyone.

Although he really didn't intend to be that way, his disposition wavered between sullen and terrified. He spent most of his time moping around like a moon-sick idiot. His brother had given up on him in disgust; Maria Garavelli and Caesare Aldanto only knew he was pining over a girl and being unusually peculiar about it.

Caesare was being more than patient, he was being condescending—which Marco was overly sensitive to just now.

Maria, having failed to jolly him out of it, had taken to snapping at him frequently. They repeated the same scene at least twice a day. It usually started with him glooming about in her path, and Maria stumbling around him, until she finally lost her temper—

Then she'd explode, canaler's cap shoved back on her dark hair, strong hands on hips, dark eyes narrowed with annoyed frustration—

"*Dammit Marco, can't you get the hell out of my way?*"

Even the memory made him wince.

She snapped, he sulked, they both got resentful, and Caesare sighed.

The problem was they didn't know the *half* of what he'd gotten into.

Marco, who was just home from work at Ventuccio's booth on the Piazza San Marco, huddled in a soft plush-covered chair in Aldanto's living room. He had lit one lamp, on the right side of the window tonight—that was to tell Maria that all was well—but had left the rest of the room in gray gloom. He was curled around the knot of anguish that seemed to have settled into his gut for good. Every time he looked up, the very room seemed to breathe reproach at him.

There was frost on the window—bitter cold it was out there. Here he was, warm and dry and eating good—he *could* have been out in the Jesolo marshes, freezing his butt off, but he wasn't, thanks to Caesare Aldanto. He could have been shivering in Benito's attic, or in their little barren apartment in Cannaregio—hell he could have been *dead*, but he wasn't, again thanks to Aldanto.

Caesare had taken him and Benito under his protection. He had protected them and then taken them into his own home. He'd been feeding them and housing them and keeping them safe because the town was in a turmoil and that was the only way he could be certain they *were* safe. And now Marco had gone and compromised the whole damned setup *and* compromised Caesare himself.

Maria was right. He *was* an ingrate.

He was more miserable than he'd ever been in his life; more miserable than the time he'd hidden out in the marshes, because that had only been physical misery—more miserable than when his mother had been killed, because that was a clean-cut loss. This—this tangle of lies and half-truths he'd woven into a trap binding him *and* Aldanto—this mess had him so turned inside-out—that it was a wonder he even remembered what day it was.

Oh, Angelina, he thought mournfully, *if only I'd never seen you.*

It had seemed so innocent, sending that love poem to Angelina Dorma. She wouldn't know who had sent it, so what harm could possibly come of it? But Angelina had *assumed* it had come from Aldanto, because *she* was in love with Caesare. Not surprising, that. Caesare Aldanto was a *man,* not a lovesick boy. Caesare Aldanto was urbane and sophisticated and, to top it off, tall, golden-haired—in a city full of short, dark folk—and as handsome as a sculpture of Apollo. No girl would think twice about Marco with Caesare Aldanto in the same city. Marco didn't *blame* Angela—and truth to tell, he hadn't really expected her to respond to the poems so strongly.

But she had; and she had come to her own conclusions about them. She'd caught Marco delivering a third love-poem. She'd got him so twisted around with the way she'd acted towards him that all he could think about was that she'd guessed about his own passion and she was being *Case Vecchie* and coy. He'd been so bemused he hadn't left her until long after dark . . .

Caesare—still recovering from the fever—Maria and Benito had all been in a fine case over him by then, worrying that he'd been caught by Montagnards, caught and maybe been tortured or killed.

But he was so full of Angelina and how she'd guessed at the identity of the author of the poems, and sought him out, that all he could feel was resentment that they were *hovering* over him so much.

It was only after he'd read her note—then reread it and reread it—that he realized that she'd guessed wrong. She'd figured that the author was Caesare, and he was the errand-boy. And she'd set him such a tempting little trap, too—offered to have Dorma sponsor and fund him into the Accademia, and make his dream of becoming a doctor come true, so that he could be conveniently close to deliver more such messages. So tempting; he could at least see and talk to her, any time he wanted. He could also have his other dream—all he needed to do was to keep up the lie, to keep writing those poems and pretending Caesare was sending them. That was all. Just as simple as Original Sin and just as seductive.

And now he was afraid to tell Caesare, because he'd been such a fool, and worse, got them tangled up with a romantic *Case Vecchie* girl, one with power and connections. He was afraid to tell Maria because—because she was Maria. She was capable and clever and she'd laugh him into a little puddle of mortification and *then* she'd kill him, if Caesare didn't beat her to it. And he *couldn't* tell Benito. Benito was put out enough over the notion of his brother taking a sudden interest in girls—"going stupid on him" was what Benito had said.

Hell, he'd gone stupid all right. So stupid he couldn't see his way straight anymore. And that was dangerous for him, and for all of them, with the town in a dither over the magical killings.

Marco himself was sure that the killings were Montagnard work, not "magical" in the least. Sure as death and taxes; and Caesare was ex-Montagnard and knew too damned many Montagnard secrets. For that matter so did Marco.

And the city was simmering with suspicions. He, Marco, might be sure the wicked Viscontis were moving again. But if you got three people together you got eight opinions. Strega or Jews were the most common suspects, of course, but the Council of Ten and the agents of Rome were accused too. Of course there was no certainty who might or might not be in one of the factions, so opinions were voiced very carefully.

Complications were *not* what Caesare needed right now. Yet "complications" were exactly what Marco knew he'd gotten them into. And this left him unable to tell the truth. Because the truth hurt so damn much, and he couldn't force it past the lump in his throat and the ache in his gut.

But he *had* to tell somebody; had to get some good advice before what was already worse became disastrous. He could reason out that much. Somebody older, but not too much older; somebody with experience with nobility. Somebody who knew how girls thought, wild and romantic *Case Vecchie* girls in particular.

A face swam into his mind, surrounded with a faint shimmer of hope, almost like a halo.

Rafael—Rafael might help him to think straight again. Rafael de Tomaso was a student. He was, Lord knew, smarter than Marco was—and a little older, more experienced. He dealt with *Case Vecchie* families all the time in the form of his fellow students. And he was old enough to know how to handle girls. Maybe even how to handle *angry* girls.

Yes. *He'd* be willing to give advice. *He* was the right person to see.

Marco made up his mind to go and find Rafael right then and there, before he got faint-hearted again.

He jumped up out of the chair and padded across the soft carpet to the bottom of the stairway, listening carefully at the foot of the stair for the faint sounds of Aldanto dozing in the bedroom above. Caesare had been sleeping a lot the past couple of weeks, since Brunelli wasn't using him much lately . . . although Marco was beginning to realize that Caesare Aldanto had plenty of other irons in the fire.

Poor Caesare. Damn near everyone's hand was against him now—or would be if they knew what he was. And now one of the kids he'd taken in had gone and messed up his life even more, and he didn't even *guess* the danger that kid had put him in. Marco felt like a total traitor.

Benito was in the spare bedroom downstairs, sprawled on his back half-draped across the foot of the bed and upside down, trying to puzzle his way through one of Marco's books and making heavy work of it. This one had illustrations, though, which was probably what was keeping Benito's attention.

He writhed around at Marco's soft footfall.

"I've got to go out; an hour maybe. I'll be back by dark, *si*?"

"Why?" Benito's dark face looked sullen; rebellious. Not only was he mad about Marco getting mixed up with girls, but Marco had had it out with him over obeying Caesare and treating him with respect. Benito had been smart-mouthed and Marco had finally backed the boy up against the wall and threatened honest-to-God serious mayhem if Benito didn't shape up. Benito was still smoldering with resentment, and Marco *still* wasn't sure the lecture had taken.

"I've got to see Rafael. I've got to take some of Sophia's herbs for him. One she says will give him a deeper red than madder root. I promised him some and I've never taken them."

Benito's expression cleared. He nodded and his brown eyes got friendly again, because it wasn't a girl that was taking Marco out, and it wasn't one of Aldanto's errands. "*Si*. Reckon he can make something off them?"

"Probably, what with all the painters at the Accademia. He isn't much better off than we are, you know? He deserves a break."

"Just you best *be* back by dark," Benito admonished, shaking a tangle of brown hair out of his eyes only to have it fall back in again. "Or Maria'll have the skin off you."

Talk about pot calling kettle! Marco bit back a retort. He dug a bundle of herbs out of the box under the bed, noting wryly that Benito was far more respectful of Maria than Caesare, even now, after all Marco had told him. One of these days Benito was going to push Caesare Aldanto too far, and his awakening would be abrupt and rude. And probably involve any number of bruises.

"I'll be back," he promised, shoving the packets into his pack, huddling on his cotte and shrugging the pack strap over his shoulder. "And probably before Maria is in."

He slipped into the dark hallway, walking quietly out of habit, and eased the front door open so as not to wake Caesare. The last rays of the evening sun were not quite able to penetrate the clouds, and Venice of the bridges and waterways looked bleak, shabby and ill-used. There was snow coming to the Alps. Marco could smell it in the air and shivered inside his woolen shirt and canvas cloak. The grayed-out gloomy bleakness suited Marco down to his toe-nails and it was just dark enough that if he kept his head down and muffled in his scarf, it was unlikely he would be recognized. Foot traffic was light; what with the bitter wind blowing, anybody with cash was hiring gondolas even this early in the evening. That suited him too.

He'd almost made it down the water-stairs when somebody called his name. Recognizing the voice, he swore to himself, but stopped on the steps above the landing. Rowing to his night tie-up was Tonio della Sendoro—and clinging to Tonio's prow was a kid.

Marco sighed and padded down the last three stairs to wait for Tonio to toss him a cold, stiff line.

"*Ciao,* Tonio," he greeted the canaler, once he'd gotten the gondola tied. "Got another one for me?"

Tonio nodded, his face a comical mixture of relief and reluctance. "Her Papa says her ear hurts—she's been crying since yesterday and he can't get her to stop. Her name's Leonora."

No last name. Not that Marco was surprised. He rather doubted that Tonio was even telling the parents exactly *who* he was taking their sick kids to. They probably suspected Strega. That would be bad enough. But to take them to see one of Maria Garavelli's pet bridge-boys, who were probably thieves, or something worse, and were definitely going to come to no good end? The idea would have appalled them. They would have laughed at Tonio for the very suggestion.

The ragged little girl huddled on Tonio's halfdeck was still crying; the kind of monotonous half-exhausted sobbing that tore Marco's heart right out of his chest. He eased down onto the gondola in the over-cautious fashion of one not very used to being on a small boat, then slid along the worn boards and crouched beside her so that his face was level with hers.

"Come here, little one." He held out hand coaxingly. "It's all right, Leonora. I'm going to make it better."

She stopped crying, stared at him for a minute, then sidled over to him and didn't resist when he gathered her into his arms, trying to warm that thin little body with his own. Children trusted him. So did dogs.

He murmured nonsense at her while he gently felt along the line of her jaw and checked for fever. Relief washed over him when he found neither a swollen gland nor a temperature elevated beyond what he would expect in a kid who'd been crying in pain for a day or more. With every kid brought to him, he expected to find one too sick for his knowledge or experience to help. Then what would he do?

Ah, he knew what he would do. Tell Tonio the child needed real help—and if the parents couldn't afford it, tell him about Claudia and her Strega healer. And let the parents decide whether it was worth the risk of having Strega strings attached to their child's soul.

Or maybe kidnap the child and take it there himself, and take the damnation onto his own soul . . .

This one—like all the others so far, thank God—was an easy one. Infection. A scratch just inside the little ear gone septic. He went back up to his rooms and fetched some dead-nettle tea. He mixed it with a little of Tonio's grappa, poured into a spoon and heated it to just-bearable over Tonio's little boat stove. This he poured into Leonora's ear. She cried out briefly, but then was still. Then he heated a small pot of dead-nettle tea, along with a pinch of aromatic pine resin, scrounged from the timberyard.

He gave her a pebble. "Now, honey, you suck on this pebble, and sniff that steam up." Her nose was a bit stuffy, but the inhalation would clear that if he was right. The ear would drain and the pain would suddenly go. He and Tonio watched.

He could see it in her face—the sheer wonder of the moment when the pain went away. Looking at him like *he* was an angel. He blushed and his heart melted a bit more.

"Now," he said softly and mock-sternly, "you have to promise me something. When the wind blows and it's cold, you will keep your scarf tied around your ears good and tight, you hear? Otherwise your ear'll start to hurt again."

The tiny girl gazed at him from eyes so big they seemed to take up half of her tear-streaked face. "Don't got no scarf," she protested.

He sighed again, and reached under his coat collar to pull yet another of Benito's "souvenirs" off his own neck. That was the fourth one used so far—two gone for bandages and one as a sling. Benito must surely think he was *eating* the damned things—it was a good thing they weren't the silk ones Benito liked to sport; his brother would have strangled him in his sleep.

He tied the scarf under her chin, making sure both ears were covered. "*Now* you have. Promise?"

She nodded, then unexpectedly threw her arms around his neck and kissed him messily. He hugged her back, and she squirmed out of his grasp to go and crouch at Tonio's feet. He knew he was still blushing a little, but he was feeling better than he had all day, kind of warm inside. She was a little sweetie—a lot nicer than the last one, who'd kicked him. He got gingerly to his knees and edged carefully off the pitching boat onto solid land, tucking his chilled hands under his arms as soon as he got there.

Tonio cleared his throat, and Marco knew what was coming next.

"Dammit Tonio, I've said I won't take anything about a hundred times—and I damn sure won't take anything this time either. You folks haven't any more to spare than I do, and I haven't done a damn thing this kid's papa couldn't have done if he knew how!"

"But he didn't, did he—"

"So you tell him and he will." Marco set his chin stubbornly. "And don't you go bleating debts or imperiled souls at me either. There is nothing magical about this, and by the Lion of Saint Mark, even if there was, then surely Christ himself would have blessed it. He said 'Let the children come to me,' after all. I don't believe in counting favors. I do what I can. Let the accounting be set in God's hands."

"That's true enough, may be—" Tonio replied, just as stubbornly,

"—but this baby's papa *does* believe in the payment of debts. He may be poor, but he's proud and honest."

That just about described all the boatmen, caulkers and fishermen of Venice. Only the rich and the rogues had other standards. "Oh, hell—" Marco sighed, pulled the rope loose, and stood up holding it in both hands, braced against the tug of the sluggish water and the icy wind on the boat. "All right, I tell you what. If you people are so worried about debt, here's what you do. When there's a few lira to spare, have the people I've helped put it in some kind of common pot against the day when I *can't* help one of these children and they need a *real* chirurgeon. I suppose you might as well hold the pot, Tonio, since you're always the one bringing them here. If they do that, I figure we're even. *Si?*" That should solve two problems—theirs and his.

Tonio's face still looked stormy, but he must have reckoned that that was the only concession he was going to get out of Marco. "*Si,*" he agreed, after a long moment of stubborn silence.

He signaled to Marco to toss back the rope and poled back out into the current.

Marco headed back along the walkway, resuming his interrupted journey. His leather-soled boots made no sound on the damp wood as he kept to a warming trot. No bare feet in *this* weather, not for him or Benito—Aldanto had bought them boots when he caught them without foot-coverings. Another undeserved kindness.

Sounds were few above the wind; the occasional murmur of voices from above, the slap of waves on boats and buildings, the ever-present creaking of wood, canalers calling out to each other down on the water. Cold—God, it was cold. *Weather for sickness, that's for certain; in the swamp, down on the canals, weather for dying, too.* Winter would be bad this year, he thought.

Funny, this business with Tonio della Sendoro. It had started when Marco caught Rafael de Tomaso with a cut hand going septic and forced him to let Marco clean it out. Then de Tomaso had brought him a child with a bad case of the fever. Then Tonio had gotten into the act. Always children, though, never adults. Eleven, no, twelve of them so far. Marco couldn't resist a sick child—not even when they kicked or bit.

Soft heart to match my soft head.

No matter. Marco knew damned well he could no more see a

child in pain and walk on, without doing something about it, than he could stop breathing.

Well, one thing for sure, no matter how badly he'd messed things up with Caesare Aldanto, there were a dozen poor boat-people or fisher-folk babies he'd made a bit healthier.

From across the Canale di Cannaregio, on the Ghetto side, the three priests watched the boy trotting away. Then, their eyes followed the gondola as it made its way up the Canale and turned into a smaller canal which entered the heart of the Cannaregio sector of the city.

"That boy has become a bit of a blessing for this poor neighborhood," said Diego approvingly. "That's at least the seventh child I know of that he's given medical attention."

"Nine," grunted Pierre. "That I know of. Good treatment, too, by all accounts."

Eneko's expression was grim; not sharing any of the approval so evident in the faces of his companions. "He's also the same boy who brought that message to me from Caesare Aldanto. That despicable offer I told you about."

Pierre and Diego's eyes widened. "*Aldanto?*" choked Pierre. "Are you certain?" asked Diego.

Eneko nodded. "Quite certain. I was struck at the time, by the incongruity. Between the villainy of Aldanto and the boy's own face—the face of an angel, almost."

"But . . ." Pierre lapsed into silence, for a moment. Then: "I don't believe Aldanto is guilty of black magic, true enough. But I don't doubt he's guilty of almost any other crime. Treacherous to the core, by all accounts. A pure mercenary." He pointed a finger toward the distance into which the boy had disappeared. "Whereas he . . . He *refuses* to accept any payment, Eneko. I've spoken to that canaler myself. Tonio is his name."

"It just doesn't make sense," added Diego, shaking his head.

"No, it doesn't," mused Eneko. "Which is precisely what interests me the most. *Why* is such a boy working for such a man? Or—perhaps more important—why has such a man taken such a boy under his wing?" He cocked his head at his two companions. "Aldanto is indeed, as Pierre said, 'a pure mercenary.' So what is his mercenary reason in this instance?"

His two companions looked at each other. Pierre shrugged;

Diego sighed. "I suppose this means you want me to investigate something *else*."

Eneko chuckled. "I don't think it will be as bad as all that, Diego. If the boy is a healer—" Eneko pointed across the canal at the Cannaregio district. "You've met Father Mascoli. I introduced you to him just a few weeks ago. Ask him first. If the boy is as well known in this area as all that, as a lay doctor, Mascoli will know who he is."

"The Cannaregio," muttered the Castillian. "The Ghetto's reputation is bad, but overrated. There are other places in Cannaregio whose reputation is . . . not."

"I'll protect you," said Pierre stoutly. "From sin, of course. Footpads—you're on your own."

Eneko clucked. "The only danger you'll face in the Cannaregio is from cutpurses. And since neither of you has a purse . . ."

He ignored the glares coming his way. Insouciantly: "Righteousness, brothers. Always the best armor."

Chapter 32

Marco made good time across to Dorsoduro; he'd have at least an hour with Rafael before he had to head back. He was glad to get there; the overcast had given birth to flurries of cold rain, and his nose felt numb.

If Rafael was there—

The Al Caraveillo tavern was the likeliest spot to find him; Marco poked his head in the door and got hit in the face with the light and the noise. It was almost as bad as a physical blow after the chill gray of the canalside. It took him a moment to adjust to it.

But when he finally did, he breathed a prayer of thanks to the Saints—for at a table in the rear, book propped up in front of him and huge orange cat spread out like a rug on his lap, was a tall, thin dark-haired young man wearing an Accademia cotte.

"—so that's the whole mess," Marco concluded miserably. He slumped on his hard wooden chair, staring at his own clenched hands, surrounded by the clutter of artwork, books, and other paraphernalia of a student and artist's life that filled the tiny room that made up Rafael's lodgings. The lanky student across from him lounged on his unmade bed, chewing his lip thoughtfully.

Marco had laid out the whole story—saving only Aldanto's exact identity and what he was involved with. Rafael de Tomaso had simply been told that Aldanto was a man with enemies—a *lot* of enemies. That was enough for Rafael to add into his calculations, without his knowing enough for the information to be a danger to Caesare. At least de Tomaso hadn't laughed at him.

"You've got yourself a problem, all right," Rafael said finally, putting his hands behind his head and staring at the ceiling. "A bad one. The Dormas are rising in influence; rising fast, from what I hear. I'm almost certain that Petro Dorma is in the Council of Ten already. From the little I know, Angelina Dorma would be a very bad enemy for your friend to have. And if you go through with this charade, she'll find out eventually. When she does she will want *his* hide as much as yours. Her older brother Petro's a calm one, sure. Still, it *is* a family thing—and, like I said, Council of Ten. A Lord of the Nightwatch, for sure."

"I figured," Marco replied dismally.

"You weren't planning on trying to carry it off, were you?'

"For about five minutes, maybe," Marco admitted. "After that— dammit, Rafael, it isn't *right*, that's all I can say. It isn't fair, even if I *could* make it work."

Rafael de Tomaso smiled; a kindly smile, as if he were giving Marco credit for honesty. "How much of *your* hide are you willing to part with?"

The lump rose in Marco's throat, nearly choking his words. "All of it," he said at last. "She's going to hate me forever, no matter what happens. If there's a way to keep my friend out of it, I'll take it and take my lumps."

"You got some place you could go to get out of sight for a couple of weeks? Long enough to let things cool down?"

Marco thought, as best he could. Not Aldanto's place. Not the apartment in Cannaregio that he and Benito had shared; that would be the first place a searcher would look. Claudia and Valentina?

They'd take him in—no doubt of it. But Claudia was a Strega *and* a thief on top of that—Benito had confirmed that, all of it. The two singers had been Benito's protectors and mentors in his early days on his own, Claudia more than Valentina, but he knew most of what there was to know about both of them. Claudia had been "courting" Marco ever since she'd found out he wanted to be a doctor, dangling a secret Strega-run healer school in front of him. He was mightily afraid that his resolution not to get involved with any more religious or factional fanatics would crumble under the slightest pressure at this point. It would be such a logical move; cut ties to Caesare, get under the protection of somebody else, drop out of sight—and get his dream into the bargain.

So easy . . .

No! He wouldn't even think about it. "Easy" usually had strings attached that wouldn't show up until later. And what if the Strega used him to get at Caesare or Benito—or Maria and her boatmen friends?

The Jesolo marshes? Back into the muddy *velme* and hide in *barene*?

He gave that one a second thought and then a third. Maybe not such a bad notion. He could move a hide into old Gianni's territory, it might still be open with Gianni dead by Marco's knife. Even if it wasn't, no marsh-locos would fool with the man who'd killed Gianni. They'd leave him alone, maybe clear out altogether themselves. There were a fair number of food plants there, and some good fishing spots. It was cold, sure; but he could take blankets and medicine out with him. He could tough it out for two weeks or so. Maybe getting back to the basics of surviving would clear out his head.

"I think maybe I got a place," he answered Rafael slowly. "Why?"

"I think if I were you, this is what I'd do—and first thing is, you aren't going *tell* anybody anything; you're going to *write* to them—"

It was almost dawn. Benito was so dead asleep he didn't even stir when Marco slipped out of bed. Marco hadn't slept more than a few minutes all night, lying there in the bed with every muscle so tight with nerves that they were ready to cramp. He dressed quickly in the dark, putting on every bit of clothing he possessed here; not daring to light a lamp lest he wake Benito. His pack was back in the Cannaregio apartment, already made up with the clothing he'd left there and the blankets from that bed.

There were other things there, too; things he'd bought—a spare knife, a tinderbox, fishhooks and line, and lures. He'd been afraid to bring the pack here, lest somebody catch him at it and try to stop him.

The Jesolo marshes had been a really good notion—except that he hadn't any money to buy the gear he needed to survive. In the end he'd had to get back to their apartment in Cannaregio, retrieve his precious books—and sell them. He'd already spent all the money he had saved on the goods he'd traded with Sophia for herbs to treat Caesare's fever. His books were all he had left in the way of portable wealth. It had damn near broken his heart all over again to part with them. But this was his only choice. He couldn't live for weeks out there without supplies and cold-weather gear, not in wintertime. He knew that Chiano and Sophia would have stripped his hideout of everything useful once they were certain he wasn't likely to be coming back to the marsh.

And maybe he'd have to stay out there for longer than a couple of weeks. The more he'd thought about it last night, the more logical *that* seemed. He'd just about talked himself into staying out there—unless his plan worked; the *other* plan he'd thought of, lying in the dark last night—

Now he crept to the spare room, one careful, hushed step at a time. He had to get into Aldanto's medicine-chest for the last of what he needed.

He hated to steal, but he wasn't sure Sophia had been able to collect any more artemisia in the marshes, even if he'd had the money to pay for it, and Aldanto had enough to cure a dozen fevers—or to kill four men. Marco was glad there was a night-lamp left burning in the room, else he'd probably have broken something and roused the whole house. The herb was right out in front, in neat twists of paper. Marco knew exactly how many there were, since he'd weighed and made the twists himself. It was, he supposed, something he'd traded for. Still, Marco took half of them; neither Aldanto nor Maria was likely to need it, and Marco might very well before the winter was over. If the fever got him, he'd need it for sure. He stuffed the packets into his pocket, and stole out.

Now he crept quietly into the kitchen; ran his hands along the shelf until he found the old bread and a bit of cheese, then found the round, hard bulk of the wine carafe the same way. First thing that Aldanto did when he wandered downstairs in the morning was to take some watered wine, so that was where Marco's letter to him would go.

Dear Caesare; I am a Bigger Fool than you ever thought I was. I've gone and got Both of us into Trouble, it began, and went on from there. It had been a torture to write, and Marco wasn't entirely clear on what he'd put down. He'd fought down the ache in his gut and the swelling in his throat all through writing it, so it wasn't exactly a miracle of coherency. But it did lay out the whole sordid story, and finished by telling Caesare not to go looking for him. He rather doubted Caesare would want to waste the time looking for such a fool as he was, but—better assure him that Marco was going to be hidden where nobody was likely to be able to find him.

Maria's letter was shorter by about three pages; that was going to her cubbyhole at Giaccomo's. It occurred to him, belatedly, that she wasn't going to be able to read it anyway. But he owed her some explanation.

He wasn't going to leave a letter for Benito. Best not to.

Although it caused him a physical pain as sharp as Gianni's knife to do so, he left Angelina's letter folded up inside Caesare's under the wine carafe, so Caesare would be able to see for himself how Angelina had woven a fantasy around him.

His throat and stomach were hurting again, but he forced the bread and cheese down. He wouldn't be getting any more of *that* in the swamp. There was no way of keeping anything for more than a day or two in the marshes anyway. If it didn't go moldy it drew vermin. From now on anything he ate—not that food was real attractive at the moment—he'd have to catch or find it *when* he wanted to eat.

He'd oiled the hinges of the door last night; now he eased down the hallway, and slid back all of the locks and bolts as carefully as he could. He froze half a dozen times, agonizing over the slightest sound, and finally inched through the door, opened just enough so that he could slip through. The sharp-edged cold hit him hard, waking him completely. He closed the door and relocked it. He couldn't do the bolts of course, but at least the door was locked. He posted the key gently back under it. Then he went softly down the water-stairs and sneaked past old Minna's and Tonio's and Maria's empty gondolas all tied up at the bottom. The gondolas stayed silent, their occupants tucked up in all the blankets they owned. Except for Maria, who was tucked up with Caesare—

He stomach lurched. *Oh, Angelina!*

Now came the hardest part of all—

He knew Angelina would never be up this early; the *Case Vecchie* kept hours like Caesare's. He trotted down the wet walkways, watching carefully for slippery pools, as the sun began turning the edge of the sky a bloody red. No fog this morning, but it was as cold as Brunelli's heart, and there might be more rain or even sleet before the day was over. The wind was cutting, cold and bitter. There were a few hearty souls about, even this early: boatmen, folk on their way to work or coming home from it. The cold kept the stink down; the sharp breeze smelled mostly of smoke and wet wool.

Once he thought he saw Claudia's raven head with her bold red scarf tied about her hair to confine it—so he quickly chose another way. Claudia could be damnably persuasive when she wanted to be. And he didn't want to be talked out of the only honorable course he had left.

Dorma's doorkeeper wasn't even awake—thank the Lord. Marco managed to slip his sealed letter to Angelina into the hollow block she had shown him to leave her private *billets-doux* in. *Billets-doux* she thought had come from the fascinating, dangerous Caesare. This was no love letter. It was, however, five pages long—and ended with a poem so that she'd *believe* it really was him who had written the others.

Now she'd hate him forever. It couldn't be helped. It wasn't in agreement with Valdosta honor that he leave Caesare entangled in a lie, nor that he let Angelina continue to believe that same lie.

So why didn't he feel better?

Now to Cannaregio, for his pack, then Giaccomo's.

Lying staring into the dark, he'd made some hard decisions last night. Given all the trouble he'd caused him, the best thing he could do for Caesare Aldanto was to cut his ties with the man. *All* of his ties, including the job with the Ventuccios, so not even *they* could hold that over his head.

He sniffed in the cold, his eyes burning and watering—surely from the early-morning woodsmoke—and rubbed his eyes and nose across his sleeve.

Woodsmoke. Sure. Be honest with yourself, Marco Valdosta, even if you've lied to everyone else.

This was hurting more than he'd ever thought it would. For a little while he'd had a family. A weird family, but a family all the same. It hurt to cut loose.

And he *had* to cut loose; and do it before he managed to do something that couldn't be repaired.

Benito could still be useful to Caesare, and if he ever needed anything Marco could supply, Marco could send it surreptitiously through Benito. Honor could still be satisfied that way.

But he needed some way—if he was ever able to poke his nose back into the city—to keep himself housed and fed. And, maybe, maybe, save enough to sneak into the Accademia . . . perhaps with yet another changed name. If he could find some way to make enough money—

Medicinal herbs weren't all that could be found in the marshes, after all. The other things that were abundant enough were bones. And the way Marco figured it, if someone was superstitious enough to want relics or charms, well, *he* might as well get the benefit of the money being thrown away. He only knew of one person, though, who might know where he could safely dispose of "smuggled" "relics."

Giaccomo. Who scared the hell out of him.

Giaccomo's was just open; Marco went up to the front porch and through the door, open and aboveboard. He walked, barefoot because he'd stowed his socks and boots in his pack, silently and oh-so-carefully across the wooden expanse of floor. He gave over Maria's sealed letter, then asked of the man behind the bar in a soft and *very* respectful voice, if Milord Giaccomo might be willing to talk with him on business. Jeppo left the bar in the care of one of the other helpers and vanished briefly. As it happened, Milord Giaccomo evidently hadn't gone to bed yet—and was apparently willing to see the frequent bearer of so much of Aldanto's coin. Jeppo returned and directed Marco with a silent jerk of his thumb. The office.

The door to the office was next to the bar. Facing Giaccomo scared the liver out of him; to sit quietly at Giaccomo's invitation all alone in the cluttered cubbyhole while the dim gray light smudged the dirty windowpanes, and stammer out his offer, took all of the courage he had left. Giaccomo sat behind his desk, tall, balding—and *big*, most of it not fat—and looked at him hard and appraisingly, melting away the last of Marco's bravery.

"You want to sell relics, huh?" he asked Marco bluntly. "Why?"

Marco could hardly think under that cold, cold stare—he stammered something about needing a lot of money, and didn't elaborate.

"What?"

"Saints b-bones. Saint Theodoro," Marco stuttered. "Saint's bones" were fairly common—a cure and a protection for everything from pox to plague. Caesare had once said that it was a good thing that the saints had such numerous and big bones, the rate the city used them. "And . . . and some fragments of Saint Gerado's skull . . ." Skull fragments were more precious. But still quite commonplace.

"That won't get you much money in a hurry." Giaccomo continued to stare at him, jaw clamping shut on each word, eyes murky.

"Don't need it in a hurry. Just need to put it t-together. I can get you Strega herbs and charms, also."

"Huh." The way the big man kept staring at him, Marco imagined he could see all the way through him. He wondered what Giaccomo was thinking; the man's opaque eyes didn't reveal even a hint of his thoughts.

"Well, I don't deal magic, Christian or otherwise."

"Oh." Marco's plan for independence—and the Accademia— collapsed. "I'm sorry to have bothered you, milord. I guess it wasn't too good a notion."

He rose, awkwardly, and started for the door.

"Boy—"

Marco turned, a thread of fear down his spine. Giaccomo wasn't anybody to trifle with. He wondered if he'd passed the invisible bounds beyond which Giaccomo allowed no one he dealt with to trespass. Giaccomo had a way of dealing with trouble, or potential trouble. It ended in the canal, with a rock tied to one ankle. Splash, gone. He wondered if he looked as deathly white as he felt.

"Don't you go making that offer anywhere else—"

Marco gulped. He wasn't quite sure what the look on Giaccomo's face meant, but he thought he'd better answer with the truth. Or part of it.

"I w-wasn't going to, milord." he replied. "You were the only one. I got more sense than to deal with anybody but you. Milord, I got to be going, please, milord. You likely won't be seeing me again. Ever. That's a promise."

He meant that. It would be better for everybody at this point if he went back to the swamp and stayed there. Ties cut clean.

Giaccomo looked—funny. His eyebrows were up near where his hairline used to be. The big man looked a little confused. And oddly troubled. But he let him go, with only: "The town is full of spies, boy. Agents for the Council of Ten, the Servants of the Trinity, and even the Grand Metropolitan in Rome. This sort of business will get you burned at the stake for witchcraft, or beheaded for grave robbing . . . If you're lucky. The brethren who run the real thing . . ."

He shook his head. "Go. You stay out of it, boy. Especially with these magical murders happening. Everyone from the Church to the Doge wants to catch someone. Any scapegoat will do. That's how it works."

Chapter 33

"That's the fifth murder," said the grim-faced Brother Uriel. "That we know of. This cannot be allowed to go on. We must find the guilty party."

Erik dragged his attention from the burned, shriveled remains of the body on the floor and stared at the monk. Of all the company of Servants of the Holy Trinity in Venice, Uriel was the one Erik found the most acceptable. Nobody could claim to actually *like* Brother Uriel. But you had to respect him. He was rigid and intolerant, yes. But also scrupulous, and one of the few Servants of the Holy Trinity who seemed to care little for hierarchy. He was certainly not one of Abbot Sachs's favorites. It seemed to make no difference to Uriel.

Manfred yawned and stretched. It was predawn. They—as a group—were only here together because they, and the guard, were the only ones who had not been asleep when the Schiopettieri runner came in. Erik had been drilling with Manfred. Brother Uriel had been having a fasting vigil in the chapel for some obscure saint. The Schiopettieri had sent a boat for them. But they were far, far too late.

Uriel began prayers for the soul of the departed. Erik stepped back and examined the room. There was a small, still hot, furnace. Many tools. Small delicate tools. "What is this place?" he asked of the woman who had called out the Schiopettieri. She was still standing, wringing her hands.

"It's . . . it's Signor Mantelli's workshop." She pointed weakly at the burned crisp on the stone-flagged floor. "He . . . he was a goldsmith."

"He lived here?" asked a tall, slim elegant man who, though he wore the signs of hasty dressing, also wore the air of command. The man had just arrived. From his appearance, Erik suspected he was one of the Lords of the Nightwatch—and was *not* pleased to find Knights and a Servant of the Holy Trinity there ahead of him.

The woman bowed respectfully. Whoever the man was, he commanded both respect and fear from her. "Upstairs, Lord Calenti. I . . . I was housekeeper to him." A tear began to trickle down her cheek. "I can't believe it. I just can't believe it. And I never had a chance to tell him that I was sorry. . . ."

The respectfully addressed lord pounced on this. "For what, signora?"

She wrung her hands. "It was a silly thing, Your Honor. He shouted at me because he said I'd stolen a cap of his. A knitted one. It was his favorite. I would never steal, Your Honor. On my father's grave, I swear it! But he was angry. And I was angry. I said . . . many harsh things. He was good man even if he did drink too much."

The Venetian lord patted her shoulder. "There, there, signora. We all say things we afterward regret. I think you should go upstairs and have a glass of your late master's wine. He has family here?"

She shook her head. "No, Your Honor. He is—was—from Padua."

The Venetian lord nodded, and gently guided her to the door.

When it had closed firmly behind her, he turned to the two Schiopettieri standing by the entrance. "Seal this place. Allow no one in, and detain all those who try. They will have to be questioned."

The lord turned to Erik. "Pardon me, Sir Knight. This has now become a matter for the Republic. When the good monk has finished his prayers, I must ask you to leave. To be frank, I am not quite sure why you were summoned in the first place."

Because Abbot Sachs has been spreading bribes among the Schiopettieri, thought Erik sourly. But he saw no reason to contest the matter with more than a shrug. "It seems a bit late for us to do anything, anyway. As soon as Brother Uriel has finished his devotions, we'll go. But I suspect Abbot Sachs will want to come and exorcise and bless the place as well as scour it for witch-sign."

Lord Calenti nodded. "He may apply to me."

That's going to go down really well, thought Erik. But he said nothing. It was left to Manfred to ask the questions starting to trouble Erik. "Lord Calenti. Just what was this man doing that's worrying you? Other than bursting into flames and doing a lot of screaming, that is."

The tall, slim Venetian's eyes narrowed. He looked at the two of them very carefully, obviously considering things. He must have decided that telling them was either innocuous . . . or might carry a message to the people who were involved that he was closing in on them. "Treason," he said grimly, pointing to the workbench and an open mold. "He was a coiner."

At this point, Brother Uriel stood up. "I am finished."

The Venetian lord nodded. "His soul is at rest." The way he said it sounded as if he regretted the fact.

Brother Uriel turned on him. "His soul is in torment! Can you not feel the pain? Something evil, evil beyond your comprehension devoured his very life." The monk shuddered. "The last time I felt the uncontained taint of this much evil was when we clashed with the forces of Lithuania outside Grudziadz. There is great evil afoot in your city."

"I will leave you to deal with matters of the spirit," said the Venetian stiffly. "The Republic must deal with secular affairs. Please leave now."

Lord Calenti looked now as if he regretted telling them anything about the victim, and motioned to the Schiopettieri to see them out.

The dawn was just blushing a translucent cloud-framed sky when they stepped out. Obviously the courtesy of a vessel was not going to be offered to them. In the distance a bell began sound.

Uriel sighed. "Another mess that the Servants of the Trinity are ill-able to deal with. I never though it possible . . . but I wish I was back in the marshes and forests, facing the evils of the Grand Duke of Lithuania's minions—instead of being in this misbegotten and supposedly Christian city. At least there it was clear who our enemies were."

Manfred looked speculatively at the stiff, upright monk. The man was plainly distressed by what he'd encountered. "Just what is going on here, Brother?" he asked. "Why are we even involved here in Venice?"

Brother Uriel shook his head. "You had better ask Father Sachs that," he said heavily. "I am not privy to the inner councils of my order, or yours. I only know that the scryers, including Sister Ursula, have by means of their holy magics foreseen that we have some role to play here in Venice. I do not know why my own abbot sent me to join Abbot Sachs's men. I only know that great evil is afoot in this city. The abbot may claim there is witchcraft everywhere in Venice. I only know what my eyes have seen and my spirit felt."

Erik scowled. "I can understand the Servants of the Holy Trinity. But why the Knights? We are the militant order. Keeping us sitting here is a waste of military power, never mind the fact that we don't really have a clear reason to be staying on at all."

Uriel looked grim. "We have orders to stay until the evil is rooted out. As long as need be. Those orders are not for us to question."

"Maybe not—but with people being killed like this the whole town is a powder keg. Likely to blow up beneath us. And we certainly don't seem to have reduced the level of evil here."

Brother Uriel took a deep breath of the morning air. "True. Look, there is a church over there. I have need of a few moments in prayer and silence. I will return later." He walked off with long determined strides.

Manfred stretched. "Well. That just leaves you and me. How about we walk and take some air, and maybe a sop of new bread and a glass of wine. This day seems pretty old already."

Erik nodded. "Why must they keep on ringing that bell? Every morning it rings for at least half an hour."

"The Marangona," said Manfred. "It's supposed to get the workers to the Arsenal."

"Why? Do they stop ringing it when they all get there?" asked Erik irritably. He was feeling a need to get back to his roots. To the clean open air of Iceland or Vinland. This city with all its great buildings seemed cramped and oppressive. "And what was all that excitement from that Venetian lord about?"

Manfred shook his head. "Intrigue, Erik. Italian intrigue, by Venetians who are the masters of it."

There was an open tavern. The two went in. Manfred ordered wine and flaps of the local bread, in what was, day-by-day, becoming better Italian. Erik had little doubt where he was learning it from. But, on the other hand, at least Francesca was safer than any random street-women that Manfred might have amused himself with. Erik found it awkward, owing someone he should be protecting Manfred from, for their lives. They walked back outside and stood in the chilly morning. The promised sun failed them. But the crisp air off the sea was clean.

"I don't understand about the intrigue, Manfred."

Manfred grinned. "You wouldn't. You understand battle, Erik. This is something else." He took a deep pull from the wine goblet. "This is about what really makes treason happen."

Eric shook his head. "Treason . . . Loyalty? Idealism? Ambition?"

Manfred grinned. "Ignorant Icelander. Money, of course."

Erik grimaced.

"It's like this," Manfred explained. "The Venetians know that money and treason go hand-in-hand. They also know that you can't spend anything in Venice except ducats."

Erik shrugged. "Even trading with the *skraelings* we use them. They like the hole in the middle because they can string them like beads."

"Uh huh. The mostly widely used coin with the purest gold in Europe. Even the best from the imperial mint at Mainz is not as good. The same coin you use trading in Vinland . . . except here it has no hole in it." Manfred pulled out a coin. "See. If you're a foreign trader, the bankers at the foot of the Rialto bridge won't release your coin until your harbor tax is paid. The hole punched out. Any Venetian must on the order of the Doge exchange holed coins for entire ones. On which they pay tax. You can't spend foreign coin in Venice without it going through the bankers and the *Capi di Contrada*—their tax collectors. And the Doge's council keeps track of foreign money coming in. They have a good idea of just what is happening by the flow of money. That's why a coiner is a problem. He can melt pure Venetian gold and recast it without the hole."

Erik thought it through. "You could bring in goods, or offer bills of exchange."

"True. And you can bet the Doge's council watches those too. I suppose jewelry might offer a gap. But money is what's usually wanted. Hard cash. Money for weapons. Money for bribes. Money to reward adherents."

Erik looked askance at Manfred. "How do you know this?"

Manfred grinned. "Francesca. We talk sometimes too, you know. Quite a bit, actually. She's a very clever woman. I was thinking of passing this on to Charles Fredrik. Come on, drink up. We can stop at Casa Louise on the way. I want to tell her about all of this."

Chapter 34

The marsh and the wind swallowed up sound, and the rushes closed them almost into a small room, which was just as well. Chiano howled with laughter, his eyes vanishing in his wrinkles; Marco prayed at that moment that lightning would hit him and reduce him to cinder. It would hurt a lot less than what he was feeling now. He tucked his cold, wet feet under him, huddled under his cotte, and wished he was on the moon. Or dead. Or something.

"Shut up, ye old *bastardo*—" Sophia scolded sharply, her face crinkling up in anger as she pushed a stray bit of gray hair under her knitted cap; Marco had brought her that the last time he'd come. "Have some pity on the boy. Maybe it's baby-love, but it hurts all th' same—and a young one ain't never been hurt that bad before." She turned to Marco, huddled on one corner of the raft. "Marco-lad, don't ye let him get to ye. I ain't saying ye did right t' leave—but I ain't sayn' ye did wrong neither."

Marco made a helpless gesture. To *these* two, his protectors and friends, he could tell everything—and he had. It had lessened some of the burden, at least until Chiano had started laughing at him. "I—Sophia, after the mess I got him in, I *can't* face Caesare, and I can't keep on being a burden to him, either."

"I thought you was working for the *Casa* Ventuccio. Real work, I mean, not make-work."

"I was."

"That don't sound much like being a burden t' me."

"I—" He hadn't thought of it quite that way. Sure, he and Benito

326

had been living on Aldanto's bounty lately, but they'd been keeping watch over him while he was sick. *And* helping to get him out of the tangle that illness had put him in. And it had been his savings and Maria's that had bought part of the medicine that had kept Caesare alive. He'd bankrupted himself for Caesare's sake, and hadn't grudged it. He'd lost several more weeks' salary too, staying with Caesare to watch him and watch out for him, and hadn't grudged that either. Maybe he *had* been pulling his own weight.

"And who's a-going take care of them sick canaler kids if ye're hiding out here?"

That was one thing he hadn't thought of. Not likely Tonio would take them to some strange Strega—Marco was risk enough.

"Don' ye go slamming no doors behind ye," Sophia admonished him gently. "Now, getting out of sight 'til that aristo girl can forget your face, that's no bad notion. But staying here? No, Marco-lad; ye don't belong out here. Stay just long enough to get your head straight—then ye go back, an' take yer licks from that Caesare fellow. Ye learned before, ye can't run from trouble."

Sophia was right. That was *exactly* what he'd been trying to do—he'd been trying to run from all his troubles, and rationalizing the running.

"Yes, milady," Marco said humbly, feeling lower than a swan's tail.

She shoved his shoulder; but not in an unkindly fashion, "Get along with ye! Milady! Huh!" She snickered, then turned businesslike. "Where ye going park your raft?"

"I figured at the edge of Gianni's old territory, right by the path near that big hummock with the patch of thatch-rush growing out of it."

"Good enough. Get on with it. We'll keep an eye out for ye."

Chiano waited until Marco was off down the trail and into the reeds; out of sight and hearing. Then he slipped off the raft onto one of the "secret paths" of firm ground that wound all through the swamp. He generally moored both his raft and Sophia's up against one of these strips of "solid" earth—they weren't really *visible* since most of them were usually covered in water about a handspan deep.

"Where ye goin'?" Sophia asked sharply.

"Going see to our guest," Chiano replied. She shut up at that;

shut up and just watched him with caution. Chiano had changed in the past months.

Yes, indeed, he had. Or rather, begun acting more like the person he really was—ever since the news of Gino Despini's death. The more news that trickled out of Venice, the more he was allowing the cloak of deception to slip. From his mind even more than from the minds of others.

He balanced his way along the narrow, water-covered trails, so used to following them he did it unconsciously, so used to the cold water he never noticed his numb feet. Yes, Chiano had been changing.

For the first time in years he was himself—Luciano Marina. *Dottore* Marina. Strega Grand Master. Grimas.

Fool Grand Master! Beaten, nearly dead. Fleeing for his life. Wounded and damaged. Even his mind confused, abused and lost . . . in that conflict. He still didn't know who had done it, or why—was afraid to know, in truth.

He'd ended up in the marshes and he'd survived. Barely. Perhaps his magical skills had helped. Perhaps the Goddess had held her hand over him, despite his pride and foolishness, as he wandered amnesiac for months among the other loco in the Jesolo. That had been—long ago. It had taken time for the Strega master to begin to return; humbled but alive.

And when he had, then he'd cursed the fate that left him so stripped of all position, possessions, and contacts as to have to *stay* here. He'd joined up with Sophia some time before Marco had come to them; how much time, he wasn't sure. His memory of that period was . . . vague.

Sophia'd had the gift of healing that he lacked, though he had the knowledge. Together, they'd formed the only source for medicine the swamp folk knew, and he'd done his best to follow the healing path among the crazed and the impoverished losers who lived here.

And now . . . well, perhaps she who was Hecate, Artemis, and Ishtar needed him back. There was a yearning to go back. His position both in the Accademia and Marciana Library had brought prestige, and power. But most of all he yearned for the books.

And—he had learned a great deal. Humility, for one. But also, the need for greater stringency in the service of the Goddess. The

Dottore Marina he remembered had been too vain; yet, also, not proud enough. Too peacock *soft.*

His mind turned to the boy. The boy did not even begin to realize he bore the mark of the winged lion, which had been obvious to Luciano's Strega-trained eye from the moment the boy had stumbled into their lives. Well, the guardian of the lagoons and marshes who had welcomed the gentle Saint Mark was ever so in its choices. They were good vessels. He had to admit that he, Luciano Marina, was a flawed vessel. Still . . . The boy had come back here, and he carried with him the feeling of danger. Danger and darkness far greater than could be linked to one life or death. But Luciano also felt the potential for something else.

Luciano approached the islet cautiously through the mist, making no sound in the water; he'd left Harrow trancing-out on the mushrooms he'd fed to him.

His caution was needless; Harrow was deaf and blind to everything around him. Except Luciano's voice, and magic.

Harrow was having another vision. This one was, like the others, beginning with a face; a woman's face. She started out young, then flickered from girl to woman to crone and back again. It was the Goddess, of course. She had come to instruct him again. Harrow felt both exalted and humbled; and excited, with the kind of near-sexual excitement he'd felt only when he'd completed an assignment for Duke Visconti. But he wasn't supposed to be thinking of that. He was supposed to be making himself worthy to be the vessel of the Goddess.

"Harrow—" said the Goddess, her hollow, echoing voice riveting his attention upon her. "You have much to atone for. Are you ready?"

"Yes," replied Harrow thinly, bowing his head as her eyes became too bright to look upon. Those eyes—they seemed to see right into the core of him.

"So let it be."

There was a sound like a great wind, and Harrow was alone in the dark.

Or was he? No—no, there was someone coming. Or forming rather, out of the dark and the mist. Another woman.

For a moment he thought it might be another avatar of the

Goddess. Then with a chill of real fear he recognized her. Lorendana Valdosta—once a Montagnard agent herself and dead at the hands of the Visconti's assassins these five years gone. He knew she was dead, and for a certainty. He'd been there when Aleri had given the order; and Bespi himself had slid in the blade while Lorendana's new lover Aldanto held her silent and immobile.

She had been the key Montagnard information-drop in Venice, but she had also been loose-tongued and incredibly reckless. Never less so, Bespi had realized later, than when she'd personally insulted Duke Filippo Visconti by spurning his advances. That knowledge had been the thing, more than any other, which had finally crystallized Bespi's growing disillusionment with the Milanese. He had uncaringly killed a woman for being—so he'd been told—a danger to the cause. The knowledge that he'd actually killed her for no more reason than the duke's personal disgruntlement, when it finally came to him, had been . . . unbearable. He'd realized then that he'd been as gullible as the woman he'd murdered.

She didn't look too gullible now—

"Bespi," a voice said . . . seemingly inside his head. "*I see you—*"

He blocked his ears, but it did no good. The ghostly voice cut right through him; the almond eyes did the same. She was stark-naked, her well-formed ivory flesh floating in a cloud of smoke and fog and midnight-black hair, obliquely slanted black eyes cold as the grave—she aroused no desire with her weird nudity; he'd never wanted a woman *less.*

Bespi. You carry my curse. Do you wish to be free of it?

A low moan came from his throat.

My curse shall follow you wherever you go. Her eyes grew until they filled his entire field of vision, black and like looking into hell. He felt ghostly hands running down his arms, leaving chill trails behind them. *When you sleep, I shall be there—waiting. When you wake, I shall follow; in all your comings, in all your goings, I shall be one step behind you, making you careless, making you nervous, until one day you will make a mistake—then my fingers will close about your throat—*

"Wait!" he yelled. Panic snatched at him now. Dread he had never felt in dealing with the living, or the soon-to-be-dead, closed around his heart and squeezed it like an invisible hand reaching through his chest-wall. He panted. Whimpered . . . "I'll do anything you want!"

The eyes receded and again she floated before him in her cloud of smoke and hair and magic. *Then guard my sons.*

That caught him off guard. "Huh?" he replied stupidly, unable to fathom the puzzle.

My sons live, Harrow. Bespi who was. Guard them. Guard them well. Keep them from harm. Keep the Montagnards from their throats. Only then my curse will leave you.

"I don't—I mean I don't even know what they look like. How . . . how do I find them!"

There—she pointed and something began forming out of the smoke and the dark beside her. The foggy image of an adolescent— sixteen, seventeen, maybe. A dead ringer for Lorendana. *That is Marco.*

Bespi/Harrow gasped as he recognized the boy. The one who had killed Gianni! The boy with the great *reasons!* Harrow could now understand why he had been witness to the sight.

And there—

Beside the first, a boy about two years younger; Carlo Sforza as a kid.

That is Benito. Guard them, Harrow. Your life on it, or you will carry my curse forever.

He had barely sworn to it, when she faded away and his grasp on consciousness went with her.

Luciano was well pleased with himself. That had been one of the better vision-quests he'd sent Harrow on. The former assassin hadn't fought him, he had responded beautifully to all the suggestions. He hoped the sending of Marco's brother was right. He'd only seen the boy once, but somehow it had seemed a good touch. These were just small magics, true. But he did not dare to try greater magic than this. Not without calling the sort of attention that he didn't want onto himself.

Harrow came around gradually. He wasn't a particularly pretty sight, with half his head scarred and the rest of him splotchy with burned skin. He coughed a good deal too: a gift from the smoke and the water he'd breathed in. But he was functional; indeed, he'd healed better and faster than Luciano had thought likely. The new vessel of the Goddess sat up slowly, uncurling from his nest of reeds and rags and old blankets. He blinked at the sun, and then at Luciano, his dilated eyes not focusing properly.

"Well?" asked Luciano.

"I got—a thing—I got to do," the man said through stiff lips, eyes still hazed with the drug.

"The Goddess gave you a task, huh?"

"But I don't—I don't—I got to take care of a couple of children—" His pupils were still dilated, but there was a certain despair in his voice. Luciano kept his satisfaction shuttered behind his own stony expression as he crouched down next to Harrow in the reeds.

"So?"

"But—how the hell am I going find her children?"

"*What* children? Whose children?"

"Valdosta. Marco and Benito Valdosta." If Harrow was confused about why the *Goddess* would be concerned over the welfare of Lorendana's two children, he wasn't showing it. But then Harrow had never been strong on logic. "How the hell am I going to find them?"

Luciano spread his arms wide with his hands palm-upwards and looked to the sky, taking on dignity and power as he deepened his voice. This was the part he played the best— He knew, thanks to another very minor piece of magic, that the former Montagnard assassin now saw him haloed in a haze of dim white light. Every time he took that particular pose, Harrow would see him glowing with the power of the Goddess. "Praise be the Goddess. Blessed are the vessels of her will. Her ways are beyond all mortal understanding."

He lowered his eyes to meet Harrow's. "She has you in Her plan, Harrow; She's had you there from the start of the world. She weaves the threads of destiny on her loom! Marco Valdosta is right here, Harrow; in the swamp. He's hiding out, an' he's scared. He damn-well needs protecting; he's a good child and this here is a bad place. But he's nervous and he's touchy; he won't let nobody near him, except them as he knows, like me and Sophia. You want to watch over him, fine. That's the Goddess's will. But if you show yourself, he'll run, I can promise that. If he even *guesses* you're there, he'll run. You want to keep him from running further and right into more trouble, you stay right out of sight."

As Harrow nodded understanding, Luciano rose and stepped off the islet into the knee-deep murky water of the swamp. Harrow followed, showing no more discomfort than Luciano.

"Come on, then—I'll show you where to keep watch on him without him knowing you're there."

Marco's hands ached with the cold as he worked without really thinking about what he was doing. He was trying to hold his mind in a kind of numb limbo, as numb as the rest of him was getting. He was doing his best to avoid thinking, to just exist. The cold and the damp were making his nose run and the slap of water and the hushing of wind in the reeds and the little sounds he was making were punctuated by his sniffles.

His raft and hideout had been where he'd left them—and as he'd expected—they'd been stripped. The hidey was still in surprisingly good shape, all things considered. Marco was grateful. He hadn't had much other good luck lately.

Even with the water level in the swamp at high water, it had been cruel, hard work to pole the raft out of his old territory and into Gianni's.

Gianni had ruled one of the best territories in the marsh. There was an unobstructed view of the city across the water and a nice stock of food plants as well as two really good fishing holes and a couple of solid islets. Marco's arms and back were screaming with pain before he got his home to its new location and, if he hadn't been working, he'd have been three-quarters frozen. As it was he was soaked to the skin and glad of the change of dry clothes in his pack. He had moored the raft up against the islet. With the camouflaging hideout over it, it would look like an extension of the island.

The sun was a dim, gray disk above the horizon when he'd gotten set up properly. Despite the cold, he'd been sweating with exertion; even his feet were almost warm. He'd been up since before dawn and by now it seemed as if it should be nearly nightfall, not barely morning.

From the islet he gathered rushes and sedge to weatherproof the hideout against the winter rains and winds. Then it was nothing but drudge-work. Crouch over the framework and interlace the vegetation into it. Grass, then sedge, then reeds, then grass again until it was an untidy but relatively windproof mound. With only his hands moving, evening coming on and the wind chilling him, he'd lost all the heat he'd gained by the time he was ready to thread new tall reeds into the top of the bushy hammock to renew its disguise. It was well towards full darkness when he'd finished to his satisfaction.

He was exhausted and cold all the way through, still soaked to the skin and more than ready for the sleep he'd lost last night. But he hadn't forgotten his old lessons. He made more trips to the center of the islet for old dry grasses, stuffing the cavity beneath the hideout with them. He crawled under the basketlike hideout and stripped, putting his soggy clothing between the "mattress" of dry grasses and his bottom blanket, to dry while he slept. Then he curled up into his grass-and-blanket nest to shiver himself to almost-warmth, then sleep the sleep of the utterly exhausted. It was a far cry from the cozy bed he'd left in Aldanto's apartment. If he hadn't been so cold and tired, he might have cried himself to sleep.

As he returned to his own islet, wading through the reeds, Luciano did not notice the sudden swirl in the nearby deep water, as if a large fish had been attacked by a larger and was making a desperate escape. Nor did he notice the undine, a short time later, slowly raising her head above water and studying him as he made his way back to the camp he shared with Sophia.

A small streak of blood dripped from the undine's sharp-toothed mouth. The mouth gaped wide, expressing satisfaction. Then the undine slid beneath the surface of the water and was gone.

Chapter 35

When the shaman's human form had returned sufficiently to enable him to speak, the grand duke leaned forward from his throne and touched the shoulder of the man squatting before him. Then, brought the fingers to his heavy lips and tasted the water which soaked the shaman's fur cloak. The taste was that of the stinking waters of the Jesolo marshes; that, and some blood.

"Well?"

The grand duke's shaman shook his head. The gesture was not one of uncertainty; it was one of fear. The man's lips were trembling.

"It is dangerous, lord. The Strega is not powerful, but he knows a great deal. Even now. And so long as he remains in the Jesolo, he has protectors." The shaman winced, rubbing his shoulder. As always, the shape-change had healed the wound, but the pain lingered. The undine's teeth had been sharp and jagged.

"The priest? Did you find him? I need to know where he goes when he leaves his quarters."

The shaman hesitated; tried to control his trembling lips. This question was far more dangerous than any undine. "I sensed him, lord, yes. Impossible not to, anywhere in Venice. Even in the marshes, I could sense him. Though not strongly. His presence is very strong anywhere in the vicinity of the Ghetto."

The shaman paused, hoping that answer would satisfy his master. He kept his eyes lowered, his shoulders hunched under the heavy cloak. At all costs, he wished to avoid the grand duke's gaze. Jagiellon's eyes were . . . frightening.

"Do not annoy me, slave. Or I will send you back into the forests of Karelen with your shape-changing powers severely stunted. Difficult to be a shaman without a hide. I will eat your skin."

The shaman was frozen, for a moment. The grand duke's threat was not an idle one; not in the least. The shaman had seen his master eat a retainer's skin thrice before. The first time, the skin had belonged to the shaman's predecessor. The grand duke had required the shaman to taste the meal first, before Jagiellon devoured the remainder, on the off chance that a fanatic might have poisoned his own skin before displeasing the ruler of Lithuania with his incompetence.

"It is *dangerous*, lord," whined the shaman. "For you as much as me. The priest is much less knowledgeable than the Strega, but— he is very strong. Very strong!" The shaman rubbed his temples with both hands; brackish water soaked through the fingers. "It hurt my head just being near him."

A massive hand seized the shaman's shaggy hair and jerked his head up. "*Look at me.*"

Despite his terror, the shaman dared not disobey. For all that he desperately desired to close his eyes, he met the grand duke's stare.

The moment lasted for . . . the shaman knew not how long. It seemed endless. But, eventually, the grand duke relinquished his iron grip and allowed the shaman's head to sag forward.

"I will tolerate your cowardice. For the moment. There is some truth to what you say. The priest is, indeed, very strong."

The grand duke's huge hands tightened on the armrests of his throne. He swiveled his massive head and stared at the window facing to the south. As was true of all the windows in Jagiellon's private chambers, this one was covered with heavy drapes. The drapes, dark red against the dark brown wooden walls, gave the room an almost funereal atmosphere.

"I have already punished those who did not prevent his mission to Venice," said the grand duke, so softly it almost seemed as if he were speaking to himself. "Intolerable incompetence. The man himself asked leave to go to the Holy Land; and the Grand Metropolitan is a weakling. It should have been easy to arrange."

The shaman relaxed a bit. As was always true with Jagiellon's underlings, the news of another's punishment came as a great relief. The grand duke needed punishment in his diet as much as food, and he ate both in prodigious quantities. Still, he was not exactly a glutton. One or two Lithuanian agents in Rome dead—most likely by poison or knife; possibly by magic—meant less chance of a shaman's skin being fried in Vilna.

The shaman even made so bold as to speak. "For all his strength, lord, the priest is groping in the dark. Best to leave him there, until it is too late. Whereas, if you strike at him . . . and the thing is mishandled or goes awry . . ."

Ensconced in his heavy robes of office, the body of the grand duke filled the chair to overflowing. When the body shifted, as it did now, the sturdy piece of furniture creaked alarmingly.

With as much alarm, if not more, the shaman studied that shifting form surreptitiously, from under lowered eyelids. Suggesting that the grand duke might be contemplating error, as the shaman was now doing, was risky.

The shaman was relieved to see that the shifting seemed more a matter of a heavy body adjusting its weight than of one gathering itself for the attack. The grand duke's obesity, as the shaman had many occasions to recall, was deceptive. Beneath the rolls of fat lay slabs of muscle whose power went beyond the human. And while Jagiellon was now a great sorcerer in his own right, the ruler of Lithuania was partial to more physical means of expressing his displeasure. As a prince, before the fat which came upon his body after the *change*, Jagiellon had been a famous warrior.

"Um." Jagiellon said no more than that, for a few minutes. Throughout that time, the shaman squatted silently, unmoving, his eyes hidden under the lowered brow and the great mane of shaggy hair. Trying to make himself as inconspicuous as possible.

"You may be right," mused the grand duke, eventually. "It is certainly true that when I let the Woden escape, the results were . . . unfortunate. I had thought the Lion's slumber to be a heavier thing."

The shaman dared to speak again. "That was the strength of the priest at work, Lord. He is *dangerous*."

"Yes." Again, silence. "Impervious to seduction also, it seems. I had hopes for that tool, but she is proving less useful than desired."

There was a slight edge to the last words. From long experience, the shaman knew that a death sentence had just been passed. He felt a small regret. The tool in question was as beautiful as she was evasive. Thus far, unlike the other female in Venice, she had managed to retain her own soul. But the shaman knew it would have been only a matter of time before Jagiellon broke her to his will. After which, as was his way, he would allow his chief underlings to enjoy the woman.

But the regret was small, and fleeting. There would be other beautiful women. Being in service to Jagiellon was as rewarding as it was perilous.

Still . . .

"She may be of use yet, Lord," murmured the shaman. "If she has failed in that task, she has succeeded in many others."

Again, the great body shifted; and, again, the shaman grew tense. But, again, it was simply an obese ruler's discomfort.

"True. We will see. In the meanwhile, I have decided you are correct. We will continue the murders, but keep the Woden on a tight leash. And make no attempt, for the moment, to remove either the mage or the priest. Time is on my side, after all. Venice grows more ragged by the day. So long as the priest remains ignorant and the mage remains too terrified to act . . . good enough."

The grand duke planted his hands on the arm rests of the chair and heaved his great, gross body erect. "Leave now."

The shaman bobbed his head, rose, and scuttled from the room. He left behind him a trail of foul-smelling water, in addition to the pool which had collected before the grand duke's throne where he had squatted. But the shaman was not concerned about that. Jagiellon was not fastidious. Not in the least.

When the door closed behind him, the shaman finally heaved the great sigh of relief he had been suppressing. He was always relieved when he left Jagiellon's presence, of course. But never more so than when he could hear the heavy robes slithering to the floor and smell, behind him, the coming transformation.

Moving as rapidly as he could without actually running, he scurried down the corridors of the palace in Vilna. It would take the shaman some time to reach his room, for he had deliberately chosen quarters as far away as possible from those of Jagiellon. As far away, in fact, as the immense and sprawling palace permitted.

The distance was still not enough, as far as the shaman was concerned. The stench was getting stronger by the moment, seeming to follow him like a hound. None of the various guards whom he passed noticed it, of course. They did not possess the shaman's other senses.

Chernobog was feeding.

Chapter 36

Benito hadn't worried when he'd awakened and seen that Marco's bed was empty. Marco had been going to work early, the past few weeks, working in a frenzy of earnest activity all day, and leaving work late. Old man Ventuccio himself had come down out of his office to see the handiwork of his new clerk. Too bad Marco hadn't been there at the time; he'd been out at lunch, and nobody thought to mention it to him when he came back. Of course, the other clerks were probably jealous—half of them were Ventuccio hangers-on anyway, worthless cousins who weren't expected to accomplish much for their salary.

Benito thought he knew why Marco had been working so hard—he might be hoping to get an advance on his wages. He'd spent all the cash he'd saved on Caesare, and in a week the rent was due on their apartment in Cannaregio. A runner earned about a quarter of what a clerk earned; Benito couldn't pay it. And if Marco couldn't raise the ready, it was back to the leaky attics for both of them, unless Aldanto would let them stay on. Which wasn't really likely. Maria was getting an impatient and irritated look whenever her eyes happened to fall on them. She'd been snapping at Marco for being underfoot, and it was clear to Benito that they'd worn out their welcome once Aldanto had recovered from the fever. He had a fair notion that it was Caesare overruling Maria that was keeping him and Marco in the apartment.

And that despite Benito's being smart-mouthed with both of them.

With Marco too, which Marco hadn't much noticed, but he *had*

noticed Benito's attitude with Aldanto. *That* had gotten a rise out
of him, more than Benito had intended.

He'd backed—no, *slammed*—Benito into the wall the night
before last; and his face had been so cold, so tortured—

*"You listen to me, Benito, you listen to me good. You're messing
with fire, I'll tell you once and not again! Caesare's an aristocrat,
he's quiet—but he's killed more people than you have hair, and you'd
better think about that hard before you smart him off another time.
I don't know why he's putting up with you, but I won't, not any more!
I'll beat you black and blue next time—because I'd rather you were
beaten up than dead. Remember he's a trained assassin. Remember
who trained him, and that they murdered Mama before you open
your mouth to Caesare again."*

He'd sulked for the rest of that day and most of the next, not
speaking to Marco. But he *had* thought about it, and he'd come
to the reluctant conclusion that Marco had been right. Even if
Marco *was* more than a bit touched about some girl. So he'd started
to make friendly noises at his brother again.

Thus, all-in-all, he didn't think twice about Marco being gone.
But when Marco wasn't *at* work, and didn't show up there by the
time Benito got sent out with his first message, he began to worry
just a little.

He came around the corner of Ventuccio's on his second run
of the day and saw a familiar gondola tied up at the base of the
stairs with a lurch of foreboding. No mistaking that particular tilt
of a weather-beaten hat—that was Maria's gondola down there,
and with Maria in it. And where Maria was—

"Man to see you, boy," was the curt greeting at the door; sure
enough, behind Benito's supervisor stood—

Caesare Aldanto. Wearing that impassive mask that said *trouble*.

"Benito . . ." Caesare barely waited for Ned Ventuccio to get out
of earshot before starting in, and Benito backed up a pace or two,
until his back was against the office wall. "Benito, have you seen
your brother this morning?"

Benito decided to play innocent. "You mean he ain't here?" he
replied, making his eyes big and round.

Aldanto was not fooled—and the flash of annoyance in *his* eyes
told Benito that he was not in the mood for this sort of nonsense.

Aw, hell—Marco's in trouble—

"You know damned well he hasn't been here," Aldanto hissed,

grabbing Benito's arm before he could dart out of reach. "Your brother's in a mess—now I want to know *what* it is and *where* he is."

"I don't know, M'lord Caesare, honest—" Lord the strength in that hand! Benito belatedly began to think about what Marco had told him when he'd given him that lecture—about what Caesare was—and what he could do. And he began to wonder—

What if the man had turned his coat a second time? If he was planning to use Benito to get to Marco, and sell Marco back to the Montagnards? Marco was worth plenty to the right people.

Paranoid, that was plain paranoid; there'd been no hint of any such thing.

But—if the Montagnards threatened Maria? Would he buy safety for Maria with Marco's life? He might, oh God, Aldanto might . . .

"Boy, I want you back in the apartment—" Aldanto was saying. "I've made it right with the Ventuccios." Benito had missed what had gone before; God, this did *not* sound good. There was no threat that Benito could read in Aldanto's face, but dare he take the chance that he *could* read an experienced agent?

Aldanto still had his arm in that iron grip, and was pulling him out of the door with him. Benito's mind was going like a scrap of drift in a strong current. He couldn't take the chance; no way. He had to get away from Caesare if he could.

Besides, if Marco was really in trouble, Benito could likely help him better than some Milan-born foreigner or even a canaler like Maria could; he *knew* the town, and knew most of the dark ways. And there was always Valentina and Claudia to call on if he had to.

They were out on the balcony now, Benito playing docile, and Aldanto loosed his grip just enough.

Benito whipped around, putting all his weight behind a wicked blow with his elbow, and he'd aimed a bit lower than Aldanto's midsection—aimed at something more personal.

Hit it, too; dead on target.

Caesare was wide-open and completely taken by surprise.

He doubled over with a painful wheeze, and loosened his grip on Benito's arm.

Benito lit out like a scalded cat, heading around the balcony and straight for the bridge.

Aldanto started yelling—recovering faster than Benito had figured he would, and began running after him. But Benito had gotten a good twenty feet worth of a head start, and that was all he needed. He made the bridge supports and jumped for the crossbeams, swarming up into the scaffolding like one of Venice's feral cats. From there he made it to the rooftops and, as he knew from long experience, there was no way an adult was going to be able to follow him up there— not unless the adult was another roof-walking thief like Valentina.

It was cold up there, and doubly dangerous with the wind so strong and unexpected patches of wet everywhere, and smoke blowing into his face when he least expected it. Benito didn't stop for breath, though, not until he'd gotten halfway across Castello. Then he slumped in a warm spot between two chimneys for a bit of a rest and a bit of a think.

Marco *was* in trouble—that much was certain. Either with Aldanto or on his own. And Benito was going to have to see what he could do about it—if he could find out what the trouble *was*.

The last person Marco had talked to—that he knew of—was Rafael de Tomaso. Benito reckoned he'd better pay *that* fellow a little visit.

So best to lie low for a bit, then get across the Grand Canal to Dorsoduro. He'd been to Rafael's room once; and Benito figured he knew of a way in that wasn't by the door.

Katerina looked out of the high window of one of towers of *Casa* Montescue at the gathering dusk. It was a slaty, gray evening. The lagoon was gray too, chopped and flecked with white. It was going to be bitter out there tonight. Still, she had no choice.

Well . . . she could become a courtesan. Francesca had managed to make that—occupation—seem even less attractive than Kat had thought possible. And she hadn't thought it was in the least bit attractive to begin with.

Still—at least she'd get to spend miserable evenings indoors. And it wasn't as if she'd ever met any one man she felt she'd like to be tied to. But it would kill her grandfather. Kat Montescue was a realist, though: one day she might just have no choices. And at least a courtesan had *some* choices and more independence than most wives could dream of. And unlike many *Case Vecchie*, she did have one of the essential requirements for being a courtesan and not just a whore. She was literate. Still, the idea of multiple lovers . . . many of them old and corpulent, was repugnant, to say the least. Francesca could put a bold face on it, but the idea still frightened Kat. When she'd been a girl, she'd always thought that she'd marry a young and handsome man. The trouble was, in Venice, most of the young and handsome *Case Vecchie* were off in various trading colonies of the Venetian Republic. Of course some of the older men—like Lord Calenti—were still attractive, at least in their own opinion.

She pulled a wry face. This was all foolishness! She might have the education and literacy, but that was hardly sufficient. She didn't have the lush beauty of someone like Francesca; not even close. So . . . it would be out in the dark on a nasty night again, and there was an end to it.

Lodovico came in, rubbing his hands and looking worried. "What did you think of Lord Calenti's visit, *cara mia*?"

Kat bit her lip. She could hardly tell her grandfather that she thought the man had too high an opinion of himself, and that she'd always thought there was something vaguely *slimy* about Calenti. Although she allowed that, other than being so obviously vain, he had been pleasant enough. A surprising visitor, but pleasant withal. Alessandra had been in an absolute fury when she'd discovered that one of Venice's most eligible bachelors had come on a private call on Milord Montescue—and not one involving her.

"I don't understand why he came, Grandpapa." Calenti had been perfunctorily polite to Kat, nothing more. So he certainly hadn't come to see about her.

Or had he?

Kat hadn't considered *that* possibility, she suddenly realized. *Casa* Calenti had plenty of money, but they were not really *Case Vecchie*. For them, a dowry would not be as important as the social advancement involved in marrying a girl from what was still, despite their current misfortune, one of Venice's handful of most prestigious families.

Lodovico pulled a face. "I don't know how to tell you this . . ."

Kat waited, blood draining to the pit of her stomach.

Lodovico continued. "He wanted a small parcel of documents transported to Constantinople."

Kat, her hasty assumptions knocked asunder, could only manage to shake her head. *"Him?"*

Lodovico Montescue nodded. "He offered me a great deal of money for it."

Kat sighed. "I wish you hadn't, Grandpapa."

Her grandfather hugged her, smiling. "Katerina. I *didn't* accept it. In fact, I rather indignantly refused. Does the man think me a fool? It's either spying, treason, or a trap."

Kat's eyes narrowed. "A trap."

Lodovico chuckled. "The Council of Ten will assume we are clean as driven snow." He scowled fiercely. "And I told him not to offer my granddaughter his slip-slop compliments either."

Katerina went down to her room to change into her warmest clothes in a far more cheerful frame of mind. Yes. Lord Calenti would be just the man to set such a trap.

The cheerfulness lasted until she was out on the dark water, battling the wind and the waves. Deliveries, she'd shifted to the daytime. But collections from Captain Della Tomasso were always at night, always before moonrise, and always off Guidecca. Della Tomasso was definitely a fence, definitely a messenger for spies, a smuggler . . . and their lifeline. He was a careful, taciturn man. And they owned his ship.

She hit a wave amidships, and it splashed and slopped over the gunwale. It was a good idea keeping the relationship between the illegal cargoes that Captain Della Tomasso carried and the *Casa* Montescue as far apart as possible. The old devil would load a legal cargo of salt, beeswax, and hides at the Montescue warehouse not seventy-five yards from Kat's bedroom tomorrow morning. Of course his coaster would be clean as a whistle while the *Capi di Contrada* were about at the warehouse. Of course they couldn't chance passing incriminating parcels to-and-fro there. But Kat wished to hell—by her half-frozen hands—that she could meet him somewhere closer to the Casa.

Chapter 37

Old habits woke Marco with the first hint of dawn—he'd been so exhausted otherwise that he'd have managed to sleep through to the afternoon. He'd spent a good part of the night with his teeth chattering hard enough to splinter, until exhaustion put him to sleep for another hour or so. He stuck his head out from under the hideout, still shivering, and peered around in the gray light. No fog this morning, though the sky was going to be overcast. He pulled his head back in, and checked his clothes where he'd put them under his bottom blanket. As he'd hoped, they were reasonably dry, water driven out by the heat of his body. He beat the worst of the dried mud out of them, and pulled them on, wrapped a blanket around himself, pulled his cotte on over it all, and crawled back out into the day.

He hopped from the edge of his raft onto the edge of the islet—which was an exposed and weathered ledge of rock, and a lot more solid than many a landing back in town. He wriggled his way in to the center of the islet, having to carefully pull his blanket and clothing loose when branches snagged them, lest he leave tell-tale bits of yarn behind, or rip holes in clothing he didn't have the wherewithal to repair. He was looking for a place where he would be well hidden by the reeds and rushes—at least hidden from the casual observer. He finally found a dry spot, one well padded by the accumulation of many years of dead reeds, and made himself a little hollow to sit in. He reckoned it would do well enough; he hunched down into the hollow, hugged his knees to his chest, and settled down to the unpleasant task of confronting everything he wanted to avoid thinking about.

Take it one step at a time—

All this time, he'd been casually saying to himself: "Caesare will kill me for this." Looking at the mess he'd made of things in the cold light of dawn, and soberly recollecting his own lecture to Benito—*might* he?

He might, Marco thought reluctantly. *And be justified. If Casa Dorma take offense . . . he could hand Petro Dorma my head, and get himself out of it. I've made myself into a pretty expensive liability.*

But *would* he? Marco looked at it from all the angles he could think of, and finally decided that he probably wouldn't. Aldanto never did get that drastic without having several reasons for doing it. To be brutally frank, Aldanto was too much of a professional to waste anything, even the time and effort it would take to dispose of a stupid child.

And Maria would probably get upset if Aldanto actually killed Marco. For all that the girl doted on her lover, and had the usual canaler's tough outlook on life, Marco didn't think that she really approved of Caesare's . . . profession. And he thought that, underneath the temper, she was actually quite fond of him and Benito.

But just to be on the safe side—

Rafael had suggested he hide out here about two weeks, then come back into town. *Get hold of Benito first—give him a note for Caesare. Use the old Montagnard codes, and flat ask him if he thinks I'm better gotten out of the way, permanent-like. Then make a counteroffer. Say—say that I'll do what he wants me to do; come in, stay here, or leave Venice altogether.*

The last wouldn't be easy, or desirable from his point of view, but he'd do it; he couldn't go north—but south, maybe? Or maybe hire on as a hand on an Outremer-bound ship?

That was a possibility. The sailors had seemed pretty rough characters, but basically good people, when he'd met a couple at Ventuccio's. But—

He had a fairly shrewd notion of what some of the duties of a very junior (and passable-looking) sign-on might well include, and he wasn't altogether sure he could stomach the job. Better that, though, than dead. No such thing as a "fate worse than death" in Marco's book—except maybe a fate involving a lengthy interrogation at the hands of Montagnards, the Servants of the Holy Trinity, or Ricardo Brunelli—or Caesare Aldanto.

But Benito—if he left Venice, he'd have to leave Benito. No good could come to a fourteen-year-old kid in a strange place like Acre or Ascalon, or more-or-less trapped on an eastbound ship.

That would leave him more alone than he'd ever been.

He swallowed hard, and wiped his sleeve across his eyes. So be it. For Benito's sake, he'd do just about anything. Including take on that lengthy interrogation.

But figure Caesare wanted him back in; in a lot of ways that was the worst case. Si, *I'll go in, I take my licks. God knows what he'll do. Probably beat the liver out of me. Be worse if he didn't, in some ways. He won't be trusting me with much, anyway, not after the way I've messed up. Don't blame him. I wouldn't trust me, either.*

So. Be humble; be respectful. Take orders, follow 'em to the letter, and *earn* the respect back. *Even if it takes years.*

Thank God he'd told the truth—at least he'd cut the thing with Angelina short, before it had landed them in more tangles than could be cut loose.

Give up on the notion of the Accademia—too close to the Dorma, especially with Dorma cousins going there. Hang it up; stay content with being Ventuccio's third-rank clerk. At least that paid the bills.

Stay clear of anyplace Angelina might show, unless Caesare ordered different.

Keep clear of the Strega, too. That meant Valentina and Claudia and Barducci's tavern—again, unless Caesare ordered differently.

Going back meant more than facing Caesare—it meant figuring a way to pay the damn bills with no money. Rent was paid until the end of the month—but that was only one week away. Borrow? From whom? Maria didn't have any to spare. *Not* Caesare—

Marco gnawed his lip, and thought and thought himself into a circle. *No choice. Has to be Caesare. Or beg an advance from Ventuccio. Have to eat humble pie twice. Charity. Hell.*

Sometimes it seemed as if it would be a lot easier to find one of the marsh bandits and taunt them into killing him; God knew it wouldn't take much. But he hadn't fought and fought and fought to stay alive this long just to take the easy way out.

Last possibility—that Caesare would tell him to stay. That Caesare would trust to the Jesolo marshes to kill him, rather than killing him outright. Well, wasn't staying what Marco had figured on doing in the first place?

All right, if Caesare told him to stay in the marshes—well, Marco would stay. At least this time he'd arrived equipped to do a little better than just survive. Not much, but a little. So long as he could keep clear of the bandits, he'd manage. And he and Benito could go back to the old routine—at least he'd be near enough to keep in touch.

Now—the Montagnards—have I screwed up there too?

Benito waded through mud and freezing water; over his ankles mostly, sometimes up to his knees. His legs were numb, his teeth were chattering so hard he couldn't stop them, and his nose was running. He kept looking over his shoulder, feeling like he was being watched, but seeing nothing but the waving weeds that stood higher than his head. There was a path here, of a sort, and he was doing his best to follow it. If he hadn't been so determined to find his brother, he'd have turned tail and run for home a long time ago.

Rafael de Tomaso had told him the whole messy story, and had admitted that he had advised Marco to go and hide out for a week or two until the thing could blow over. Benito had gotten a flash of inspiration right then, and hadn't waited to hear more—he'd lit off over the roofs again—

It had taken him half an hour to reach the apartment in Cannaregio—

To discover Marco's belongings stripped, right down to the books. The fact that it was *only* Marco's things ruled out thieves. Stuff gone, plus hiding, added up to "marshes" to Benito.

So he put on every shred of shirt and cotte he had, and two pairs of pants, and made for the roofs again.

He had to get down to the roadways by the time he reached Castello. By then he had gotten the notion that it might just be a good idea to let Maria and Caesare know where Marco had gone, and to let them know he was headed out after him.

Damn fool Rafael, he'd cursed, more than once. *Damn marshes almost killed Marco before this—hell, it could do it now! Damn fool city-dweller, thinks living in the Jesolo in wintertime, in the middle of the Aqua alta, is like living in the city—*

So he'd looked around for a boatman, knowing that boat-folk

stuck together, knowing that what he told one would be halfway across town by midmorning.

"Hey!" he'd yelled at the first head that poked out of a small pirogue's cabin to peer at him, bleary-eyed, in the dawnlight. "Hey—you know Maria Garavelli?"

"Might," said the bargee; old, of dubious gender.

"Look, you find her, you tell her Marco's headed out into the Jesolo marshes and Benito's gone after him." Then he added, shrewdly, "There's money in it."

The whole canaler had popped out of the hidey then, and the creature was jerking at his tie-rope as Benito continued his run down to the sandbars off the eastern point of Castello and the "path" Marco had told him about. He hoped he was right about the tide. You could only get across there at dead-low.

Marco had talked so casually about walking in among the islands and out into the Jesolo. Benito was finding out now that it was anything but easy. For one thing, he could hardly tell where he was going, what with the reeds being so high. For another, it was hard to follow this so-called "path." It was prone to having deep wash-outs where least expected. He was wet to his collar, and mired to his waist, and it was a good thing that wool clothing stayed warm when wet, or he'd have been frozen into an icicle by now. The swamp was eerily silent, the only sounds being the splashing and sucking noises of his own passage and the murmur of a breeze in the reeds. It was *damned* cold. And it smelled to high heaven. Worst of all, Benito wasn't entirely certain that he wasn't lost.

"Marco?" he called, hoping that he was close enough to the area Marco had described Chiano and Sophia living in. He hoped that his brother would be the one to hear him. One heard horrible stories about the marsh-folk. "Marco?"

Harrow crouched in the cover of the reeds and rushes on the little muck-and-reed hummock Luciano Marina had led him to, watching the boy. Or rather, what he could see of the boy, which from this angle was only the top of his head. So far, this business of guarding Lorendana's kids had been absurdly easy. He'd stayed under cover most of yesterday, watching the boy work on his hideout until he seemed finished, then watching the hideout after the boy crawled into it to sleep. Then Luciano Marina had come to bring him some food and told *him* to get some sleep. He'd gone back to his hiding place near Luciano's raft. When dawn arrived, so had Luciano Marina. The Strega had given him something to chew on—"keeps the cold away," he'd said—and sent him back to his watching-place.

So far all that the boy had done was to make a pocket-sized fire and boil a pot of water for drinking. Other than that, he'd sat on the island for the past hour or more, hidden in the reeds, not moving. Harrow chewed the bitter-tasting, woody stuff Luciano Marina had given him. It made his head buzz pleasantly, and did, indeed, keep the cold away. He wondered what the kid was up to. Meditating? Neither Luciano Marina nor the vision of Lorendana had said anything about the boy being mystical. But it was a possibility, given the Goddess's interest in him.

Well, whatever, it was certainly proving to be a lot easier than he'd thought it was going to be—

He was too well trained to jump at the sudden sound of a shout, echoing across the marsh. It was the voice of a boy calling out a name, echoing out of the depths of the swamp.

"Marco?" It was so distorted he couldn't really tell what direction it was coming from. "Marco?"

Someone was looking for young Valdosta! He focused his attention on the boy just in time to see him slide off the islet and into the reeds, fast as a lizard and nearly as silently. Harrow saw the weeds shake once—and the boy was gone.

Saints!

That was *Benito's* voice, echoing among the islets. If Marco could hear him, it was damn sure others could. For all of his younger brother's savvy about the streets and canals of Venice, Benito had no real understanding of the dangers which lurked in the marshes.

Marco slid off the islet, skidding on sharp-edged, rustling grass, slipping on icy mud patches. He splashed down onto the path, ignoring the knifelike cold of the water, and then began moving as quickly and quietly as he could. He wove through the reeds, hoping he'd get to his brother before anyone else did. But he must get there without getting ambushed himself. Marco made scarcely more noise than a snake, keeping his feet under the icy water to avoid splashing, slipping between the clumps of dry, rattling rushes rather than forcing his way through them. Benito's one hope was that at this time of year, most of the really bad locos were deeper into the marsh than this.

He burst into a tiny clearing unexpectedly, knife at the ready, practically on top of the kid.

"Marco!"

Benito flung himself at his brother, heedless of the knife Marco held, looking well and truly frightened. He clung to him as they both teetered in icy, knee-deep, mud-clouded water. Marco returned the embrace, relieved almost to the point of tears to find him safe.

"Benito—" He hugged him hard. "Thank God—thank God you're all right!"

Then Marco looked up from the kid clinging to him, to see that they had been surrounded on three sides.

It was the Squalos; a banditti gang of marsh locos. A bad bunch, too. Mostly younger than the general run of the swamp folk; late teens to early thirties. Rumor had it they worked for slavers. When supplies of suitable bodies in town ran low, bodies tended to start disappearing from the swamp.

There were ten of them, ragged, dirty, and predatory. They had spaced themselves in a rough ovoid, standing on high spots at irregular intervals between the reed hummocks, at distances from fifteen to twenty feet from the two boys, except on the side bordering the deep water. Feral eyes gazed hungrily at them from within tangles of filthy hair and beard.

They were in deep trouble.

Marco slipped his spare knife from his belt, feeling the hilt like a slip of ice in his hand, and passed it wordlessly to Benito. Then he shifted his own knife to his left hand and felt in his pocket for his sling and a stone. He got the stone into the pocket of the sling one-handed, and without taking his attention off the gang. With the sling loose and ready in his right hand, he shifted his weight from side to side, planting himself a little more firmly in the treacherous, icy mud. And prayed his numb feet wouldn't fail him.

"Hear ye finished off Big Gianni, Marco."

One of the least ragged of the gang members stepped forward. Marco recognized the leader, Grimaldi, by his shock of wild reddish hair.

"Hear yer got pretty good wi' that sticker." The redhead made a vaguely threatening gesture with his own thin-bladed knife.

Marco's hopes rose a little—if he could somehow convince them to go one-on-one with him, they *might* have a chance. Benito

would, anyway, if he could talk the kid into running for it while
the gang's attention was on the fight.

"Good enough to take *you*, Grimaldi," he said, raising the knife
defiantly. "You want to dance?"

"Maybe, maybe—" the filth-caked, scrawny gang leader replied,
swaying a little where he stood, knee-deep in muddy water, wisps
of greasy red hair weaving around his face.

"What's the matter, Grim? What's matter? You *scared*?" Marco
taunted, as the blood drained out of Benito's face and his eyes got
big and frightened. "I'm not a kid anymore, that it? Afraid to take
me on *now*?"

"Marco—" Benito hissed, tugging urgently at his soggy sleeve.
"Marco, I don't think that's too smart—"

The gang leader hesitated—and his own followers began jeering at him, waving their arms around and making obscene ges-
tures. Under cover of their catcalls, Marco whispered harshly to
his younger brother.

"Benito—don't *argue*. For once, don't. I know what I'm doing,
dammit! When you figure they're all watching me, you light out
for deep water. You swim—"

"No! I'm not leavin' you!"

"You'll damn well do as I say!"

"No way!"

"*Shut up!*" Grimaldi roared, effectively silencing all of them. He
sloshed forward a pace or two and grinned. "I ain't afraid, Marco,
but I ain't stupid, neither. I ain't gonna get myself cut up for
nothin'—not when we can take both o' ye, an' make a little bargain with the Dandelo buyers for two nice young eunuchs—" His
knife described a fast nasty low flick.

He sloshed forward another step—his last.

Marco's right hand blurred, and Grimaldi toppled sideways into
the mud, wearing a rather surprised expression, a rock imbedded
in his temple.

There was a moment of stunned silence, then the rest of the
gang surged forward like a feeding-frenzy of weasels.

Harrow lost the boy as soon as he slid into the reeds. It took
him longer than he liked to get to the place where the boy had
vanished. If this had been the mountains, or a forest or a city—
even a weird city like Venice—he'd have had no trouble tracking

the kid. Here in this foul wilderness he was at something of a loss. He floundered around in the mud, feeling unnaturally helpless. Fine vessel of the Goddess, *he* was—he couldn't even keep track of a dumb kid!

Then he heard the shouting; there was enough noise so that he had no trouble pinpointing the source even through the misleading echoes out there. It sounded like trouble; and where there was trouble, he somehow had no doubt he'd find the boy.

But getting there . . . was a painfully slow process; he literally had to feel his way, step by cold, slippery step. Waterweeds reached out for him, snagging him, so that he had to fight his way through them. The noise echoed ahead of him, driving him into a frenzy of anxiety as he floundered on, past treacherous washouts and deposits of mud and silty sand that sucked at him.

Until he was suddenly and unexpectedly in the clearing.

He blinked—there was the boy—no, *two* boys, standing at bay, side by side on a hummock of flattened reeds. They were holding off—barely—a gang of mud-smeared, tattered marsh-vermin. One boy was Marco—

Merda!

The other was Benito!

Harrow saw the pattern of the Goddess's weave. It was too much to be coincidence; first the vision, then Marco just *happening* to be holing up out in this Godforsaken slime-pit—and now the *other* boy also turning up—

But the boys weren't doing well. They'd accounted for one of the crazies, now floating bloody-headed within arm's reach of Harrow. But the others were going to overpower them before much longer. Marco had an ugly slash across his ribs that was bleeding freely and soaking into a long red stain along the front of his mud-spotted tan cotte. And even as Harrow moved to grab a piece of driftwood to use as a weapon, one of the crazies started to bring down a boathook, aimed at the younger boy's head.

"*Benito!*"

Harrow saw the horror in Marco's eyes as the boy saw it coming, and before Benito could turn, the older boy shoved him out of the way and took the blow himself.

The deadly hook missed, but the boy took the full force of the pole on his unprotected head. The pole broke—the boy sank to his knees—

And Harrow waded into the fray from behind, roaring in a kind of berserker rage, wielding his driftwood club like the sword of an avenging angel. The ex-Montagnard assassin used a blade by preference, but he was every bit as expert with a cudgel. His first blow landed on a skull with enough force to cave it in. Thereafter, his opponents warned and trying to fend him off, he shifted to the short and savage thrusts of an expert brawler and killer. One throat crushed; a rib cage splintered; a diaphragm ruptured—two more sent sprawling by vicious kicks. The rest fled in a panic and faded into the swamp; leaving behind four floating bodies and another crawling into the reeds coughing blood as he went.

There was a sudden absolute silence.

The younger boy had flung himself at his brother when Marco had gone down, and was holding him somewhat erect. He looked around with wild eyes when the quietude suddenly registered with him.

His eyes fastened on Harrow. He paled—

And put himself as a frail bulwark of protection between the one-time Montagnard assassin and his semi-conscious brother.

Harrow was struck dumb by a thought that approached a revelation. *Those two—they'd die for each other. My own brother might have killed someone for me . . . But he wouldn't have been willing to die for me.*

Coming from the mercenary background that he did, Harrow had never known much affection or loyalty. His mother had been a Swiss mercenary's whore. She'd reared the boys as a way of making a living. A poor substitute for the kind of living a daughter would have brought her, but a living. Bespi had never experienced that kind of attachment. He wouldn't have believed anyone who told him it existed. But here it was, and unmistakable. Those two boys would willingly give their lives for each other.

He held himself absolutely still, not wanting to frighten the younger boy further.

They might have remained that way forever, except for Marco. The boy began struggling to his feet, distracting his brother, so Harrow was able to transfer the crude club he held to his left hand and take a step or two closer. At that, Benito jerked around, knife at the ready, but the older boy forestalled him, putting a restraining hand on his shoulder.

Harrow met the disconcertingly direct eyes of the older boy with what he hoped was an expression of good-will.

"N-no, 'sfine, Ben—"

The words were slurred, but there was sense in the black eyes that met his.

"—'f he meant us trouble, he wouldn't have waded in to help us."

Marco used his younger brother's shoulder to hold himself upright, and held out his right hand. "Marco—" he hesitated a moment "—Valdosta . . . dunno who you are, but—thanks."

Harrow looked from the outstretched, muddy hand, to the candid, honest face, with its expression of simple, pure gratitude. He stretched out his own hand almost timidly to take the boy's, finding himself moved to the point of having an unfamiliar lump in his throat.

This boy was—*good*. That was the only way Harrow could put it. Honest, and *good*. Small wonder the Goddess wanted this thread for her loom. It was a precious golden thread, one which would lift the other colors in the weave into brightness. Harrow had never known anyone he could have called simply . . . "good."

And—so Harrow had often been told—the good die young.

Resolve flared in eyes. *Not this one.* As an assassin, one of the most deadly killers the Visconti had ever unleashed for the Montagnard cause, he had felt an almost sexual pleasure when he had fulfilled his missions. When he'd killed. Now a similar but richer feeling came, displacing the old. He was the vessel of the Goddess. And he was full, full to overflowing. He was only distantly aware of the impression of a great winged shadow, passing over all of them. The Montagnards brought death to serve their purposes. The Goddess conserved life. Purpose and *reasons* flooded into Harrow. *Not this one! Death will not take him while I watch over him.*

Marco swayed in sudden dizziness, and Harrow sloshed through the churned-up mud to take his other arm and help keep him steady; Benito tensed, then relaxed again when he realized that Harrow was going to help, not hurt them.

"Which way from here?" the vessel of the Goddess croaked, finding his voice with difficulty.

Marco fought down dizziness as he grayed-out a little; heard the battered, burnt-faced stranger ask: "Which way from here?"

"We've got to get him out of here—back to Venice, back where it's warm and they can look after him," Benito replied, hesitantly. "There's probably people out looking for him by now—and he ain't in any shape to stay out here, anyway."

Marco gave in to the inevitable, too sick and dizzy and in too much pain to argue. "The path's—through those two hummocks," he said, nodding his head in the right direction and setting off a skull-filling ache by doing so. The three of them stumbled off down the rim-path, making slow work of it—especially since they had to stop twice to let him throw up what little there was in his stomach. He concentrated on getting one foot set in front of the other. That was just about all he was up to at this point; that, and keeping from passing out altogether.

He was still survival-oriented enough to be aware that now that they were in the clear, they were attracting the attention of the marsh dwellers with boats—some of whom were more dangerous than the Squalos. He tried to warn the other two, but his tongue seemed to have swollen up and it was hard to talk.

But the walls of the Arsenal were in sight now, crumbling and water-logged brick-and-wood, looming up over their heads. Things began to whirl. . . . He couldn't possibly see the Piazza San Marco from here, but he would swear he saw the pillar and the lion . . . and the open book. He struggled to read the words. . . .

"Don't fall over yet, Marco!" Benito's voice. Pleading. "Don't die on me, brother!"

By an effort of will, the whirling world steadied briefly.

There was a shout from behind; just as a small boat came around the Castello point. An errant beam of sunlight glinted off blond hair in the bow, and there was another, darker figure waving at them frantically from the stern.

And there was ominous splashing growing nearer behind them.

The stranger on Marco's left suddenly dropped his arm, and Marco and Benito staggered as Marco overbalanced.

Then things got very blurred and very confusing.

The stranger bellowed behind them, and there was the sound of blows, and cries of anger and pain; Benito began hauling him along as fast as they could stumble through the weeds and muck. Then he was in waist-deep water, with the sides of a gondola under his hands, and he was simultaneously scrambling and being pulled aboard. That was . . . Maria Garavelli cursing under her breath beside his head.

And then a gun went off practically in his ear.

He tumbled onto the bottom slats and lay there, frozen, and wet, and hurting; shivering so hard he could hardly think, with shouting going on over his head, and another shot.

Then they were under a winged leonine shadow as consciousness slipped away.

When he came to again, it was to the sight of Maria standing on the stern, moving the gondola with steady easy strokes. Benito wrapped a blanket around him and helped him to sit up. It was a good thing Benito was supporting him; he was shivering so hard now that he couldn't sit on his own.

"He all right?"

There was worry in Maria's voice; *that* surprised him.

"He need help? Lord—he's bleeding, ain't he! Caesare—"

Aldanto was down on the slats beside him, without Marco seeing how he had got there. He shut his eyes as much to hide his shame as to fight the waves of dizziness. Amazingly gentle hands probed his hurts.

"Cut along the ribs—looks worse than it is. But this crack on the skull—"

Marco swayed and nearly lost his grip on consciousness and his stomach, when those hands touched the place where the boathook pole had broken over his head. The pain was incredible; it was followed by a combined wave of nausea and disorientation. The hands steadied him, then tilted his chin up.

"Open your eyes."

He didn't dare to disobey; felt himself flush, then pale. The blue eyes that bored into his weren't the dangerous, cold eyes he'd seen before—but they were not happy eyes.

"Not good, I'd judge."

"So what's that mean?" Maria asked harshly.

"Mostly that it's his turn to be put to bed, and he isn't going to be moving from there for a while. You—"

Caesare was speaking to *him* now, and Marco wanted to die at the gentle tone of his voice.

"—have caused us a great deal of trouble, young man."

"I—I didn't mean to—I just—I just wanted—" He felt, and

fought down, a lump of shamed tears. No, no he *would* not cry! "—I made such a mess out of things, I figured you were better off if I went away somewhere. I didn't *mean* to bring you more trouble! I tried to find some way I could get you out of it, and get out from under your feet, and when that didn't work I just tried to do what was right—"

"If I had thought differently," Aldanto said, slowly, deliberately, "you'd be out there entertaining the locos right now. There are more than a few things I want to have out with you, but it's nothing that can't wait."

Then he got up, and took a second oar to help Maria, ignoring Marco's presence on the bottom slats.

But that wasn't the end of his humiliation—every few feet along the canals, it seemed, they were hailed, either from other boats or from the canalside.

"*Si*, he's okay," Maria called back, cheerfully, "*Si*, we got 'im—"

Apparently *everybody* in town knew what a fool he'd made of himself. There were calls of "Hooo—so *that's* the loverboy? Eh, throw him back, Maria, he's just a piddly one!" With every passing minute, Marco felt worse. Finally he just shut his eyes and huddled in the blanket, ignoring the catcalls and concentrating on his aching head.

Because, as if that humiliation wasn't enough, there were more than a few of those on canalside who *didn't* shout—shadowy figures whom Caesare simply nodded to in a peculiar way. And Marco recognized one or two as being Giaccomo's.

Giaccomo—that meant money—

—a *lot* of money. Out of Caesare's pocket.

Marco wanted to die.

The ribald and rude comments were coming thick and fast now, as they headed into the Grand Canal. Maria was beginning to enjoy herself, from the sound of her voice. Aldanto, however, remained ominously silent. Marco opened his eyes once or twice, but couldn't bear the sunlight—or the sight of that marble-still profile.

The third time he looked up, his eyes met something altogether unexpected. Aldanto had shifted forward, and instead of his benefactor, Marco found himself staring across the water at another gondola.

There was a girl in that elderly nondescript vessel, rowing it with consummate ease. From under the hood curled carroty-red hair. She had a generous mouth, a tip-tilted nose—merry eyes, wonderful hazel eyes—

She wasn't beautiful, like Angelina Dorma. But those eyes held a quick intelligence worth more and promising more than mere beauty.

Those eyes met his across the Grand Canal, and the grin on that face softened to a smile of genuine sympathy, and then into a look of utter dumbfounded amazement.

Which was maybe not surprising, if she felt the shock of recognition that Marco was feeling. Because even if he'd never seen her before, he *knew* her; knew how the corners of her eyes would crinkle when she laughed, knew how she'd twist a lock of hair around one finger when she was thinking hard, knew how her hand would feel, warm and strong, and calloused with work, in his.

In that moment he forgot Angelina Dorma, forgot his aching head, forgot his humiliation. He stretched out his hand without realizing he'd done so—saw she was doing the same, like an image in a mirror.

And then his eyes blurred, and vision deserted him. When his eyes cleared, she was gone, and there was no sign that she'd ever even been there. And he was left staring at the crowded canal, not even knowing *who* she could be.

Before he could gather his wits, they were pulling up to the tie-up in Castello. He managed to crawl under his own power onto the landing, but when he stood up, he didn't gray out, he blacked out for a minute.

When he came to, he had Maria on the one side of him, and Caesare on the other, with Benito scrambling up the stairs ahead of them. They got him up the stairs, Lord and Saints, *that* was a job—he was so dizzy he could hardly help them at all. Aldanto had to all but carry him the last few feet. Then he vanished, while Marco leaned against the wall in the hallway and panted with pain.

Maria, it was, who got him into the kitchen; ignoring his feeble attempts to stop her, she stripped him down to his pants with complete disregard for his embarrassment. She cleaned the ugly slash along his ribs, poured raw grappa in it. That burned and brought tears to his eyes. Then she bandaged him up; then cleaned the marsh-muck off of him as best she could without getting him into water. Then she handed him a pair of clean breeches and waited with her back turned and her arms crossed for him to strip off the dirty ones and finally bundled him up into bed, stopping his protests with a glass of unwatered wine.

He was so cold, so cold all the way through, that he couldn't even shiver anymore. And his thoughts kept going around like rats in a cage. Only one stayed any length of time—

"Maria—" he said, trying to get her attention more than once, "Maria—"

Until finally she gave an exasperated sigh and answered, "What now?"

"Maria—" he groped after words, not certain he hadn't hallucinated the whole thing. "On the Grand Canal—there was this girl, in a boat—a gondola. Maria, please, I *got to* find out who she is!"

She stared at him then, stared, and then started a grin that looked fit to break her face in half. "A girl. In a boat." She started to laugh, like she'd never stop. "A girl in a boat. Saint Zaccharia! Oh, all the Saints! Damn, it's almost worth the mess you've got us into!"

She leaned on the doorframe, tears coming to her eyes, she was laughing so hard.

Then she left him, without an answer.

Left him to turn over and stare at the wall, and hurt, inside and out. Left him to think about how he'd lost everything that really meant anything—especially Aldanto's respect. About how the whole town knew what a fool he was. About how he'd never live *that* down.

And to think about how everything he'd meant to turn out right had gone so profoundly wrong; how he owed Caesare more than ever. Left him to brood and try to figure a way out of this mire of debt, until his head went around in circles—

He was going into the reaction that follows injury. Sophia had told him . . . He tried desperately to recapture her words. . . . It was all vague. He knew about that somewhere deep down, but he didn't much care anymore. He wouldn't ask for any more help, not if he died of it. Maybe if he died, if they found him quiet and cold in a couple of hours, maybe they'd all forgive him *then*.

He entertained the bleak fantasy of their reaction to his demise for a few minutes before he dropped off to sleep. .

Chapter 38

Francesca looked out of her window onto the Grand Canal. "It will be nice here in spring. Not as nice as on the Ligurian coast, but still pretty." She spoke calmly, conversationally—as if Erik had not come bursting in here three minutes back, looking for Manfred.

Now he was sitting here, being as polite as if in any Venetian lady's salon. And feeling utterly ill at ease.

Erik swallowed. Francesca always left him not really sure of his ground. She was so . . . alien to him. Different from his expectations, especially after that first meeting. By the time the second one occurred, he was floundering. Francesca's new residence could, he supposed, be technically referred to as a "bordello." But it was like no bordello Erik had ever seen. There was no salon downstairs where half-naked women lounged for the inspection of the customers. In fact—other than, presumably, in the privacy of their own very spacious and luxurious apartments—the women were always extremely well dressed. And not flirtatious in the least, in the blatant manner that Erik expected from "whores."

Erik glanced around, trying to keep himself from fidgeting. Francesca's apartment was on the third floor of the Casa Louise. It had a large salon and a balcony and windows—real glass windows—looking out over the hustle and bustle of the Grand Canal. As always when he arrived to round up Manfred, she had greeted him like a lady when he came in the door—and, as always now, she was dressed like one.

Well . . . a lady with a taste in low-cut upthrust bodices. Erik found it nearly as distracting as her nudity had been. While they waited for Manfred to get dressed, Francesca—as always—engaged Erik in genteel conversation. He had found her intelligent, well-read, and with a political background that made him feel naïve. To his back-country Icelandic-Vinlander values, a whore was a whore. A lady was a lady. The concept of a "courtesan" was new to him, and he still wasn't sure how to deal with it. Or how to protect his charge from her. Or even—a very new and heretical thought, this—whether his charge *needed* to be protected from her.

"You can't really stop him, you know."

How had she known what he'd been thinking about? Well, it was no use beating about the bush. Despite his warnings, either Manfred had said something to her or her very quick mind had picked it up. "I must," Erik said stiffly. "It is my duty to care for him. To keep him under my eye and train and protect him . . . from entanglements too."

Francesca laughed musically. "Poor Erik! He must be a great trial to you."

It was all Erik could do to keep himself from agreeing. Manfred was a tearaway. There was no getting away from it. Half the taverns and a fair number of the women in the Empire could testify to that. "I do what I have to do, madame."

She gurgled. "The title is premature, Erik. But it is correct. I shall either be a madame or simply retire with considerable wealth after a career as a courtesan. Perhaps marry one of my clients, at the end—some plump, cheerful rich old merchant looking to stay cheerful in his dotage. I have no long-term designs on young Manfred. He is amusing and . . . energetic. He is also young. His fancy will turn elsewhere, and some sweet young thing can be very grateful that I have polished him a little." She patted Erik on the arm gently. He tried very hard not to be distracted by her soft skin. "He is safer here, with me, than on the street. The owners of this building take great precautions. There are mistresses of men from all factions, and courtesans who could entertain a man who is Montagnard tonight and one who is a Petrine legate tomorrow. This is one of the safest places in all Venice."

There was some shouting and catcalling down on the canal below.

"Ah." Francesca smiled. "They must have found him."

"Who?"

Francesca moved to open the doors onto the balcony. "Someone has been spending a great deal of money looking for a youngster who got himself into trouble with a girl. If my informant is to be believed, with one of the daughters of the *Casa* Dorma no less! It is a long and complicated romantic story."

Erik blinked. "Do you know everything?"

Francesca dimpled. "I do my best."

They'd gone out onto the balcony as the gondola which was drawing the comments drew near.

"Ah. That must be him. The dark-haired one in the bow."

Erik looked. And saw a very recognizable handsome blond-haired man also in the gondola. "Do you also know who the blond fellow is?"

Francesca looked amused. "Of course. Caesare Aldanto. Once of Milan. Reputed to have once been a Montagnard agent. A sellsword under the shadow of the hand of none other than Ricardo Brunelli."

"He's also the man who is directly responsible for us meeting you, Francesca," said Erik dryly.

She smiled again and turned him back to the warm apartment. "Then I owe him. But I don't think I'll tell him. So, he set up that . . ."

"Fiasco. It would have been different if Manfred hadn't deliberately fooled me and been there too. I would have probably been dead—certainly injured. Your 'sellsword' is awfully good with that sword of his. So he takes orders from Ricardo Brunelli. Who is this Brunelli? By your tone he is a big cheese here in Venice." Erik hoped his tone did not betray the fact that he intended to see the cheese sliced down to size.

"Have you found Erik a girl, my demoiselle?" asked Manfred, who had finally come out of the bedroom, giving Eric a brief glimpse of a rumpled large brass bed.

Francesca turned to him. "Manfred, did you dress *entirely* by guess? Come here! Let me fix your collar. Your friend has ambitions on killing the head of the house Brunelli."

Manfred was obviously better informed than he was. Probably by Francesca. "Ha. You don't start low, do you, Erik?"

"Who is he, Manfred? It appears he's the bastard who set me up to be killed at the House of the Red Cat."

Francesca smiled, as she neatly twitched the neckband of

Manfred's shirt into shape. "He is the man who believes he will be the next Doge."

"I don't think you can do that, Erik," said Manfred seriously. "I don't think even my—the Emperor—could stop the Venetians hanging the lot of us."

"Besides," said Francesca, "Aldanto is reputed to be for sale, confidentially, to the highest bidder. It may have had nothing to do with Brunelli."

"He sounds like the sort to have influence with these Venetian Schiopettieri."

Francesca shook her head. "Not really. Any of the *Signori di Notte* could have done it. But Brunelli is not one of them."

Manfred stretched. "I know you don't like the idea, Erik. But I still think you need look no further than our dear abbot."

Erik shrugged. "Sachs says he sent Pellmann to me with a message that the raid was off. Pellmann has enough of a grudge against me to not deliver it. I'm not a North German *Ritter*."

"And you didn't beat him, so he didn't respect you," said Manfred with a grin. "You're a callous brute, Erik. How could you treat the man like that? No wonder he ran off."

Francesca laughed. "And what the two of you do not see is that that does not add up. Aldanto being the organizer of that ambush, and the time at which the Schiopettieri arrived, adds up to two things: money and influence. Venetian influence. How would this Pellmann have access to either? He was not a Venetian, was he?"

"Pomeranian," said Erik. "Couldn't even make himself understood in the local dialect. Despised all Southerners, and Venetians most of all."

Francesca sighed. "I think you will find he's dead."

Manfred snorted. "Well, that's no loss to the world. Unless sharing Von Tieman's squire-orderly is worse, Erik?"

Erik shook his head. "No. He's a nice enough old fellow. A bit slow upstairs. Probably from all those slaps around the head Von Tieman gives him. He's pathetically grateful that I don't. But why kill Pellmann? And if it wasn't him, arranging it in a piece of spite, who was it? It can't be the abbot, Manfred. Me being wounded or killed or even captured in a raid by the local constabulary on a brothel would have shamed the Knights—and by extension, the Servants."

Manfred shook his head. "Believe me. If they had caught you, the abbot would have been the first person to be *shocked* that you were there. It was a set-up, I tell you."

"I don't believe it," said Erik, stubbornly. "I have opposed him, true—in a relatively minor matter—but surely that's not worth the effort and money such a plot would take. He could just send me home."

Manfred grinned. "Heh. I'd be sent off on the next boat. Just think. No Uncle Erik to ride herd on me."

Erik didn't say anything. Francesca was there. But he smiled and shook his head. His duty was to protect Manfred. There were certain steps he would have to take if the abbot tried to send him away. A signet ring to be used. In dire emergencies.

"Well, the thought of my running wild has shut Erik up. He's even forgotten he's come to hale me away for guard duty. Goodbye, my sweet. Until tomorrow."

Francesca shook her head. "Not until Thursday, Manfred, as you well know."

A look of pouting hurt spread over Manfred's face. "I wish you'd give this up. I thought you loved me."

She smiled, and patted his cheek. "And I do! But not exclusively."

He put his bulky arms around her waist and drew her close, his face growing sulky.

Francesca gave him a quick, easy kiss, but her hands were on his chest gently pushing him away. "Please, Manfred. You could not begin to afford keeping me for yourself, and you know it as well as I do. So enjoy what we have."

"But . . . Francesca," he pouted.

"Thursday. Build up your strength." Her next kiss was firm, and dismissive.

On their way back, observing Manfred's clumping steps from the corner of his eye, Erik found himself fighting down a smile. For once—*ha!*—even the happy-go-lucky imperial prince seemed to have met a woman who confounded him.

Perhaps sensing his companion's humor, Manfred shrugged thick shoulders. "What can I do?" he demanded, in a tone which was half-amused and half-exasperated. "Next to Francesca, all the other women in this town are just . . . *boring.*"

His still-young face seemed, for just a moment, even younger than it was. "It's not fair! I'm being *ruined* for a normal life of whoremongering." Blackly: "You watch! Before you know it, she'll be *reading* to me in bed."

Erik held his tongue. But he finally decided Francesca was right. Maybe some young girl out there—some eventual princess—*would* thank her for the training she was giving Manfred. He was far too used to getting his own way; with women as much as anything else. Being stymied and befuddled was undoubtedly good for the royal young lout.

As a guardian and a warrior-mentor, Erik still regretted the incident that had led Manfred into consorting with Francesca. Because of the debt between them, he hadn't been able to deal with it as decisively as he usually would have. But . . .

Yes, there was truth in what she'd said. He simply *couldn't* watch the young hellion twenty-four hours a day. Manfred was as safe with Francesca as in the Imperial embassy . . . from which Manfred had found at least three unofficial exits. If he could leave, then anyone could enter too. Erik had pointed this out to the abbot, to be told that the rite of enclosure precluded it. All Erik could say was that the rite appeared—as testified by Manfred's presence in the Casa Louise—to be ineffectual.

And, he supposed, just as he was seeing to some aspects of the education of the future Duke of Brittany and possible heir to the Holy Roman Emperor's throne, Francesca was also. Erik blushed a little. These were certainly areas he was ignorant of. And besides that, she was knowledgeable about other things which Erik knew little about—such as the political intrigue that seemed to be the heart of the Venetian Republic. The Italians seemed to relish it. It left him puzzled and with a feeling of distaste. But this was what Manfred would have to deal with when Erik went back to Iceland and thence to Vinland.

Chapter 39

Benito hadn't missed the subtle little signals Aldanto was passing to those shadow-lurkers canalside. Benito knew those shadows, knew them for Giaccomo's. Knew how much they cost. Was totaling up that cost in his head, and coming to a sum that scared the socks off of him.

All that—for Marco?

Oh, hell.

He began doing some very hard thinking about the time they hit the Grand Canal. He'd made up his mind by the time they reached the house in Castello.

Aldanto helped to get Marco as far as the kitchen, then let Maria take over; he headed for the sitting room, and stood looking out of the window in the dim sunlight, arms crossed over his chest, handsome face brooding and worried. Benito made himself a silent shadow following him.

"M'lord—" he said quietly, as soon as they were alone.

Aldanto started—barely visibly; controlling an automatic reaction of defense. Benito's quick eyes caught it all, and his evaluation of Caesare rose considerably.

Damn—he's good. If he can pull his reaction after all this—he's damned good. Better'n anybody I've ever seen.

"What?" the man said shortly, obviously not in a mood for more nonsense.

"M'lord," he said soberly, as Caesare regarded him over one shoulder. "I—I'm sorry about the—" he gestured, flushing, "—where I hit you."

"You're *sorry*?" The ex-Montagnard was actually speechless.

"M'lord—listen a minute, please? I didn't know what to think. Thought maybe you might have—well—Marco might be worth a bit, to the right people."

"Thought I might have turned my coat again, is that it?" Aldanto looked very odd; a little amused, and maybe a little understanding.

"M'lord, I didn't blame you—I was thinking maybe somebody's been leaning on you. If I was you, reckon I'd swap a kid for Maria, if I had to—hard choice, but—that's the way I'd be doing it." Benito kept his eyes on Aldanto, and thought he saw a thoughtful gleam there.

"So—hey, I thought, you didn't have Marco, you might use me to get to Marco. So I let you have it where it could count, so as I could scat."

"I'm afraid, boy," Caesare said quietly, "that this once you were wrong."

Benito preferred not to think about what that peculiarly phrased sentence might mean if he examined it too closely.

"Look, m'lord, I told you—you got a hard choice to make, you make the best one you can. Happens I was wrong this time—but I'm sorry, hey? Now—" Benito got down to business. "I think my brother cost you more than you could afford, no? I've got eyes—and I know what Giaccomo's rates are—"

Aldanto's own eyes narrowed speculatively, but he said nothing.

"M'lord Caesare, I used to figure there was one person worth spending all I had to keep alive, and that was my brother. Now, I figure there's two—"

He felt, more than heard, Maria come in behind him. That was all right; nothing he was going to say now that he didn't want Maria to hear. "Well, maybe three, except Maria back there can take care of herself, I reckon. But the other one's you. We owe you, m'lord."

Aldanto turned to face him fully. "I may be able to salvage something from Marco's poetry," he said dryly. "I wish he'd told me about it earlier." He shifted his weight to one foot. "But what is the point of telling me something I know?"

"It's this, m'lord—Marco, he's *good*, ye know? I'm *not* good—I'm trouble. I don't know how, but the Dell'este—my grandfather—always knew that, even when I was a kid. 'You take care of Marco,' he told me. 'The good ones need us bad ones to keep them safe.'"

Aldanto's right eyebrow rose markedly. "I'm not exactly popular with the Duke of Ferrara, boy. How do you think he'd feel about the company you're keeping now?"

Benito shrugged. "That's not my problem. He just told me I was to take care of Marco."

Aldanto looked pensive, but he said nothing. Benito continued, nervously, but determined. "M'lord, I—" he waved his hands helplessly "—I guess what I want to say is this. You got into this mess because of us. It cost you. You didn't have to do it. Well I'm guessing. But I figure you might need help. Well, from now on, you say, and I'll do. Whatever. However. For as long as you like. And there's some things I'm not too shabby at."

The eyebrow stayed up. Caesare made no pretence that he didn't understand what Benito was talking about. "And if I say—no noise?"

Benito remembered a certain window, and a certain escapade that no longer seemed so clever, and the shadowy men on the canalside walkways—and shuddered. "Then it'll be quiet, m'lord. *Real* quiet. Babies wouldn't wake up."

"And how long can I expect this sudden fit of virtue to last?" Caesare asked with heavy irony.

"It'll last, m'lord, long as you got use for me. Though, I reckon—" Benito grinned suddenly, engagingly, "you'll have to crack me over the ear, now and again. Claudia used to—about once a week."

Caesare's eyes narrowed a little as he studied Benito. The boy held steady beneath that merciless gaze, neither dropping his own eyes, nor shifting so much as an inch. Finally Aldanto nodded in apparent satisfaction.

"You'll do as I say? *Exactly* as I say? No arguments?"

"Yes m'lord. No arguments, m'lord. I can spot a professional when I see one, m'lord. Happen you could teach me more than a bit, no? I learn quick, even Valentina says so. One other thing, though—Marco, he went an' spent all the rent money on your medicine, and both of us had to leave work to help out here, so there's nothing saved." Benito was *not* averse to rubbing that in, just to remind Aldanto that they'd already bankrupted themselves for *him*, and that debt could work both ways.

He got a bit of satisfaction when this time he definitely saw Caesare wince. "Money's a bit tight."

Benito shrugged. "I understand. Giaccomo's boys don't come cheap. But we're broke. So we either got to stay here, or hit the attics again. Happens the attics are no bad notion; you've got to get over the roofs to get in them—hard for folks to sneak up on you."

Aldanto shook his head, closing his eyes for a moment.

"Mercy—" he mumbled, "—*what* have I let myself in for this time?"

He cast a glance behind Benito. "Maria—you've got some stake in this too—"

Benito didn't look around, but heard Maria flop down in a chair behind him.

"I think it's no bad idea," she said. "Let them stay here. Lots of comings and goings—maybe not all by doors—confuse the hell out of any watchers."

Aldanto looked over at Benito again, and Benito had the peculiar feeling of seeing someone quite near his own age looking at him out of those adult eyes for one brief flash.

"Hey, the attics ain't so bad," he gave a token protest. "I lived there two years. You get some heat from the house and if you keep quiet you don't get found out and have to move too often. Better than the marshes by a long way."

Aldanto shook his head. "I'd rather you were where I could see you."

Benito shrugged. "Well, if you let us stay, we stay. But we've got jobs. We'll kick in."

"You'd better." That was Maria, behind him.

Caesare shook his head again. Sighed. "Well then, Benito Valdosta, I think we may have a bargain even if my bones tell me it may well be a partnership made in Hell."

Benito just grinned "Hey, not for *you*, m'lord. But for people acting unfriendly-like? Against a team like the three of us, you, me, and Maria, m'lord Caesare? They haven't a chance!"

Harrow had panicked at first, when he'd seen *who* was picking up the boys—he'd broken out of the knot of fighting loco he'd tipped into the water and struggled vainly to get to the gondola before it could carry the boys off. The treacherous bottom had betrayed him. By the time he'd hauled himself out of the wash-out the two boys were aboard the gondola and being sculled away, back into the shadowed bowels of the city.

Then recollection came to him, and he edged past the brawl back into depths of the swamp, comforted by this new evidence of the Goddess's intervention. Aldanto was *former* Montagnard; a man with an assassin's knowledge, a snake's cunning, an eel's ways, a duelist's defenses. If the Montagnards were after the boys, what better protection could they have than that of the man who knew most about the ways the Visconti operated, from firsthand experience?

But the Goddess had charged him with watching over them—and Aldanto was only one man; he couldn't be everywhere at once, and he couldn't spend all his time awake. So. That meant Harrow should return to the city—

Luciano was pleased with his convert's plans. Secretly. The man responded well to manipulation. It was necessary to rant at Harrow about the folly of them until he was hoarse—but Harrow simply held his peace until Luciano ran out of words and then repeated his intentions.

"I'm going back in," he said simply. "The Goddess put it on me, the job's not done till *She* says so. She said to watch the boys, so I'm watching the boys."

Luciano sighed, "Can't argue with Her, or you," he said glumly, concealing his triumph. "But you got any notion *where* you're going?"

Harrow nodded, slowly. "Know where Aldanto lives; know lots of watchin' holes around Castello—"

"You just go to the boy's friends if you run into trouble, hear me? Claudia—that's th' main one. Singer—"

"—works out of Barducci's tavern, lives second floor. You told me that already." Harrow did *not* add what he was thinking—that he probably could teach this Strega more than a few things about covert work. He had little respect for female agents; most of them were damned little use out of bed. He was itching to get out and get moving—Luciano had given him some other drug that cleared his mind and fired his feeling of purpose to a near-obsession, and every moment spent dallying only made the urge to get into place stronger.

"All right, get moving," Luciano growled. "I can see you've no more interest nor purpose out here."

Harrow did not wait to hear anything more.

Chapter 40

Petro Dorma refolded the letter. And bestowed it and the bundle of poems . . . in his own desk. He ignored his sister's gasp of outrage. He'd had years of practice.

"You . . . you give that back to me!" yelled Angelina, her face red. "I brought it here so you could deal with the little upstart. If you won't, I'll get someone who will!"

Petro took a deep breath. "Angelina, you have been carrying on a clandestine correspondence with this . . . love-starved puppy. You know as well as I do that half the *Case Vecchie* would send an unmarried virgin off to a nunnery for that. Your fury seems to be entirely directed at this unfortunate and obviously besotted young Marco Felluci not because he wrote you some very inaccurate if flattering poems, but because you thought the poems came from someone else. Would you care to tell me who this 'Caesare' your young swain refers to is?"

Angelina Dorma looked sullen. "Give me back my letters."

"No." Petro looked at his sister. Almost twenty years younger than he and still a child when their father had died, she'd been pampered. His mother had needed someone to turn to and spoil and—well, so had he. She could be very taking, very sweet, even now. When she'd been younger he'd never had the heart to refuse her anything. He'd seen giving her whatever she'd desired as a way of making up for her missing out on having Papa. He'd always felt guilty about that. He'd been twenty-five, already making his own way in the world, marked and shaped by Ernesto Dorma's hand. She'd been six. Now he was beginning to realize that he and his mother had been the ones who'd missed Ernesto. Angelina had hardly known him. He'd been his father's shadow. Angelina, of course, had not been allowed to go to the dockyards and timberyards.

"Angelina. That is Caesare *Aldanto*, isn't it?"

Her out-thrust lower lip confirmed it.

"He's a bad man, Angelina," Petro said gently. "An adventurer of the worst sort, not some kind of hero. The Signori di Notte have suspicions about at least two of those duels he's fought. Only Ricardo Brunelli's personal intervention has kept him out in the taverns. Keep away from him, little sister."

She flounced out, angrily.

Sighing, Petro sat back in his chair and looked at the stack of papers on his desk. These magical murders were generating more paperwork than answers. He still felt they were no closer to knowing just who was behind them. Problems generated by Angelina's wild behavior were something he didn't need on top of it. He knew she was—along with a crowd of the wealthy and spoiled of Venice—slipping off to various taverns. He'd done it himself once upon a time. There had always been a couple of *Case Vecchie* girls who were no better than they should be among the crowd. Looking for thrills, looking for excitement. Enjoying being the "wild ones" able to retreat under the family mantle when real trouble came around. It was something of a shock to realize that was what his sister had become. He'd have to do something about it. Perhaps her aunt . . . he sighed. Better to deal with the immediate problems she would be causing. He rang a bell. A footman came hastily. "Tell Bruno and Giampaulo I want to see them. Now."

The two Dorma cousins came in, looking wary. Petro didn't summon people often.

Petro looked them up and down. Both were dressed with some flamboyance. Both carried rapiers. "And to what do we owe this sartorial elegance, gentlemen?" he asked dryly.

"We . . . we were just going out," said Bruno with attempted nonchalance.

"To see some—a . . . friend," said Giampaulo uneasily.

"Ah?" Petro tilted his head inquiringly. "Who?"

"Oh . . . um . . . just a friend." Bruno said airily. "You, you wouldn't know him."

"I see," said Petro affably. "With swords only, or were you planning to take a horsewhip along?"

They looked uneasily at each other. Said nothing.

Petro shook his head. "You will both forget about it."

"He insulted our honor!" said Bruno hotly.

Giampaulo was slightly more fulsome. "We can't tolerate some lowlife bringing shame on our house, Petro! This Felluci has made *Casa* Dorma—and your sister specifically!—the laughingstock of Venice!"

Petro's brow lowered. "May I remind you both that she is my sister and that I am the head of Dorma. Not you. I'll decide what needs to be done—if *anything* needs to be done. And if either of you think of taking over my authority . . . you can try being a Dorma factor in Outremer this year. Or Negroponte may have need of hotheads. I don't. I specifically forbade any dueling. And I promise you if I find out you've disobeyed me—and I will find out, don't think I won't—I'll leave you to rot in the Doge's dungeons. Is that clear? Who else was involved in this?"

Giampaulo and Bruno glanced at each other. Their shoulders slumped. "Bonaldo and Michael," muttered Bruno.

"I suggest you waste no time in passing this on to them. The less we do the less scandal there will be. At the moment only Angelina and this boy . . . and you four are involved. By the time you were finished half of Venice would know all the details and my sister and my house would truly be a laughingstock. I won't have it. Is that clear?"

Both of them looked sulky, wary. Nodded.

"Don't even think of trying to circumvent me," said Petro quietly. "I may just have saved your foolish lives. I wonder if Angelina mentioned that this Felluci is the duelist Aldanto's messenger?"

Petro had the satisfaction of seeing the two cousins go abruptly pale.

Chapter 41

Chiano brooded over the little fire while Sophia grilled fish he'd coaxed into his net for dinner. He thought about how Harrow had slipped away into the marsh so easily he might have been born here; the man made scarcely a rustle in the reeds. What he'd done to mold the creature that had come into his hands into the man now called Harrow had used a smidgeon of magic, a great deal of knowledge he'd gleaned from Sophia about the properties of the plants of the Jesolo, and all his manipulation.

Face the facts, old man, you used him. To protect Marco, yes, but he'd made Harrow into a mere tool for that protection . . .

He was a tool before you got him. He just didn't know it. You gave him that much; self-knowledge. There are those who'd give anything for that.

And there were those who would—and did—give anything to have the luxury of denial, too. He hadn't given Harrow a choice.

How many choices did I have? None, if he was to give Marco a protector. And Marco *had* to have a protector, if he was to grow into the power the Lion's Shadow promised for him. He was close now, close to accepting the Winged Mantle; Chiano had sensed it. But Marco had to live to grow into that power, and—

And Venice is suddenly a world more dangerous than it was before. And you, old man, aren't there.

Self-knowledge. . . .

He'd had the luxury, not of denial, but of absence of that knowledge for a long time, courtesy of those who had ambushed him in the very corridors of the Accademia, coshed him, and dropped him into a canal. Him! *Dottore* Marina! And he hadn't even remembered *that* much until recently! All those experiments with drugs and hallucinations—*he* knew enough to be able to tell the difference between a real vision and a hallucination—hadn't been to gather the Word of the Goddess. It had been to jar loose his own memories from the confused mist the blow to the head had sent them into.

At first, when he came here, all he'd known for certain was what old Sophia had told him—that the undines had brought him to her, that they had told her he was their friend and that they had rescued him when *someone* had tried to kill him. They didn't know who; the men had worn steel armor, and that had prevented their magic and his own from saving him. They knew he was a magician, a powerful magician, one who was the friend of water creatures in particular, but that was all they knew. That, and his name, which meant nothing to him as he was, and nothing to an old herb-witch living in the Jesolo.

Sophia had decided—and told him—that he must have some powerful enemy in the city to have earned such treatment, and he had caught fear from her. For the longest time he hadn't wanted to know; it seemed safer when he didn't. And he particularly didn't want to use magic. Sophia had told him that magicians could tell where other magicians were using magic, and even who it was that was doing it—as if there would be any other magician in the Jesolo!

But when nothing happened, and no one came seeking him, then he dared, a little at a time. He dared first a little magic, a very little magic, something that he remembered bits of, that Sophia knew bits of, to call the undines to him. And it worked; they came out of friendship more than anything else, but stayed because he *could* feed them tidbits of power out of his own stores. It was the undines who came often enough for his tidbits and stayed to chase fish into his traps. It was the undines, also, who frightened the locos sufficiently, with their clawed hands and shark-tooth smiles, that he and Sophia were left unmolested. They could even, at need, make dangerous locos like the late Big Gianni feel threatened enough that he *could* have made Big Gianni back off from Marco if he'd been there when it needed doing.

And finally he tried getting those memories back of who, exactly, *Dottore* Marina was, and what he could do.

"Here," Sophia said, nudging him. "Better eat."

He accepted the piece of grilled fish from her and ate it mechanically.

It was a good thing that it was the memories of danger that came back first, and not the ones he had just gotten over the last few days, or his enemies would have surely found him. *Someone* had paid for very, very skilled bravos, dressed head-to-foot in fine chain mail, to ambush him within the Accademia itself. His defensive magics, the ones he could do without thinking, had all been of the sort to use against another mage or a creature of magic. When striking cold steel, they had fizzled and died, like a wet firework. That was all he remembered; the blow to his head that must have followed blanked out everything else.

For a while at least.

He had struggled since then, trying to put a face on the faceless enemy. Who could have hired these men? Obviously someone conversant enough with magic to know exactly how to disable a *Magister Magus*, a Grimas, a master of all three of the *stregheria* traditions. He had enemies, but none that virulent. Some were political; he was—had been—the spokesperson, not only for the Strega but also the rest of the non-Christian mages, the Jews and Moslems and that bizarre little fellow allegedly from the Qin empire. He had managed to get a single voice out of that chaos of conflicting personalities, even though for the most part it was like trying to herd cats and just as thankless a task. But the Strega were little more than an afterthought in the politics of Venice; he couldn't think of anyone who would consider him a political threat.

What did that leave? A mystery, a faceless threat, and somehow that unnerved him, unmanned him, and left him determined to hide out here and depend on no more than the little dribs and drabs of magic it took to just stay alive.

But then that poor child had shown up, running from faceless enemies himself, men who had killed his mother. And on him, guiding him—the Lion's Shadow, the sign that Chiano had not—then—recognized for what it was, because he himself was not aware that he was the wearer of the Winged Mantle. He only knew that Marco *could* be a magician if he chose, and through Marco, he himself could work the magic that would elevate life in the swamp above mere survival.

Until now. Until now . . .

Now he knew what he was—the force through which the Protector, the Soul of Venice could work, a Soul that went right back through the Romans and to the first Etruscan fishermen who had plied the Jesolo. The Soul that now took the shape of the Winged Lion of Saint Mark, but who was older than even *Dottore* Marina could guess. And the Shadow he had seen on young Marco was not just the shadow of potential power, it was the Shadow of the Lion, showing that Marco—if he lived, if he grew into and accepted his power—would be the next to wear the Winged Mantle. Marco might even—Chiano was not sure about this yet—be the first to assume the Lion's Crown as well, something which no one had done in centuries.

Now he knew why he had lived—because the Shadow had dispersed his attackers with the brush of its wings that called up terror, and called the undines up the canal to rescue him before the assassins could complete their business. Because the Shadow had told the undines to take him to Sophia, deep into the Jesolo, where he could live and regain his memories.

But there was no reason to follow Marco into the city, to go back. Was there? The boy had Harrow to protect him. He didn't need Chiano, nor did anyone else.

Except—

Except for the stories that came drifting into the Jesolo like mist, like the echoes of bells from the city, the stories that spoke of the sinister and cruel acts of the Servants of the Trinity—

Who would burn you, if they could take you, Chiano—

And of a monster who prowled the waterways and killed—

And what business is that of yours?

The shadow of wings brushed through his mind, reminding him that—yes, it was his business. It threatened the city. It was not just politics, but *evil*, that had sent him into the canal that night, not merely to serve as a warning to those who might think to challenge it but to rid the city of its protector.

Dottore Marina would have scoffed and taken up the gauntlet. Chiano had come too close to death. Chiano was afraid.

The truth is—

The truth was, he didn't know enough.

That's easily remedied, some small inner voice told him. He sighed. Yes, it was—except he was afraid of the remedy.

No more softness!

He stood up abruptly, and jumped down off the raft. It was not quite sunset; there was still time for magic. Sophia paid no attention. By now, she was used to the way he would just get up and go off somewhere without a word.

Sophia was more than a little *loco* herself. Odd behavior meant little or nothing to her.

There were places, even in the Jesolo, where there was pure water. Springs bubbled up from beneath the marsh, rainwater collected— you could find it, if you knew where to look. Anyone who was friend to the undines could find it without difficulty at all.

It had rained last night. Chiano waded out onto a thread of a path that took him to a place among the hummocks where he had left a bowl to collect water. It would be fresh and sweet and pure— exactly what he needed for scrying, since he would use something other than the *stregheria* rite, which would surely pinpoint him to anyone who was looking for him.

Dottore Marina did not need to go through an elaborate ritual to invoke and erect a Circle of Power and Protection anymore; he just *thought* a few key words, and it sprang up around him. Invisible to most eyes, and only barely visible to those with the Inner Sight, it ringed him with the Inner Fires that would screen his probing from those watching for magic. Holding his hands over the bowl of pure water as he squatted beside it in the dying light of day, he breathed another invocation, and watched patiently. As the last of the sun vanished, and the first rays of the moon touched the surface, it misted over, then cleared, showing him the once-familiar canals and walkways of his city.

Show me the threat, he commanded silently. *Show me the peril to my city.*

He had hoped to see nothing. But the water misted and cleared immediately, and showed him, in rapid succession—a voluptuous woman with red-gold hair—

Lucrezia Brunelli—

—her brother, Ricardo—

—a sour-faced, fanatic-eyed man in a cassock with three crosses emblazoned on it—

An abbot of the Servants? But who? I don't recognize him—

A woman in the habit of a nun of the Servants.

Whose eyes were—lifeless. Then something looked out of them. At him. And saw him. And *knew him!*

And last, before he could react to that flicker of malevolent recognition, the darkened canal, with something swimming below the surface.

He bent nearer, closer to the water, trying to make out what it was.

It was coming out.

It sent one clawed hand, then another, to fasten into the stones of the canalside. Then it heaved itself up out of the water faster than a striking adder, and it turned, and it *looked* at him!

He screamed, and involuntarily thrashed at the water, breaking the spell. Just in time.

One moment more, and it would have been through the water-mirror, meant only for scrying, and at his throat, feeding on his life.

And his soul.

Reflexively, Luciano called up all of his defenses until he lay, panting, within a cocoon of power. Oh, anyone looking would See him now—but it didn't matter. Not after that. *They* knew he was out here, and it wouldn't take long for them to find him. How many undines would die protecting him?

For a very long time he couldn't think, he could only sit and shiver with fear that turned his bowels to water. As the moon climbed higher in the sky, he sat, and shook, and even wept unashamedly.

Not to me! This can't come to me! I'm too old, too tired—

But on his shoulders rested the Winged Mantle. He felt it, though it was invisible. There was no one else. Marco was untrained and unaware and could not take the Mantle in any case until Chiano was dead. The Mantle had come to *him* on the death of his predecessor—irony of ironies, it had been a little Hypatian priest-mage, out of a bastard branch of one of the four Old Families, and not one of the Strega.

No, Chiano was the bearer, for the good of Venice. If there had been anyone in all of Venice fit to wear it, it would have gone to him, or her, the moment his body hit the water, senseless, and he would have died. Extraordinary measures had been taken to ensure that he did not. Marco no doubt had the Mark, even then, but he hadn't the training, had no one to train him, and in any case was too young for the weight. The weight of the Mantle, even, much less the Crown.

His denial turned to a plea. *Please—not now. Please, not to me.*

But the answer was still the same. There was no other.

The night had never seemed so dark. . . .

Then, the shadow of a wing brushed him, and a quiet filled him. He made his mind very still, then, and waited.

There is no other, my child, said a voice as deep as the seas, as vast as the night sky. *But I will be with you. Your soul will survive.*

His soul . . . not his body, perhaps, but his soul.

It was enough; enough for him to find a small scrap of courage left, to drag together the rags of his sense of self, and to find a little more courage, a little more heart. And finally, what was left of his dignity.

He dismissed his protections with a word, and walked back to what had been his home, and would not be for much longer. Sophia looked up as he rejoined her on their combined rafts. Her eyes widened a little, as if he somehow looked different, now.

Perhaps he did.

For a moment he gazed out over the water towards the city, towards his fate.

"It's time, Sophia," he said at last. "It's time to go back."

Sophia smiled at him, shifting the wrinkles. And shook her head. "It's time you went back, Chiano. But this is my place, now," she said with finality.

Chapter 42

After he lowered his pack onto the cot which would henceforth serve him as a bed, Eneko Lopez heaved a sigh of relief. "Thank God," he murmured, as his eyes made a quick survey of his new living quarters. The survey was very brief, for the simple reason that there was very little to survey in the first place. The room was tiny, as small as any cell he had inhabited in his years as a monk. Except for the cot and a small chest at the foot of it which would serve to store his few belongings, the only other item of furniture was a writing table in front of the room's one small window and a chair. Other than that, the room was bare except for a crucifix hanging on the wall above the cot.

"I'll miss the library," he murmured. "But nothing else."

His two companions smiled. Diego motioned with his head toward the open window. "The smell from the canals is bad at times, here in the Ghetto."

"Not half as bad as the stench in *Casa* Brunelli," growled Pierre. "What did you give as your reason for changing quarters?"

"I simply told Ricardo Brunelli that my work in the Ghetto had progressed to the point where I needed to live there. Which is true enough, as far as it goes."

"You should have—"

"Oh, Pierre—do stop!" snapped Eneko. "We have enough problems on our hands without offending the Brunellis unnecessarily. Any more than I have already by spurning that infernal Lucrezia's constant advances."

Pierre, as usual, was stubborn. "'Infernal' is right," he growled.

"Pierre . . . *please*. You admit yourself that you've never been able to detect any sense of a witch about her."

"You're making too much of that," retorted Pierre. "My talent has definite limits, Eneko. What I said was that I could not detect any *demonic possession* in the woman. That's what a 'witch' is, after all. That does not mean she can't be as vile as any of Satan's minions."

"That the woman is evil I don't doubt for an instant," replied Eneko, shrugging. "But we have not a shred of evidence to think she is in any way connected to the events in Venice which brought us here. And, given the position of the Brunellis, I can see no logical reason why she would be."

"You yourself have said 'evil needs no reason,'" pointed out Pierre.

Eneko sighed. "Savoy mule! Let there be an end to it, Pierre, at least for now. We must concentrate on the matter at hand."

"On that," interjected Diego, "there is news. Perhaps, I should say."

At Lopez's cocked eyebrow, Diego elaborated. "I have discovered the identity of that boy you asked about. The local healer who also works for Caesare Aldanto. His name—so it is said, at least—is 'Marco Felluci.' And he doesn't simply work for Aldanto, he lives with him. He and another boy named Benito. Along with Aldanto's woman, a canaler by the name of Maria Garavelli."

Lopez's eyes widened a bit. "Are the two boys related? Brothers, perhaps?"

Diego shook his head. "Not according to the information I've been able to collect. The other's last name is Oro. And I've seen him, once. He doesn't resemble Marco in the least. The only similarity between the two boys is that, according to rumor, they are both orphans."

Lopez studied him for a moment. "But . . . you are, I suspect, wondering the same thing that I am."

Diego nodded. "It seems odd, yes. For Aldanto to take two boys under his wing . . . and he just spent a large sum rescuing the boy Marco."

"From what?"

Pierre chuckled. "From an absurd romantic complication." He proceeded to give Lopez a quick sketch of what he and Diego had learned from local canalers about what had quickly become a rather famous little episode.

Eneko smiled. "Love poems, eh?" Slowly, he sat down on the chair. "It *is* odd. Why should a mercenary like Aldanto go to such lengths to shelter two waifs? Two orphans—presumably penniless. One of whom, at least, does not seem to have the temperament one would expect from a protégé of Aldanto. Healing poor children—for no payment—love poems. Even leaving aside that angel face."

"And the names," added Diego. Eneko nodded. "Yes. Marco and Benito are common names, of course. Still . . ."

"One moment," said Diego. He left the room and returned shortly with a scarf in his hand. "I obtained this from the little girl whom we saw the boy treat that time. She was reluctant to part with it, but . . ."

Lopez couldn't refrain from wincing. Another coin gone, from the few they had in their possession. But he did not utter any protest. Like Diego, he thought the money well spent.

"Yes," he said forcefully. "With that scarf, we can discover the boy's past. As much, at least, as that scarf was a part of it."

Pierre, unlike his two companions, was not well versed in sacred magic. "Unreliable . . ." he murmured. "Possibly even risky."

Diego shook his head. "Not in the least, Pierre. This is not like scrying, which another mage could detect and distort. Nor is it as difficult—almost impossible, really—as foretelling the future. The past is done, immutable. What Eneko proposes is simply an aspect of—" Diego, who had a bit of the pedant in him, began what was clearly going to be a long-winded description of the principles of contagion as applied to sacred magic. But Eneko cut him short.

"Enough!" he chuckled. "Pierre wants to hear it less than I do." To Pierre: "It can be done. Trust me. Will you join us in prayer?" He cast his eyes about their new home. "Since I am going to be living here, working here—" He raised his eyebrow significantly. "—and worshipping here, it should be cleansed first. And Diego, you may pretend ignorance, but you know very well how to ritually cleanse a dwelling."

Diego groaned. "I'll get a broom."

"A prayer of intention, first," Pierre said, with a laugh of his own.

The ritual cleansing didn't take long; to be honest, although the room was physically filthy, there wasn't much in the way of negativity to chase from it, and nothing at all of evil. The smells might be dreadful, but the spiritual atmosphere was clean. There was a practicality to a ritual cleansing—following the principle of "as above, so below," you *cleaned;* you cleaned everything, floor to ceiling, in order to set a barrier of protection permanently in place, but you cleaned with intention, prayer, and the magic to flush away the "dirt" you couldn't see along with what you could. Diego was very good at floors.

One of the reasons Eneko had chosen this particular room was because of a peculiarity of alignment: the four corners were exactly pointing to the four cardinal directions. By nailing a bit of wood into each corner to serve as a shelf for the tiny statues of the Archangels Michael, Gabriel, Raphael, and Uriel he had brought, he recreated, in miniature, a ritual chapel. Like Hagia Sophia on the other side of town, like the ritual chapels of Hypatians everywhere, by the time he and Pierre finished blessing it, setting up the boundary-spells, blessing it again, this was sacred ground, protected from evil.

"Ah!" Eneko said, stretching his arms and shaking out his hands when they were done. "I much prefer *this* sort of comfort to anything *Casa* Brunelli offered."

"I can't say as I blame you," Pierre replied. Diego just shrugged and picked up the scarf, which they had left lying on the cot.

"If you're going to do this, you might as well get it over with," he said, holding it out to Eneko gingerly, as if it was a viper.

Eneko just smiled and dug a flat bowl out of his belongings, while Pierre went out to find a water-seller. He returned with a cask of potable water which he set up in the corner beneath the statue of Gabriel and tapped. "Strange that in a city *on* the water, you can't drink any of it," he remarked.

"No stranger than being on a ship, surrounded by water," Diego countered. "For that matter, would *you* drink water from the Loire in Orleans?"

"Ah . . . no. Here you are, Eneko." Pierre had filled the flat bowl with clean water and put it on the floor where the two of them knelt on either side of it. Eneko murmured a blessing over it, and Pierre blessed salt and cast it over the top of the water. Then, holding an end of the scarf each, the two mages bent over the bowl, while Diego peered at it from his perch on the cot.

While Pierre readied the bowl to reflect the images that came to it, Eneko used a thread of power to "talk" to the scarf. *Show us where you have been*, was the gist of his spell, and in a moment, a mist passed over the face of the water, and images appeared there, looking exactly like reflections.

Except these reflections were of nothing that was in the room.

The scarf itself was not very old, which was just as well; Eneko hurried past the silkworm, the weavers, the dandy (prone to getting recklessly drunk in foolish places) who had owned it, until he came to the moment that Benito Oro plucked it from the drunk's neck.

"Ah—" said Diego, with interest. Now they settled down to watch in earnest.

When the work was finished, the magic dispelled, and the blessed water scattered around the room, Eneko chuckled again. "The Marco boy may be an innocent, but his young companion Benito is certainly not. Which, unfortunately, leaves us knowing not much more than we did before. Since the scarf was stolen only a few days before Marco gave it to the child."

He rose to his feet. "Still, there is enough here to warrant further effort. Diego, I need to make a trip. It will use up most of what we have, until we get another disbursement of funds from the Grand Metropolitan. But well worth it, perhaps."

Pierre had risen to his feet also. "It will do us good to live on alms for a while, anyway."

Diego, still seated on the cot, cast a questioning look upward. "A trip? Where? And to do what?"

When Lopez told him, Diego sighed. "And what makes you think the old man will allow you the privilege? He's ferocious on that subject, by all accounts."

Lopez handed him the scarf. "I will give him this. Then tell him how the younger boy acquired it and what the older one did with it. If our suspicion—say better, surmise—is correct, he will allow me to see the portrait."

"If there is one," demurred Pierre. "He may have burned whatever existed."

"Oh, I doubt that," said Lopez softly. "It is one thing for a man to disown his daughter and cast her out. It is another thing entirely to burn his own memories."

❀　　　❀　　　❀

"It appears that Marco has come to no permanent harm in his sojourn in the marshes," said Antimo, carefully. "The money you've been sending Aldanto to keep the boys was well spent. Although—" For a moment, Bartelozzi's prim mouth pursed with distaste. "Needless to say, he's been letting everyone think that it was *his* money which rescued Marco."

The Old Fox chuckled wryly. "You expected *Caesare Aldanto* to be truthful and modest?"

Antimo shrugged, acknowledging the truth in the little jest. "However, there is another aspect of the new situation you need to consider, milord. A quite unforeseen one. It appears the boys have acquired *another* protector besides Aldanto—and one who is every bit as skilled, and in some ways perhaps even more dangerous."

Dell'este put his hands behind his head and rocked back on his chair. "They seem to have a talent for attracting supporters and defenders. That is a valuable trait for the Dell'este," he said cheerfully. "You might even say: a family custom."

Antimo looked at him. A steady unblinking basilisk stare.

The Old Fox sighed. "All right, Antimo. Who is it?"

"Fortunato Bespi."

The chair came down with a thump. The Old Fox looked anything but cheerful. Then he shook his head sharply.

"All right, Antimo. You've succeeded! For once you have brought me a piece of information that was so totally unexpected I was at a loss. Bespi! Who would have thought it? All reports claimed he was dead. That he should turn up protecting Lorendana's children is . . . bizarre."

There was a long silence. The duke sat quietly. After a moment, he turned his lined old face away from Bartelozzi and stared blindly at a far wall. Moisture welled in his eyes, and, eventually, slowly, a tear found its way down one cheek.

At length Antimo Bartelozzi cleared his throat. "What do you wish done about the matter, milord?"

The Old Fox rubbed his eyes and took a deep breath. "*Nothing*," he said harshly. "Lorendana made her choices. It may be that I failed her as a father. She was a very beautiful child, Antimo. Maybe I indulged her more than I should have. But, nonetheless, she made her own decisions. She lived by them and she died by them. Bespi was a fanatic. Had he murdered her for money, I would

have had him assassinated at the time as a message: Killing a
Dell'este for money guarantees you will not live to spend it. But
Bespi killed to orders, because he was a single-minded fanatic. I
would have done as well to have my revenge on a knife. Still true."

He peered at Bartelozzi, his eyes once again as sharp and dry
as usual. "Tell me this, however: are you certain that Bespi guards
them?"

The agent nodded. "Yes, milord. He could have killed both boys
in the swamp as easily as he could two chickens. You know that
as well as I. Bespi is—deadly. And I've watched him myself since
he returned to the city. A mother hen puts in far less effort caring for its chicks. *You* know, my lord, how a fanatical foe can turn
into the most loyal of defenders, if you can change their hearts."

The Old Fox looked at the man who had many years ago been
sent to kill him. "I know that, Antimo," he said quietly.

There was silence, for a moment. Then the Duke of Ferrara
clapped his hands in a quick and decisive gesture. "Enough! I trust
your judgment. Now, let us turn to the general situation in Venice.
The Council of Ten: what of Calenti?"

Antimo shook himself back to the present. "Lord Calenti remains
apparently neutral, milord. But . . . we have discovered he has been
having a very discreet liaison with Lucrezia Brunelli."

The Old Fox raised an eyebrow. "She's a busy woman. She must
have to apportion her time carefully. She's been linked to several
other people whom we have watched. Well . . . does this lean him
toward the Metropolitans?"

The agent shook his head. "Based on Lucrezia's other . . .
paramours . . . I would guess that the tendency is *not* in favor of
her brother's party. Lucrezia is her own woman. Ricardo Brunelli
thinks his sister draws her suitors to him. But of the ardent suitors
and possible lovers we know of—quite a number have Montagnard
sympathies or contacts. Count Badoero, for example."

"A bad egg if there ever was one," said the Old Fox. "Lord Calenti
will bear watching. And what of Petro Dorma? Have there been
any repercussions from Marco's foray into poetry?"

Antimo shook his head. "No, milord. Apparently, Lord Dorma
stifled the usual 'young bravo' sentiment within his own house
quite decisively. I have to say I'm growing increasingly impressed
by the man. I think he remains our best bet among the Council
of Ten."

The Old Fox reached for his quill. "So am I. Well, then. Let us see if we can arrange a little warming of relations between the Dell'este and Dorma. I think the blade that is my grandson Marco has been tempered. It is time to start using it. Let us see if my enemies dare to move openly—when the head of a reborn *Casa* Valdosta stands forth in Venice under his rightful name."

Antimo looked perturbed. "He may be killed, milord."

The Old Fox shrugged. "If he is, then we will know he was poorly tempered steel," he said quietly.

When Eneko returned from Ferrara, he said nothing to his companions at first. He simply unwrapped the small parcel he brought with him, and showed them what it contained.

Diego hissed. "Dear God, what a resemblance."

"There is a much larger portrait at Dell'este, in which the resemblance is even more striking. But the duke gave me this miniature."

"Why?" asked Pierre.

Eneko smiled. "I asked him that same question myself. A most interesting answer he gave me. 'You must remember the mother, most of all.'"

"I don't understand," said Diego, frowning.

Eneko placed the miniature on his little writing desk. "'Old Fox,' indeed," he murmured. "I shall keep the portrait here at all times. To remind me that *both* boys had the same mother." He turned back to his companions. "And what was *she*, brothers? An evil woman or a good one? Or simply a mother?"

Diego stared at the portrait, still confused. But Pierre nodded. "Indeed so. The portrait is a reminder to us. A warning, perhaps—of the danger of pride."

"She was indeed a proud woman, by all accounts," mused Diego.

Eneko shook his head firmly. "You misunderstand. The duke was warning us of the danger of *our* pride." He smiled grimly. "Canny old man. That is indeed the downfall of theologians."

His eyes went back and forth from Pierre to Diego. "We will do nothing with this knowledge, for the time being. That, too, the old man made me swear. The children are safer for the moment with their identity concealed, obviously. But when the time comes—remember, brothers. There were *two* sons, produced by the same mother."

"God works in mysterious ways," said Diego solemnly.

"Oh, nonsense!" chuckled Pierre. "Not in this instance. Any Savoyard can tell you the trick. Always keep a second string for your bow."

PART IV
March, 1538 A.D.

Chapter 43

Humiliation, Marco was learning, was a very different thing from shame.

Shame gripped your gut and made you sick. Humiliation made you wish you were dead. Shame had made him run. Humiliation made him hide. He hid at his job behind a facade of the drabbest clothing in his wardrobe and a bulwark of work. He was fast becoming one of the most put-upon clerks in the office, because he courted, volunteered for, the most tedious and boring tasks available. And he hid after work anywhere but home, once he made his check to see if Caesare had a job for him. He visited his friend the art student as much as he could without becoming a nuisance, which actually wasn't that difficult at the moment. When Rafael wasn't studying, he needed models to draw from, and Marco had absolutely no objection to stripping down to his smallclothes and holding still until he turned blue, so long as no one was teasing him about Angelina.

And when he wasn't visiting Rafael, he hid in books, or, increasingly, in the tiny church of Saint Raphaella—and somehow the confluence of names seemed appropriate. He didn't seek out the priest, Brother Mascoli, and he didn't let the priest catch sight of him. He simply sat in the back, and thought, until it was almost dark, and only then did he go home.

Here, at least, his thoughts weren't so much about humiliation as humility itself, and not at all about Angelina.

Over and over he thought about what the priest had told him, and tried to come up with counterarguments. He couldn't.

Moreover, the more he saw of the militant Pauline faction, the less he liked them. They were arrogant, the most of them, and pride was arguably the most deadly of the sins, since it led to so many of the others. And oh, they were angry—he scarcely ever saw a Sot or a Knot without a frown on his face—and that was not only another deadly sin, but one that led straight to murder and mayhem. You couldn't keep that much anger pent up for long without it boiling over, and when it did, someone always got hurt. Perhaps the Petrines were soft, and perhaps they were inclined to another deadly sin, that of sloth, but at least no one was ever hurt by a slothful layabout with a deadly weapon.

The Paulines were right about one thing: there was such a thing as real evil, and oft times the Petrines preferred to pretend there wasn't in the hopes that it would get bored and go away. But not all Petrines. Not the priest here, for instance . . . no, that sort of thing was the besetting sin of those whose wealth and power allowed them to insulate themselves from the rest of the world. The ones who scoffed at the stories of the canal monster because no one *they* knew had been attacked by it. Well . . . except for the financier killed the previous summer. But that had been months ago, and most of Venice's elite seemed to have convinced itself that his murder was the work of a simple maniac. A disgruntled debtor, no doubt. Only ignorant and superstitious peasants would credit such a thing as "magical murder" or a mysterious monster in the canals.

But, being honest with himself, Marco could not be at all certain that Paulines sufficiently insulated by wealth and position from their sweating peasants would not have said the same thing, had the monster prowled the back alleys of Milan instead of the canals of Venice.

So, on long afternoons before darkness fell, Marco sat on a bench in the darkest corner against the wall at the rear of the church and looked at the crude statue of Saint Raphaella, and wondered what he should do. He didn't want to ask for a sign—who was he that a saint should give him a sign? He blushed to think that he had asked one of Saint Peter—*Saint Peter!*—those months ago in the swamp.

He'd come here again after another day of making triplicate copies of tedious documents, knowing that his friend was studying for an examination and Caesare was out on some mysterious business or other. The church had been darkening steadily for the past several moments, and he would have to go soon—

With a start, he realized that Brother Mascoli was in the church—was coming towards him—

Was coming at him.

Jesu! Has the man eyes like a cat?

"Marco, I need you," the priest said, as Marco started to get up, to get away, before the man could confront him. Mascoli grabbed him by the arm before Marco could protest, or even think of anything to say. "Don't argue with me, boy. I need you. *They* need you, and they asked for you by name."

"Who did?" Marco squeaked.

"You'll see," Brother Mascoli said, and dragged him up to the altar, around to his own quarters, and out a tiny back door.

It was, as it transpired, a water-door, which let onto a mere thread of a canal. Handy for poor canal-folk to bring in their sick and injured by night? Handy, too for smuggling—

In this case, handy for something else entirely, for something that was the last thing Marco would have expected. He stared down at the three faces in the water. Three pale green faces, looking up at him and the priest, their fishy eyes reflecting the light from a torch set up in a sconce on the wall, their emerald-green hair like water-weeds streaming and waving in the water around them. And it reflected upon a fourth face, so pale there was hardly any green to it, eyes closed, webbed fingers clasped over a hideous wound in its—her—stomach.

Marco turned on Brother Mascoli. "Those are *undines!*" he said accusingly.

"And this—if you will notice—is enclosed within the church walls," he replied, waving at what Marco had taken to be a canal. It wasn't. Now that the priest had drawn his attention to it, he saw that it was part of the church proper, beneath the roof, a crucifix mounted on the back with another Presence-Light beneath it on a shelf that served for an altar. A sort of watery chapel, apparently.

"Technically, since I bless this place three times daily, *this* is Holy Water," Brother Mascoli continued. "They may not be human, but they've passed the test of faith. And they asked for you by name. *I* can't heal her, but they think you can."

"Me?" Marco's voice went up another octave.

"*You*," said a sibilant voice from below. "*We have seen you with our brother, among the reeds. You have the light and the power. We cannot reach him in time—you must heal our sister!"*

He couldn't help himself; he knelt down on the water-stair and looked at the terrible gash that crossed the undine's torso from left nipple to the top of her right hip, and a spasm of sympathetic pain closed around his throat. How could *anyone* heal that? How could the poor thing still be alive?

The wounded undine's eyes opened, and he was caught in her gaze. She moaned pitifully, and held out webbed fingers to him. *"Please,"* came the faintest of whispers.

Blessed Maria— It was more than a spasm of sympathy now; he swallowed down actual tears.

"But—" he directed, not a protest, but a plea of his own to Brother Mascoli. "I don't know how—"

"They're magic creatures, Marco. You probably couldn't heal a human slashed like that, but they're as much spirit as flesh—" Brother Mascoli began, then shook his head. "Just do what I do." He looked down at one of the uninjured undines. "Little sister, you're going to have to help. I may need you to act as a catalyst; the boy's never done magic as far as he knows."

One of the undines separated herself from the injured one, leaving the other two to support their sister in the water. *"I am ready,"* she said, undulating over to Marco, and sliding up onto the water-step beside his feet. He couldn't help noticing when she spoke that she had long, sharp claws on those graceful green hands—and a mouth full of sharklike teeth. Looking at those teeth . . .

Marco almost shuddered. The "our brother" the undine had referred to could only be Chiano. He'd always known old Chiano had a special relationship with the undines in the Jesolo. The marsh locos had always been afraid of Chiano. Marco had thought it was only because of some vague fear of Chiano's magic, but now—looking at those teeth—he suspected that at least marsh locos had learned the hard way not to fool around with a friend of the undines.

Brother Mascoli turned Marco to face the opening of the water-chapel that led to the canal, "Holy Angel Gabriel—"

He nudged Marco who realized suddenly that this was a prayer, and he was expected to follow. "Holy Angel Gabriel," he repeated obediently, echoed by the undine at his feet.

Jesu—it's a prayer—I'd better put some feeling into it. All it took was a single glance at the poor creature at his feet to do that.

"You who brought the word of God—to the Blessed Virgin Mary—who guard the waters—and those who dwell therein—we beseech and pray thee—to guard our circle—and guide our work."

He'd been concentrating on putting his heart into the words and he hadn't really thought about what the prayer might do—and it came as a shock when the area of the opening suddenly filled with a flare of green light so bright it made the torch pale. It certainly made Marco start back with surprise, but Brother Mascoli only grunted with what sounded like satisfaction and turned Marco to the right to face the blank wall of the chapel, and began another prayer. "Holy Angel Michael—you who guard the world with a flaming sword—and all the creatures born of fire—we beseech and pray thee—"

This time when the flash of red light came, Marco was, more or less, ready for it. He turned on his own this time, beginning to get the idea. The angel was Raphael this time—"who guard the air and those who dwell therein"—and the flash was of blue light along the wall with the crucifix mounted on it. And last of all, they faced the wall behind them and invoked the Angel Uriel, the keeper of the creatures of the earth, and were greeted with a flash of pure golden light practically at their noses.

Brother Mascoli once again turned Marco to face the altar. *"In nomine Patri, et Filius, et Spiritus Sanctus, fiat lux!"* he intoned, with Marco only a fraction of a second behind him, and a blinding white light enveloped the entire water-chapel for a moment, to die down to a faint curtain of light between them and the outside world.

And if Marco doubted that—there was the evidence of his own ears. There was no sound coming from out there—nothing of the echoes of voices and the splash of water, of the bumping of boats against the mooring and the slap of feet on the walkways. Nothing.

Brother Mascoli gave another grunt of satisfaction. "All right, Marco, the rest is simple. Kneel down beside our little sister there—"

Too caught up now to even think of protesting, Marco knelt on the step beside the undine at his feet. She placed her hands in the water, just over the injured one's, once again clasped desperately over her wound.

"Just put your hands over hers—" the priest directed.

Marco shivered at the order—shivered once again at the touch of the cool flesh under his, cooler than a human's could ever be, and—scaled? Yes, those were scales under his fingers.

Brother Mascoli bent over and completed the stack with his own hands. "Now," he said in Marco's ear. "Just pray. Pray to Saint Raphaella and Saint Hypatia, to give you the power to heal this child of God—"

How—he thought, but he obeyed, closing his eyes and putting every bit of concentration he had into a fervent, even desperate, plea. He barely noticed one of the scaled hands slip from beneath his and come to rest just over his heart. Instead he concentrated on an image that came to him from nowhere, of the dreadful wound being un-made, sealing up, closing over, leaving the flesh sweet and unmarked, linking that image to his prayer in a way he *felt* was right—

And then he felt something else entirely.

An upwelling within himself, first a trickle of warmth and life and energy, then a rivulet, then a stream, then a gush—energy that was somehow *green*, although he could not have said why, that flowed from somewhere into him, and down through his chest and into his arms and out his hands, which grew warm as it passed through them. Startled, he opened his eyes, and saw, to his open-mouthed astonishment, that it wasn't some trick of his imagination. His hands *were* glowing with a green light the color of sunlight passing through early leaves, and the light was sinking down and spreading over the wounded undine.

And the wound was closing, exactly as he had imagined it.

There were two—*beings*—of light, one to his right, and one to his left, hovering weightlessly over the water. They were vaguely human-shaped, but too bright and at the same time too diffuse to really make out anything else. They each held a hand over his head, and he knew, somehow, that this was the source of that energy that was coursing through him. Brother Mascoli and the other undine were caught fast in some sort of trance; their eyes were shut fast.

This is for your eyes only, little brother. He sensed, somehow, that the being to his right was smiling at him, that the words came from—him? Her?

Both. And neither. Meaningless, little brother. God's spirits have no gender.

He didn't know whether to be elated—to have at last that sign he had not dared hope for—or to be ashamed that he had doubted and had waited so long to *use* this thing he'd been given. He decided he had to be both.

And neither. Could the infant Tintoretto have painted a fresco? Some things must wait upon . . . maturity.

Embarrassment, the too familiar taste of humiliation at his own stupidity, his own failures; then, suddenly, the sweeter taste of something altogether different. Humility.

Of course. Sometimes, old Chiano had said, you have to wait until you're ready. . . .

Exactly. Now—concentrate, little brother. We cannot remain much longer.

He closed his eyes again and focused his attention, until the flow of what he now knew was pure, simple *power* began to ebb; from a rush, to a stream, from a stream, to a rivulet, from a rivulet, to a trickle, and then it was gone.

He opened his eyes, and pulled back his hands.

The only light came, once again, from the torch in the sconce overhead. The water-chapel was utterly unchanged. But in the water, a miracle opened her eyes in wonder.

The wound was gone, exactly as he had imagined it, leaving not so much as a scar.

The newly healed undine clapped her hands with joy, and to Marco's intense embarrassment, leapt out of the water to plant wet and strangely hard lips on his cheek, as her sister who had sat at his side did the same on his other cheek.

"Well done, Marco," said Brother Mascoli heartily—but with overtones of weariness. A moment later, Marco had to put out a hand on the step to steady himself, for when he tried to stand, he was nearly bowled over by the same weariness.

The undines made a move in the direction of the water-entrance, and Brother Mascoli called out to them while Marco was still trying to get to his feet. "A moment, little sisters—who did this to you?"

The one who had been wounded turned back, although her three companions shook their heads in warning.

"It's all right—I haven't dispelled the circle," Mascoli assured them. "It's safe enough to use a True Name."

"*We do not know the True Name, Elder Brother,*" the wounded one said solemnly. "*Only that it is a thing of water or land or fire as it chooses to be, that it is a thing that is a stranger here, and that*—" she hesitated. "*We think that it was once a god.*"

Marco looked up at Brother Mascoli to see his reaction, and a shiver of fear came over him. Brother Mascoli was as white as foam.

But within a moment he had gotten hold of himself, and made a gesture of cutting in the air. With a rapid flurry of thanks, the undines plunged under the surface, and disappeared, presumably out into the canal, and from there, into cleaner water elsewhere.

"Now," Brother Mascoli said, putting a hand under Marco's elbow to help him up, "You, my young mage, are not going elsewhere until you learn the *right* way to do what we just cobbled together."

"Yes sir," Marco said. He knew the look on the priest's face. He might just as well try to argue with the Lion of Saint Mark. Brother Mascoli drew him in through the water-door and sat him down at a little work table, then pulled out a dismayingly heavy book. "First of all, you *always* cast a circle of protection. The only reason we got away with not doing so this time is because the church is within a permanent circle that only needs to be invoked, and . . ."

It was going to be a long evening. But at least he wouldn't be thinking about Angelina for a while.

Or so he thought, until he finally returned home the next day. It was a shock to see her. Especially this close, and *here* of all places. Marco didn't know what to say when he almost bumped into Angelina Dorma. . . . Here in Caesare's apartment—coming out of Caesare's bedroom. Not wearing an awful lot of clothing. Also, by the slight sway, anything but sober. Marco had stammered something incoherent, and bolted for the room he and Benito shared, her somewhat guilty laughter ringing in his ears.

In the security of the room he tried to work through the confusion of his feelings. She wasn't his. Never had been, the truth be told. He had no reason to feel torn up like this. After all, Angelina was just another daydream. She'd been nothing like his dream girl. Her face lacked the character, humor and . . . a certain *something* of the girl he'd seen on the Grand Canal the day he'd been brought back from the Jesolo marshes. But he had still kept Angelina on something of a pedestal . . . which she'd climbed off and into Caesare's bed. He needed to be alone to think this lot over.

Then he realized he wasn't even alone now. Benito was sitting on the far side of the bed, looking at him with a quizzical, slightly worried expression on his round face. For all that Benito was younger than he was, sometimes he looked older. And . . . at least there was no need to explain. "How long?"

"Quite a while now." Benito answered, sotto voce. "Started up seeing her while you were still in bed with that knock on the head. Seems like he took the opening you had made once he realized she was interested. They don't meet here hardly at all, though, so I was hoping you'd never find out."

Marco shook his head, trying to clear it. "Um. So what are you doing here?"

"Same as you. Old man Ventuccio gave us a half holiday because he's got a grandson to carry on the family name, in case you forgot. Only I didn't come in by the door, and I didn't drop in to see a friend at the Accademia." Benito grinned impishly. "Thought I'd catch up on my sleep 'cause I got things to do tonight."

"Oh." Marco paused. "What about Maria?"

Benito look a little uncomfortable. "She's gone on a long trip out to Murano. Got some more glassware for that ceremonial galley to fetch. You know what Maria's like. They trust her. When she's away is a good time for us to stay away, brother. Aldanto . . . entertains visitors."

Marco swallowed. "More?" he asked in a small voice.

Benito nodded. "Couple or two or three. There's Signora Selmi. Her husband is one of the captains in the galley fleet. And there's this one I don't know. Little prisms-and-prunes mouth with a mole on her left cheek. She's wild. Doesn't come often but when she does . . . we even had old Camipini coming over later to complain about the noise—when Maria was home. Lord and Saints! I thought the fat was in the fire then!"

Marco felt as if he might faint. Benito *had* said that Caesare played the field with women. But . . . "Do you think I should warn Angelina?" he asked quietly, his loyalties torn.

Benito snorted. "Marco, big brother, Grandpapa was right. You do need someone to look after you. Like me. Now listen good. Your precious Angelina is a wild girl. She's trouble, Marco. That's a bad crowd she runs with, and I don't think Caesare is her first time either. You just leave her to Caesare. He knows how to deal with girls like that. You don't."

Marco stood up, biting his lip. Then, nodded. "You're right, brother. This time, anyway. I need to go out. I'll see you."

Benito stood up too, stretching. "I'll tag along for company. I think we ought to leave quietly by the window. We can go and see Claudia and Valentina. Unless you'd rather go looking for that dream girl of yours?"

Marco wanted to be alone, but Benito obviously had no intention of letting him be. "At least my dream girl is not like that," he said quietly.

Benito muttered something. Marco didn't quite catch it, and didn't want to ask him to repeat it. But it could have been "In your dreams, brother." Instead he swung out of the window heading for the ornamental casement Benito always said was like a ladder. A slippery ladder that the city's pigeons used for other purposes, in Marco's opinion. Once they were away up on a roof, overlooking the canal, Benito leaned back against the chimney stack. "Right, brother. What am I looking for again? Let's hear the lyrical description."

Marco panted. "Stop teasing me."

Benito grinned impishly. "Oh, that's right. I remember now. Amazing what even I can remember when I've only heard it three thousand times. 'She has curly red-carroty hair. She has a generous mouth, a tip-tilted nose—merry eyes, wonderful hazel eyes.' And she's your soul mate. You knew the minute your eyes met."

"You're a cynic, little brother."

"At least I'm not a fool."

Benito regretted it the moment he'd said it. He found that look of Marco's one of the hardest things to deal with. That clear look that seemed to see right into you. He squirmed slightly under the gaze. Marco didn't even seem to be aware that he was doing it. After a while, as if from a distance, Marco said: "It's good to be a fool sometimes, Benito. And you will be too, one day."

"Yeah. When hell freezes over, Marco," said Benito, feeling uncomfortable. "Come on, let's go down. I got a tip today and my pocket'll run to a couple of *toresani*. Or maybe some *Muset* and beans."

Marco sighed, but stood up. "Do you ever think of anything but food, brother?"

"Do you ever think of anything but girls?" It was an unfair comment, and Benito knew it. He was starting to think quite a lot about girls himself, nowadays. And Marco thought, if anything, about too much. He cared for the whole world, especially sick canal-brats. Benito . . . well he cared for his brother Marco. And . . . well . . . Maria. He'd like to earn her respect sometime. And Caesare. He owed them.

Chapter 44

Katerina Montescue was in a foul mood. It was all very well forming an instant *rapport* with someone across a crowded canal. But . . .

She'd always thought that if she ever married, she'd have to marry money. Then she'd seen him. Establishing who he was had proved easy enough. At least three people had asked her if she'd seen him, when they'd been looking for him. She'd been rather frightened to discover just how many of the canal boatmen knew her.

So: his name was Marco Felluci. A few casual questions began to paint a broader canvas. A clerk for Ventuccio. And something of a healer. Respected by the bargees and canalers—people who didn't give respect or liking easily. And a boy with friends. Friends prepared to spend money to find him when he went missing. She hadn't needed that information to tell her he was a good man. She knew that the moment she saw him.

So . . . he was only a clerk. It hadn't taken her long to realize that being *Case Vecchie* was less important to her than being happy.

So. She'd be poor, then. Why not? She was practiced at it by now, wasn't she? They'd have a little house and she'd wash, and clean and cook. Easier work—less dangerous, too—than what she'd been doing, after all. And if they needed more money than he could make as a clerk, Katerina could always take Francesca up on her offer to work as a special gondolier for Casa Louise.

She must learn more about cooking. . . . How to make cheap meals. They'd have children and his work would bring him promotion and . . .

Insane. She couldn't do it! Not that she cared herself about remaining *Case Vecchie*—well, not much, anyway—but if she abandoned her family *Casa* Montescue would collapse. Without her dealing in the gray goods coming in with Captain Della Tomasso, the *Casa* would fall apart. Be bankrupt before the summer. Her grandfather—who had borne so much, with such Montescue pride and fortitude—would die if the *Casa* were sold. And it wasn't just him. All the servants and family retainers, many of whom had spent their lives in service to Montescue—for generations, some of them—would be cast adrift also.

Katerina Montescue had responsibilities as well as longings and desires. She couldn't simply toss over the one for the other.

And, besides—she had no idea how to meet him anyway. Neither of her two personas, either as "the Spook" or as Katerina Montescue, would ever come into contact with a clerk who worked, no doubt, in a back room at Ventuccio. A dark back room where his eyes would go . . .

What to do? What to do?

Francesca. Yes! I'll talk to Francesca about it. The very next time I see her!

Katerina's face went through an odd little play of expressions. "Oh," she murmured to herself. "That's tonight, isn't it?"

And that was *another* problem! For a moment, Katerina almost burst into a pure shriek of frustration at society's quirks.

"Are you going to get dressed or aren't you?" snapped Alessandra, peering around the door.

Guilt and the reason for being so out of sorts returned Kat to the real world. "I'm coming."

"Well hurry up," said Alessandra irritably. "We go out so little that you don't have to be late when we do have the chance. You'll never find a man—not that you've got a chance without a dowry—cooped up here."

Kat began to hastily dress her hair. "I'll be there in five minutes."

"You're not wearing that dowdy old green thing to go to La Fenice, are you?" Alessandra demanded. Kat's sister-in-law was clad in a Venetian lace-trimmed gown of golden-yellow silk. Katerina shuddered to think where the money had come from. Alessandra, on the other hand, looked truly shocked at her sister-in-law's dusty-green taffeta.

"Yes. Now go away and let me finish." It was last year's style and last year's dress. And in Venice among the *Case Vecchie*, death was better than being out of fashion. It was just too bad. Katerina had learned this much if nothing else: there were many more important things in life than silk.

"We won't wait!" threatened Alessandra.

I wish, thought Kat. But she held her tongue and simply closed the door. Took out a string of "pearls" that wouldn't stand too close an inspection. Glass and fishscale . . . A poor replacement for what had been her birthright. She shook herself. It was no use getting upset about any of it. She had no idea if she'd ever get to meet him. Or if he was married already. But wait, that canal-brat, Benito! She'd seen him, now and then, wearing Ventuccio livery. Perhaps he would help her—

"KATERINA!" It was an old voice, the timbre going, but still strong.

"Coming, Grandpapa."

Katerina had that feeling in her stomach which more commonly accompanied a over-sufficiency of sugar-plums. Her stomach . . . well, she just felt sick. She was *used* to doing dangerous things— alone at night. Going to dark and insalubrious places to meet possibly very unpleasant people.

This was somehow worse. Kat swallowed, looking around at the slow butterfly swirl of the haut monde of Venice socializing. The public masques were events where the people came as much to be seen, as to see the performance. She wished desperately she'd never agreed to do this.

It had not seemed unreasonable when she was sitting talking to Francesca. It was very different here under the glitter of the candelabras. "Introduce me to your grandfather at the interval at the masque at La Fenice. It's something of a public place, and I have not yet acquired the cachet for exclusive soirees or recitals at private camerata. He's still a man of influence, you know, and highly respected. *Crème de la crème,* in Venetian society. It will do me a great deal of good just to be seen talking to him."

Kat understood the logic. In truth, all that visibly set the cour-tesans at such events apart from the matrons and virgin daugh-ters of Venice was the lower cut to their dresses. And the more well-known and reputable men that a courtesan could draw around her, the more her acceptability grew.

The problem for Kat, however, was that there was a fine social line "respectable" women did not cross. *Men* openly talked and flirted with the courtesans at these events. Women didn't. So Kat needed to make the introduction in as discreet and unnoticed a manner a possible.

Unfortunately, *this* night—when she desperately wanted Alessandra to do her usual disappearing trick—her sister-in-law seemed to be glued to her. Kat had tried to shed Alessandra and stick to her grandfather, which was normally not that difficult. But tonight the swirling crowd had peeled off Lodovico Montescue somewhere along the line, while Alessandra remained by her side at every moment.

There was Francesca. The daring chaperon-hat with the peacock feather made her easy to find. As usual, the courtesan dressed with a flair that separated her from the lesser birds of paradise.

What to do, what to do . . .

At last, Alessandra had caught sight of Lucrezia Brunelli and hastened away from Kat. Kat tried desperately to spot her grandfather. She gritted her teeth. Now or never. She'd find him and drag the old man over to the chaperon-hat she could see bobbing over there by one of the ornamental pillars. And then she'd trip over a flounce or something. She just hoped that Lodovico would not be as scathingly rude as he could be.

First off she must get rid of this prosy bore. "I'm afraid I have no real interest, signor," she said cuttingly, to a well-meaning if prosy *curti* who was attempting to explain the work of the new painter, Robusti. "Excuse me. I must go and find my grandfather. There is someone I wish him to meet."

The truth was easy enough when the person you were talking to didn't know just what you were talking about! She walked away, edging her way through the knots of people, quite differently from the way she'd seen Francesca sashay her cleavage through the crowd. Unfortunately she hadn't spotted Lodovico. Her grandfather had a commanding presence, so it was easy to forget he was not actually very tall.

She spent the next while in fruitless search. Well, she'd go over to Francesca and at least show she'd tried. The play would be starting soon. At least Francesca's hat was easily visible.

As Kat came around the ornamental pillar she heard Francesca's laughter. It was a liquid and musical sound. "Most amusing, Signor

Montescue," she said, and the courtesan rapped Lodovico's knuckles gently with her ivory fan. And he was only one of the cortege she had gathered. Her flirtation with Lodovico done, Francesca turned her head and made a quip of some kind to a couple of priests standing next to her. The little crowd immediately burst into laughter. "Oh, how very well said," choked one of the priests, managing even in that short phrase to convey a thick Savoyard accent.

Kat caught her jaw. Most of the men gathered about Francesca were typical of what showed up from the great merchant-houses of Venice at these events. They were *old*. Middle-aged, at the very least. The youngest of the Venetians was Petro Dorma, who was almost forty—and, with his short stature and bald head, hardly the image of a romantic swain.

The only exception were the two men in clerical garb, who seemed even younger than Dorma. And quite a bit more slender and physically fit. Kat was a little puzzled by their presence in the crowd surrounding Francesca. Not because they were clerics. There were several high-ranked members of the Church present at the masque, and Kat knew that at least one of them, Bishop Capuletti, was notorious for being a libertine. But the clerics who came to these events were generally *Case Vecchie* themselves—whereas these two, judging from their plain and simple garb, seemed to be nothing more than simple priests. One of them, judging from that heavy Savoyard accent, no more than a villager in his origins.

The sight of those mostly pot-bellied men brought home to Katerina that despite the wealth and comparative liberty they enjoyed . . . there were certain disadvantages to being a courtesan. She slipped her arm into her grandfather's. "I have been looking for you everywhere, Grandpapa." Kat smiled at Francesca, who dimpled just slightly in reply—lowering her lashes a touch. "Won't you introduce me to your fascinating lady-friend?"

"Er." Lodovico Montescue, not accustomed to being at a loss for words, was caught a bit short this time. "Signorina Francesca de Chevreuse. This is my granddaughter Katerina."

Kat bowed and extended a hand. "I am delighted to make your acquaintance," she said demurely, almost managing to keep a straight face.

Lodovico's discomfiture was relieved by the ringing of the bell to signal that the masque was about to begin. It didn't stop him bowing very low to Francesca in parting.

As they walked to their seats, Lodovico shook his head at his granddaughter. "Minx. How could you do that to me? Making me introduce you!"

Kat pinched his arm. "Ha. You can talk to her but I cannot? Ha."

Lodovico sighed. "Our society is a hypocritical one, my girl. I must protect you from gossip-mongers or I would be very tempted to take you to talk with her. She is a very intelligent woman. Cultured. Understands the vagaries of politics. That's a rare coin. It attracts men."

Kat smiled up at him. "And her cleavage has nothing to do with it."

The encounter with Francesca had left Lodovico in rare good mood. He chuckled. "This is Venice, my girl. We are an ostentatious people. We like to display our . . . endowments."

Kat chuckled. "She has enough 'wealth' to display in that respect, that's certain." Despite the humor, she found herself torn between gratification that Francesca had succeeded in charming her grandfather—and an irrational jealousy of sorts. He was her grandfather! Not a man chasing a woman! She suppressed the ungracious thought. It was nice to see him take an interest in something other than their troubles and his dreams of vengeance on the Valdosta, she supposed.

Perhaps he read her mind. "Ah. My Kat. I must admit she made me forget my age too."

They sat, and Kat noticed that Alessandra was looking frozen-faced at the stage. Alessandra pointedly ignored their arrival. Kat wondered—not with much interest—what had got up her sister-in-law's nose. Well, one of the misfortunes of being cloistered in the same house as Alessandra, was that sooner or later Kat would be told. Quite probably with histrionics.

After the masque was over, Lodovico insisted on remaining for a while. That was unusual. Then he took up an offer to join a number of the *Case Vecchie* at private soiree at the camerata of Lord D'selmi. As a rule, Kat's grandfather preferred to keep his appearances at these social gatherings to the bare minimum required by the demands of status. Tonight, however, he seemed much more energetic than usual. Kat noted that the invitation to proceed to the *Casa* D'selmi had included Francesca. Seeing him join the crowd which gathered around Francesca there—quite a bit larger, now, that crowd—Kat almost choked. Partly from amusement, partly from chagrin bordering on outrage.

My own grandfather! That woman is shameless! So is he!

Eventually, humor won the engagement. Kat smiled and turned away from the sight of her grandfather flirting suavely with Francesca. *At least he's not glaring at the walls, planning revenge on Valdosta.*

She sighed. Not that Lodovico Montescue could afford Francesca, these days, any more than he could afford to pay capable spies and assassins.

The evening wore on. The camerata sparkled with silver, candle-light and fine Venetian glassware. Katerina wished she could say the same of the intelligence of the boring, fat old *curti* who had backed her up against a wall and was now attempting to talk her to sleep with his self-praise. There was Lucrezia Brunelli, laughing to her own court of gallants—who were no younger and no less corpulent than the ones gathered about Francesca—her hair gleaming as if it had been spun out of coppery gold. Katerina didn't envy her for suitors . . . and if rumor were to be believed, lovers. All she envied Lucrezia for was the ability to escape being trapped by a idiot with breath like old anchovies, too many chins, and his interminable tales of his not-really-so-clever little swindles in the Levant.

Kat was amused to see that—for once!—the crowd of men gathered about Lucrezia was not the largest in the palace. It was not small, of course, but it was definitely smaller than the little mob surrounding Francesca. Smaller, and—a lot less noisy. Lucrezia was *slightly* more beautiful than Francesca, Kat supposed. The beautiful lady of *Casa* Brunelli was also famous for her intelligence and witty repartee. But Kat had overheard that repartee, in times past, and had always found it fundamentally hard-edged. Nasty, in truth— a matter of scoring points in a contest. Whereas, judging from the relaxed and boisterous laughter coming from Francesca's gathering, the men there were discovering Kat's friend to be more convivial company. Francesca's sense of humor was . . . genuinely funny. Her jests were jests, not barbs; and as often as not likely to be directed at herself rather than others.

So, as the fat old *curti* droned on and on, Kat paid him as little attention as possible. She was observing the subtle contest going on between two beautiful women elsewhere. And found herself enjoying the fact that Francesca was clearly emerging the winner— judging, at least, from the frequent and angry little glances Lucrezia Brunelli sent her way.

Relief came from a strange and unexpected quarter. And relief was even less welcome than the old geezer's breath had been. As happens at such large gatherings, the slow swirl of the crowd eventually brought someone new in front of her.

The minute that Kat saw his face, she recognized it. It was not a face you forgot. The aquiline nose, the single line of forbidding brow; the aura of power and dominance quite out of keeping with the man's height. He was dressed with plain severity, which was also out of keeping with the Venetian nobles and merchants. The same garb, she recognized, as that of the two priests in the crowd around Francesca. Someone had commented on it. Someone had murmered "political influence." It worried her.

He obviously worried the fat old toad, too. "Goo . . . good evening, Senor Lopez."

The foreigner favored the toad with a faint lift of his eyebrow line. "Ah, Signor Della Galbo. I have been to see you on a number occasions at your home. You were either away or indisposed. I am glad to find you here when you are neither."

"Uh. Yes, of course, signor." Little beads of sweat had started out of many-chinned toad's florid face. "But it's really getting late, and I must be off. Call upon me at my home. Excuse me, M'lady Montescue." He vanished with a speed that was almost astonishing for one so portly.

Katerina found herself fully in the eagle-eyed gaze of Senor Lopez. "My apologies, signorina. I did not mean to interrupt your discussion with Signor Della Galbo." He bowed. "My name is Eneko Lopez de Onez y Guipúzcoa. I am a stranger and guest here in your midst."

Kat curtseyed and held out her hand in the accepted manner, restraining a strong instinctive desire to run like hell. She wished she could equally restrain the cold sweat on her hand. Maybe this Lopez expected all women who were introduced to him to have cold-fish hands. "Katerina Montescue. I trust you are enjoying Venice?"

He certainly showed no reaction to her clammy hand as he bowed low and kissed it in a practiced courtly manner. "Alas, no." An almost-smile touched the face. "I find it damp. But that is inevitable in a city with so many canals. And one does God's work where God wills. Now, if you will excuse me, Signorina Montescue?"

"With pleasure!" Kat fled. He recognized her—she was sure he did!

She found she'd escaped one unpleasant thing, only to have to deal with another. "Well, well, well!" said Alessandra, archly. "Got a suitor I see. Signor Della Galbo is quite a catch. But better keep your hands off that fascinating Spaniard. Lucrezia has marked him as hers."

Kat shuddered. "She's welcome to him. And she can have Della Galbo too, with pleasure. Alessandra, he's fifty-five if he's a day. He's old enough be my grandfather, never mind my father! And he is fat, gross, and stupid, and his breath smells."

"But he's got money, darling," said Alessandra with a little moue. "Pots and pots of it. And you, I obviously need to remind you, haven't got any. You'd be lucky to even get such an attractive offer. He'd at best want you to be his mistress if you weren't *Case Vecchie*, and him *nouveau riche*. Or are you going to run off and marry some commoner? You just do your duty and . . . well you can always have a lover on the quiet. So long as you're discreet."

"If that's the choice, yes. I'll run off as soon as possible." The thought of "doing her duty" with that . . . made her feel nauseated. Best change the subject. "Who was the other man, that your *friend* Lucrezia has got her hooks into?"

"My *cousin* Lucrezia Brunelli . . . That was Ricardo's guest from Spain. Castilian nobility. Well—Basque, actually. A rising man in the Church, with friends in Rome. An envoy plenipotentiary from the Grand Metropolitan himself, people say."

Kat swallowed. The Petrine church had its agents too. This was probably one of them. The Petrines were more tolerant than the Paulines, but in the factional fighting . . . well, people were ground between them. Whole cities were ground. If the rumor her grand-father had told her was true, Ferrara could be next. The Po River city had played a delicate balance between Venice and Rome, against Milan and the North . . . And sometimes the other way around.

She was relieved to see her grandfather stumping up. "Let's go home. The conversation's turned to politics, and the more I listen to these fools the angrier I get," said the old man, his grizzled eyebrows lowered in an angry frown. "Except for Petro Dorma—and Francesca de Chevreuse, from the little she said—they're all a lot of sheep. Bah. The Republic of Venice must stand for the Republic of Venice. Not for Milan, or Rome, anyone else. Come. I want to go home."

Predictably, Alessandra pouted. "The night's still young. I'll come home later. I want to meet some of those knights from Germany. They're supposed to be here later."

"You'll come home now," growled the old man. He turned his lowered brow on Katerina. "As for you, young lady. I won't have you associating with the likes of that Della Galbo. He's nothing but a cheap crook. Even the slave-trading Dandelos are not as low. I want you home, too."

"Grandpapa, I'm only too glad to obey you," said Kat from under lowered lashes. "I couldn't stand him."

The thunderous brow lightened. "You're a minx, girl. Now, let's get out and find a gondola to take us home. The Montescue have been here. Shown face. Shown we are still *Case Vecchie*." The pride in that old voice was as deep as the ocean and as hard as granite.

Chapter 45

Lopez followed the Montescues out of the palace, keeping far enough back not to be noticed. As the family began embarking onto their gondola, he emerged onto the steps. A moment later, his two companions joined him.

"A very nice voice, she has, even with the tremor of fear in it," said Lopez quietly. "I recognized it from the counseling session I had with her last year."

"You should be ashamed of yourself, Eneko," chuckled Diego. "Frightening girls the way you do."

Lopez shrugged slightly. "The encounter was quite accidental. Her small sins cause her to fear the suspicion of great ones. Of which, as it happens, I am quite sure she is guiltless. She is involved somehow with the evil which is coiling within this city, but she is not one of its vessels."

Diego turned his head to peer down the canal where the Montescue gondola had vanished. "I agree. If Satan were *that* capable, old friend, we would long ago have vanished into the maw of the Antichrist."

Lopez rubbed his bad leg. "Bad today," he muttered. "Come, brothers. Since the Grand Metropolitan has seen fit to dole out some more funds, let us employ a gondola for a change."

After they climbed into the gondola, Diego returned to the subject. "How involved do you think she is, Eneko? And in what manner?"

The gondola was just pulling into the Grand Canal. The Basque priest stared thoughtfully at the statue of the winged lion in the

Piazza San Marco, quite visible in the moonlight. "Has it struck you yet, brothers, how many odd coincidences we have stumbled across since we arrived here in Venice?"

Diego and Pierre glanced at each other. Pierre shrugged. "What coincidences?" asked Diego.

"One. The *coincidence* that I happened to witness Katerina Montescue and Benito Valdosta—yes, it was he; I'm sure of it now that I've had a glimpse of him—engaged in mysterious activity on the same evening and in the same locale that the Woden casket was brought to Venice. Two. The *coincidence* that those two had met each other in the first place. Three. The *coincidence* that we happened to find lodgings in a part of the city which would enable us to observe the older brother Marco engaged in charitable work. Four. The *coincidence* that Katerina Montescue—"

"Enough, enough!" chuckled Diego. "Odd, I admit. But what's the rhyme and reason to any of it?"

"I wish Francis were here," mused Eneko. "If he weren't needed in Mainz . . ." He shook his head. "Francis is more versed than I am in those aspects of sacred magic which deal with pagan powers and spirits. The whole subject remains a bitter bone of contention among theologians, you know. Are pagan demons such as Chernobog independent beings—or are they simply so many manifestations of Satan?"

"If you start talking about how many angels can dance on the head of a pin, I will pitch you overboard," growled Pierre.

Diego chuckled. "It's not as silly as it seems, Pierre," reproved the Castilian lightheartedly. "The issue is not whether two or twenty angels can dance on the head of a pin. It's a dispute over the nature of angels in the first place. Are they immaterial or, in some manner, corporeal. If the former, then an infinite number of angels can dance on a pin. If the latter, then the number—whatever it is; and no one cares about *that*—is nevertheless finite. So you see—"

"Overboard," growled Pierre. "The both of you."

"Desist, Diego," chuckled Eneko. "The Savoyard grows surly. As to the subject we *were* discussing, I have no definite opinion myself. But . . . there are too many coincidences. Something is at work here."

"What?" asked Diego. "Not the Lion, surely. You have said yourself that it can only be summoned by one who knows the ancient rituals—pagan rituals, mind—which none of us do."

Eneko shrugged. "And what exactly *is* this creature, this being?" He ran fingers through his close-cropped hair. "I don't know, Diego. While I was living at *Casa* Brunelli I scoured that magnificent library. There wasn't much, but . . . there are these occasional references to the *Shadow* of the Lion, as well as to the Lion itself.

"I tend to believe that these ancient pagan spirits have a life of their own. Are not simply constructs of Satan. And, if so, they have their own ancient rules and customs. Savage ones, often enough. Still . . . I think Chernobog is constrained himself, by those rules. Must operate indirectly, subtly, lest he rouse the Lion himself. But in so doing, I think . . ."

He gazed out over the Grand Canal, observing the shadows cast by the moonlight. "Too many coincidences," he repeated firmly.

Then, he shook his head. "But that is all speculation. For the moment, we must concentrate on matters we can get a grip on." He smiled faintly. "In a manner of speaking. So I think it is now time to have a discussion with that other young lady. The one you and Pierre spent most of the evening with. Set it up for me, Diego, if you would be so kind."

Lopez's Castilian companion chuckled again. "You are bound and determined to place me in the way of mortal sin, aren't you?"

Lopez smiled wryly. "I prefer to think of it as a kindness on my part. Personally, I think forcing you to spend time with the formidable Francesca de Chevreuse is all to the good. It will give you something to do penance over, when we finally make our pilgrimage to the Holy Land."

"Very *long* penance, I'm afraid," mourned Diego. "Her flesh I can resist easily enough. But the woman's *mind*—" He sighed. "So tempting."

"Why don't you tell me about it in the morning, Alessandra," Kat yawned, looking pointedly at the door and then at her bed.

Of course, Alessandra refused the invitation to go and leave Madelena to undress Katerina. "How could you, Katerina? We've got our reputation to consider! You spoke to that . . . that . . . *puttana*!" she spat. "And how could Grandpapa go and join that throng around that cheap woman? Lucrezia was furious. Three of her cicebeos left her and went and hung about that . . . that . . . scarlet . . ."

"I doubt very much if Francesca de Chevreuse is 'cheap,' "

interrupted Kat, pushing Alessandra towards the door. "And she seems nice—which, frankly, is not something you can say about Lucrezia Brunelli. Now, good night."

"She's a slut!"

"And you and Lucrezia both seem to be jealous. Why? Now go away, do. I don't care."

Chapter 46

There was, thank the Lord, plenty of light from the windows and walkways above to let Marco see where he was going, and to show him the footing on the ledge that led to the hole.

The fact was that he really didn't want to be here at all.

But for some reason that maybe only God knew, that strange scarred man had followed him out of the Jesolo after saving both him and Benito from the Squalos gang. And, presumably for that same reason, he had decided to set himself up as a kind of watchdog or bodyguard for the two of them. Marco felt a certain guilty responsibility for the man's well-being. They had abandoned him when Aldanto and Maria had come to their rescue.

So here he was, clinging to the ledge above the waterline, with a bundle and a message to deliver and only the haziest notion if the man was still *in* there.

If he hadn't been so nervous, he might never have noticed the stranger at all. But Marco was desperately afraid that his last escapade had drawn unwelcome attention to the entire Aldanto ménage, attention that would *have* to include the Montagnards. And if anyone who had ever known Lorendana Valdosta got a good look at him—well, there'd be no doubt whose kid he was.

So he'd been watching every shadow, and thinking out every footstep ever since he'd emerged shakily from his sickbed—and he'd seen the man ghosting along, fifty feet behind as he went to work one morning. And no matter how he'd changed his course, there the man was. Then he'd watch from the dirty window of the Ventuccio offices as the man shadowed Benito on his first run of the morning. He was ready to rush out to attack the man himself out of sheer terror when he moved across a patch of sunlight—

It was at that point, when he got a brief but very good look at the man's scarred face, that he'd recognized him as the mysterious stranger who'd saved them.

That night he'd spotted the man slipping into the foundation hole across the canal.

And now, when he watched carefully, he could catch the stranger at his comings and goings—and *very* rarely, at trailing them. He thought that after a few days the man would get tired of it and go away—loco folk from the Jesolo weren't known for long attention spans. But he hadn't, and Marco realized that he was going to have to do something about the fact that he was there, and was apparently not going to give up on his self-appointed task.

First—tell Caesare, so that Aldanto didn't kill the stranger, thinking he was a threat. That was easiest done in the morning, before Aldanto was completely awake and thinking.

Marco had planned his approach carefully the previous morning, waiting until Aldanto had gotten his first glass of watered wine and was starting his second before accosting him.

"Caesare," he started hesitantly, "there's something you should know."

Before Caesare could do more than look apprehensive, Marco had plowed onward. "That man I told you about? The one in the marshes? The one that helped Benito and me?"

Aldanto nodded slowly, putting the goblet down on the table and absently running a hand through his tangled golden mane.

"He's here in the city," Marco said shortly. "Hiding out in that rundown building of Gasparsi's. I've seen him."

Aldanto didn't move, much, but he went from sleepy and a little bored to startled awake, wary, and alert. Marco continued before he had a chance to interrupt.

"He's right across the canal, holed up in the foundation under Gasparsi's place," Marco said, words tumbling over each other as he tried to get them all out. "Please, Caesare, I don't think he means any harm. I think he's guarding us, me and Benito. He's been following me to work, and I saw him following Benito on his runs. I think maybe he's trying to keep us safe. He's saved us once. I don't know why he did, I don't know why he's watching us, only—please, Caesare, please don't kill him."

Aldanto regarded Marco dubiously for a moment before replying. "You have strange choices in friends, boy." He picked up his goblet, and studied Marco over the rim of it.

Marco hadn't the faintest notion how to reply to that, so, in keeping with his recent decision to keep his mouth shut when he didn't know what to say, he'd remained silent.

"How sure are you of this—friend?" Aldanto asked, when even *he* seemed to find the silence had gone on too long.

Marco had to shake his head. "I'm not. I told you, I don't know why he helped us in the first place. I don't know why he's here now. I thought maybe—he's crazy, sort of. I thought he'd get tired and go away, but he hasn't. I don't know what to tell you, Caesare— but I just don't think he means *us* anything but good."

Caesare relaxed back into his chair, a thought-crease between his brows. Marco remained patiently standing by the table, wishing with all his heart that he hadn't been such a great fool this winter as to destroy any trust Aldanto had in him.

"I didn't even know that this watchdog of yours was there," Caesare said at last, cradling his wine goblet in both hands, as if taking warmth from it. "That argues for a—certain level of expertise. That is a very bad sign."

"If he wanted us he could have killed us a dozen times by now," Marco whispered humbly. "He could have just stood back in the marshes, and we'd have been dead and nobody the wiser."

"True." Caesare continued to brood over the wine goblet. "There would be no point in his watching you that I can see. If he wanted to take you to use against me he should have made his move by now. Which makes me think you might be right about him."

Marco heaved a completely internal sigh of relief.

"Now I can't for a moment imagine why this man should have decided to attach himself to you and your brother, but *since* he has, and since he seems to have some useful skills—" He paused, and raised one golden eyebrow significantly. "—and since he seems to have appointed himself as your bodyguard gratis—"

Marco flushed, and hung his head. He knew Aldanto was still desperately short of money, and he knew that the reason was because he had spent vast sums of money trying to find Marco when Aldanto and Maria had thought he was in trouble. Money that hadn't been his to spend. Brunelli money, Marco assumed. Or money from Bishop Capuletti, which amounted to the same thing.

"—well, I'm not inclined to look this particular gift horse in the mouth," Aldanto concluded. "But I hope he has the sense to realize that I am inclined to strike first and ask questions like 'friend or foe' afterwards. And I want you to stay out of his reach after this."

"Yes, Caesare," Marco backed out of the kitchen hastily. "Thank you, Caesare."

But here he was. Because he felt a responsibility to warn the man. And because he felt he owed him something besides a warning, he carried a bundle.

Word had gotten out from Tonio that, well, actually, it was that bridge-boy of Maria Garavelli's who had doctored their children. And if the parents had any doubts, the children didn't. That appeared to have overcome many an adult's doubt. Ever since his return from the swamp, Marco had found himself overwhelmed with new patients. Quite a few of them didn't even come through Tonio any more. The boat-folk, ignoring Marco's vehement protests that he *did not* want to be paid for doctoring their kids, had taken to leaving things in Maria's gondola or with Giaccomo. Things that Marco had no earthly use for—a woolen cloak, five sizes too big, laboriously knitted out of the remnants of five different lots and colors of yarn, half a blanket, candle-ends, a homemade oil stove of the kind used on boats, a bunch of fresh chestnuts off an incoming barge, a bundle of *boccalao* . . . and more.

A lot of it they couldn't use, and Maria couldn't sell or trade the stuff without going to a world of time and effort that she couldn't spare. But if the stranger had come out of the Jesolo, he was even poorer than the poorest canaler. These odds and ends could mean a great deal to him. So that was the thing Marco meant to do—see that the man was in some sort of comfort. It was a small payback for their lives. He'd gotten a few coppers doing some odd jobs on his day off, and those had gone for a bit of food for the man, flour and salt and oil, and some dried salt fish, all bundled in with the rest.

"Milord?" Marco called into the darkness of the partially flooded foundations of the building, wondering if the man could hear him—or if he was even there. He turned away for a moment to look out uneasily over the canal behind him—

"I'm no milord, boy," came a harsh whisper from right beside him.

Marco jumped and nearly fell backwards in the canal. A long arm snaked out of the darkness and steadied him.

"M-m-milord, I—" Marco stuttered.

"I told you, boy," the ragged, battered stranger said, a little less harshly, as he emerged from the darkness of the foundation cavern, "I'm no *milord*. Call me Harrow. Why have you come here?"

"I—came to thank you. Also to warn you. Aldanto says: 'Don't cross his path or bring him trouble.' Um . . . and I came to bring you a few things I thought maybe you could use. Food and some warm stuff. It's not a lot and it's not good. But it is something."

The stranger looked puzzled. "Why?" Then he nodded. "Thank you, Marco Valdosta."

Marco nearly fell backwards out of the entry hole again.

"How—" he started

"You look just like your mother. Now go, Marco. And be careful not to come here again. It is not safe." And without another word he turned and walked back into the darkness with Marco's gift.

Harrow waded back into the blackness, knowing his way even in the pitch-dark, the stale water slimy around his ankles. After a short while, he felt and heard dry gravel crunching under his feet. Harrow struck tinder and lit the tiny fire of dry debris. By the flickering light he carefully surveyed the place that was now his home.

He'd lived in worse. By some freak or other, the back end of the ruined bottom story was still above water level and relatively dry, a kind of rubble-floored cave. You had to get at the dry part by wading through ankle-deep, stagnant water, but it wasn't bad, certainly not as bad as the swamp.

Mind you, it was no palace, either. Water condensed on the walls and ceilings above the sunken area, dripping down constantly, so that the air always smelled damp. And with stale canal water coming in with every tide, it often smelled of more than damp. But there were feral cats down here, which kept the place free of vermin. Harrow had always admired cats. And he held them almost sacred now, for cats—black cats in particular—were the special darlings of the Goddess. There was a mama-cat with a young litter laired up down here that Harrow had begun luring in with patience and bits of food. He had hopes he could tame the young ones enough for them to stay with him.

For the rest, he had a bed of sorts, made up of a couple of blankets and armfuls of dry rushes brought in from the swamp. Certainly no one ventured down here, so anything he managed to acquire was safe. It wasn't much. He sat down on the bed and opened the bundle.

What the boy had given him tonight was very welcome. The little fire was guttering and so rather than waste his meager fuel supply he lit one of the tallow candle-ends Marco had given to him. After pulling the new cloak over his chilled body, he examined each little prize with care. Then he stowed it all away within reach of his pallet so that he'd be able to find the stuff if he needed it in the dark.

He re-made his bed to add the new coverings to the top and the rags that the boy had brought as padding underneath; then Harrow blew out the candle-stub and lay back on the pallet, staring into the darkness. Thinking.

Thinking mostly about his past. Thinking about his life as Fortunato Bespi. It was mostly a life he would rather have forgotten. A time when he had been one of the most deadly killers and workers of mayhem that Duke Visconti had ever recruited into his Montagnard agents. He'd served the Montagnard cause, for which he'd done much . . . that was to the superficial look, evil. He had done it all with a clear conscience, knowing the cause was good. Now—in the light of hindsight—he could see that the "cause" was no more than a thin cover for the ambitions of the only one he'd ever really served. Filippo Visconti.

Harrow felt his scarred lip curling into a stiff and soundless snarl, thinking of the Duke of Milan's treachery and the willingness of his tool Francesco Aleri to further that treachery.

But, soon enough, he pushed the anger aside. The Goddess had given him other work, after all.

His thoughts turned to young Marco. The boy's . . . considerateness . . . shone through every item in that bundle. Duke Visconti had carelessly handed out gold—of which he had plenty. This boy had next to nothing. There'd been nothing careless in that bundle. The kid was unlike anyone Harrow had ever known before; he was—kind, that was it. Compassionate in a way that Harrow didn't really understand, and could only admire from a distance. The younger boy—*that* one he understood, but the older one—never. Marco's type was the sort he could appreciate, but never emulate. But he understood why the Goddess might have a purpose for the child of such an unlikely woman as Lorendana Valdosta.

Well, I can't be like that, he thought somberly. *But I can do what the Goddess put on me; I can help that boy survive to do some good. That ought to count for something.*

He settled himself a bit more comfortably, and thought about the warning the boy had delivered. *That* was something he hadn't thought of; he hadn't considered Caesare Aldanto except as a fellow guardian.

Better make sure not to ever let him get a look at me, he decided thoughtfully. *Even as scarred up as I am, he might recognize me. And he won't be seeing Harrow—he'll be seeing Fortunato Bespi. A threat. And I know damned well how Caesare Aldanto responds to threats.*

Then he grinned in the dark, his lips curling like stiff, old leather. *No threats from me, Caesare Aldanto, we're on the same side, as it happens. Just like old times. But Francesco . . . you bastard, you—*

His grin turned into a feral snarl. *Let's just see you try and get past Caesare and me together, Milord Francesco Aleri. Let's just see you get at the boy through me. I might leave enough for Caesare Aldanto to play with, after.*

Chapter 47

Marco had another mission tonight, besides that of dealing with the man who called himself Harrow. He'd had a suspicion for some time that there was something not quite right in the Ventuccio books; today that suspicion had become a certainty. And it was something that might well be very valuable to Caesare Aldanto. Maybe valuable enough to repay what Aldanto had spent for his sake.

When he locked the front door and listened for signs of life in the apartment beyond, he heard footsteps in the kitchen; shod footsteps with a certain lightness to them. Only one of the four living in this apartment wore shoes on a regular basis; so Caesare was home, and puttering about in the kitchen again. Well enough. Marco always preferred to accost him back there, it was a friendlier place—small, tiled in a cheerful terracotta, and always warm—than the sitting room.

He padded down the hall to the rear of the apartment and stood, quiet as you please, in the doorway of the kitchen, waiting for Caesare to notice him. He'd been trying to imitate the wallpaper ever since the disaster of this winter, doing his level best to become invisible whenever he was in the apartment. He'd evidently gotten quite successful at it, for Aldanto got halfway through his finocchio soup before he noticed Marco standing there, twisting his cap nervously in his hands.

"Marco, I almost didn't see you! Are you hungry? There's enough for you if—" He looked, then looked again, and frowned. "Have you got something on your mind?"

"It's—something I think you ought to know, Milord Caesare," Marco replied quietly, edging into the cone of light cast by the oil lamp above the table.

"Lord, boy, *don't* tell me you've been writing poetry again," Aldanto groaned, putting both the bread and the spoon down. "It's been a long day; I don't think I could handle another romantic crisis."

Marco blushed, but took heart at the ghost of good humor in Aldanto's eye. "No, Caesare, it's—there's something funny going on at Ventuccio."

Aldanto grimaced, and shoved his chair back a bit. "Marco, I'd be very much surprised if there *wasn't* 'something funny' going on there. Half this damn town smuggles."

"It isn't that—I mean, they *tell* us what not to see, if you catch my meaning." Marco bit his lip as he struggled to communicate what he had discovered in a way that Aldanto would understand. "This is something else; it's different. I'd swear on my life it's something that Ventuccio doesn't know is going on. It's something I sort of ran into in the books. I don't think anybody else would notice, because nobody else remembers these things like I do."

Now Caesare looked serious, and very much interested. He quirked one finger at Marco. "Come over here and sit where I can see you—"

Marco obeyed, pulling out the chair next to Aldanto's and plopping into it. Aldanto shoved his food aside and clasped his hands quietly on the table before him. Marco imitated his pose without really thinking about it.

Aldanto took a deep breath. "I've got good cause to know about that memory of yours; I don't know that I've ever seen *it* play tricks. So what is it that you've uncovered?"

"About twice a month," Marco replied, picking his words with care, "there are three or four fewer tax stamp receipts than there are items on the bill of lading inventory, which is when things go into the warehouse. But there's exactly the same number as on the warehousing inventory, when things go out. There's no discrepancy in the bill of lading and what's been paid for, and no calls for reimbursement from clients, so there's no reason for Ventuccio to go back-checking the books; so far as *they* figure, they've been paid in full, everything's okay. The way things go is this—the bill of lading gets checked off at the warehouse door when the ship gets unloaded. That's the first time they make a count. Then the Doge's official in charge of duties inspects the goods, stamps each thing when it comes back out again; that's the second time. That way nobody can swipe stuff from the warehouse with the tax stamp on it an' resell it."

"Huh." Aldanto looked *very* thoughtful. "So—somebody is bringing something *in*, paying Ventuccio for it, then 'losing' it before it gets duty paid on it."

Marco nodded. "Or before it gets inspected. That's what it looks like to me, milord."

"Do you know who—or even what?"

Marco nodded again. "Spices. Or so it claims to be. About three, four little spice casks at a time."

Aldanto chewed his lip. "Not much is it?" he said after a pause.

Marco's head bobbed. "Enough to make a real difference to *somebody*, I'd think. Spices aren't cheap. And maybe they just don't want those casks looked at."

Caesare brooded for a bit. "You've been doing your damnedest to act and think like a responsible adult, lately," he said, and Marco flushed painfully, lowering his eyes to his clasped hands. "I'm minded to see if you can take an adult task. It just might be worth what you cost me."

Marco looked up at him in a flare of sudden hope.

Caesare smiled sourly. "You'll be fishing in dangerous waters, Marco, I want you to know that. This might be something one of the younger Ventuccios is running without the knowledge of the Family—it's maybe something worth enough money that at least one of the parties involved is going to be willing to kill to protect it. You're going to have to be very, very cautious, and very, very smart."

"You want me to find out who's involved," Marco stated. "And you figure that I've gotten enough sense beat into me to take the risk and come out on top. *If* I keep my head."

Caesare nodded, and coughed a little self-consciously. "And you know why. I sell information, and I don't much care who I sell it to, or how many times I sell it. If you take care, you should be all right, but this will *probably* cost you your job, no matter what—"

Marco shrugged. "It was *you* got me the job in the first place," he pointed out. "Reckon I can scrounge another one somewhere.

Maybe Maria can have a word with Milord Giaccomo; maybe
Milord Giaccomo could use a pencil pusher, or knows someone
who could—"

"Oh no, boy—" Aldanto got a real, unfeigned smile on his face.
"No, you won't have to go hunting up another job; you're going
to have enough to worry about, come summer. I had a word with
Milady Dorma this afternoon—"

Marco blushed very hotly, knowing quite well that the "word"
was likely to have been pillow talk.

"—and it seems she's talked her formidable older brother into
giving you full Dorma sponsorship into the Accademia. Think you
can handle *that* assignment, Milord Almost-A-Doctor Valdosta?"

Marco's jaw dropped, and he stared at Aldanto like a brain-sick
fool. Never, *never* in all his wildest dreams, had he thought for a
moment that Angelina Dorma would follow through on her half-
promise once he'd revealed how he'd deceived her with his poetry,
poems she'd thought came from Caesare Aldanto.

"Now I want you to *listen* to me, Marco Valdosta," Aldanto
continued, staring so hard into Marco's eyes that it felt like he was
trying to inscribe his words directly onto Marco's brain. "This is
good sense, good advice I'm giving you. Put your dreams and
idealism in your pocket for a minute and *listen* to me just as
carefully as you can."

"Yes," Marco said, dazed.

"Dorma," Caesare said with force, "is going to expect you to
become their House Physician; that's the price you will personally be paying for their gift. You're going to become fairly well-
off; you'll *have* to be, you'll be an associate of the Family. Now I
know you want to help out Maria's friends; that's very nice, it's
very admirable—but you *aren't* going to be able to help the poor
by being poor yourself. Be smart; take what comes your way and
use it. Once in the Family you will be in a position to *get* that
medical help to the canalers. Dorma seems to have a certain sense
of noble responsibility." His tone was wry; cynical. "You can play
on that *if* you play *their* game by *their* rules. And that's the way
to get what you want in this world. So *don't* blow the chance you've
been given; it's been my experience that you don't often get more
than one."

Marco got his jaw back in place, swallowed, and nodded. "You're
right, Caesare, I know you're right. The world's like that. And you've

been—real good to me and Benito. Better than you had any reason to, and I can't say as I've done much to deserve it. I just wish—" He swallowed again. "—I just wish I could do something to give you a shot at what you've always wanted. *You* wouldn't screw it up."

Aldanto turned his eyes on him. Pulled a wry face and shook his head.

That strange look lasted only a second—then Aldanto was back to his old self.

"One more thing," he continued, pulling his interrupted dinner back towards him, and toying with the bread. "You've been granted two ways to prove you've learned your lessons and to pay me back for the trouble you caused. One—to find out what's going on at Ventuccio. Two—to become my channel into Dorma and the Accademia, to be my eyes and ears and keep me informed. *You* know what kind of information I'm likely to find interesting. So—"

"Don't blow it," Marco completed for him, still a little bemused by the turn in his fortunes.

Caesare actually chuckled. "Right," he said, resuming his meal.

"Caesare—would it be all right if I wrote to my grandfather and told him about going to the Accademia, do you think?" Marco asked hesitantly, as he shoved his chair away from the table and prepared to leave.

Aldanto considered the possible ramifications for a moment; Marco could almost see the thoughts behind the eyes. "I can't see where it could do any harm," he finally replied. "It might ease his mind about you. Go ahead."

Marco hesitated at the doorway. "Thank you," he said shyly, feeling that he was likely to be glowing with gratitude and happiness.

"For what?" Caesare asked, weary, but amused. "Oh, go on, Marco. If you're not hungry, go and read, or to bed. Get out of here—you keep reminding me of how old and corrupt I am."

Marco bobbed his head awkwardly and scooted back to the room he shared with Benito. The kid wasn't back from his mysterious errand with Maria—but Marco wasn't overly worried about him. This wasn't the first time he'd been out on a night-run with Maria. It was no doubt dangerous—but less so than roof-walking with his old mentor Claudia, the singer-thief. And possibly even less dangerous than what Marco was going to attempt.

So Marco undressed and climbed into bed—and for the first time in months, the dreams he dreamed were bright.

He thought out a plan of action the next morning on the way to work, grateful beyond words for the presence of Harrow on his backtrail so that he was able to spare a bit of his mind to *make* plans. The very first thing to do was to try to find out if this was an overall scam, or limited to one particular ship—which was what he thought likeliest, given the frequency.

He waved to Tonio on the canal below, who waved back; the man was much friendlier now that Marco was accepting "payment" for his doctoring. There was, thank God, less of that, now that the killing season of cold was over. Marco hadn't needed his cotte for weeks; the only *bad* part about the weather warming was that the canals were beginning to smell. Then would come summer; plague-time.

Well—that was to come; *now* was for bare feet on the walkways, and heads bared to the spring breeze, and a general feeling of cheer all around that another winter had been lived through. And the laxness that came with spring-born laziness just might make it possible for Marco to find out his information undetected.

He was early to work; scooting in through the peeling wooden doorway literally as soon as Niccolo Ventuccio unlocked it. The early morning sun wasn't yet high enough to penetrate into the lower levels, so he had to trot around the dusty, cluttered outer office, lighting all the clerk's lamps. That was usually Niccolo's job— but the Ventuccio cousin didn't look at all displeased at the junior clerk's enthusiasm. He gave Marco an approving nod and left the outer office, to take up his position at the runner's desk in the next office over.

Marco had reason for being so early; he was early enough to make an undisturbed, though hasty, check through the import lists by ship. He soon discovered that only one, the caique *Jaila*, a regular on the Black Sea run, ever carried the spice shipments that had the discrepancies. And only one captain, Alessandro Montello, had been at her helm since the discrepancies started.

This was quickly and quietly done. By the time anyone else came in, Marco was at his desk, copying the inventories from the galliot *Albiona* into the appropriate books. One or two of his fellow clerks jibed at him for working so hard; Marco looked up from his copying and grinned slightly. "What do you expect," he countered, "when a fellow is so ugly no girl will look at him? A fellow's got to do *something* to take his mind off—what he ain't getting."

Matteo Feruzzi rolled his dark eyes expressively as he settled onto his tall stool behind his slanted desk. "Father and Saints, Marco—if you ain't getting nothing it's because you ain't looking! Half them canaler girls is makin' big eyes at you—and the only reason the rest of them ain't is because their fathers would beat them black and blue if they did." Matteo snorted, scratching his curly head. "Ugly! Hell, I wisht I was as 'ugly' as you! Maybe Rosa wouldn't be giving me such a hard time!"

Marco blushed and ducked his head. *He* knew why the canaler girls were giving him the eye—not because he was desirable; because he was notorious. The boat-folk had been alerted when he'd gone "missing"—and all of them knew the outcome. He was just grateful that his fellow-workers *didn't*; they were landers, and canalers didn't spill canal-gossip to landers. And it seemed Marco was semi-adopted now—because the boat-folk *hadn't* told the landers about what a fool he'd been.

And for all of that, he *still* hadn't seen THE GIRL since that awful day. He'd looked—oh, how he'd looked!—but he'd not seen her once. His only possible aid, Maria, had been unable—or unwilling—to identify her. Marco sighed, recollecting the peculiar jolting his heart had taken when he'd seen her—she'd shaken Angelina Dorma clean out of his head, and herself in.

Well, he couldn't think about her now; he had a ticklish job ahead of him.

Matteo chuckled at Marco's blush, not knowing what had caused it. He was about to toss another jibe in his direction when Christophoro Ventuccio stalked through the outer office on the way to his inner sanctum, and all four clerkly heads bent quickly over their assignments.

For the next bit of information, Marco had to wait until the appropriate book came into his hands legitimately—though he'd agreed to take on the lengthy *Albiona* inventory with the notion of getting at that book in mind. This East-run round ship had sprung a leak in her hold and had as a consequence sustained a bit of spoilage to chalk off on the loss sheets. And *that* was the book Marco wanted in his hands; the "Spoilage, Refund, and Salvage" book—because if *he* was the captain covering tracks, that's where *he'd* have hidden those little spice casks.

And sure enough—there they were; and no one else ever seemed to have quite as much spoilage in such a specific area as Captain Alessandro Montello of the *Jaila*.

It *looked* legitimate; all properly logged, and with no loss on the Ventuccio ledgers. The only thing that the captain had forgotten—were the casks themselves.

The miniature barrels that spices were shipped in were unlike any other such containers in that they were *not* tarred to make them waterproof. Tar ruined the delicate flavor of the spices. They were very carefully *waxed* instead; caulked with hemp and coated with beeswax, inside and out.

This made them very valuable, no matter that they were so small. Cooks liked them to hold flour and sugar and salt. For that matter—a good many used the casks, with the wax coating burnished into their wood until it glowed, as workbaskets, and for a dozen other semi-ornamental purposes.

So even if the spice inside had somehow spoiled, through leakage, or rot, or insect contamination, the *cask* had a resale value. Yet none of those casks from the *Jaila*'s inventory ever appeared on the "Salvage" side of the blotter.

And no one seemed to be interested in claiming back part of the value from the company that imported the spice for them. And *that* was very odd indeed.

And it was in the "Spoilage, Refund, and Salvage" book that Marco found out who had ordered and paid for the "spoiled" spices—and who had apparently been so careless, or generous, as to absorb the entire loss.

Casa Badoero. Spice merchants on Murano.

The next day, and the next, Marco kept strictly to legitimate business, waiting for an opportunity for him to get at the packets of tax-stamps.

The Venetian tax-stamps, placed on an article that had had its duty paid in full, were distributed by a small army of officials, *Capi di Contrada*, who had to report to the Doge and the Council of Ten. The stamps themselves were green paper seals, signed by the officiating *capi*, and each was wax-sealed and stamped twice with a unique number. They were intended to be split into two parts, each half bearing the same number. The first part was sealed with lead and wire to the taxed goods. The second part was torn off and returned, after counting at the Doge's palace, to the appropriate importer as evidence that he had paid his tax-duties to both the Republic of Venice and the Doge. The stamps came in from the Doge's palace in bundles and were kept in the cubbyholes of the tax desk, one hole for each day of the month. At the end of the month some luckless clerk got to check them against the warehousing inventory and file them away. Marco was too junior to be entrusted with such a task—but Matteo Feruzzi wasn't.

Sure enough, at month's end Matteo got stuck with the job. And Matteo *never* had lunch at his desk. Marco waited until lunchtime, when Matteo had gone off to lunch with Rosa and the office was deserted, to make his move.

He slid over to Matteo's desk, counted the little packets and purloined the one representing the twelfth of the month, the day the spice shipments from the *Jaila* had been collected by the Badoero representative. He thumbed through the little slips as quickly as he could, not daring to take the packet out of the office, hovering over in a corner next to the filthy glass window where the light was best. Finally he came to the Badoero slips, and got the name of the officer in charge puzzled out.

Capi Marco Tiepolo.

Chapter 48

Benito was in as cheerful a mood as he'd ever been in his life. Maria was so pleased with the way he'd been handling himself that she had decided to take him further into her confidence.

Well . . . she'd been damned desperate. But it was a start. Lately, being liked and noticed by Maria had mysteriously become important to him.

She'd flagged him down with the little signal they'd worked out that meant she needed to talk to him somewhere where they weren't likely to be observed. He finished his current run in double-time; then, when there didn't seem to be anybody about, ducked under the second bridge at the Rio de San Martino. He eased his way along the ledge at water level.

And there was Maria, holding her gondola steady against the pull of the canal current.

"*Ker-whick-a*," Benito chirped, seeing the flash of her eyes as she looked in his direction. He skipped over to the side of the boat, keeping his balance on the ledge with careless ease. "What's it you need, Maria?"

"I got a problem," she said in a low, strained voice. "Giaccomo sent me to pick up a payment for him—only after I'd got it, something spooked the Schiopettieri. They're all over the damned water and they're stopping gondolas—"

"And if they find you with a bag of coin—" Benito didn't have to finish the sentence. "Huh. Caesare'd have a helluva time prying you away from the Doge's torturers. Pass it over, Maria. I got to go by Giaccomo's anyhow. They won't stop a runner

436

in House livery, and even if they do, they won't touch Ventuccio money."

"If there's *one lira* missin'—"

Benito pouted, hurt. "C'mon, Maria, Ventuccio trusts me with cash!"

"I ain't as stupid as Ventuccio," Maria replied, but with no real force. "Here."

She pulled a flat packet out of her skirts, a packet that chinked and was surprisingly heavy. Benito raised a surprised eyebrow. Silver at the least—maybe gold. Something *had* gone amiss if Giaccomo had sent Maria out to make a pickup of this much coin in broad daylight.

He slipped the package inside his own shirt. "Keep heading up the canal," he suggested. "If it's *you* they're looking for, an' lookin' for you to head for Giaccomo's, that ought to throw 'em off the scent."

She snorted, and pushed off from the bank. "Tell me m'own job, landsman," she replied scornfully. "Just *you* tend to what I give you."

"*Si*, milady," Benito executed a mocking little bow, then danced back along the ledge to the first water-stair up to a walkway.

Behind him he heard Maria swear half-heartedly at him, and grinned.

Julio Destre had been trailing that canaler Maria for hours— just as the Dandelos had paid him to do. Then he saw her duck under the bridge—and a moment later, saw that bridge-brat Benito do the same.

He snickered to himself. Keeping tabs on the brat after he dropped out of the bridge-gangs and into "respectability" had been well worth his while, after all.

"Jewel" Destre had graduated from bridge-brat to street bravo in the two years since he and Benito had last tangled. He sported a cheap rapier (that he used like a club) and silk scarves and a constant sneer. There were dozens like Jewel on the walkways of Venice, and "work" enough to keep all of them in grappa and scarves, if you weren't too particular about who you worked for. Jewel certainly wasn't. The *Casa* Dandelo might derive its money from slave-trading but their ducats spent like anyone else's.

No one had ever beaten Jewel at anything—no one but bridge-brat Benito, that is. Benito had gotten to Jewel's girl, gotten her off the walkways and out of the gang, *into* the purview of his mentor Claudia.

Which wasn't what the brat had intended, but before you could say "surprise" Lola had gotten installed in an acting-group and acquired a very wealthy patron. And had *no* further need or desire for Jewel and his gang.

It still rankled. Jewel had never forgiven Benito for the way the little bastard had humiliated him. So this looked like a chance to pay Benito back *and* turn a little profit by way of a couple of Dandelo bonuses.

He watched Benito moving in the shadows under the bridge. He squinted, but couldn't make out anything more than a brief exchange with someone in the gondola—just a meeting of a pair of shadows within the shadows. Then Benito squirted out again and scrambled up the water-stairs and on over towards Cannaregio.

So. Maria had transferred whatever it was she'd picked up to the boy's hands—likely because of the Schiopettieri stirring on the water.

He grinned viciously with absolute satisfaction, and headed up the walkway on the brat's backtrail. In a few more moments, he'd have whatever it was Maria had been carrying, and he'd have the boy as well to sell to the Dandelos. Without balls. He was a good age for a trainee eunuch.

Harrow spotted the swarthy bullyboy trailing Benito with almost no effort whatsoever. The scar-faced low-life was so clumsy in his attempts to shadow the boy that Harrow snorted in contempt. This inept street brawler wouldn't have lasted five minutes as a Montagnard agent.

Once Harrow saw that the boy was on the Calle del Arco, Harrow had a fairly good notion where he was bound: Giaccomo's. That boat-woman must have passed something on to him.

The bravo evidently had a shrewd notion where Benito was going as well, since he increased his pace a trifle. It looked to Harrow like he was planning on ambushing the boy down in one of the *sotoportego* that Benito would use as a shortcut on his way to Giaccomo's. Harrow gave up trying to be inconspicuous—there wasn't anyone much in this decaying part of town anyway—and hastened his own steps.

He was almost too late. He hesitated a moment at the shadows next to the Gallina bridge, his eyes momentarily unable to adjust to the darkness of the *sotoportego* after the dazzle of sun in the piazza. Then he heard Benito shout in anger and defiance—and a second time, in pain.

He saw a bulkier shadow in the darkness of the overbuilt alley ahead of him, and that was all his trained body needed to respond with precision and accuracy.

A few heartbeats later the bully was unconscious at Harrow's feet, and Benito, huddled beyond, was peering up at the face of his rescuer with shock and stunned recognition.

Harrow gave him no chance to say a word. "Move, boy," he said gruffly. "And next time don't go down dark places without checking to see if someone's following."

The boy gulped, and scrambled to his feet, favoring his right arm. "Yessir!" he gasped, and scrambled down to his destination as if someone had set his tail on fire.

Harrow saw him get into a gondola twenty yards farther on. Good. He was safer on the water.

Harrow considered the body at his feet, thoughtfully prodding it with one toe. He rubbed his knuckles absently; he'd almost forgotten to pull that last punch; and if he hadn't the bravo wouldn't be breathing. He wasn't sure why he'd held back, now; he was mostly inclined to knife the bastard and push him into the canal—

But that wouldn't keep others of his type from dogging the boy's footsteps. On the other hand, if he made an example of this bravo, he might well save Benito and himself some future trouble.

Some half hour later, Jewel dragged himself, aching in every bone, from the cold, foul water of the Rio del Panada. He was lighter by his sword, dagger, purse, and cloak—at least the terrible, scarred madman had slapped him awake before tossing him in. He clung to the ledge that ran around the canal edge, clinging to the step of someone's water-door. He clung desperately to the sun-warmed, rotting wood, not thinking much past the moment. He hadn't swallowed any of the canal water; but he was bruised all over. The crazy man hadn't smashed bones. He'd shown he was perfectly capable of doing so. Jewel was just grateful to be alive enough to hurt and shiver.

Never, for the rest of his life, would Jewel forget that masklike face, those mad eyes. Or the carefully enunciated words, spoken in a voice like the croak of a marsh-bird.

"Touch that boy again," the mysterious attacker had warned, "and the next time you land in the canal we'll see how well you swim without knees and elbows."

"Katerina!"

Katerina looked up from the water, wary, startled. The last thing she wanted was to be recognized. It was that scamp, Benito. He had blood running out of his nose, and looked pale and frightened. Common sense said she should paddle away immediately. It was bad enough doing runs in daylight without extra trouble.

She stopped and he scrambled hastily into the boat. "Give me a lift a bit away from here. Please."

She sculled steadily as he attempted to staunch the flow of blood from his nose. "You going to bring trouble on me?"

"No. Trouble just got itself beaten up." Benito paused. "But— yes. You'd better let me off. Schiopettieri are doing checks of all vessels. You got anything . . ."

"We're inside the cordon," she said scornfully. "Don't you know anything? Now where were you going?"

"Giaccomo's," he said, gratefully.

Chapter 49

One casual question to two independent sources—Jeppo at Giaccomo's, and Barducci's cook Katia—had given Marco one simple, and odd, fact. The cheapest place in town for spices *wasn't* Badoero's. To the contrary, their prices were, if anything, more expensive. It was, however, the place of choice for wealthy women of Venice to buy their spices.

Rafael de Tomaso had been Marco's source on *Capi* Tiepolo. Marco had had plenty of reason to visit his new friend—his good news, for one: some seaweed you could apparently boil up and make a suspension medium for paints to achieve a marbling effect. It was one of those things Marco had picked up from one of his boat-people patients, when he'd mentioned painting. They claimed their father had done it, and he was a seaman from the far-off League of Armagh. That might be true. You could find blood of many origins on the waterways of Venice. But Rafael had been wildly excited by the idea, and begged him to find out more. So here he was with a bunch of dried seaweed. And while Marco was visiting, he'd asked Rafael if he could find out something about *Capi* Marco Tiepolo's background. The Tiepolo were, after all, an aristocratic family.

Though the Accademia student had been a little puzzled by the question, he agreed—especially after Marco told him that if it became any trouble to find out, he wasn't to bother. As things turned out, it was easy for him to resolve with a couple of casual questions to his own patron, carefully spaced out over several days.

It seemed that *Capi* Tiepolo was a bastard son of Count Badoero, who held large estates outside of Venetian territory in Padua. Padua . . . wooing—and being wooed—by Milan. The Badoero on Murano were cousins of the count, which meant they were allied with the Montagnard-leaning faction in Venetian politics—and friendly with the Pauline orders like the Servants of the Holy Trinity.

Yet . . . most curiously, *Capi* Tiepolo himself was apparently one of Bishop Pietro Capuletti's protégés. Which in the tangled weave of Venice's politics should have made him . . . an adherent of Rome and the Grand Metropolitan, as the Capuletti positioned themselves with the Brunelli Family. Bishop Capuletti, in fact, was the Doge's representative at the Accademia.

This was all very complicated.

Well, that sure as hell explains the Badoero connection, if nothing else, Marco thought to himself, as he hurried to reach Della Elmo's before the lunch-time crowd did. *But it surely doesn't explain this. There's a connection here I'm missing, and it's a Family connection, or politics, maybe. It's not enough to give Caesare—yet—*

He scampered in at the back entrance; Michelo Viero, one of the barman's helpers, had agreed to let Marco take his place at noon for the next several days. It hadn't been hard to persuade him, not when Marco had offered to split the tips for the privilege of doing his work for him. Michelo had no notion who or what Marco was; Marco let him think he was a student with some gambling debts to pay and a short time to pay them in. And Lord and Saints knew that a few of the patrons of the Della Elmo's Trattoria were quite good tippers. It was close to the San Marco, and it was fashionable right now.

Marco joined the milling lot of a half-dozen other boys in the shabby back hall, claiming Michelo's apron from its wooden hook and bobbing awkwardly to the burly owner. "Michelo still got th' bad ankle?" the square-faced man asked gruffly.

"Yes, milord," Marco replied, scuffing his bare feet in the sawdust on the wooden floor. "Says he's mortal sorry, milord, but it's still swole up."

The man actually cracked a smile. "I ain't, boy. You lookin' for a job, you check by here regular. I get an opening, you got a place."

Marco contrived to look grateful. "M-my thanks, milord," he stammered, and slipped past him onto the floor of the tavern proper.

After that it was nothing but scurry and scramble and keep his head down so that nobody could see his face long enough to recognize him later; bringing orders of food and drink to tables, clearing away the dishes after, bringing more drink when called for—and keeping his ears open.

For Elmo's Trattoria was where the second sons of the Families met—and where they met, there was gossip aplenty. And where there was gossip—

Lord, it was wearing him down, though. He leaned around a patron's bulk to snag the empty plates before the man could yell for them to be taken away. He was beginning to be very grateful for his sit-down job at Ventuccio's. He was so tired when he got home at night that he was bolting a little dinner, going straight to bed, and sleeping like a stone. Aldanto had been worried enough by this anomalous behavior that he'd actually asked Marco if he was all right—which surprised him. He'd explained—he thought; his mind wasn't too clear on anything after sundown anymore. At least Aldanto seemed satisfied.

Two days ago he'd learned that Count Badoero was one of Lucrezia Brunelli's more ardent suitors, and as such, was not popular at Elmo's. He was certainly the target of enough gossip.

From Luciano Delmi's idle comment yesterday, had come the news that Accademia must be awash with new gold the way Bishop Capuletti was spending it. And someone had said suspiciously, cattishly, that they wondered where it was being minted. That was the problem with subversion here in Venice. *Venice ducats.* Unpunched winged-lion-faced ducats were just not freely available outside the city. The gold refined and smelted here was definably, noticeably purer than coin from Florence or Milan. The magical blessing of the molds gave the coins a faint but delicate bouquet . . . cinnamony lavender. A fake coin was not worth passing.

Any attempt at subversion here in the Republic of Venice was expensive. There were just too many noble families you'd have to buy. Anyone spending that kind of gold was due a visit from the Council of Ten's agents.

Then somebody asked if the *Casa* Badoero was still courting the Milanese. The scar-seamed merchant considered the question thoughtfully before replying with the carefully worded bit of information that no, it was too late for courting.

And just as Marco was hauling a load of dishes to the back, he got the final key piece from Mario Pellagio. Marco overheard mention that the *Signori Di Notte* were looking for some ideas on who had killed Veronica Mantelli. And Delmi's unknown companion had said they need look no further than whoever was bringing the new supply of black lotos into the city. It was just an unrelated comment . . . except the rich and beautiful Signorina Mantelli had been prominent among Lucrezia Brunelli's set.

If there was one thing that could get you into real trouble with the Doge and the *Signori di Notte* and their Schiopettieri it was black lotos from Turkey. When they'd collected the tiny blue lotos in the marshes for Sophia's concoctions, Chiano had explained. From the magical lotos that had stolen the wits of Ulysses' men in Libya had come the two strains. The blue lotos was a rare, wild plant in the marshes of the Mediterranean coast—doubtless spread by sailors over the years. The blue was a mild hallucinogenic and soporific, and difficult to harvest in quantity. But somewhere within the Pontus mountains the plant had been bred, and magically altered. Black lotos. Twenty times as powerful . . . before refining. The magically refined drug had become a plague not twenty years back. Then it had been freely for sale. Doge Marco Gradenigo had utterly banned its import and sale, and agents of the Council of Ten had quietly killed importers. So. It was back. And back in the wealthiest circles. People who went a-spice-buying on Murano. People who had ample *Venice ducats*.

Ducats to buy support . . . inside the Accademia where the sons of Venice's nobles were an available target.

Marco's head buzzed, and his gut went tight with excitement. So—*Accademia* might be involved in this new Milanese policy!

Or *part* of the Accademia was. Marco was no longer so naïve as to figure that what one priest wanted, the rest did too. Assuming, of course—which those at Elmo's did—that the bishop's superiors were aware of his loyalties. Which might, or might not, have been the truth. In *either* case, it was something Caesare Aldanto would find fascinating indeed.

Marco hustled the last of the dishes into the kitchen, took off his apron, and hung it up for the last time. He had what he needed; time to give Michelo his job back. Now only one thing remained; for Marco to verify with his own eyes exactly what was going on down at the Ventuccio warehouse and how it was being conducted.

❀   ❀   ❀

Aldanto was beginning to have a feeling of déjà vu every time he looked up from dinner to see Marco hovering like a shadow around the kitchen door.

"Something wrong, Marco?" he asked, beginning to have that too-familiar sinking feeling. The last time the boy had had that look on his face, that—watcher—had moved in across the canal. And the time before—

The time before was what had gotten them all *into* this mess.

"Caesare—" the boy hesitated, then brought his hands out from behind his back. "This is for you."

Aldanto took the slim package from the boy; a long and narrow, heavy thing, wrapped in oiled silk. He unwrapped it, and nearly dropped it in surprise.

It was a fine—a *very* fine—*main gauche*, the like of which Caesare hadn't seen, much less owned, since his Milan days. Light-rippling oystershell folded Damascus steel; perfection from tip to sharkskin handle—balanced so well in his hand that it already felt part of him. Unmistakably Ferrarese workmanship. For nearly a century now, since Duke Andrea Dell'este had had the foresight and cunning to recruit steelworkers from the East and swordsmiths from Spain, and brought them together, Ferrara blades had become the standards whereby all other swords were judged.

He was so surprised that his first thought was that the boy must have stolen it. The Lord knew it wasn't the kind of thing the boy could afford! But Marco spoke before he could voice that unworthy thought.

"It—it's from my grandfather, milord," he said, his face and voice sounding strained. "He says it's by way of thanking you. He sent me one for Milord Dorma too—seems he wrote and told him who my mother was!"

"He *what*?" Aldanto tightened his hand involuntarily on the knife hilt.

"He says," Marco continued, "that he thinks *Casa* Dorma ought to know, and that I'm safer with them knowing, because they'll put me where hurting me would cause a vendetta no one wants. 'Hide in plain sight,' is what he says."

"The man has a point," Aldanto conceded, thinking better of the notion. Relaxing again, he checked the weapon for maker's marks, and sure enough, on the blade near the quillions found the tiny Dell'este symbol. The old man was a shrewd one, all right—he hadn't kept his smallish city intact and largely independent while sitting between three powerful forces by being stupid. He had a real instinct for which way to jump. Besides, if Dorma now knew what station the boy *really* was, the obligations would be turned around. Dorma would now be in the position to negotiate favorably with the guardians of the Po River and the roads to Bologna and Rome.

Marco was the son of an undutiful younger daughter of the House of Dell'este. But the Dell'este honor was legendary. It ran as deep as the heavens were wide. No trading family would want such an enemy. Marco would no longer be the object of charity, and the Dorma would actually wind up *owing Aldanto* for bringing the boy to their attention. Altogether a nice little turn of events— especially considering that he was being paid by Dell'este to watch over the boys.

"He says," Marco continued, looking a little relieved but still plainly under strain, "it's by way of a bribe, milord, for you to keep Benito. He says he doesn't think we better let Dorma know about Benito at all, not that he's my brother."

Aldanto thought about young Milord Lightfingers loose in Dorma and shuddered. "I think he's right." Besides, the boy might just be a main chance.

Marco carefully calculated his day off to coincide with the day that the Badoero hirelings picked up their consignment from the Ventuccio warehouse. By dawn he was down at the warehouse dock, ready and willing to run just about any errand for anybody. This wasn't the first time he'd been here—he'd played runner before, when he wasn't playing waiter's helper at Elmo's. He wanted his face to be a familiar one on the dock, so that he wouldn't stand out if *Capi* Tiepolo became suspicious. He even had Ventuccio permission to be out here; they thought he was strapped for cash, and he was supposedly earning the extra odd penny by running on his day off.

He'd run enough of those errands by noon that no one thought or looked at him twice when he settled into a bit of shade and looked to be taking a rest break. The sun was hot down here on the dock; there wasn't a bit of breeze to be had, and Marco was sweating freely. One friendly fellow offered Marco the last of his wine as he went back on shift, and Marco accepted gratefully. He wasn't having to feign near-exhaustion; he *was* exhausted. He was mortally glad that the remainder of his self-imposed assignment was going to allow him to sit out here, in the shade of a barrel, and pretend to get splinters out of his hands while he watched the Badoero barge being loaded twenty feet away.

The barge was a neat little thing; newly painted and prosperous looking. The boatman who manned her did *not*, however, look like the run-of-the-mill canaler.

In point of fact, that carefully dirtied cotte looked far too new; the man's complexion was something less than weathered—and those hands pushed pencils far more often than the pole of a skip. Marco would be willing to bet money on it. This was no canaler, hired *or* permanent retainer. This was likely one of the younger members of the Family.

This notion was confirmed when *Capi* Tiepolo put in his appearance. There was something very similar about the cast of the nose and the shape of the ears of both the good father and the boatman. Even in inbred Venice, features *that* similar usually spelled a blood-relationship.

It didn't take long to load the tiny casks onto the small barge; Marco didn't bother to get any closer than he was. He wasn't planning on trying to see if the articles were stamped or not. He was doing what only *he* could, with his perfect memory.

Even amid the bustle of the dock, he was keeping absolute track of *exactly* how many spice casks—and *only* the spice casks, nothing else—were going into the bottom of that barge.

Three days later, when the bundle of tax stamps came in, Marco had his answer. Three more casks had gone into the barge than there were stamps for.

That night he intended to give Caesare Aldanto his full report—but that afternoon he got an unexpected surprise.

A creamy white and carefully calligraphied note from the House of Dorma.

Marco finished his report to Aldanto, given while he was finishing his dinner in the kitchen, and Caesare was both impressed and surprised. The lad had handled himself like a professional—

Like an adult. He'd thought out what he needed to know, he'd planned how to get it without blowing his cover, and he'd executed that plan carefully, coolly, and patiently. Aldanto pondered the boy's information, and concluded that no matter how you looked at it, it was going to be worth a great deal to *both* sides of this messy and treacherous game he played. He nodded to himself, then looked up to see that the boy was still standing in the doorway, looking vaguely distressed.

Aldanto's approval did nothing to ease the boy's agitation; if anything, it seemed worse. "Marco, is there something wrong?"

"Caesare—" The boy looked absolutely desperate. "I—got this today—"

He handed a square of creamy vellum to Aldanto; feeling a terrible foreboding, Caesare opened it.

It proved to be nothing more than a simple invitation for Marco—and a friend, if he chose—to come to dinner at Dorma, to be introduced to the Family.

Aldanto heaved a sigh of relief. "One may guess," he said, handing the invitation back to Marco, "That Milord Petro Dorma has received your grandfather's letter." The boy's expression didn't change. "So what on earth is *wrong*?"

"It's—it's *me*, Caesare," the boy blurted unhappily. "I was a child the last time I was in a noble's household. I don't know . . . how to act, what to say, what to wear . . ."

He looked at Caesare with a pleading panic he hadn't shown even when he'd known his life hung in the balance. "Please, Caesare," he whispered, "I don't know how to do this!"

Caesare restrained his urge to laugh with a control he hadn't suspected he had. "You want me to help coach you, is that it?"

Marco nodded so hard Caesare thought his head was going to come off. He sighed.

"All right, young milord—let's see if we can create a gentleman out of you." He smiled dryly. "You *may* wish yourself back in the swamp before this is over!" Inwardly he smiled. This might be tedious, but it would be valuable.

Chapter 50

"I don't believe we've met before, Father Lopez, although I've seen you several times at the Doge's soirees." Francesca glanced at Pierre and Diego, who were sitting in their own chairs in her salon not far from the Basque priest. "I'm acquainted with your two companions, somewhat, from the last such event." She pointed at Diego, and then Pierre. "He has an excellent wit, and the other laughs quite nicely. But I suspect you didn't come here to engage in humorous repartee. Nor, I'm quite sure, for the other reason gentlemen pay me a visit."

Lopez smiled. "Call me Eneko, if you would. The first thing I'd like to dispense with is formality."

"Good enough. Call me Francesca. The name 'de Chevreuse' is a false one, anyway—as I'm sure you are already aware."

Diego cocked his head. "Why are you sure of that? You've gone to considerable trouble to establish the name."

Francesca snorted. "Please! Father Lop—Eneko, rather, is a special envoy from the Grand Metropolitan in Rome. No one seems quite sure what he—and the two of you—are doing here in Venice, although I suspect Metropolitan Michael knows. You seem to spend most of your time in the Ghetto, which is largely *terra incognita* to the Venetian *haut monde*. Charitable work, it's said."

"That is, indeed, what we have been mostly doing," interjected Pierre.

" 'Mostly,' " mused Francesca, arching an eyebrow. "That leaves—?" She answered her own question almost at once.

"Investigation. That's what it leaves. Most people think you're trying to ferret out Strega witchcraft."

"And you don't?" asked Eneko.

"The idea's nonsense," replied Francesca. "First, why bother? The Strega have been in Venice for centuries, with no one any the worse for it. Second, you've been here for many months now. 'Ferreting out' Strega so-called witches in the Ghetto wouldn't take more than a few weeks, for any but the most incompetent of clerical magic-workers. Which you are—don't deny it—and I don't think the Grand Metropolitan chose to send fumblers."

Eneko nodded, accepting the compliment. "I thank you for that. Although I must admit I've wondered at our own 'competence.' The saints know we've had a difficult time ferreting out what we *did* come to find."

Francesca sighed. "Which, I suppose, was not *my* true identity."

Diego cleared his throat. "Ah . . . no. As it happens, Francesca—Marie-Françoise de Guemadeuc, to use the name you were born with—we uncovered that little secret within a few weeks of learning of your existence."

"My condolences," murmured Eneko. "I can't say I approved of your family, but I would not wish such cruelty and destruction on anyone."

Francesca stared at him. She was a little shaken. "You learned *that* quickly?"

Diego began to say something but Eneko waved him silent with a little motion of his hand. "It is time for a full introduction, I think. Francesca, let me explain who we *really* are." He nodded toward Pierre and Diego. "By 'we' I include more than just the three of us. There are some others sworn to our cause. Most of them—which is not many; a half-dozen—still in Toulouse or Orleans. Another, Francis, now resides in Mainz. All of us, at one time, were students at the University in Orleans. That is where we first met, and forged our brotherhood. Which explains, of course, our intimate knowledge of Aquitainian affairs."

Francesca's lips twisted into a wry little grimace. "I wouldn't have thought Orleans—anywhere in Aquitaine—would make a good breeding ground for the creation of brotherhoods and the forging of causes. Except those leading to personal advancement, which—" She gave all three of them a quick inspection. "—does not seem to be the case here."

Pierre chuckled harshly. Diego's chuckle was a softer and warmer thing. Eneko simply smiled, a bit grimly.

"To the contrary, Francesca, Aquitaine explains much. It was there that all of us finally realized—and accepted—the extent of the rot within the Church. By which I mean the *Petrine* branch."

For a moment, Francesca's jaws tightened. "Do tell," she murmured. "I believe it took the Metropolitan of Orleans five seconds to decide to excommunicate my father. As much time as it took to fill both his hands with gold coin."

Her ensuing chuckle was even harsher than Pierre's. "I must say it's refreshing to hear this from a Petrine cleric. At least, I *assume* you consider yourself such. Difficult to imagine the Grand Metropolitan of Rome sending a Pauline envoy to Venice."

"Petrine through-and-through," agreed Eneko. "In fact, we have a close relationship with the Hypatian Order."

Hearing that, Francesca's eyes widened. In the complex welter of Church institutions, the Hypatian Order was considered— certainly by Paulines—the most extreme of the organized Petrine currents. Although they were generally regarded as ineffective and relatively harmless—

"Oh, God," she croaked. "Don't tell me." She sighed again, and this time far more deeply. "I was *afraid* you weren't really all that interested in my personal identity."

She rose abruptly, walked to the doors opening on to the balcony, and began to open them. She had a sudden need for fresh air.

"Don't," commanded Eneko. "Please, Francesca. We took great pains not to have our visit here noticed by anyone. If you open those doors—at night, with this room well lit—"

She closed her eyes, lowered her head, still clutching the door handles. "Please," she whispered. "All of that is behind me."

"Don't be stupid," said the Basque. "That's simply cowardice speaking. You are not a coward—far from it. And you don't even mean it, anyway."

She turned her head, staring at him. "Yes, I do," she insisted. In a very soft voice; which, she realized, didn't sound as if she really meant it.

The Basque's grin, when it came, was astonishing in its sheer charisma. Francesca got her first real glimpse of the personality which had forged this little band of . . . brothers.

"You *adore* the world of politics, Francesca," continued Lopez, still grinning. "All this—" He made a little circling motion with his finger, indicating the plush surroundings. "—is really fraud and fakery. You enjoy wealth, I'm sure, but is that really why you chose this life?"

"I didn't 'choose'—"

"Of course, you did! A woman as beautiful and intelligent and charming as yourself could have easily—long since—settled yourself into a nice comfortable situation."

"In fact, the Comte du Roure," added Diego, "asked you to marry him—the night before you fled with your mother to Avignon."

Francesca almost spat. "He was forty years old—and looked seventy—and almost as stupid as the hogs on his estates. He would have shut me up in that great ugly castle of his until he died. Which couldn't possibly have been soon enough."

Suddenly, she burst into laughter. "You're a shrewd bastard, Eneko. Pardon the expression. The Saints know, I've met few enough priests in my life who can see past the harlotry."

Again, she sighed heavily. But she found it easy enough to release the door handles and walk back to her chaise. "Yes, you're right," she admitted. "My fondest memories, as a girl, were the times I spent at the dinner table discussing the political affairs of the world with my father and his friends. I didn't realize at the time, of course, how deadly those affairs could become."

She plumped herself back in the chaise, making no effort to maintain her usual languid and seductive manner of sitting. "God help us all. You—*that's* what you're doing here, isn't it? You intend to organize a new Petrine order. The equivalent of the Servants of the Holy Trinity—say better, a *challenge* to the Sots."

"I prefer to think of it as a challenge to the Petrines, Francesca." All traces of humor left Eneko's face. "Who have grown soft, lazy—even corrupt, and not just in Aquitaine. The accusations leveled by the Servants of the Holy Trinity have far too much truth in them, as you well know. I leave aside their frenzied gibberish about heathens. I speak of the rest."

"I'll still take the Petrines over the Paulines," growled Francesca. "Any day of the month."

Eneko shook his head. "If things continue as they have, you will eventually not have a choice. The Paulines have been gaining in strength for a century, at least. Soon enough—if nothing is done—

they will dominate the entire Church." Seeing the courtesan's little frown of protest, he pressed on. "It is *inevitable*, Francesca. For centuries, now, the Paulines have been the shield of Christendom. Their power and influence ultimately derives from that simple fact. So long as the Petrine church is willing to loll about in comfort, here in the soft and summery south, and allow the Paulines to wage the battle against the Evil One, the Paulines will continue to wax in strength."

He shrugged. "And deserve to, in all truth. Or would, except . . . their own theological errors leave them prone to a different kind of corruption. One which is, in the end, far more dangerous than simple avarice and sloth." Eneko paused, for a moment. "Indeed, I fear they have already fallen into that pit. The Servants, at least— leading elements within them, I should say—if not yet the Knights. But the Knights have become, more and more, simply the tools of the Servants."

Francesca stared at him for a moment, her hands making little movements on her thighs. Like caresses, only firmer—as if she were drying her hands before lifting a heavy weight.

"What do you want from *me*?" she asked abruptly. "I'm a whore, Eneko, not a theologian or a paladin."

"I did not use that term," he said mildly.

"Use it, then!" she snapped. "If you want something from me, speak plainly."

"I will not use the term, Francesca, for the simple reason that if I believed it I would not be here at all. Neither that term nor the term 'harlot.'" He smiled thinly. "I can accept a 'lady of easy virtue.' Easy virtue is still virtue, after all."

Again, Francesca burst into laughter. "God, I'd hate to argue theology with you! The Grand Metropolitan must tremble at the sight of you coming."

Eneko winced. "It is true, I suspect, that the Grand Metropolitan . . . Well. I seem to make him a bit nervous."

"I can imagine!"

"Which is why he sent me here, of course," continued Eneko. "You might think of this as something of a test."

Diego cleared his throat. "Probably best not to ask whether the Grand Metropolitan hopes we succeed or fail. I'm not sure he knows himself."

Francesca smiled. "I could guess . . ." The smile went away and she sat up straight. "All right, Eneko. But the 'lady of easy virtue' *still* needs to know what you want from her."

"You must understand the severe limits we are working within, Francesca. There are only three of us here in Venice. The Grand Metropolitan has provided us with some funds, but . . . nothing extravagant, I assure you." For a moment, his face grew pinched. "Which is why, to my regret, I was at first forced to accept the hospitality of *Casa* Brunelli. Diego and Pierre were not invited, so they found lodgings in a poor hostel, as I have now."

"Not to my regret," growled Pierre. "The hostel stinks—but not half as bad as Brunelli. The evil in that house practically saturates the stones."

Eneko's lips were very thin. "Indeed. But let's not get side-tracked, for the moment. In addition to our financial constraints, Francesca, we are also—more and more every day, it seems—being watched by spies. It has become difficult for us to move about, outside of the Ghetto, without being observed."

He raised his hand in a little gesture of reassurance. "We managed well enough tonight, I assure you. But when the time comes—which it surely will, before too many more months have passed—when we need to contact certain critical persons, we will not be able to do so directly. We need you to serve as our conduit."

"'Certain critical persons,'" husked Francesca. "Who?"

"Petro Dorma, for one."

Francesca tried to keep from smiling. Not entirely with success. "That should not be, ah, too difficult. Who else?"

Eneko was silent for a moment, studying her. "You know perfectly well 'who else,' Francesca. When the crisis comes, the actions of the Holy Roman Emperor will be decisive. My own contact with the Emperor is circuitous and would take far too long to set into motion when the time arrives. And besides, I suspect I will be preoccupied with other matters. Whereas you—*you* are but one step removed from Charles Fredrik."

Francesca froze. Diego coughed into his fist, discreetly. "The Hohenstauffen dynasty," he murmured, "has perhaps dipped too often into that well for the subterfuge to work as nicely as it did once. And the Earl of Carnac is a rather distinctive young man. And . . . well, as it happens, I met him once." Hastily: "I'm sure he doesn't remember. He was only sixteen at the time, visiting Orleans with his mother.

And, ah, quite drunk. Sad to say, the lad fell into bad company—roistering students, the city's plagued with them—and, ah . . ."

Francesca rolled her eyes. "I can imagine," she muttered. She brought her eyes back to meet Eneko's. "He doesn't even know that *I* know who he is. I'm his whore, not his confidant."

The Basque priest's gaze remained level. He said nothing. After a moment, Francesca looked aside. "I suppose I'm being a bit disingenuous."

"More than a bit, I think. The earl trusts you, Francesca."

The look which came on Francesca's face made her seem much younger, for an instant. "I think he does," she said, almost in a whisper. "Why is that?"

Eneko's gaze was still level. Francesca sighed again. "I'm a disgrace to the Aquitaine," she muttered. "What kind of respectable whore can be trusted?"

Still, level. Francesca threw up her hands. "All right, then! Damn you. I'll do it." She rallied briefly: "When the time comes, not before. And how will I know *that*?"

Still, level. Francesca glared at Diego and Pierre. "Does he *ever* glance aside?"

The Basque's two companions grinned. "Welcome to our brotherhood, Francesca," said Pierre. Diego coughed behind his fist. "In a manner of speaking," he added.

As they were about to leave, Francesca placed her hand on the door and held it shut. "This will cost you, Eneko."

He smiled. "Not in coin, I trust."

"Coin I'm not short of," she snorted. She glanced at Pierre. "Although I'm a little shorter now than I was. Your Savoyard here is not the only one who can smell the stink coming from *Casa Brunelli*. I hired a bodyguard a week ago, after the Doge's last soiree. I do believe Lucrezia Brunelli has placed me on her list of enemies, and she's got a reputation. At least two courtesans have been murdered in Venice in the past year, both of whom apparently attracted too much attention from her."

The three priests frowned simultaneously. "We did not notice any bodyguard, coming in," said Diego.

Francesca smiled. "He's very good. Cost me plenty, but it was worth it. Another Aquitaine, unfortunately. So he insisted on coin rather than, ah, taking part of his payment in trade."

"How long do you intend to keep poking me, Francesca?" asked Eneko. His tone was very mild. "It's quite pointless. I have no doubt you will set a record for the longest stay in purgatory, when the time comes. Purgatory is not my concern."

She made a face. "No, it wouldn't be. And how stupid can I be to get involved with a priest who doesn't care about my sins?" Stubbornly: "It'll still cost you. And you know the payment I want."

The Basque nodded. "Trust. Confidence. To play a part—as you thought you did once, as a girl—in the great affairs of the world. Sitting again at your father's table, excited by knowledge; excited, even more, by the feeling that your knowledge *mattered*."

She lowered her head and removed her hand from the door, squeezing her eyes shut to hold in the sudden tears. "Thank you." Then, in a very small voice: "Forgive me, Father, for my sins."

Eneko placed a hand on her head and kissed her forehead. "Not so many sins as all that, child." He chuckled into the glamorous hair. "Well . . . many sins, I admit. Or, at least, the same sin oft repeated. But, in the end, not such a great one, as sins go."

Pierre scowled. "It's still sinful, and you should give it up," the Savoyard grumbled. "But . . ."

Diego smiled. "He's a witch-smeller, you know. It's quite a rare talent. But that's really why he kept insisting on kissing your hand at the Doge's palace."

Francesca's eyes were quite dry, now. She peered at Pierre intently. "And?"

The Savoyard looked away. "You should *still* give it up," he insisted. "But . . . there's nothing here in the way of that stench coming from *Casa* Brunelli and the Imperial embassy."

"Enough, Pierre," commanded Eneko. To Francesca: "I will keep our end of the bargain, Francesca. Be sure of it. Whatever we discover will be passed along to you." Slyly: "This will be quite an adventure, you know?"

After she closed the door behind them, Francesca leaned her forehead against the ornately carved wood. She could still feel the slight moisture from the priest's kiss. And was not really surprised, when she thought about it, that Eneko Lopez did not have dry lips. Whatever his vows—and Francesca was certain he kept them— she didn't doubt for a moment that the Basque was also the most passionate man she'd ever met.

"Quite an adventure," she murmured. "Idiot woman!"

But when she pushed herself away from the door, she was smiling. And did not even try to deny, to herself, that she felt as if she'd shed years as well as sins.

The effect translated immediately into action. Francesca had been trying to decide for days . . .

She went directly to her little writing table and penned a note. Quickly, for all the impeccable handwriting. Then, sealed it with wax and went back to the door.

Her bodyguard was standing in front of her, not more than an instant after she opened the door. Francesca had no idea where he'd come from. Nor did she care—that was what he was being paid for, after all.

"Have this taken to *Casa* Montescue, Louis. No—better yet, take it yourself. I'll be safe enough here tonight and I want to be certain it goes directly to the person addressed. Let no one else see it. Understood?"

Louis examined the name on the note and nodded. "Easy enough," he said, and was gone. Francesca watched him leave, wondering if she'd hear any sound at all.

She didn't, of course. Louis Marillac had come *highly* recommended.

The next evening, when she opened the door, the man who entered made no attempt to walk quietly. Not that he clumped, even as big as he was. The noise his feet made was more in the way of a shuffle. As if he were trying to disguise embarrassment.

"Mademoiselle de Chevreuse," he said, bowing and kissing her hand. "I was delighted to receive your invitation to pay you a visit, of course. Didn't feel I could refuse. But—"

"Please, come in!" Smoothly, Francesca closed the door and guided him into a chair. "And I insist you call me Francesca."

The man cleared his throat. "Francesca, then. But—"

He fell silent, obviously groping for words. "I must explain—"

"You need explain nothing." Francesca smiled and laid a hand on his shoulder. "I asked you to come, did I not? I am well aware of the straightened financial circumstances you are suffering from at the moment. I simply wanted the pleasure of your company, that's all."

The man stared up at her; his eyes disbelieving, at first. Then, slowly, the stiffness in his face began to ease. "It's been a long time," he murmured.

"Too long, I think." Francesca took his hands and lifted him out of the chair. "Come."

Quite some time later, as he stared at the ceiling of the bedroom, the man's face had lost all of its customary sternness. "I haven't felt this good in years."

"Not so old as all that, eh?" She lifted herself on one elbow and smiled down at him, running her hand across his wide chest.

He rolled his head on the pillow and met her gaze. "What *do* you want from me, Francesca?"

"I want you to think about the future, for a change. That's all, Lodovico. Your grand-daughter is my best friend. Your—obsessions—are not good. Neither for her nor for you."

For a moment, the old man's face grew fierce. Then, he chuckled. "I make no promises. But . . . yes, I'll think about it."

"You'll do more than *think* about it, you old vendettist!" Francesca laughed. "If you've got any coins to spend, I'll expect you to spend them on *me*. I dare say I'm a lot more capable at what I do than those incompetent assassins and spies you've been wasting your money on."

He grimaced. "True enough. And what else?"

She studied him for a moment. "Does there need to be anything else, Lodovico? Your company has been quite a pleasure, I assure you. It's not often I meet a man who understands—or cares—how a woman's body works."

"There's *always* something else, Francesca." He placed a hand on hers and gave it a little squeeze. "That's not intended as an insult. I sometimes think courtesans are less predatory than anyone. But there's *always* something else."

"As you say: 'true enough.'" She sat up in the bed. "I've decided I love Venice, Lodovico. And when something I love is threatened by enemies, I believe in taking steps."

"Well said!" he growled. A moment later, he was sitting up beside her. "Tell me what you know. If there's a threat—" The growl became a rumble, as if an old lion was awakening.

"*There's* your 'what else,' Lodovico," she whispered, placing a hand back on that great wide chest and giving it a caress. "There's still a lot of muscle there, you know?"

Chapter 51

"It smells like a trap, that's for sure," Erik said to Manfred, as they strode along the loggia. "Maybe Sachs is right."

Manfred felt his broadsword. "If it is, they'll regret it."

Erik looked at the abundant cover of the loggia. "If they don't shoot us from a distance. But why us? I mean, we never introduced ourselves to that *Signori di Notte,* that one time we met him when the coiner got burned. But that message was specifically for us. Sealed with what the doorman assured me is the signet of Lord Calenti."

Manfred shrugged. "Search me," he said. "You might as well ask me 'why here?' At least it's daytime and there are a lot of people around this Accademia place. Too many with books if you ask me . . ."

"You're a fraud, Manfred. You were so busy reading in that embassy library, you didn't even hear me come in."

Manfred grinned. "My father's duniwasals say it's a sissy accomplishment. I don't think they wanted me to read or cipher or tally, so they can skive out of paying their hearth-loyalties. But with Francesca being a walking library I've had to do some reading up, or look a buffoon. It's not so bad now that I don't have some damned whiny tutor rabbiting at me about it. Where do we go now?"

"Through there, I think."

They walked through into a courtyard and then across to the described door.

Erik loosened his broadsword and checked the hatchet under

the small round buckler strapped to his right forearm. Being left-handed had its negative points, but in combat it did have the advantage of discomfitting his enemies. Harder for them to deal with. It gave him an edge.

He pushed the door open fast. . . .

It was a pleasant enough chamber. And Lord Calenti did not appear to be waiting in ambush. He was perusing a huge pile of papers instead, very much alone, unless someone was balancing on the window frame behind these draperies. The Venetian was very grave-looking however, when he looked up to see who had thrust his door open. "Ah. Come in."

He stood up. "Gentlemen, I owe you an apology. I have come to realize that this treason nearly had the Knights . . . and myself . . . as unwitting dupes. Accounts are a more powerful tool than all the spies in the world. Now, about the incident at the House of the Red Cat . . ."

He paused. "I . . . I . . . My God . . . Luc . . ." His eyes bulged and he screamed. The hair on Erik's neck stood up. It was the same terrible shriek they'd heard on the night that Father Maggiore had been killed. He heard the hiss of Manfred's broadsword being drawn. He didn't even know how his own came to be in his hand.

"Reverse the blade!" yelled Manfred. "A crucifix!"

Erik did it. He began to walk forward. It was like pushing against the tide . . . the air seemed to be full of carillons of bells, all discordant. Sparks leaped and hissed from the steel. The words of the Lord's Prayer came instinctively to his lips.

To his right, Erik could see Manfred advancing also. Lord Calenti was tearing at his clothes; his face was contorted into the same terrible rictus of a smile they had seen on Father Maggiore. The flames and the cruel, vicious laughter began together with a maelstrom wind that plucked the papers up in a snowstorm. The velvet-seated chair skittered across the room; the writing table was hurled at them. It all stopped just short.

And still they continued to advance. A glance showed that Manfred's steel armor was almost purple with the sheen of crackling lightning. So was his own, Erik realized. The discordant bells were coming to a cracked and furious crescendo. He could scarcely hear his own chanting. They dropped to their knees on either side of the naked and burning man . . .

And there was silence. Blessed silence. And the flames died as if they'd never been . . . except for the ruin they'd left behind. Then Lord Calenti began to scream. It was a healthy, joyful sound, comparatively. It was merely the scream of a badly burned human in extreme pain.

At this point, Erik realized that they had an enormous audience. Students were peering in at the window, crowding in through the door. Awestruck and horrified faces gaped at them.

"Call a doctor!" yelled Erik at the crowd. "We need a chirurgeon here, fast!"

A man pushed his way forward through the crowd. Unlike most of the gaping young watchers, he was weather-beaten and wrinkled. He joined the knights at the side of the now moaning Lord Calenti, who was curled up in a fetal position on the floor of the ruined salon. The crowd was pressing forward, threatening to overwhelm them. Manfred got to his feet. "Back!" he shouted. "All of you out of here! Out!"

His bull-like bellows were accompanied by sharp swats with the flat of his broadsword, first on heads and then on behinds. So he was obeyed. Obeyed with alacrity—the fact that Manfred was able to wield that huge and deadly weapon in such a light and casual manner, causing no more damage that a schoolmistress with a switch, was even more frightening than the great blade itself.

"And fetch us a priest!" he bellowed after the retreating students. "We may need one."

Erik had stayed with the lean, wrinkle-faced man who was gently examining Lord Calenti. "Will he live?" he asked quietly, surveying the burned, whimpering man.

The weather-beaten man shrugged. "Might do. Might not. He'll need skilled nursing, and lots of fluids. He's going to be terribly disfigured even if he does live. Hell on a man who thought of himself as the ladies' delight. But I think you saved his soul. He should be grateful for that at least, even if he dies. It was devouring him. Here. Help me with these."

From a battered pouch at his waist he produced two poultices of neatly folded leaves, thick with some unguent. "I was taking these to someone else. Treatment for healing skin, not fresh burns, so they're not ideal, but they'll do. They'll sooth and keep the infection out of his face."

They were in the final stages of applying them to Lord Calenti's ruined face when a man in an elegantly tailored cardinal's red, with beautifully coiffured hair burst into the room. Despite the horror of the scene, the bishop's eyes were first drawn to the healer. His eyes grew as wide as saucers.

"Marina!" he choked. "What—what are *you* doing here? You've been gone for—I thought they said there was a doctor with him!"

The lean, weather-beaten man stood up, dislike written loud on his features. "And I thought they'd gone to fetch a *priest*, Bishop Capuletti, not a scavenger. I learned a thing or two about healing on my pilgrimage, and I was on hand. But I've done what I can. Get one of the Accademia's cadaver-masters if you prefer. I'm out of here. I don't like the smell—and I don't mean that of burnt flesh and parchment."

The bishop merely snorted dismissively as the weather-beaten man left. When he'd gone, he turned to the knights. "Pilgrimage, my foot! More likely, that Luciano Marina went to learn the dark arts from the devil himself. Now. One of you had better go and fetch a doctor, and the other find someone to send for the other *Signori di Notte*. And get me someone to tidy this room." He looked at the confetti confusion of parchment. "Might as well throw this lot away."

Erik shook his head. "I'm sorry, Monsignor. I think we should stay with him. Whatever attacked him may come back."

The bishop patted his crucifix-hung chain. "I will deal with it. I am, in case you cannot see, your superior in the Church."

Erik shook his head again. "Dealing with this magic requires steel, Monsignor. Not just holiness."

"So—as he is going to live and we don't need your priestly services, why don't you trot off to do the errands," said Manfred, with all the arrogance of an nineteen-year-old prince crammed into his voice. Because of Manfred's size and the fact that he'd seen a lot, Erik tended to forget his age. Sometimes however, like now, it showed.

The bishop goggled, his ever-so-white face suffusing with choler.

Erik thought he'd better intervene. "That's enough, Manfred! Go and bellow for someone at the door. I'll collect these papers. Lord Calenti seemed to ascribe some importance to them. Perhaps they'll mean something to one of the other *Signori di Notte*."

Bishop Capuletti sniffed. "They're just bills of lading and accounts from the bankers at the Rialto bridge," he said, in voice like iced vinegar. He deliberately ground one underfoot.

Erik calmly picked it up and smoothed it. It was indeed nothing more than a partly burned bill of lading. A spice-cargo from Acre. It seemed to be innocuous enough. Loading. Unloading. Damages. Signed by the captain and bearing official looking seals. The bishop snatched at it. Erik held it away.

Manfred watched as Erik lifted the piece of paper out of the portly bishop's reach. He'd known Erik for the better part of eight months now, and he knew the danger signals. He'd better be ready to intervene. Erik was easygoing and rational a lot of time. Hard to anger. But the Icelander had a rigid code of right and wrong—and the bishop had overstepped it. Erik would not let little things like the future stand in his way.

"A man has nearly died for what is contained in these pieces of paper." Erik's voice was absolutely level, utterly expressionless. "You will treat them with respect." Erik's gray-blue eyes bored into the red-clad prelate with an implacable stare. That look would have sent a ravening lion creeping off quietly to its lair.

The bishop, about to make some stinging comment, looked into those eyes. He shut his mouth. Raised his hands pacifically without even thinking about it.

Seeing Bishop Capuletti wilt, Manfred relaxed. Manfred knew himself to be much quicker to anger. But Erik, when he finally got angry, didn't cool easily. The famous Norse fury of ancient times didn't lurk all that far beneath the civilized and pious surface.

Relief in the shape of a doctor and a worried-looking Schiopettieri arrived.

"Ah! Father Belgio!" squeaked the prelate. "As you are both an ordained priest and a doctor, er . . . I think I'd better go and confer with the Accademia authorities." He left hastily, without his dignity—but with his head.

Manfred turned his attention to the doctor-priest. The Schiopettieri had taken one horrified look, a second to confirm just who the burned man was, and had followed the bishop's example of a hasty exit. Hopefully he was going to call someone more senior. The doctor, on the other hand, had knelt by the fetal-ball of burned man. He looked at the poultices.

"Where did these come from?"

"A weathered and wrinkled fellow called . . . Marina, apparently,"

Erik answered. "Your bishop didn't like him much. Do we take them off?"

The doctor-priest shook his head. "No. I wonder if he knows what he is dealing with? Someone . . . a woman . . . has imbued those with a great healing and soothing power. I sense the work of one of the neutrals . . . one of the ancient nature spirits about them. They may do more good than I can. Now. This man has been spiritually attacked as well as physically hurt. The physical hurt is great, but the spiritual hurt is greater. His life is like a guttering candle flame. This not a consecrated place, so we will need circles of exclusion and the evocation of guardians to secure and defend him. Are either of you skilled in the working of magic?"

Both Erik and Manfred hastily shook their heads.

The doctor-priest sighed; shook his head. The gesture seemed one of slight puzzlement. "Your auras . . . Never mind. Take these."

He dug into his bag and came up with a censer, salt, and a bottle of water. He hesitated a moment. "Water. Yes." He looked carefully at Erik. "Water. There is much latent force in you." He turned on Manfred. "And you can take the salt. It is . . . right. Neither of you must ever take fire or air." The enigmatic doctor-priest then placed candlesticks around the Venetian lord.

"*Fiat lux!*" The doctor-priest's voice, so gentle a few moments before, now commanded.

And there was light. The censer in his hand began to smoke.

"Let that which cannot abide, depart! In the name of Jesus, in the name of the Holy Spirit . . ."

He led them, praying, in the ninefold circle . . . of smoke, sprinkled salt, and water.

Then, when that was done and they were enclosed in a wall of smoke, they went to work under the doctor-priest's direction. First unguent, then poultices and then, as gently as possible, they rolled Calenti onto a blanket the doctor-priest had brought. As they worked the priest led them through various psalms.

Father Belgio called on names of power, evoking guardianship and protection on the burned lord. Then he led them in thanking and dismissing the Guardians and the wall of shifting smoke was gone . . . to reveal Abbot Sachs, Sister Ursula, several knights, and three people who were obviously Venetian nobility. All of whom wore expressions of irritation, worry, and perplexity in varying degrees.

"What in Heaven's name have you been doing in there?" demanded Sachs.

"God's work, brother," answered Father Belgio tranquilly. "Lord Calenti can be moved now. It is God's will that he should live, at least for now. And these brave knights saw to it that he was spared."

"But what were you *doing*?" demanded Sister Ursula. "We tried to reach you, to break in, but to no avail! Abbot Sachs and I are two of the most skilled practitioners of Christian magic in the Servants of the Holy Trinity!"

Father Belgio smiled tiredly. "I am a simple healer, and one whose gift it is to be sensitive to certain occult forces. A minor magician only." He looked at Erik and Manfred. "I can only think that some of the primitive nature forces lent their aid. They are capricious . . . And I am exhausted. Can some stout fellows be called to carry poor Lord Calenti to the chapel? I think it best that he be nursed there."

"Will he live?" demanded Ursula. She shuddered. "Burns are dreadful. I fear them." Manfred noticed that the nun's hands were balled into such tight fists that her knuckles were strained white. She looked ready to faint. It was the first time he'd seen the ice-woman display as much as a trace of any emotion.

Belgio nodded. "If it is God's will."

"We will accompany him to the chapel and pray. It was surely the hand of the Lord and his apostle Paul that brought the Knights of Holy Trinity here today," said Sachs.

"Actually, it was that letter from Lord Calenti, Abbot. The one you thought was a trap," said Erik, yawning.

"It is still God's work," insisted Sachs.

Manfred found himself yawning in sympathy. He suddenly felt drained.

Two sturdy-looking Schiopettieri took up the corners of the blanket and lifted Lord Calenti. He whimpered faintly. One of the worried looking Venetian noblemen cleared his throat. "May we talk to you about it?"

Manfred looked at Erik. The Icelander showed no signs of following the procession. "What do you say, Erik? A glass of wine would be nice."

Erik swayed slightly. "Some of that grappa might be even better."

Two of the Venetians looked a trifle taken aback. The third, a shorter balding man who was considerably younger than the others, smiled. "Why not? Lord Calenti is in good hands. There does not appear to be anything further to do here. Let us go and sit these good knights down, give them a well-earned glass and see what they have to say."

An alarm bell rang in Erik's head. *Nothing more to do here?* He looked hastily around the salon. Someone had righted the desk and taken away the smashed chair. They'd also taken away the laboriously gathered partially burned bills of lading and accounts from the bankers. Only two or three badly burned fragments, which must have been within the circle, still lay on the floor.

"Do you know what happened to the bills that were here? A whole stack of them? In that corner?"

The three shook their heads. "They will doubtless have been taken somewhere for safekeeping," said one, as Manfred gathered up the three remaining fragments.

"Not just thrown away?"

The balding, slightly plump man laughed. "In Venice! Never. We are a republic of traders. And that means records. Half the reason we make a profit out of you northerners is poor bookkeeping on your part. Come. There is a tavern just around the corner. Zianetti's. I remember it well!"

They walked to the tavern past knots of worried, peering students. In silence, except for the bald-headed nobleman quietly informing Erik and Manfred that he was Petro Dorma. He did not mention the names of the other two Venetian lords.

Inside Zianetti's, Dorma secured a room at the back. Once everyone was seated, he poured the strong Italian brandy which was already on the table.

"Now," said oldest of the three. "Tell us what happened."

Erik shrugged. "The doorman at the Imperial embassy received a note from a runner. The note was sealed with Lord Calenti's official seal. It was addressed to us, by name, but it was taken to Abbot Sachs who was meeting with the knight-proctors. They called us in."

"I expected them to haul us over the coals, like we were bad children," said Manfred with a grin.

"The abbot told me to open the letter and read it to the assembled proctors," said Erik, managing not to smile at Manfred's accurate assessment. "Lord Calenti asked us, and only the two of us, to please come to his rooms here before Sext. He said it was of greatest importance. Since it was then well past Terce, we left immediately, on the abbot's instruction. A party of knights followed some ways behind us, so as not to frighten anyone who might be attempting an ambush."

Manfred shrugged. "It looks as if someone tried to kill him before he spoke to the Knights."

"All he did manage to say to us was that he'd uncovered treason that almost had the Knights—and himself—as unwitting dupes. And that accounts are a more powerful tool than all the spies in the world. Then he started to say something about the incident at the House of the Red Cat, but the attack came before he got out more than a few words."

The three looked startled, obviously recognizing the name of the bordello. So Erik had to recount that episode. He edited it, cutting Francesca's part out entirely. He could still feel his face glowing despite that.

"Well, we can find out where those orders came from," said the eldest. He was plainly familiar with the near-dockyard bordello, which led Erik to suspect that he was—or had been—an officer of the Venetian fleet. Probably an admiral, judging from the man's easy assumption of authority. The main clientele of the House of the Red Cat were naval officers; common seamen frequented less expensive brothels.

"And I'll talk to Doge Foscari," said the second nobleman. "At least we know the Knights are not part of this conspiracy."

"I'm going to try to track down these accounts," announced the bald-headed Dorma. "Any idea what they're about?"

Erik shook his head. "I only saw one. A bill of lading. A cargo of various spices, and the damages."

"And there are these pieces," Manfred handed over the pitiful scraps of burned parchment. "I can't make anything of them."

Dorma examined them. "It's a tally of punched ducats being released to merchants in payment for goods. Probably a copy. I'll try to track down the original, but there are thousands of pages to go through. Unless I know where to start . . ."

The second one was a list of punched ducats exchanged for the whole ducats used in the city. *Had* been a list, at any rate. What was left of it contained only the names of two merchant houses, with no amounts surviving, and a third amount—with the name itself no longer readable.

The third scrap was simply a *Capi di Contrada* seal on a piece of paper.

The three signori thanked Manfred and Erik and left them to finish their drinks. Manfred chugged his and called for a second. Erik sat sipping. "Well. I owe you an apology. I heard the bells this time. Not very musical, are they?"

Manfred scowled. "You said it was inside my head after I was flung away onto that flimsy chair. You know they complained to me about breaking that chair? *Ha.* And I could have saved that whiny old Servant of the Trinity as well. Only that force seemed much stronger."

Erik smiled. "There were two of us this time. Come on. Drink up. Time we got back."

Manfred shrugged. "They'll never notice if we don't. Erik, I've a need to accumulate a few sins to confess."

Erik shook his head, hiding a reluctant smile behind his hand. "Get up, before I turf you off the bench."

They were crossing the campo, under the eyes of the bunches of students still buzzing with hushed talk, when a woman came running up to them.

People, Erik had noticed—particularly the Venetians—tended to avoid the Knights. That was hardly surprising. The likes of Von Stublau were likely to knock anyone who got in their way into the nearest canal. So a young woman running up to them was something of a surprise. To judge by Manfred's expression—even if by her dress she was a serving-maid—it was a welcome change. She was pretty enough.

She curtseyed hastily, nearly dropping the bundle she bore. "Pardon your honors, the students says you are the ones who saved M'lord Calenti?"

Manfred bowed. "We are, signorina."

"Ooh! From demons seventeen feet tall with horns and lots of teeth! And dancing naked witches with six breasts—like dogs. And I heard the whole building was destroyed and Legions of Cherubim, not that I understand why fat baby angels can fight well, but Father Pietro always tells us they do. Then there were those with trumpets and the whole city shook. And the winged lion itself stirred in the piazza. And there was a rain of blood—" Her eyes sparkled, as she tilted her head, quizzical for more juicy details.

Even Manfred was gobstopped. "Er. No . . . It wasn't quite like that. . . ."

Well, if they weren't going to oblige, she'd help out. "And poor Lord Calenti, him so handsome and all, he fought like a tiger before he got so burned by the devils. They burned the clothes right off his back, with their pitchforks and I don't know why they say that because surely it must have got the clothes in the front, but that would have got his privates, or at least showed his smalls and he has such elegant knitted smalls." She giggled coyly. "Not that a girl like me would know anything about that."

"Er," Erik began.

That was quite enough interruption. "So when Signora Elena said she needed someone to take m'lord his best nightshirt, because he was too sick to move, and Silvia and Maria were both too scared to come for fear of demons, and all the boys at the Accademia ogling them, and I don't know why because Maria's been walking out with that rough Samarro boy—and what's a few noble students compared to that?—I said I would take it. Only then Signora couldn't find it and I've had to bring him his second best and it hasn't got nearly such nice embroidery, and now I don't know where to find him, and none of these students want to tell me."

They probably couldn't get a word in edgeways, thought Erik. "The chapel," he said, hastily, pointing.

"Thank your honors," she said, curtseying again. Then, peering at Manfred, "You're awfully handsome, your honor. And so big, too." Squeaking and giggling at her own temerity, she scuttled off towards the chapel.

"It's not that funny." Manfred shook his head at Erik, whose steel armor—proof against great dark magics—was in danger of being shaken apart internally.

Erik snorted, his shoulders still shaking. "You fancied her and she fancied you. I don't see the problem. Just the girl for you to take home to your mother."

Manfred raised his eyes to heaven. "Hah. Funny, funny. Icelander sense of humor. Cowpat in the face."

"That's Vinlanders," grinned Erik. In the aftermath of the terrible encounter, and with the grappa burning in his veins, he was feeling unusually silly. "Icelanders are more likely to put sheep droppings in your stew."

"Huh. I'll watch out for 'olives' in ragout while you're arou—" Manfred stopped suddenly.

His face had gone serious. "Erik, that's the third victim that we know of that had just lost a piece of clothing. Remember old Maggiore was complaining about his cassock. And that coiner's housekeeper and his favorite cap. And now a nightshirt."

Erik's felt the blood drain from his face. "I've heard of this. Mammets with the victim's hair and clothing . . . We better tell Sachs."

Manfred pulled a wry face. "If we can persuade him to listen."

Erik shrugged and began to walk on. "If not, we can perhaps get Calenti to give us a lead on who could have got hold of one of his nightshirts."

"Do you think he's going to live?" asked Manfred. "Those are major burns."

Erik nodded. "He'll live. Just as long as he is in the care of that priest. He's a good healer, that man."

Chapter 52

Maria stared at the two golden hairs in her work-calloused hand. She stared at them, not for the first time, or the third time, or the thirty-third time. It couldn't be true.

Both hairs came from Caesare's pillow. And they certainly weren't his—or hers.

They didn't even come from the same head! One was much coarser, yellower and had a dark root; the other finer and more wavy.

There had to be some other explanation. There had to be. Only . . . it was hard to work out what it was. Her heart and mind felt as if they were tearing each other apart. This wasn't the first time she'd been suspicious. But this was the first time she'd had hard evidence.

"Whatcha starin' at, Maria?" Benito had come in, unobserved. She had thought she had the place to herself. The little scamp had probably come in the third-story window. He'd have to give that up one day. He had turned fifteen over the winter and he wasn't so little any more.

Hastily she thrust her hand into her skirt pocket before Benito could see. "None of your business!" she snapped.

Benito looked hurt. "Hey, come on, Maria. You can trust me. I carried that 'cargo' to Giaccomo's for you, right? And I got a bloody nose from Jewel as well as my ribs nearly kicked in—and I still got it there for you. Not one lira missing."

She felt herself floundering. He wasn't a bad kid, really. She had to talk to someone. If she talked to one of the cousins . . . they'd

471

try to kill Caesare. Benito—and Marco too—had proved themselves both trustworthy and honest. But Marco was so . . . so good, even if he was nearer her own age. Benito she could at least talk to, about this sort of thing. He was more worldly than Marco. Marco's interest in girls was real but so—innocent. Sending them love poems! On the other hand, she'd seen Benito doing some experiments in heavy kissing with one of the Sarispelli girls. Those two girls were heading one way. . . .

She took a deep breath and rushed her fences. "Benito, do you think Caesare could be seeing some other woman?"

He looked as if she'd just smacked him in the face with a wet fish. But only for a moment. "Na! There ain't no one in Venice as pretty as you."

She snorted and took a swing at him. She'd noticed that hesitation. But his reply still gave her a smile. "You were born to be hung, Benito. I ain't pretty! Now, according to that Sarispelli girl, if only you could kiss as sweet as you talk, you'd be inside the pants of every girl in town."

Benito felt himself blushing. He had thought that he didn't do that anymore. Still, she'd spotted that hesitation. *Merda.* Women didn't feel the same way about this as men did. Well, except for Marco. But Caesare just did what a real man did. Played the field. At the same time he also felt for Maria. She so *wanted* Caesare. But there was no way she'd keep him except as a part-time lover.

And the funny thing was that Maria Garavelli *was* pretty. She was more than just pretty. She was . . . Maria. Tough as nails. She had to be, as a woman alone, working small cargos on the canals. But there was a gentle side to her too. She really was quite something, compared to, say, Lisa Sarispelli who was only a year younger than Maria, but good only for kissing, and . . . well a bit of fumbling experimentation. Maria was worth ten of her. Maria was working so hard with her speech, and getting Marco to teach her to read now . . . All to try to raise herself up to Caesare's level. To keep him. Regretfully, Benito knew that there was just no way she could do it. Caesare . . . well, he and Marco owed him. But Benito could sense that Caesare had ambitions that went a long way beyond a canaler wife. It would all come apart one day. And Benito didn't want to be around when it happened. Best to try to lead off the subject.

"I'm workin' on the kissing," Benito said, with a shrug. "I mean, how's a fellow supposed to get better without getting some experience?"

Maria snorted. Benito noticed she was smiling, however. "Just be careful it don't end up with her up the spout or you with the French pox, 'Nito."

She walked off. When she was well gone, Benito exhaled. Long and slow. He'd better have a word with Caesare about this. Men had to stick together.

Maria was too preoccupied to be keeping a proper lookout. Normally this was what she did well. Nobody could sneak up on her. It was a lesson a woman learned quickly out on the water . . . or else. Especially on a foggy morning like this. She knew she wasn't looking out properly . . .

But Caesare's infidelity was preying on her mind. Should she confront him? Did she hope it was just a once-off? Just pretend it had never happened. So many times she'd said to herself: *Just enjoy now. Don't even dream about tomorrow. Just be grateful for what you have got, now.* He was so beautiful. So refined. She was just a canal girl. . . .

Something bumped into her boat. Maria nearly dropped her paddle and jumped overboard. To her relief it was only a hooded girl in an even shabbier gondola than her own.

"Idiot! Look where you're going!" snapped Maria.

The girl held up a hand apologetically. "Sorry. This fog. I misjudged the distance. I just wanted to ask you something."

Maria had placed her now. Working nights—as she did sometimes for Giaccomo's cargos—she'd seen her before. Also, lately, in the early mornings. She was the one the canalers called "the Spook." Someone who sculled a gondola like she was canal born and bred, but nobody knew her. She was nobody's family. Looking at that dress under the hooded cloak, Maria guessed it was because she wasn't anyone's family.

The dress was old, but had once been very good. Too good for canal. And word was out on the water that you stayed clear of her. Word was she had connections that could get you hurt. Strega. Maria tensed. She really didn't need any more trouble now.

"Yeah? What?" she asked warily. *She can't be more than a year older than me,* thought Maria. *And I've got bigger shoulders. I could tip her into the water and hit her over the head with a paddle. In this fog, nobody'd be the wiser. Hear what it was she wanted and if it was trouble . . . In her heart of hearts she wondered if she could do it.*

The girl smiled uneasily. "Well, um, you go to Giaccomo's quite a lot."

Here came trouble. Maria tensed. Nodded but didn't say anything. Messing with Giaccomo's cargos meant trouble. And you didn't cross Giaccomo.

The girl continued. "I'm looking for a party that goes there sometimes. Only . . . I don't want to go there myself. Could you give him a message from me?"

Maria relaxed, slightly. "Depends. Who?"

"Well, his name is Benito. He's a kid—about fifteen, maybe sixteen. Dark curly hair. Round face. He's a runner with Ventuccio."

Suspicion leapt into Maria's mind. Was this woman somehow tied to whoever had tried to kill Marco? With the mess their mother had been involved in? Could be. Could be! It would explain the oddities.

"Might know him. Why?"

Even in the fog, Maria could see that the other girl was blushing. "Just . . . wanted to see him. That's all," she said airily "He's . . . he's a friend of mine. I'll be around Campo San Felice between seven and half-past most nights."

Somehow Maria restrained the bubble of laughter. That Benito! She'd have to warn him to stay clear of this girl. "Yeah. I'll tell him. Who do I say? Benito's got so many girls chasing him he'll need a clue."

The girl shook her head. "He's a kid! I mean . . . um . . . just tell him Kat wants to see him. It's not about business or anything," she said hastily. "Just . . . want to ask him something."

"Uh huh. Kat who?" Benito wasn't *that* much of a kid.

The girl looked faintly alarmed and taken aback. "Just Kat. Er. Kat Felluci."

Kat was surprised to see the canaler's eyes narrow like that. Then she remembered. It had been all over the canals. What a stupid name to choose for herself . . . it had just come from silly daydreams and just not being able to come up with a different name on the spur of the moment. She flicked her oar and sent the gondola off into the fog to hide her burning face.

※　　　※　　　※

Caesare hadn't been in when Maria had rowed her reluctant way to the water-door. She still hadn't made up her mind what to do about Caesare, but she'd been bracing herself to meet him. So—of course—he wasn't there. Both Marco and Benito were, however.

It set her off-balance not having Caesare there. All day she'd been making up her mind just what to say to him. And then changing it. She hadn't even had time to wonder too much about the girl's choice of surname. It obviously wasn't hers. . . . It could be coincidence. It wasn't that rare a name. Or she might know Marco.

"Met one of your girlfriends today, Benito."

Benito looked suitably embarrassed. "Aw. She's not really that. She's just . . ."

"Someone to practice kissing on?" she teased. "I didn't know about this one. She's a big girl, too."

Benito looked startled. "Huh? Who?"

Maria gave a wry smile. "Kat. Or that is what she calls herself."

"Kat?" Benito looked puzzled.

"Wears a hood," said Maria, taking a glass of wine from Marco. He was considerate like that. "And works nights, mostly. Girl from a good family by the way she dresses."

Light dawned on Benito. "Oh, *that* Kat! She's no girlfriend of mine!" he added hastily.

Marco looked amused. "I didn't know you were into the petticoat-line yet, Benito."

Benito looked a little shamefaced about growing up, thought Maria. "Um. Well, Kat's no girlfriend of mine. I've just done some work for her."

Maria shook her head. "Word is out on the water that she ain't someone you should mix with, Benito. Trouble. Anyway, she said you could find her at Campo San Felice between seven and half-past most evenings."

"I know she's to be steered clear of now, but, well, I didn't know then," admitted Benito with shrug. "Valentina and Claudia both warned me off."

Marco's amusement had entirely drained away. "If they did that I hope you listened to them, and have stayed away from her?"

Benito looked uncomfortable. "I figured out she was the kind of girl you don't mess around with, but well, you know when I had that spot of bother with Jewel?"

"Uh huh."

"Well after that marsh-loco showed up and beat him to a pulp, I was running on, but kind of sore and a bit spooked. And there she was and she owed me a favor, maybe. So I got her to give me a lift to Giaccomo's. She knew exactly where the Schiopettieri were working."

Maria swallowed her wine. "That's scary in itself. And that explains why she's looking for you at Giaccomo's. Anyway, do you know when . . . Caesare will be back?" She was irritated at herself for allowing that hesitation and hurt to show in her voice when she mentioned his name.

"Won't be in tonight," said Benito.

Maria was proud of her casual tone this time around. "Oh. Well, I'm pooped. I'm going to catch some shut-eye. He didn't say where he was going, did he?"

Benito laughed. "He never does, Maria."

She nodded and headed up the stairs.

Benito did however know where he was meeting Caesare. He had work to do for him. He felt a little uncomfortable about the evasions. Caesare had said it was best to give her time to get over it. And Benito supposed he knew. But Maria, trying to keep the misery out of her voice when she said Caesare's name, made him feel uncomfortable. Even a little miserable himself.

"Benito, who is this 'Kat'?" asked Marco. "And what's bothering Maria?"

"Kat? Just a girl I know. Got the sharpest tongue in Venice. I ran into her by accident, brother, and I'm keeping clear of her. I'll stay away from Giaccomo's for the next while."

"And Maria?"

Benito shrugged his shoulders. "She's worried about competition."

Marco pinched his lips. "Oh." He sighed. "I don't know what to do about it, because we owe him. But it's not right, brother."

Benito shrugged again. "A man's got to do what a man's got to do, Marco. And it's not our affair, huh?"

Marco sighed again. "It's not right."

Benito felt uncomfortable—as he frequently did when Marco

drew the moral line. "Yeah. Well, nothing we can do about it. It's kind of your fault, Marco." That was unfair and he knew it. Caesare had always played the field. Just that Angelina in the last few months had been somewhat "in-your-face" to Marco. But that too seemed to be tapering off. As if the sheer heat of it was burning it out. "Anyway, I've got to go out. I'll see you later," he said hastily.

"I don't trust you, Aldanto." He could see the swarthy, heavy-bodied man was ready to leap like a cat. Whether it was at Caesare's throat or away, Benito couldn't be certain.

By Caesare's posture, Benito could tell that he too was keyed up. Small movements betrayed him. Benito, hiding in the deep shadows, on the roof across the alley, prided himself that he'd learned well from Caesare. He could even read his mentor. But Caesare's voice was dead-steady. "The feeling is mutual, Francesco Aleri. But it's business."

"You are not welcome back."

Caesare snorted. "I'm not coming back. And if I happen to die, some very interesting information will be forwarded to Ricardo Brunelli."

It was the heavy-set Francesco's turn to snort. "You've got nothing. We've changed things since your time."

Back on the shadowy rooftop Benito squinted, trying to absorb the details of his face. So, the man was a Montagnard agent. Well, his official title was "Milanese Trade Ambassador-at-Large." Benito knew that from delivering the initial message to the man at the German hotel next to the Rialto.

There was a flash of teeth from Caesare. "Everything?" he asked slyly. "Even your sleepers?"

Aleri gave a short bark of laughter "You don't know who those are. You were never on that part of the operation."

"Ah, but on the other hand—Lorendana Valdosta was," purred Caesare. "Now, why don't we talk business. In there. You've got the Dandelos in your pocket."

The two walked into the small shrine and, to Benito's frustration, he could hear no more than the indistinct murmur of their voices, no matter how hard he strained his ears. It had been something of a shock to hear his mother's name. But obviously Caesare had gotten something useful out of Marco's careful writings. Well, he was glad they'd paid something back.

Minutes later, the two emerged and went their separate ways. Benito waited a good minute before slipping away like a ghost.

A good minute after that, Harrow moved. Marco was at least asleep, safe. But this younger boy! He was old Dell'este reborn, if rumors about the old duke were to be believed. Harrow found Benito's preference for roofs made him hard even for an experienced former-agent to track. Basically Harrow had to try to second-guess him. Either he was a good guesser or the Goddess was doing more than her fair share of intervention. He'd get lost in the alleyways and then catch sight of Benito . . . against all probability. Harrow had decided that if the Goddess wanted the boy followed she'd make sure he succeeded. Marco was easier. For this Harrow was devoutly grateful. But he was also glad he'd followed the younger boy tonight . . . first into the hotel and then to this rendezvous. Obviously, the Goddess had meant him to witness this. Obviously, also, Aldanto hadn't meant Benito to be here. But just from following him, Harrow knew that Benito wasn't good at doing what he was supposed to do.

This meeting was a worrying one. He'd been sure that a meeting between Aldanto and Aleri could only be short, sharp—and end with Aleri dead. In his former life as Fortunato Bespi he'd seen both men's swordsmanship. Aldanto had the edge. Aldanto was perhaps the best he'd ever seen. So: what was this all about? No good, he'd bet. Interesting to hear Lorendana Valdosta's name. It had nearly startled him into moving. That had to be the Goddess's hand again. She watched Montagnards too.

Chapter 53

Luciano Marina had not expected to just move back to his old life. He thought he'd manage to scavenge a living around the Calle Farnese. What he hadn't realized was that the death of Gino Despini had left an empty hole at the center of Venice's Strega community. After Marina's disappearance, Despini had done his best to keep the city's Strega solid. But with Despini killed . . . by a still unknown hand . . . The Strega in the city were terrified—which, Luciano was now convinced, had been the purpose of the murder. And now that the Servants of the Holy Trinity were stirring up talk of burning out the whole of the Ghetto, being in a visible position of leadership was something all other Strega were shying away from.

He hadn't realized it when he slipped into Itzaak ben Joseph's shop, hoping to scrounge a few coins to start a life in the city. He had little enough to offer. Some medicinal herbs, a couple of twists of blue lotos, a little fly agaric, and his patchy memory . . .

He'd not expected Itzaak to peer at him warily, when he gave the old greeting, and once he recognized the face, fall on his neck. "Grimas! You have returned to save us in our hour of need."

Dressed in new clothes, and walking around in the city which had once been his home, he'd felt ready to chance his arm. Appointments to the Accademia were in the hands of the Council of Ten. But the Marciana Library warden-positions were within the gift of the Doge. And, given Luciano's past history with Giorgio Foscari, the Doge's majordomo had been persuaded to arrange an interview.

❀   ❀   ❀

Luciano had been shocked to see how much Doge Foscari had aged. Still, he'd bowed low and hoped the Doge would remember him. He had, after all, provided working diagrams of several of the clockwork devices Foscari loved.

"Your Grace will perhaps remember the water-clock designs I obtained for you?"

It had indeed rung a bell with the old man. "Where have you been, *Dottore* Marina?" asked the old man querulously. "The idiots in library now never set anything out clearly."

"Doge Foscari, several years ago I undertook a brief journey to Fruili. On the way I was set upon, beaten and left for dead by bandits. It took me some months to recover under the care of a traveling monk. I could not remember who I was or where I came from. I'd been robbed of everything that gave any indication of my home or my station. The monk was on his way to the Holy Land. So, not knowing what else to do, I went there with him on foot. My memory was miraculously restored at the church of the Holy Sepulcher in Jerusalem. Now I have returned, a wiser and— I think—better man. But I must find employment. Does Your Grace need anyone in the Marciana?"

The Doge pointed a bony finger at him. "I need *you* there. I need more designs for my collection of mechanical marvels. All I ever get these days is reports of yet another ship lost. We've even lost galleys. Do you know when last—except at war—the Republic lost a galley? And now we have lost five to separate storms." His voice quavered slightly. "Send me some interesting plans for mechanical devices. You must have seen some things on your pilgrimage to inspire you."

Luciano accepted readily. It would be a short step from the Marciana to occasional lecturing slots at the Accademia. Marina was confident that within six months he would be able to regain his position in the Accademia.

Now that he was back, back in the heart of the academic and Strega worlds, the fragmented patches of memory were uniting. He nearly had it all back now. And his fear was growing steadily.

Strega were dying. And there was something very rotten at the Accademia. Money—lots of it, in a student community. Students were always broke. But from somewhere a river of coin was pouring in to the worst and most thuggish young noblemen. And knowing some of the families, it wasn't coming from their parents. There were also—unless he misread it totally—at least two cases of black lotos addiction among the students. Where was that coming from? Who would dare trade in the cursed stuff?

And these terrible magical murders. Naturally, many people blamed the Strega for the killings. But, leaving aside the fact that Strega themselves had numbered among the victims, anyone familiar with the principles of magic would understand that these killings could not possibly be the work of Strega. Everything about the murders shrieked *demonism*.

The community was almost paralyzed with fear. And his carefully placed scrying spells . . . revealed nothing. Nothing more than several sources of darkness . . . and some ice. And something trying to get to him, personally. A creature of the water; perhaps a monster, perhaps a shape-changer. It might not appear to be more than an unrestful period, with trade being bad, disease rife, and factional stresses high—but magically, Venice was under siege.

Still. Something *was* stirring on the side of Venice also. One of the old pagan "neutral powers." Something the Strega treated with great respect, even if they did not fully understand it. The Lion of Saint Mark . . . It was stirring if not fully awake. Demons were not the only ones who could work indirectly, and in mysterious ways.

Luciano had fully accepted that the Shadow of the Lion was at work when he spotted young Rafael de Tomaso. De Tomaso's mother had raised her son in the Strega tradition. Luciano, in fact, had been there at the coming-of-age ceremony as one of the sponsors. Even if the young artist hadn't known Grand Master Marina by sight . . . He, Luciano, knew that boy.

He had expected to see him at the Accademia. What he *hadn't* expect to see was Marco Valdosta walking beside him, deep in conversation. When he saw Marco, Luciano studied the crowd in the campo. Long and carefully. It had taken him nearly fifteen minutes to spot Harrow in the shadows by the loggia.

Circles within circles. Coincidences that shouldn't happen. The Lion casting its shadow . . . He was certain of it now. The knowledge brought courage with it.

He was standing looking at the scene, his attention absorbed, when someone spoke to him. Snarled at him, rather. He turned to see yet another familiar face. One much less welcome than Marco's. Especially now that he was a bishop.

Recognition was plainly mutual. "Are you deaf?" demanded Pietro Capuletti. "I asked you what you're doing here?"

Luciano smiled wryly. "Admiring the campo. It's a more attractive view than a fat fellow in red."

Capuletti's face hardened. "Your tongue will get you into a great deal of trouble with the Church. We want to know what you are doing back in Venice."

Luciano wondered who the "we" was. Luciano distrusted Pietro Capuletti. He'd been a sneaky boy and Luciano Marina would bet he was an even more devious man.

He also wondered if Pietro was still puppy-dogging after Lucrezia Brunelli. He was a fool, and always had been. There had never been any chance Lucrezia would have married him, even after he became a bishop. No Capuletti was ever going to be important enough to *marry* a Brunelli. Run errands for them, yes. Get fat on the crumbs from their table, yes. But *curti* like the Brunelli would never settle for lesser *curti*.

"As I've told you before, I've been on a pilgrimage to Jerusalem, and now that I've returned I intend to re-establish myself here at the Accademia." He smiled urbanely. "Don't try to threaten me, Pietro. I have many friends in the Church. More than ever, after Jerusalem." Let Capuletti sweat that one. Many pilgrims took vows of anonymity. A trip to Jerusalem, instead of wandering mindless in the Jesolo marshes, would have certainly given him some church contacts—perhaps of great importance.

"Ha." The bishop left without a further word, his anger proclaimed in his flaming cheeks and pursed little mouth.

Chapter 54

The rain was hissing down on the water. At a time when all sensible canal people—anyone with any sense at all—were indoors in front of a fire, maybe with a nice hot glass of mulled wine, Maria was out in the wet. But . . . things were rather tense between her and Caesare, right now. And he'd asked her to do this especially. And she really wanted to show him that she did love him. The last two weeks had been horrible. Left her sick to her stomach with a mixed mess of emotions.

He'd been so hurt when she had accused him. That hair might have blown in the window or something. Didn't she trust him? And, then, he'd been loving and attentive once he'd gotten over being distant and hurt.

She was still suspicious. But . . . she loved him. How could she let him go? So here she was getting soaked to the skin. She must be the only person on the water right now.

But, no. There was another gondola on the canal. As it went by without so much as a greeting from the other paddler, Maria realized that she knew her. That wasn't really surprising—she knew most of the boat people. And if anyone would be out in the half dark and rain, it would be "the Spook."

Maria was grateful, at least, that her destination wasn't all the way out to Guidecca to drop letters with Captain Della Tomasso this time. Tonight her rendezvous was comparatively close. Too close to the *Casa* Dandelo and the reek of its warehouses for comfort. You could smell the slaves even in the clean rain-washed air.

She pulled into the little landing. Good. There was no one around yet. She must be early. She shivered. She moved down off the stern to the duck-boards and sat down, huddled against the gunwale.

Someone loomed suddenly through the rainy darkness.

"Well, let's have it," grumbled Maria. "I'm wet and cold and I want to get home."

And then someone else jumped onto the stern behind her.

Maria stood up hastily, reaching for her knife. "Hey! *Figlio* . . ." Bright lights and stars exploded in her skull. But not before she'd seen that it had been Luciano Matteoni jumping onto the stern of the boat.

When she awoke it was to the betraying stench of the *Casa* Dandelo. But all she wanted to do was to be sick and pray the pain in her head stopped. Once she'd cast up everything that was inside her onto the rotten straw, blessed oblivion came again.

When she gradually awoke again . . . naked, cold, still sore, lying on the filthy straw a scant few inches from her own vomit . . . she was leg-shackled too. It was then that the true horror of situation dawned on her.

Casa Dandelo.

Slave traders.

Officially, they were not permitted to touch hide nor hair of Venetian citizens. Officially, their "cargo" was checked. The poor of Venice knew the truth: the Doge and the *Case Vecchie* turned a blind eye. The Dandelos took what they could and if the slave might complain to the *Capi di Contrada* signing the cargo outbound on ship . . . they took out the tongue that might wag. Or beat the victim senseless. Either way, the Dandelos never released any of those who found their way into their clutches. They brought a lot of money into Venice, and Venice looked the other way. After all, it was only the poor and unwanted who ended up in their clutches. The Dandelos didn't want a fuss. As far as the officials of Venice were concerned, their depredations were nearly the equivalent of "human garbage" collection. So long as it stayed that way, the Council of Ten and the *Signori di Notte* left them to it.

So: who would notice if she was gone? Well, Caesare would be waiting for his message. He'd panic.

A short, dark-visaged, thick-bodied man looked in at her. Instinct made her cover her nakedness. But this man wasn't interested. You could see it in his look. Merchandise. She was no more appealing to him than a bale of cotton would be. *Calm now. Try to talk your way out.* "Let me out. I've got friends with contacts. Ricardo Brunelli . . ."

The slaver grave a sardonic snort. "You wouldn't believe how many cousins of the Doge go through here. Anyway, the party wanted to know when you were awake." He turned and walked off.

"Can I have some water?" Maria called after him.

"If the man says so."

She was left to her fears. The minutes passed slowly.

The man who now entered walked like a cat. He was very like Caesare in that way. "I've got some questions for you about Caesare Aldanto. I will get answers. If I get good enough answers you'll go free."

And Caesare would die. "You can burn in hell, *figlio di una puttana.*"

His hand twitched. "You are lucky there are bars between us woman," he snarled. "Any more lip from you and I'll see that *you* end up as a whore in Aleppo, servicing a hundred fresh-from-the-desert rancid camel drivers a night. You think you're tough. You might last a year."

She spat at him.

He wiped the spittle away from his face. "It seems you need to think about it. Let's see how well you spit after a day of being dry."

Tonio's whistle woke Marco. Sick child. Must be very sick to call Marco out of bed. Marco seemed to be suffering from a lack of sleep these days. He'd been to see Rafael the night before. He'd been for another private meeting with Milord Petro Dorma last night. He liked the balding, chubby, perpetually worried-looking Petro. He also got the feeling that, although Dorma would be funding his studies at the Accademia, Petro was using him as a window into the world of the tradesmen and canalers.

Again, Tonio whistled. Louder. Eyes bleary, Marco fumbled about, dragging on clothes. By the lack of light coming in through the shutter crack it was very early.

Tonio whistled again; louder still. He'd have the whole neighborhood awake in a minute. Benito thrust open the shutters.

"He's coming," he said crossly to the boatman below on the dark water.

Tonio beckoned. "You too," he said.

The two of them, both more-or-less dressed, legged down the dark stairs.

"Who is sick?" demanded Marco, his herb bag in hand. His eyes were still half focused. It was still half dark.

Tonio pointed to the gondola attached to his vessel by a rope. "Couple of the night fishermen picked it up on the tide-wash. They brought it to us."

Marco recognized the boat now. Maria's. A terrible sinking feeling hit his gut.

"Maria?"

Tonio shrugged. "Maybe she fell overboard."

"Get real, Tonio!" snapped Benito. "Maria wouldn't even know how to fall off a boat, any more than you do. She was born on one."

Tonio shrugged. "Accidents happen," he said grimly. "Sometimes people help them to happen. You'd better go tell that fancy-man sellsword of hers." There was disapproval in the canaler's voice.

Benito took a deep breath. "Yeah. We'd better."

Caesare took it with a rigid face, allowing not one trace of emotion to show. "She'll be at the bottom of a canal with weights on her feet, I'm afraid. I should never have let her go out last night, in that rain. But she said they were relying on her. She said she'd overnight at Murano, if the rain got worse. I didn't worry too much . . ."

He shook his head, regretfully. "Leave me alone, please. I need some time."

"Sure, Caesare," said Benito quietly.

"Can I bring you a glass of wine, Caesare?" asked Marco.

Caesare smiled wanly. "No. Just leave me alone, please."

Benito and Marco went downstairs again. Marco found the emptiness and helplessness hard to bear. Benito snuffled slightly. It was a long quiet morning. Neither of them had it in themselves to go to work. Caesare had not come down, but they felt they should be on hand, perhaps . . .

The bells had just rung Sext when Marco decided he'd had enough. "Benito, I'm going across to Rafael."

"I'll tag along, if that's all right."

Marco understood the feeling. He didn't really like the idea of Benito being out and about and maybe in danger either.

"You're sure she's dead?" asked Rafael

Marco shrugged. "How can we be sure? But what else? They found her vessel, not her."

Rafael pursed his lips; looked at them thoughtfully for a while. "I do know someone who might be able to tell you if she's alive or dead. It is a little magical skill that he has. Do you have any of her clothing?"

Marco shook his head. Benito fished in his pockets. "Scarf she's been wearing?" he asked, pulling it out.

"That should work. Come on. He's over at the Marciana Library this morning."

Luciano looked up from the book he'd been peering at. The ink was old and fading. His eyes were tired. And there coming toward him was a sight for sore eyes: Rafael de Tomaso and Marco and Marco's brother. Well, it was time he made formal contact. He looked back among the stacks. There was Harrow. The boy was still protected.

Here, in between the books, he felt safe. Walking out to see Rafael, Marco had felt naked . . . as if they might be the next victims. Because he was utterly certain Maria hadn't disappeared by accident.

Still, he'd nearly fallen over his own jaw when Rafael brought them face-to-face with Chiano. Chiano wearing a fine cloak, and now calling himself *Dottore* Luciano Marina—but still unmistakably Chiano.

"Hello, Marco," his Jesolo guardian said with a smile.

It was Rafael's turn to look dumbfounded. "You know each other?"

For an answer, Marco embraced Luciano. "Better than you could dream, Rafael. And Sophia?" he asked. Seeing Luciano brought it back to him. He'd been forgetting a debt. He longed to see her, especially right now.

"She's still in the marshes, boy. Won't leave. Says it it's where she belongs, now. I went to see her a few days back. Misses you. You were always better with her medicines and potions than I was.

So—what brings you here? I am delighted to see you, of course, but you came looking for me."

They explained.

Luciano looked grim. "The town is awash with trouble. Give me that scarf." He stretched both hands out, palms up.

Benito laid the scarf across them.

They waited.

Luciano shuddered briefly.

Took a deep breath.

"She is alive," he said slowly. "Hush. This is a library!"

"Sorry. We're just relieved."

"Don't be," said Luciano grimly. "All I can tell further is that she is a prisoner, and surrounded by water."

Benito took a deep breath himself. "Right! Well, we'll get a search organized. I'll get back to Caesare and have a word with all the runners. Marco, you could maybe get hold of Tonio. Get the canalers to look for anything."

Rafael smiled. "Your little brother's quite an organizer, Marco."

Marco took Luciano's hands. "Thank you, old friend. We'll find her. And even if she is in danger—we have friends." Turning to Rafael he smiled. "You don't want to try living with Benito, Rafael. He organizes himself out of all the bad chores. But Maria's important to him. She's important to me too, but Benito thinks the world of her, though he won't admit it. Anyway, I must go. Thank you both from the bottom of my heart."

Maria knew every detail of her cell by now. There wasn't much to learn. Three cubits by six, rusty iron bar-gate, and stone floor and walls. On the floor, moldy straw. On the walls, prayers and curses written in what could only be excrement. This was just one of some ten cells on this level. Solitary confinement for trouble-makers and "specials," according to her neighbor. He claimed to be a wealthy cargo-master from Sicily, who had missed his ship and got himself into one bar brawl too many. He'd been mugged, robbed of everything but his breeches—and now these *porco cane* had taken even those.

There was no water. No place or container to relieve herself in. And a jailor who threatened to beat the pair of them if she spoke to her neighbor again. It wasn't worth it.

God, she was thirsty. And . . . eventually she had to use one of the corners of the cell. No wonder this place stank.

"How sure can you be of this, Marco?" asked Caesare. "I mean, as I said to Benito, these charlatans prey on the fact that it's hard to accept that someone you love is dead."

"He's no charlatan," said Marco, quietly. "He's the man who kept me alive in the marshes. I know you don't want to start hoping, Caesare. But he's a real magician. If he says she's alive, then she is."

Caesare stood up. "Then we'd better look for her. I'll get word out to some of my contacts. I'd better see Giaccomo. She did a lot of work for him."

Benito could be heard panting up the stairs. He was hot, tired, and enthusiastic. "I got her cousin Luigi and Fredrico. The Arsenalotti will be looking for her too. And I stopped by and woke up Claudia and Valentina. Once they'd gotten over it, they started to look too. We'll have everybody but the Schiopettieri out looking for her."

Marco smiled. It was best to be able to do something. "Well, now that you're back, you can go out again. Stick with Caesare, Benito. He's going to get to his contacts—but he might be the reason someone snatched Maria. I'm going to see if I can get Tonio to take me around to some of my 'patients.' I can get the bargees and boat-people looking too."

Benito stood up from the chair he'd flopped into. "Well, the other thing you could try is to stop by and see Kat. She's that 'Spook' I told you about. She has some contacts in among the Strega, I think. I was going to, but I'll be with Caesare. If you get a chance, go to Campo San Felice between seven and half past. She always wears a hooded cloak and she's got a shabby gondola. Anyway, just ask if her name is Kat and tell her you're my brother. Stick with Tonio if you can, Brother. I'm nervous about you being alone out there."

"I'll probably have my shadow, anyway."

"That you will," said Caesare grimly. "I don't want anyone on my back trail on this venture. You go out first."

They went their various ways. By the late afternoon, it seemed as if half of Venice was looking for Maria.

☙   ☙   ☙

Maria was sitting in the one place that no one could go looking. And she didn't know for sure that anyone was looking for her.

"Are you ready to talk yet, sweetie?" asked her persecutor from the night before. The light was better now and she could see him clearly. She took in the details of his heavy-set face and his dress. He wore well-to-do merchant clothes. And, unlike the slave-warder's disinterest, his eyes roamed her naked body with an unpleasant eagerness.

He turned to the warder. "Take her out of there. Give her a smock and put her in the 'interview' room. We'll have some wine and some food."

Maria behaved herself when the slave-warder let her out. She was quiet and submissive, putting on the slave-smock when she was told to. She knew that this wasn't the time to try anything. She hobbled her shackled way along to a room off the passage.

The room was bare. Except for two chairs and a small table. "Sit." There was a mug of wine and a plate of pasta on the table.

She sat. He sat down across from her.

"Taste your wine."

The devil will let me have a sip and then take it away from me, she thought. She took the mug and drained it. It was cheap raw strong red wine. And there was a lot of it.

"That was stupid, but predictable," said her interrogator, with a horrible smugness. "That was a lot of wine on an empty stomach. Which is what I wanted you to have, but I thought I'd have to persuade you. Now, I want answers. You might as well give them to me. Even if I have to take them out of you with pain, I'm going to get them. If I get them . . . I'll have them let you go."

The wine burned in her stomach. It might have been his intent to get her drunk, but it did lend her some courage. And heaven knew she needed it right now. Somehow his calmness was more unnerving than shouted threats. "How about some more of that wine?" she said with an assumption of casualness.

Without any warning he hit her. Hard. A stinging openhanded slap that rocked her head back. Maria tasted blood. Put her hand to her cheek. The speed and sheer violence of it left her huddling back in her seat with a little whimper of pain.

"Don't play games with me, bitch," he hissed. "You'll lose."

Chapter 55

Marco loitered around the edge of the Campo San Felice. This was stupid. How was he supposed to recognize this "Kat"? He'd been here ten minutes now, and had seen two old men manhandling a barge, and a solitary gondola going past without stopping. It wasn't much of a description to go on. *A shabby gondola and a woman wearing a hooded cloak.* This was a depressing waste of time.

Kat was depressed. It had been just over two weeks since she'd run into that woman who said she'd pass a message on to Benito. Huh. Imagine thinking Benito was her lover! She'd been at the Campo San Felice dead on time every night, except last Wednesday. Finally, two days ago, she'd ventured into Giaccomo's. He wasn't there. And one of Giaccomo's flunkies had quietly asked her to leave.

It had been a quiet request. But it was backed up with a potential threat. Clearly enough, some people had grown suspicious of the cargoes carried by "the Spook," and Giaccomo didn't feel he needed the possible complications of having her on the premises.

She'd tried Barducci's also. Those two singers had simply given her the wall-eye when she'd asked after Benito. She'd left a message with them, but she was willing to bet he'd never get that message. The only option that was left now was to go into Ventuccio's and ask to speak to Marco Felluci. . . .

She'd give it a few more days, but she was certain that Benito wasn't going to be there. She'd seen that canaler-woman last night, her head bent against the rain. But, in that downpour, Kat couldn't really have asked if she'd seen Benito lately. Not really the right time for a chat—nor the right area for it, either. You seldom found anyone hanging around *Casa* Dandelo. Not that you weren't safe enough on the water, but still . . .

She sculled towards the Campo San Felice. She couldn't see anyone. But then last time she hadn't seen Benito either.

The sky held the last translucent skeins of vermilion cloud. The sun was gone and that first whisper of the night-breeze brought the sound of distant laughter with it. The zephyr had picked up the scent of the sea from over the barrier lidi. For a moment, it carried Marco away. Back to the time centuries ago when the first refugees from barbarian invaders had smelled that same breeze, and had seen, perhaps for the first time, the swampy Rialto islands not just as refuge but also as a place of beauty. Venice had been loved, was loved. As much as a place of bricks, mortar and marble facing, the city of the winged lion was a great ancient repository of hopes and dreams. A place the barbarians had never managed to conquer. A city of love and lovers.

Then, cutting through the rippled, reflected last splendors of the day, came a gondola. Moving silently along the canal between the gothic-fronted buildings, sliding across the water, the dip and sway of the gondolier was as easy and graceful as a dancer's movements.

Marco looked across the water into the eyes of his kindred spirit.

The grace, romance, and beauty of the moment ended in a splash. His dream girl, her eyes locked on his, hit a mooring pole, dropped her oar, lost her balance and fell—fortunately—down onto her own duckboards.

The gondola was close to shore and Marco managed the jump without even thinking about it.

"Are you all right?" he asked anxiously.

"Fine." said Kat, sitting up, her face blazing. "Er. See if you can grab my oar."

He leaned over the side and pulled it inboard.

Kat seized the moment to pull herself together. What an absolute idiot he must think her. What a complete fool! And what a way to meet him! She'd have wanted to put on some better clothes.

Maybe some belladonna to widen her eyes . . . She must talk to Francesca about it.

One minute ago, she'd been sculling easily, putting minimal effort into it. The next she'd lost her concentration; lost her balance; lost her dignity; lost her oar . . . what should she say? Reality was with her, now. He might turn out to be a lot less likable than her imagination had painted him.

He pulled the oar onto the gondola; then, offered her a hand. "I'm sorry," he said smiling. "Maria says it's really bad manners to board a boat without permission. But I thought you might be hurt."

Whoever "Maria" is, she's going to have to go.

Now that he was up close, Kat found herself tongue-tied for the first time in her life. She settled for smiling at him. God, he was handsome. No. That was the wrong word. He wasn't ruggedly handsome. He was beautiful. No wonder this Maria was chasing him.

"You've hurt your hand!" he exclaimed.

There was indeed a thin trickle of blood running down her hand and onto her cuff. Kat looked at it and looked away. She really didn't like blood. "Oh, it's nothing," she said hastily.

"Here." He held out a tentative hand. "Let me see to it. . . . Signorina. I'm hoping to be a doctor one day."

"It's fine. Really."

He smiled. "I won't hurt you. I promise."

God in heaven, he could cut the hand right off if he wanted to. Well, if he wanted her as a practice patient she could have lots of injuries. Lots. If he wanted to lie her down on the duckboards—

Her mind shied away from that line of thought. She held out the hand.

He was gentle and surprisingly professional about it. "Just a scratch, I think. If you would just come over there to the light I could clean it and bandage it quickly."

"Thank you," she said, wishing he hadn't let go of her hand. "And I think we'd better tie up because we're drifting."

Two minutes later, the hand was neatly and professionally bandaged; the ragged scratch cleaned out. "There. Good as new within two days."

"And how do I find the doctor if it needs further attention?" She did her best to make the question sound casual.

"Oh. Well, I spend quite a lot of time over at Zianetti's near the Accademia."

So all this time hanging around Giaccomo's and even venturing into Barducci's had been vain endeavor! "Well . . . I'll find you there." *If have to invent an injury.* "What's your name?"

"Marco. Ah, Felluci." He bit his lip; then: "Well, I'd like to ask you to have a glass of wine with me, but I've got to wait for someone for Benito. Then we've got to go back to looking for Maria."

That explained it. He worked with Benito! What could be more natural than the scamp would send his friend off to see what she wanted. And what a friend to choose! But if this "Maria" was a girlfriend, then she—Kat Montescue—was going to do her best to make sure she stayed lost. "And this 'Benito,' did he tell you who you were to wait for?" she asked, managing to keep a straight face.

Marco shook his head. "Someone called 'Kat.' He's been avoiding her because she's trouble, but with Maria gone missing . . ."

It was Kat's turn to bite her lip. *"Trouble," was she? Well, there was some justification to that that description. She'd partly orchestrated it herself, and, well, she did have dangerous associates. The story Benito brought back couldn't have enhanced a saint's reputation, she'd bet.*

Then the humor of it all got through to her.

She has the most delicious laughter in the whole world, thought Marco. *I could listen to it forever, even though I don't see what is so funny.*

Finally she stopped laughing. "Sorry . . . *I'm Kat.*" And she started laughing again.

Marco found himself drowning both in her laughter and his own embarrassment. And yet, as bad as that embarrassment was, it was all right: He'd finally got to meet her. *He'd kill Benito! Either Benito had known and had been keeping his brother from another entanglement—for which he couldn't really be blamed, after the last time.*

No. Benito must not have worked out that Marco's "dream girl" and Benito's "trouble" were one and the same. But at least he'd found her. Now if he could keep from putting his foot in his mouth while he talked to her. Maybe he could even find out where she lived. She was everything Angelina was not. While he'd worshipped the ground Angelina walked on, and dreamed one day of kissing her hand . . . this girl made him want to fold her in his arms and . . . well, better stop these thoughts dead right there . . .

"I'm sorry. I'm sure they didn't mean it," he said humbly.

Kat smiled broadly. "I'm sure they did!" she said. "And they were right too, but I promise, not to you."

Marco had put two and two together. "Um. The girl you sent the message to Benito with. You haven't seen her, have you? We're looking for her."

Ah. So that was Maria. "Yes," said Kat, thinking back to the driving rain of last night. After her experience in the church she'd given up taking shelter. "But not today."

"She went missing yesterday," said Marco. "Caesare is worried sick."

"Who is this 'Caesare'?" asked Kat carefully.

He smiled again, and it did odd things to her insides. "Oh, sorry. Caesare Aldanto. Her . . . her boyfriend."

Relief was like the sun coming out. "She's not your girlfriend, then?"

He looked surprised. "Maria? She's crazy about Caesare. She wouldn't even look twice at me." He looked slightly sheepish. "Um, I . . . I'm not involved with anyone right now."

"Well, I'm not either." *There. What an opening.* "Although I have had several suitors." *That seemed important to say too.*

"I'm not surprised," he said warmly. "But about Maria. When did you last see her? We . . . we've had word she's a prisoner somewhere."

Kat cocked her head, put a finger to her jaw. "It was long after Vespers, but before midnight. Maybe a hundred yards from the *Casa Dandelo.* I . . . wanted to ask her about Benito. But it was raining too hard."

"I'd better go and tell Caesare. Why did you want to see Benito? I can give him a message."

"Oh . . . I, um, just wanted him to get hold of a friend of his for me," said Kat airily. "It's all right now. How about I take you to where I saw her?"

"You haven't got other work to do?" asked Marco. "I want to talk to you, but if you've got work . . ."

Her heart warmed. *He was an ordinary working man, after all.*

And a considerate one. She wished the Montescue could somehow sponsor him to do what he should be doing: medical studies. Already he was worth six of any Case Vecchie *scion-doctors she'd ever met. But unless her father came home laden with half the jewels of the Indies, there was no way.* Casa Montescue *limped on from day to day as it was. Extra expenses just couldn't be borne. Only yesterday her grandfather had said to her that he didn't know how they'd have managed without her.* "No. Nothing this evening. I'd be happy to help."

They rowed along and Kat found that conversation was as easy as breathing. It was obviously his interest, so she led him to talk about medicine. The more he talked, the more Kat decided that her first look had led her unerringly. He wasn't—unlike most of the elderly roués at the occasional functions the *Casa* Montescue still attended—at all inclined towards over-the-line flattery and flirtation. Instead he talked with passion about medicine. About what could be done.

"By the way—how do you know that this Maria is definitely alive?" she asked, as they neared the *Casa* Dandelo.

Marco pursed his lips. "Well, you wouldn't know him but we went to see Luciano Mariana—"

"But I do know him! He was my tutor! But—he went away, years ago. I was afraid he was dead."

Marco pauses. "Um. Well. They say he's just got back from Jerusalem. I know him well, too, from—from earlier. I owe him my life in part. Anyway, he's—ah—good at divining. And he says she's alive, a prisoner and surrounded by water. We've got half the town looking for her."

Kat pointed to the mess of heavily barred old buildings, isolated on their own islet across the Rio della Crea. "*Casa* Dandelo. That's where she'll be. Nobody knows what happens there."

Marco pulled a wry face. "You don't have any contacts?"

She shook her head emphatically. "I'd sooner sell black lotos," she said with distaste.

"Yes. It's a disgrace to the Republic," said Marco grimly.

She got the feeling that if he were the Doge for a day, the *Casa* Dandelo would be among the first festering sores to go. "Come on, let's go find Benito and this Caesare."

They actually found an irritated-looking Caesare and a still-eager Benito within two hundred yards.

"*Ciao*, Kat. I see Marco's got you working too," said Benito cheerfully. "Listen, old Beppi saw her at the corner of the Canale di Cannaregio. She was definitely heading for this part of town."

Caesare shook his head. "After which she could have been taken anywhere."

Marco smiled. "Except that Kat saw her too. Right near the *Casa* Dandelo. That's where we reckon she must be."

Caesare nodded. "I suppose it's possible. We can't get in there. Well, I'll get the Capuletti. One of them is *Capi di Contrada* for the Dandelo shipments. Relax. They won't be able to take her out. She's a citizen of the Republic. Now I think we ought to go back, maybe stop at Giaccomo's in case there is a message or a ransom demand."

"Let's just go on down to the *Casa* Dandelo. Please," pleaded Benito. "See if any of Marco's patients are about. Or you could go back—I'll go on. Case the joint."

So, little Benito did care about someone. He'd talked about a brother once. But obviously this Maria was important to him. It was odd to realize that she'd met this Caesare Aldanto too. He'd been at a rather raffish ridotto she'd found reason to leave early. His partner, with whom he'd been flirting outrageously, was definitely Case Vecchie. *A masked blond. Not his Maria—who, to judge by their one meeting—was canaler through and through.* "I'll give you a lift down. Quicker than walking. And safer, too."

Benito laughed. "Not many would want to mix it with Caesare, Kat."

There was admiration in that voice. *He needs to be more selective about his role models,* thought Kat. *But what would a wharf-and-canal brat know of such things? Well, enough to choose one good loyal friend at least, it seemed.*

Marco was all agreement about going back down to the Rio della Crea outside the *Casa* Dandelo. However, Caesare put his foot down firmly. "You leave the Dandelos alone. Come. We'll go back to the house. Get some food. You two will stay there. I'm going to see the Capuletti."

"I'll take you," offered Kat. At least that way she'd be able to find out where he lived. But she still worried about their loyalty to this Caesare. Obviously what he said went.

"Your loyalty is misplaced," said Maria's questioner. "How do you think we knew exactly where to find you? He wanted to be rid of you so he made a deal with us. He's the pig who betrayed you. What do you owe someone like that?"

Maria's head was spinning a little. She'd had a lot of strong unwatered wine on an empty stomach. The blows hadn't helped either. "Can't tell you what I don't know," she said sullenly. "Caesare kept his business private." *He was lying. They weren't going to let her go. No matter what she told them.*

Her questioner sat back. "It's going to be a long night. But you are going to tell me everything you do know." He leaned forward. His hands shot out and he grabbed her by the throat. The strength in those hands was terrifying. And she'd learned by now that resistance only made him worse. "Understa—"

Someone started screaming. A terrible, awful scream, even by slave-trader standards. At least her tormenter let go of her.

By the sounds of it, pandemonium was breaking loose. Yelling and panic around the screams.

The slaver who had brought her in here said: "Ask questions later, signor. She goes back to the cell! There's trouble out there." He pulled her to her feet and thrust her, stumbling in her hobbling leg-irons, out of the door. It was here that the wine came to her rescue. She tripped and fell against the wall, into a little alcove, intended by some long ago builder for a saint's shrine. Maybe the place was still blessed.

The stampede of panicked prisoners and warders thus missed her. But her warder and her questioner were swept off with the mob. The screaming had turned to a terrible laughter. Looking over her shoulder, she could see her interrogator glaring back at her. He was shouting something, but the words couldn't be made out over the general din. A moment later, the stampeding crowd had taken him out of sight.

Hurriedly, Maria got to her feet and went the other away, moving toward the horrible sound, half-laughter, half-screaming. The sound made her scalp crawl, but that was the only direction in which she might escape. Fortunately, before too long she found an unlocked door and pushed her way in.

She was apparently inside *Casa* Dandelo's warehouse area. She made sure the door was shut behind her and then plunged into the cluttered, cavernous interior. Maria wasn't moving very fast. Leg-irons didn't help. Neither did being a little drunk and completely lost in a strange building. She wanted down, but the only staircase she found went up. Not having any choice, she climbed the stairs, struggling with the leg-irons.

The staircase led to a heavy, iron-reinforced door—which obviously was normally bolted and locked from the outside. But now it was ajar. Maria stepped through and out of one world and into another. This place was soft with carpets and rich hangings. This was the living quarters of the slavers.

For a moment she hesitated. Then, hearing voices behind her, she stepped into the first room and held the door handle up. It was dark in here.

She heard the bolts being shot. She—and the other slaves—were being safely locked in. Only . . . she was already on this side of the door. It had been panic and drunken luck that had gotten her this far. But one thing she was determined on—she wasn't going back. She'd kill anyone who tried to take her. She felt about the darkened room for a weapon. She decided the shutter-bar would do as well as anything else. She shuffled—so as not to clank her leg-irons—over to the crack of light and lifted the bar. The shutters swung open. Moonlight touched the canal below.

To young Benito the climb down would have been a joke. To her . . . with leg-irons and a bit dizzy with wine, hunger and fear . . . it seemed impossible.

She heard voices, and her determination returned. She could just jump, taking the shutter-bar with her. Whatever else, at least she'd be outside and with a weapon.

Taking a deep breath, she struggled up onto the sill and jumped.

Moments later, she realized she should have thought about swimming in leg-irons first.

It took all her strength to haul herself out of the canal on the far side, and onto the walkway. Then spotting a nearby alley, she crawled toward it, too exhausted to walk. She could only hope that all their attention was distracted by the riot going on in the building. She could only bless whatever had caused the commotion in the first place.

Maria crawled on, into the alley and then down it, keeping to the shadows. If somebody found her now, in this part of town, she'd be dead meat. Or—worse—returned to the *Casa* Dandelo. At length the alley ended next to a canal.

She was so tired and turned around. This could be Canale di Cannaregio. Oh, God. She was such a long, *long* way from home.

If only she could spot a boatman she could trust. But the barge moving slowly along the water was not familiar.

Then a gondola came into view . . . a bit scruffy . . . It was that Kat! A moment of indecision, mostly due to sheer exhaustion, and Maria called out.

By the startled look on her face, Kat was not used to being greeted or summoned. But she peered; and as soon as she saw who it was she came in, pulled up and hauled the manacled Maria into her boat. Maria was so exhausted she simply tumbled onto the duck boards. Kat pushed off hastily. "Marco, Benito, and your Caesare have been looking for you. Let's get away from here, before someone else finds you."

Maria groaned. "Ow. Yes. The farther from the Dandelos the better."

Kat looked down at her. "I told them that's where you'd be. You're in a bad way. Do you know if the Dandelos are looking for you?"

Maria shook her head. "Dunno. Probably. But they may not have figured out that I got out of the building already."

Kat exhaled. "I think . . . I'd better take you to my home. We are close. Get you off the water and out of that slave-smock. But you must promise me you won't tell anyone where I live."

"Promise," said Maria tiredly. "Swear to God. Just keep me away from those Dandelo *bastardos.*"

Kat took a deep breath. "You'll be safe enough. I swear. Just pull that canvas over yourself." And she bent to the oar. "I think we'll try for speed rather than being unobtrusive right now. They could take me for you, and then we'd both be for it."

She concentrated on her sculling. Then, panting a little, glanced over her shoulder. "There are a few boats in the distance. They're too far off to see us in the moonlight but when we get to the *Casa,* you must move as fast as you can. Please."

Maria tensed her tired body. "Won't they just follow us?"

Kat snorted. "Not . . . huh . . . likely." They bumped against a tiny landing. Kat leaped forward and dropped a painter over a pole. She turned and helped Maria up and they staggered up the stairs. Kat rapped a hasty pattern on the water-door.

Maria heard the bolts slide. She and Kat half-fell and were half-dragged within by a white-haired old man with "family retainer" written all over his wrinkles.

The bolts sliding home were a wonderfully secure sound. But as Maria slumped against the wall and felt the suspicious angry gaze of the old man wash over her, she wondered whether this was security or worse trouble. The old man had a wheel-lock pistol in his belt and looked ready to use it. "And now, Signorina Katerina! What's this?" He pointed at Maria as if she were a long-dead alley-cat. "Milord won't be pleased. Trouble." His tone would have rimed boiling minestrone with ice.

Kat wasn't pleased either. "Oh, Giuseppe! Stop behaving like an old woman. As if I didn't learn half my troublemaking from you in the first place! See if you can find something to cut this chain with. And if you see Madelena, ask her for some food, some wine, and some hot water. We'll be in my room. Please."

The old man shook his head doubtfully, as Kat helped Maria to her feet. "Ai, signorina. You are like your father all over again. Still, the master won't be pleased."

"Then we won't tell him," responded Kat quietly, but firmly. "He has enough worries already. Now get Madelena for me, Giuseppe, do. Please."

He nodded and turned away. His rolling gait as he left—still muttering—said that this family retainer was an old seaman. Kat led Maria down a succession of corridors, up a staircase, down another corridor and into a bedroom. By the time they got there, the leg-irons felt like lead weights.

Chapter 56

Maria realized that the bedroom she'd swayed into was the finest she'd ever seen. Or must *once* have been very fine. But there were subtle signs of decay everywhere. The gilt-trimmed mirrors were old and fogged. The silken hangings on the carved bedstead were slightly tattered. The beautiful cassone had a little chip in it.

"Sit here on the bed." Kat thrust her gently onto it. Maria sat. Obedient, bewildered, but at least no longer terrified. Benito certainly picked his girlfriends! Kat went to the dressing table, took a branch of candles and lit them at the wall sconce. She rummaged in the closet and came out with a gown of some sort before returning to the bed. "My God! Your poor knees!"

"I crawled. From the *Casa* Dandelo to where you found me. It was better than staying there," said Maria quietly.

Kat took a deep breath. "Well, you're safe now. Lord. I wish Marco was here. He's so good at doctoring. Let's get you out of that smock anyway."

Marco? Maria's tired mind took a moment to work this one out as she managed to stand and hold her arms up to allow Kat take off the coarse slave-smock. *Marco . . . Marco?* By the worshipful tone, Benito had lost his *Case Vecchie* girlfriend! Well, it was keeping her alive. And Marco was a good soul. Too good for comfort, at times. But he would at least be nice to her, even if he was still daydreaming about his "girl in a boat."

The dress Kat dropped over her was soft twilled . . . silk.

From the doorway came a horrified squeak. "Katerina! You can't dress some slave-girl in your best taffeta!" The little bright-beady-eyed old woman with the tray of food and wine looked utterly horrified.

Kat clicked her tongue. "Madelena, just leave me to my business. And she's *not* a slave." To Maria: "It's not a new dress. But we've got to get you back to . . . to Caesare and they won't be looking for someone dressed in clothes like these. Put the tray down, Madelena, and get me some hot water. Do. Please."

Madelena set the tray down, pinching her lips with disapproval. Then she took a deep breath and, with the attitude of a stern taskmistress, shook a bony finger at Kat. "You can't do this, Milady Katerina! I'm going to go and talk to the master, no matter what old Giuseppe says."

Kat hugged the old lady. "Please, Madelena. He's asleep by now. And this is the honor of the *Casa* at stake here. Papa would have told me to do this."

The old lady sighed. "I wish he would come home." But she turned and went out.

Kat shook her head as she lifted the hem of the newly loaned dress above Maria's raw and bleeding knees. "Sorry. My old nurse, and my father's too. She won't accept that he's never going to get back, or that I'm not five years old any more. If I set this tray here on the bed, do you think you could eat a little? And maybe drink a glass of wine? You're as pale as a sheet. I'll try to clean up these knees. I'm not much of a doctor, I'm afraid. And it is not much in the way of food either."

Maria looked at the tray. Bread, the crumb finer and whiter than any she'd ever eaten. Slices of prosecco, salume, taleggio cheese, some early melon, something wrapped in pastry, olives, a tiny sweet cake bursting with raisins and almond slivers, dusted with sugar. Huh. Kat's ideas of "not much"! *Case Vecchie* ideas.

Maria sighed. This was Caesare's background. This was the world he belonged in. It was a world that left her feeling like a fish on a mountaintop. "Why are you doing this?" she asked quietly.

Kat shrugged. "Honor. I promised I'd help to find you."

Both the old man and old woman bustled in, arguing. "Hush!" snapped Kat. "You'll wake the house. And I do *not* want Alessandra here!"

That shut them both up. Madelena had brought a crock of warm water, cloths, soap. Giuseppe had in hand a small fine-toothed saw and a huge pair of pliers. He set to work on the chain. "You'll need a blacksmith to break the locks, or cut through the shackles. But if we cut the chain you can walk properly," he said. "Or run if you have to. You a local girl, missy?"

Maria nodded. "Born and bred." By his walk he was a seaman. All caulkers did a stint with the Republic's galleys and, as often as not, other vessels. "My family are caulkers."

She was right in her guess. That brought a look of frosty approval to the old man's face. "So what are you doing in slave clothes and slave chains?"

Maria shrugged. "The Dandelos don't care much where they get their slaves."

Giuseppe nodded, his face growing heavy with anger. "This time you were right, signorina. We must talk to milord about this. He can take it up with the *Signori di Notte* or even the Doge. This ought to be stopped!"

Kat sighed. "Do some more sawing, Giuseppe. I can just hear Grandpapa saying: 'Well, Your Grace, my granddaughter was just out for a little midnight row, on her own, when she found this runaway slave who happened to be a citizen of the Republic. Now, that's not allowed, Your Grace. Yes, my seventeen-year-old grand-daughter is often out alone at midnight. For starters, the Dandelos and their allies would laugh us out of the council. How could we prove Maria was a captive of theirs? For seconds, we don't need any attention. We have too much business of our own we don't need examined too closely."

"It still ought to be stopped," grumbled Giuseppe, going on sawing.

Madelena said nothing. She just snorted. But Maria noticed that she was more gentle about the cleaning. Maria sipped at the wine and tried to work out just how Kat was planning to get her home. The wine too was fine. A vintage red. Unless she was completely turned around this was one of the old great houses that looked onto the lagoon, towards the mainland. That was a long way from home, if the Dandelos were out looking for her. And they would be, for a certainty. They wouldn't want a citizen well known to canalers and Arsenalotti to escape their clutches and tell her story. That could cause them a lot of trouble.

Getting Maria home if the Dandelos were combing the canals could be tricky, thought Kat. But from the moment she dropped the dress over Maria's head, Kat realized that this was, potentially, a very beautiful woman. True, her jaw was very square and firm. But it simply enhanced the strength of those dark features. The dress suited Maria far better than it had her. Out of her baggy canaler's clothing, which was all that Kat had ever seen Maria wearing, it was obvious that the canaler girl's figure was . . . female. Decidedly so, in fact.

Giuseppe had cut his way through the chains for the second time and left to return the tools. Maria now had two heavy iron anklets. But, if need be, she could run. And she could walk normally. "Madelena, we need to dress her hair up. Do you think you could steal one of those Spanish combs from Alessandra's dressing room?"

The old woman smiled evilly. Madelena loathed Alessandra. The feeling was mutual. Alessandra detested a servant she could not dismiss. At least once a week, Alessandra accused Madelena of anything from theft to poisoning. Perhaps once—long ago—the war between them had sparked out of jealousy of a new wife for an old nurse. But especially after the death of Alessandra's baby, it had degenerated into simple warfare. "I'll bring some of her makeup too, Katerina." She got up and went out.

Kat surveyed Maria, weighing up the possibilities. "Shoes will be a problem. But the rest will be easy." She grinned at Maria. "Let me do that lacing on your bodice. No *Case Vecchie* is going to be at a party unlaced. Or at least they'd get someone to lace them again afterwards. If you keep your feet tucked under you and don't talk, we can do a remarkably fine pair of ladies going home for the night after a party."

Maria took an embarrassed look at her feet. "They're too big," she said wretchedly. She began to cry.

Kat hugged her. "It's all right. It's all right."

Maria gave a determined sniff. "I don't cry. I'm a canaler. I don't cry. I get even," she said gruffly. Then she sobbed. "But I've got very big feet. Canaler feet. And he's so fine."

No one could possibly have recognized Maria Garavelli the canaler and "Spook" the night-cargo runner, in the two finely arrayed and made-up Venetian *Case Vecchie* ladies who made their way through the maze of passages to the front of the house. Giuseppe bowed. "The gondola will be here in a few moments, signorinas."

Maria felt . . . odd. She could hardly recognize the elegant woman in the mirror in the hall. Her hair was dressed up onto an ornate comb, her face heavily made up, her cheeks and lips red, her eyes widened with belladona. In one hand was a fan of lacquered sticks and silk. In the other a little reticule . . . in which rested the comforting solid bulk of a pistol. It was a small and very finely made wheel-lock, the kind of weapon which only extremely wealthy people could afford. Kat had one identical to it in her own somewhat larger purse. Maria hoped that Kat knew how to use hers; she had only the sketchiest notion herself.

"If you see anyone," said Kat, "flirt with the fan—like this—over your mouth and nose. It makes it very hard to recognize you."

Maria tried it, looking at the stranger with the fan in the mirror.

"You're a natural," said Kat with a grin. Maria was quite relieved to see that expression. It was the only familiar thing about her rescuer: that wide-mouthed grin. Kat didn't smile that often. But it transformed her face when she did. Maria saw the smile change to a frown.

"And where are you going?" demanded the cause of the frown. The willowy-figured woman who had come into the hall looked every inch a wealthy *Case Vecchie*. Maria guessed her at mid to late twenties. Her complexion was as flawless as a master of the paintbrush and rouge pot could make it, except that she had a little mole on her cheek, just above the rosebud mouth. It seemed to accentuate the perfection. Her hair too was a lustrous black, dressed into a perfect frame for her face. She looked as sour as vinegar, despite her beauty.

"*Out*, Alessandra." Kat's face had closed down. There was now no expression on it at all. "Family business."

Alessandra looked as if she'd just swallowed a cup of gall. "What nonsense!" she snapped. "This trollop is no family of ours. And why is she wearing your best gown?"

"My mother's family. And Maria spilt wine on her gown. It's in that bag." Kat pointed to the bag at their feet. It actually contained a hooded cloak.

Alessandra sniffed. "Oh. I didn't know we had anything to do with them." Her expression said she didn't want to know either. She let them leave and get into the waiting gondola—which was *not* shabby—without a word.

Only when they were well away down the canal did Kat give

way to helpless laughter. "Oh, she is such a snob! If she'd noticed the comb in your hair, we'd have been for it."

"Or my feet," said Maria, tucking them under the folds of the dress. "Who is she?"

"My dear sister-in-law," answered Kat. "And my mother's family were just merchants. Not even *curti*. She pretends they don't exist."

Maria sat back tiredly against the squabs. "Who *are* you, Kat?"

Kat shook her head. "Best if I don't say. Not that I don't trust you, but, well, what you don't know can't slip out even by accident. And remember: you promised."

Maria nodded. It felt odd with all her hair piled up. "Even wild horses wouldn't drag it out of me. But I owe you."

Kat shrugged. "I promised I'd help."

They waited next to Alberto's barge. "He's trustworthy?" Kat asked for the third time.

"He's fine." Maria soothed. "He's Tonio's brother and a sort of cousin of mine." Here, out of her place, Kat was as uneasy as Maria has been in Kat's home. "They could be watching the building, as they know who Caesare is. I'm sorry I lost the water-door key when they took my clothes, because we could row up safely enough. But two ladies walking down our calle at this time of night would be in danger—even if the Dandelos aren't watching. So—best if Alberto fetches them. Can your gondolier be trusted to get you back?"

Kat nodded. "They do work for the family. And old Giuseppe knows who took us. Pietro would be insane to come back without me. Besides I have my little friend in here." She patted the reticule. "I can shoot. Quite well."

There was the sound of running footsteps. They both hastily reached for their reticules. Maria was still struggling with the fussy little catch when she heard Benito's voice. "Maria! Maria!"

He bounced over the barge and looked down at the two of them, and their patient gondolier. Benito was obviously a little startled to find himself staring into the muzzle of Kat's hand-cannon, but he didn't let it stop him. "Maria?" he asked incredulously.

"Who else, Benito?" said Maria tiredly. "Where's Caesare?"

Benito swung down onto the deck. He grabbed Maria and did a fierce little jig. Then he hugged her. Benito never even touched her, normally. Not that she had encouraged it, but . . .

"He's seeing the Capuletti. In case the Dandelos had you. Marco is off with Rafael over around Accademia looking for you. They were going to some Marina guy, the one who told us you were alive but a prisoner, to see if he could tell them anything else. They left me alone here to hold the fort. I reckon they both knew that way I wouldn't go back to the *Casa* Dandelo. That Kat said to Marco they must have you. And here you turn up looking like the queen of Sheba! Where have you been? We've been worried sick!"

For an answer Maria lifted her dress to reveal her bare feet and the iron anklets. " '*That Kat*' was right. *Casa* Dandelo. I escaped. And Kat saved my bacon. I owe her, so you treat her with respect, see."

"Oh she's not so bad," said Benito with a grin. "Got a snappy tongue when she's cross though. She brought us back here, but Rafael was waiting, so Marco went off with him, and she left. So who's the friend with the cannon?"

Maria realized that Kat was hiding behind her fan. "Just a friend, little sneaker. Leave her alone. Katerina—I'll get these clothes back to you. And . . . thank you. Thank you a million times. You ever need to find me, you leave a message with Giaccomo. I'll tell him. I owe you. Go carefully, huh?"

Kat nodded, without taking the fan from her face. And—with her other hand, still holding the pistol—pointed to the bag on the duckboards.

"Good idea," said Maria. "You take care now, see." She took out the hooded cloak and pulled it over her borrowed finery.

The gondolier had pulled the boat next to the walkway and the two of them alighted. The gondola pulled away.

Maria waved. Kat, having returned the pistol to the reticule, waved back.

"Mighty silent friend, that," said Benito curiously.

Maria yawned. "Be a good thing if *you* buttoned your lip sometimes, Benito. Let's get home. I can't wait to bathe myself." She could hardly believe that he hadn't recognized Kat. But then, looking in a mirror, she'd hardly recognized herself in these clothes.

"She reminded me of someone," said Benito. "But I can't think who. I don't know any posh women like that. But I hardly even recognized you in those clothes." He hesitated. Then, speaking much less brashly than usual, almost shyly: "You're real pretty when you dress up nice, Maria Garavelli. *Real* pretty."

Maria swatted his ear. Gently, though. She was quite sorry Caesare hadn't seen her in Kat's best gown. She was tempted to hang on to it for long enough to model it for him, but on reflection that wasn't a good idea. For Kat's safety, it would be best if she revealed as little about her part in this as possible.

Chapter 57

When Father Mascoli saw the three figures entering his little chapel in the Cannaregio, he sighed. "Come into the back," he said. "I don't want to discuss the matter out here."

He led them through the door behind the statue of Saint Raphaella and into his private quarters. Then, seeing them pause, he waved his hand. "*Further* in the back," he muttered. "We need someplace that I'm certain is safe."

He opened the water-door at the rear of his cell and led them into the small water-chapel beyond. There was just enough room for four men to stand there.

The three other priests examined the chapel with interest. Their interest was aroused further when the heads of two undines broke the water and gazed at them. The undines' eyes seemed wary— or perhaps simply watchful. Both of them were female.

"It's all right," said Mascoli. "These are . . . friends." There was just a slight hesitation before the last word.

The undines studied the three strange priests, their eyes spending most of their time examining the shortest one. "*I hope so*," hissed one of them. Pointing at the short priest: "*That one could be dangerous. Very powerful.*"

The priest in question pulled a wry face. The solid eyebrow line twisted into an S-shape. "First time I've ever been called that. Even before my leg got mangled."

"She's not speaking of your physical strength, Father Lopez," replied Mascoli, almost snapping. "As you well know."

"He likes to practice modesty," said one of the other priests,

510

his Savoyard accent very pronounced. "Good thing, too. He'd be insufferable otherwise. I'm Pierre, by the way. The other one is Diego."

Despite the tension of the moment, Mascoli chuckled. "Well said. All right, then. I assume you've come because you heard the news about *Dottore* Marina. Reappearing in Venice—out of nowhere, it seems—after all these years."

Lopez nodded. "We need to speak with him. But it would be dangerous—very dangerous—to do so openly. We thought . . ."

"I can place you in touch with him," agreed Mascoli. "But for the moment, at least, I think you should have no direct contact at all. I doubt if Marina would agree, in any event. He is very frightened by the state of things in Venice." Mascoli nodded toward the undines. "The *dottore* has a special relationship with them. They can serve as the messengers."

"*Difficult,*" hissed one of the undines. The tone of her voice was distinctly unhappy. "*The stupid* dottore *has gone too far from the water.*"

"*Not safe,*" hissed the other.

Diego eyed them curiously. "From the rumors which have been swirling through the city for months, the water is the *most* dangerous place to be. Because of the so-called 'canal monster.'"

The undines gaped shark-toothed grins. "*Dangerous for most. Dangerous for us, even. Not dangerous for the* dottore." One of the undines sank below the surface for a moment, then came up gushing water out of her mouth in an undine version of laughter. "*The* dottore *eat that one easily.*"

"That makes sense," murmured Eneko. "A Grimas would be vulnerable to steel-clad enemies. Another great sorcerer; the most powerful of demons. And not much else."

Mascoli cocked his head in a quizzical gesture. As close as he was to the undines, he had no doubt at all that the rumors of a "canal monster" were quite accurate. "And what makes you think this thing is *not* a most powerful demon."

"Doesn't make sense," replied Lopez. "The thing—whatever it is—is a servant of Chernobog. I'm quite sure of it, now. Chernobog would have lamed it in some manner. Broken it to his service."

Mascoli ran his hand across his bald pate, grimacing ruefully. "You move in a strange world, Father Lopez. That thing is quite too powerful for my taste, thank you."

Lopez shrugged. "I did not say it wasn't dangerous. I am simply pointing out that it is, in the end, nothing more than a tool in the hands of another. It is that *other* that I am truly concerned about."

He looked down at the undines, moving slowly in the waters of the chapel. "Very well. Would you take this message to *Dottore* Marina: Tell him to concentrate all his efforts on finding the Lion. We will see to the rest."

The undine's mouth gaped wide. "*And who is 'we'?*" demanded one.

"He's a special envoy from the Grand Metropolitan of Rome," explained Diego.

The undine's mouth gaped wide again. "That means precious little to her," murmured Mascoli. The bald priest squatted by the edge of the water. "Just tell him that they are friends of mine. And I trust them."

A moment later, in a little swirl, one of the undines was gone. The other remained, swimming slowly through the water-chapel.

Father Mascoli stood up. "I hope Sister Evangelina is not mistaken." He gave Eneko a hard look.

The Basque priest smiled and spread his hands. "I could give you assurances of my own, Father Mascoli. But would they really mean very much? In the end, you must make your own decision."

"I already have. Doesn't mean I have to like it. I'm just a simple priest, Father Lopez." Mascoli pointed a finger at the still-swirling surface of the water-chapel. "These waters here are quite deep enough for me. "I tend to my flock—in whatever form they appear. I'm Hypatian—"

He gave the Basque another hard look, as if saying: *as you are supposed to be.* "I don't make judgments. Let God judge. That's His business, not mine. God has given me the gift to make it so that evil can't freely enter here, so anything that enters freely deserves my help."

Pierre had opened his mouth when Mascoli proclaimed his unwillingness to make judgments as if to protest, but closed it after that last sentence, looking far more satisfied.

Mascoli led the way out of the water-chapel. Once in his cell, with the water-door closed, he paused at the entrance to the main chapel. "There are still other waters too deep for me," he added, facing Lopez. "The Marco boy you asked about."

"Valdosta."

Mascoli winced. "That secret is getting too frayed, I fear."

"What 'secret'?" demanded Pierre. "Dell'este sent word to *Casa Dorma*. From there, it is spreading like fire."

"Not quite that," demurred Diego. "But it *is* spreading. I fear Petro Dorma has spies in his household."

Mascoli looked even more unhappy than ever. "The boy is— has the potential, I should say—to be a powerful user of magic in his own right, Father Lopez. Especially healing magic. I will not be able to train him properly much longer. I am reaching the limits of my own talent and knowledge."

Eneko nodded. "Consider the bargain made, Father Mascoli. But . . ." He hesitated. The Basque priest seemed to be experiencing one of his few moment of uncertainty. "In truth, I am not well versed in the healing arts myself." After another pause, grudgingly: "Nor, I confess, is that a branch of magic in which my own talents are particularly, ah—"

Pierre snorted. Diego laughed. "Ask a Viking berserk to be a nursemaid, Mascoli—you'd do better."

Lopez glared at him. His companion responded with an insouciant smile. "It's the truth, Eneko. You know it as well as I do." To Mascoli: "I will be glad to assist you with the boy's training. And, if all goes well, in a few months others of our brotherhood should be arriving in Venice. At least two of them—Francis, in particular—are superb with healing magic."

"Thank you," said Mascoli softly. "I have become very fond of Marco." He studied Eneko for a moment. "Does this—ah, Viking berserk—magic of yours extend to protective spells? Or is it simply a specialty in smiting the ungodly?"

Lopez's glare at Diego was in full flower now. "See what you've done?" he demanded. "My reputation was bad enough already."

Diego simply smiled. After a moment, sighing, the Basque looked at Mascoli.

"What do you desire, Father?"

Mascoli groped for words. "I would like—something—don't know what—to protect the brothers somehow. A shield of some sort, I suppose. Marco is swimming in those same deep waters, whether he knows it or not. And Benito—" He rolled his eyes; he couldn't help it. "Benito dives into every bottomless pool he can find. And dives to the bottom of everything else as well."

Pierre grinned at this assessment of the younger brother, but
sobered as Eneko shook his head. "At this point, that would be
more dangerous than anything. I don't think the enemy—not
Chernobog, at least—has any sense yet of the potential danger to
him which rests in those two boys. A shield of the sort you're
suggesting would just draw his attention. Attention which, for the
moment, I would much prefer centered on *Dottore* Marina."

He glanced at the crucifix on the wall. "But I think something
else might be of use. The boys already have a guardian. Two of
them, in fact, if my suspicion is correct. I can place a finding spell
of sorts on them—not a geas, something much more delicate—
which would . . ." It was his turn to grope for words. "Enable the
guardians to find them very easily, and know where to bring them
in case of trouble. Think of it as lubricating an axle, if you will,
and perhaps giving the cart a push over the rough spots."

Diego winced at the crude analogy. Pierre, on the other hand,
beamed from ear to ear. "We'll make you a good Savoyard yet!"

They heard the sound of the church door opening. "Wait here,"
said Father Mascoli. "I'll let you know when you can leave without being observed."

But he was back within a short time. Behind him came a woman
whose face could not be seen because of the cowl over her head.
But that she was a woman there could be little doubt, even under
the heavy and utilitarian clothing.

"And now this," muttered Mascoli. "What *have* you gotten me
into to, Lopez?"

The woman swept back the cowl. Francesca's smiling face appeared.
Even without her usual elaborate coiffure and cosmetics, the
woman's beauty seemed quite out of place in Father Mascoli's austere living quarters.

"Nice to see you again, Eneko," she said. "You've heard the news
about *Dottore* Marina, I imagine?"

Lopez nodded. "I assume you have more tidbits to share," he
added, with a wry smile.

"Does a chicken have feathers?" snorted Francesca. She glanced
around the small room. "Is there anywhere a bit more commo-
dious? I have quite a few 'tidbits,' in fact."

Sighing, Mascoli opened the water-door and led the way back
into the water-chapel. "There's no place to sit, I'm afraid."

"No matter," responded Francesca cheerily. "We'll squat. I have very strong legs."

Once in the water-chapel, she spotted the undine immediately. "Oh, thank heaven! Another female."

The priests' faces grew stiff. "You have nothing to fear—" Pierre began to growl.

"Nonsense," snapped Francesca. "And why would I be afraid of a mortal sin in a Hypatian chapel, anyway? The peril lies elsewhere. Men don't know how to gossip properly."

The undine's mouth gaped wide. "*Truth!*" She swam to the side. "*Did you hear—*"

Chapter 58

It was dark, and it was dangerous, and Benito was so happy he could hardly stand himself. If it hadn't been too risky to chance *any* sound, he'd have been singing. Or humming, anyway.

He was upside-down, hanging by his knees from one of the dozens of timbers supporting *Casa* Dandelo's leaky, half-rotten roof—the kind of position he'd held so many times in the past that he was almost as comfortable upside-down as he was on his feet. Hidden by the darkness, three stories beneath him the canal-water lapped quietly against the foundations of *Casa* Dandelo, but there was not much else in the way of sound. There wasn't even so much as a breeze to make the timbers of the building sway and creak, which made it all the more imperative that *he* keep silent.

He was sawing most of the way through the bolts that held the metal grilles and bars protecting the slave-quarters' upper-story windows. *Most* of the way, not all; just enough so that someone who was determined on a breakout had only to give a good hard pull to break the grilles free—but from inside or outside, to everything but a close inspection, all was secure. To really hurt the slavers you had to hit them where it counted most—the pocket. That meant slave breakouts . . . for which Benito was now cheerfully preparing the way.

He grinned to himself, working the cable saw carefully, slowly, back and forth on the bolt currently under his fingers. Valentina had threatened his life if he lost that *very* expensive saw—but had been quite willing to lend Benito the tiny thief's tool when she heard *whose* place it was going to be used on. Little more than a bit of wire with two handles, it would cut through damn near any metal, and was making short work of *Casa* Dandelo's soft iron bolts.

It was as black as the inside of a cat tonight, no moon, nary a star showing through the clouds of a warm, overcast spring night. No matter. Benito hadn't ever needed to *see*, to know what he was about. Valentina and Claudia had taught him to work blind. It was *best* working blind in some ways: the darkest nights were a thief's best friends.

One: case the place till you know it like the inside of your mouth. Two: take it slow. Three: go by feel and know by feel.

Those were Claudia's rules for nightwork. She might have added the one Benito was abiding by tonight.

Four: have you a lookout.

And Lord and Saints—*what* a lookout!

Down there somewhere on the canal below him, hidden in the darkest shadows and straining eyes and ears against the thick blackness, was no less a personage than Maria Garavelli—and a more unlikely banditry pairing than himself and Maria was hard to imagine.

The greater wonder was that *Maria* had come to *him* to ask for his help.

Runners had lunch after the rest of Venice; not the least because runners were often sent to fetch lunches and drink for their employers. It made for a long morning and a rumbling stomach, but Benito had gotten used to it. Besides, it meant that the rest of the afternoon until knock-off time was that much shorter.

And you could pick up some nice stuff at half-price from vendors anxious to unload what was left, now that the noontime crowd was fed. So this afternoon Benito had been pleasing his palate with several slabs of castagnaccio that were only slightly old. He was pleasing his hide with warm spring sunshine, and his mind was at ease with the fact that his behind was firmly planted on the upper steps of the *Casa* Ventuccio. He had a good view of the canal from there, and no one hassled a kid in Ventuccio-livery there—so long as he kept his butt near enough to the edge of the steps that he didn't impede traffic.

He had been dangling his feet over the edge, and had both arms draped over the lower bar of the guard rail, watching the traffic pass in the half-light below him. He was rather pleased that he knew a good many of those passing by name—even if those good folk would hardly appreciate the "honor." He watched, feeling his back and shoulders ache in sympathy, as Gianni and Tomaso labored against the current, poling what looked to be a nice little cargo of barrels of some kind up the canal. He noted one of the younger Baldasini boys go by, riding in one of the family boats, and old man Mario in a hire-boat going in the opposite direction. And he saw a double handful of canalers he recognized besides Gianni, and rather wished he had his brother's incredible memory. There might be valuable information there if he only could remember who he saw going where. The one real pity about having his lunch break late, was that he and Marco couldn't sit together.

He hadn't had a decent talk with Marco since Maria's return from captivity. Marco had gotten back from looking for Luciano Marina even later than Caesare had returned from his visit to *Casa* Capuletti. Marco, at least, had been sober. Benito sighed. Marco was walking around with that moonstruck look on his face again. Doubtless yet another girl. Benito couldn't understand it. Girls were . . . interesting. But not this walk-into-walls-and-die-for-you stuff. And what did he mean by that "One person's trouble is another person's delight"? Benito sighed again. More trouble for Benito and the rest of them no doubt. But right now the sun was warm and the chestnut-flour castagnaccio was superb.

He was halfway through his lunch when he saw Maria tie up down below. So far as *he* knew she had no business with *Casa* Ventuccio today, so he wasn't much surprised when she strolled up the steps and planted herself beside him; feet dangling, like his, over the edge, the rest of her hugging the bottom railing.

"Bite?" he said, offering her a piece of castagnaccio to be sociable. It didn't pay to be less than polite to Maria at any time—but most especially Benito walked softly these days. What with her being short-fused and in a muddle over Caesare Aldanto, and them being short of cash, and Benito's brother more than half the cause of both—and now this Dandelo thing—

"No," she said shortly. "I ate."

He shrugged. She'd say her say when she was ready; he wasn't about to push her.

He kept watch on her out the corner of his eye all the same. After living these months with Caesare Aldanto, Benito knew Maria

Garavelli about as well as he knew anybody—and the storm warnings were definitely out. The sleeves of her dark blue dress were pushed up over her elbows, which only happened when she was nervy; her battered hat was pulled down low on her forehead, like she was trying to keep her eyes from being read. But Benito was close enough for a good view, and he could see that her square jaw was tensed, her dark eyes gone darker with brooding, her broad shoulders hunched, her fists clenching and unclenching—storm-warnings for sure.

Well, she and Caesare had "celebrated" her return from captivity in the *Casa* Dandelo two days ago with an almighty fight. Things definitely hadn't been right between the two of them lately. He should talk it through with Marco, but he'd barely seen Marco since the night Maria had gotten back.

"You've got the sneak thief's ways, Benito Valdosta," she said at last, softly, so softly her voice hardly carried to Benito.

Benito tensed up himself; in all of Venice only Alberto Ventuccio, Maria Garavelli, and Caesare Aldanto knew his real name, his and Marco's. Only *they* knew that Marco Felluci and Benito Oro were real brothers; were Marco and Benito of the *Case Vecchie*, the last of the *longi* family Valdosta. Only those three knew that the boys had fled from assassins who had killed their mother, and were still very probably under death sentence from Duke Visconti for the things their dead mother Lorendana might have told them and the names and faces they knew. Even the Ventuccio cousins didn't know.

For Maria Garavelli to be using his *real* name—this was *serious*.

"I ain't no sneak thief," he said shortly. "'Less Caesare wants a job done. It don't pay, 'cept to buy a piece of rope at nubbing cheat. Unless you're *real* good." He thought of Valentina, of Claudia, their skills and bravado, with raw envy. "I'm good; I ain't that good."

"What if I wanted you to turn sneak thief for a bit . . . for me?" came the unexpected question.

"*Huh?* For you?" he responded, turning to stare at her, his jaw slack with surprise.

She moved her head slowly to meet his astonished gaze. "*Casa* Dandelo," she said tersely.

He nodded, understanding her then. *Somebody*—Montagnards, likely—had kidnapped the redoubtable Maria Garavelli; had kidnapped her, and truly, *truly*, frightened her, something Benito had never thought possible. She said that nothing else had happened. Benito believed her, but most of the canalers didn't. They assumed Maria had been molested, maybe raped, and was lying about it out of shame.

That assumption was fueling the seething anger which was steadily building among the canalers and the Arsenalotti. Most of Venice's working poor had no love for the Dandelos at the best of times. Now that the Dandelos had crossed the line by messing with a well-known citizen of the Republic . . . a poor one, true, but a canaler, not a vagrant . . .

There was going to be an explosion soon, Benito thought. And a lot bigger one than the initial rash of attacks on Dandelo retainers who had been unlucky enough to be caught in the open when the news of Maria's escape—and the identity of her captors—had raced through the city. Four Dandelo hangers-on, one of them a distant relation of the family, had been stabbed or beaten to death in two separate incidents within hours. After that, all the Dandelos and their retainers had hastily retreated to their fortresslike building to wait out the storm.

The canalers and Arsenalotti were now waiting to see what measures, if any, the authorities would take against the Dandelos for their flagrant transgression of the unspoken "rules." So far, however, all the signs were that the Signori di Notte intended to remain carefully blind to what the Dandelos had been up to. In which case . . . all hell was going to break loose, soon enough.

Maria herself, it seemed, had already waited long enough. She intended to start her own vendetta—*now!*—and she'd come to Benito first. He felt a strange, great thrill at that fact.

"*Si!*" Benito replied. He owed them too. Maria gave him hell sometimes, but he was fond of her. Kind of like a sister, except sometimes she made him think unsisterly things. Ever since he'd seen her in those *Case Vecchie* clothes . . . he'd realized she was beautiful. Not that she was interested in anyone but Caesare, of course. "*Si*, Maria, you got me. You say, how and when."

The hunched shoulders relaxed a bit; she favored him with a ghost of a smile. "Knew you wasn't *all* bad," she said, grabbing the railing and pulling herself to her feet.

Benito wasn't all fool, either; *he* knew where his primary loyalty lay—with the man he'd privately chosen as his model and mentor, Caesare Aldanto. When Benito had arrived at Caesare's Castello apartment—which they all called "home" now—that afternoon, he'd first checked to make sure that Marco and Maria weren't home. Caesare was sitting reading. Benito felt no qualms about disturbing him with a terse report of Maria's attempt to recruit him.

The warm, comfortable sitting room seemed to turn cold as Aldanto's expression chilled. Aldanto's hands tightened a little on the sheaf of papers he was holding; his blue eyes went cloudy. Benito knew *him* now, too—knew by those slight signs that Aldanto was not happy with this little piece of news.

Benito clasped his hands in front of him and tried to look older than his fifteen years—older, and capable; capable enough to run with Maria. Maybe even to ride herd a little on Maria.

"Caesare—" he offered, then before Aldanto could speak to forbid him to help, "you *know* I'm not bad at roof-walking. You've seen me; you've set me jobs yourself. You know if I tell her 'no' she's just going to go it alone. Let me help, huh? Happens I can keep her out of real bad trouble. Happens if she's got me along, she maybe won't go *looking* for bad trouble so damn hard, figuring she's got to keep me out of it."

A good hit, that last; Maria was likely to feel at least a little bit responsible for Benito, if only because she was maybe two years older than him. That was the line Valentina had taken when he was along on one of her jobs, and she was one of the *least* responsible people Benito knew. Aldanto tilted his head to the side and looked thoughtful when Benito had finished, then put the papers down on the couch to one side of him, crossing his arms over his chest and tapping his lips with one long, aristocratic finger. "How about if I tell *you* to keep her out of trouble?" he asked finally.

Benito winced. *That* was nothing less than an impossibility, as Aldanto should very well know. "Ask me to fly. I've got a better chance."

Aldanto managed a quirk of the right corner of his mouth. "I'm afraid you're probably right. I should know better than to ask you to do something no one else can." He stared at Benito, then stared *though* him; thinking, and thinking hard. "All right; go ahead and give her a hand. See if you can't keep her from being totally suicidal."

Benito grinned and shrugged; so far as *he* could see, both he *and* Maria had won. He'd told Caesare—and he hadn't been forbidden to help or ordered to hinder. What little conscience he had was clear, and he was free to indulge in the kind of hell-raising he adored *with* Aldanto's tacit approval—

He prepared to turn and scoot down the hall to vanish into the downstairs bedroom he shared with Marco, when Aldanto stopped him with a lifted finger.

"But—" he said, with the tone that told Benito that disobedience would cost more than Benito would *ever* want to pay, "I expect you to keep me informed. *Completely* informed. Chapter and verse on *what* she's doing, and *when*, and *how*. And I want it *in advance*; and *well* in advance."

Benito stifled a sigh of disappointment.

"*Si*, milord," he agreed, hoping his reluctance didn't show too much. Because he knew what *that* meant. Maybe he wasn't going to have to try to stop Maria—but now he was honor-bound to *keep* her from trying to do the kind of things *he'd* like to pull. And what that meant, mostly, was keeping things quiet. Damn. "Quiet" wasn't half the fun.

Hey, this one didn't work out too bad, Benito thought, inching along the rough beam to the opposite corner of the grille and ignoring the splinter he got in a palm. Pain was for later. He attacked the next bolt.

Quiet—and nothing to connect me or Maria to the mess when all hell breaks loose. Caesare was happy enough about that. We're here earlier than planned but I told him every detail. And we've been doing well tonight; this is two more windows than I'd figured likely to cut when we planned this.

He had gotten this bolt nearly sawed through when a feral cat yowled from the invisible canal below him. She did a good cat-yowl. . . . It was somewhere to his right, which meant upstream.

Maria had spotted possible trouble.

Benito coiled up the cable saw and stowed it safely away in the buttoned pocket of his breeches, making *damn* sure the button was fastened and the saw *in* there. Then he inched, still hanging upside-down, back along the support beam until he met the cross-brace. He switched to it, using both hands and legs, taking it slowly and carefully to avoid making the wood creak, until he reached the end that met the roof, where the gutter was. The drainpipes and gutterwork on *Casa* Dandelo Isle were sound, even if most of the rest of the building wasn't; Dandelo got most of its potable water from rain.

Might ask Marco if there's something we could drop into the roof-tank, give them all the heaves and trots. Benito grinned again in the darkness—he had a fair notion Maria would like that idea real well. It was another quiet one—which would please Caesare. And it was an idea that would cost the Dandelo's money, real hard-cash money—cash for the doctors, for clean water when they figured out what the cause was, and for somebody to come clean and purge the system. That pleased Benito—and there was always a chance that the fear of plague or sickness in *Casa* Dandelo would flush some of the Montagnard agents out of their safe-house and maybe into the hands of the Schiopettieri. Hmm—another thought; if they had any human cargo in there, they might have to find another place for the captives. And that would give the slaves a chance to escape. That pleased Benito even more; he didn't have much in the way of moral scruples, but he was flat against slaving.

He continued to think about this new plan as he grabbed the edge of the gutter and hauled himself up onto the roof with its aid. The metal groaned a little, and he froze, but nothing further untoward happened. He continued easing himself up over the edge. He crawled from that point along the roof-edge, feeling his way and moving slowly to avoid any more noise, until he found the outside corner of the roof and the place where the gutter met the drainpipe. He stopped, taking stock with his ears, and nodded after a bit. The echoes from the water lapping against the building were right for where he thought he was; and he thought he could make out the sable pit of the Grand Canal, a blacker blot in the night-shadows ahead of him. He should be right on the point of *Casa* Dandelo where the building fronted Rio della Crea—and Maria should be right below him, holding her gondola steady against the pull of the current.

"*Woo ooo*," he called softly, and was rewarded with a yowl almost directly below. He eased himself over the edge of the roof, dangling blindly for a little until he got his legs around the pipe, then shinnied silently down the drainpipe. It went in through the wall to a tank within, but in a full stretch he could reach the narrow ledge that ran around the edge of the islet.

"*Woo ooo*," he chirped, struggling to hold his balance on the cold, slippery, slimy ledge, as he positioned himself with his back to the wall. Come high tide, this would be underwater, and it tended to collect unsavory stuff. He was having to hold to the drainpipe above him with both hands; the ledge was barely two inches wide.

Meeeow, came the answer, and the soft bump of a boat-nose against the ledge beside him, black blot against the reflective water. Benito squirmed about like a real cat, grabbed the gondola's nose with both hands and leapfrogged aboard her before Maria had a chance to say a word.

He felt his way down off the nose, worked his way past the barrels occupying the slats of the bottom, and sat down on the worn boards of foredeck, knowing *she* knew he'd gotten aboard safely by the gondola's movement. He heard and felt her heave with the oar, moving the gondola into the current of the Grand Canal. There was a tense moment as they passed the bulk of the residential side of *Casa* Dandelo, but it stayed quiet, with hardly a light showing anywhere in the building. Then they were past, down into Cannaregio, where Maria had legitimate—well, sort of—business. A barrel delivery from Giaccomo, and not all the barrels were empty. This wasn't the first night she'd had him along on the skip to help—nor would it be the last, hoped Benito. Maria's company grew on you, away from Caesare.

Make it look like business as usual, and that's what everybody is going to figure, was another of Valentina's maxims.

When they finished this delivery, they'd head home by way of Barducci's. Benito would pass Valentina her little tool under cover of buying her a drink, and that would be her signal to spread the word tonight along certain channels that *Casa* Dandelo was no longer as impregnable as the Dandelos thought.

Benito grinned yet again as he picked the splinter from his climb out of his palm with his teeth. *Figure as many as two of the slaves hit them—and they'll fall out. With a small pry bar, anyone could pry them loose. Lord and Saints—I damn sure wouldn't want to be the fellow responsible for those grilles!* he thought, smugly.

He heard Maria start to whistle through her teeth, and guessed she was thinking the same thing.

Well, that was a little more off the tot-board for what he and Marco owed to Maria and Caesare. A good night's work, profitable for everybody—except *Casa* Dandelo.

Chapter 59

"Message for you, Maria," said Jeppo laconically, as they unloaded the barrels at Giaccomo's. "That Spook came here for you. The boss don't like her here. Giaccomo's real nervous about that 'magic' crowd. She ain't a good contact to do business with."

"I owe her," said Maria shortly, pushing her hair back from a sweaty brow. "Ain't business. But I got stuff to give back to her. What's the message?"

"Said she'd be over at Zianetti's tonight."

"Uh huh." Maria sighed. "All the way over to Accademia tonight."

Jeppo grinned. Twitched a thumb at Benito. "You better teach the apprentice to row."

Zianetti's was never as noisy as Barducci's. There'd been trouble years ago about a tavern in the middle of the Accademia area disturbing students—who were of course the ones who made the disturbance, and not the ones who complained. So Zianetti's wasn't a music place. The food was good and relatively cheap. The drink slightly more expensive than elsewhere. This simple recipe kept those intent on serious drinking going elsewhere, while making sure there were always customers. The big common room had been split up into a succession of smaller rooms, so rowdy argument— about everything from politics to paints—was limited to the crew who could fit in the smaller salons. Benito found it too quiet for his taste.

He and Maria looked into several rooms before finding Kat in one of the smaller back ones.

With Marco.

Oh, great. *One man's trouble is another man's delight.* It made sense now. And by the way Marco looked at that snappy-mouthed smuggler-girl, this was *real* trouble. What on earth did Marco see in her, besides someone shrewish enough to give Maria words? He had to grant—now that he could see her coppery curly hair—that she was prettier than he remembered. And sort of aglow. Her cheeks were flushed and her eyes sparkling.

Wonder if she's stuck on Marco too? he thought. *That'd be a change! Normally the girls who want Marco don't even get noticed by him, and he's all eyes for the ones who don't know he's alive.*

"Hey, *ciao*, Kat," said Maria cheerfully, leaning over their table. "What brings you to a dump like this? Got no music. And the wine is expensive."

Benito flopped down next to them. Maria was pleased to see Kat. That was obvious. Great. Now he had a brother *and* Maria to get away from trouble. Caesare didn't know how right he'd been in telling Benito to be her minder.

Kat dimpled. "The company is good though. Listen—a word of warning. There's going to be a Schiopettieri sweep through the town tonight."

Benito shivered. If they hadn't gone early they'd have been caught up in it.

Maria sat down abruptly, scowling. "*Bastardos!* They're just trying to intimidate anyone from hitting the Dandelos." She stared at Kat, the scowl turning into a crease of puzzlement. "How do you know this stuff, Kat?"

Kat's face took on a guarded look. "Business. Let's just leave it out of this."

Benito got to his feet. "I'd better go over to Claudia and Valentina. I've got something to give back—uh, to deliver to them."

Maria nodded. "*Si.* I'll take you. Quicker. Look Kat, I've got a bundle I need to get to you."

"I'll be here on Thursday." She glanced shyly across at Marco. He nodded.

Like that was it? thought Benito grimly. *Have to break this up.* "You'd better come with us, Marco. Hear Claudia's got some . . . doctor who wants to talk to you."

Marco stood up, reluctantly. "I suppose so." He smiled at Kat. "Thursday then."

She drained her wine, and stood up. "I might as well go too. Time I got home."

They walked out. As they got to the door there was something of a press of older men. Benito realized he recognized one of them. It was the short, red-haired man with the single line of dark eyebrow . . . who had seen them that first early morning outside the Imperial embassy—and then again when they'd recovered Kat's parcel. He was the Spaniard who had been staying with Ricardo Brunelli.

The redhead looked across the crowd . . . his eagle eyes taking them all in. The eyes narrowed and he began to push towards them.

"I've got to get out of here," said Kat, genuine fear in her voice.

But there was a real crowd at the door. A masque must have finished across at La Fenice, and this was the drink-after-the-show bunch. "Follow me." Benito dropped to his knees and began squirming between legs. He collected a few slaps on the rump, and by the squawks behind him, so did a few of the others. But they were out in a minute, all of them.

"It'll take more than a crowd to stop that man," said Marco. Sure enough the redhead was outside the inn, peering into the night. And, as luck would have it, he'd come out closer to the canal.

Benito didn't know this area as well as he did some the richer areas he'd cased along the Grand Canal. But knew it well enough. "We can just nip up that alley. If the tide is out enough we can walk along the ledge around to where the gondolas are moored."

The alley a few yards from the corner of Zianetti's stank just like what it was often used for. They moved down the dark curve of it quietly. And then, Maria—who happened to be in the lead—stopped them. Outlined by lights on the far side of the canal, at the mouth of the alley, were two people . . . kissing passionately.

"*Merda*," whispered Maria. "*Him!*"

Benito recognized the man too. It was that Milanese trade mission fellow he'd taken the message to at the German Hotel. The one he'd seen Caesare in the alley with afterward. The fellow had a very recognizable profile, even in bad light.

"There are some stairs back there," whispered Kat.

Benito thought he was good at managing without light, but she was obviously as good as a real cat. They went back a few yards and up the little walled staircase. There they crouched and waited. Sure enough, someone came past beneath them.

The person stopped a few yards further on. And then turned and walked far more quietly back.

"That's the *figlio di una puttana* who questioned me in the *Casa Dandelo*," hissed Maria.

"Who? Senor Lopez?" whispered Kat. "The man who saw us at Zianetti's and chased us? You mean it was *you* he was after?"

"No." whispered Maria. "I'm talking about the man kissing the woman. I've never seen that Lopez fellow in my life before. Who is he, anyway?"

Benito heard Kat take a deep breath, and whisper nervously. "He pretends he's just a visitor to Venice. But I think he's a witch-finder from the Grand Metropolitan in Rome, hunting Strega."

"I thought the Petrines believed in tolerance of other religions?" whispered Marco.

Kat snorted quietly. "Did he look tolerant?"

Benito had to agree. He didn't. Determined; powerful, yes. Tolerant, no.

"You don't know the other man? The one at the end of the alley? Or the woman?" Whispered Maria, before they got bogged down in theology.

"No," said Kat.

Benito actually bit his tongue to stop himself from saying "Francesco Aleri." He must talk to Caesare. He didn't have a clue who the woman was.

Kat bit her tongue. She had no idea who the man was. But the silhouette of Lucrezia Brunelli's hairdo was unmistakable.

And from the foot of the stairs someone rasped. "All right, Lorendana's kids. Aleri and the other guy have gone. You can go home."

Kat hadn't realized she'd been holding Marco's hand. She felt him relax. Whoever this was, he wasn't bad. "Thanks, Harrow," said Marco.

The relieving party said nothing, just walked away up the alley. So they all got up and left too. Two minutes later she was out on the Grand Canal. Why was Lopez after her? The thought was scary. She'd better prompt Giuseppe to not have her at home to any visiting Spaniards. And she'd take the long way home to avoid the sweep.

❀　　　❀　　　❀

Maria worked her oar in silence for a while. Then she said "Marco, what did your Spook say?"

"Kat? She's not 'mine.'" Marco sounded almost wistful about it. "She's a wonderful girl, isn't she? And you heard what she said . . ."

Maria clicked her tongue in irritation. "Tch. Lord and Saints, Marco. Not Kat. That burned-face troll that follows you around! Ugliest guardian angel in the universe."

"Oh. Harrow." Marco shrugged. "He's just somebody who—knew our mother."

"And the other name?" asked Maria, intently. "Aleri?"

"Well," said Marco thoughtfully. "There was a high-up Montagnard in mother's time by that name. Francesco Aleri."

Benito wished like hell Marco's memory was less good. He really had to talk to Caesare about this before Maria went in like a bull in a china shop. Aleri would have to die. But Maria must be kept well clear. Best to change the subject before Marco remembered something else inconvenient. "So now you're crazy about Kat, Marco. What happened to the dream girl in the boat?"

Marco laughed happily. "Kat *is* the dream girl in the boat, Benito."

There was a long moment of silence from both Maria and Benito. Benito wound his jaw back up. Bossy-boots Kat, with too big a mouth, and a tongue that could scour brass?

"*What!?*" he croaked—in unison with Maria.

Late that night, there came a knock on Eneko's door. When the priest opened it onto the dimly lit Ghetto alley, a burly man with a badly scarred and burned face seized the Basque by the lapel of his cassock and forced his way inside. Then kicked the door shut behind him.

Eneko made no attempt to resist. The man's strength was enormous.

"Why are you following the boys?" the man rasped.

"I'm not," replied Eneko calmly.

"You've been watching them," snarled the scar-faced man. "I've seen you—you and the other two. And tonight, at Zianetti's—"

Eneko laughed softly. "I wasn't trying to talk to *them*. I wanted to talk to the girl they were with. The one they call 'Kat.'"

The man released the cassock and stepped back a pace. "Why?" he demanded.

"None of your concern," said Eneko, shaking his head. "But I will tell you that I mean her no harm. I simply wanted to pass a message on to another through her. Unfortunately, she left too quickly."

The man grunted. "The whore."

Eneko cocked his head. "That's not a term I use. But . . . if we're speaking of the same woman, I wonder how *you* know who she is."

The man took another pace back. "I'm charged with protecting the boys. I watch everything—everyone—they come into contact with."

"Charged by whom?" asked Eneko mildly.

The man shook his head. "None of your concern." He turned on his heel and left, not bothering to close the door.

Eneko followed, standing in the entrance. "Stop," he said softly. The man, now halfway down the alley, paused and looked over his shoulder.

"Should you ever have need," said Eneko, "I will help you with your task. Those boys are vitally important."

The man's eyes seemed to widen a bit. "Smart, for a priest." Then he was gone, moving more quickly and silently than Eneko would have imagined such a scarred lump of a man could possibly do.

When he turned back into his room and closed the door, he found Pierre and Diego already there. The door to the adjoining cells was open. Pierre held a cudgel in his hand.

Seeing the cudgel, Eneko clucked. "We are *not* a militant order, Pierre."

"Define your terms," came the instant retort. "And remember that I'm a Savoyard peasant, not a theologian."

Chapter 60

Swords clashed in a high-speed flurrying dance of steel. Not for the first time, Manfred wondered how Erik could be so damned quick. The edges were blunt, there were buttons on the points, and they wore quilted jackets. So why did Erik always leave him feeling he had been half skinned and half beaten? He put in another determined rush. If he was going to feel like that, so was Erik.

"Hold." A voice commanded. They put up the practice swords. "You must go to Abbot Sachs's chambers." Von Stublau looked sour enough to curdle milk. "He has some Venetian lord to see you." He looked disdainfully at the training rapiers. "Pah. Too light for a knightly weapon."

"But very fashionable," said Manfred with a grin, knowing this would irritate the surly Altmark knight.

"Enough, Manfred," said Erik before the slow-thinking knight had time to respond to Manfred's lure. "We train with broadswords on the pells, *Ritter*. But these give us more of a chance to learn how to respond to a live opponent. Come Manfred, the abbot and this Venetian lord won't thank us for keeping him waiting. Help me out of this jacket. We need to get some kind of mask also, if we're to do this 'fencing' properly."

Manfred pulled the quilted jacket off his mentor, and turned so that Erik could do the same for him. "We're neglecting the legs, too. We need a trainer, Erik. A master of this Italian bravura style. I'll ask Francesca."

Erik turned hastily, to see if the supposedly celibate knight-squire had an audience. But fortunately Von Stublau had left. "It's not a bad idea, Manfred. I don't care what Von Stublau says—for marine warfare, anyway, armor is history."

"I like armor myself," grumbled Manfred, as they made their way up to the abbot's rooms. "But I'll admit having a horse to carry it helps."

The Venetian waiting for them with the abbot was the balding one of that group of *Signori di Notte* that they'd met after they'd saved Lord Calenti from being magically murdered.

Abbot Sachs was doing his best to be pleasant. It sat ill with the cleric. "Ah, *Ritters*. Signor Petro Dorma has requested specifically to speak to you two."

"You were quite correct in your surmise," said Dorma. "Each of these vile murders—except possibly one, where the fire destroyed the entire building it was in and therefore we can't be certain—has been found to have recently involved a missing item of clothing."

"Mammet witchcraft!" barked Sachs.

Petro Dorma cleared his throat. "Well, the expert on magic I have spoken to says there are several other possibilities. But I wanted to thank you gentlemen for your efforts on behalf of my fellow *Signori* . . . and also to tell you the sad news about Father Belgio and Lord Calenti. Despite our hopes, Lord Calenti died last night. And in a separate type of murder, someone killed Father Belgio as well."

"Father Belgio was not killed by magic?" asked Erik, intent.

Petro Dorma shook his head. "No. Just straight assassination. A misericord pushed in behind the ear while he slept. A thoroughly professional killing."

"Why?" Manfred demanded. "He didn't seem the sort of man to attract enemies."

Sachs snorted. "He was a man of God. That's enough for these Godless Strega."

Petro Dorma's expression was pained, for an instant. "We have had Strega murders from time to time, Abbot. Poison, not steel, is their way. We're following several lines of inquiry. That is only one of them."

Dorma paused for a moment, studying Erik and Manfred. "I came for another reason, as well. There was another magical murder last night. In the slave quarters of *Casa* Dandelo, of all places! According to my investigator who examined the scene, once again the victim had lost—or claimed to other prisoners to have lost—all of his clothing." Petro Dorma frowned. "Whoever murders these people by whatever demonic means, and for whatever reason, there is certainly no respect for rank. From Lord Calenti, to a slave."

Again, Dorma paused. Then: "But the reason I asked Abbot Sachs to speak to the two of you is tangential to the murder. Rumors are flying all over Venice that the Dandelos abducted a citizen into slavery, just before the killing. A canaler by the name of Maria Garavelli. She apparently took advantage of the confusion caused by the magical murder to make her escape."

Erik's jaws tightened. In the months since he had arrived in Venice, he had developed a detestation for the type of chattel slavery tolerated in the Republic—throughout most of the Mediterranean, in fact. Slavery had been legally abolished in the Holy Roman Empire for more than a century. And while it was still officially practiced in his own League of Armagh, Celtic and Norse thralldom had little of the sheer brutality and degradation of the Mediterranean variety of servitude.

"I'll bet that's causing a stir," snorted Manfred.

Dorma pulled a wry face. "To call it a 'stir' is to understate the matter considerably. Bad enough that the Dandelos tried to enslave a legal citizen. To make matters worse, the girl is a well-known canaler from a large family of caulkers at the Arsenal."

Manfred whistled softly. "All hell's going to break loose, then. They abducted a daughter of the *Arsenalotti*? Are they insane?"

"I have no idea what motivated the fools. They are trying to deny everything. But the facts seem well enough established." Dorma scowled. "And, at this point, I no longer care what their reasons might have been. If the authorities do not act decisively—" He nodded at Manfred. "As you say, 'all hell will break loose.' "

By now, Erik understood Dorma's purpose. "And you want us— Manfred and me—to be part of the, ah, what shall I call it?"

" 'Punitive expedition' will do quite nicely," said Dorma firmly. "Yes, exactly. There are enough factional tensions in the city. If some Knights of the Holy Trinity are involved in the affair, no one will be able to claim the raid was done for partisan purposes." He glanced at Sachs. "The Dandelos are known to have Montagnard leanings."

Erik was a bit puzzled by the abbot's apparent willingness to go along with Dorma's plan. But Sachs cleared up the mystery immediately.

When the abbot spoke, he almost seemed to be choking on the words. "Naturally, Lord Dorma. Given the recent unpleasantness . . . misapprehensions of the Knights' motives . . ."

Erik almost laughed. *You mean the mess you've stirred up with your idiot witch-hunts.*

"Both the servants and Knights of the Trinity are only too pleased to help serve God and your Venice," finished the abbot, lamely. "Eh, *Ritters?*"

Erik nodded. "It would be our pleasure."

Manfred bowed deeply. Which was a good thing, thought Erik. It helped to hide his grin.

Dorma bowed in return. "Thank you. If you would be ready by Lauds, tomorrow morning, I will have some of my Schiopettieri come to meet you here. I'll take my leave now." He sighed. "Affairs of state, business, and at the moment, family. The last are the worst, believe me!"

Sachs motioned to the two knights to stay, and showed his guest out. When he returned, his face was sour.

"A silly business, asking knights to serve as common policemen. But . . ." He shrugged irritably. "You are to make yourselves available for Lord Dorma. Whatever he wants. You are dismissed."

Erik was not surprised to find Petro Dorma waiting for them around the corner. He had been certain that Dorma had said as little as possible in the presence of Sachs.

"You'd like more than just the two of us, I imagine."

The Venetian lord nodded. "Yes, please. At least half a dozen, as heavily armed as possible." He smiled grimly. "I want to over-awe the Dandelos from the very beginning. And for that purpose, Knights of the Holy Trinity will serve far better than Schiopettieri."

He hesitated. "Of course, I do not expect you to do anything which would jeopardize your good standing with the abbot."

Manfred snorted. Erik just smiled. "We were told 'whatever Lord Dorma wants.' That seems clear enough." He and Manfred exchanged glances.

"Von Gherens, for sure," said Manfred. "Let him pick the others. Except I'd like Gerhard Bach along."

Erik's smile widened. "Bach, eh? Yes, I agree."

Dorma looked back and forth from one to the other, his eyes expressing a slight question.

"Gerhard Bach's our gunnery expert," explained Manfred cheerfully. "He's got a new little bombard he's been dying to test under field conditions."

Dorma seemed to choke a little. Then, after a moment, grinned himself. "A bombard, you say . . . Well, why not? The main door to *Casa* Dandelo may not open quickly enough."

"I can *guarantee* it won't open quickly enough," growled Erik. "No matter how fast they try."

"I must talk to Francesca," said Erik, as they walked down the passage after parting company with Dorma. "We've got some time. And—" He glanced at Manfred. "At this time of day she won't be, ah, occupied."

Manfred looked at him with some amusement. "So long as it's only talk. But why?"

Erik shrugged. "Because she understands all this intrigue and I do not. And it is my task to keep you safe in it."

"The way I see it," said Manfred, going into the breech, "these 'Strega' are not in the clear at all when it comes to Father Belgio's murder. They can hire their killing done as well as anyone else."

Francesca smiled at him the way a teacher smiles at a bright pupil . . . who has managed half the answer. She ruffled his hair and neatly evaded his arm, going to sit instead on the arm of Erik's chair. "True. But as you rightly point out, so could anyone else— if it was paid for. But," she held up an elegantly manicured hand, "it would have to be a *rich* anyone. The Church does not take kindly to its clerics being assassinated. And beside the chance of excommunication, their investigators are ferocious. This was professionally done, and that doesn't come cheap. And there are very few who do it well."

She paused, thinking. "If it was paid for . . . well, the first name that springs to mind is your blond friend Caesare Aldanto. Or, as a second choice, Giuliano Dell'Arta. Although Giuliano probably makes more as swordmaster than he does killing people. Both of them have powerful protectors, and are pretty much immune to Petro Dorma. If it was done to further the aims of the factions,

Bruno Di Netto is Rome's man. The Metropolitan's chief executioner in Venice. Francisco Aleri is in charge of Milan's—and he has the whole Montagnard faction at his command. They ship men in and out. The Republic's Council of Ten . . . well, they keep their secrets. So do the imperials, although I suspect Count DeMarien or Von Stemitz." She smiled. "Enough, Erik?"

"There are how many factions?" said Erik, weakly.

She smiled. "In Venice? Where there are three people together, at least five factions are gathered! The Venetian Republic is worse than elsewhere because Venice sits a jewel between so many interests. It is the key to the Mediterranean. And the key to the East. Emeric, the King of Hungary, Milan, Rome, the Holy Roman Emperor . . . all want Venice—or, at least, the riches which pour through the city. The Ilkhan Mongols have their own interests, also, as do the Greeks. Even the Grand Duke of Lithuania . . . just to stir up trouble, or to flank the Holy Roman Empire. And that is without the interests of the Church and its various factions, and the Strega, and the Jews. I think the latter just want a quiet life, but both factions have money for whoever will offer to leave them alone." She laughed throatily. "It's a quiet little town. I love it, even more than I did my native Orleans."

Erik sighed. "I want to go back to Iceland. At least you only had to worry about someone trying to kill you. This is all too complicated for me."

Manfred smiled. "Why don't we get some lessons from this swordmaster's *salle*? I don't think us going to visit this Caesare Aldanto fellow is a good idea."

Erik drew a deep breath. "*I* still think a visit is called for."

Francesca laughed. "What ill came of it, Erik? I thought it was the Italians who believed in vendetta?"

Manfred laughed. "Compared to Icelandic clan feudists? Not even in the same league, Francesca! And Erik's got humiliation to avenge as well as a simple attempt on his life. Aldanto's the man responsible for getting him under your sweet thighs, don't forget."

Francesca chucked the unfortunate Erik under the chin. "Poor man. It must have been *so* hard for you."

Erik got hastily to his feet, amid Manfred's guffaws. "I think it's time we talked to Von Gherens."

"Coward," grinned Manfred. "*You* talk to him. I'm going to stay here and take my punishment like a man."

❀   ❀   ❀

Von Gherens was willing. So were the four young *Ritters* he spoke to.

Gerhard Bach was downright avid.

Fortunately, the abbot was sequestered in private discussion with Sister Ursula when the Schiopettieri barge arrived at the embassy in mid-afternoon. Erik thought Sachs would probably have had a fit if he'd seen eight armored knights wrestling a bombard into the Venetian vessel. Even a small one.

The knight-proctor Von Stublau *did* pitch a fit. But with the official authority of Sachs on his side—as attested to vehemently by Manfred and Erik—Von Gherens simply ignored Von Stublau's protestations.

"Take it up with the abbot!" snapped Von Gherens. "Better make it quick, too. We're leaving."

Fuming angrily, the Prussian knight-proctor stormed back into the embassy. Von Gherens, grinning, turned to his knights and said: "Let's go. Just in case Von Stublau develops the nerve to interrupt Sachs and Sister Ursula."

"He'd better knock first," muttered Manfred, not *quite* under his breath. Two of the younger knights chuckled softly. Erik frowned.

"That's in very bad taste," he growled.

"Not as bad as Sister Ursula, I'll bet," responded Manfred cheerfully. The two young knights burst into outright laughter.

Erik sighed. Once again, reproving Manfred had proven to be as useful as pouring naphtha on a bonfire. . . .

The barge carrying Erik and Manfred met up with the rest of Dorma's flotilla not far from *Casa* Dandelo. It was quite an impressive show of force, even before the Knights and their bombard arrived: three barges packed with Schiopettieri, and another three coming behind. The last three, to Erik's surprise, were empty except for skeleton crews. He wondered as to their purpose.

As soon as Dorma's barge came alongside, Petro hopped into Erik's vessel. The easy and nimble way he moved reminded Erik how young Lord Dorma was—not yet forty, he'd heard—for a high Venetian notable. The man's bald head, pudgy build, and judicious manner normally made him seem older.

"I'll ride the rest of the way with you," Petro announced, smiling.

"I believe I should, since I'm officially in charge of this—ah, I believe we're still calling it an 'investigation.' And you'll be spearheading the—ah, I believe I'll call it an 'entry.'"

He eyed the little bombard. "Can you fire that from the bow of the boat?"

Gerhard Bach looked indignant. "Are you cra—" He broke off, coughing, as if he'd just remembered he was addressing a high-ranking Venetian official rather than a young knight-squire. "Ah, no. Sir. That'd be a *very* bad idea. The recoil would probably hull the barge. It's not designed to be a gun platform."

Dorma frowned. "Then how—"

"I'll figure something out," replied Bach cheerily.

Dorma shrugged. "I leave the matter in your capable hands, then." He turned to Erik. "Any questions?"

Erik looked at him uncertainly. *Yes. How in the hell did you ever get the Council of Ten to agree to this—much less the Doge?* But he decided that question would be impolitic. If rumor was to be believed, Dorma himself was a member of that secretive body. As for the Doge . . .

Petro coughed. "I might mention that the Doge has given me his blessing. Well. In a manner of speaking."

Again, he eyed the bombard. "I told him we needed to test a new mechanism. He was quite engrossed in his clocks at the time. I took his wave as a gesture of assent. It seemed a reasonable interpretation."

Erik nodded solemnly. It seemed a reasonable response. And less likely to get him in trouble than any words he could think of.

Manfred, as usual, suffered no such inhibitions. "Foscari'll probably have a heart attack when he finds out. On the other hand—" the big young knight swept his arm in a half-circle "—I think you're about to become the most popular official in Venice."

Erik and Dorma turned their heads, following Manfred's gesture. Erik was startled to see the size of the crowd that had already formed alongside the canal, with more and more people pouring in from little side streets. And as the flotilla passed by a small side canal, he could see that it was full of gondolas. All of them were packed with onlookers, for all the world as if they were going on a family promenade. As soon as Lord Dorma's flotilla passed the mouth of the canal, the much larger flotilla of gondolas came following behind.

At first, Erik was surprised that the crowd was so quiet. Almost completely silent, in fact. But before long he understood. Venice's canalers and working classes were still not sure about the nature and purpose of Dorma's flotilla. True, it *looked* as if . . .

But the Venetian authorities had a long history of looking the other way, when it came to the transgressions of the Dandelos. So who could be sure that this would not just turn out to be another empty gesture?

"They're wondering about us," murmured Manfred. "Look at 'em whispering back and forth, all through that mob. On the one hand, the Knights are supposed to be nothing but tools for the Emperor—which means the Montagnards, to them. On the other hand . . ."

He examined his fellow Knights, standing in the barge, and grinned. "We *are* a rather fearsome lot to be hauling around just for show."

Erik wasn't sure whether to smile or frown. Once again, Francesca's influence on Manfred was showing. Not so many weeks ago, Manfred wouldn't have been able to analyze a foreign crowd so surely and readily. For that matter—not so many weeks ago—the thought of doing so would never even have crossed his mind. *Wine, women, and song*, it had been—and very lightly on the "song." Since he'd met that one particular woman, however . . .

He doesn't even drink *that much anymore. Will wonders never cease?*

But he had no time to pursue the thought further. The grim and imposing edifice of *Casa* Dandelo loomed ahead of them. Even at a distance, it was obvious the Dandelos had forted up. There was not a person to be seen anywhere in the immediate vicinity.

Except one.

"What in the name of God is that boy doing?" demanded Von Gherens. "Crazy kid!"

Erik stared at the small figure perched on one of the timbers holding up the roof of *Casa* Dandelo. "Perched" like a bat, not a bird. The kid was hanging upside down.

"I guess he wanted the best possible view," said Manfred. He loosened his great sword in its scabbard. "So let's not disappoint him."

Chapter 61

Benito's eyes were riveted on the bombard nestled in the hold of the barge, with three of the knights squatting next to it. From Benito's vantage point, high atop *Casa* Dandelo, he could see the bombard clearly. But he knew that from the angle of Dandelo observers below, the bombard would still be invisible.

That, as much as anything, finally convinced Benito that Dorma's expedition was *serious.* Like most canalers and lower-class Venetians, his first reaction on hearing the news that Lord Dorma was going to "inspect" *Casa* Dandelo was jeering. *Oh, sure. Dorma'll trot through the place and come out announcing that all is well.*

But the bombard . . . hidden from sight . . .

And—the fact that there were Knights in the expedition. If Benito had lost his childhood enthusiasm for his mother's Montagnard cause, he still retained a certain romantic image of the Knights. The champions of Christendom; defenders of the right; bold and brave and true. If the image was tarnished—and had been tarnished even more by the general behavior of the Knights in Venice over the past year—it was still there, lurking in the corners of his mind.

Besides, not *all* of the Knights were simply lackeys for the Servants. Was there a canaler in Venice who hadn't heard the story, by now, of how some of the Knights—one in particular—had defied their abbot when he ordered a girl and some children hauled out of a church and put to the inquisition? Benito had heard that story several times over the past months, in several different places and from several different pairs of lips.

The stories varied in detail, of course, as city rumors will. Except on one point: all of them agreed that the knight who had first defied the abbot was a Nordic wolfman of some sort. A young blond maniac, who had been ready to carve his fellow knights into bloody pieces over an issue of law and principle.

The barge was closer now. If they hadn't been wearing helmets, Benito could have seen individual faces. Eagerly, he scrutinized what little he could see of the Knights past their helmets and nose guards. Which was not much, unfortunately.

Then Benito noticed that one of the knights—one of the three standing in the bow of the barge—was a very big man. And he remembered that, according to some of the stories he had heard, the blond one had been aided by a supposed giant.

I wonder if...

At that moment, one of the knights standing next to the very big one unclasped his helmet and removed it. Then, quickly wiped his forehead and brushed back his long hair; in the way that a warrior will just before battle, to make sure that his hair will not slide forward in the helmet and obscure his view.

His very long and very *blond* hair...

The knight glanced up at Benito as he did so. Then, after shaking his head in bemusement—*crazy kid!*—replaced the helmet. The whole thing had not taken more than a moment, but long enough for Benito to see the knight's face clearly.

A face that seemed a thing made entirely of angles and sharp planes, for all its obvious youth.

Yes! It's got *to be him! I'm sure of it!*

Benito's excitement was cresting. Suddenly, he was *certain* that this expedition was no thing of "show." Not in the least little bit.

I've got to see it!

He made up his mind right then. Curling quickly back into an upright position, he planted his feet firmly on the crossbeam of the roof. Then, looking across the canal to the rooftop across the way where Maria was perched, watching him, gave her a quick and cheerful wave. And a thumbs-up.

Moving quickly, before Maria could have time to start yelling orders at him to cease and desist, Benito took out the little prybar he had brought with him—just in case—and began working at the iron bars of the small window he was squatting beside. Those were some of the iron bars he had sawn through two nights earlier, and it was quick work to pry a couple of them loose. Benito glanced down to make sure no one would get hit, and pitched the bars into the waters of the canal below.

Then, he paused. *Better wait until . . .* He looked at the barge holding the knights. He could see Petro Dorma also. Benito recognized him from his many public appearances. The Lord of the Nightwatch was perched in the very tip of the bow, preparing to offload. The barge had almost reached the *Casa* Dandelo.

A moment later, the barge came alongside the wharf. Lord Dorma and the three knights in the bow hopped off and strode to the main door of *Casa* Dandelo. One of the knights—the big one—began pounding on the door. Lord Dorma was shouting something.

Benito couldn't make out the exact words. Mostly because he was doing his best to close his ears entirely, so he could claim later that he hadn't heard Maria's—now very loud and profane— shouted orders at him to *stop what you're going, you crazy little bastard!*

He grinned wryly. Well . . . he *was* pretty little, and he was certainly a bastard. "Crazy," on the other hand . . .

I prefer to think of it as "bold."

Maria's cursing could probably be heard in the Jesolo by now. *Get away from that window, you blankety-blank stupid little blankety-blank . . . what do you think you're* doing?!

Benito avoided looking at her—his eyes were fixed on the bombard, which several of the knights were wrestling onto the wharf—but he did give her an assuring little wave. *Relax, Maria. I know what I'm doing.*

A complete lie, of course. Even Benito thought what he was about to do was at least half insane. *Voluntarily* entering the lair of the Dandelos?

But . . . *I have* got *to see this!*

Lord Dorma shouted something which sounded very . . . final. Then he and the three knights at the front stepped back. The other knights, by now, had nestled the bombard against a heavy stone abutment on the wharf. One of them took out a smoking slow match—

They must have already loaded it.

—and the bombard went off with a BOOM. Even though Benito was expecting it, the noise startled him. So did the sound of the heavy front door of *Casa* Dandelo being turned into splinters. Not so much from the cannonball, which had simply shattered the lock, but from the weight and fury of half a dozen armored knights slamming into it.

Maria's shrieking orders and curses at Benito could be heard in the *Alps*, by now. He gave her a last little wave and plunged through the window, into the darkness of *Casa* Dandelo.

The room he found himself in was some kind of storage area. Everything was very dark, but he could see the dim outlines of a door on the opposite side. Stumbling over various carelessly stacked crates, holding God-knows-what, he scrambled to the door. Then, tested it cautiously. Despite the recklessness of his project, he hadn't lost the fine details of burglary work.

To his relief, the door wasn't locked or bolted on the other side. He opened it slowly, carefully, peeking out into the corridor beyond.

There was no one in the corridor. To his left, the corridor dead-ended a few yards away. Three other doors on that side seemed to be the same type as the door he was opening—old, decayed, apparently little used; the kind of doors which led to nothing beyond rooms for storing mostly unwanted items. By pure luck, he had chosen a perfect entry route into the Dandelo building.

To his right, the corridor angled almost immediately to the left. He couldn't see what lay beyond that bend. But he could hear a furious ruckus coming from somewhere below. The excitement he wanted to watch, obviously.

Hurriedly, not wanting to miss *any* of it, Benito almost lunged out of the storage room and scurried to the bend of the corridor. The lighting was so bad—just one sconce at the very end of the corridor—that he tripped over an unseen obstacle lying on the floor and wound up sprawling around the bend instead of creeping unnoticed.

Fortunately—

There was no one. The bend led immediately to a flight of stone stairs leading downward to a landing and then curving to the left again.

The noise was louder now. So was—the stench.

Benito almost gagged. Maria had told him how badly *Casa* Dandelo reeked of the effluvia of slave trading. But he hadn't quite believed her. Breathing through his mouth, and trying to breathe as little as possible, Benito pranced down the stairs. For all the speed with which he negotiated the steps and the landing, he made almost no noise at all.

There was no one on the landing, either. But then Benito got careless. The noise coming up from the fracas below was *very* loud, now. Men shouting at each other. Benito was suddenly terrified that he would miss *everything.* So, abandoning what little caution he still retained, he raced from the landing down the stairs. As he neared the bottom of the steeply inclined staircase, he could see that it ended in a balcony overlooking a large room. He covered the last three steps in a single bound, landing on the balcony in a crouch and then eagerly leaning over the stone railing.

Below, in the large entrance hall of *Casa* Dandelo, he could see Petro Dorma, backed by all of the knights, almost face-to-face with Angelo Dandelo, the head of the House. Dandelo was backed in turn by more than a dozen of his own retainers, all of them armed. Most with cudgels and knives, but at least two with halberds and another two with arquebuses.

The two men seemed to have finished shouting at each other. Dorma was turning his head, clearly on the verge of issuing orders which—just as clearly, from the tension of the knights and the arquebus-armed Schiopettieri standing behind *them*—no! spreading to the sides, ready to fire—was going to cause all hell to break loose!

Benito was ecstatic. *Sure enough! He had a grandstand view!*

Unfortunately . . . so did the four Dandelo retainers who were *also* perched on the balcony, not more than ten feet away from him. All of them large, angry looking—and armed with cudgels.

The moment was . . . tense. Benito stared at the Dandelo goons. They stared at him.

What to do? What to do? Two of the Dandelos were starting to move toward him.

Fortunately for Benito, his abrupt arrival had also been noticed by one of the knights standing next to Dorma. The very large one, with a very large voice.

"Hold!" came the bass bellow. Wide-eyed, Benito stared down at him. The very large knight had taken a step toward the balcony, pointing a very large (and armored) finger at the advancing Dandelo goons. *"Hold right there! You men are under arrest!"*

The very large and armored finger now pointed imperiously at Benito. *"You have your orders, Knight-Squire Crazykid!"* The finger swept back—as imperiously as ever—to the Dandelo goons on the balcony. *"Arrest them! Don't let them escape!"*

One of the Dandelo retainers standing not far from the very large knight began to shout some sort of protest. The knight—moving *way* faster than Benito would have believed he could—slammed a very large and armored fist into the man's face. The Dandelo was flattened instantly. Blood everywhere. Benito wasn't sure, but . . . he thought the blow had broken the man's neck as well as crushed his head.

Knight-Squire Crazykid? Arrest them? Don't let them go?

Fortunately, Benito was no stranger to brazening his way out of jams. He drew his little knife and brandished it like a sword. What the hell. "Knight-Squire Crazykid"—slurred in that terrible accent—*did* sound a bit German.

"Stop!" he shouted at the goons on the balcony. "I'll kill any man who tries to escape!" He took two steps toward them. "God and the Right!"

Before he got out the last words, an arquebus went off with a roar on the floor below. Then, two more. The four Dandelos on the balcony took off like antelopes. In an instant, they had disappeared up another set of stairs.

Benito looked over the balcony. Both of the Dandelos holding arquebuses were down. One of them clearly dead, his chest a bloody ruin; the other, groaning and holding his side. Blood was pouring through his fingers.

Benito hadn't seen it, but he was sure that the Dandelos had made some threatening move with the firearms and the Schiopettieri had cut loose with their own. Now, with the Dandelos armed with nothing beyond cudgels and edged weapons . . .

Against Knights of the Holy Trinity?!

The stampede was already starting. When the very large knight whipped out his sword and bellowed *"Dia a coir!"* the stampede turned into a rout. Dandelo retainers raced out of the entry hall, seeking escape anywhere they could find it.

Most of them made it, but five were corralled by the Knights or Schiopettieri. Angelo Dandelo didn't even get two steps. He *tried* to make his escape, but the blond knight seized him by the scruff of the neck and drove him to the floor by kicking in the back of his knee. None too gently, with an armored boot.

Benito practically howled with glee. But his pleasure ended

abruptly, when he noticed that the very large knight was glaring up at him.

Again, the imperious finger. Again, the booming basso voice. *"You! Come down here!"*

Benito danced back and forth. The staircase he'd come down from was just behind him, after all. Benito was sure he could outrun that big knight, especially since he'd have to come all the way from the floor below . . . clanking in heavy armor up a staircase that was at an angle from where Benito was standing on the balcony. . . .

He was *sure* he could make his escape.

On the other hand—

—if he didn't—

Benito glanced down at the Dandelo who'd been struck by the knight's fist. Um. Yes. His neck *was* broken.

"RIGHT NOW, KID!!"

Meekly, Benito trotted over to the staircase indicated—*even that damned finger looks like it could break bones*—and came down the stairs.

"Yes, sir! I'm coming!"

When he arrived before the very large knight, it seemed as if *everyone* was glaring at him. Most of the knights with reproof, the Schiopettieri with anger, Petro Dorma with the stern face of official Venice.

Well . . . everyone except the blond knight and the big one. The blond was still holding Angelo Dandelo down. He just glanced at Benito and shook his head, the way a man will when confronted with the crazy act of a crazy kid.

The big knight's heavy and square face was half hidden behind the nose guard of his helmet. But Benito saw it very clearly when he . . . winked at him.

"Who are you?" demanded Petro Dorma. "And what are you doing here?"

For some reason, the large knight's wink returned all of Benito's usual self-confidence. Although he did manage to restrain his usual swagger.

"I'm Benito Oro," he announced. Then, angrily: "It was my friend Maria the bastards grabbed! That's why I'm here!" The angry tone faded into something more sullen. "I just . . . wanted to make sure, that's all."

Dorma sighed. Then, exchanged glances with the blond knight.

Benito heard the blond knight mutter something to Dorma. He wasn't sure, but he thought it was "From the mouths of babes."

Dorma's mouth quirked into a little smile. "And why not? All right, young Benito. Since you're here anyway, you can be my— ah, let's call it witness for the canalers. How's that?"

Benito nodded his head, eagerly.

The eagerness faded, when he felt a very large hand close on his shoulder. The hand squeezed a bit. Just a bit. Benito felt like he was caught in a vise.

"I'll look after the kid, Lord Dorma," rumbled the voice. "Have no fear."

Dorma's quirky smile turned into something a lot broader. "Oh, I don't." He gave Benito a genuine *official stare.*

"I don't believe there's any reason to fear. Is there, boy?"

The very large hand squeezed a bit more. Benito's head-nodding became very eager.

The next two hours were sheer joy. Benito accompanied Lord Dorma and his entourage as they went through every room—every closet—of *Casa* Dandelo. Those locks on slave pens for which Angelo had keys in his possession were unlocked. Those which he didn't, were smashed open.

Every slave was inspected. Then, records demanded.

Every slave for whom Dandelo had no records was immediately freed and escorted away by Schiopettieri. Then, Lord Dorma made a notation of the fine. In every instance, he fined *Casa* Dandelo the maximum permitted by Venetian law.

Every slave for whom Dandelo had *inadequate* records was also freed—with the same maximum fine.

Lord Dorma's concept of "adequate records" was . . . strict.

Manfred's was . . . Teutonic. Erik's was . . . Viking.

"The ink is smudged here," announced Dorma. "Can't be read at all," snorted Manfred. "I say she's a free woman," growled Erik.

Dorma hesitated a moment, then nodded. Scribble, scribble. *Maximum fine.*

"He doesn't *quite* resemble the description," mused Dorma. "To say the least!" boomed Manfred. "An inch too short," sneered Erik. "No resemblance at all. He's a free man."

Scribble, scribble. *Maximum fine.*

"Does that hair look black to you, *Ritters*?" queried Dorma. Half a dozen helmeted heads shook back and forth in firm disavowal. "Brown," stated Manfred firmly. "Practically blond!" barked Erik.

Dorma nodded again. "He's free, then." Scribble, scribble. *Maximum fine.*

Angelo Dandelo stopped even trying to protest, halfway through the process. Partly because of the split lip he had from his first—and very profane—protest. The blond knight had been no more gentle with his (armored) backhand than he'd been earlier with his boot. *You'll show respect for the Lord of the Nightwatch, damn you. Next time you'll spit teeth. The time after that you'll spit guts. Try me, you fucking slaver bastard.*

But, mostly, because Dandelo was not a fool. Protest was pointless. The Dandelos had misgauged the political situation, and misgauged it badly. Lord Dorma's place in it, most of all. And they were now going to pay the heavy price which Venice's often ruthless politics exacted from losers. Dorma would leave them just enough slaves—the ones who were incontrovertibly legal—to keep them from outright bankruptcy. But by the end of day, *Casa* Dandelo would be almost penniless and politically humbled.

It was late afternoon before Benito emerged from *Casa* Dandelo. He came out at the very end, with Lord Dorma and the knights. The very large one's hand was still on his shoulder, but it had long since stopped squeezing.

By now it seemed that half of Venice must have gathered to watch. Quite a bit more than half, probably, of the canalers and Arsenalotti. The roar of the mob was almost deafening. No one had any doubts any longer—not after seeing the procession of freed slaves who had emerged from *Casa* Dandelo for the past hour or so, and been escorted by the Schiopettieri into the waiting empty barges.

Dorma led the way onto the last barge. Unsure what to do now, Benito let the large knight propel him into the barge also.

"Better come with us, Knight-Squire Crazykid," he said. "You *don't* want to be left alone on *Casa* Dandelo's wharf tonight."

"My name's Benito."

The very large knight grinned. The square blocky teeth were visible even under the helmet. "Benito, then. It was still a crazy thing to do."

"You should talk, Manfred," chuckled the blond knight standing next to them. He removed the helmet and shook his long, very pale blond hair in the breeze. "God, I hate helmets." Then, smiling at Benito: "I'm Erik Hakkonsen, by the way. And you are insane."

But the words were spoken in a very friendly tone, and Benito found himself meeting the smile with a grin.

"I just couldn't help it, that's all. And I wouldn't have missed that for anything."

The very large knight—Manfred, he was apparently named—now removed his helmet also. Benito was almost shocked when he saw how young he was. *He's not much older than me. Can't be more than eighteen.*

The barge pulled away from the wharf and began heading across the canal. The mob on the other side was packed like sardines, all of them waving and shouting.

"*LORD DORMA! LORD DORMA!*" And more than a few: "*Doge Dorma!*"

The knight named Erik stared, apparently taken aback by the crowd's frenzied applause. Oddly, the young knight named Manfred didn't seem surprised at all.

"Just like Francesca predicted," he mused. "I do believe Venetian politics just went through an earthquake."

"I'm letting you off here," Petro Dorma said to Benito, as the barge was almost across the canal.

At that moment, a young woman suddenly pushed her way to the forefront of the mob. Her eyes seemed a little wild. As soon as she caught sight of Benito, her square jaw tightened like a clamp. Then . . .

"That's an incredible command of profanity, she's got," said Manfred cheerily. "And the way your girlfriend's shaking her fist at you doesn't bode well for your future."

"She's *not* my girlfriend," growled Benito.

Manfred's already huge grin got bigger. "Could have fooled me!" He eyed the shrieking young woman. "In my experience—okay, it's limited, I admit—but still . . ." The grin faded a little, and the next words came softly. "Young Benito, I think only a woman in love gets *that* angry at a man."

"You're crazy!" snapped Benito.

They were almost at the edge of the canal. With as little effort as if he were picking up a toddler, Manfred hoisted Benito by the armpits and began to deposit him off the barge.

"Maybe so," he whispered. "But if she isn't, you're the one who's crazy, not me. Damn, but she's gorgeous."

Benito stared at the furious eyes that Manfred's huge hands were depositing him before, to meet his punishment. The square jaw, the red face, the thick hair swinging wildly—almost as wildly as the fist—the broad shoulders.

Damn. She is *gorgeous.*

The thought vanished as soon as Maria's hand cracked his face. And it stayed away while she shook him by the shoulders—slapped him again; not as hard, but twice—and finished cursing him. But it returned, in a flood, when she seized him and hugged him close, sobbing softly in his hair and kissing his cheek.

"God damn you, Benito, don't *ever* scare me like that again."

"I'm sorry, Maria," he mumbled. "But . . ."

He didn't know how to respond. He was too confused. *Damn, but you're gorgeous* seemed . . . crazy. But he couldn't think of anything else to say. Not a damn thing that didn't seem . . . crazier.

Chapter 62

When Antimo brought the news of Dorma's raid on the Dandelos to the Duke of Ferrara, Dell'este rose from his chair and went to the window. There he remained, for some time, staring toward Venice.

"How much money have we received so far from the Emperor, through Baron Trolliger's private agents?"

"We'll have enough to hire the condottieri we need."

"Secretly?"

"Yes, milord. Since you'll be commanding the army yourself, I've not had to negotiate with any well-known great captains. Just a large number of small companies. Neither Visconti nor Sforza will be able to keep track of the numbers involved. Ferrara will field twice the force the Milanese are expecting. I'm quite sure of it."

"Careless on their part," mused Dell'este. "But I'm not surprised. Filippo Visconti has always been too arrogant, and Sforza has grown complacent with success." He was silent for a moment. Then gave the windowsill a little tap. "So. Everything else is in place. We have the army we need, and it seems as if Venice has finally found a leader worthy of the name. There remains, only—Valdosta."

When he turned back, the face of the Old Fox seemed to have no expression at all. But Antimo knew his master far too well to be fooled.

"The sword, then?"

The duke nodded. "Yes. Send it. The time has come. At last."

The Old Fox's right hand curled into a loose fist, as if an expert swordsman held a blade in his hand. Still, there was no expression in his face. But, again, Antimo was not fooled. And so, as he had done so many other times and in so many other ways, he gave help again to his master.

"They murdered your daughter, hounded your grandchildren. Did their best to soil the name of Dell'este. Plotted and schemed to destroy Ferrara and Venice both."

The duke's lips peeled back into a snarl. Had he been there to see the sight, Carlo Sforza—the famous "Wolf of the North"—would have finally recognized what he was about to face.

But Sforza was not there; nor were his master Visconti's spies. And the moment was brief, in any event. Soon enough, the Old Fox was back.

"So they did," he murmured, smiling thinly. "And in so doing, did nothing more—in the end—than sharpen my blades." His eyes moved to the rack of swords. "There are no finer blades in the world, Antimo, than those of Dell'este."

PART V
May, 1538 A.D.

Chapter 63

The summons to Dorma had come often that spring. Petro seemed to enjoy talking to him, and they would be sending him to the Accademia in the summer.

This Friday morning it was different.

Petro Dorma was sitting—as usual—in his inner sanctum. The balding man's face, usually serious, was downright solemn. Across his desk lay an open box containing a naked sword on a sheet of scarlet silk it had plainly been wrapped in. It was an old hand-and-a-half-blade, made in a style a century out of date now. The blue-silver folded Damascus steel was as rippling mirror bright as if it had left the maker yesterday. Only the golden hilt showed the signs of years of careful devoted polishing. Wordlessly, Petro Dorma held out the letter.

It didn't take Marco long to read it.

I send into the keeping of House Dorma one of the honor-blades of Dell'este, in token of the bond now between us. Young Marco will know how it is to be cared for.

"Your grandfather says you know how to care for this sword."

Marco nodded, not able to speak. There was a hidden message there from Duke Dell'este, a message Milord Petro could not possibly read. But Marco knew—and the implications turned his life upside down in the single span of time it had taken Petro to free the blade from its silk wrapping.

Petro Dorma was no fool, of course. If he could not read the message, still, he knew that one was there—and that it must be

555

portentous for his house. So he took Marco's nod at face value, and set the sword back down in its silken nest.

Dell'este steel—Dell'este honor. There is no going back now. Not for Grandfather. Not for the Old Fox.

"Tell me what you need," Dorma said simply. "I gather this isn't the sort of thing you just leave in the armory or hang on the wall."

"A—p-place," Marco stammered. "I need a place for it, somewhere where it's safe, but where it can be seen by—by—" He flushed. "By the House-head. You, milord. You're—supposed to be reminded by it, milord."

Petro nodded thoughtfully. "Will that do?" he asked, pointing behind and to Marco's right.

There was an alcove between two windows, an alcove currently holding an unimpressive sculpture of the Madonna. The alcove was approximately a foot wider than the blade was long.

"Yes, milord," Marco said immediately. "Yes. Milord—that's perfect."

A few days later, the thing was done. And he was summoned into Dorma's presence again.

Marco held his breath, and with all the concentration he could command, placed the century-old hand-and-a-half sword reverently in the cradle of the special rack he'd asked Milord Petro to have made.

Marco stepped back two paces to scan his handiwork with an apprehensive and critical eye.

He'd inspected and cleaned the blade of the sword that morning, that being a small ritual in and of itself. Somewhere in his earlier conversations he'd told Petro that in Venice's damp climate, he'd have to inspect the blade once or twice a week, and that he preferred *not* to have to move it too far from its resting place.

He'd been a little apprehensive about that, since this was clearly the Head of Dorma's private—and very special—sanctuary. But Petro had nodded his acceptance of that, gravely, and then he'd taken the undyed tassel off the hilt, keeping it, *not* giving it to a servant to be dealt with.

This morning he'd returned the tassel to Marco, now the deep and unmistakable midnight-blue of Dorma's house colors. That was all Marco had needed. The ancient sword was now ready to take its place in the heart of Dorma.

He knelt again, and reached out to adjust the blade so that the silk tassels hung side-by-side from the hilt, neither obscuring the other. The Valdosta-scarlet and Dorma-blue tassels hung gracefully, shining as only heavy silk could.

Dorma colors. Dell'este colors. Ferrara's steel.

Marco wore all of them, now. A *main gauche* and rapier of more modern design on his belt, sent by the duke. And—on his right hand, a signet ring. A new-cut signet, with an old design. The lion's head seal of *Casa* Valdosta.

He would be hidden no longer. After all these years, the secret life in the marshes and the canals, Valdosta had returned to take his rightful place in Venice.

"It is your grandfather's opinion—which I share—that you would now be far safer in the public eye, where harming you would be noticed and acted upon. You must come to live here in the *Casa* Dorma." Petro Dorma's gaze weighed and measured Marco before he added—

"Both of you."

It took all the eloquence that Marco possessed to convince Petro that he did not want Benito—not-entirely-ex-thief, bridge-brat Benito—inside *Casa* Dorma. At least not for now.

"Caesare Aldanto's the only one who can control him, milord." He pleaded earnestly. "I can't. And you might as well try to tell the tide not to come in, for all he'll heed you. Caesare Aldanto can keep him safe until he develops a little more sense."

Marco clenched his hands in anguish on the arms of the chair. "Please, milord—Lord and Saints know I love him, but I know him. He's Dell'este blood—but wolf Sforza blood also. He's been on the street since he was a kid. Bridge-brat taught; it'd be like trying to tame a wild kitten. Tell Caesare to bring him around to being civilized. If anybody can make Benito see sense, it'll be Caesare Aldanto."

Petro Dorma scowled at the mention of Aldanto's name, then nodded again—this time reluctantly. "I can't say that I like it, but you know your brother." His mouth firmed. "That makes it all the more important that we fulfill our obligations toward you, Marco." He surveyed Marco's clothing with a critical eye. "And one of the first things will be an appropriate wardrobe. I'll have my mother see to that—"

But in the end it had been Angelina, not Rosanna, who had outfitted him. Petro's mother, Rosanna, was indisposed, and Marco had yet to actually see her except at meals. She seemed ill, and looked as frail as a creature of lace and spun glass. He much doubted she'd seen *him*, not really; he'd kept his head down and his eyes fixed on his plate, and he never spoke. That *wasn't* because Dorma cousins were unfriendly; mostly it was because he didn't know what to say. The intricacies of polite social conversation were still a mystery to him. And what could he talk *about*, anyway? How to survive in the marshes? The best ways to break into a house?

So he kept his mouth shut, and let the Dorma cousins steer him though the maze of dancing, religion, and etiquette lessons; let Angelina guide him through what it meant to be a House scion; let Caesare Aldanto *try* to show him how to keep himself alive with that Valdosta steel—

And let Angelina outfit him. In leather, silk, wool, and finest linen. Clothing he hadn't worn since that long ago childhood in Ferrara, the kind where the cost of one pair of boots would outfit a canaler for years.

The silk of a sleeve slid caressingly along his arm as he adjusted the positioning of the *basse taille* enameled sword-rest by a fraction of an inch. The stand itself was adequate—the best Petro could do on short notice. The cabinet maker had been given a more exact design, and instructions to paint the stand with no fewer than twenty coats of varnish. *That* kind of work took time, and Marco was content to wait for it.

The walnut half-moon table it stood on, though, was perfect. Rescued from the Dorma attics, its neat marquetry could have come from the hand of a master craftsman. Perhaps it had come from Ferrara too—Rosanna Dorma had brought some furnishings with her from their estates outside Vicenza. Iron from Vicenza went to the forges of Ferrara and the Dell'este craftsmen marked only their steel.

Marco looked again at the old sword and shivered. The second sword of Dell'este, that he'd last seen on its own rest just below the *first* sword. It brought with it levels of meaning as intricate and interleaved as the folded and refolded steel that made up the blade.

"The sword of Duke Dell'este is the soul of House Dell'este," the old duke had said, with Marco kneeling attentively beside him.

"This sword—" Marco had turned wide eyes on his grandfather—"is as old as Ferrara?!" He could not imagine it: the tally of years made him dizzy to contemplate.

"Not Ferrara and not this sword," Grandfather had sighed. "The Dell'este were swordsmiths ... back when the Etruscans first came across the mountains to the flatlands of the east. The first soul of Dell'este was forged in Felsina. The second in hiding in Motena. The third was made in the marshes we reclaimed to make Ferrara's wealth. Each time we have made two. As strong and with the new skills that the Dell'este alone can give to the great blades. Some call it magic . . ." The old man had smiled, dryly. "The witchfinders suspect us. But if there is magic, it is in the blood and bone and steel of the Dell'este. Sometimes . . . when the House Dell'este is threatened—in uncertain times—it is sometimes wise to send a second soul out with an heir to seek a new home, so that the Dell'este line will continue. This is the third blade that—"

Beside him, Benito wriggled and yawned audibly.

"Father, this is boring me to tears." Lorendana had complained. "I can hardly imagine the boys—"

"Exactly," Grandfather had snapped. "You can hardly imagine anything. Exercising your mind is evidently beyond you." He rose to his feet, his face gone cold with anger, and pointed to the door behind her. "Go, get out of here, and take your impertinence with you."

That was what Grandfather had meant, sending the sword. That things were deteriorating in Ferrara. That he feared for the House Dell'este, and was taking steps to ensure its survival. But he, Marco Valdosta, was merely the child of a daughter of the house. Things must be dire indeed . . . that he, Marco, was now a recognized heir.

Dell'este honor. The Dell'este soul-sword. He wanted to heal people, not cut them down. But honor demanded he must do as the House Dell'este needed.

Petro Dorma couldn't know these things, but he had evidently understood that the coming of the sword meant far, far more than mere courtesy to a new ally, a new powerful trade partner, or even the Family that had assumed guardianship of his grandsons.

"You realize—we've had to change our original plans about you." Petro spoke reluctantly, as if he regretted having to tell this to Marco. "We were going to sponsor you into the Accademia in anticipation that you would eventually replace Doctor Rigannio. He's getting old, he's been hinting for some time that we should start thinking about finding an 'assistant.' But now—"

Petro shrugged, helplessly.

"I'm sorry, Marco, but it's really out of the question. It simply isn't done, having a son of one Family serving another Family, even in so honored a position as Family physician. Oh, I see no reason why you can't study medicine, so go right ahead, and we'll go through with our sponsorship and support. But—"

Marco nodded. "I understand, milord," he'd said quietly. "That's just the way it is."

Dell'este honor.

Dell'este *responsibilities*.

There was no running away from this. And he had learned, finally, the folly of running. Even Caesare didn't run from problems—because he had taken on responsibilities. So there would be no "Doctor Marco" living canalside, helping the canalers and the poorest of the canalsiders.

Still . . . Doctor Rigannio, a kindly man, had been letting him *be* something of an assistant, in the past month or so that he'd been visiting Dorma. Now that he was here he spent more time with him, so long as it was within the House. And Rigannio'd been listening, carefully, to what Marco had poured out to him about Sophia's cures. That information—slowly, carefully, and with no clues as to the source—was something Doctor Rigannio had taken to leaking back into the Accademia. It *wasn't* heretical; and Marco had already seen evidence that it was coming back down to canalside, as the herb-hunters were pointed to new plants, and the results coming into the apothecaries. So he'd done that much good.

And there was something else. He'd been *watching* these aristocrats, and from the inside vantage point. No one thought any the worse of the *Casa* heads for having hobbies—some of them pretty odd. Old man Renzi cultivated entertainers. Bruno Bruschi studied Venetian insect life. Carlo di Zecchilo played the flute. Angelo Ponetti made lace, for God's sake! As long as it didn't obsess you, the way the Doge's clockwork toys did, a hobby was actually considered genteel.

There was no reason why the head of an old *Case Vecchie* family like the Valdosta *couldn't* indulge himself in a hobby of medicine. And if he chose to treat the impoverished canalers and canalsiders, well, the medical establishment would be relieved that he wasn't taking away potentially *paying* patients, and his peers would consider it no more than mildly eccentric. He could work it out with the priests by explaining that he was discharging religious obligations. As for having the time to do this, he'd been watching Petro; and yes, he was *busy*, but he did have some leisure time. It was possible.

And the opportunity to so indulge himself—the training to be able to do so—would have come without any strings attached other than those of duty to his family. Not Strega, not Dorma. There were other ramifications—of potential benefit to both Valdosta and Aldanto. He could earn loyalty and gratitude for Valdosta down along canalside that no amount of money could buy. He could earn *friends* for his Family, and ears for Caesare Aldanto.

"I'm kind of lost here," he had been saying to his patients, or his patients' parents. They knew by his accent that he wasn't canalside born, though what they made of him, he couldn't guess. "I don't *know* canalside. I need friends in the trade, friends who'd tell me when somebody's setting up to cheat me or hurt me. Not spies, Lord and Saints, no! Just friends—who'll give me a ride now and again, give me warning if there's a bullyboy on my tail, and tell me the common gossip everybody knows, but nobody else would tell *me*. That's help, honest help, worth more than silver, worth more than enough to clear any debt."

Those who'd insisted on paying him with goods instead of that asked-for help, he'd had leave the stuff in front of Harrow's hole. It kept disappearing, so he assumed Harrow was getting most of it. He doubted anyone else was. That part of Castello had become mysteriously free from crime of late . . .

He sighed, and got to his feet. It was hard, trying to think out all the ramifications of something. He was so used to living one day at a time, not thinking beyond the needs of the season. Now—

Now it was time for dancing lessons. Pah. Dancing lessons. He'd been here a week and needed to get out and see Kat. But he wasn't sure what to tell her. She was a commoner, a smuggler. He was now one of the *Case Vecchie*. How was she going to take that? She was the greatest darling in nature. But touchy about her home. It must be very simple and poor and she didn't seem to want him to know where it was.

How would he handle that, now? How would he handle *any-thing*?

He didn't know. All he knew was the meaning of the sword, there in its rightful place.

Dell'este steel. Dell'este honor. It had been returned to him. He had no choice but to honor it. Nor, he discovered, probing his heart, did he have any desire not to honor it.

Chapter 64

Light flickered up ahead as a door opened and closed. A figure entered the corridor. "Who is it?" snapped an elderly female voice in irritation.

"Your pardon, milady," Marco said humbly, "I'm afraid I took a wrong turn somewhere."

He paused in the unfamiliar stuffy, darkened corridor. Marco realized that, with his mind preoccupied with the conversation just finished with Petro, he'd gotten lost. This area of *Casa* Dorma was part of the Family's living quarters—and, apparently, an old and poorly maintained one. The perfume in the single lamp along this stretch of hallway could not mask the faint odor of mildew, nor the olive origin of the oil it burned.

Marco's night sight had always been good; he had no difficulty seeing who it was that had accosted him. Milady Rosanna Dorma—Petro's mother—and she didn't look well. Her skin was grayish, a vein throbbed in her temple, and her eyes seemed to be all pupil. She was pressing her right hand to her temple, and supporting herself against the corridor wall with her left. Prudence said that he should go back and leave her alone. Concern and the healing instinct said she was in no shape to be *left* alone. He moved quickly to her side, footsteps sounding hollow in the uncarpeted corridor, intending to ask if he could be of service to her, since he'd inadvertently intruded on her privacy.

But she began trembling the moment he came into view, staring at him as if he was a thing out of nightmare. She crowded back against the corridor wall—and when he held out his hand to steady her, she shrieked, spasmed, and fell to the floor.

Prudence dictated that he find help: Doctor Rigannio, or Petro Dorma.

And by the time I find help she may be dead—

He was on his knees beside her in an eye-blink, then cradling her in his arms to protect her from injuring herself with the convulsions she was suffering. He held her head against his shoulder, and pinioned her wrists in one long hand. She was so frail, it took next to nothing to restrain her.

"*Ernesto!*" she cried shrilly. "Ernesto, no! Not again! Dear God, not *again!*" She writhed in his arms, trying to free her hands, trying to reach for something.

Dilated eyes, racing pulse, clammy skin. Sweat beading the brow, and hallucinations. By that throbbing vein in the temple, probably a blinding headache. Symptoms tumbled together in his mind and formed an answer.

Lotos dreams. He'd seen it in the Jesolo with blue-lotos addicts. Either induced, or flashback; it didn't matter which. And in a patient as obviously weakened as this one was, if someone didn't *do* something, *now*—she was in very real danger of never coming out again.

And if he left her alone to get help—she was in very real danger of hurting, or even killing herself.

There was only one choice; try and talk her though it. He'd done it more than once, with Luciano. If he could just get her attention fixed on him—

"Rosanna—" *Now* was not the time for "Milady Dorma"; she wouldn't respond to that. He slipped her farther down so that she was lying against his upright knee and slapped her cheek, lightly. "Rosanna, say something. Tell me you hear me." He slapped her other cheek. "Tell me! Talk to me!"

Her eyes wandered, seeing things he couldn't; tears poured down her ashen cheeks.

"Rosanna! Talk to me!" He shook her, and dredged up her few, hysterical words, looking for a clue to get into her dream. "Rosanna, if you *don't* talk to me, Ernesto will get very *angry* with you!"

Her eyes focused on him for a moment. "L-Lorendana? Lorendana

Valdosta?" She faltered, her face twisted, her mouth a slash of pain. "Lorendana, stop them! They're your friends—they're killing Ernesto—"

God and Saints—she thought he was his mother. That must have been what threw her into this in the first place! Ernesto—that must have been Ernesto Dorma, Petro's father. He'd wondered about the portrait in the study, so like Petro, but plainly older; Petro had identified it, then said something about his father dying from an accidental fall.

Gods—could she have seen something no one else did? Is that why—never mind. Whatever it was, it couldn't have involved my mother. She was murdered months before Ernesto Dorma died. I'll get her out of this first, then worry about Dorma secrets.

There were only two ways of dealing with lotos dreams—*direct* the dream, or break it—

And somehow Marco knew if he directed the dream from the nightmare she was in into something pleasant, she'd never leave it again.

"Ernesto is *dead*, Rosanna," he said savagely. "He's been dead more than a year. You *know* he's dead. And you can't change the past. You think you can, but the past you create is a *lie*. And Ernesto doesn't *like* lies, Rosanna."

Her eyes widened, and she whimpered in the back of her throat. He continued on, as stern and unyielding as Saint Chrysostom, his morning's religion lesson giving him another weapon to break her out of her hallucination. "He's very *angry* with you, Rosanna. You're muddying his trip through purgatory, trying to hold on to him like this. He sent me to tell you that if you *really* loved him, you'd let him go!"

She cried out in denial, freed her hands from his, and tried to push him away. At the end of the corridor another door opened and closed, and there was the sound of a footstep—two. Marco didn't dare look up—he had Rosanna's attention now, and if he broke eye contact with her, he'd lose it.

"No—" she moaned, as a gasp from the direction of the door reached him; he heard running footsteps. "No, Ernesto would never say that! Ernesto wouldn't—"

"He would, and he did—you're *hurting* him, Rosanna, you're holding him back."

Angelina's voice, sharp and shrill. "*What are you doing with my—*"

"Shut *up*, Angelina," he hissed, regaining Rosanna's wandering attention by shaking her again. "Get the doctor—"

She at least had enough sense not to argue with him. Running feet retreated, and the door slammed against the wall as witness to her hasty passage.

Rosanna beat at his face and chest with hard, bony fists; her blows were wild, but she got him a good one in the nose and just under the left eye. Marco tried not to wince; ghosts feel no pain.

"I don't believe it!" She was crying. "I don't believe *you*! Ernesto would never believe such—"

"Ernesto is in purgatory. Do you want to be responsible for dragging him down?" The religion lesson having given him the barb to use on her, and forced to be cruel by desperation, he dug it in. "Do *you* want to be the one who forces him to stay there longer? If you die, if you lose yourself in opium dreams, Rosanna, that's what will happen, and it will *all be your fault.*"

"*NO!*" She shoved him away, hard enough that he lost his hold on her, and he lost his balance as well. He hit his head on the wall with a sickening *crack*, and saw stars.

He struggled against the darkness, still not able to see but fighting off the dazzle, and more footsteps pounded up the corridor. As his eyes cleared he was shoved summarily out of the way by Doctor Rigannio, and a wiry woman he recognized as Rosanna's maid. A hand grabbing his elbow helped him to stand; when he turned to render thanks, he found himself staring into Angelina Dorma's profoundly unhappy, dark-circled eyes.

He froze, unsure of what to say, as behind him he could hear her mother's muffled sobs, and the comforting murmur of her maid.

He stood that way for an eternity. Angelina reached out toward his face, as if to touch his swelling nose, then stopped herself. She seemed at as much of a loss as he was.

"Marco—"

He turned, grateful for a chance to look away.

"Marco, whatever you did, it was right," Doctor Rigannio said, getting painfully to his feet, while the maid held Rosanna against her shoulder, letting her cry herself into calmness. "You broke her out of her hallucination—"

"She thought I was someone she knew," Marco said carefully,

not sure how much of his background the House had been told. "My mother, I guess, and she knew that my mother is dead. I guess she never got a good look at me before this. I think I might have thrown her *into* the hallucination in the first place. I—I'm sorry. I certainly didn't mean it."

"Of course you didn't," the doctor said smoothly, one eye on Rosanna as her maid helped her to rise. Rosanna turned a tear-streaked face toward the sound of their voices, and blinked.

"Who are you? she asked, voice hoarse with strain.

"This is Marco Valdosta, Rosanna," Doctor Rigannio interposed smoothly. "You remember; Petro told you. He's going to the Accademia under Dorma sponsorship. He is a grandson of Duke Dell'este of Ferrara. The duke has made some trade agreements with us in return."

She turned away from her maid and looked at him with wondering eyes. "Marco Valdosta—you must be Lorendana's boy. She had two, I heard."

He bowed to her. "Yes, milady." The mention of Benito made him nervous.

"It's uncanny," she said, "you look just like her."

"So I've been told, milady."

"I—" Her eyes clouded for a moment, then cleared and she drew herself up, taking on a dignity and poise that reminded him sharply of his grandfather, and a beauty that had nothing to do with tear-swollen eyes, blanched cheeks and trembling hands. "I believe I owe you a debt of gratitude."

He interrupted her gently. "Milady, you owe me nothing. You were ill, I simply stayed with you until Angelina could bring the doctor. That *is*, or will be, my duty—I'm studying medicine after all." He was amazed at himself; he sounded *years* older and he wondered where the words were coming from.

They were evidently the right ones. She flushed a little and lowered her gaze.

"Rosanna, you should go rest," the doctor prompted.

"Yes," she replied vaguely. "Yes, I should. Forgive me."

As the corridor door opened and closed behind them, Doctor Rigannio cursed savagely. "Angelina, where is she getting it?" He stopped then, as if only now realizing that there was an outsider not *of* Dorma standing awkwardly at his elbow, privy to every word he said.

Marco cleared his throat. "It's none of my business, Doctor Rigannio, but—that looked like a lotos flashback to me."

The doctor pivoted, face blank with surprise. "Lotos *flashback*? What in the name of God is *that*?"

Marco flushed and stammered: "If y-you take enough lotos, it changes your head. Even if you never t-take it again, you can get thrown into hallucinations by any strong stimulus." He shrugged. "That's why a lot of Jesolo-marsh folk are crazy. Stuck in lotos dreams."

Doctor Rigannio closed his eyes and cursed again. "So *that's* why—thank you, Marco. Again. I trust we can rely on your discretion?"

Marco managed a feeble smile. "What discretion, milord? Milady Rosanna had a dizzy spell and I just stayed with her until you came. Nothing terrible and she certainly didn't say anything except to thank me."

"Good boy." The doctor clapped him on the shoulder and he staggered a little. "I'll go see what needs to be done."

That left him alone in the corridor with Angelina.

Now she wouldn't look at him.

"You've heard enough that you might as well know all of it," she said bitterly, staring at the polished wooden floor, twisting the hem of her shawl in white hands. "When Father died she took it badly—she'd been in love with him, really in love, and she couldn't bear to be without him. She started taking lotos so she could see him." Angelina looked up finally and gestured her helplessness.

"Where was she getting it?" Marco asked.

Angelina's eyes blazed. "Caesare Aldanto," she spat—and burst into tears.

Once again Marco wound up sitting on the floor of the corridor with a lady of Dorma in his arms—this one crying into his shoulder all the things she did not dare tell mother or brother. About how she still loved Aldanto—and hated him. About how her mother's manservant, Paulo, had been the go-between. About how she'd put two and two together when she realized that Paulo had known *exactly* where to take her the first time she'd met with Caesare—which could only mean he'd been there many times before.

And that she was pregnant with Caesare's baby.

None of this—except for the business with Rosanna and the lotos—was any surprise to Marco. It was pretty obvious from her intermittent hysterics that Angelina was "not herself" and adding those frequent visits to Caesare gave anybody good cause.

But that she thought the man was the source of the drug— Lord and Saints.

He didn't know quite what to say or do, so he just let her cry herself out—something she evidently needed—then helped her to tidy herself and helped her to her feet.

"Thank you, Marco," she said, shyly, a little ashamed. "I didn't mean—"

"That's what friends are for," he told her. "We *are* friends, aren't we?"

"I'd hoped so—but after—"

He shrugged. "I learned things from that whole mess—and it got me *here*, didn't it?" He delicately declined to mention how much that fiasco had placed him in Aldanto's debt.

"Then we *are* friends." She offered him her hand with a sweet smile that could *still* make his heart jump a little, even if he wasn't in love with her anymore. He took it, squeezed it—and they parted.

The dancing lessons were worse than ever. Even if his mind hadn't been elsewhere, Marco would have found the intricate precision of the steps hard to remember and follow. It was odd, in a way, given that his memory was normally so perfect. Why should he have so much difficulty with this, when he didn't with herbal remedies and cargo lists?

In the end, listening to the dance master's shrill and humorless criticisms, Marco decided his memory was being sabotaged by itself. He and Chiano used to dance little jigs sometimes, in the marshes, without ever worrying about whether the "steps" were proper and correct. Remembering the cheerful and raucous jibes of Sophia which accompanied those moments of gaiety, he smiled.

"*Marco!*" shrilled the dance-master. "You're *not* supposed to smile during this dance! *This* dance is a very solemn—"

Marco sighed. *There are ways in which my old life was a lot easier . . .*

Chapter 65

When Marco was summoned to Petro Dorma's office at sunset, he assumed it was due to the near-disaster with Rosanna in the private corridor the day before. This time Marco followed the servant to the top of his house with only a little trepidation. He had, he thought, handled the whole mess fairly well.

The east windows framed a sky that was indigo blue, spangled with tiny crystal star-beads. The west held the sun dying a bloody death. Petro was a dark silhouette against the red.

Marco cleared his throat. "You sent for me, Milord Dorma?"

Petro did not turn around. "It seems," he said dryly, "that you have fallen into the muck-pit of Dorma secrets. Doctor Rigannio told me a bit—'Gelina told me more." He sighed. "It seems to me the older and more honorable the House, the deeper and darker its closet. Almost as if our 'honor' were a reaction to this."

He seemed to be waiting for a response.

"Every House has secrets," Marco replied carefully. "You know more'n—more than a few things that neither the Valdosta nor the Dell'este could be proud of. You can trust me, Petro."

Now Petro turned, though he was still nothing more than a sable shape to Marco. "Well. I will admit I have been toying with this notion for a while, but—I didn't quite know how to phrase this delicately, yet I also did not want you to have any deceptions about what I was going to offer. Angelina told you, she says, that she's—"

"Expecting," Marco supplied.

"And who the father is." Petro coughed. "We are in something of a dilemma. It just isn't done for a *Case Vecchie* daughter to have an—unacknowledged child. Yet we can *hardly* look to Caesare Aldanto as a husband. It would seem best for Angelina to make a marriage, but frankly, there wasn't anyone she wanted to confide in—really, no one she truly didn't find repugnant even for a titular husband." He paused, significantly. "Until today."

Marco was considerably less of a fool than he had been half a year ago, but this was still a shock.

"You mean—" He gulped. "You mean me."

"It would be of great benefit to Dorma," Petro admitted frankly. "A marriage with Valdosta would get us out of an awkward situation—and not incidentally, give us a chance to negotiate for a better access to Ferrara's steel trade." His voice was wry. "I do have to think first of Dorma as a whole before I think of Angelina—but if I can benefit both . . ."

Marco fought for solid ground. "Was this Angelina's idea, not yours?"

Petro tapped his chest. "I suggested it after she told me about this afternoon. She seemed to welcome the idea. She does like you, Marco—and so do I. I'd be quite pleased to have you further tied to my House."

Marco was floundering. He could have Angelina Dorma, the girl he'd once dreamed of—and if he kept his mouth shut, she'd continue to blame Caesare for her mother's addiction. That would, eventually, break the hold Caesare had on her heart. Which would please Maria, and maybe Caesare too. It would save the *Casa* Dorma from a potentially damning scandal. Marco could read between Petro's careful words. Finding a husband for Angelina that wouldn't drag the family down was going to be hard, to say nothing of expensive. And he, Marco Valdosta, owed the Dorma. For protection as much as advancement. He owed Caesare. He owed Maria too.

But what about Kat? His heart felt like it would break.

Dell'este honor.

He'd followed the dictates of his heart before. The result had been disaster.

Dell'este honor demanded payback. And he might be in love with Kat . . . yet he still had no idea if she was in love with *him.*

More than anything, at that moment, Marco wanted to talk to Kat. *Desperately.* But he had no idea how to reach her before their appointment on Thursday. He didn't know where she lived—even her last name.

Everything *hurt*.

He was almost gasping like a fish out of water, now. His mind, reeling, tried to find a point of solidity somewhere. The only one which came was—

Honor. Family honor.

Marco had a feeling that if he saw Kat again, family honor might just crumble. But honor demanded that he did see her. Didn't it?

"Milord—three things," he said carefully, choosing his words and somehow managing not to stammer. "The first is—I need to think about this. There's someone—never mind. I'd like to get out of the House for a while."

His mind slipped into a medical track, seeking comfort in the familiar. "For your mother . . . I'll suggest a few things that I know of to Doctor Rigannio. But while he's trying them, it might be a good idea anyway if Milady Rosanna wouldn't be in a position to see me."

Petro nodded. "Certainly. I didn't expect an immediate answer. But please keep in mind . . . Marriage can't wait too long, Marco. Angelina's three months pregnant already. Closer to four months, I suspect. As for the other, a place away from my mother could be arranged—but not back with Aldanto. Did you have anything in mind?"

"Well—my friend, Rafael de Tomaso, was talking about there being a suite of rooms at a boarding house not far from Zianetti's. He was kind of wishing he knew somebody he could trust to split it with him. I *think* he was hinting at me. He's Father Bellini's protégé, in art."

Petro nodded again. "A good choice. I think we can arrange that. What else?"

This was daring, but— "Caesare Aldanto isn't where Milady got her drugs. There isn't much he *hasn't* done, but that's not one of them." He coughed a little, shamed, but offered the confession to balance the secrets he'd stumbled on. "A while back, I think I found out where the introit of lotos shipments was. This was about two months ago. This . . . problem with your mother has been going on for some time longer than that hasn't it? And Caesare Aldanto didn't know about the lotos sales then. So . . . I can't *prove* it, not yet, but—it wasn't him."

"So?" Petro's voice was neutral.

"Before I say anything to Milady Angelina, I want to be able to prove to her that it *wasn't* Caesare. I want everything clean between us."

Dell'este honor.

He sighed. "I want her making her choices without any lies. I messed her up with lies before; I don't want to do it again. If she knows the truth—she might make different choices. And that's her right."

Petro folded his arms across his chest; the sky behind him deepened to blue and the first stars sprinkled across it. "I can respect that," he said, a certain warmth coming into his voice. "I can respect that and I can understand that. Of course as the head of family, I can tell you that Aldanto will never be acceptable to Dorma. And you know that I serve as one of the *Signori di Notte.* Since Lord Calenti's death we know the damned lotos trade has started up again. Even if it was not my mother, I'd want to know. Because it is . . . I want to know badly. Very well—you seek your proofs and I'll see about getting you moved out of Dorma so that you can have your time to think. But please. The wedding has to be soon."

"Thank you, milord," Marco replied quietly and turned to go.

"Marco—"

He stopped and turned back.

He could just see Petro's smile in the blue dusk.

"You are part of our secrets. Therefore, you are part of us. Whatever decision you make regarding a marriage to my sister— welcome to *Casa* Dorma, Marco."

Marco was in a daze after he left *Casa* Dorma. Now that he was no longer in the presence of Petro Dorma, the Head of the House, matters of family responsibility and honor seemed less overwhelming. His personal hopes and desires loomed far larger.

I have to talk to someone!

But who? He considered Benito, but ruled him out almost immediately. His younger brother's advice on this matter would be useless, or even worse.

Rafael, perhaps. Marco needed to speak to him anyway, on the subject of the lodgings.

But, as he made his way through the narrow streets, dark now that evening had fallen, Rafael's advice on the matter seemed less and less attractive. Marco couldn't help but remember that the *last* time he'd taken Rafael's advice on a matter of the heart, the results had been . . . mixed, to say the least. For all of Rafael's self-confidence and ease, the truth was that he was still too young himself to really understand what would be the right course.

Thoughts of Rafael, however, triggered thoughts of Chiano. Or *Dottore* Luciano Marina, as he was now. *Chiano will have good advice.*

Marco didn't know where Chiano lived. But he was sure that Rafael did. The student would be reluctant to tell him, since Marco was not another Strega. But that he would, Marco had no doubt. He would just have to be persuasive.

At the moment, Marco was certain he could persuade a stone to talk. Compared to everything else, persuasion seemed the easiest task in the world.

Chapter 66

This has all been too easy.

Luciano Marina had worked his way back into his old life so smoothly that he was worried. Granted, he had not attempted to reach most of his former adherents among the Strega. Granted also, he had not practiced *any* magic without so many protections that the air was thick with them, literally. *Still.*

He had made some contacts . . . carefully, and a very few. Claudia and Valentina, a pair of Strega entertainers whose eyes and ears were always open and who had, in their turn, contacts everywhere. Itzaak ben Joseph, a Kabbalistic mage and goldsmith, whose clients ranged from the *Casa Vecchie* to a very recent arrival at Casa Louise, who—as Luciano alone knew, thanks to Itzaak—had up to that moment been a popular "entertainer" at the House of the Red Cat. Sister Evangelina and Father Mascoli of the Order of Saint Hypatia, who had always been friendly to the Strega. Father Palladio, who taught anatomy to the students of medicine at the Accademia. He would very much have liked to have more trusted contacts among his fellow Strega. Sadly, though they were well intentioned they were often lamentably loose tongued.

That was probably why poor Despini had been found floating. He had, said old rumor, been alerted to something very evil coming to Venice; he had certainly made the attempt to fill in the gap in Strega leadership that Luciano's own disappearance had left.

But the first rumor—that Despini had learned of something very evil with its eye on the pearl that was Venice . . . *Very evil.* As evil as that which Marina had seen in his vision? If so, that evil had

575

a name, and it was a thing that Luciano was not prepared to confront. Not yet.

The Lion was stirring, true, and no longer in slumber. But neither was it awake yet—and waking it was a major and very dangerous ceremony, which also required the presence of . . . certain persons. Without the Lion, Luciano could do very little against the black evil that threatened Venice.

He shivered. He hated even to think the name of that evil, for fear of attracting *its* attention.

He had not moved back into his former set of rooms in the complex of buildings that loosely comprised the Accademia. For one thing, they were already occupied by someone else; for another, moving back into them would be like issuing a challenge. Instead, Luciano Marina—using his true name, since he saw no reason not to, being as he was assumed to be dead—had taken this little furnished room. Comfortable enough, with the advantage of having a back door even the landlord didn't know about, a door that had been paneled over until Luciano divined its presence and surreptitiously restored it. It let out into a private courtyard, but if Luciano had to escape some night, he wasn't going to be too particular about whose sensibilities he offended at the time. This sort of arrangement of doors and windows being paneled over happened all the time, when men of wealth fell on hard times and had to sell or lease their former manors, which then were carved up into individual dwellings. It had even happened to *Casa Vecchie* families. Even *Casa Longi.*

Poor little Katerina. The fortunes of the Montescues had not prospered in the time he'd been gone, although there was a part of that which could be laid at the old man's door, wasting endless amounts of money on that stupid attempt to destroy *Casa* Valdosta, root and branch.

Old fool.

But Luciano, now huddled over his brazier as the evening mists crept in and the air grew cold and damp, did not have a great deal of time or pity to waste on his former pupil and her family. He was collecting information, and he needed as much of it as he could gather, as fast as he could bring it in.

He had questions, but there was one thing that he had *no* doubt of. The hand of true evil was stretched towards Venice, and it had at least one finger firmly planted within the city.

Finger? Call it a claw, a talon.

Who, for a start. Who was the nun with the dead eyes? If there was a vessel for that talon, it was surely her, but who was she? To what Order did she belong? The Servants of the Trinity? If that was so, then how could such a *creature* have gotten into the ranks of those most fully dedicated to fighting it at all costs? How could they possibly miss the signs of such evil?

What? What was the monster he had seen in the scrying-mirror, the thing that was surely a servant of the Great Evil if not another vessel for it—the monster that was killing in such a horrible manner, the monster that could seemingly reach any-one, anywhere?

Why? What was the ultimate plan here? Luciano was quite certain by now that the Great Evil lurking behind these machinations took the form of the Grand Duke of Lithuania. But *why* was the duke so interested in Venice? At a glance, there seemed no logic to it.

And, a very, very urgent question—*when?* There would be an attack on the city, of that Luciano was now also certain. So—*when?* Who would be the major players?

His vision had shown him some of those players: Lucrezia Brunelli and her brother Ricardo, the nun, another churchman who was certainly wearing the cassock of the Servants of the Trinity. Another question, just how many plots were there building to a climax, and how many of them were interwoven? What he had seen was—he thought—the sources of danger to Venice; which, since these things were of necessity biased towards the attitude of the seeker, meant *Venice as he knew it.* Now, Lucrezia and Ricardo could, together or separately, have plans for Venice involving alli-ances outside the borders of the city-state that would certainly destroy the fabric of the city as he knew it, but did that mean they were allied to the Great Evil? And if they were, did they know it? The Sots—

Well, the Sots and presumably the Knots, fanatical Paulines as they were, would be only too happy to purge the city with fire and the sword of anything that was not of their own rigidly defined Christian path. That would *certainly* destroy Venice, but that did not mean they were allied with the Great Evil.

Ah, but one did not need to be allied with or a part of some-thing to serve it.

What could he do? Well, he could, at the *least,* move to protect a few people, who had no protections of their own. Little Kat, for instance. He had once held that Hypatian medal of hers in his own two hands, and that once was enough for him to invest it with far more power than the mere wardings it contained. Now that he knew the reality of . . . *It* . . . in his city, he could do something specific.

But first, his protections.

He moved his bits of furniture against the wall, picked up the rug—a sadly worn import from Persia—and flipped it over. No one but another mage would ever have guessed what he'd had bonded onto the back of this old rug.

A pentagram within a protective circle, formed of bitumen mixed with blessed salt—courtesy of Sister Evangelina—and the pulverized dust of pearls and gemstones, frankincense, myrrh-gum, ambergris, copal resin, and cinnabar. A coating of artist's varnish sealed it and allowed it to be painted over with the appropriate symbols, then sealed again. Before he went to work, Luciano went over the entire diagram with his nose mere inches from the painted cloth, looking for cracks and flaws. Today there were none; had there been any, he would have immediately repaired them. Never mind that the energies were supposed to be able to flow across any such defects; in these circumstances, he dared not take any chances. Once he was done, he blew out all the lanterns in his room but one, set up his tiny altar in the middle of the pentacle, then blew out that final lamp before feeling his way to the altar.

He lit a single candle on the altar, with a spark of magic.

He cast his circle three times three, with each element—salt for earth, incense for air, a candle-flame for fire, and water. Then he traced it again, three times three, with his ritual white dagger, made, not of human bone as the Paulines claimed, but the leg bone of a fine buck-deer. And again, three times three, with the *black* dagger, carved of obsidian-glass from the heart of a volcano. When he was done, a faintly glowing border followed the outermost line of his circle.

He took up the bowl of water and whispered a blessing over it, then held it up to the east. "Guardian of the spirits of the water, guardian of the creatures of the water, I summon thee from thy dwelling place in the Uttermost East to stand as Watchtower, to witness my rites and guard my work."

As he flicked a single drop of water towards the east, a pillar of blue light sprang up out of nowhere, reaching from floor to ceiling, as if it was some arcane support pillar.

He turned to his right, to the west, and took up the candle. "Guardian of the spirits of fire, guardian of the creatures of fire, I summon thee. . . ."

When his invocations were complete, four tall pillars of light—blue, red, green, and yellow—stood within his glowing circle, which was now a glowing floor-to-ceiling wall stretching in a curve along the curve of the painted circle on the rug. But his protections were not yet complete, for now he would do what no Christian mage ever dared. He would invoke his deity. The Goddess, not the God—he had a sense that the monster he had seen might once have been linked in to some northern deity—Odin, perhaps, or Thor. It might be . . . impolitic . . . to invoke the Lord at the moment. Let Him decide whether or not to act on His own; there was no point in trying to force His hand.

He faced the altar, with the triple-moon sculpture of hammered bronze, and the ancient Cretan axe that was also Her symbol. "Lady of the night, Lady of the moon, you who have been Isis, Astarte, Tiamet, Diana, Artemis, Aphrodite, Rhiannon, Inana, I call and invoke thee to witness my work and guard my rituals—"

He didn't necessarily expect a response; you could invoke all you wanted, but whether or not She chose to bless you with Her presence was up to Her. But this time—

This time, with no warning at all, the inside of his circle was flooded with powerful, silvery light. The Lady of the moon not only approved, but She was minded to take a hand.

Thank you, he whispered, feeling much humbled, and bent over his scrying bowl. He had to find Kat. Then he had to fence her in with a subtle web of power that would cut any thrice-damned Odin-creature to ribbons before it even knew the protections were there.

And then—well, he would see what occurred to him.

He was startled by a knock on the door. He wasn't expecting any visitors at all. But, since the knock had consisted of the special signal he'd told his few confidants to use—two short, two long, three short, one long—he went to the door and opened it immediately.

He was more than startled to see Marco standing there. "How—"

"Rafael told me," said Marco. The boy's face seemed full of suppressed anguish. "Please, Chiano—I *have* to talk to you."

After Luciano heard what Marco had to say, he rubbed his face wearily. "Is happiness so much to ask for?" he murmured.

But he did not dwell on the matter. He had asked the Goddess that question many times, in his life. He would ask it no longer. *No more softness!*

"Marco," he said quietly, "Venice is in the gravest danger. At such a time, you must think of your responsibilities. You don't even know this canaler-girl's surname. You know nothing about her family—or even, to be honest, she herself."

Marco's face was set in a stubborn cast. Luciano sighed. "Speak to the girl if you must, before you make your final decision. But I will tell you this, boy. I can think of nothing you could do which would strengthen Venice more than to weld Valdosta reborn—and Dell'este—to the house of Dorma."

Except a marriage between Valdosta and Montescue, came the whimsical thought. But Marina dismissed the notion as a ridiculous fancy. Lodovico Montescue would disrupt any such wedding by having the groom assassinated as he walked to the altar.

"The Valdosta name, which is still a powerful thing, would give weight to Petro Dorma's position. And, as I'm sure you've come to realize yourself, he's the best of the lot. Potentially, the leadership which Venice will need—does need, already."

Marco hung his head. He was listening, at least. Marina started to add more, but decided not to do so. Anything more, at this point, would be counterproductive. Marco Valdosta had a fierce sense of honor. Give the boy time, and he would make the right decision.

"I've got to talk to Kat," he whispered. When he lifted his head, his eyes were blurred with tears. The sight was heart-breaking.

"Talk to her then," said Luciano. "But please, Marco—remember your responsibilities."

It was time to change the subject. "So. When are you being officially presented to the city?"

Marco smiled wanly. "Tomorrow night, at the Doge's Levee."

"Splendid!"

"I think I'd rather go anywhere else," muttered Marco. "Even the Jesolo."

Chapter 67

Kat was whistling. A terrible un-genteel habit, as Alessandra told her frequently. Right now the thought of that made her want to whistle louder. She wanted to practice being un-genteel. And besides, happiness was bubbling up in her.

Her joy seemed to be affecting everything. The last cargo had come through, perfectly. The Montescue's tiny share as part of a *Colleganza* of a wood shipment to Alexandria had paid off handsomely, the merchant having come up with a return cargo of ivory . . . which had caught the current fashion for marquetry just in the upswing. It had made them a tidy profit. Not enough to tow the *Casa* Montescue out of the river tick but enough to make it seem as if there might—eventually—be a light on the horizon.

And she'd be seeing Marco again on Thursday. She hugged herself. Two days. She should have made it sooner. But, well, she didn't want it to appear too much as if she was chasing him.

Even the thought of tonight's levee at the Doge's palace could not upset her. If Senor Lopez was there and wanted to talk to her . . . well, he had no real evidence. Mind you, even the thought of that eagle gaze was enough to put a damper on her mood. He wasn't the sort who needed "evidence." She shook off the thought and took her mind back to Marco Felluci. It wasn't hard. And the thoughts were pleasant as she waited for Madelena to come down and help her dress for the levee.

A levee at the Doge's palace . . . Marco was so nervous he could hardly think straight. All the *haut monde* of Venice would be there,

Case Vecchie, rising merchant houses, distinguished foreign visitors, ambassadors and nobility. All the power and glitter of Venice. Marco had looked across the piazza past the winged lion of Saint Mark at the colonnaded Gothic palace often. But to be *inside*?!

The inside was a place of confusion, light, and above all, people. Musicians—no mean performers either—played in a side salon. Nobody kept quiet for them, however; people simply continued their light inconsequential chatter and laughter. If anyone had dared treat Valentina and Claudia's music thus! Marco was introduced to yet another *Case Vecchie* family head. He bowed politely for the . . . he'd lost count. No wonder the *Case Vecchie* went slumming at Barducci's.

"Valdosta, eh?" said the florid Count Antonelli. "That's one of the old names we haven't heard for a while. Where have you been, boy?"

"With his grandfather, Duke Dell'este," interposed Petro Dorma smoothly.

The Count nodded. "So, boy—which way is Ferrara leaning? Venice, Milan . . . or Rome?"

Yes, these were worrying times. Ferrara had for the better part of century stood by Venice, but keeping its independence. Then the Venetians had demanded the salt pans, and Ferrara had balked and called on Rome—and even, for a time, threatened alliance with Milan. Who, for its part, had sent no less of a condottiere than Carlo Sforza to pay a friendly visit to Ferrara . . . a visit to which, Marco suspected, he ultimately owed his brother.

It had all blown over, eventually. But . . . by the presence of that sword in the *Casa* Dorma, the storm was brewing again.

Marco was not prepared for the direct question. For the simplest reason: he had no idea what the old duke was planning to do.

"My grandfather keeps his own council, milord."

"Yes, but . . ."

"I see the majordomo is beckoning to us, Count Antonelli," interrupted Petro. "Pardon us. I must find my sister and take my new ward to be presented to the Doge."

Petro steered Marco away across the salon to where Angelina was talking to a tall, beautifully made up woman with a neat little mole above her rosebud mouth, standing in the circle that surrounded Lucrezia Brunelli. They were laughing. The woman gave Marco a very considering look as Petro snagged his sister and led them off to meet Doge Foscari.

Kat was preparing herself for the sheer delight of giving Signor Sergio Della Galbo the finest put-down of his obnoxious life. The fat *curti* had cornered her again. But knowing how her grandfather felt, and having met her soulmate, Katerina Montescue was going to tell this disgusting old roué where to get off. In training for a life as Katerina Felluci she was going to use some choice canaler terms she'd picked up from Maria.

And then her grandfather came storming up, towing Alessandra. His lined face was as pale as his snowy linen. His eyes bulged. Alessandra was looking terrified and wasn't even protesting. "Come," was all the old man said. Very quietly.

Della Galbo protested. "Get lost, worm!" snapped Kat, pushing past him to her grandfather. She slid an arm around the old man. "What is wrong, Grandpapa?" she asked, worried. The last time she seen him like this was when they'd brought the news of Alessandra's baby's death. Normally, if he was angry, the whole countryside knew about it.

"*Valdosta.*" He spat the name out as if it were a curse. "They're *not* all dead, girl. I told you some of the vermin still survived. But I never thought I'd see them here, bold as brass, under the protection of *Casa* Dorma." He pointed.

She was glad she had her arm around the solid if elderly stanchion of her grandfather. Walking, head bent forward in the listening pose she knew so well, had studied so lovingly . . . was Marco Felluci. He was listening to Petro Dorma and that horrible spoiled brat, Angelina Dorma. Marco was not wearing Ventuccio livery, or old canaler clothes. He was dressed in a silk shirt, and fine hose, with a cloak that could have bought Maria's gondola. There was gold on his finger.

"Who—who is *that*?" she asked, in a small wooden voice, feeling stupid, stunned, her world in chaos.

Her grandfather hissed like a leaky kettle. "Calls himself 'Marco Valdosta.' They claim he's been in Ferrara. With the Dell'este. That's another Valdosta lie. I'm quite sure he's the same one I tried to have assassinated here in Venice last year—and failed, I'm sorry to say."

For a moment, Kat thought she might faint.

"Now come," growled Lodovico. "We're going home."

Kat sat on her bed. She had neither the will, nor, it seemed, the ability to do more than stare at the wall. Madelena had fussed her charge into a nightgown. Gently and quietly this once, seeing Katerina behaving like some porcelain doll, obedient but mechanical, and silent.

Even Alessandra coming in to her room didn't excite any reaction. Madelena crossed herself.

Alessandra was big with excitement. "Well! What a scene. I thought the old fool was going to drop dead on us. That Valdosta's not bad looking, is he? Although I prefer more rugged men, myself. Still, that Angelina Dorma seems pleased enough with her catch."

"*WHAT!?*"

Alessandra prattled on. "They say she's getting married to the Valdosta boy. Lucrezia said it has to be pretty soon, because she's already carrying his baby."

The roaring in Katerina's ears refused to be stilled. Even Alessandra noticed. "What's wrong?"

"Nothing." Lead was lighter. "I feel sick."

"Are you pregnant?" said Alessandra, eager for more fuel.

This was enough to penetrate Kat's armor of confusion and misery. "No!" she snapped. "But if I left it to you, half the town would say I was. And I'll bet all this gossip is just as true as my pregnancy."

Alessandra shrugged and turned her shoulder. She sniffed. "And I suppose Grandfather isn't talking about finding a decent assassin to get rid of the brat."

"Be real, Alessandra," said Katerina a terrible sinking feeling in her gut. . . . *He could. He hated the Valdosta name bitterly.* "Like we need to open warfare with Dorma. Or even Duke Dell'este."

Alessandra shrugged an elegant shoulder. "I suggested he hire Aldanto. He could do it quietly."

"Caesare! Ha! He knows Mar . . . Valdosta too well," a curious mix of fear and misery betrayed Kat into speaking before she thought.

Alessandra pounced on her. "And how do *you* know Caesare Aldanto? You keep away from him Katerina." She laughed. A humorless, bitter sound. "He's too strong a meat for *you.*"

Alessandra turned and walked out, with a parting snort.

It took Kat a few minutes of mulling to suddenly wonder. How did her sister-in-law—married at seventeen from a cloistered background into a sheltered and restrictive *Case Vecchie* family—know someone like Caesare Aldanto at all?

Sleep was not going to come tonight. She got up and put on a dressing gown, and went up to her grandfather's study.

He was sitting there staring at his tallies. He wasn't looking, just staring. He didn't even see her come in. She had to put an arm around his shoulder before he noticed her.

He sighed. "Ah Katerina, *cara mia*. I had begun to see some small hope from the *Casa* Montescue. A future for you, a dowry." He sighed again. "Now . . . Valdosta."

She hugged the hunched shoulders. "Grandpapa . . . I know they are our enemy . . . but I've never asked . . . why?"

He snorted. "Never wanted to make me angry by even mentioning the name, is what you mean." He rubbed his face wearily. "The two houses were once allies—even friends. We go back far into the history of the Venice. Luciano—that was Luciano Valdosta—he used to joke that it was a Valdosta and Montescue that witnessed the meeting between Saint Mark and the winged Lion. He said the Montescue was busy stealing Saint Mark's fish and the Valdosta, not to be outdone, was stealing the whole boat . . . Luciano and me. We were like that." The old man twisted his fingers over each other. "People used to say 'Luci and Lodo'—here comes trouble."

Lodovico Montescue sighed. "It wasn't really like that. I used to get us into trouble and Luciano would get us out. He was a good man . . . deep down. Not like his son, Fabio." The old face was contorted into a scowl. "Luciano would have married my sister: your great-aunt Fiorenza. But he got involved with the Montagnards from Milan. He and I had a fight. The first time ever . . . It's a long story. But then he married Viviana. And there was bad blood between us and the two houses didn't speak.

"But I missed him, truth to tell. There wasn't a day when I didn't think I'd been stupid. I even sent a message over once. It came back, torn up. Then, when Luciano was killed in a freak accident over at the boatyard . . . I went to the funeral. To pay my respects to a man I loved. And that little pig Fabio screamed at me and denounced me for killing his father. Right there in the church! He swore revenge. I was angry, true. But—out of respect for the Church and for Luciano—I didn't throttle him right there. I should have. He paid us back with black magic. You can put the death of your mother, your aunt Rosa, your brother, and even my grandson down to him. Even a baby at his door.

"He fled to Ferrara with that silly foreign-born wife of his before I could take action. The *Signori di Notte* and the Doge claimed it was plague, but I didn't believe it for a moment. Then Fabio got himself killed in a fight with some mercenary. But that wife of his continued the vendetta when she came back here, I'm sure of it. Very low she was then, thinking she could get away with her Montagnard activities by pretending to be a mere shopkeeper. She and her Montagnard friends organized against our house. I'm sure they're responsible for your father's disappearance."

Even as angry as Kat was at anything remotely "Valdosta," her grandfather's theories seemed . . . well, insane.

He sighed. Ruffled her hair. "I suppose it all sounds insane. And . . . perhaps it is. At least, that's what—ah, a good friend of mine tells me. She may well be right. But if I've given up the vendetta—not that we could afford one against Dell'este as well as Valdosta anyway—I haven't given up my sentiments. Now, be off to bed, minx."

Kat went. But not to sleep. Before dawn she dressed in her canal-going clothes and hooded cloak and went out.

"I missed you at the levee tonight," yawned Francesca, tying up her robe. As she led Kat into the salon, the courtesan glanced at the window, still covered with curtains. The sun was just beginning to rise and its light, filtered through the expensive cloth, bathed the room in a soft velvety glow. "Or last night, I suppose I should say. I just got home myself, and was about to go to bed."

The courtesan examined Kat's clothing and grinned sleepily. "Congratulations, by the way. How in the world did you manage to talk your way into Casa Louise dressed like *that?*"

Abashed, now that she was actually inside Francesca's apartment, Kat glanced uneasily at the door to Francesca's bedroom. The door was open.

Francesca's grin widened, and became less sleepy. "Relax. I don't usually entertain my clients here any longer. Except Manfred, of course, since I refuse to smuggle myself past that gaggle of knights at the embassy. And . . . one other, who wants to keep our liaison a secret from his closest relative."

Kat tried to find the right words. Then, when she couldn't find any words at all, burst into tears.

Francesca's grin vanished. "Come, come, little one," she crooned, folding Kat into an embrace the way a mother or a big sister might, "it can't be *that* bad."

"*Yes it can!*" wailed Kat. And proceeded, in the ensuing time of babbled words, to prove her point. Or try to, at least.

By the time she was done, Francesca was standing at the window, looking at the canal below through a curtain she had drawn partly aside with a finger.

"You could probably nip it in the bud, you know," the courtesan mused. "This budding marriage between *Casa* Dorma and *Casa* Valdosta, I mean."

She removed her finger, allowing the curtain to sway back into place, and cocked her head toward Kat. "I heard the rumors myself, last night. A marriage of convenience, driven partly by politics and partly by the crude fact that Angelina Dorma is pregnant. Nothing more than that."

"Nothing *more!*?" choked Kat. "It's still a *marriage*, Francesca! And—" She choked again. Then, in a whisper: "Pregnant? By Marco?"

Francesca shrugged. "That seems to be the assumption. Myself, I wouldn't—"

"That bastard!" shrilled Kat. "That—"

"*Katerina!*"

The sharpness in Francesca's tone jolted her. "Yes?"

The courtesan was frowning. "Before you get *too* carried away with your own self-righteousness . . . A question: Did *you* ever tell this young man exactly who *you* were?"

Kat's face closed down. "No."

"Why not?"

After a moment, between tight lips: "Because."

Francesca chuckled dryly. "Ah, right. '*Because.*' Oh, you Venetian *Case Vecchie*! How quick you are to condemn others for your own sins."

Kat couldn't meet that sarcastic gaze. "My grandfather . . ." she whispered, trying to summon up a protest.

" 'Your grandfather,' " mimicked Francesca. "And you think Marco Valdosta isn't *also* thinking of a grandfather? A grandfather in a desperate position of his own, you know. Which an alliance with *Casa* Dorma in Venice would go a long way toward improving."

But Kat was in no mood to be calm and objective, much less charitable. "It's because she's pregnant," she hissed. "That *bastard*. Telling me—while he was—with her—"

"Go home, Kat," said Francesca wearily. "I'm tired, and you are obviously not willing to *think*. If you were, you might realize—"

"I'm not listening to any more!" snapped Kat, jumping to her feet. "I *hate* him!" She rushed for the entrance.

"Don't slam the door on your—"

Kat slammed the door on the way out.

Ugo Boldoni's poor little church was thinly attended for Lauds. It was not hard for him to spot an extra person in a hooded cloak, who waited until his early morning parishioners had left. He went back into the church where Katerina was waiting.

"And now, Katerina?" he asked the white-faced young woman who was standing chewing her lip, looking at the ground.

Katerina half-mumbled the next words. "Ugo, you're the only priest that I've known since we were both children . . . I need to find something out. I need to find out if someone is getting married."

Father Boldoni shrugged. "The banns will be read."

Kat shook her head. "I need to know now. I need to know . . . is . . . Marco Valdosta marrying Angelina Dorma?

"Not in my parish."

"Oh." Kat took another deep breath. "Well, can you find out for me? Please. I need to know *now*. Please."

Ugo took pity on her. "As it happens, I was at the palace of the Metropolitan only yesterday. Having a meeting about witchcraft— with Senor Eneko Lopez, as it happens, that Basque priest who seems to terrify everyone." He chuckled dryly. "I'll admit he some-how manages to be, simultaneously, one of the most frightening and inspiring men I've ever met. In the course of it, Lord Petro Dorma did come in to make some enquiries about the marriage of his sister. Soon."

"To . . . whom? And . . . and they're getting married in a hurry? W-why?" she faltered.

Ugo shrugged again. "I am the priest of a poor parish. They didn't confide in me. But I imagine for the usual reasons, Katerina. Is she a friend of yours?" Then the thought struck him. "Or—is he? I thought the Valdosta name was bad word with the *Casa* Montescue."

"I *hate* both of them," said Kat between clenched teeth and stormed out, not even genuflecting to the altar as she left.

Before Kat went back to her bed there was one last job to do. She stopped at Giaccomo's and left a brief note, before going home. Her chin was held high.

Chapter 68

Marco sat, patiently. Well, impatiently. Kat had always been on time. Unlike Angelina. He'd only been a couple of weeks in *Casa* Dorma, and her attitude to time was already grating him. Almost everything was held up slightly for Angelina. She'd be late for her own funeral. Kat—he got the feeling—wouldn't ever be late without reason.

So Marco sat and sipped his wine, making it last.

And Kat just never showed. He waited. He *had* to talk to her. Petro was doing his best not to be impatient, but well, the days of Angelina's pregnancy were ticking past. You could claim a six-month child but not less than that.

It was quarter to twelve, and Marco was about to abandon hope, when Maria came in. Marco had "dressed down" for the occasion but still his appearance caused Maria to snort—half derision, half admiration. "Mighty smart. Mighty fine," she said dryly. "Where's the young girl sitting on your knee, Marco Valdosta?"

Marco blushed. "I was waiting for Kat. But not to sit down on my knee. I . . . I have to talk to her."

Maria smiled. "Well, she sent you a note. Which is why I'm here instead of in my bed. See. Them—those—reading lessons are paying off. I can manage your name at least. I just picked it up at Giaccomo's. Figured you'd be here tonight."

Of course. He'd known he could rely on Kat. And to send him a note to explain was just like her. A world apart from Angelina. Angelina only seemed good at thinking of herself. No worries about that with Kat.

❀　　❀　　❀

590

Maria could see worries were weighing on the boy. But he lightened up with that scroll . . . Kat was good for him. And they were both *Case Vecchie* now. Funny, it did far more than a year's living with Caesare had done to convince Maria that nobles were just human too. Because, if she had it right, Marco's blood ought to be blue. She'd seen it. It was definitely just ordinary red. Maria watched as Marco cracked the wafer. Unrolled the scroll.

And she watched his face change . . . Marco had a very open face. First surprise. Then hurt. And then his face closed down. He rolled the scroll up again and stood up.

"I'm probably getting married in the next few days," he said abruptly.

Maria felt as if her eyes would pop out. "What! To Kat?"

"To Angelina Dorma." His voice was expressionless.

Maria floundered. "But . . . but . . ." *Those Dorma bastards wanted to lock him in! Well, she owed Kat.* "That's far too soon, Marco," she said, firmly. Her mind raced. *She'd have to get Benito in on this. The damn scamp didn't approve of Kat, for some stupid reason. But anything—anything!—was better than Angelina. Even if she had to tell Benito that Kat was also* Case Vecchie. *He'd been pestering her to reveal the identity of her posh friend. . . .*

"I can't. She's nearly four months pregnant," said Marco, woodenly.

Maria caught her jaw. "Ah . . . who's the father?" she croaked.

Marco paused. Looked her straight in the eye. "I am," he said in a dead level voice.

And he turned and walked out.

Petro Dorma looked grim. "I'm sorry, Marco. Only the *Signori di Notte* knew, until an hour before. That means somehow someone must have bought one of them. But the Badoero were gone."

Marco felt flattened. Caesare's ploy hadn't worked. Caesare had been sure if Petro could arrest the Badoero they'd confess, quickly enough to tell just whom the real go-between was. He had ascribed Angelina's accusation to spite.

"Of course Paulo knew the way here. He was Ernesto Dorma's confidential runner. I did some business with Ernesto. Commercial information. Valuable if not glamorous. And for heaven's sake, yes. Marry Angelina Dorma," he'd said. His words were fresh in Marco's mind.

Petro sighed. "Well, we're no closer, Marco. We still don't know how my mother got the stuff—even if we know where she used to. You don't feel you could just . . ."

"Marry Angelina now," said Marco quietly. "Yes."

Petro breathed a sigh of relief. "Well. Thank you, Marco. I can't deny I am pleased. . . . She always was father's favorite. We lost my other sister in the plague . . . And 'Gelina got . . . rather spoiled by Mother too after that. She's used to getting her own way. But, well, she'll be handsomely dowered. And we'll be happy to have you as part of the family."

He smiled. "Dorma is not as old as Valdosta, but we're prosperous. And, well, I predict that the Republic is going to have a rough time in the next few years. The Doge is old, the succession is not as clear cut as Ricardo Brunelli imagines it is." He patted Marco on the shoulder. "I trust you, Marco. I trust that Dell'este honor. I trust the name 'Valdosta' too. It was a proud one in my father's time. I'd rather have it with Dorma than against us, and many of the *longi Case Vecchie* will rally to it."

Marco had never thought of his name as a political point. "Never rich though," he said quietly.

"Oh, not lately. But the family used to work with another *Casa*—the Montescue—in my grandfather's time. Organizing *Colleganzas*. I can still remember my grandfather cursing them and saying it seemed like they could do nothing wrong. Like the shadow of the Lion was on them. Anyway, to practical details. I've spoken to the Metropolitan. He has agreed to let pass with just one reading of the banns. The wedding itself . . . will be something of a political affair, Marco. I want it clear in a lot of minds that the Valdosta are under the protection of the *Casa* Dorma. So the guest list will not be friends. In fact, some of them may have had a hand in your mother's death."

He paused, took a turn around the table. Took a deep breath. "Your sudden 'reappearance' has started just a little buzz about 'witchcraft.' I need to squash that. Would you be prepared to take a test of faith from Father Sachs of the Servants of the Holy Trinity before the service?"

Marco nodded. He was, after all, no heretic, and knew no reason to fear . . . except knowing that Sophia and Luciano used Strega magic in their healing and that some of the herbs he'd dealt in were "blessed." Even the frightening Pauline monks could find no real stain on his soul, surely? Like this wedding, it was nothing to be afraid of.

Dorma studied him for a moment. "The sooner we can do this wedding the better, Marco. I've already quietly cleared the way. If you are certain . . ."

Marco shrugged. He could hear a little voice somewhere inside shrieking at him—*too fast! too fast! you haven't even talked to Kat!*—but he ignored it resolutely. Kat's letter had been . . . harsh and angry.

"Yes, I'm certain." His voice sounded hollow. "Do it tomorrow, if you wish."

Again, Dorma heaved a sigh of relief. Then, shook his head and smiled. "That'd be a bit rushed, Marco. How about the day after tomorrow?"

When Marco nodded his head, even his head felt hollow.

"You seen Kat?"

Benito knew Maria's work patterns well enough to know she'd deliberately waited around to speak to him this morning. He shook his head. "Not in a while. Since that night at Zianetti's. She keeps herself to herself, does that Kat."

Maria sighed. "I need to talk to her. Even if Caesare says to leave her alone."

Curiosity and protective instinct rose in Benito. He'd promised Caesare . . . "What about?"

"Nothing to do with you," Maria snapped. She paused, looking uncomfortable. "Well, I guess he *is* your brother."

Benito had it now. "Marco's getting married has nothing to do with Kat, Maria. It's . . . it's *Case Vecchie* stuff. They don't marry for love. It's all for politics and money. Caesare explained. Kat's . . . she's trouble. A canal girl. Marco can't . . . He doesn't have that choice. And . . . Oh hell. Don't cry, Maria."

Maria sniffed determinedly. "You don't know everything, Benito Valdosta. More like, you know very little."

Benito handed over an embroidered handkerchief that had belonged to a *Case Vecchie* lady only yesterday. You had to keep your hand in even if you weren't going to make a regular thing of the snatch. He offered a cautious pat, and was rewarded by a roundhouse swing. She was feeling better. "*Si.* I don't like it much either, Maria. But Dorma will look after Marco. And I don't know where to look for Kat."

Maria shook her head. "I've been to her house. Twice. The first time I left a note under the water-door."

Benito cleared his throat, unsure what to say. He'd been helping her with her reading and writing now that Marco had moved out. Maria wasn't stupid. But like most women—except courtesans—she was illiterate. She could tally like anything. But her writing was still limited to her name and a few words.

"I kept it simple," she snapped. "But she didn't come, so I went around. The old man said she wasn't there. I was kind of hoping you'd seen her. Or might know where else to look. I've *got* to talk to her before Marco goes off—idiot!—and gets married."

Benito shook his head. "I'll keep an eye out for her. But it's too late, Maria. It's as good as done. I wondered if I should have gone, but Marco said 'stay away.' He's having the test of faith before the wedding tomorrow—an' he didn't want me around. Besides . . . he said it wasn't like it was going to be a real marriage or anything."

Maria looked stormy. "You should have stopped him, Benito! *You* could have stopped him."

Benito felt uncomfortable. That had been his first, irrational reaction. But he'd talked it over with Caesare . . . "You don't understand."

Maria lifted her square chin. "I do understand, Benito Valdosta. Maybe *you* will one day."

She turned and left, slamming the door behind her.

Caesare, when he came down a few minutes later, was in a far better mood. "I had word last night that the job you pulled for me getting that door open over at the Accademia has paid off handsomely. First time I've ever been paid by two separate parties for the same job. You'll need to do a spot of running for me this evening. I can't really go to either place. But there'll be a bit of coin in it for you, Benito."

Benito grinned. "That was a piece of cake. Cloister doorlocks aren't much."

Caesare shook his head. "Forget you were ever there. Don't make a noise about how you got that coin, when you spend it."

Benito nodded. "Actually, I'm not going to spend it. I'm going to invest it."

This brought a snort of amusement from Caesare. "Spoken like a true Veneze. And what great venture are you becoming an investor in? Second-hand scarf business?"

"Nah," said Benito. "A couple of us over at Ventuccio . . . we wanted to get in with a *Colleganza* for the galley convoy. We've got an insider hot tip. Silver is right up in Outremer right now. We can make a killing. You want in, milord?"

Caesare laughed. "A killing! No, boy. I don't think I'll put money on that convoy."

"It's a great-galley convoy! Safe as houses. Come on, Caesare. You've got real money. We 'uns'll get a tiny share."

That hooded look came over Caesare. "No."

Uncomfortable now, Benito decided to change the subject. "I've been thinking," he said, looking at the stack of three bright ducats on the table, his reward for the two collection runs well done. "I should put two o' these into the housekeeping." Maria managed the finances of the house. And Benito had heard her swearing about them enough lately.

Caesare shook his head, and pushed the ducats toward him. "Put them in your pocket. You just keep your mouth shut about this windfall, Benito. You don't even tell Maria. I'll sort out housekeeping."

Benito nodded. Still, it was enough to get him thinking about his two shadowy pickups. Both in the same part of town. And both, unless one of Caesare's male clients had an odd taste in scent, female. One had been using a nun's habit for disguise. He totally failed to see the other. But he'd smelt her.

Chapter 69

"I'm terrified of weddings, Erik," said Manfred grumpily. "You catch deadly diseases at them. And with Sachs there, I won't be able to do the good part . . . you know. Get drunk afterwards."

Erik snorted. He had to wear full armor for the occasion again. That worried him more than a mere wedding ceremony. "What deadly disease?"

"Matrimony. You can die of boredom, I've been told."

Erik snorted again. "I am going to save that up and tell your wife. And then you are going to be in trouble. Deep trouble. Manfred, he asked for us specifically. It is that Venetian grandee, Dorma, whom we helped with the Dandelos. His sister is getting married. It's a compliment. Sachs is delighted."

Manfred traced the outline of the caryatid on Erik's bedpost. "So we're going. Erik, I sent a private message off to my uncle yesterday. I asked Von Stemitz to take it with him on his trip to Mainz. Whatever Sachs and the knight-bishops are doing keeping the Knights of the Trinity in Venice . . . it isn't in the Emperor's interest. The last thing Charles Fredrik wants is to be involved in a civil war down here in Italy, no matter what these Montagnard-Pauline fanatics think about one Holy Roman Emperor over all the Christian world. We have the Aquitaines on our western flank, the damned Grand Duke of Lithuania on our northeastern flank and the King of Hungary on the southeastern—with both of them creeping down into the Black Sea. We need trouble to the south in Italy like we need a hole in the head. He should know about the situation here."

Erik nodded, hiding a grin. Francesca's influence was considerable. She plainly enjoyed this game of politics, and Manfred, too lazy and too obstinate to do it when driven, was letting his private parts lead him into this. Perhaps Charles Fredrik should hire her as an instructor of heirs. "Yes. The Knights are supposed to be independent soldiers of Christ, defenders of Christendom. But they're perceived by many—most, probably—to be the arm militant of the Empire, not the Church. And I get the feeling that the reality is the other way around. They're trying to use the Empire as the political arm of their faction of the Church. Some of the leaders of the Knights, anyway—along with the Servants, I don't doubt."

Manfred nodded in turn. "Power games. Charles Fredrik needs to rein them in."

Erik could almost see him taking it down in his mind. He'd bet he'd repeat it to Francesca within the next few days. Erik sighed quietly. It was all very well Erik's father telling him to stay out of politics. "Your loyalty is to the *Godar* Hohenstauffen, boy. Let them enjoy their wrangles." If Manfred was going to survive, he had to understand these wrangles, as much as he had to understand swordplay.

"So." Erik poked him in the ribs. "What are you lolling around for? We have to be at the church for the test of faith before this wedding. We've got barely an hour before Abbot Sachs is going to be squalling for his escort."

Manfred stood up. "Easy on those ribs. Between you and the hammering they take from Giuliano at the *salle d'armes* of his, I'm too tender for Francesca to appreciate me."

Erik began hauling out the quilted underclothes for their armor. Well suited to armor; ill suited to Venetian summer. "And we're no closer to finding out whether he had anything to do with killing Father Belgio yet," he grumbled. More brightly: "But my rapier-work is coming on."

"Yes, Giuliano said you were better than a blind drunken cow with a rapier handle up its butt . . . but only just." Manfred retreated, grinning, out of the door, bellowing for Erik's squire-orderly as he went.

He left Erik to his preparations and reflections. Giuliano insulted them both copiously. But he had rapidly moved them under his own, personal tuition. Very few attained that. And while Manfred's weapons of choice would always be dictated by his strength, they were both picking up techniques . . . techniques that could kill armored, broad-sword-wielding knights. Lessons that should be part of their armory of skills. It was high time the Knights of the Holy Trinity stopped playing religious politics and moved into the real world.

Politics and religion. Marco looked at the assembled people in the chapel. They were a cross section of the powers of Venice, not "wedding-guests" in the normal sense of the term. Everyone who was anyone was there. The Doge had graced the occasion with his elderly presence. Ricardo Brunelli and his legendarily beautiful sister Lucrezia were there too. The head of the Ventuccio—who looked at Marco as if he'd never seen him before. Other *Case Vecchie* he'd really never seen before, making their appearance, coming to examine the Valdosta.

And plenty of non-Venetian folk, too:

The peacocky condottiere Aldo Frescata. The head of the Milanese "trade delegation," Francesco Aleri. Marco looked him over very, very carefully. Yes. He was the man they'd seen at the mouth of the alleyway. The man Maria said had taken her prisoner, who was in cahoots with the *Casa* Dandelo. Who was probably the director of the Montagnard spies and assassins. Maybe even the man who'd had Mama killed. They greeted each other with urbane politeness and every appearance of disinterest. It left him feeling a bit sick and unconsciously putting his hand onto the hilt of his rapier.

Petro Dorma was making sure that the whole of the power of Venice—of the entire region—saw Marco, knew that he had the Doge's blessing, and also that he had passed this test of faith. The Servants of the Holy Trinity, too, were glorying in this display of power. A nun and several gray-clad monks were doing the slow rounds, sprinkling holy water, chanting psalms. The air was heavy with holy incense. Bishop Capuletti, resplendent in his robes, there to conduct the wedding ceremony later, looked faintly put-out.

Then the bells began their solemn tolling. And the chapel was hushed. In the front of the chapel the abbot had the chalice, the bread, sword and bible arrayed. Obedient to the nudge from Petro, Marco walked forward. The monks began their chanting plainsong. Both fear and misery suddenly knotted his stomach. By the poisonous look that the abbot had given him, he clearly thought

Marco ought to fail. And even if he didn't . . . he was going to be married to Angelina. He should make best of it.

Oh Kat—

If he even began to know where to find her . . . He'd spent the morning in futile wandering. Asking around. Being treated with *Case Vecchie* respect. He'd spotted Harrow in the distance, but even attempting to reach him to ask him had failed.

Too late now. He bit his lip and walked up and knelt before the altar.

Petro Dorma breathed a sigh of relief. He was fond of Angelina. But he was no fool. She was trouble. The last thing he'd ever expected was for her to catch someone who would be of value to Dorma. A nobleman short of money, perhaps. Almost certainly someone who would be a liability to Dorma—like Caesare Aldanto. Marco Valdosta was an innocent, and in some ways Petro felt almost guilty about catching him this way. But he had to look after Angelina. The boy had no idea just how much the name "Valdosta" counted for among the older *Case Vecchie.*

And among the populace, perhaps even more so. The Valdosta Family was *old*. True, Marco's father had been a wild young man, who married an out-of-town Ferrarese woman too involved in politics for her own good. But Luciano, the paternal grandfather, had been enormously popular. And the Dell'este connection . . .

The Old Fox might be in trouble right now, with Venice, Rome, and Milan all wanting his steel works. But he was a cunning old man. Ferrara might just hold its own. The Republic's Council of Ten, as Petro had reason to know, were warming again towards their one-time ally. Alliances changed. And the Old Fox knew that Dorma's shipyards needed good steel. And the Dell'este could use an accommodation with the Republic to ship to the east again. If Ferrara survived the gathering condottieri and internal factions, well, then Marco would be rich and powerful. Even if the boy were not old *Case Vecchie*, Dorma would have welcomed the alliance. Petro just hoped Angelina wouldn't drive Marco mad with indiscreet, expensive-to-hush affairs.

Petro sighed again. His duty as her brother would be to help out. He settled back in the pew and watched the ceremony. Unlike Marco, he had no qualms about the test of faith. The boy's goodness was patently obvious. He'd bet the lad had not a hint of a stain on his soul. Unlike himself. When it was over he got up and went to collect Angelina.

To his relief and amazement, she was ready.

Marco knew his normally excellent memory was . . . having trouble. He was . . . married? Standing accepting congratulations from the Powers-that-be . . . from Lucrezia Brunelli herself. "My, but Angelina caught herself a handsome one," cooed the legendary beauty, taking his hands in hers. She tickled his palm with one of her fingers. "You look . . . almost familiar. Have I met you before?"

Marco swallowed. Not all the lessons in etiquette had taught him how to deal with this. *Yeah, I met you on the back stairs of Casa Brunelli, with you in a fury because you'd failed to seduce Senor Lopez. . . .*

Was not the right thing to say. "No, m'lady."

She laughed. "Come now, Marco! We're going to be . . . *friends,* aren't we? Call me Lucrezia." Then she continued—in an entirely different tone. "Well, I wish you a happy married life. You and *dear* Angelina."

Bishop Capuletti, who had just approached them, looked like he might consider making that a very short life, if he had the opportunity.

PART VI
June, 1538 A.D.

Chapter 70

It was about a month after the wedding before Maria finally got a chance to see Kat.

The Arsenal was working flat out. It was always like that, anyway, this time of year. The convoy for the Golden Horn would leave in a week and the last-minute outfitting was still going on. Now, with a war looming, there was additional work getting the navy's galleys ready.

A couple of cousins waved to Maria as she rowed in with the load of brass nails from Seino's. "Maria, we need a piece of *trompe l'oiel* work for the admiral's cabin fetched from the Botega Giorgione," said the foreman, when she'd off-loaded. He pulled a sour face. "The admiral sent it back because of the cherubs. So they've held it back to the last minute. They're not punishing Admiral Niccolo. They're punishing us. But do you think they can see that?"

Great. That meant into town. Again. Well, she'd see if she could fit a trip to Giaccomo's into her rounds. They said trade was tight in Venice lately, because of the political situation, and you could see signs of it. But not right now. She felt she was being run off her feet, or more like rowed off her shoulders. "Consider it done, Paulo."

He patted her shoulder. "We trust you, Garavelli."

Yeah. They trusted her. The boatyard work was reliable, but for real money she still relied on Giaccomo. And the trouble with the squeeze on trade on the Po, the Vinland trade, and Genoa trying to muscle Venice . . . everyone was poorer and everything was more expensive. Which didn't worry those who had a lot coming in.

The trouble was—since she'd been living with Caesare, she'd gotten used to those little luxuries, like sleeping warm and dry. But they seemed so short of money, especially with Marco not putting in anymore. Caesare seemed really tight.

She was in a brown study about it as she sculled along to Giaccomo's. It took her a good moment to realize the *"Psst!"* from the gondola resting against the poles was addressed at her. It was Kat. She looked drawn and miserable.

"Been lookin' for you for days," said Maria.

"I went to the mainland," Kat replied dully. "We still own a small farm there. It's mortgaged to the hilt, so we can't sell it. And then Giuseppe didn't give me your note until Madelena decided it might stop me . . ."

"Crying into your breakfast," finished Maria. Kat didn't look like she'd eaten or slept much in the last ten days.

Kat nodded.

Maria snorted. "She must have been pretty desperate."

Kat shrugged. "She always told me men were like that. I didn't believe her."

There was a time for sympathy. There was also a time for no mercy. This, decided Maria, was the latter. "Like what?"

"False!" spat Kat. "Cheating, lying, and false. Making up to . . . becoming *engaged* to someone when they say they're not even involved with anyone. Not even seeing anyone."

Maria shook her head. "I don't know what maggot you've got in your head. The only other woman young Marco has 'seen' in the last three months is me. Unless you are talking about women he passed in the street! And he hasn't 'made up' to me. That's for damned sure."

"So how come he suddenly *married* Angelina Dorma?" demanded Kat savagely. "Just suddenly, huh?"

Maria shrugged. "Because she's *more* than three months pregnant."

Kat stood there gawping like a carp, abruptly out of water. Eventually she managed a small "oh."

"Yes. 'Oh.' Marco is so 'good' it almost shines out of him. He's done this because he felt it was the right thing to do. I wanted you to help me to talk him out of it. That's why I tried so hard to get hold of you. He doesn't love her, and never did. He had a 'she's a gorgeous *Case Vecchie* girl' crush on her. She didn't even know *he* was *Case Vecchie*. She's a tramp. But . . . well, it's too late now."

"Are you sure . . . about it all . . . about the baby?"

Maria nodded. "He's a terrible liar. He might lie to save someone else pain, but not himself. And he told me straight out. I'm sorry, Kat."

Now it was time for comforting. Maria hitched the gondola, and climbed over and held Kat for some time. The chiming of bells suddenly started Maria back into a realization of her duties.

"Hell. I've got to move. I'm supposed to have that picture back there for them as soon as possible! Look, you must go and see Benito. Talk to him. Confirm what I said. You can find him outside Ventuccio's just after lunch. I've got to go."

Lunchtime for runners saw Benito draped in his usual spot over the lower railing of the Ventuccio stairs, absorbing lunch and sunlight at the same time. He was blind and deaf to the traffic into Ventuccio behind him, intent as he was on his study of the canal below, until an elegantly-booted foot nudged his leg.

"Hey, kid," drawled a smooth voice, rich with amusement. "How's the trade?"

Benito looked up sharply from his afternoon perusal of the traffic and stared, his mouth full of bread. He *knew* that voice!

Wiry and thin, dark hair falling in a mass of curls to below his shoulders, Mercutio Laivetti leaned elegantly on the walkway rail beside him, grinning, looking very like a younger, darker, shorter version of Caesare Aldanto. Benito took in the slightly exotic cut of his clothing, the well-worn hilt of his rapier, the sun-darkened state of his complexion at a glance, before bursting out with his reply.

"Mercutio!" he exclaimed, scrabbling to his feet, and throwing his arms around the older boy—boy still, for Mercutio was only a year or two older than his brother, Marco. "Where've you *been*? I was thinkin' the Dandelos got you!"

Mercutio laughed and ruffled Benito's hair, but did not attempt to extract himself from the younger boy's embrace. "Had to make a trip to the East, kid—for my health." Benito let him go and backed up a step, looking up at him in perplexity. Mercutio tapped

Benito's nose with a playful fingertip. "Not to make a story out of it, laddie, but my dear father turned me in to the Schiopettieri. Hopped a ship one step ahead of 'em, and worked my way to Turkey and back. Didn't have much time for goodbyes."

Benito grinned in delight. "Truth."

Mercutio turned his expression to one of unwonted seriousness, and placed his hand solemnly on his satin-covered chest in the general vicinity of his heart. "Truth." Then he dropped the pose, put his arm around Benito's shoulders, and returned the boy's embrace. "So what you been up to, kid? Still roofwalking?"

Benito grinned. "Some. Mostly been running. Do an odd job for Claudia and Valentina, for—'nother fellow. Out-of-towner. Landsman but a good fellow. Some for a canaler too, but that's been a special—"

He broke off, not wanting to talk about Maria to Mercutio, for some odd reason. He finished a bit lamely: "I've been helping, like. Mostly running for Ventuccio these days."

"Ventuccio?" Mercutio pursed his lips in surprise. The sun struck red lights from his hair, green sparks from his hazel eyes. "Come up in the world, have we?"

Benito flushed with pleasure. "Hey, ain't no big thing. And it's mostly on account of that fellow, the one I do a bit of odd work for. *He* got me the job. I been staying with him."

Mercutio grew silent, a silence punctuated by the distant clamor of voices on the canal below, the splashing of poles, the regular spat of wavelets on Ventuccio foundations. "Benito—" Mercutio's expression darkened, and his grip on Benito's shoulders tightened. "Benito, this feller—he isn't messing with you, is he?"

Benito's open-mouthed shock seemed to reassure the older boy, even before he spluttered out his reply. "*Him?* Hell no, not in a million years! He likes *girls.* Got him one, too. 'Member Maria Garavelli?"

Mercutio's eyebrows rose, and his tense expression relaxed. "Milady Hellcat herself? An *out-of-town landsman*? Lord and Saints, I don't know whether to congratulate the man, or pity him! Who *is* this paragon?"

"Name of Aldanto," Benito replied. "Caesare Aldanto."

"That's not a name I know." The questions in Mercutio's eyes gave Benito momentary qualms, and he belatedly began to pick his words with care.

"Aristo, Capuletti bastard, half German," Benito said, sticking to the "official" story. "They pay him to keep himself quiet and do a job or two for 'em."

"To *not* make an embarrassment of himself, and to do what Milord Capuletti doesn't want to dirty his fingers with, hmm?" Mercutio mused. "I can see where a smart kid like you could be useful to him. Is he treating you all right?"

Benito nodded vigorously. "As good as you. 'Cept he tries to keep me *outa* trouble."

Mercutio laughed. "Then *I've* got no quarrel with him. And how are my old pair of nemeses, Miladies Valentina and Claudia?"

Benito hid another grin. Claudia did not approve of Mercutio Laivetti, and Valentina approved of him even less. *She* considered *him* far too reckless, far too careless; which, to Benito, seemed rather a case of pot calling kettle. She hadn't liked it when Benito had taken to hanging around with the older boy—she'd liked it even less when Mercutio had included him in on some of his escapades.

But Mercutio was something special—a kind of substitute brother; while Benito's brother was out of reach in the Jesolo, he'd given Benito someone to tag after, look up to, try to imitate. He'd initiated Benito into the no-longer-quite-so-mysterious ways of Girls—or rather, Women—just prior to his disappearance. And he'd been something of a protector when there was trouble and Claudia wasn't around.

Truth to be told, Mercutio was a great deal that Marco was *not*. He took risks Marco would not even have thought of, and took them laughingly. Marco was so serious—and Benito grew tired of seriousness, now and again.

It was Mercutio's easy, careless good humor that attracted Benito the most. Mercutio could always find something to laugh at, even when the job went wrong. Mostly, though, nothing went wrong in Mercutio's hands, and he did everything with a flair and style that Benito could only envy.

"Claudia's okay—but ye'll never guess who Valentina's playin' footsie with," Benito replied, smirking.

"Ricardo Brunelli?" Mercutio laughed.

"Less likely'n that."

"Less likely—the only man less likely would be a Schiopettieri—" He stopped dead at Benito's widening grin. "You *can't* be serious!"

"Dead serious."

"Dip me in batter and call me fried fish! If Valentina's a-bedding with a Schiopettieri, can Judgment Day be far behind?" Mercutio's eyes were wide and gleeful. "I can see I've been missing *far* more than I dreamed!" He let Benito go, and regarded him with a lifted eyebrow and a grin that practically sparkled. "I can see that getting caught up is going to cost me at least the price of a dinner. So tell me, my young wage earner—when do your employers release you for the day?"

Chapter 71

The girl approaching the bench of Ventuccio runners was an enigma. She was definitely money. Her hair and clothes said that. If she hadn't been here, in the working part of the Ventuccio warehouse, Benito would have said she was *Case Vecchie*. There was something vaguely familiar about her. Benito chewed his thumbnail and wondered what brought her to Ventuccio.

She walked up to Ambrosino Ventuccio's desk like she owned him, the desk, and all of Ventuccio, and didn't need to flaunt the fact. The saturnine Ventuccio cousin sat up sharp when he saw her, and put what he was doing aside. She spoke quietly to him for a moment, too quietly for Benito to hear what she was saying, although he strained his ears unashamedly. But then she turned away from Ambrosino towards the bench and crooked her finger, beckoning. Beckoning *Benito*.

He jumped up and bounced over to her. Ambrosino Ventuccio looked him up and down, speculation in his no-color eyes, then cleared his throat. "Milady Montescue needs a runner—for something special," he said, slowly. "She wants somebody as knows where Marco Felluci went. I told her that he's not here any more, that he got proper leave to go, so he's not in any trouble with us. Then she wanted to speak to you, about him."

"Yes, milady," Benito said quickly. "Milady, I—" He gulped. He recognized the hairdo now. This was the woman who had brought Maria home. She smiled at him. His mouth must have fallen open in response. Only one person had that wide a smile . . . And standing as she was, only he could see her put a finger to her lips.

Digesting this one was going to take more than a few seconds. He wasn't quite sure what to say about Marco, and looked at Ambrosino for some clue. It was no *secret*—at least, he'd not been told it was—that Marco Valdosta was now openly under Dorma protection and sponsorship. But it wasn't something that too many people knew yet, either, outside the *Case Vecchie* circles. Ambrosino knew, but that didn't mean he wanted the other runners to know.

"Why don't you and the milady take a walk, kid," Ambrosino said. "Make this the last run of the day. The Montescue are still a great house."

Lord and Saints—*That* "Montescue?" The ones that owned the huge palace and shipyard down on the landward side of Cannaregio? It wasn't in the best of repair maybe, but still. They were *Case Vecchie. Case Vecchie longi!*

"—and it can't hurt to tell her what she wants to know."

"Yes, milord." Benito replied faintly. "Milady?"

She led him out, into the late-afternoon bustle and clamor on the shadowed walkway, maintaining a strained and complete silence. They moved with the flow of the crowd all the way down to the bridge, without her saying a word.

Finally, she stopped in the little alcove where the bridge met the walkway, a nook built in the side of the building so that people with long burdens to maneuver off the bridge onto the walkway could do so. She finally faced him there, and cleared her throat awkwardly. "Maria said I must talk to you."

Benito shook his head, still unbelieving. "Kat . . . *Montescue?*"

She grimaced. "Katerina Montescue, when I'm wearing these clothes. Kat the Spook when I'm . . . like you know me."

Benito swallowed. "But why? How . . ."

She shrugged. "Some things family have to do. And the Montescue are . . . few. There is nobody else. And I grew up playing around the boatyard. Playing in the boats. My mama wasn't *Case Vecchie.* The Negri aren't even *curti.* They're new money. Grandpapa Negri still rowed his own boat. I think Mama encouraged me to be a tomboy because . . . because it upset the Montescue cousins." She pulled a rueful face. "Back when there were some."

That left an awkward silence. "Um. Seeing as old Ambrosino said I could take off now . . . shall we go and have a glass of wine. Er. I gotta explain to you . . . 'Marco Felluci' is really . . ."

"Marco Valdosta," said Katerina sadly. "Come on. You're right. I could use a whole bottle of grappa, never mind a glass of wine." She pulled a wry face. "Except I don't like it. Somewhere quiet, Benito. I'm sticking the Montescue name out into public view enough just doing this. Maria said it was important. So important she posted a note under our water-door. Her writing's not great." That produced an almost-smile. "It took Giuseppe until this morning to give it to me. He thought he was protecting me. Madelena had a fight with him about it and made him come and deliver it."

Benito didn't know who these people were. But he knew a private place, close enough. He nodded. "Follow me." He led off to a little wine-cellar a hundred yards off. Inside it was dark and smoky, and still further privacy was offered by little cubicles. The sound was oddly damped within. "Traders use this place for negotiations. The partitions are double walled and filled with wool."

Kat and he sat down and the padrone wordlessly brought them a carafe of wine and a bowl of anchovy-stuffed olives. "Supposed to make you thirsty," said Benito, cheerfully taking three. "Now . . . if you already know that Marco is Marco Valdosta, what else can I tell you?"

Kat chewed her lip. "I . . . sent him a very angry letter, when I found out he was getting married to Angelina Dorma. I thought, I, I, well, he, I mean, er . . ."

Benito had to help out. There was some fun in seeing Kat tongue-tied, but he felt sorry for her anyway. And it was too late now, even if she was Katerina Montescue and not Kat "Trouble" the Spook. "Was two-timing you?"

"Yes," she said, her voice hardly audible. "Maria—I saw her early this morning—said it absolutely wasn't like that. She said I had to talk to you. Even if it was too late now. It's taken me all day to screw up the courage to walk into Ventuccio and ask for you."

Benito took a deep breath. He didn't really know how to handle this. But honesty to his brother seemed only fair, especially as Maria had already muddied the waters. Women! They made things complicated.

"Marco wasn't seeing Angelina when he was seeing you. He . . . well, never mind, but I promise, word of honor, swear to God, he never even saw her face in the last three months. Not until he moved into Dorma."

"I know," said Kat, dully. "And he's married now. Anyway it would never have worked. He's Valdosta. I'm Montescue. Our Families are enemies to the death. And I suppose it was the honorable thing for him to do, even if they had split up. He had to marry her. She was carrying his baby."

Benito choked on his wine. He spluttered.

"*What!?*"

Kat looked around anxiously. No one appeared to be staring at a red-faced Katerina Montescue and a tousle-haired teenager who was still gawping like a fish out of water. *Marco . . . Marco had always been rather protective of Benito. Kat couldn't see why, because she'd bet his co-worker knew all about where babies came from when he was still in his own cradle. Still, it was par for the course. Very like Marco. She'd bet that Dorma bitch had seduced him. Her hands crooked into claws.*

Benito finally got control of his larynx. "Who told you that?"

"Maria. Marco told her."

Benito shook his head. "Marco is the ultimate prize idiot. He needs a minder."

"Accidents happen," said Kat, stiffly.

Benito snorted. "Not unless Marco is the male equivalent of the Virgin Mary. And I've known him all my life. He's only half a saint. The other half is pure idiot, I promise."

He seemed so absolutely certain. "So who is the father then?" Kat demanded.

Benito looked at her, then away; then shook his head. "Let's just say Marco is paying his debts."

She had to know. "Benito, I'm not joking. If I have to spend the whole of the *Casa* Montescue's strongbox on a truth-spell, I'll get that answer. There isn't much in the strong box—but we can borrow." *And some things are more important than money.*

Benito shrugged. "It's too late, Kat. I know Marco. It is a question of honor. He's made his decision. He'll live by it."

Kat sighed. *She should have trusted her heart and gone and talked him out of it.* "He made it after he got that stupid letter from me." *Well, marriages could be annulled. It wasn't easy, but once she had the real father . . .* "I need to know who the father is, Benito. I'll find out. Every Strega scryer in this town relies on us. So you might as well tell me."

Benito shook his head. "Who did Marco tell that he was the father? There's your answer. And it is no help to you, Kat."

Marco told Maria. . . . "Caesare?" she asked, weakly.

Benito nodded. "After Marco's silly love poems made Caesare know the *Case Vecchie* girl had the hots for him, he made a move."

She'd even seen them together, she now realized. At that ridotto—true, Angelina had been masked, but the hair was recognizable. "Maria?" she asked, already knowing the answer.

"Doesn't know. I mean, she was after Caesare about him having another woman. But she doesn't know who, or even for sure. Hey—you leave her out of this, Kat! Look, there is no way the Dorma would have taken Aldanto. He's an ex-Montagnard. Forget about Marco. All you can do is wreck his life, and wreck Maria's. I know my brother. He won't back out. I'm sorry . . ."

Kat's head was whirling. She put it in her hands.

"Have some wine," said Benito gently, pushing the glass to her.

She took the wine. The harsh ruby liquid slopped a little. "You're his *brother*!?" There was a small sameness about the mouth, and in mannerisms . . .

Benito nodded. "I don't think we have the same father," he said wryly. "But yes, I'm Marco's brother. And believe me, Kat. Best thing you can do is leave him to get on with life with Angelina Dorma."

"Your name is *Valdosta*?"

Benito nodded. "Benito Valdosta. But I don't advertise it. After Mama was killed we went into hiding. Marco took off into the Jesolo. I lived in an attic and was a sneak thief. Then someone tried to kill Marco, about a year ago. Assassin. Professional. So I took him to Caesare."

"Someone tried to *kill* him?"

"Yes. Marco kind of assumed it was someone from the Council of Ten. But later we decided maybe it was the Montagnards."

Kat closed her eyes. "Dear God!" *That was Grandpapa!*

"He didn't even get hurt," said Benito reassuringly, but she wasn't listening anymore. She stared into nothing for a moment. Then she stood up.

"Don't ever tell anyone your name," she said harshly. "Never. Not anyone. Or go to Dorma for protection. And whatever you do, don't tell Aldanto." And she walked away.

Giaccomo was watching them out the corner of his eye, so Benito was doing his damnedest to act virtuous.

"—I can't believe it," Mercutio said, leaning back in his chair against the wall, and sipping at his brandy, his eyes alight with laughter. Jeppo cleared away their plates, with an odd look at Benito, but didn't say anything. Benito concentrated on being *very* well behaved. This was Giaccomo's after all, and if he *did* anything, Maria would hear about it. He wasn't even drinking brandy, though Mercutio had offered it, he was sticking to wine. Watered wine. He'd have a halo at this rate.

Outside Giaccomo's open door there were canalers lounging on his porch, mugs and glasses in hand, enjoying the balmy evening. He and Mercutio had the taproom pretty much to themselves.

"I just can't believe it'" Mercutio repeated, chuckling. "I leave this town, and the *very next day* all hell breaks loose! And me not here to help it along!" He shook his head mockingly. "I can see I've got a lot of lost time to make up—"

Suddenly he leaned forward, and his tone grew conspiratorial. "That's where you come in, kid. If you want in. Because I need a lookout and a housebreaker for a little piece of work."

Benito brightened. "'Course I want in!" He replied softly. "What'd you take me for? What's the action?"

Mercutio's eyes flamed with glee. "Who's the richest, *dumbest* man in this city?"

Benito snorted. "No contest. The Doge."

"And what does he love above power, wealth, women—everything?"

"His clockwork toys," Benito supplied.

"Now—what would he do, do you think, if he'd gone and built a *wonderful* toy just to send to Rome as a kind of present for the Grand Metropolitan—and he'd sent it to the jeweler to get all gilded and prettied up, and get sparklies put on it—and somebody—borrowed it? And told him he'd get it back *only* if he left a *great* deal of money in a particular place—and *didn't* tell anyone about it. *And* told him if he *did* bring in the Schiopettieri, he'd get his beautiful clockwork toy back in a million pieces?" Mercutio settled back in his chair with a smile of smug satisfaction.

"He's just dumb enough to do it," Benito acknowledged, answering Mercutio's smile with one of his own. "When and where?"

"Tonight, if you're game. Jeweler just opposite the bridge."

"Schiopettieri?" Benito asked.

"Got a distractor. Gave Jewel Destre a Turkish-made coat like this'n when he drooled over it. *He* thought I was groveling." Mercutio chuckled. "Then this afternoon I sent a couple messages to him and Giancarlo Polo concerning the coat and Jewel's manhood. Send one more and I'll guarantee they'll play knife-talk on the bridge tonight."

Benito chuckled evilly. "An' if anybody *sees* anythin', all they'll notice is the coat. So if anybody comes lookin' for a thief—they go for Jewel. *Si.* What is this thing of the Doge's anyway? A timepiece?"

Mercutio snickered. "I *heard* it's a clockwork whale he put together for his bath."

Benito snickered at the notion of a grown man playing with bath toys. "Let's do it," he said.

Chapter 72

There were more ways in to any building than by the door, and Benito knew most of them. He and Mercutio began their operation with him going over the roof and down an air-shaft. The air-shaft was very narrow. A year ago, Benito would have slid down it easily. Today—even though Benito didn't have an ounce of fat on him, he was already showing the stocky and muscular physique of his presumed father, Carlo Sforza. It was a tight fit.

But the air-shaft gave access to a window that was never locked. The window gave on a storeroom holding cleaning supplies, and the storeroom was shared by both the jeweler in question and his neighbor, a perfumer.

Benito opened the outer door to Mercutio, just as all hell broke loose on the bridge.

Mercutio flitted in, Benito out. Crouched in the shadows by the door he kept eyes and ears peeled for the approach of *anyone.* Innocents could make as much trouble as Schiopettieri if they noticed the boy in the shadows, or that the door was cracked open.

Across the canal on the bridge, torches were flaring, waving wildly; there was clamor of young male voices, shouting, cursing. A girl's scream cut across the babble like a knife through cheese— a scream of outrage and anger, not panic, and the hoarse croak of a young male in pain followed it.

And Benito saw, weaving through the walkways and heading up the stairs to a bridge, a string of bobbing lights moving at the speed of a man doing a fast trot.

Schiopettieri.

"Mercutio!" he whispered. A slim shadow flitted out the door, shutting it with agonizing care to avoid the clicking of the latch, a sound that would *carry*, even with the riot going on across the water. A bundle under Mercutio's arm told Benito everything he needed to know.

He grinned, as Mercutio took off at a trot, heading away from the Rialto bridge. Benito lagged a bit; his job to guard Mercutio's backtrail, delay any Schiopettieri.

Perfect, he thought with exultation. *Worked this 'un timed as perfect as any of the Doge's contraptions—*

And that was when everything fell apart.

People were looking out of windows, coming out of compartments with walkway entrances, moving toward the bridge, attracted to the ruckus like rats attracted to food. He and Mercutio had counted on that, too—it would cover *their* trail—

An old man, looking angry, popped out of a shop door in his nightshirt, halfway between Mercutio and the bridge. He was holding something down by his side; Benito didn't even think about what it might be, just noted his presence and his anger, and planned to avoid him. He looked like he'd been disturbed and wasn't happy about it—he probably had a cudgel, and he'd take out his pique on anyone jostling him. A lantern carried by someone hurrying toward the fight flared up and caught the gaudy patchwork of the Turkish coat Mercutio wore.

And the man let out an angry yell.

"You punk bastard!" he screamed, raising his hand. "Break *my* windows, will you! *I'll* give you 'protection'—"

Too late, Benito saw what the man held was a matchlock arquebus. Too late he yelled at Mercutio to duck.

Too late, as the arquebus went off with a roar, right in Mercutio's astonished face. His head exploded, blood fountaining as he fell.

Benito screamed, his cry lost in the screams coming from the bridge, the screams of those around the madman and his victim. "Mercutio!" he shrieked, and tried to push his way toward his friend, past people running *away* from the carnage. But something seized on him from behind, and when he struggled, hit him once, scientifically, behind the right ear, sending him into darkness.

He woke with an awful headache, and looked up into the eyes of the eagle. When his head stopped whirling quite so much he realized that it was the man with the solid line of eyebrow . . . who had seen him and Kat hide from the Schiopettieri and return to retrieve that package. Who had chased them down the alley outside Zianetti's. Senor Lopez. He was wearing a simple monk's habit. Benito pulled away in fear.

"Lie still!" snapped the man. There was such command in the voice that Benito did. Lopez's hands explored his scalp. Gently. "Well, your skull appears intact. Now lie still. You were noticed. The Schiopettieri are casting around for you. Your burned-face rescuer couldn't stick about." He pulled a blanket over Benito. Moments later the voice of the law could be heard.

" . . . a boy. Rumor has it he lives somewhere in this area of the city. Dark curly hair."

Then the voice of Lopez. "There are thousands of boys in Venice with dark curly hair. Doubtless I have this one hidden under a blanket in my cubicle." This was said in an absolutely level voice.

Respect in the voice. " . . . just wondered if you'd seen him, Father Lopez."

"I did. When I see him again, I will tell him you are looking for him," said Lopez.

Benito lay still, trapped between the terror of the Schiopettieri and horror about Mercutio's death.

A minute later, Lopez returned. "Schiopettieri are looking for you. Now. Explain to me what happened. Your burned-faced friend simply deposited you at my door and left."

Benito sat up, frightened. "I don't know what you're talking about. Mercutio, my friend . . ."

"With the Turkish waistcoat? The Schiopettieri say he is dead. Killed in the fracas." Lopez took a deep breath. "I am here to save a city, not to look after little sneak thieves. You are a piece in this puzzle, Benito Valdosta. You and your brother Marco and Katerina Montescue."

Benito started in fear. "How did you know—" He shrank back a little. It was always said that the Montagnards had killed their mother, had hunted Marco. Benito had always believed that himself. But what if . . . it had been the Metropolitans . . . even possibly this man, or agents of the Council of Ten. Those shadowy agents no one knew.

And Mercutio was dead. His mind just kept coming back to it.

Dead . . . What was it that Valentina had said . . . *He'll end up dead, and in two days Venice will have forgotten even his name.*

Mercutio was dead. Dead. The whole of his face blown off. Dead.

Lopez shook him. Benito swung a fist at the Spaniard. "He's dead! Mercutio is dead!"

Lopez sighed. "Go on. Get out of here. You have that young fool's death on your mind. Perhaps we can talk when you are no longer a boy."

As he staggered out onto the street, Benito was vaguely aware that there was something very wrong about that scary priest. Ricardo Brunelli's guest, at one time, now living in the Ghetto. A Legate of the Grand Metropolitan . . . being attired as a monk and manning a confession booth in Dorsoduro . . . waiting for some great happening. But his mind was too full of the death of Mercutio.

He charged down the cobbles to Aldanto's, wiping hot, angry eyes with his fists. He only slowed when he got to their house, because he had to talk to the gate-guard, and he *wouldn't* be crying in front of anyone, not if he died for it. So he composed himself— holding his sorrow and his rage under tightest of masks; opened the door with his key—

Started to. The door opened at the first rattle of key in lock, and he found himself looking at Aldanto himself.

He just stared, frozen.

"You're late," Aldanto had said, grabbing his arm and hauling him inside. "You should have been back—"

"*Let me go!*" Benito snarled, voice crackling again, pulling his arm away so fast his shirt sleeve nearly tore.

Aldanto gave him a startled look, then a measured one. He let go of Benito's arm and turned back to the door, careful to throw all the locks—and only then turned back to Benito.

"What happened?" he asked quietly, neutrally.

He'd told himself, over and over, that he was *not* going to tell Aldanto what had happened.

But Caesare was a skillful interrogator; Benito couldn't resist the steady barrage of quiet questions, not when Aldanto was between him and the door. Syllable by tortured syllable, the handsome blond dragged the night's escapade out of him, as Benito stared at the floor, smoldering sullenly, determined *not* to break down a second time. He got to know every crack and cranny of the entryway floor before it was over.

Silence. Then, "I'm sorry," Aldanto said quietly. "I'm sorry about your friend."

Benito looked up. Aldanto's face was unreadable, but his eyes were murky with thought, memory, something. He looked *past* Benito for a moment.

"But you know very well," he said, noncommittally, "that was a damned fool stunt."

Benito snarled and made a dash for the stairs. Aldanto made no move to stop him. He tore up the stairs, stubbing his toes twice, getting up and resuming his run—got to Caesare's bedroom and through it, not caring if Maria was in the bed—to the roof-trap and out, slamming it behind him—

And out onto the roof, into the dark, the night, the sheltering night, where he huddled beside the chimney and cried and cried and cried. . . .

Dawn brought the return of sense, the return of thought.

Valentina was right, he thought bleakly. *She told me and told me. Must have been a million times. She told me Mercutio was a fool. She told me he wouldn't see twenty. She was right. Him and his ideas—"gonna be rich and famous." So what's he come to? Blown away 'cause some ol' fool thinks he's Jewel. And ain't nobody going to remember him but me.*

He crouched on his haunches, both arms wrapped around his knees, rocking back and forth and shivering a little. *Ain't nobody going to remember him but me. Could have been me. Could have been. Been coasting on my luck, just like Mercutio. Only one day the luck runs out . . .*

He stared off across the roofs, to the steeples and turrets of the Accademia. *Marco maybe got it right.*

He sniffed, and rubbed his cold, tender nose on his sleeve. *What have I done? What the hell good am I doing for him, or even for Caesare? The Dell'este has gone and made an heir to the house. And Marco . . . poor fish, doesn't even begin to know how to be sneaky. Just honest—and honest could wind up with him just as dead as Mama. There's gotta be somethin' I can do. There's got to be . . .*

His thoughts went around and around like that for some time until he heard voices below, and saw Maria shutting the door beneath his perch, saw her hop into her gondola and row it away into a shiny patch of sun and past, into the shadows on the canal.

He knew Aldanto would be up.

He unwound himself and crept on hands and knees to the trapdoor; lifted it, and let himself down into the apartment.

"I wondered if you'd gone," said a voice behind him as he dropped.

He turned. Aldanto sat on the edge of the rumpled bed, eyes half-closed, but not at all sleepy, fishy-smelling breeze coming in the open window and ruffling his hair.

"No, Caesare," Benito replied uncertainly. "I've—been thinking."

He could *feel* Aldanto considering him from under those half-closed lids; weighing him.

"You've been thinking?"

"I'm a fool. Lucky, but—Mercutio was lucky for a while."

"And you saw what riding luck got him."

"*Si.*"

"And what do you propose to do about this revelation?"

Benito couldn't stand looking at that expressionless face. He dropped his eyes to his own feet; bare, callused, dirty, and covered with little scratches. "Don't know, Caesare," he muttered. "Just—*you* need help, m'brother needs help—and I don't how— what to do. I just—want do it smart, that's all. I want to be able t' *do* things. An' if somebody decides to put a hole in me—"

He looked up again, his chin firming stubbornly, a kind of smoldering anger in the bottom of his stomach.

"—if somebody decides to put a hole in me, I *don't* want it to be for *no damn reason!*"

Aldanto licked his lips a trifle, his eyes no longer hooded. "You're asking my advice."

"*Si,*" Benito said. "I'm asking. And I'll take it. I ain't going to be a fool any more."

"Dorma," Aldanto replied.

Benito wrinkled his nose doubtfully. "Milord? What's Dorma got to do—"

"Petro Dorma has been made aware of the fact that there are two Valdosta boys in Venice. It is only because of my effort and Marco's that he hasn't had his people out to bring you in regardless of your wishes in the matter." Was that a hint of smile? If so, it was gone before Benito had a chance to identify the expression.

"We persuaded him that until *you* wanted the shelter of Dorma's patronage, it would be—a less than successful venture. He continues to inquire about you. He has a very strong sense of obligation—" It *was* a hint of a smile. "—has Milord Dorma. He's a powerful, influential man. Keeps quiet, but has a following. I wouldn't mind knowing what happens at Dorma. You have eyes that see things that your brother doesn't."

"But—Marco, he wants to be a doctor," Benito felt moved to protest. "I ain't smart, not that smart—what am I supposed to do?"

"What did your grandfather tell you to do? I know he sent you a note not long ago."

Benito remembered, as clearly as if he had Marco's perfect memory, the words of his granther's note. *It is your duty to take care of Marco. He has no talent for lying, no ability to deceive. This is not altogether bad, as there should be one in every generation who understands and believes in Dell'este Honor. But those who believe in the Honor need those who understand the price of Honor to care for them.*

"He told me to take care of Marco."

"Why you?" said Aldanto quietly.

"Because I'm *not* good—and the good ones need bad ones to watch out for 'em." That may not have been what the duke had said, but it was what he *meant*.

"Ferrara is being squeezed. The Dell'este have not a sure ally in the world. The old Duke is a canny old fox. But Marco could become the Head of the Dell'este in exile." Aldanto spoke intently, his blue eyes boring into Benito's. "What then?"

Benito thought about the duke; the clever, canny duke, who understood expediency—and Marco, who did not—and shivered.

Aldanto leaned back on his pillows a little. "So. You see."

Benito nodded, slowly.

"Then, young milord, I advise you to go to Petro Dorma. And I advise you to ask him to train you in the ways of business. And I further advise you to *learn*, Benito Valdosta. Apply yourself as devotedly as you did to learning to pick a lock."

"*Si*," Benito said, in a small humble voice. He turned, and started to go—then turned back for a moment. "Caesare—"

Aldanto simply raised one golden eyebrow.

"We're still in your debt. You call it in, any time—I pay it. Roofwalking too."

"I'll hold you to that," said Caesare, bleakly.

Benito nodded. And he picked his way carefully down the staircase, and out the door, into the dawn sunshine.

He sat on the doorstep of Dorma for a very long time before the doorkeeper opened the outer protective grate for the day. The doorkeeper was a withered old man who stared at him with a pride far more in keeping with a House Head than that of a doorkeeper.

"Away with you, boy," he grated, looking down his nose as Benito scrambled to his feet, and clasped his hands behind him. "We don't need idlers or beggars. If you're looking for work, present yourself at the kitchen."

"Pardon, sir," Benito interrupted, looking out of the corner of his eye at the huge pile that was Dorma, and feeling more than a little apprehensive at what he was getting himself into. "Your pardon—but—I've got a message. For Milord Dorma."

"Well?" The ancient drew himself up and sniffed disdainfully. But his disdain was short-lived.

"Caesare Aldanto sent me, sir. If it's convenient . . . I'm supposed to speak to Milord Petro. I'm—" He gulped, and watched the surprise flood the old man's face. "I'm Benito Valdosta. Marco's brother. I think Milord Petro wants to see me."

Chapter 73

"Who in the name of God is this *Francesca*?" demanded the Holy Roman Emperor. He held up the second of the two letters Count Von Stemitz had brought with him from Venice. The letter was quite a bit longer than the first, which consisted of a single page.

The count cleared his throat. Then, cleared it again. "Ah. Well, as it happens, Your Majesty, your nephew has taken up with a Venetian courtesan. For quite some time now. He's kept the liaison more or less secret from Abbot Sachs and his coterie. But Erik Hakkonsen quietly informed me of the situation early on."

"Hakkonsen *allowed* this to continue?" demanded the Emperor, his heavy brows so low that his dark blue eyes seemed a deep purple.

"Well . . . yes, Your Majesty." Again, Von Stemitz cleared his throat. "Actually, in an odd sort of way, I get the feeling Hakkonsen rather approves of the arrangement."

The Emperor's brows lifted. "I'll be damned," he grunted. "I didn't think the young Icelander was that smart. His father—God rot his soul—would have beaten me black and blue."

"It was a simpler world in those days, Your Majesty. If you'll permit me the liberty of saying so."

"Indeed it was," sighed Charles Fredrik. "Jagiellon's father was a brute, and the uncle he usurped the throne from was even worse. But they weren't as ambitious." He fanned his face with the sheaf of papers held in his left hand. "Not to mention that accursed Emeric of Hungary. Either he or Jagiellon would be bad enough. To have *both* of them coming to power within a year of each other . . ."

He sighed again and picked up the single sheet of paper which contained Manfred's letter to him. Then, hefted it a bit, as if he were weighing the one letter against the other.

"They say essentially the same thing. But this *Francesca's* so-called 'addendum' is ten times longer, twenty times more sophisticated, and lays out in fine detail all of the nuances Manfred missed."

"I thought Manfred's letter was quite thoughtful," said the count, rallying for the moment to the young prince's behalf.

The Emperor snorted. "For an eighteen-year-old boy who's never given any evidence in the past of thinking past the next tavern or whorehouse, the letter's a bloody miracle." He squinted at Francesca's letter. "Still—there's nothing in Manfred's letter we didn't know a year ago. Whereas *this* one . . ."

"She claims to be from the Aquitaine. I tend to believe the claim, even though I'm certain the name she uses is fraudulent."

"Oh, I don't doubt she's from the Aquitaine," mused the Emperor. "Nobody else in the world—not even Italians—has that subtle and convoluted way of looking at things." His eyes left the letter and drifted toward the narrow window. An arrow-slit, that window had been once. Probably half the arrows fired from it, over the centuries, had been aimed at Aquitainian besiegers.

"I'd be a lot happier if I knew *exactly* who she was."

The third man in the room coughed discreetly. The Emperor and Von Stemitz moved their eyes to gaze on him.

"Her real name is Marie-Françoise de Guemadeuc," said the priest. "You can be certain of it. We investigated quite thoroughly."

The count grimaced. "A bad business, that was. Even by the standards of the Aquitaine."

The Emperor's expression was a study in contradiction—as if he were both relieved and disturbed at the same time. "You are certain, Francis?" he demanded.

"Yes, Your Majesty." The priest nodded at the letter in the Emperor's hands. "My brothers in Venice have even more at stake in this matter than you. Their lives, in the end."

"True enough," admitted Charles Fredrik. His brows lowered again. "Which is perhaps the part about this that bothers me the most. You had given me no indication, prior to this moment, that your . . . 'brotherhood' was involved at all with my nephew."

Father Francis spread his hands. "And we are not, Your Majesty. Not directly, at least. But, you may recall, I *did* tell you—

several times, in fact—that we had established a line of communication with you which was less circuitous than the letters I receive from Father Lopez through our brothers in the Aquitaine."

"'Less circuitous!'" barked the Emperor. He jiggled the letter in his hand. "That's a delicate way of putting it!"

Father Francis did not seem abashed. "Well. Yes, it is. We *have* taken solemn vows, after all."

After a moment's worth of imperial glowering, Charles Fredrik's heavy chest began to heave with soft laughter. "I'll give you this much, Francis. You have a better wit than the damned Sots." The amusement passed. "Let's hope that extended to your wits also."

He laid the letter back on the table, planted his thick hands on the armrests of the chair, and levered himself to his feet. Then, almost marching, went to the window and gazed out. There was not much to see, beyond the lights of the sleeping city.

"I agree with this Francesca's assessment of the situation," the Emperor announced abruptly. "The troubles in Venice have been carefully orchestrated to leave the city helpless and at odds with itself—while Jagiellon has moved to precipitate a war in northern Italy. A war whose sole purpose is the destruction of Venice itself."

Von Stemitz had not actually read Francesca's letter. She had given it to him already sealed. "That seems a bit farfetched, Your Majesty, if you'll forgive me saying so. Why would anyone want to *destroy* Venice? The city is the key to the wealth of the East."

Before Charles Fredrik could answer, the count made a little waving motion with his hand, forestalling objections. "Oh, to be sure—Duke Visconti wishes Venice all the ill in the world. But he wants to *control* the city, not ruin it. And how could he do it, anyway? Venice is an island and its fleet is far more powerful than anything Milan and its allies could muster—" He broke off suddenly.

"Unless Emeric of Hungary comes onto the scene," finished the Emperor. "Which he surely would if it appeared that Venice was falling into ruin."

"But—" Von Stemitz was clearly groping, his face tight with confusion.

"Think," commanded the Emperor. He spread his arms wide. "But think on the *largest* scale, because that's how—I'm certain of it now—Jagiellon is thinking." He turned away from the window entirely. "At first glance, of course, Jagiellon would seem to be the least likely source of trouble in the Adriatic. The Grand Duchy of Lithuania and Poland is very far from Venice, and has no common border with it. No apparent source for mutual conflict." He shrugged heavily. "Not even the commercial rivalry which periodically agitates the Hungarians and the Genoese and the Greeks in Constantinople."

"Exactly. So why in the world—"

"Who *is* the great rival of Lithuania?" interrupted the Emperor.

Von Stemitz frowned. "We are, of course. The Holy Roman Empire."

"Precisely. And what will happen if Venice is destroyed? Who will fill the sudden power vacuum in northern Italy and the Adriatic? Not Milan!"

Von Stemitz stared at him. Then, slowly, the count's face began to clear. And seemed, as well, to grow slightly pale.

"Precisely," grunted Charles Fredrik. "Grand Duke Jagiellon's reputation for insensate brutality is well earned, Count. But I think that's as much of a maneuver as anything else he does. Don't be fooled by it. He is also a consummate manipulator; a schemer, quite unlike his father. A man—we'll call him that, for the moment— who would prefer to let others bleed themselves to death, if at all possible, while he marshals his forces elsewhere."

Von Stemitz spoke in a whisper. "If Venice . . . is destroyed, the Holy Roman Empire will have no choice. If you don't intervene— with direct military force—the Hungarians surely will. And— and—"

"And with Lithuania and the borderlands to deal with already, I cannot also afford to see a more powerful Kingdom of Hungary— especially not one which has a toehold in Italy. *Especially* not with a man on the throne like Emeric, who doesn't quite have Jagiellon's reputation—outside of Hungary, that is—but comes in a very close second."

"There'd be war between the Empire and Hungary!"

Charles Fredrik nodded. "For a certainty. With—for a certainty— Milan and Rome sucked into the vortex as well. All of north Italy. Genoa also, be sure of it—soon enough, the Greeks as well." He turned his head, staring out of the arrow slit again. "Within a year . . ." he mused. "Within a year, half of my army would be mired in north Italy. Leaving Jagiellon free to strike elsewhere."

"Where, do you think?" asked Father Francis.

The Emperor swiveled his head back and fixed his eyes on Eneko Lopez's companion. "I don't know," he said. "You'll find out for me."

Father Francis's head jerked a little. Then, slowly, a small smile came to his face and he lowered his head. The gesture was almost— not quite—a bow. "Thank you, Your Majesty," he said softly.

The Emperor chuckled. "Not just yet, Francis. We still have to spike this plot of Jagiellon's in Venice. And you *still* have to get the agreement of the Grand Metropolitan in Rome before you can form a new order. What are you going to call it, by the way?"

Francis hesitated. "We haven't really decided, Your Majesty. Most of us lean toward the 'Society of Hypatia.'"

"Eneko Lopez also?"

"No, actually—he doesn't seem to like the name. He—"

"Smart man!" barked the Emperor. "Within a year, your enemies will be calling you 'the Shits.' What does he favor?"

"The Society of Chrysostom."

The Emperor stroked his thick beard. "Better. Better. Still . . . they'll shorten it to something like 'the Socks.' Then, within a week, to 'the smelly Socks.' Be certain of it." He paused. Then: "Call yourselves the Society of the Word," he stated. Firmly, even imperiously.

Francis seemed to bridle. The Emperor barked a little laugh. "Don't be stupid, Francis! Allow me the luxury of command in small things, if you would—since you *do* need my permission to operate in imperial territory. My cooperation, in fact, even if it is kept at a certain official distance."

Francis' stiff shoulders eased. "True, Your Majesty." A little crease appeared between his eyebrows. "But I don't see how calling ourselves—" The crease disappeared into a much deeper one. "Your Majesty! 'The Swords?' We are *not* a militant order."

The most powerful man in Europe simply stared at him. And, after a moment, the priest looked away.

When Antimo finished his report, the Duke of Ferrara rose from his chair and moved over to the blade-rack along the wall. There, for a moment, his eyes ranged admiringly over the blades before he selected one and took it down from its rack.

"Benito has made his decision, has he?" mused the Old Fox. He hefted the dagger in his hand, holding it with an expert grip. "The *main gauche*, Antimo. Not so glorious as the sword, of course. A plebeian sort of weapon." His left hand glided through a quick motion. "But, in the end, it's often the blade sinister which spills the enemy's guts on the field."

Dell'este replaced the dagger and turned back to Bartelozzi. "Show in Baron Trolliger now, if you would. I assume he's brought the rest of the money with him."

Antimo nodded. "Enough to hire all the condottieri we'll need." Smiling grimly: "Ferrara will seem like a veritable military giant, when the war erupts."

The Old Fox shook his head. "Don't fool yourself, Antimo. The great swords will remain in the hands of the Emperor and the Grand Duke and the King of Hungary. But for the needs of the moment, here in northern Italy?" Again, his left hand made that swift, expert motion. "Ferrara will be Charles Fredrik's *main gauche*."

PART VII
August, 1538 A.D.

Chapter 74

When Manfred strode into Erik's chamber, the Icelander was struggling with a letter. Erik had met up with an Icelander pilgrim, and the chance to send a letter home was a rare one. Now he just had to choose his words with some care. There was always a chance the letter might not get home. There were things going on that he didn't want to tell the world about. Besides, there was Manfred's identity to be kept secret. He was tempted to write in runic, but that would convince any curious person this was full of secrets worth reading—or destroying if they could not read it.

"We need some air, Erik," said Manfred loudly.

Something about that tone stopped Erik from saying he had a letter to finish first. He put the letter carefully aside, the quill balanced across the inkpot.

They walked out. Full summer was coming and the smell rising off the canals was as unpleasant as the shimmering water was beautiful. Manfred picked a spot where they could lean against a wall in the shade. "Count Von Stemitz just came back from his visit to the Emperor. Who is now in *Innsbruck*, by the way."

Manfred snorted. "Yes—Innsbruck. He never leaves Mainz if he can help it! Which means . . ." Manfred glowered at nothing in particular—or the world in general. "Von Stemitz brought a reply for me from Charles Fredrik."

Manfred took a deep breath. "And he sent me this also."

It was a plain heavy gold ring, set with a polished bloodstone.

Erik raised an eyebrow. Plainly there was more to the ring than mere jewelry.

"Charles Fredrik is like the Doge," said Manfred. "He likes mechanical gadgets." He pressed the ring on the inside, under the stone, with a knife point. The bezels opened. And Manfred took the bloodstone out. He handed it to Erik. Upside down.

It was an imperial seal.

"He trusts you," Erik said mildly. The seal could be cut by any competent forger . . . but wouldn't be. The curse the Church magicians had laid on misuse was as much threat as the weight of the Emperor's anger. Neither was something even kings would take lightly.

Manfred slammed his meaty fist into his palm. "Damn it! I don't want this, Erik. I was enjoying Venice. Look what Francesca has got me into!"

"Here." Erik handed over the seal, carefully. "You'd better put it back into the ring. I suppose he was impressed by your new-found grasp of Venetian intrigue?"

"He's made me his privy emissary plenipotentiary to deal with the Venetian situation as it unfolds." The Breton prince ground his teeth. "He says that other rumblings have also reached him. He's having a tourney in Innsbruck, and will find reason to remain there with considerable force for some months."

Manfred sighed. "There's more," he continued. "My uncle has also discovered that there are a further one thousand, two hundred Knights of the Holy Trinity apparently on their way to Trieste. He wants to know why, and says if need be I must remind them that they hold the charter for their monasteries on imperial sufferance."

Erik reviewed a map in his mind. "Having the Emperor champing on the other side of the Brenner pass is going to be of no use if the Knights are in Trieste. They can get here a lot faster than he can. But Manfred, whatever is going on—invasion of this place is insanity. They're water people. Even ten thousand knights would just be drowned."

Manfred shook his head. "There's more to it than just straight invasion. But right now . . . well, their second fleet left a few weeks ago and the town is pretty thin of people, Erik. And now I have to find out what is going on. Damn Francesca. Damn Charles Fredrik."

Erik was amused. He noticed that Manfred was complaining but showing no signs of evading the orders. He was changing as he grew. And Erik had to admit quite a lot of that was due to the time he spent with Francesca. "Why don't you ask Francesca? Subtly, of course."

"I'm going to," said Manfred. "If anything good has come out of this it's that my uncle has sent me a pouch of jewels . . . that can be spent unobtrusively, which ducats can't. I was running low on money. I'm going to damn well spend some of his on wine and a specific woman. Oh, he sent instruction for *you*, too. 'Take any heads you feel necessary. I'll sign bits of paper for them later.' You want to start with that idiot Sachs? Although that would give Charles Fredrik more trouble with the Church than he wants."

Erik smiled dryly. "I don't think the Venetians would like it much either. Charles Fredrik is forgetting his writ doesn't run here."

A bell began to toll, furiously, over at the piazza. "Sounds like a fire or something. We'd better get back."

This was Venice. Word, racing like wildfire along the canals and alleys, beat them back to the embassy. The doorman greeted them with "Milan and Verona have embargoed Venetian barges coming up the Po and the Adige!"

Manfred took a deep breath. "It's starting," he said to Erik.

When Erik got back up to his room he found the quill pen had been moved. Slightly—but enough for him to notice. He hoped they'd enjoyed his letter regarding his wishes of best health for his sisters.

Francesca pulled a wry face. "Men always think there is a profit to be made from war." She looked at the emerald Manfred had given her. "There is, but for very few. For most, even the whores in an army's tail, war is a drain."

She sighed. "Now it seems you want me to become one of those who make a profit out of it."

Manfred showed he'd learned a great deal—about tact, at least. "In this particular case, you can bet that the Holy Roman Emperor does not want war."

Francesca looked speculatively at him. "And how would you know, Manfred?"

Manfred chuckled. "I've met Charles Fredrik a couple of times. He's an old woman who likes to stay in Mainz and fiddle with his map collection. He hates changing borders."

Erik had to admit it was masterfully done. He didn't know if it would fool someone like Francesca. But as they'd learned from Giuliano, the Venetian fencing-master, bravura was sometimes enough. This time it looked like Giuliano was right. But there was also the double feint . . .

Francesca nodded. "True. The Emperor has small running wars on the northern and eastern borders, but he has a reputation for not bestirring himself. And I'll bet the Empire is richer for it."

"There is a time for war," said Erik, mildly.

Francesca looked sharply at him. "Those who don't know you, Erik, are fooled by that tone of yours. Yes, there is a time for war. There are enemies who will use a desire for peace to weaken and devour you. And if I have to put my finger on what is happening here, these are the moves being enacted now. Have you noticed any shipping coming in?"

Manfred shrugged. "I don't really pay any attention."

Erik was far more geared to noticing vessels. "Lateen-rigged coasters. I haven't seen any bigger round ships for a week or so."

Francesca dimpled at him. "Trade has been down for the last while. You can bet the Spleto pirates are at work. By now I think there is a blockade. And how convenient all of this is, just after the spring convoys leave. The better part of eight thousand men at arms are out of the city. The cream of Venice's fighting boatmen. The Arsenalotti are still here of course, but my next prediction of trouble would be in the next biggest concentration of young disaffected men in the city. The Accademia and the various Scuolo. They'll build up pressure, trying to get Venice to start fighting from within."

She looked thoughtfully at the two. "Someone—or possibly several someones—is trying to orchestrate all this. The magical murders are part of the plot, I'm sure of it. You can tell your uncle Charles Fredrik that he's too early. The whole thing won't come to the boil until late summer."

Her reference to the Emperor as Manfred's uncle brought an instant silence to the room. Erik and Manfred were as rigid as boards.

"How the hell did you know?" demanded Manfred. "I didn't tell her, Erik—I swear!"

Francesca shrugged. "You're a Breton nobleman. Important enough to keep your identity and the fact you have a bodyguard secret. You have contacts with the Imperial Court—high enough to know fine details of the Emperor's movements. You have kept your own first name. I know a great deal about the royal houses of Europe. A Breton—with the same name as the Duke of Brittany's son, familiar with the court at Mainz. There are other possibilities . . . But none that have Erik ready to kill me."

Startled, Manfred looked over and saw that Erik had his heavy-bladed Shetland dagger in hand. He moved to block the way between the Icelander and the courtesan.

"You can't, Erik. You can't."

"I may have to," said Erik quietly.

"Not without killing me first."

Francesca stepped past Manfred. "I'm not a fool, Erik. I needed to do this to establish trust. If I intended to betray Manfred and sell this information . . . I would have kept quiet."

Erik digested this for a few seconds. Then he put the knife into the sheath in his boot. "I'll have to pass on who you are, and what you look like, to Charles Fredrik. And to my kin. You realize that . . . if harm comes to Manfred through this, nowhere on earth will be safe for you. Not even the court of the Grand Duke of Lithuania. You might still get away from the Emperor's assassins. But the Hohenstaffen *Godar* are ours. *Linn gu linn*. We avenge them. We always do."

Francesca patted him on the arm. "Nowhere is safe anyway. Be practical, Erik. If I sold Manfred's secret, I'd be well paid. But I'd also probably be killed before nightfall. Those who would use it, don't want to advertise who they are, and the answer could be obtained from me by torture. Now, instead of giving me half the information and forcing me to guess the rest . . . why don't you tell me as much as you can?"

She smiled sweetly at Manfred. "It'll cost you another emerald, my dear, but I'm sure I can put together a few more pieces. Once we know just who is moving with what intent you can tell your uncle how to counter it."

They sat and replayed incidents and pieces of the Venetian puzzle. When they came to the coiner incident, Francesca—who had simply listened up to this point—stopped them.

"A mold for forging coins? Coins are *stamped*, not molded. The blanks are molded, presumably without holes. They are then stamped with iron dies. Those dies are heavily guarded. Counted daily. Your lord Calenti spotted that, not the molds."

"Well, I presume the coiner was one of the conspirators—with access to the Venetian mint. So we can assume whatever is murdering these men magically is opposed to this conspiracy."

Francesca shrugged. "Conspirators fall out. Particularly about money. And different conspiracies fight one another too."

Erik groaned. "I wish I was back in Iceland! The clan feuds were murderous, true, but at least they weren't subtle. 'Your great-grandfather raped my great-grandmother.' *Chop.* 'Your third cousin twice removed stole a pig from my aunt's husband's father's second wife's—' "

Francesca patted him sympathetically. "I conclude several things. And the first is that Iceland is more complicated than you claim. The second is that the Knights of the Trinity are tied up in this. So probably is that Woden-casket. You've been here for more than a year, on what was originally supposed to have been a mere 'visit.' "

"And I cannot see the reason for it," said Erik gloomily.

Francesca continued. "The next point is that attack at the brothel was intended to get rid of *you*, Erik. Either dead, or maimed, or disgraced and sent home—or any combination thereof. This means someone already knows who Manfred is, and has known for a long time. I just thought I might point this out before you decide to kill *me* for it. I would guess they want Manfred dead at the hands of a Venetian. Venetian *Case Vecchie*, and with your uncle playing right into their hands looking for vengeance on Venice."

Manfred chuckled. "And after that? They just gave up?"

Francesca ruffled his hair. "Either they decided that both of you would be better killed at once, or they found out that Erik's departure would cause the Emperor to act immediately. Or, even simpler, after getting a taste of Erik's mayhem they decided it was just too risky."

Erik sighed. "You're lucky Abbot Sachs isn't listening to you, Francesca. He'd have *you* burned for witchcraft. Speaking of which, we're supposed to be involved in a witch-hunt tonight—over at the Accademia."

Chapter 75

The footsteps outside the door to his room were familiar ones, so Marco didn't start—or reach for his knife—when a voice hailed him.

"Hey, Marco—"

Marco Valdosta stretched out his leg and pulled the closed door open with his foot.

"Rafael, I thought you were in class." He raised an inquiring eyebrow at his tall, skinny roommate.

Suite-mate, actually, Lord and Saints. Still hard to believe that I'm actually in the Accademia, that I'm rooming with Rafael. Easier than believing I'm "married" and that my wife has gone to stay at a family estate in Fruili, rather than spend time with me. And the worst of it is that it suits me. I've tried . . . But the more I see of Angelina . . . I must have been crazy.

Rafael shrugged his shoulders, barely rippling the gray-black material of his cotte, and put his parchments behind the bookcase beside him. "The model got sick, so they threw us out."

"Not surprising, if she had to look at you for too long."

Rafael grimaced at him. "Thanks a lot! I like you, too. You coming across to Zianetti's for a glass of wine and a bite?"

It was Marco's turn to grimace. "No thanks. I . . . I don't like to go there much."

Rafael shrugged again. "I said to Luciano I'd try to bring you along. He's got some of those herbs from someone—Sophia?—for you."

Marco got to his feet. "I wish he'd picked some other tavern."

"You'll get over her," said Rafael awkwardly.

Marco sighed. "I used to think that."

Rafael patted him on the shoulder. "You will. Just give it time. These things blur eventually."

Marco shook his head, then pulled on his cloak. "It's been months since I saw her last. Time just seems to bring Kat into closer focus."

They walked in silence down the alley and across the campo to Zianetti's. They took up residence in one of the smaller back rooms and soon brought conversation around to happier topics, before they were joined by Luciano Marina. He looked tired and grim. "We must meet in private in the future. Things are getting too risky. Even the Jesolo marshes are less dangerous these days."

Marco's blank look made Luciano smile. "Even for you, young lord. For us more ordinary Strega it is dangerous enough."

Marco swallowed and looked at Rafael . . . Who nodded slightly. "I didn't realize . . ."

"We'd like to keep it that way," said Luciano. "Persecution is stepping up. Why a trade blockade should be our fault, I do not know."

Rafael shrugged. "The magical murders are easy enough to blame on the Strega. Except several of the victims have been among us."

Luciano pulled out a cloth bundle from underneath his cloak. "Anyway, here are some of the herbs that you wanted from Sophia. She misses you. Sends her love."

He stood up. "I've got things to do. Don't get caught up with the Church while carrying these herbs. It'll challenge even Petro Dorma to explain some of them."

A moment later he was gone. Marco and Rafael finished their wine in silence before following after.

As they headed across the torch-lit campo, Rafael coughed apologetically. "If you think it better to find other digs . . . well, I'll understand. It's not that safe these days to associate with the old faith."

"Safer than running into Filippo Recchia," Marco replied bitterly. "By comparison the Church inquisition is dull and gentle, and they aren't after me all the time."

Rafael frowned sympathetically. "*Si*—you managing to avoid the bully? Is there anything I can do?"

Marco shook his head when Rafael looked like he was going

to say more. "Don't worry about it; there's nothing either of us can do about him. I've dealt with worse."

"The problem with Filippo Recchia . . ." Rafael shrugged. "The Recchia are a rising house. Before you arrived on the scene, Marco, Recchia had been the pack leader. But this new kid on the block . . . it's the old story. The Valdosta family is where the Recchia *wish* they were—and Filippo's young enough and stupid enough to let the resentment show."

"My disadvantage is Filippo's obvious physical prowess—which he shows off every chance he gets. Every other *Case Vecchie* boy learned to fence. I know how to *fight*—I'd kill Filippo in a real street brawl—but not how to fence. And Filippo's pushing it for all it's worth. Still, I'm not worried about it. As I said, I've dealt with worse before, and—"

The relative quiet of the night was torn by the explosive boom of an arquebus. The sharper crack of wheel-lock pistols followed. A yell of "*A rescue! Students! A rescue!*"

"That was Luciano's voice!" exclaimed Rafael.

They ran toward the noise, which was now an out-and-out riot, involving an influx of students pouring out of the taverns and lodging houses. Half of the Accademia were going to be there before them.

Half of the people in this "Accademia" must be involved by now, thought Erik. *What a God-forsaken mess.*

They were supposed to have moved in quietly and seized the entire group. Alive, for questioning. To that end, Abbot Sachs had insisted on cudgels instead of swords. Well . . . as they burst the door open, he'd had half a second's worth of seeing the group busy with some sort of ritual, when the candles had blown out and all hell had broken loose.

Von Linksdorf had obviously triggered some kind of trap. Not only had the candles gone out abruptly, but a rigged arquebus had proved that steel armor might be effective against pagan magic, but it was damned useless against black powder. Von Linksdorf had been hammered flat by the heavy bullet.

In the charge and chaos that followed, the Knights had learned two more things. First, there was another exit—which they hadn't known about. Second, the pagans were not intent on being arrested without a struggle. And they were not only armed, but at least two of them were apparently wealthy enough to possess pistols.

The melee had burst onto the narrow, mostly dark street, and some clever pagan had called for a rescue . . . in a place where attacks and brawls were not uncommon, and students were the frequent victims of attacks. Knights on horseback, in open fields, dealing with lesser armed and less-armored foes were a deadly force. Here, in the narrow confines, armor was perhaps good for stopping knife thrusts and cudgel blows. Otherwise, it simply slowed them down and hampered movement.

"God and Saint Paul!" shouted Sachs. "Slaughter the pagans! Slaughter them all! God will know his own!"

A branch of candles appeared on a balcony. "*HOLD!*"

The voice was elderly but full of power. "*Stand! Put up your weapons!*"

Erik looked up and recognized Michael, the Metropolitan of Venice. Bishop Capuletti was standing beside him, staring down on them.

In the distance he could hear the rattles of the Schiopettieri.

Erik sighed and lowered his cudgel. *What a mess Sachs has gotten us into. Again.*

"What a mess." Petro Dorma, here in his role of Lord of the Nightwatch, was not smiling on anyone. Neither was the Metropolitan.

"I have forty-three of the scions of wealth, nobility, and gentry— including my own brother-in-law—arrested for affray. I have twelve monks, Servants of the Holy Trinity, involved in the same incident. I have nineteen belted Knights and Squires of the Holy Trinity in custody. I have three dead bodies to explain, as well as a number of injuries. Two of the dead are students of good family. There can be very little doubt that this will come before the Doge in the morning. He is going to ask me hard questions. I want answers, gentlemen."

"How dare you arrest us?" demanded Abbot Sachs. "We are the Church!"

Metropolitan Michael looked as if he might just have apoplexy on the spot and add to the death-toll. "*You* are the Church? *In my See!?*"

The old cleric rose to his feet, trembling with fury and speaking between clenched teeth. "Lock this idiot away, *Signor di Notte.* Lock him away and throw away the key. The Church is no man's! It is God's."

Bishop Capuletti bleated. "But, Metropolitan! They do but root out witchcraft. . . ."

Sachs was not so mild. "Petrine son of—"

"*Silence!*" bellowed Petro Dorma. "Let us not allow our tempers to betray us. I will remind you once, Abbot—once, not twice—that this is *Venice.* Here—in *this* city—I am the authority. *Not you.* And tonight it is my duty to uphold the law, without fear or favor."

He leaned back in his chair, bracing himself with both hands clenching the arm rests. "You will be released, Abbot, under your own cognizance, as soon as I have ascertained the facts. And I imagine *most* of the other Knights and Servants. But three people are dead—and one of them is Andrea Ghiazza, the son of the Count of Lissa. Dead with his head half severed. One of your knights has a bloody sword. At the very least, I must hold him in custody until he can face the judges."

Erik, standing with Manfred toward the rear of the crowd, cast a glance at the knight in question. Hans Dussel, that was. The young Saxon was a hothead. Erik hadn't seen it happen, but he was quite sure Dussel had seized Von Linksdorf's sword after the Prussian fell, mortally wounded by the arquebus. The Prussian officer had been the only Knight Sachs had allowed to carry a sword.

Abbot Sachs drew himself up. "He was a pagan man-witch and would have died in the fire! He was engaged in black magic ritual—"

One of the students yelled "Rubbish! He was in the taproom at Zianetti's with us. We came to see what was going on!"

Dorma lifted a hand. "My men or myself will take statements from each of you. Weapons will be confiscated, and returned if they do not show evidence of being used in this civil disturbance. You will all doubtless be appearing before the justices at the Doge's palace tomorrow."

They were taken, one at a time, to speak to Petro or to one of his officers. Not surprisingly, Marco found himself taken in to see Petro. His brother-in-law shook his head. "At least *someone* I can rely on. Tell me what actually happened."

So Marco did, omitting the fact that he knew who had called out. "So when we got there, there was this knight, bleeding from a pistol shot in the arm. I stopped the bleeding. Then Rafael and I went on to try and help Andrea. We were too late. The truth is, it would have been too late at any time. His neck was cut half through."

Petro took his head in hands. "What a mess! Half the *Case Vecchie* families in Venice caught up in this mess. These damned German fanatics. I've been trying to be evenhanded, but the city would be better off if we could get rid of them. Even witches are less destructive and divisive." It was the first time that Marco had heard Petro express any factional sentiment.

"So . . ." Marco said cautiously. "Who does Dorma—that is *we*—stand behind?"

Petro gave him the first smile he'd seen on Dorma's face that evening. "Nobody. We stand for *Venice*. If that means we must put up with fanatics, we do. But Venice is not anyone's lapdog. Not Rome's, not Milan's. Not the Holy Roman Empire's either, and I feel they too must be dabbling in this lot. The winged lion stands alone." He sighed. "Anyway. I'll see you tomorrow. In your case, it will be a token appearance. Angelina's due in town overnight. Come to Dorma for the night, at least. I'm worried about 'Gelina. She seems very moody these days—worse than usual."

Marco held out his hands, palm up, to Petro. "She's unhappy. Pregnancy can cause moodiness. But I am—always—her friend."

Petro sighed. "Given that you're married to Angelina, I can't say I'm unhappy to hear you say these things. But she's always been unsettled, moody. The pregnancy has just made it worse. But right now I think she needs a friend more than anything else in the world." Petro massaged his temple as if his head hurt.

"It'll be better once the baby's here," he told Petro earnestly. And then felt a lurch in his stomach, himself.

Lord and Saints. Me and Angelina, married, even if it's only in name. When I want—now—

What he wanted would not satisfy anything or anyone but himself. What he wanted was time—to turn time back. Time for himself, and Kat.

Benito had told him he'd seen her. Marco knew now that she'd written that letter believing that . . . well, he could understand how she must have felt.

Lord, Kat. If I'd had any choice—

But he hadn't had a choice. And now it was too late. He couldn't back out of this, not now. Not ever.

He still wanted to see her. Talk to her. But Benito had said that while she understood . . . she didn't want to see him. Not now. Not ever. A clean break was best. He could understand and respect that. Chains of family and honor . . .

"I can't say I blame you for staying roommates with that friend of yours over at the Accademia," Petro continued, looking up with a wry twist to his mouth. "There are times lately when I wish I could move out of Venice entirely. By the way, those herbs you brought do seem to be helping Mother."

It was an oblique sort of "thank you," but neither of them particularly wanted to openly allude to Rosanna's addiction to black lotos—and that the only thing that could help the addiction was the substitution of the less potent blue lotos. Hopefully, the addict could slowly be weaned off that.

"I'm glad Doctor Rigannio was willing to trust me," Marco replied.

Petro smiled faintly. "He *was* rather dubious at first, but you've convinced him that you know what you're talking about. In fact, he's invented an 'old herb-doctor' to account for the things you brought him, and he's been leaking the information over to the Accademia since the remedy seems effective."

"I'm glad to hear it. That—stuff—it's still a problem," Marco said soberly. "Nothing seems to keep people away from it, once they start. You'd think people'd have learned by now." He shrugged. Petro shook his head.

"People never seem to learn—"

By his face, unguarded for a moment, Marco could read the unspoken words—

Not even Mother.

Petro Dorma sighed. "But we've still got to try to help them." He stood up and went to a nearby window, looking out over the Bacino San Marco. Instead of the usual forest of masts it stood near-empty.

Marco knew a dismissal when he saw one; he stood likewise, edged past Petro to the door, made the right noises, and took his leave.

❀   ❀   ❀

The justices thanked him for rendering medical assistance to the injured, and dismissed him. It still left Marco shaking inside. Did they realize that he was the child of Lorendana Valdosta, who had planned to give their Venice to Milan? The world changed with one's perspectives. He'd spent years dreading that court . . . those justices . . .

And now it was "thank you, Signor Valdosta." Dorma's influence was not small, and the Valdosta name itself seemed to be a good and popular one. Well, except with Filippo Recchia. And that woman at the soiree at Gian Cecchi's palazzo. Signora Katerina Montescue, who had turned away rather than be introduced. Snooty. Even the Brunellis were more friendly. Lucrezia to the extent that he avoided her. What did the most courted and supposedly most beautiful woman in Venice find attractive about him? Or did she pursue all men like this? Maybe the stories weren't exaggerated!

He and Rafael walked back to their rooms, in companionable silence.

Two bedrooms and a sitting room. And even if it isn't Dorma, it's a world away from anything I've ever had before. Yeah, and I'm earning my way. So, tonight I will be nice to Angelina. Still, Benito and I keep paying the rent for that little pit over in Cannaregio. We need some place nobody knows about. And these days, with the allowance we get, we can afford it.

He felt guilty about the money. Benito had paid last month. What spare he had, he'd actually spent on food that he'd given to Tonio for some of the children. The trade was thin. And canal-people were getting thinner. The kids were the first to suffer.

Chapter 76

Trade was thin. Maria felt her ribs. So was she. Nothing coming downriver. A trickle of expensive food coming in from Fruili. Nothing but some local fish coming in from the sea. There was just no work available. She rowed along slowly. Other boatmen were sitting idle too. She might as well go home. At least it would be cool.

She pondered over relationships in general, and hers in particular. Lately all she and Caesare seemed to do was fight. It had been different back when they had first gotten together. Even once he'd established a relationship with his protector, Ricardo Brunelli, he been gentle . . . caring. For a while.

Yes. In those early days, he'd been quite different. Back when they'd been arranging the smuggling chambers he'd been a darling. She sighed. They'd yet to see a profit from that. Her cousins had painstakingly cut the chambers in the keels, had put up the secret *Colleganza* that paid for the cargo . . . And not one of those galleys had come back. The Garavelli clan were the poorer for it, and . . .

Well, nobody actually *said* it was her fault.

She sighed again. Most of their conflict came down to money, really. Well—except their quarrels about Kat. Caesare seemed to have a real animus against Kat. He'd told Maria to stay away from her, that she was a *Case Vecchie* bitch. How had he known she was *Case Vecchie*? She hadn't mentioned it.

"How's trade?" Tonio had come up alongside while she was in her brown study.

"Slow, Tonio," she said. "We need to take some kind of action, but the Doge is just sitting on things."

"He can afford to. We can't. I got some more sick kids for young Marco. Fancy him turning out to be a Valdosta. A good *Casa* that, in his grandpa's day."

"He's still seeing kids . . . Why am I telling you this? You know."

Tonio shrugged. "*Si.* I'll go there this evening. But likely enough he'll say 'they need more food.' And that's what I want to talk about, Maria Garavelli. He's the only *Case Vecchie* we know to talk to. You know him special-well. He's tied in with Dorma. They're a good house; look after their people—and Petro Dorma was the only one who stood up to the Dandelos. Dorma's got influence now, lots of it. You tell him the *popli minuta* want the Doge to stop playing with his toys and sitting on his ass. Boats are only going as far as Ferrara . . ."

Maria snorted. "You're behind the times, Tonio. Ferrara is being attacked by condottieri from Bologna and Milan. Nothing's going up the Po at all."

"*Merda.*" Tonio spat into the canal. "Why don't we at least go to the help of the Old Fox? The Duke Dell'este was a good friend to Venice, back before we argued about the salt pans. What's a few salt pans? We need trade."

Maria laughed wryly. "We need you on the Council of Ten, Tonio."

The lean Tonio acknowledged a hit. "Yeah. Well. You tell Marco, huh. His grandfather. He should listen."

Maria pushed off. "You tell him, Tonio. You'll see him before me."

Tonio looked uncomfortable. "*Si.* But he's got respect for you, see. You and that fancy man of yours. Tell him."

Maria sighed. "I'll tell him, Tonio. But I don't think there is much he can do."

She rowed on up the canal, heading home. She'd tell Marco when she next saw him. She'd promised, and a canaler's word was always good. But she'd also tell Benito. He came to see her more often.

She smiled for a moment, thinking of Benito. He was quite a boy, although she wouldn't tell him that. Effective. Not like Marco, who might be a saint, but would still be seeing good in people while they slit his throat.

The canal by the water-door was limpid, with not even a ripple around the floating bits of garbage. She tied up quietly. Maybe Caesare would be home and they could spend the afternoon in lovemaking . . . like they used to do. The idea was attractive. Distracting.

She went in quietly.

And it rapidly became apparent that an afternoon's lovemaking had been on someone else's mind too. The panting and begging said they'd been at it for a while.

Her mind in a furious turmoil, Maria went up the stairs three at a time. Threw the door open. She'd . . . timed her entry well. Caesare was so preoccupied in thrusting up into his kneeling mount that he didn't even realize Maria was there for a moment.

Maria took in the white body, slightly pendulous breasts, the long elegant neck and perfect face complete with tiny mole above her mouth. The face was flushed and prim mouth wide. It was a double shock. The last time Maria had seen her, she, Maria, had had one of the woman's Spanish combs in her hair. Seeing Kat's sister-in-law here . . .

Maria—having got this far—suddenly realized she didn't know quite what to do next.

She picked up the ewer and flung it at them, as one might at a pair of dogs.

The water had the same effect.

"My hair!" shrieked Alessandra.

Caesare abruptly parted from her, grabbed for his rapier. "Maria! What the hell are you doing here?"

"I live here, remember? Or maybe you forget. Like your promise that you were faithful to me? That you loved me?"

The woman, now with a sheet around herself, snapped. "Get out, you little dockside *puttana*! He's *my* lover. He's been mine for years! Long before he met *you*."

"Get out, Maria. We can deal with this later." Caesare's voice was dangerously even.

Maria's reply was not. "For you and me, there *is* no later, Caesare Aldanto! We're finished. Finished, you hear me? *FINISHED!*"

Caesare advanced on her. Stark naked except for his sword. "Get out. Get out now."

"Or what!? Or you're going to kill me?" She snarled back. Right now she didn't care.

She'd forgotten how fast and strong he was. He grabbed her arm and spun her round and pulled it up behind her back, his sword arm around her throat. He hauled her painfully, half off her feet, down the stairs, ignoring her struggles and screams. "*Shut up, you bitch.* Or I'll give you something to scream about." He took two fingers off the sword hilt and put them around the chain around her neck. With a sharp, flesh-tearing jerk he snapped it, tinkling the keys to the apartment onto the steps. He pushed her past the steps, thrusting her into the barred gate. He picked up the water-door key.

"You're going to get out of that door, now. And stay out," he said grimly. "Love *you*? A canal girl? I never did, but you were very useful. Now you're not. Get out, stay out and keep quiet. I'm warning you. I never do that twice."

Maria felt something break inside her. A tiny voice that seemed to belong to someone else said, "Unlock the door then."

And as she stepped out into the summer brightness of Venice, she heard Alessandra's mocking laughter echoing down the stairs that used to be hers.

Chapter 77

Benito was sick of it. His "transfer" to the *Case Vecchie* world was going to drive him mad. It was all very well for Marco, learning things he was interested in. So far he hadn't even seen a Dorma cousin he was interested in getting into the pants of, let alone spend time in endless social chitchat with. Dorma was treating him like a child.

For crying out loud. He was fifteen now! A mere year and a half younger than Marco—who was already married! On the canals or even on the ships, at sixteen you did a man's work. Only among the soft *Case Vecchie* did they give you another five years to grow up. Yeah sure, the house was at sixes-and-sevens with Angelina showing signs of being ready to pop.

He would take off again tonight. Seeing Maria always cheered him up. In the months since he moved in here, he'd been back to visit more frequently than Marco had.

So he would be absent without leave again tonight from the soiree. They couldn't sing anyway, compared to Valentina and Claudia. He'd slip off to Barducci's instead.

Kat listened to the singing coming out of Barducci's. The place was less crowded than usual. Times were hard in Venice . . . although right now the *Casa* Montescue were having a run of unprecedented luck. The coaster they used for transfers of gray merchandise coming in from the east hadn't had any cargos of stuff out of Ascalon for a while. But its every-second-day run to Trieste was turning in a real profit, for the first time ever. And the little caique was one of

651

the few ships they still owned outright. Covertly, it was true. And
Captain Della Tomasso was as crooked as a dog's hind leg and ran
various dubious operations. But right now his legal cargoes, which
belonged to the Montescue and were just supposed to break even,
were making a small fortune.

For the first time in nearly two months, the caique *Margerita*
had met a galliot that had made it through the blockade. Kat had
a parcel from Ascalon to collect. Delivery to run. She had it easier
than the galliot captain, however. He would turn in a fat profit,
true—but he was also having to face an interview with the Council
of Ten tonight . . . and the address to the Grand Council tomorrow. All Venice wanted to know what was happening. It was a hard
summer for trade for most people.

Captain Della Tomasso had news that he couldn't pass on to
most folk. And for once he was dying to talk. "The Dalmatian
pirates, a fleet from Ancona, and Genoan fleet are in the gulf. No
sign of the galleys from the Golden Horn or the western fleet."

Three years ago, Papa had parted with the western fleet at Bruges.
Even hearing it mentioned brought a pang to Kat. "The city's not
safe at night. Keep your crew aboard if you can. There was another
magical murder yesterday and the factions are blaming each other.
There'll be knife-fights tonight."

Della Tomasso was a bad man, who ran a smelly evil-crewed little
ship. Kat met him on dark nights off Guidecca. He never showed
the slightest concern for anything except money. She realized he was
tense too, with the first inquiry he'd ever made—in two years of
collections. "You going to be all right, Kat?"

"Yeah. I'll be fine," she said. "I'll stay on the lagoon, not go
through town, and deliver in the early morning. When do you sail?"

"I'm running some messages. As soon as they arrive . . ." He
snorted. "For the churchmen, would you believe it?"

Kat chuckled. "Doubtless the Metropolitan came to you personally."

"Nah. This German bunch. There's a lot more of them sitting
in Trieste." Della Tomasso looked vaguely alarmed. "I never said
that."

"Who am I going to tell, Captain?" asked Kat dryly. "Anyway,
the wind's getting up. I'd better go."

Della Tomasso nodded. "Stiff land breeze coming. Maybe a
storm, later."

The row up the Guidecca canal against the wind was a stiff one. After a while, Kat decided that even the risks of rowing quietly through town were worth it. It would cut her distance in half and avoid rowing against the wind. There was definitely a storm coming.

Benito walked out of Barducci's. The place had been thin on company, and full of uneasy knots of people. Even the music that Valentina and Claudia chose tonight had been careful. Things were just too explosive in town. Rumors were circulating that a small galliot had arrived from down-gulf, bringing news of the block-ading fleets. Rumor had everyone from the King of Sicily to the Ilkhan intervening.

"We should side with Milan." "We must call on Rome." "A pact with Emeric of Hungary." Ha. According to what Benito had been able to pick up at *Casa* Dorma, the *Case Vecchie* were in the same confused state. And the Doge wasn't doing a coherent job of leading.

Benito shimmied up an ornamental pillar, grabbed a cornice and headed for the rooftops. The streets weren't safe tonight; and why take a gondola, when he was short of exercise and liked the view from up here anyway? Mind you, it wouldn't be pleasant up here for too long. The wind was starting to blow.

He came down to canal level to cross a bridge over the Rio di Muti when he noticed a familiar gondola tied up there. A lousy mooring—a rotten old pole, half under the bridge shadows.

Maria? What was she doing here? This was way off her usual routes.

There was something in the bottom of the boat. Very cautiously, Benito pulled the mooring. The something in the bottom of the boat sat up, a bright sliver of steel in her hand.

"Maria Garavelli?" said Benito incredulously. "What are you doing here?"

"'Nito? Are . . . are you looking for me?" There was a curious pitiful hopefulness in her voice.

"No . . . I was just going past." Benito took a liberty. He climbed into Maria's boat. You didn't do that without permission. Benito knew then that something was seriously wrong. She didn't react. "What's up? What are you doing here, Maria?"

Scudding clouds cleared the moon-crescent, shining down on Maria's face. Those were tear tracks. Benito ignored the knife still in her hand, moved uneasily down the rocking boat and hugged her. She clung to him. This wasn't like Maria. He'd never seen her like this. She was always so tough. Even when she'd gotten away from the Dandelos...

"What are you doing out here, Maria?" he asked for the third time, gently.

"I..." She sniffed. "I've got nowhere else to go, Benito."

Benito had a sinking feeling in his gut. He knew the answer before he even asked. "Caesare... the apartment...?"

She swallowed. "He threw me out. I came home this afternoon... he was making love to another woman."

Benito didn't know what to say, so he just held her. It was the right thing to do. "He said... he never loved me. He used me, Benito. He *used* me. And I loved him. I wanted him so badly. Am I so ugly?"

"Lord and Saints no! You're really... well, when I saw you in that outfit of Kat's I thought you were one of the most beautiful women in town."

"You're a smooth talker, Benito Valdosta." But she didn't let go of him.

"No, it's truth." A dash of the old Benito audacity returned. "You feel pretty good too."

This didn't get him the slap it would've normally earned him. She leaned against him instead. It made the gondola rock, dangerously. "I'm too thin and my feet are too big."

Benito clicked his tongue. "Now what man is going to look at your feet?"

"So what do you look at, Benito?"

Benito realized he was in dangerous and unfamiliar waters. "Um. I like your eyes." He was aware of curves pressed against him.

"And what do you like about my eyes?"

"Uh, the way they spit fire when I look any lower down. Um. Not too low." He hoped turning it into a joke would at least ease things.

She pushed him away. The moon was out again, and a small, sad smile trembled at her lips. She tugged at the cords of her bodice-lacing. His eyes almost popped out of his head as she spilled her breasts out of her bodice. The white curves were hypnotic. The nipples stood out sharply in the moonlight. "You mean these?"

"Uh. Y... yes," stammered Benito.

Maria's voice was still sad, questioning, doubtful. "Benito. I need someone to make love to me. To kiss my breasts. To tell me they're beautiful. To tell me he wants me . . ."

Benito Valdosta found himself suddenly very dry in the mouth. "They're really really beautiful. They're . . . they're . . ." His biblical lessons with the Dorma pastor came to his rescue. "They're like twin does, it's, it's . . . from the Song of Solomon," he said thickly.

She smiled a little. "Come and kiss them now, Benito." She lay back on the duckboards, and pulled him down with her.

Benito found himself exploring a nipple gently with his tongue, her belly with a fumbling hand. He was both more excited and more . . . *awkward feeling* . . . than he could ever remember. This was no young boy's eagerness. Even Benito understood that for the first time in his life he was seized by a man's passion. Not for any girl, but for a particular woman. *Maria!* He was almost desperate in his desire to please her.

Gently! he told himself. But Maria was having none of it. She was caught up in her own passion—and a more furious one even than his. Her hands were tugging at his breeches cord. The boat rocked wildly as he attempted to help.

"You'll have us over, you fool!"

That sounded so like the old Maria, that Benito paused. "We shouldn't be doing this. . . ." His body was betraying his mouth.

"I asked you to, Benito," she said, a hand guiding. "I need . . . aaha!"

And after that there was no more talking for some time. Nothing coherent, at any rate.

"I think there's more water in the boat than in the canal," Maria said, laughing softly. "Ooh. I am going to have bruises. Duckboard stripes on my behind." *The arms that held him tight didn't seem perturbed.*

Benito felt the trickle of water down his neck. "I think some of it is because it's raining."

"Oh, hell. These are my only clothes."

Benito stretched, feeling her underneath him, muscled yet soft. "Um. Well, I've got some ideas about that. You can't sleep out here."

"I haven't got anywhere else, Benito," said Maria. "I'm not going back to the Garavellis'. The cousins were very unhappy about my moving in with . . . with Caesare anyway. I'll sleep under bridges. Take me a few days to find my feet, get together money for a place to stay."

"What I was going to say is . . ." The next words came out in a rush: "There is our—Marco's and my old place—in Cannaregio. It's got no windows and it's pretty noisy, but well, it's a roof. Got some spare stuff there, too."

She was silent for a few moments. "I don't want to be beholden." There was a shutdown in that voice. Pure canaler pride.

Benito shifted position slightly, shivering. The wind and drifts of rain had taken the heat out of what had been a sultry summer evening.

"Maria," he said quietly, gently. "You don't *owe* me anything. Marco and I, we put a lot into paying back the debt we owed to Caesare. Strikes me we probably owed you just as big a debt. We kind of thought we were paying both of you back. But it wasn't really like that, was it? We are beholden to you. Our place ain't much, but until you get sorted out . . . it's yours. You're already wet. It's going to get colder. Marco would never forgive me if I left you out here." He kissed her cheek. Then, awkwardly: "There's no conditions attached . . . or anything like that. It's yours."

She sighed. "Benito Valdosta. You can be just like your brother, sometimes."

Benito snorted. "Yeah. But I lie down and it goes away. Marco's my conscience. I'm just Benito—the practical one, and trouble. Come on. I'm getting cold, and you must be too."

"I've got a warm heavy blanket on top. But my back is tired of being wet. Let's see if we can sit up without having this thing over."

They managed. Maria saw to her lacing. "Benito," she said. "I'm sorry. I . . . used you. I needed someone and I used you."

Benito shrugged, smiling widely. "I didn't exactly mind! Actually . . ." His smile changed into something very shy. "It was wonderful. We men don't feel the way women do about it."

Maria snorted. She sounded almost her old self. "I've noticed! So. Was it better than with that Sarispelli girl?"

"Uh." Now Benito was embarrassed. "It was—very different. And, yes, much better." He suspected his face was bright red. "The truth is, Maria," he said very softly, "I think . . . well. There's nobody like you. Not for me, anyway."

Maria stared at him, for a moment. Then she snorted again. "Benito. Sometimes you say *exactly* the right thing. Whereabouts in Cannaregio is your place?"

Kat cursed the rain. If there was one thing about her night-trips she hated more than anything else, it was getting wet. But she'd decided to never shelter in a church again! Under San Trovaso bridge was safer than San Trovaso itself.

When the rain slacked off, she headed on down the canal. She decided she'd been right to come through town. It was safe enough. There were few people about and they were hurrying to their destinations before they got caught by the rain again. The torch-bearers were scattered and lights from unshuttered windows were few.

She was not prepared for the shout from a torch-bearer. "He's dead! Quickly! Come quickly. Bring lights. The bishop is dead!"

Shutters flew open. Lights spilled onto the rain-wet *fondamenta*, and the canal.

Kat put her head down and sculled. And as she did so, she saw a man slip from the shadows into the *sotoportego*. But in the momentary glance she saw him clearly. She started, and their eyes met. Then she hunched her face down and sculled. When she next looked he was gone, and she was into the comparative safety of the Grand Canal.

There was no doubt about one thing. She'd seen Eneko Lopez and he'd seen her. And neither of them, not her nor the creepy Spaniard, had wanted to be caught on the scene.

"It's not much of a place," said Benito anxiously. Surveying the tiny room by the candlelight, it looked even smaller and dingier than he remembered.

Maria smiled at him. Her hair was wetly plastered about her head. Somehow, this and the candlelight made her definite features stand out. The firm chin; the straight nose and broad cheek-bones.

"It looks like heaven compared to the boat in this weather. Going to have some baling to do in the morning." She shivered. "So. How about you help me light this fire?"

"Sure." He knelt in front of the prepared kindling and took a candle to light it. "There's some dry gear here." He pointed to the cupboard. "Boys' clothes, I'm afraid. But they're dry. You should fit into them. And we've got blankets. And there's some wine. Some grappa. Some almond biscotti. But that's all the food, I'm afraid."

He blew on the fire. It caught, sending small tongues of smoky flame to nibble at the bigger twigs. He turned around to see her still standing there, dripping. Those were tears adding to the wetness. He went across to hug her. "What's wrong?"

"Nothing. Well, everything. I was going to say 'you're a good kid, Benito Valdosta.'" She sighed. "Only you're not a kid any more and I'm not as strong as I thought I was. Can . . . can you stay a while?"

"Sure," said Benito, letting go of her and going to the cupboard. He unstoppered the bottle of grappa with his teeth; then poured a generous dollop into a cracked mug and took it to her. "Here. Get yourself outside this. Let me get you out of those wet clothes."

Her teeth chattered against the edge of the mug. She drank. "I can deal with it myself."

Benito went on loosening the laces. "I saw it all earlier, Maria. Do it yourself if you like. But I want you out of that wet stuff, wrapped in a blanket, eating biscotti in front of the fire in two minutes or I'll do it for you."

This drew a smile. "Help me, then. You can be really bossy, Benito Valdosta."

"Uh-huh. And who do you think I learned it from?"

She laughed. "Well. You'd also better get out of that wet stuff before *I* help *you*."

Benito took a deep breath. He wasn't naïve enough not to see certain inevitable consequences coming. And . . . he was quite shocked when he understood how much he wanted them to.

This can't be happening! cried out some little corner of himself. *You idiot! You'll turn into a fool like your brother!*

The rest of him, however, as his hands drifted across Maria's shoulders and back—so feminine, for all the muscle—had a different opinion.

Shut up . . . boy.

The next hours seemed almost like a dream to Benito. In a bed, well lit by candlelight, Maria was not the fierce and dimly seen rutter she had been in the bottom of a gondola, lit by nothing more than a crescent moon. There was nothing of the hard canaler left in her now. She was soft, rounded, smooth—more velvety and gorgeous than anything Benito had ever imagined.

The muscle was still there. The strong arms and legs coiled around him in passion gave proof of that often enough. But Benito barely noticed. His entire existence seemed nothing but a world of warmth, wetness, softness, all aglow with candlelight and his own dreams, finally boiling to the surface.

The first time he told her he loved her, Maria didn't even scowl at him. Indeed, she smiled.

"You don't have to say that, Benito," she murmured softly.

"I wanted to," he insisted. Feeling a bit of the old street savvy wailing somewhere in his heart—*you idiot!*—but not much. Hardly any, in truth.

Maria shook her head. "Please—don't. The word is cheap. Caesare showered me with it like false coins. I don't want to hear it any more."

So he subsided, for a time, distracted easily enough by Maria's next wave of passion. She might not want to hear the word with her ears, but every other part of her body seemed eager to listen. Besides, it was hard to stay poetic with Maria. She made him laugh too much.

When she wasn't criticizing him, that is. Usually both at the same time.

"What *did* that silly Sarispelli teach you, anyway?" she grumbled at one point. "I'm not a wooden plank being nailed on a ship, you know? And that thing of yours is way too big for a nail in the first place."

By now, Benito was relaxed enough to give an honest answer. "Hey, she's nice. I don't think she really knew any more than I did."

"Guess not," agreed Maria.

Benito was even relaxed enough to be smart instead of street-savvy stupid. "Show me, then. Please."

"Good boy," gurgled Maria happily, and proceeded to do so. Some time later, as she cried out with pleasure—much louder than she had before—Benito whispered the words again. Moaned them, rather, since he was awash in his own ecstasy.

Maria slapped the back of his head, sure enough. But, that done, the same hand which slapped began to caress and clutch. And stroked him, softly and steadily, as they lay in each others' arms afterward, pooled in their own moisture.

"That stinking bastard Aldanto was good for something," Maria whispered. "I give it to you as a gift."

"I love you," he whispered back.

She didn't slap him, this time. But her hand came up and closed his mouth. "Don't, Benito. Please. Tonight is too special, for both of us. Just let it be what it is, that's all."

He never spoke the words again that night, even though it lasted almost until dawn. Before he finally fell asleep, not long after Maria, he raised himself on one elbow and gazed down upon her nude body lying next to him. He had never seen anything so beautiful in his life, and knew that he never would. Fifteen years old be damned. Some things are certain.

Still, he didn't say the words, even though she was no longer awake to rebuke him. In some obscure way, he couldn't.

He puzzled at the problem, for a bit. Just as he drifted into slumber, it came to him. He could never steal anything from Maria, he realized. Not even words of love.

Chapter 78

"We have the dagger. It's a Ferrara-steel blade with scarlet and blue tassels," said Retired Admiral Dourso, one of Petro's fellow *Signori di Notte*. "We have the witnesses—one who saw him lurking in the alley, and two who heard him utter angry threats at the bishop. You were there. It was the night he was arrested in that affray with the Knights and Servants of the Trinity."

Petro Dorma took a deep breath. "Bishop Capuletti was killed at about midnight?"

The admiral nodded. "The body was still warm when it was found, just before midnight. The clothes were barely wet. I'm sorry, Petro. I must take Marco Valdosta into custody."

Petro shook his head at his older colleague. "Admiral, I haven't had much sleep. I must tell you that some hours after midnight, I became an uncle."

It took the salt-and-pepper-haired admiral a few moments to work this out. "Valdosta's child?"

Petro thought the little girl looked very like its father. But that was another matter for later. "My sister, Angelina, has had a daughter, yes. The child is rather premature."

"Congratulations, Petro, but . . ."

"The birth was attended by the Doctor Rigannio, a midwife, my mother, Countess Marangoni—*and* Marco Valdosta. He assisted as he is learning to be a doctor. Angelina went into labor just before midnight, at the soiree at the *Casa* Antorini. Which, as you know, is near the Oratio del Cruciferi."

Petro walked over to the sideboard and poured each of them

a glass of Vin Santo. He handed the admiral one of the Venetian-ware glasses. "So. Unless you wish to accuse my ward of witch-craft and having a doppelganger, I suggest you look elsewhere for a murderer. The time and distances traveled make it unlikely. The witnesses who actually saw him help with Angelina make it impossible."

When the admiral had left, Petro sat with his head in his hands. Someone had set out to deliberately incriminate Marco. It was pure luck that he had a cast-iron alibi. This was plainly an attack on Dorma. Somehow the deliberations of Council of Ten must have leaked. This lot was bad enough . . . without that Angelina had spent half her labor demanding that Caesare Aldanto be brought to her, and already this morning had summoned him to her bedside to demand the same.

An hour later the admiral was back. "Not Marco Valdosta. His brother."

Benito was struggling to wake up. Having his room at Dorma—which he'd been back in for less than two hours—invaded by Petro, another *Signor di Notte*, and two Schiopettieri was something of a shock.

It was even more of a shock when they wanted to know where the hell he'd been last night.

They didn't find his refusal to answer at all satisfactory.

"Benito Valdosta. I must ask you to dress and come with us," said the salt-and-pepper-haired ex-admiral turned *Signor di Notte*. "You will be charged with the murder of Bishop Pietro Capuletti."

"Ha!" Kat's grandfather came into the breakfast salon, where Kat was picking at a bowl of frumenty. "I told you, girl! Blood will out! They've arrested that damned Valdosta boy for murder!"

Kat's chair went flying. The fragile bowl was dropped, shatter-ing on the fine intarsia floor as she leapt to her feet. She felt blood drain from her face. "What?"

The old man rubbed his hands in glee, ignoring the destruc-tion. "That Valdosta-pig. I went to see Dourso this morning. Just checking things out for you, girl. And he was just on his way to arrest Marco Valdosta. For the murder of Bishop Pietro Capuletti. Ha!"

"*Did you do this?*" she demanded furiously. "Did you engineer this, Grandpapa?"

Lodovico Montescue shook his leonine old head. "I *wish* it were my doing. But they'll have his head, anyway," he said with great satisfaction.

Kat stared at him. "He wasn't even born when you had your stupid fight! You crazy old man! He doesn't even know who you are!" She stormed out.

"Katerina! Where are you going?" He hurried after her as fast as his old legs could manage.

Over her shoulder, Kat snapped: "To hand myself over to the justices at the Doge's palazzo, for murdering Bishop Capuletti."

"Stop, Katerina! You can't do tha—" His voice was cut off by the great front door closing. A passing gondolier answered her hail. And Kat, in a turmoil of emotion, set off to rescue Marco.

Marco Valdosta stared incredulously at his brother-in-law. "You just let them take him away?"

Petro threw up his hands helplessly. "He has witnesses. A Ferrara-made knife with house tassels. I'll swear it's not Benito's. But it looks bad. And then your brother refuses to say where he was last night."

Marco steepled his long slim fingers. "Ten to one he'll have been doing something for Caesare Aldanto. Probably with Maria."

Dorma leaned forward. "Who is this Maria?"

There was no sense in pulling punches. "She's a canal-girl—the one who was abducted by the Dandelos. She lives with Caesare Aldanto. He's worth asking about this. If anyone will help Benito, it's him."

"I'll have some of my people go out and fetch him." He stopped Marco's reply. "You will stay right here, Marco. Under my eye. You'll accompany me to hear the galliot captain address the Senate at midday. You *will* be seen. This is intended as an attack on Dorma. I wish I knew by whom."

Marco shook his head. "The knife is too obvious, Petro. Why would he leave it behind?"

"Exactly," said Petro. "But they'll claim it was wrestled from his grasp by the dying man."

Marco took a deep breath. "Who are these witnesses, Petro? And tell me about this knife."

"By the description, the knife is one with the *main gauche* you and Benito carry. As for the witnesses, it's a Filippo Recchia and Vittorio Toromelli. Boys from respectable rising families."

Petro Dorma was one of the most phlegmatic of the *Case Vecchie*. He was totally unprepared for Marco's harsh laughter. He positively gaped.

Marco stood up. "Petro, I think we can deal with this *and* find out for you exactly who is trying to get at you. Can we arrange to see the justices before the Senate address?"

"It should be possible, yes," said Petro. "Why?"

Marco smiled like a shark. "They came here looking for me first, right? Recchia and his buddy Toromelli know me. I'm willing to bet they don't know Benito. They know I have a younger brother. But he doesn't show up at the Accademia. And he hasn't been to any major functions with you."

"We're trying to polish out the rough spots," said Petro with a smile. "He's been to three private soirees. He should have been at last night's one. That would have been the first time you were 'on show' together."

"They claimed they saw me. Then, when you provided an alibi for me . . . they changed it hastily to Benito. We're going to trap them. They don't know that we don't even look alike."

Dorma realized that Marco was right. *They don't look alike, not in the least. If I hadn't known—if Duke Dell'este had not warned me—I never would have guessed they were brothers. Even half-brothers.*

Petro sat back in his chair and rubbed his hands. "That's not all," he said. "They claim to have heard you swearing revenge on the night of that abortive raid by the Knots on that supposed Strega circle. Except for the time when you were in with me—alone without anyone to claim to have listened—you were with the injured. Including a Knight of the Holy Trinity."

He rose and began pacing slowly about. "I wonder if the injured have been called as witnesses? I'll ask the abbot to send that knight to the justices. Sachs should agree—he wants back into my good books after that fiasco at the Accademia."

Dorma rang a bell, and then he wrote a hasty note. The runner came up and was dispatched.

"Well, I think we shall go across to the Doge's palace."

"Good," said Marco, grimly. "Because I have another string to this bow. If that blade is like this one, if we can get it to Ferrara, then my grandfather can tell us exactly who it was sold to. I *want* them."

Petro looked at the intent, pacing Marco. "I've never seen you like this before, my boy."

"They threaten my *family*, Petro. Filippo Recchia has let his little grudge against me put Benito in prison for murder. I won't allow that. If necessary I will kill him and his friend myself. Because I can if I have to. Or I will pay Aldanto to do it."

Petro stared at his young brother-in-law. He had never seen Marco in such a state, and was just realizing that the years in the marshes had left an imprint. A rather savage one. "I glad we're family, Valdosta," he said wryly.

The Piazza San Marco was already crowded. All ten of the justices were in their chambers. Most of the senators were also there in the palace. It was not hard for someone of Petro Dorma's standing to ask the chief justice with two of his colleagues to have a preliminary hearing on the holding in captivity of the suspected murderer Benito Valdosta, with a couple of eminent senators for witnesses. "This affair is political," explained Petro. "We are likely to take political actions this afternoon, so this may have a bearing."

Two Schiopettieri were sent off to find Masters Filippo Recchia and Vittorio Toromelli. Marco was able to direct them to a couple of likely taverns. Another three were sent to round up another five boys of between Marco and Benito's age.

They waited on them and the arrival of the Knights of the Holy Trinity.

Abbot Sachs looked thin on patience. He didn't get up when Erik entered but remained at his piled scriptorium. "I have all this correspondence from our courier out of Trieste, and now this note from Dorma. It seems better-natured than our last encounter. And we could still use the man's good graces. He wants Von Gherens and any other of the Knights or Servants of the Holy Trinity who were with the injured in that raid of ours at the Accademia. Go, *Ritter*. Take Von Gherens. He is up on his feet again. Brother Uriel helped attend him too, along with that student. Take Uriel along. Go." He shooed.

Erik was only too glad to go. The embassy had been full of things going on for the last while that he wasn't on top of—and whose consequences for Manfred worried him. He wanted out, for both of them. He didn't ask permission to take Manfred. He could always claim that he'd needed Manfred to support Von Gherens. So what if Manfred had been safe at the embassy—actually, with Francesca—that night?

The palace was crowded, but a couple of Schiopettieri were waiting for them at the doors, and escorted them to Petro Dorma, who was sitting with a couple of the Venetian justices, and a stripling Erik recognized. It was Dorma's ward. Yes, he had been there at the raid. Von Gherens probably owed his leg to the boy, and one of the students probably his life. Erik hadn't put two and two together at the time. There had been other things on his mind.

Petro Dorma greeted them. "So Abbot Sachs was not able to come personally? A pity. But never mind. We need you as witnesses to the truth or falsehood of a particularly unpleasant accusation. We are questioning statements allegedly made by this young man. Do any of you recognize him?" He pointed at his ward. Uriel, Von Gherens and Erik all nodded.

Dorma smiled. "Right. If you don't mind, could you wait in the antechamber? You will be called one at a time. I've sent for some wine."

Manfred brightened visibly. "I'll stay here and look after the wine," he said cheerfully. "I wasn't there."

Dorma smiled humorlessly. "I suspect the 'Accusers' might well not have been there, either. This way, gentlemen."

Filippo Recchia, the handsome and wealthy champion fencer, looked sulky, angry, and just a little overawed. His sycophant Vittorio just looked terrified. They were led one at a time to bear witness. Dorma insisted they each testify separately.

Recchia spoke first, his face stiff but seemingly calm. "He was angry. He said to that friend of his, Rafael de Tomaso. 'I wish we'd killed all of these German monks and knights. I wish we could get rid of Bishop Capuletti. I would do it myself if I had half the chance.'"

One of the Justices pointed at Marco: "And it was definitely this man who said that?"

Both Filippo, and then Vittorio, confirmed the statement. *Yes. They knew him well. Would recognize him with certainty.*

"But it was not him you saw lurking in the alley next to the Fondamenta Pruili," the justice asked Recchia.

"I thought so, Your Honor, but I realized I must be mistaken and it must be his brother."

"Ah. But you saw him well enough to recognize him?"

Recchia crossed himself. "My oath on it."

"Thank you. Stand down, Signor Recchia."

Marco watched as the first of the knights was called. What if he were part of this conspiracy? Fear of the Knots and their reputation rose in his throat as the young blond knight with the chiseled features took the stand.

Unnecessarily, it seemed. "No. He was with us all the time from when the Schiopettieri arrived, until we were summoned individually."

"And did he at any stage say anything about killing anyone?"

The knight, Erik Hakkonsen, frowned. "No. Definitely not. He said very little. His attention was on the wounded. A good young fellow. An innocent bystander who came to provide assistance, that's all. The Knights of the Holy Trinity are in his debt."

"And do you remember these two?"

The blond knight pointed at Vittorio. "Him. He was very drunk. Kept singing. Some of your Schiopettieri would remember him."

The justices then called the next witness, Von Gherens, who seconded Hakkonsen's statements and echoed his praise of Marco.

Then Brother Uriel came along. As usual he didn't mince his words. "They swore they heard *what*?" he demanded. When told again, he snorted derisively. "Absolute lies. They've broken their oath sworn on the Holy Bible. Get your Metropolitan to excommunicate them."

Vittorio went pale, but Filippo laughed. "Who do you believe? Good Venetians—or foreigners and half-bloods like this Valdosta? He's mongrel Ferrarese, not Venetian. And Ferrara will be history soon."

The chief justice just shook his head. "Signor Recchia. Come through to the next room and point out the younger Valdosta. You did see him clearly, did you not?"

"It wasn't daylight, but I saw him clearly enough to think it was Marco Valdosta at first." Recchia spoke with supreme confidence.

❀   ❀   ❀

The confidence disappeared when he saw the six young men, all wearing Dorma-blue.

"He's not here . . ."

"Indeed, he is," countered the chief justice sternly. "Point him out, put your hand on his shoulder."

Eventually Recchia chose the tallest. A young man with straight dark hair. "Him. He's Valdosta."

The young man accused got a very alarmed look on his face. "I am not!" he protested. "I'm Enrico Battista. Everyone will tell you so! I'm just a pastry cook."

Benito, curly-haired, stocky Benito, who had been through very little sleep, arrested for murder, thrust in jail, hauled out and made to dress in Dorma livery by two Schiopettieri and wait while this . . . *figlio di una puttana* lied about him, started laughing. And then, before anyone could intervene, he hopped forward and grabbed Filippo Recchia by the silk shirtfront. Marco watched as Benito kneed straight-nosed, handsome Filippo champion-of-the-fencing-salle-Recchia in the testicles—and then punched his face, once, twice, as he bent forward.

Marco noticed that the huge, solid young knight who had wandered in put his glass down and clapped. Once, twice, before the Schiopettieri dragged Benito off Recchia.

The chief justice managed to keep an absolute straight face. He was possibly the only one in the chamber to do so. "Perjury and the bearing of false witness, especially in such a serious case as this is a serious offense, with which you will be charged, Filippo Recchia and Vittorio Toromelli. Your false testimony also places you under extreme suspicion of being party to the murder. . . ."

"I was in Zianetti's!" choked Recchia, still clutching his groin. "I can prove it. I was nowhere near the scene. I just heard about the dagger and—"

"Enough." The chief justice silenced him. "Benito Valdosta. Brawling in public places carries certain penalties. You are hereby fined one ducat, considering the extreme provocation. When that is paid you are free to go." Then he paused. "Wait. There is still the matter of the dagger and your whereabouts last night."

"Ahem." Petro cleared his throat. "The dagger was a transparent attempt to put blame on Valdosta. Anyone could buy one and color the tassels. Only a fool would use such a weapon—and leave it on the scene, eh, Your Honor? In my opinion, it's a base political thrust at Dorma, as the Valdosta boys are my wards and my kin."

Again, he cleared his throat. "As for the refusal to say where he was, Your Honor . . . a gentleman's obligations, you understand . . . a young lady by the name of Maria—no last names, please!—surely no one will insist . . ."

Marco watched his younger brother blush absolutely puce. "How the hell did *you* know?" Benito demanded.

Not even the chief justice could keep a straight face any more.

The door to the chamber burst open. Marco saw an extremely distraught, sobbing *Case Vecchie* woman standing there. It took him a few moments of incredulous staring to realize that it was Kat.

"I . . ." She swallowed. "I've come to confess! I murdered Bishop Capuletti. On the Fondamenta Pruili—last night, just before midnight."

The chief justice looked at her "Ah. The mysterious Maria."

She looked at him in puzzlement. "No. Katerina Montescue."

A look of wary understanding dawned across the chief justice's face. He was, after all, a man of about sixty who knew a great deal about the wrangles of the various families of the *Case Vecchie.* He looked at Benito "Valdosta . . ." Then at Kat. "And you would be Lodovico Montescue's granddaughter?" His voice held both understanding and trepidation.

Kat nodded.

The chief justice shook his head. "No wonder . . ." He sighed. "I suppose I can expect old Lodovico here any minute with real murder in mind?"

The Campanile bell chimed. When it was still, the chief justice continued. "But right now I am going to listen to the captain of that galliot. Out. All of you except Recchia and Toromelli. They can remain with the Schiopettieri until I return." He looked at Benito. "You might have been safer in jail, boy."

Chapter 79

The passage outside was full of people. Anyone with the least excuse was hurrying to the great council chamber. Marco, as the oldest Valdosta, was supposed to be there. So was Petro Dorma.

Marco was instead engaged in hugging Kat.

Petro took a deep breath. "I suppose, as Angelina's brother and head of *Casa* Dorma, I should ask for an explanation. Or at least a formal introduction." He sounded resigned.

Flushing a little, Marco broke from Kat. "Petro. This is Kat. This is the woman I . . . I would have married, if I hadn't married your sister."

"Oh." Petro had the grace to look a little embarrassed.

"Don't worry," said Kat. "There is nothing between us." She sounded slightly wistful.

"Um. Yes. I suppose I'd better go and listen to the captain and hear what the Doge has to say," said Petro, uncomfortably.

Katerina smiled. "We're under blockade by the Genoese, the Dalmatian pirates out of the Narenta, and a fleet up from Ancona— presumably supplied by Rome. There is no sign of either the eastern or western fleets. The captain came island hopping from Ascalon, and sneaked up the coast at night, having heard about the blockade in Corfu. Which is more than he will tell you."

It was Petro Dorma's turn to smile. "And as I helped to draft the Doge's response, I don't need to listen to that either."

"On the other hand," Kat added, no longer smiling, "I can tell you who killed Bishop Capuletti."

"She . . . never . . ."—pant—"did it, Dorma." It was Lodovico

670

Montescue, red faced, with rivulets of sweat on his choleric face. He looked ready to keel over.

"Grandpapa!"

"Away from him . . . girl." The old man went off into a paroxysm of coughing. Benito, quicker on the uptake than most, grabbed a chair from against the wall and sat the old man down on it. "Thank you. You're a good lad. Listen, Dorma. My granddaughter knows nothing about this . . . killing."

"I do." Kat said firmly.

Lodovico shook his head. "She's got a maggot in her head about this Marco Valdosta here. But leave my granddaughter out of this. I've forsworn my vengeance against *Casa* Valdosta anyway."

Marco stepped forward. "Kat isn't implicated. And I won't let her be. Not while I'm alive."

Lodovico looked at him in some surprise. "What? Who made you free of my granddaughter's name? But that's well said, for a Valdosta," he granted, grudgingly.

Petro laughed. "They're none of them guilty, Montescue. It was an attempt to falsely implicate them, and through them, me. We don't know who killed the bishop . . ."

"I told you," interrupted Kat. "*I do.* I saw him just after the killing. It was that Spaniard. Senor Eneko Lopez."

Petro Dorma put his hand over his eyes. "You saw him actually do it?"

"Well, no," admitted Kat. "I saw him running away from the scene."

Petro looked at her with absolutely no expression. "If I asked what you were doing there just before midnight . . . would I regret it?"

Marco beat Lodovico to the punch. "Yes. Just leave it please, Petro. We'll follow it up through that dagger. If we need to, we'll take action. Forget the court. We can even call Aldanto in if need be."

Lodovico looked at him very speculatively. But he nodded approvingly. Started to speak . . . But his words were lost in the thunderous applause from the piazza.

When the cheering had died down Kat asked: "What's happening?

Lodovico smiled crookedly. "I think, Katerina, that Venice just went to war. If they have any sense they'll pick off our enemies one by one."

Dorma nodded approvingly. "Correct. The Scaligers in Verona first. We need Fruili secure."

"The other vultures will try to attack the Republic on other fronts when we're engaged."

Dorma nodded again. "That's why I'm supposed to organize the formation of a militia. Angelina's been at me to engage Caesare Aldanto to head it, Marco. What do you think?"

Marco found himself in a quandary. He owed Caesare. Lord knew he'd owed Caesare. But Venice stood in danger. "He has been a soldier. He served with Sforza."

Dorma's eyes narrowed. "I read caution in what you say. I'll employ him with caution. You're very honest, Marco."

"Good," said Lodovico Montescue, his snowy brows drawing together. "Because I need to ask some honest questions which need honest answers."

Dorma sighed. "I'll leave you to ask them, Signor Montescue. Just remember, my arm is very long." This was said completely pleasantly and urbanely. Yet the feeling of power and potential threat went with it. "But now my duty to the Republic calls. I shall see you boys at the *Casa* Dorma tonight."

Lodovico Montescue watched him go. "Francesca said he was the rising man and I should throw him my support. I can believe her now." He turned to face the youngsters. "But I'll throw him my support soon enough. For the moment—Marco Valdosta, answer me honestly. What are your intentions as regards my granddaughter?"

Looking at him, Marco knew that if he said the wrong thing, no threat of Dorma or even the Doge would stop this fierce old man. "None. I'm married. I have a baby daughter. But . . ." He paused. "If that were not the case—and Kat would have me—I'd have married her, even if you or hell stood in my way. I was a fool not to have asked her the moment I saw her."

Kat leaned over him. "And if you lay just one finger on him, I'll . . . I'll . . ."

Montescue patted her arm. Smiled his crooked smile. "He's very like his grandfather Luciano. One of the good Valdostas. Gentle and soft, but good steel underneath. I tried to have you killed once, boy. My best chance came nearly two years ago now. My agents searched Ferrara, Milan, even Rome. Then I got word one had found you here in Venice. He never came back for the bounty."

"I killed the assassin," said Marco quietly. "It was an accident and I was lucky."

Lodovico snorted. "Luck? I doubt that. Any more than it was luck that enabled you to evade my spies thereafter." He coughed. "Who were, I admit, not the most competent at their trade."

His granddaughter was glaring so fiercely at him that the family resemblance, not usually that noticeable, was now obvious. Old Montescue winced.

"I gave it up entirely anyway, Kat, a few months ago. Stopped even looking for the lads. After Francesca—" He coughed again. "Well. I had a dream, also. About my boyhood friend Luciano. I woke up thinking I had ordered the death of a boy like Luciano. It was chilling."

He made a bit of a rally, presenting a stiff face to Marco. "So I called off my dogs, boy. But I still think *your* father had *my* children killed. I won't bring his sins on your head. My vendetta is over, and I have given my word. But there can be no friendship between you and Katerina, with this between us. Not even an honorable one. You have your life, and your wife. Go and live that life with your wife."

"And I respect your decision," responded Marco, just as stiffly. "But I must know one thing. Did you have my mother killed?"

The white-haired head of the *Casa* Montescue shook his head. "No. Her defenses were too good. I wasn't really hunting her, anyway. I wanted the Valdosta *sons* . . . you, in particular. Word of a Montescue. I didn't have anything to do with her death. She was involved with Montagnards, you know. The only ones who could have easily penetrated her defenses are her own people."

Marco nodded. "That's what Chiano and my brother both said. I chose not to believe them for years."

The old man struggled to his feet. Both Marco and Benito stepped forward to help. He waved Marco off. "I'll take this other Dorma lad's arm, Valdosta. I'm not ready to take yours."

Marco nodded. "I'll meet you at the foot of the winged Lion of Saint Mark, Benito. Good-bye, Kat."

Kat found herself unable to speak. Her eyes burned, but she managed a tremulous wave. They set off, leaving Marco behind in the rapidly emptying piazza. Benito provided support for the old man, who leaned on his shoulder. "Sorry, boy. That was too much for me. I ran . . . I'm too old." He sighed.

"Sir. Um. I've got a suggestion. Your granddaughter Katerina going out on these night trips on her own. It's not safe, sir." Benito ignored the poisonous look Kat gave him.

The old man sighed again. "You're right, boy. But I'm too old these days. And who else do we trust?"

"As it happens, I have someone you can trust. Absolutely. Good with a knife too, and knows how to keep a still tongue."

Old Lodovico shook his head. "Montescue can't afford any bravos, boy. Certainly not good ones. And I'm not having Kat going on these night trips with a man."

Benito smiled. "Maria is no bravo, sir, nor a man. And I reckon Kat can trust her. She owes Kat, and she doesn't forget a debt."

Kat stared at him. "Maria? But what about . . . Caesare?"

"He threw her out."

"Tell her to come to me," said Kat decisively.

Her grandfather actually managed a chuckle. That was a good sign. "Minx. We can't afford any more people."

"We can afford a roof. And food. And maybe a bit for risks."

The old man shrugged. "Find a roof that doesn't leak at Montescue these days! But you've made up your mind, Kat. I know I'm wasting my time."

"You won't regret it, sir," said Benito earnestly. "I'll get word to her, Kat. She needs a woman-friend right now. Might take her a day or two to make up her mind, huh? She's really stiff-canaler proud. But I'll talk to her. Well, can I call you a gondola?"

"Thank you. You're a good lad, Dorma."

Benito smiled. "My name is not Dorma, sir. It's Valdosta. The good one is my brother."

They were silent for a good part of the voyage. Finally Lodovico sighed. "So. I was wrong about them. But Kat . . . The Montescue will not pursue the vendetta. My promise. But he is married, Katerina. I want your promise. You will leave him alone."

Kat sighed. "It wouldn't make any difference. You don't know him. He won't do anything no matter what. Sometimes Grandpapa, I think we could choke on our own honor. And Marco is like that. Dorma tricked him into marrying that sister . . ."

"He had to do that, child," Lodovico said stiffly. "You shouldn't know about that sort of thing, but honor demands—"

"I'll bet that child has a good chance at a blond head of hair, Grandpapa!" snapped Kat angrily. "And not dyed blond like its mama, either."

A short time after, still angry, Kat was back to glaring at her grandfather. "And what's this mention you made earlier of a 'Francesca' telling you this and that? Surely—"

Lodovico's face was as stiff as a board. "My own *grandfather!*" Kat wailed. "I can't believe it!"

"I'm not so old as all that," he muttered.

"My own grandfather! I'll kill her!"

Lodovico smiled wryly. "That's the spirit, girl. Start a vendetta of your own."

Kat choked on the next threat. Her grandfather shrugged. "She got me to stop hunting him, you know. Your precious Marco, I mean."

Kat swallowed. "Well." Swallowed again. "Well. All right, then. Maybe I'll just break her leg."

Lodovico shook his head firmly. "Better to go for an arm. Good advice from an old vendettist. Her legs are awfully strong."

"My own grandfather!"

Manfred poured some more wine into his glass. He'd paid very little attention to the justice's order of eviction from the chamber. And the two Schiopettieri with the two "false witnesses" seemed very unwilling to give force to the justice's words. Steel cladding and a reputation for mayhem had some advantages.

"I think we should get back, *Ritter,*" said Brother Uriel sternly. "And not sit about idling with a glass of wine."

"*Ritter* Von Gherens needs a glass to build up his strength," said Manfred solemnly.

Von Gherens looked briefly startled, but he caught on quickly. "That's exactly what Brother Samson the Hospitaler said. I'm feeling very weak after the walk, Brother."

Uriel snorted and shook his head.

"They might as well have their glass of wine," said Erik, pacifically. "We won't get a vessel, while the half of the town is here to listen to the report from this sea captain. And Von Gherens is in no state to walk all the way home yet."

Uriel accepted this, and relaxed slightly. "True. But I do not hold with too much wine drinking. And I want to tell Father Sachs about the death of the bishop. He was of course a soft Venetian, but open to Pauline persuasion."

Manfred put a booted foot up on the bench. "Heh. But the Holy Saint Paul himself said: 'Take a bit of wine for the good of your stomach.'"

Uriel brightened. Ecclesiastical argument and knowledge of biblical quotations was his weakness. "True, but . . ."

He made no objection to them pouring him a glass, which he drank as he talked at length, and he didn't even notice them finishing the rest of the bottle before they left. Finding him and Von Gherens a gondola was by this stage possible, and Manfred kindly volunteered Erik and himself to walk.

"It's August, Manfred. August in Italy. I sweat standing still. When we've finished going to visit Francesca, which is what you intend—I can tell—we take a boat. In fact we wait five minutes and we take a boat *to* Francesca."

"Just exactly what I was going to suggest," said Manfred.

Chapter 80

Marco pulled himself back into the middle of his bed, sitting on the handsome wool blanket cross-legged and pondering the silk-wrapped, sealed package that Petro Dorma had sent over by messenger. There was more than enough light from his tiny slit-window to read the inscription on the package.

By what means the dagger had been taken from the *Signori di Notte* and whisked to Ferrara heaven only knew. Heaven and Petro Dorma.

Marco opened the outer canvas, then the box wrapped in it, tipping out the package inside. Two hand-spans long, narrow, and heavy. A *main gauche* in the new Toulouse style . . . Marco knew that before he even opened the box. He'd hefted too many blades in his time not to know the weight and balance of a knife. Even with it well wrapped and in a wooden box, he could tell.

Silk cords twisted about the final wrapping inside the box in complicated knots; red silk cords in patterns Marco knew, patterns difficult to duplicate. The final knot had been sealed with a wax stamp, imprinted with the Dell'este crest.

Hazard, those knots said, and *Be wary*. You only tied a package coming out of Ferrara with those knots when you thought there might be a possibility the package would be opened by unfriendly hands somewhere along the way.

All of which meant that *this* was the very blade that had gone upriver to Ferrara and Duke Dell'este, the town's iron-spined ruler.

The knife that had slain Bishop Pietro Capuletti. The Ferrara blade, a signed blade with the intaglio crest etched proudly on the pommel nut for all to see, pointing straight to Valdosta—and another clan, a *Venetian* clan.

House Dorma. A new Power, and rising, which made their situation more precarious than if they had been established movers-and-shakers.

Guilt by association implicated *Casa* Dorma; and most especially Petro Dorma, who had taken in two long-lost Valdosta boys and had tied silken cords of tighter binding to Marco, and so to the steel of Ferrara.

Someone had used a Ferrara *main gauche* to sever more than Pietro Capuletti's life. Someone had gone to expensive lengths to bring a signed Valdosta knife down-river to assassinate the pro-Pauline prelate.

Marco rested his elbows on his knees and stared wearily at the thing, bright on the dark wool blanket of Dalmatian weave.

I didn't expect an answer so quickly. Maybe I ought to put off untying those knots. My life's complicated enough as it is.

But the knots, and the message in them, did not permit any such evasions. Particularly not now, not when Petro Dorma needed *any* scrap of information, however hazardous, to counter the attack on their houses.

Slowly, reluctantly, Marco reached for the packet; slowly broke the seal, and gave the cords the proper twist that freed them.

The silk fell open, falling on the open oiled canvas that had contained the box. Marco pulled the silk away and the knife slipped free of it. The knife, and a tube of closely written paper. But it was the knife that held the eye: shining, beautiful in its way, like a sleeping snake.

There was more in the way of an answer than Marco had expected. He'd thought to get a simple note. Instead—instead there were several pages, all in the duke's precise hand.

Marco picked up the letters and began to read.

Petro Dorma's private study was bright as only the best room in a wealthy man's house could be; walled on two sides with clear, sparkling-clean windows and high enough to catch all the sunlight available. A beautiful Cassone. Linenfold scrollwork on the polished wooden panels on the walls, soft Turkish rugs on the floor—an expensive retreat fitting the head of one of the rising stars of Venice, both in commerce and government.

It struck Marco that despite being balding, Petro was an incongruously young man for such an important post in a republic which traditionally favored septuagenarians and octogenarians for its leaders. Although . . . not always, especially in times of crisis.

" '—purchased seven months ago by Marchioness Rosa Aleri,' " Petro read, his words dropping into the silence like pebbles into a quiet backwater. " 'Cousin to Francesco Aleri.' " He looked over the top of the letter at Marco, who was seated stiffly on the other side of the desk. "How certain can your grandfather be of this, Marco? How can he tell one knife from another?"

Marco still had the blade in his hands, and chose to show him rather than tell him. He unscrewed the pommel-nut and slid the hilt off the tang, laying bare the steel beneath. He tilted the thing in his hands so that it caught the light from Petro's windows, and touched a hesitant finger first to the tiny number etched into the metal just beneath the threads for the nut, then to the maker's mark that was cut into the steel below the quillions, where it would be visible. "This is a *signed* blade, Petro," he said softly. "Signed means special, and special means numbered. Valdosta has always kept track of what special blades went where. Of course," he added truthfully, "unless we get a blade back into our hands for sharpening or cleaning, we can't know who gets it after the original buyer."

"How many people know about this?" Petro Dorma's eyes were speculative; darkly brooding.

"That we keep track?" Marco considered his answer carefully. "Not many, outside the swordsmithy. Not many inside the swordsmithy, for that matter, except the ones making the signed blades. I don't think Mother ever knew, or if she did, she'd forgotten it. I doubt Benito was ever told about it; he wasn't really old enough when we left. The duke, me, Cousin Pauli, and whoever is working in the special forges. Maybe a dozen people altogether. *That* much I'm sure of. I'm pretty sure my grandfather was counting on me remembering."

The right corner of Petro's mouth lifted a little. "That remarkable memory of yours at work again, hmm?"

Marco nodded. "Grandfather showed me once how the signed blades were registered, when he took me through the forges. He'll remember that, I know he will. So he'll be pretty well certain I do, and probably figured that was why I sent the knife to him."

"So we have, at the very least, a tenuous link right back into the Milanese camp and as far from Senor Lopez as possible. He works for the Grand Metropolitan of Rome . . . of that much I am sure. I am not sure just what he's doing here. He and the two priests who came with him spend most of their time doing charitable work in the poorest quarters of the city, but I'm quite sure that's not his ultimate purpose. And I don't think Ricardo Brunelli really knows what Lopez is doing any more than I do. Yet if your friend Katerina is correct, it was the Petrine who was actually there. Interesting."

After a long silence Marco dared: "Well, Petro—now what?"

"I need more. Aleri seems to have disappeared—since the day before Milan began their embargo, in fact. Yes. I was having him watched." It was as close as Marco had seen Petro Dorma come to admitting that he was one of the shadowy Council of Ten that watched over the Republic's safety.

"But he evaded us. He is very good. I believe he is still here in Venice." Petro looked down at his desk. "I believe he may be sitting tight in the *Casa* Dandelo. We are watching it. But like news of Condottiere Frescata's success against the Scaligers of Verona . . . There is nothing coming out. Not that we know of."

Marco thought a while. "But the *Capi di Contrada* go in once a week to make sure there are no Venetian prisoners. And they happen to be . . ."

"Capuletti. Supposedly loyalists of Ricardo Brunelli." Petro sighed. "Leave me to it, Marco. Off you go."

So Marco went.

But he didn't go very far.

Just down two floors and over a few corridors, to another office—one not nearly so opulent as Petro's, but possibly more important to Dorma prosperity.

"—Francesco Aleri's cousin," Marco concluded; he sat back on the hard wooden chair, then continued with his own speculation. "Not enough to convict anyone, but maybe enough evidence to be embarrassing?"

"Could be." Caesare Aldanto leaned back in his own plain wooden chair and interlaced his fingers behind his blond head, looking deceptively lazy and indolent. Marco knew that pose. He also knew what it meant. Aldanto was thinking. Hard. "So why bring this news to me, Marco?"

"Because I still owe you," Marco said bluntly. "Because you may be playing Milord Petro's game, but that doesn't mean his coat'll cover you if things get *real* sticky. Because I don't know if Milord Petro will bother to tell you or not. He didn't tell me *not* to tell you, and my debt to you comes first."

Aldanto smiled, very slightly, and pointed a long index finger at him. "You're learning."

"I'm trying, Caesare," Marco replied earnestly. "'Tisn't like the Jesolo, and it is. There are still snakes, only they don't look like snakes. There are still gangs, only they don't act like gangs."

"How are you doing?" There seemed to be real warmth in Aldanto's murky blue eyes, real concern.

Of course, that *could* just be concern over the Inquisition taking up one of Caesare Aldanto's best informers, and one of the few folk who knew *who* and *what* he really was—but Marco didn't think so. As much as Aldanto could—and more than was safe or politic—he cared for Marco's welfare.

"All right, I think," Marco gave him the same answer he'd given Petro Dorma.

Aldanto laughed at that, a deep-throated chuckle. The past few months had been good to Aldanto. And he and Angelina were, if not on friendly terms, less at odds. Thanks to Marco's work, she no longer blamed *him* for her mother's perilous addiction to black lotos. There was still tension in the air whenever they met, but Marco wasn't certain what the cause was.

Could be just because it's really Caesare she wishes she had married.

That might be what kept setting her off into hysteria, seeing as she and Caesare could meet easily since Aldanto had moved into quarters on Dorma at Petro's urging.

This just brought the confusing issue of Maria . . . and Benito to mind. Marco had tried . . . four times so far in the last two days to corner his little brother on this one. The last time Benito had straight out told Marco to keep off. Caesare had not mentioned Maria.

Marco wasn't sure how Aldanto and she were doing. The fact that she hadn't moved with him to Dorma . . . He must go back to the apartment and visit her. But, at least to Marco's eyes, the suite of rooms that the new head of the Dorma-ordered militia occupied *looked* more secure than Caesare's old apartment. Marco could only hope that it was.

What Aldanto made of the situation, he couldn't tell; he could read the man a little better these days, but—well, Aldanto was Aldanto, and when he chose not to be read, there was no catching him out.

PART VIII
September, 1538 A.D.

Chapter 81

The first trickle of refugees came long before the official news from Fruili. Then a flood of folk with their scanty belongings and terror in their eyes.

Venice's condottiere Aldo Frescata had sold the North to the Scaligers of Verona. Venice was cut off. Besieged. Only a few coasting vessels were going in and out, and the only friendly port was Trieste. Passage on those ships was only for the wealthy.

Marco looked out on the piazza from an upper window in the Doge's palace. The piazza was packed, but the people were quiet and waiting.

He turned to Petro Dorma. "So. What happens now?"

Petro sighed. "A good question. We still hold the Polestine forts and Jesolo and Chioggia. And the lagoon. But even my estates in Istria might as well be on the moon. And our enemies are flooding us with refugees."

"So what are the Grand Council and the senators going to ask the Doge to do?"

Petro snorted. "Why don't we go and find out? Some of them will panic, of course, and—needless to say—others will suggest inviting various parties in to protect us."

"And you?"

Petro shrugged. "Let them come to our lagoon. The Arsenal has been readying our answer. We have better boatmen than the lot of them. Between the marshes and the water, let them try. The lion of the marshes has eaten armies before. And they know that."

"What about food?" asked Marco. Already that was starting to affect the children of the poor.

"Believe it or not, we started preparing for that nearly two months ago," said Petro quietly. "The warehouses at the Arsenal will start to issue a ration. It's not much, but we can hold out for a good while. In the meantime we're building up a fleet to go out to deal with the Gulf pirates and Ancona. The Genoans can't stay out there all winter. Our problem lies now with enemies from within."

Marco found Petro's predictions startlingly accurate. Entirely so, as he saw when the Doge came out onto the balcony to speak to the masses thronging in the piazza. Marco, along with the other three hundred and seventy *Case Vecchie* house heads, looked out from the first floor loggia. Above them Doge Foscari's old, cracked voice began to address the silent multitude.

"The news that we have stockpiled food will reassure the people," said Petro quietly.

But the Doge never got that far. "People of the Commune, of the great Republic of Venice, we stand bloodied but unbroken by the treachery of the condottiere Aldo Frescata. But the Republic is a place of free people, proud and secure in our lagoon. A war-bond will be raised to hire more men. The militia will take over the guardianship of the city, as the Schiopettieri and militia units will be prepared for the attack. Volunteers are called for, oarsmen and gunners for the new fleet. The warehou—"

There was silence. Then a great wave of muttering spread through the crowd.

Petro grabbed Marco. "We need to get up there, fast."

The two of them were halfway up the stairs while the rest of the heads of the *Case Vecchie* were still looking at each other, trying to figure out what was going on.

From the crowded piazza, standing next to Maria, Benito tried to work out what was going on. He'd come along to the piazza with her and half of Venice to hear what was going to happen now.

One minute the Doge had been addressing them; the next . . . The Doge's head slumped forward. Guards suddenly appeared in a wall around him, and he disappeared from view.

"What the hell happened?" whispered Maria, along with several thousand other people.

Benito had gone to see her again early this morning in the hope that he could persuade her to go to Kat's house. She was being damned silly about it and he couldn't work out why.

She also hadn't showed any signs of wanting a repeat of their one night together—a night's memory which, for Benito at least, had become deeply important over the past month. When he'd finally gotten up the courage to suggest it—yesterday—she'd just said: *no*. And with Maria, "no" meant "no." She treated him like a friend. Like the Maria of old, but as if he'd grown up a year or two. Well, it was true . . . He *felt* much older.

"Is it murder?" demanded Ricardo Brunelli.

Marco looked up from where he knelt next to the Doge. "He's still alive. His pulse is faint and fast, but erratic. It may just be his heart or . . ." Marco looked at Petro. "Could be poison."

Ricardo Brunelli looked at Petro Dorma and Vettor Benero, the three of them the only Senior Collegio whom the guards had permitted onto the balcony. "What now?"

Petro gestured at the crowded piazza. Already the noise was alarming from down there. "Tell them the Doge has been taken sick. And finish his speech. We all know what he was going to say."

Ricardo Brunelli gave Signor Vettor Benero a look designed to silence a mate-hunting tomcat—never mind the head of the pro-peace-with-Milan faction. Ricardo cleared his throat. Then took one of the Doge's gawping trumpeters by the ear and said: "You. Sound that thing. I want the people to listen to me."

The shrill of the trumpet, and the sight of someone standing up to address them, silenced the surging crowd. Marco was too busy applying his limited knowledge to examining the Doge to pay much attention. But it sounded—by the cheering—as if the one thing that Ricardo certainly did really well was give a speech. And, as Marco examined him, the Doge did slowly begin to recover.

" . . . *And so, my fellow Veneze, to the ships!*" Ricardo boomed.

The Doge opened his eyes. "I was going to say that."

"Quick!" said Petro, "get him to his feet. Your Excellency, can you wave to the people?"

Foscari nodded. "Of course." He tried to get up, but his frail octogenarian body was no match for Marco's restraining arm.

"It's not wise," Marco said gently.

Petro pushed him aside. "A lot more lives than his hang in the balance, Marco. The Doge is the servant of Venice first. Take one side."

So Doge Foscari was able to wave to the crowd, and reassurance rippled through it.

They would have been less reassured if they'd felt his body go limp in their arms and seen his eyes roll back as his head lolled. "Turn!" snapped Petro Dorma. And they took the Doge away, hopefully before the crowd noticed.

Down in the crowd, Benito looked up to see his brother supporting the Doge. "That's Marco!"

"Who?" said a neighbor.

"Marco Valdosta," supplied Maria.

"The new Valdosta," added another woman.

"I'd heard he was a healer," said the first with satisfaction.

"The best," said Maria, giving Benito's arm a squeeze. "I'd trust him with my life, never mind the Doge's."

"Heard he treats canal-kids," said someone else.

"What? D'you believe in unicorns, too?" chuckled a well-to-do merchant.

"You watch your mouth, mister," said a brawny bargee. "Valdosta, eh? Good name in my father's time. You know, he treated my little Leonora."

As the crowd began to disperse, Benito had the satisfaction of realizing that, at least among the common people of Venice, his brother was already well known. And well liked. Unlike Mercutio . . . Venice would not forget Marco Valdosta overnight.

He took a deep breath. "The *Capi* are taking lists of volunteers over at the foot of the columns of St. Theodoro and St. Mark. Maria, I'm going to volunteer for the galleys that are going to the Polestine forts. They haven't said so, but I think they'll make an alliance with my grandfather."

Maria looked startled. "What's Dorma going to say? What's Cae . . . *he* going to say?" She still wouldn't say Caesare's name.

Benito shrugged. "I've made up my mind."

Marco would keep the name alive. And he could get away from this situation of divided loyalties. The more he thought about Maria—and part of his mind wanted to think of very little else— the more things he kept thinking of about Caesare that bothered him. Bothered him a lot.

❋   ❋   ❋

Marco and Petro walked slowly from the Doge's chambers, where the old man lay under the care of doctors who really were the best Venice had to offer. The Doge had regained consciousness again when he was ensconced in his great pilastered bed, a tiny old man propped on mountains of snowy white pillows. He'd talked perfectly lucidly and with no sign of any impairment of his faculties for near on five minutes. And then, shuddered and lapsed into unconsciousness again.

"I'm going to volunteer for the Fruili force," said Marco abruptly.

Petro stopped dead. "Marco! You can't do that. Venice needs you *here*."

Marco shook his head. "I don't think more than two people in Venice would even notice if I vanished in a puff of smoke, Petro. Angelina's daughter has a father. Benito can take over as the Valdosta *Casa* head, and that'll please Grandfather. Benito and he are like one another. On the other hand, those refugees from Fruili are just the first. I'm going to be needed there. Besides, if I go with the galleys to the Polestine forts I'll possibly have to fight my grandfather's troops. Alliances in war are not always kind."

Petro put his hands on Marco's shoulders. "You don't understand, Marco. *Casa* Dorma itself is on quicksand. Ricardo Brunelli heads the pro-Rome Faction. He regards himself as a certain candidate for the Dogeship. Vettor Benero holds the next largest slice of support. He favors inviting Duke Visconti to share the Doge's throne." He sighed. "The third, weakest faction is mine. We stand for the Republic remaining independent. As Doge Foscari does."

He sighed again. "I tricked Ricardo Brunelli this morning. I knew, by making him speak off the cuff like that—while he was shocked—that he would have no time to turn the Doge's speech to his own purposes. That he would say what the Council had agreed to. Ricardo doesn't think fast on his feet, but he isn't stupid. He is going to work it out, and he is going to add it to his list of reasons to make Dorma an enemy of the state. And as for Benero . . . I've been trying for months to find out just how he is getting gold from the Montagnards. He wants my head, Marco. Dorma has only a few real assets: the militia, which Caesare commands for me; and you. Dorma's wealth is tied to our shipyards . . . which is tied to timber, which comes from Dalmatia. It's not going to take the wolves long to realize that if we have lost Dalmatia, Dorma has lost its wealth. Then I only have Valdosta and Dell'este."

Marco shook his head. "Grandfather's condottieri have lost Reggio nell' Emilia to the Milanese. Modena is under attack by the Bolognese. Este is under siege by Scaligers. The Dell'este . . . well everyone thinks they're finished. Even my grandfather must think so—that's why he sent the sword here. As for the Valdosta name . . . well, there is my brother. And I don't think it is worth much."

"Valdosta, you don't know your own worth," said Petro, quietly. "And I will tell you, privately, we have signed a treaty with Duke Dell'este. The galleys going to the Polestine forts are actually going to help him. He's not called 'the Old Fox' for nothing, you know."

"Petro. I know I'm Angelina's husband, and that as head of the House it is your duty to keep me safe. But I *am* going to join the militia, and go to Fruili. If the Doge dies and they elect Ricardo or Vettor Benero, the treaty with Grandfather will be broken. I've heard both of them on the subject of the Ferrarese."

Petro rubbed his forehead. "Well, yes. But while Doge Foscari hovers like this, between almost dead and fully competent—it is going to paralyze us. Every energy will go into factional fighting. If he would get better, we have a Doge. If he would lose his wits . . . the Senate would impeach him. If he died, they'd elect a new Doge. But like this . . . Venice is at her weakest."

"I wonder if that's just not exactly what someone intends," whispered Marco. "I didn't say this before, Petro, but that is like no disease I have ever heard of. The way he is completely and immediately in possession of his faculties, and then once again near death . . . I wonder if this isn't magic."

Petro took a deep breath. "I think we'll get that German abbot in to try a spot of witch-smelling and exorcism." Petro was looking at Marco's face as he said this. "Yes, yes! I don't like or trust him either. He's a damned fanatic. But he's a *Christian* fanatic."

"I wonder if we wouldn't be better off with a pagan," muttered Marco.

Petro looked sharply at him. "Don't say that to anyone else, Marco. Venice *was* the most tolerant republic in the world. These magical murders have built up feelings to the point where just the smallest thing could spark the burning of the Campo Ghetto."

❀   ❀   ❀

Benito certainly didn't have Marco's neat handwriting, thought Kat wryly.

I will be leaving with the Fleet for the Polestine forts tomorrow. Maria will be all on her own. Please, Kat, can you go and see Maria? She's in our old apartment. She won't talk about stuff with me. She won't go to you. I've tried.

Benito

There followed a postscript with directions to the apartment. Kat took a deep breath; then, went up to see her grandfather. "Grandpapa. Remember that girl that that Benito Valdosta talked to you about? I'm going to go and fetch her."

The old man smiled ruefully at her. "I've been thinking about that. And about that boy. The older one. He reminded me of Luciano. Tell me about him. Tell me about this girl. I know too little of what you do out there."

She looked warily at him. He smiled. "I won't be angry. Word of Montescue. You're the last of my blood, girl. And I'm beginning to realize I've been something of a stubborn old fool. Put the *Casa* Montescue before your safety and happiness. Without *you* there is no *Casa*."

Kat smiled back. "I am Montescue, too, Grandpapa. Except for getting wet, I enjoyed doing it."

She sat down and told him how she'd met Benito, how she'd met Maria, how she'd met Marco—and how Maria had escaped from the *Casa* Dandelo. "Old Guiseppe, he was all for calling you to take action against the Dandelo. I pointed out . . ."

"He was right! Go fetch this woman, *cara mia*. I want her here. Old Dourso needs to hear this, too."

So Kat left to go and fetch Maria, with Lodovico Montescue's blessing. It was heading towards sunset, so with luck Maria would be in the apartment. By the time she'd found her way down the narrow alley and up the dirty, narrow stairs reeking of cabbage-water, Kat was glad she'd got there before nightfall. She was also glad of the weight of the pistol in her reticule.

Maria opened the door cautiously. "Kat?" she said incredulously. "How did you find this place?"

"Benito told me. Can I come in?"

"Yeah. Of course!" Maria ushered her into the dark room. "You got trouble, Kat?"

"Not more than usual. Listen, I talked to my grandfather about you. He wants to talk to you. And I want you to come stay with me at *Casa* Montescue, at least while the war is on."

Maria put her head in her hands and shook her head fiercely. "That Benito! He doesn't know how to take 'no' for an answer. I can't do that, Kat."

"Why not? You've got a formal invitation from my grandfather."

Someone thumped on the heavy door. "Who is it?" asked Maria, walking over to the door.

"Message from Benito Valdosta."

Maria opened the door a crack . . .

To have it flung wide.

"Worked like a charm!" said the first bruiser, grabbing Maria and pushing his way inside. Another man followed him, closing the heavy door behind him.

"Oh look, Luce," said the bigger one. "There are two of them! We're gonna have us some fun first. We thought we'd have to take turns, now we got one each."

"An' one's a dainty lil' *Case Vecchie*—"

"*Matteoni filth!*" spat Maria.

"Don't hurt me! Oh please don't hurt me!" whimpered Kat, shrinking into a corner. "I've got money. Lots of money in my purse." She reached into her reticule.

The one called Luce ambled toward her, chuckling evilly. "We're gonna be paid twice, Stephano. For som'n I'd do for pleasure."

The endless practice that Giuseppe had put her through paid off. Kat gave a moment's thanks that she'd followed Giuseppe's instructions to the letter and cranked the clumsy wheel-lock mechanism before leaving her house. She didn't even try to take it out of the reticule. She simply shot straight through it.

The pistol boomed and echoed in the confined space. The noise and the smoke—not to mention having the reticule blown out of her hand—confused Kat for a moment. She just hoped Maria would do whatever needed doing next.

Maria knew what was coming just as soon as Kat reached into her reticule. In theory, at least. But she wasn't really that familiar with guns—knives were a canaler's weapon—and the noise and the smoke took her a little by surprise. She was also unprepared for the way the heavy bullet catching him square in the belly slammed Luciano Matteoni back against the wall.

But unprepared or not, Maria was no stranger to violence. The other Matteoni—Stephano, that was—his eyes wide and horrified, was still distracted by the shocking sight of Luce sagging against the wall. Maria snatched up the lamp-bowl and threw it at him. The bowl hit Stephano on the side of the head, sending him staggering; then caromed into the wall and broke. The room was plunged into darkness.

The man might be bigger and faster than Maria—and probably better with a knife—but she knew this place in the pitch darkness. She had the small knife from the slit in her skirt out in an instant, and began moving on silent bare feet toward the counter that held the water bowl. She had no illusions that she could win a straight-up knife fight with a professional Matteoni thug, but there was a cleaver next to the water bowl. One good swipe with that heavy blade . . .

And if she could get the door open, she and Kat could run.

The darkness was full of Kat's screaming and Stephano's snarls of rage. Maria shifted the knife into her left hand and lunged for the water bowl. On the way, she tripped over a body—Luce must have slumped from the wall—and cried out as she nearly brained herself on the far wall. But then she had the cleaver in her right hand.

A huge meaty hand flailing about closed on her shoulder. "Gotcha!"

Stephano's shout of triumph turned into a scream as Maria's small knife slashed at his face. Then there was a sickening thud, accompanied by the sound of splintering wood. The hand that held her in a grip of iron turned to porridge. Through the swirling mist of confusion—fury and terror and darkness—Maria realized that Kat's screams, had been screams of rage as much as fear. Kat must have picked up one of the stools and brained the thug.

"Stand back, Kat!" she shrieked. Then, pushing herself away from the Matteoni goon by the simple expedient of stabbing him with the little knife again—in the belly this time—Maria swung a ferocious blow of the cleaver. She felt the blade hack into Stephano's skull. Frenzied, she wrenched it loose and hacked again; again; again. The last blow hit something softer than a skull, and got wedged. The man's shoulder, apparently, since a moment later she felt his heavy body slumping against her legs.

Enough! The door was behind her. She pulled at it and it swung open, showing twilit Venice beyond. "Kat! Let's go!"

The two, half-falling, careened down the stairs and ran up the *Calle*. Soon enough, Kat spotted a passing gondola and yelled for it. As soon as the boatman drew alongside, they bundled in.

If the boatman thought that they were an ill-assorted pair—leaving aside the blood spattered all over Maria—he did not let on. "Where to, signorinas?"

"*Casa* Montescue," said Kat, firmly.

Kat knew that she had to be firm. She wanted to be sick. She wanted to give in to the helpless shivers. Even in this light, she could see that Maria was as pale as a sheet.

"Can't," whispered Maria.

"Just for now," said Kat. "They were hunting you, Maria. They knew exactly where to find you—and how to get you to open the door. How?"

"Caesare told them. . . . It had to have been him. Why?" Maria's voice was small, hurt by the betrayal.

"Maybe you know too much."

Maria stared at her, horror in her eyes. "I wouldn't . . ."

Kat shrugged. "A woman scorned might."

There was a long silence. "I always thought he'd come back to me. I . . . I never wanted to admit it, but I always hoped he would."

"He's not going to, Maria. That's why I want you in the *Casa* Montescue. You're safer there, for now. He won't know."

Maria laughed wildly. "Oh yes, he will! Do you know why I wouldn't come to the *Casa* Montescue? Because it's where his new mistress lives! Or his old mistress, I should maybe say. The bitch said she's known him for years—from before I met him. That means during his days with the Montagnards."

"Alessandra?" asked Kat, faintly. "My sister-in-law?"

Maria nodded. "I didn't mean to tell you."

"I thought it was Angelina Dorma."

Maria snorted. "She's just had Marco's baby."

"It's *not* Marco's," said Kat fiercely.

Maria gaped at Kat as she worked it out. Then, snorted just as fiercely.

"Sister—I think we'll kill him! Your Marco is an *idiot*."

Finally, at that point, reaction set in. All the adrenaline, possibly—almost certainly—killing two men, running away, the emotionally shocking revelations. The two girls clung to each other, sobbing their hearts out, while a stoical if puzzled gondolier took them on to the *Casa* Montescue. He did shrug, once. The city was going to war, after all. Many strange things would happen tonight.

It was Kat who stopped crying first. She swallowed. "Maria. When was Caesare in Venice first?"

Maria sniffed. "Three years back. When there was that plague outbreak."

"My brother was still alive then. It can't be true. I mean I believe you about her being there with him now, because . . . because she said things about Caesare. And she got jealous as a cat when she thought *I* might be seeing Caesare Aldanto. I wondered how she knew him. But she couldn't have been false to my brother."

"Was he ever away from home?" asked Maria, dryly.

"Naturally. He went to Istria and the Dalmatian Islands. We had property in Spleto before Emeric conquered it. And he was off to the mainland a few times . . . He always used to bring me things." Kat felt the longing for those carefree days in her voice.

Kat heard the snap of teeth from Maria. "Kat. I feel like that woman scorned you spoke about. Let's see how far jealousy will take that bitchy sister-in-law of yours. You pretend to be one of his lovers too. And we'll add Angelina. If she just pushes us once . . ."

"Why not?" said Kat viciously. "I suppose that, like us, she might just be another woman whose life has been ruined by a . . . rotten *figlio di una puttana*—but she's made my life a misery, to say nothing of old Madelena's. Madelena would kill Alessandra if she knew. My brother was the apple of Madelena's eye. Let her take one step out of line, and we'll go for her."

When they arrived at the *Casa* Montescue, their plan was ready. A whispered question to Madelena, as she opened the door, established that Alessandra was in one of the small salons upstairs. "Go get Grandfather, Madelena," Kat ordered softly. "Bring him to the corridor just outside the salon. But keep him outside the room until the right moment."

Madelena's brow creased in puzzlement. "You'll know when it comes," hissed Kat. "Just do as I say."

❀   ❀   ❀

When they entered the salon, Alessandra was inspecting her fingernails. She didn't even look up; just stared at Maria's bare feet. "Grandpapa said you'd gone out to fetch a new servant. It's about time we had some younger maids! I was going to say I need a new one, but I want someone who doesn't have dirty bare feet."

"She's not a servant, Alessandra!" snapped Kat. "She's a companion for my night expeditions."

Alessandra snorted. "It's a bit late for a duenna, isn't it? Your reputation's in tatters anyway."

"Not as much as yours, you slut," hissed Maria.

Alessandra finally looked up, straight into Maria's angry brown eyes. "You!" she screamed, leaping to her feet and retreating behind the chair. "You're supposed to be dead! Caesare—" She broke off, gasping.

Kat watched as Maria tensed that strong jaw. "Oh, Aldanto promises that about once a week," Maria said dismissively. "Doesn't he, Kat?"

Kat chuckled, as if caught by a memory which was half-fond, half-exasperated. The sort of sound a woman might make, thinking of a lover. "He *is* a liar. Not that he doesn't make up for it in bed."

Alessandra's face went from absolute white to blossoming little spots of red fury on her cheeks. "You lied to me, Katerina! You little thieving bitch!"

Kat shrugged and paid off the scores of the last six years. "You lied to me, too. You should have heard him laugh about you this afternoon."

"You lie! *You lie!*" screamed Alessandra. "*I* was with him this morning. Then he had to go to work this afternoon—God, I *hate* you. Thieving slut!"

Glancing to the side, Kat could see that her grandfather and Madelena were standing in the corridor just outside the salon. And had been there long enough, apparently, to have overheard the exchange. Just as she and Maria had planned. But . . .

The shocked, pale look on his face made her nervous. She suddenly remembered, a bit guiltily, that Lodovico Montescue was an old man, with an old man's heart.

Enough, she thought. *I'd better not let this go any further.*

"Calm down, Alessandra. I lied."

But Alessandra's mouth had a mind of its own, it seemed. "*Yesss,*" she hissed. "You lie all the time. Caesare is mine. Mine! Always has been—for *years* and *years*." She glared at Maria. "And he does what he promises for me, too. So you aren't long for this world, you bitch!"

Lodovico finally entered the room, moving shakily. "I cannot believe what I'm hearing," he whispered.

But Madelena did. The tiny little woman stalked forward, pushing past her master.

"You—*puttana*! You have betrayed the memory of your husband Alfredo!"

Alessandra was in full virago fury by now, knowing that she'd already said too much and betrayed herself. But she seemed still determined to cow them, to shock them into submission.

"Oh it wasn't just his *memory* I betrayed. Alfredo thought he was *such* a lover, but I needed a real man." She gestured crudely.

Lodovico straightened imposingly. He was a big man, with big shoulders, despite his age. "You will get out of my house," he said between gritted teeth.

Alessandra sniffed disdainfully. "Ha! As if the Montescue are going to throw me out. As if you are going to tell the world Caesare Aldanto cuckolded your precious grandson."

"If that is what I have to do to get this viper out my house's bosom, then I will," said Lodovico Montescue with a leaden voice. "You will go and you will go *now*."

"Can I throw her out for you?" offered Maria, advancing on her purposefully.

"You keep away from me, bitch!" shrilled Alessandra. "This is all your fault." And she swung wildly at Maria with an open hand.

Maria did not swing wildly, and she swung with a fist.

Kat's sister-in-law was slammed against the wall next to the window. Stunned, she put her hand to her cheek. A heavy bruise was already distinct against her fair skin. "You hit me . . . You *hit* me! You are going to *die* for this. Caesare will kill you."

Then she turned on Lodovico, still standing by the doorway. Except for the cheek where Maria's blow had landed, her face seemed as pale as a sheet. But not from fear, Kat realized. Her sister-in-law was consumed with an almost insane rage.

"Just as he killed your precious grandson!" Alessandra shrieked. "And you thought it was Valdosta or the plague. Ha!"

Everyone stood as if they had been frozen.

Lodovico's next words came in a growl. "I must know. Did he also kill your child? My pride and joy. Little Lodo? *Did he?*"

Alessandra started. "No! Even if he cried all the time." There was guilt in that voice.

"So what did you give him to keep him quiet?" asked Maria caustically. "Grappa? Henbane?"

Alessandra stared at her. Then looked away, almost furtively. "I never dosed him. Never!"

"She used to give him some stuff in a blue bottle," said Madelena suspiciously, "when she went out with him to her relatives."

Kat gaped at Alessandra. "*Laudanum?* You gave your baby opium in alcohol?"

"The bottle is still in her cupboard," said Madelena. "*She* told me it was for the wind . . ." Madelena stared at Alessandra. "Is it bad for babies?" she whispered.

Kat nodded. "Marco says it is dangerous even for adults."

There was a long silence.

Then Lodovico said: "I have changed my mind. I was going to throw you out. To go and be the harlot you were born to be. Now you will stay. And answer to the *Signori di Notte.*"

Alessandra smiled pure malice at him. "I don't think so, old man. I'll go to my dear Caesare. He's a rising man, not like the has-been *Casa* Montescue is. And he owes me for all the information about your business I've given him over the years."

Kat screamed. "No, Madelena! *NO!*"

Chapter 82

Darkness was falling like a soft shawl across a busy Venice. Out on the lagoon the bargees were busy pulling out the last of the stakes that marked the safe channels. Only an invader who knew his way could come across the lagoon.

The Arsenal would not sleep tonight. Queues of citizens waited for the issuing of weapons.

In campos across the city, citizens of the new militia were drilling under Schiopettieri instructors.

Venice was preparing to fight for her life, and also to strike back.

Harrow was wrestling with a decision. The boys had both signed up. Benito would be going off to the Polestine forts. Marco was headed for Fruili. An ugly face and a bit of hard leaning had let him see both lists. He was sure of it. His inclination said, *go with Marco*, but he was sworn to guard both boys. He couldn't be in both places at once. And the Polestine galleys would be leaving first. At last he decided to go and see Luciano Marina. The man made him uncomfortable, always appearing to have the light behind him. But suddenly it felt very urgent. Very, very urgent.

He walked into a noisy Barducci's. He'd forgotten what taverns were like. This was, if anything, noisier than usual, with people who might be going to die having that last drink at their favorite watering-hole. It fell quiet around him, as he walked across to Claudia. "Need to talk to you. Need to see someone." It was playing hell with his cover . . . but right now he felt cover was less important than decisive action. He felt the build-up of great and terrible things.

Claudia recognized him. "What the hell do you mean by coming in here, you fool," she hissed.

"Need Luciano," he croaked. "Can't find him."

Claudia looked at him. Her eyes narrowed. She put the mandola down, and got up. "Come."

She led him out of Barducci's and at a jog-trot down towards the Calle Farnese, into Cannaregio. Up to a largish salon next to the Rio San Marcoula boatyard. Luciano was at drill practice too, with the Strega's tiny but grim-faced arm-militant. To Harrow's surprise, he realized that the eleven people—a mixture of men and women—were very good. Of course they'd be at a disadvantage with brassbound wooden staves, against swords or axes.

"Come about Marco," croaked Harrow.

Luciano looked alarmed. "We've been watching over him. Our best people have met to scry his movements, his danger. The scryings show nothing."

"He's signed up to go to Fruili with the volunteer militia. And Benito is going to the Polestine. I don't know what to do."

Luciano turned on Claudia. "And you brought him here, now, about this?"

Claudia lifted her hands defensively. "He came into Barducci's. He said he needed you. You said . . . well, I thought it must be urgent."

Harrow felt as he were blundering about in a thick cottony fog. "It is urgent! Well . . . it feels it! Must come to you. Must."

A wary look came over Luciano's face. "Chalk."

"There is none here," said one of the black-clad men.

"Make a pentacle of those staves, then," snapped Luciano.

Not two minutes later the ward-candles, hastily contrived from oil lamps, burned inside the circle. Invocation was begun. Harrow watched as a nimbus of light began to dance around one slight woman. Harrow's scalp crawled.

"Treachery," she said in a hollow voice. "The inner council is betrayed. It is fogged from within. Go, Luciano. The lion's cub is in need."

Luciano's faced grew pale. "Betrayed?" he whispered. "No wonder the scrying circles have failed." He rubbed his face, looking now like a very old man. "I have been a fool."

He dropped his hand. "How could I have been so complacent?

Of course the enemy would fight us magically as well. I should have foreseen it."

"Who could do this?" demanded Claudia. "Who knows enough—" She broke off suddenly, her eyes widening.

"Lucrezia Brunelli, who else?" replied *Dottore* Marina wearily. "She advanced far enough to learn most of our secrets, before we cast her out."

He turned his head, staring to the northeast. "She is working for Grand Duke Jagiellon now, be sure of it. A second string to his bow, which I missed completely. In the end, the demon-nun Ursula and her cohorts in the Servants of the Holy Trinity are . . . not quite a diversion, but almost. A clear and obvious danger to the Strega—to all of Venice—which disguises the more subtle one. The naked dagger, distracting our eyes from the cup of poison."

He shook his head vigorously, the way a man does to clear his mind. "No time to waste! The Basque priest was right. I finally understand the Evil One's plan. And it is more horrid than I'd ever imagined."

He began striding off, gesturing for the others to follow. "And he was right about having a second string for our own bow," he murmured, too softly to be heard by anyone.

Luciano's Strega moved more cautiously than their leader, if as fast as possible, because they did not want to encounter either Schiopettieri or the new militia. The staves were relatively innocuous-looking, true. But they didn't need delays just because someone decided they looked threatening as a group. So they'd split into twos and threes, walking perhaps thirty seconds apart. Any troublesome Schiopettieri would soon find himself outnumbered. If there were too many Schiopettieri, the others would melt back and go another way.

Lodovico looked at the roughly bandaged Alessandra. The woman moaned weakly. "We need a doctor who can hold his tongue," he said grimly.

"Marco," said Maria immediately.

Kat looked at her sister-in-law and took a deep breath. "He'll be at Dorma. It's no use sending a messenger, even if we could find one tonight. Dorma won't let him come out, not to something that could be a trap."

Lodovico nodded. "Go. Bring the Valdosta boy here. Bring both of them if you can. It will give me a chance to make the apology I owe to both of them. And if she dies I want her sunk in a canal far away from here—and the younger boy has the practicality to do that. If she lives, she'll testify to the Senate about this Caesare Aldanto. The devil take the shame to the house! I want him to meet the headsman's axe. Both of you go, but take pistols, loaded and cocked. I'll stay with the hell-bitch. If she should regain consciousness, I want to hear what else she has to reveal about her treachery to my *Casa*."

Guiseppe went to get Lorenzo, he who had been their gondolier the night that Kat had smuggled Maria home. Maria found herself once again being hastily dressed from Kat's wardrobe. "Ladies" were much less likely to be interfered with, and tonight there were certain to be a fair number of drunken roisterers about. The floor-length dress, bulked with petticoats, wasn't going to show her feet. Ten minutes later they were headed for Marco at *Casa* Dorma.

Marco was packing up his books and medical gear rather more slowly than was strictly necessary. It seemed to him that Rafael was lingering similarly over his brushes and paints. Both of them were destined to join their Volunteer units in the morning. Both were headed for Fruili and would face some weeks of drilling and training before being flung into combat. Marco wanted to get back to see Benito before the boy went off with the galleys headed for Polestine. On the other hand, he didn't want to leave this apartment. It represented fulfillment of one of his dreams.

He sighed. He'd have left it on the instant to see Kat. But the head of *Casa* Montescue had made it absolutely clear. *Never again.* Petro Dorma had said the same, if less directly.

Petro Dorma was facing Katerina Montescue at that moment. He had in fact been about to step out when he had overheard the doorman saying: "No, Milady Montescue. Milord Marco Valdosta is not at home. Neither is Milord Benito."

"We'll see Petro Dorma then," said a young woman, decisively.

"Milord Petro is not available, signorinas."

Better to deal with it, he decided. Montescue was only one vote, but once that *Casa* had been a real bastion against the

Montagnards. The daughter of the house was plainly still besotted with Marco. The old man could become an enemy if this was handled wrongly. And even one vote in the Grand Council could be of huge value.

He stepped out. "I'll see them, Paolo. Escort them to the Blue Salon."

"We just need to find Marco . . ." said the other woman, nervously, in far from refined tones. She sounded like a canaler.

Petro turned his back. "I'll speak to you in the Blue Salon."

Kat thought it was a terrible shade of blue. She wanted, desperately, to see Marco again. Even if she couldn't have him. She was also afraid that she might see Angelina Dorma. Her hands crooked into claws at the thought. She might not be able to restrain herself.

But only Petro was there. "You must understand," he said gently, "that I cannot allow you to see Marco. Your grandfather would not permit it."

Kat handed him the letter that Lodovico had written. "It's addressed to Marco, but my grandfather said we could show it to you, if need be."

Petro took the letter doubtfully. It carried the Montescue seal. He cracked it open and read the brief, polite letter Lodovico had scrawled.

"Well." He bit his lip. "This puts something of a different complexion on the matter, but . . ."

"I'm not going to run off with him," snapped Kat. *Even though I would like to.* "My grandfather has discovered that he was entirely mistaken about the Valdosta involvement in our House's loss. He wants to apologize to the *Casa* Valdosta."

Her voice quavered slightly. "He is an old man and he, and they, may not live through this war. And we have someone who is injured we would like Marco to see. That's all. Word of a Montescue."

Petro nodded. "He's over at his apartment near the Accademia, packing up. He should be back soon, if you'd care to wait."

The other woman stood up, giving Petro a glimpse of her bare feet. The unexpected sight—the dress was very fine—startled him.

"We'll get him there," she said. "Come, Kat. I know where it is. You—Dorma—tell Benito that Maria says he's to come to the *Casa* Montescue. And don't you tell that stinking Caesare Aldanto."

Petro was plainly unused to being addressed like this. But he'd picked up on the name. "Maria?"

Maria nodded defiantly. "Yep. That's me. Come, Kat. We'd better move, or that woman'll likely die on us. I should have thought to stop at the Accademia on the way over."

Marco took a last look around. "Time for leaving." He started to pick up his bags. There were more of them than could be easily carried. Dorma could send someone over for the bulk of them in the morning, he decided.

Rafael nodded. "I'll walk with you as far as the Traghetto."

Laden with the things that he felt he couldn't leave behind—his books and instruments—Marco walked in awkward silence down the stairs and out into the narrow *calle*. The first inkling he had of trouble was the boom of an arquebus, followed immediately by what felt like a bull hammering into his chest. The sheer force of it winded him, knocking him down. It sprayed the precious books it had struck into the street.

"Finish him!" yelled someone. "Make sure he's dead!" A group of dark-clad figures stood up from the cover where they'd been lurking in wait.

"*Help!*" yelled Rafael. "*A rescue!*"

And to Marco's amazement a rescue came, running down the darkened street.

"*A Mercurio! Lux ferre!*"

That was Luciano's voice! The entire street danced with witch-fire, showing the mottled, scarred face of Harrow and several others with him, the weird light gleaming on brass-bound staves. The five waiting assassins were trapped in the cul-de-sac. Swords and knives were drawn to meet the challenge.

One of them ignored the fight and came on at Marco, who was struggling—with Rafael's help—to get to his feet. It was Francesco Aleri, rapier in hand.

Marco stared at his death.

"Aleri!" yelled someone. "I've come to get you."

Somehow that voice halted Marco's nemesis. "Bespi?" he asked incredulously.

"Yeah, Aleri! Me." Harrow had thrust his way through the melee. "I've come to kill you."

Marco had never seen the big Milanese "Trade Ambassador-at-

Large" look anything less than utterly confident. A few moments ago, even when the ambush had turned into a fight in which his side was outnumbered, Aleri's face had still worn that look. Now he just looked frightened. *"You're dead!"*

Harrow moved forward, a knife in either hand. "No thanks to you that I'm not. I'll have revenge now, Aleri. You're a dead man." He feinted.

Aleri had a rapier. He was, you could tell by the way he held it, skilled in its use. Harrow only had two knives. Yet Aleri was backing off—and plainly badly scared. "It was an accident," he protested.

"This isn't going to be," Harrow snarled, staring at the Milanese with mad, unblinking eyes.

Aleri made a frantic grab for Marco, while holding Harrow off with a sword.

It was a mistake. Harrow was far too good a bladesman, even with knives against a sword, for Aleri not to concentrate on him completely. The Montagnard assassin managed to stab Harrow through the belly with the rapier. Then . . .

Harrow's knives worked like a machine. Blood spouted everywhere, coating both men. The two sprawled to the ground. Aleri, still barely alive, stared at the sky; Harrow groaned once, tried to pull out the sword, and then lapsed into unconsciousness.

Maria and Kat were nearly knocked flying, first by a black-clad man and then by a man and woman with brass-bound staves.

They stepped into the little *calle* where Marco's lodgings were, pistols at the ready. The shutters were open and light was flooding into the street. Marco was kneeling beside the burnt-faced man, working on him feverishly. Even from here, Kat thought his efforts were probably pointless. The sword-hilt was flush against his body.

She and Maria rushed forward. As they kneeled next to Marco, the man half-trapped under the burned man groaned and blinked at Kat. "You'll have to kill him yourself, Lucrezia my love."

Kat winced at his wounds. The man's body was soaked in blood. Trying to avoid the horrible sight of his wounds—*she could see intestines bulging out through one of them!*—she concentrated on his face.

She knew him, she suddenly realized. This was Aleri—the man she'd seen kissing Lucrezia Brunelli at the mouth of the alley.

Plainly his blurred eyes, in this lamplight, saw her red-gold hair as being that of Lucrezia. And Lucrezia Brunelli had plainly told him to kill Marco.

She shook his shoulder, hard. A moment later, as she demanded "why!", she realized that her hand was covered in a warm wetness. Aleri's face was untouched, but Harrow's blades seemed to have cut him everywhere else.

She was only dimly aware that others were listening too, and that one of them was Petro Dorma.

"Tell me, Aleri," she shouted.

"But . . . you told me to, Lucrezia," he muttered, slurring the words. His voice sounded puzzled. "You said before Sforza gets here . . . Valdosta boy mus' die."

Kat shook him again. "More! What about Marco?"

"Lion . . ." it was a breathy whisper, followed by a gout of bloody foam. Then, silence.

Marco pushed her aside gently and felt Aleri's throat for a pulse. "He's dead," he said, after a few moments. Then he went back to Harrow.

"I wish to hell he'd stayed alive just five minutes longer," said Petro grimly. "That was the best decision of my life, to follow after you two women."

A lean Luciano, his left arm bloody, stepped forward out of the shadows. "Petro Dorma?"

Petro nodded. "Marina. You're the one who disappeared, and then came back claiming he'd been on a pilgrimage to Jerusalem."

Luciano smiled slightly. "You would know, *Signor di Notte*."

Petro's eyes narrowed. "I would also know that you are under suspicion of being a Strega mage, accused by Bishop Capuletti."

"He was quite right, for once," said Luciano calmly. "And given certain guarantees from you, I will give you your five minutes to question Aleri."

"You admit this?" Petro looked at Luciano with a mixture of suspicion and curiosity. "Most of the 'Strega' who used to have booths down on the Calle Farnese have proved to be fakes."

Luciano shrugged. "Yes, I am a real mage. A master, in fact. It is not—yet—a crime *not* to be a Christian here in Venice, you know. We practice secrecy because the threat of persecution here is very real, not because we have any evil to hide."

Petro nodded. "True, it is not a crime here in Venice . . . yet. But practicing black magic is. And at least part of the Church defines all magic which is not their own as that."

Luciano took a deep breath. "Yes. But Rome, to its credit, takes a more liberal attitude than the Pauline fanatics from the North do. And I would not be admitting this to you, if I was guilty of any 'black magic' or Venice's need was not both desperate and dire. If given your word to keep this secret—and you have a reputation for keeping that word—I will attempt some of what the Church would call 'black magic.' Necromancy, if you choose the term. I will call back this dead man's spirit and let you question him."

Petro looked carefully at Luciano. "What other conditions do you set?"

Luciano opened his palms. "None. Our scrying shows that there can be no survival for the Strega unless Venice survives. I risk the future of our faith, and my own life, by doing this. It is very dangerous for the mage."

Petro bit his lip; looked down at Aleri. "Very well. What do you need and how soon must it be done? I need to send certain messages about the information we already have."

"The sooner the better," said Luciano. "Before the soul slips too far. But I can give you ten minutes while I prepare. And one of your Schiopettieri have arrived. Use them. We can take the body up to Marco's old room."

Marco interrupted. "Use my room for that if you wish. But I need to get Harrow somewhere else. One of the hospitals." He rose, coming to stand next to Kat, and stared down at his protector. "I've done as much as I can for him here." Sighing: "He'll probably die from disease anyway—damned belly wounds—but he might not, too. God knows if anyone's tough enough to survive, it'll be him."

"Get me some paper," said Petro, as the wide-eyed Schiopettieri stepped forward. He pointed to Harrow. "And have some of your men take him to the nearest hospital."

As the Schiopettieri hurried to obey, Petro faced the others. "We can have a message to Duke Dell'este within hours. Our galleys must sail with what force we can muster in the next few hours. And no ship leaves Venice, not for the mainland or for the open sea, that could carry a message to Trieste. I don't know exactly what Aleri was talking about, but a fleet from there can only be more bad news."

Kat knew that it was a good twenty leagues to Ferrara. This could only imply that the Doge and the Council of Ten themselves had magical links to the duke. She squeezed Marco's hand. She was unaware that she had been holding it. Both their hands were bloody.

Chapter 83

Manfred lay in the position that Francesca called the "twin Camellias." Now that it was over, he reflected that this could very well give a man a permanent back injury. At the time it had seemed irresistible and exotic. Now, as he tried to disentangle his foot from a footstool, he wondered if the old-fashioned ways he had used before encountering Francesca didn't have something going for them. For one thing they were faster . . .

Francesca nibbled his earlobe. "I must eventually teach you to cultivate patience. Stallion, ha. Who needs a race horse?"

"I'm cultivating this damned footstool instead," answered Manfred. "I've got my leg stuck in the arch."

She laughed. "Like politics, it is going to take you a while to learn these things, Manfred. Now tell me, what news from across the border?"

Manfred grunted. "Two bits, my dear. My uncle's emissaries have succeeded in persuading the Aquitaines to release the Venetian ships. Their western fleet is on its way home."

"That's forty days' sailing. They won't be back in time to make any difference. Even if the fleet from the Black Sea—to which I imagine Constantinople is refusing passage—suddenly got out . . ."

"You forget how long it takes for news to travel. Charles Fredrik sent his men off to Bordeaux just as soon as he had that first letter from me. And forty days is the sailing time from Flanders. They're a week closer than that, at least. They could be as little as a week off, if you consider the time it takes to carry the news here."

She sighed. "Well, I hope this situation holds for a further few weeks. But it smells of trouble, Manfred. With the situation in Fruili . . ."

Manfred kissed an elbow. It was all he could reach. "Ah. That's my next bit of news. Emeric is poised on the border, ready to join the free-for-all orgy of destruction the Scaliger's mercenaries have loosed on the countryside. The Scaligers want to flood Venice with refugees. About the only good thing that has happened for Venice is that cunning old Duke Dell'este served the Bolognese attacking Modena such a trick they're out of it."

"He isn't called 'the Old Fox' for nothing," she chuckled. "And how did he do *this* trick?"

Manfred grinned. "My uncle says Dell'este is one of the most dangerous strategists in Christendom and Uncle has a mind to send me to study there next. He hasn't met you yet, my love. But whatever you do, don't get him into this position. He's an old man and I think Aunt Clothilde only knew one good German position. Flat on her back and thinking of the imperial heir. Let me out of this, do. The footstool and these cushions are killing my back. Not to mention the voluptuous weight of you."

She tickled him. "If you had not said the last, I would have let you up. But now you must first tell me what the Duke Dell'este did to confound the Bolognese."

"Leave off with the tickling, then! It's, uh, distracting." He continued: "While the condottiere from Ferrara was engaging the troops from Milan and Bologna—outside Modena—Dell'este himself led a band of partisans disguised as wagoneers with loot from villas in Ferrarese territory to within two leagues of Bologna. There is a big stand of pine trees there—or, I should say, there *used* to be a big stand of pines there. Those wagons had barrels of naphtha and oil in them. They set the pines into the biggest smokiest blaze imaginable.

"Then one of Dell'este's lieutenants, riding an exhausted horse and with Bolognese colors, rode up screaming '*Treachery!*' into the Bolognese rear. The cities are only eight leagues apart, you know, so they could see the smoke clearly. He said the Milanese had sneaked an attack on Bologna, while the Bolognese were distracted into attacking Modena. There's no love lost anyway between the Bolognese condottieri and the ones from Milan. Next thing there was an all-out fight between the mercenaries, with all the Bolognese levies riding home hell-for-leather."

"It's a good story. I'll let you up," conceded Francesca. "I'm amazed Sforza fell for it."

"He didn't. It was Ambroso. And I don't think I need to get up any more. Part of me is up already."

But her next statement brought him down and struggling to his feet. "Then you can bet Sforza is on his way here already. They simply want to distract the Ferrarese. Venice is the real prize. The attacks on the Ferrarese positions were designed to get Dell'este out into the countryside. They must be coming down the Po."

"What about those Venetian forts? The Polestine forts. They'll knock the hell out of a fleet of river-craft with their cannons."

Francesca bit her lip. "I would expect treachery."

Manfred reached for his clothes. "I reckon it's time I had a talk with someone in authority here in Venice. If I suggest Brunelli, Erik will have a fit—although he seems the right man, now that their Doge is hovering between lucidity and death. Who else is in their inner councils, Francesca?"

"Petro Dorma. But he has no love for the Holy Roman Empire."

Manfred shrugged his surcoat on. "I know him. He's a good enough seeming fellow. Doesn't let his feelings show, even if he does dislike us."

"He doesn't reveal too much at all. I'm certain that he's one of the Council of Ten. He is also a *Signor di Notte*. Since Lord Calenti died, he has been acting as the one in charge of them. He also heads the new militia. He has them under the command of your old friend, Caesare Aldanto."

"Oh. Well. These are for you, by the way." He handed her a bundle of parchment heavy with seals.

"What are they?"

Manfred smiled grimly. "Erik's idea. Signed and sealed warrants for the execution of Bishop Sachs and the Knight-proctors. Erik calls it insurance. And this one is from me. It's a safe conduct to an audience with Charles Fredrik."

Francesca was silent. Then she said in a rather small voice. "I have recently become fully aware of just what deep water I have waded into. You know, I did consider betraying you for a while. Not very seriously, I admit. But..."

"And my prowess as a lover convinced you otherwise?" said Manfred, hopefully.

She kissed him. "No. Well, not much. Two other reasons. The

first, of course, being Erik. I am quite unwilling to bring the wrath of that clan down on my head. I'm sure he has cousins and brothers as ferocious as himself."

Manfred nodded. "My cousin had his older brother for a mentor. He says Olaf is half troll. And I think he was only half joking." He cocked his head. "And the other reason?"

Whatever qualms Francesca might have been feeling seemed to disappear instantly. The grin she gave Manfred was not coquettish in the least—just, very cheerful. "I find that I rather enjoy deep waters."

Chapter 84

It was his last night in town . . .

Benito headed towards the old apartment in Cannaregio. Maybe—if she hadn't gone to Kat—if he played his cards right—Maria might take the fact that he was going off to war as a reason to repeat their night together. He found himself desperately hoping she would, and—almost as desperately—telling himself he was solely motivated by a manly search for pleasure.

He was unusually deep in thought, walking down the narrow *calle*. His previous life had been a humble place, but a happy one. The world had been pretty straightforward then. Now . . . for all that it was much more wealthy and luxurious, life was much more complicated. Take this business with Caesare . . . he was starting to put things into place that he really didn't like, and didn't want to believe about his hero.

He was at the foot of the narrow stairway when he looked up and saw that the door to the apartment was open. Moonlight made it look like a black pit. Benito raced up the stairs, his mind full of fear. And, as he stepped into the darkness, someone grabbed him. Someone with big meaty hands. "Knew you'd come back, bitch! You killed my cousins!"

Benito stamped down hard—as Caesare had taught him to—and struck back with an elbow with all the strength of his roof-climbing honed muscles. Straight into the pit of the stomach, by the gasp and release.

Benito had realized a while back that he was never going to be as tall as his brother. But lately he'd been getting broader. And the

713

one thing about roof-climbing was that his grip was as strong as one of those Barbary apes.

Which was a good thing, he thought, as he caught his attacker's descending arm. Whoever this was, he was as strong as one of those apes' bigger cousins. Benito snatched at his *main gauche*, cross-drawing it with his free hand. He drew it in a short vicious arc. The heavy pommel hit something, hard. The arm he was trying to hold went limp. He hit the sagging head twice more, with all the force at his disposal. As the body slumped against him, he caught his attacker by the hair, and pounded the base of his skull as hard as he could with the pommel. Then he stepped back and drew his rapier, slipping the *main gauche* into its sheath, and felt for the oil lamp.

It wasn't there. But he knew this place like the back of his hand. There were candles and a striker in the cupboard. . . .

A minute later he was looking at the carnage that had once been their apartment. His heart leapt like a fountain when he did *not* see what he had expected to see: Maria's body.

Then he realized what he *was* seeing. Two dead Matteoni brothers, with a third one—the one who had attacked him, whom he suspected had come on the scene later—slumped against the wall, staring at him with fogged eyes and a swaying head.

Since the Matteoni still alive clearly wasn't going to be moving soon—that was Giovanni, one of the Matteoni brothers' cousins—Benito took the time to examine the two dead ones. Luce and . . . Stephano, he thought. Luce had half his chest blown away. That was the work of a pistol at close range, and the only person Benito could think of who might have been at the apartment with a pistol was Kat. Whose body wasn't here either. His heart soared still further.

The other body, probably Stephano's, couldn't really be recognized at all. He looked more like a slab of meat in a butcher shop than a man. His shirt was blood-soaked from a stab wound and his head—

Benito averted his eyes, almost gagging. The man's features were completely obscured by drying blood. Brains were sagging out of the horrible head wounds. Someone—and he was pretty sure he knew just exactly what spit-fire woman could have done it, especially after he recognized the cleaver still jammed in the corpse's shoulder—had hacked his skull into shreds.

Matteoni. Caesare's errand boys.

As he finally accepted the truth about his idol, Benito felt a wave of sheer fury wash over him. The rage of a man who has been betrayed as well as wronged. He stalked towards the half-recumbent terror of the dockyards.

"Where is she?" He spoke in a voice that he scarcely recognized as his own. It was very, very cold. A voice which announced, as certainly as the tides: *I will kill you, very slowly, if I don't get answers.*

The man looked up at Benito with half-glazed eyes. What he apparently saw was not just a fifteen-year-old boy. Maybe the Ferrara-steel rapier had something to do with it. The Matteoni cowered back against the blood-spattered wall. "They got away. She—they—killed Luce and Stephano. I—I wasn't here. I was watching for Schiopettieri over on the next street. But when I saw her running away with that *Case Vecchie* bitch . . . I thought she'd come back, sooner or later."

Case Vecchie . . . who but Kat?

"Who sent you?" Benito demanded. He already knew the answer. But he had to hear it. In his heart of hearts, somewhere, he still hoped to hear it was someone else. But it was a faint hope, almost nonexistent. *How else could they have known where to find Maria?* He'd told Caesare himself, because—he'd thought it honorable and best.

"Aldanto . . . Caesare Aldanto. Said to make it look like a rape." It was said in a whisper, but it was loud enough to rock the foundations of Benito's whole world.

Three minutes later, with the surviving Matteoni lashed to the bed—and looking very surprised to find himself still alive at all— the place stripped of any weapon and the solid door firmly locked, Benito was jog-trotting in search of a gondola.

Maria's was still moored at the canalside. That was ominous. The gondola was her life.

Again, Benito felt despair seeping back in. And, again, that sudden wave of sheer rage. He had to restrain himself from stalking back into the apartment and cutting Giovanni's throat. But—

He wasn't *quite* up to cold-blooded murder, and there was nothing else to do with the man. He'd considered taking the Matteoni to the Schiopettieri and militia back on the campo. But Caesare had too much influence there. If Benito lived through this mess, then he'd take Giovanni Matteoni to Petro Dorma personally. But first he was going to the *Casa* Montescue to check that Maria was all right. And Kat, of course.

Then he was going to have to deal with Caesare. He hadn't made up his mind how he was going to do it, but it had to be done. It had him in something of a turmoil, but that wasn't going to stop him.

Soon enough, Benito found a gondolier to take him to *Casa* Montescue. He spent the entire trip locked away in the black thoughts in his mind. He was still trying to decide on the best course, when the gondolier cleared his throat, suggesting that now he'd brought the young signor here, payment and alighting would be much appreciated.

"How much?" asked Benito, feeling for his purse.

The gondolier told him.

Benito laughed savagely. "*Va'funculo!* What do you think I am? One of these poncy *Case Vecchie* idiots?"

The gondolier nodded, too dumbfounded to speak.

Benito had to acknowledge the justice of the man's assumption. "Here. That's the right sort of fare. And this," he held out a larger coin, far more than the fellow had asked for, "is for reminding me."

He alighted, and went to knock at the front door of the *Casa* Montescue.

An old man, worry written into his wrinkles greeted him. "*Si?*"

"Benito Valdosta. Here to see Milord Montescue. He must see me. About his daughter."

The old man ushered him in—and led him to a bedroom. Pacing the floor was Lodovico Montescue. His face lit up when he saw Benito.

"Ah! Young Valdosta. I didn't think they would find you so quickly. She seems to me to be getting worse."

He pointed to the bed. Benito was relieved. The woman in the bed wasn't Maria. He recognized the head on the pillow, despite the bandage. He'd seen her before. Not infrequently, visiting Caesare when Maria had been away. There was no mistaking that raven hair, the tiny mole above her mouth. He'd taken some observational sex lessons by peeking in at the window . . . something he'd never have considered doing with Maria and Caesare.

His mouth fell open. "What is *she* doing here?"

Lodovico sighed heavily. "For my sins, she is my granddaughter-in-law. She has been sleeping with your mentor, Caesare Aldanto."

Benito stuttered . . . He was trying to say *how did you know?*—but all he got out was "H–h–h–how . . ."

"She told us," said the old man. "The arrogant creature! She also told me I was a fool who had nurtured a viper in his bosom, choosing to believe my once-best friend's son a murderer, rather than to see the rot right here in my own house."

He took a deep breath. "Boy. I must tell you, I have been very wrong. I have blamed the *Casa* Valdosta for our losses, for our problems. I apologize. Fully. What small things I can do to put the past right I will do."

Benito saw that there were tears in Lodovico's eyes. He got the feeling that tears normally didn't come easily to this fierce old man.

"It's all right, milord. Honestly. Kat—your granddaughter—she's paid us back in spades. Saved my life maybe, and saved Maria's for sure. That's worth more than anything to me. Is . . . is Maria all right? And Kat, of course."

It was the old man's turn to look dumbfounded. "Yes. But—did they not send *you* here?"

Benito shook his head. "No. I . . . I thought they'd be here. At least I hoped . . ."

Worry must have colored his voice. Lodovico took him by the shoulder, gently. "They are fine, boy. They've gone to look for you at Dorma. Your brother as well, to attend to her." He pointed at the shallow-bubbly-breathing woman in the bed. "They've gone with a stout boatman and a pistol apiece."

Benito nodded. Caesare was out, organizing the new militia. Maria should be fine, going to Dorma. "My brother went across to collect his things from the Accademia. They'll be sent on to there. I'll go and see if I can find them."

The old man nodded. "Yes. But, before you go, there is something I must say to you. It makes it harder for me that you have not seen them. But . . . I must tell you that your mentor Caesare Aldanto . . ."

"I'm going to kill him," interrupted Benito, without heat, but with a grim certitude. "Or send him to face the headsman's axe."

For the first time since Benito had come in, Lodovico Montescue smiled. It was a grim sight. Grimmer than his worried frown. "Spoken like a true Valdosta! Boy—Benito, I should say, for you are clearly a boy no longer—between us we will crush him like an adder beneath a stout boot heel."

The old man seemed almost gay at the thought. "Montescue and Valdosta, together again! Ha! In the old days, nothing caused greater fear—"

He broke off, coughing a little. The cough seemed a compound of suppressed pride and rueful regret. But when he continued, his voice was calm and even. "I suppose that as we were the heart of the opposition to the Montagnards—and we'd given them good cause to fear our blades—it was inevitable that they should have sent their womanizing charmer to target my house's weakest point. I could forgive that, and the insult to my grandson—but not the deaths that she caused in my house."

He sighed. "And I suppose, given my pride, that it was inevitable that I would suspect everyone else. I just hope she doesn't die before she gives her evidence."

"What's wrong with her, milord?" asked Benito.

Lodovico pulled a wry face. "An old family servant—on hearing Alessandra's 'confession'—went for her with a fruit knife. I wouldn't have thought you could stab someone with a fruit knife, but old Madelena managed. She was like a dervish. Alessandra managed to flee to the stairs, but she was already stabbed in the chest, and the shoulder. She fell down the stairs. She hasn't regained consciousness since. Are you a doctor like your brother? Perhaps you should have a look?"

Benito laughed. "No. Marco is the only one. The healer. Me, I'm nothing much but trouble."

At last a genuine smile came to Lodovico's troubled, wrinkled countenance. "Yes. You sound like me, when I was your age. Then Luciano—your Valdosta grandfather—used to come and get me out of it."

"Well, I seem to spend my time getting Marco out of scrapes," said Benito ruefully. "And sometimes I mess that up too. I'd better get along, milord."

"Call me Lodovico. I'd like to stand in for the Valdosta grandfather you never had. And I think we will leave Alessandra to live or die. We've done what we can for her. I'm coming with you to the Accademia. The more I think about it, the more determined I am not just to wait here."

He must have seen Benito's doubtful look. He smiled. "We can take a boat, can't we? It's faster than running, young Valdosta."

❁   ❁   ❁

Marco looked at Luciano's transformation of his small lounge. It didn't look pleasant. It didn't feel pleasant, either. In fact, it made his scalp crawl.

He wasn't the only one. Rafael also looked uneasy. "He shouldn't be doing this," the artist muttered. "He's taking far too much risk. This is dangerous, Marco. *Really* dangerous, and it's gray-magic even with the best of intentions."

Maria, too, looked as if she was ready to run hastily for the nearest chapel, if not engage in a bit of impromptu witch-burning. She had all the ingrained superstition about the Strega that was part of the Christianity of the commons. Most of the ordinary priests tended to regard the Strega as direct competition for their flock, no matter what the Metropolitan said about tolerance and allowing heathens to come to God rather than dragging them to Him kicking and screaming, and as for the canalers—well. When things were going fine, the Strega were the people you went to for love-charms and luck-talismans, but when they weren't . . . the Strega just might be the people causing the problems.

Kat, on the other hand, was just pressed against Marco, a dreamy look in her eyes, as if she could not bear not to touch him—and it didn't even matter if Luciano enacted a black mass, so long as she didn't stop holding his hand. If Petro Dorma had noticed, he hadn't commented.

Luciano had the corpse hedged about with diagrams; the man was inside a pentacle, which was inside a pentagon, which was inside a circle, inside a circle, inside a circle, all drawn with blessed salt and water and traced with a dagger made of black glass.

They all . . . glowed. Could anyone but Marco and Luciano see that? Rafael, probably—if Kat did, it didn't matter to her—and from Petro Dorma's slightly puzzled, slightly skeptical expression, he saw nothing. This wasn't the pure white light that Marco was used to in working with Brother Mascoli; this was a creepy sort of purple.

But—oddly enough—before Luciano had stepped out of the pentagram and pentagon and had invoked whatever spirits he'd called that made the lines spring into life, he'd placed a crucifix very firmly around what was left of Aleri's neck.

"Marco, the powers he's calling up—" Rafael was still murmuring in Marco's ear. "You've got to be *careful* with them. You know? They're not just called on for *good* things—"

Marco's skin shivered and it felt as if a cold, dead finger was running down his spine. Oh, he knew. Luciano was just muttering his incantations, but—*Charun, Vanth, Carmina*—oh, he knew all right. These were the Dread Lords and Ladies of the Night, of the Dead, and not the sort of Powers you called on for a blessing or a healing. . . .

The corpse began to glow. Luciano's face looked as gray as the corpse's in the strange light—and was the purple witch-light growing stronger, or the room light weaker?

The latter.

As Marco glanced surreptitiously out of the corner of his eye, he watched the candle flame nearest him sinking. It wasn't *guttering*, it was sinking, diminishing, exactly as if someone had upturned a jar over it. It didn't go out, but in a few moments, it was giving off no more light than a mere coal.

No one commented; not Dorma, not Rafael, not Kat, certainly not Luciano, who was—weaving some sort of complicated knot in the air above the corpse with the point of his knife, which left a trail of sullen red light where it passed. And there was no doubt that Aleri hadn't said anything about it either. Although, to Marco's horror, the pentacle-enclosed man—corpse—was stirring. He shouldn't be. Even if Harrow hadn't killed him, Marco was a good enough physician already to know that the herbs that Luciano had stuffed down Aleri's throat should cause death all over again. The hair stood up on Marco's head; this should *not* be happening! He'd expected a ghost, or something, not that the dead body should sit up and start to move! This was *wrong*!

Aleri's voice was a weak and hollow thing. But the words were clear, even though the jaw hung loose on the face. On what was left of the face. "Who has called me back . . . ? Why am I called back . . . ? The pain . . . the agony . . . oh, Lucrezia . . ."

Luciano straightened, and became something altogether terrible. His face, corpse-gray and marble-still, took on the qualities of a death-mask. "I, Grimas Luciano Marina, servant of Triune Diana, have summoned you. She is the mistress of the earth, the dead and of rebirth. In Her name I command you; in Her name I compel you!"

The corpse made abortive moves, jerky, and uncoordinated. It brushed against the purple lines of the pentagram, and moaned. "I am not hers. Let me go . . ."

"You *are* Hers, as all things are," Luciano said sternly. "I abjure and command you. Stay you will, until She or I permit you to depart. Speak the truth and the truth only. You are bound here until you answer the questions set to you."

The lips of the dead man moved. "I . . . obey," he whispered. Sobbed.

Marco felt nauseated. How horrible could this be for Aleri's soul, trapped in a body already dead, and surely *knowing* that he faced, at absolute best, the worst that Purgatory could offer when Luciano released him?

"From which direction is the main attack on Venice coming?" demanded Marina. "And when?"

Aleri's lips moved again. The words were very faint, since they had no real breath behind them. "Word came through . . . the barges are at Bondeno. Got to be past the Polestine forts by tomorrow morning . . . got to beat th' galleys. Our people in Ferrara'll start the fires there t'night, pass in the confusion . . . Tell 'em to stop th' Trieste fleet . . ."

Petro Dorma croaked. "Ask him what the Milanese are planning to do to break through the Polestine forts?" Marco took a quick look at him—the corpse-light made everyone look awful, but the hitherto-unflappable Dorma, of the Council of Ten, was definitely—flapped. His eyes were big as saucers, and he was sweating, in spite of the funereal chill of the room.

The dead body shivered. "The Casket . . . the black nun . . . the servant and voice of Chernobog. She will deal with the forts. I warned Lucrezia. Danger, danger, danger. It hears me speak its name."

"The black nun?" Petro fumbled for the sense of this.

Luciano spat. "Sister Ursula. That 'nun' who travels with the Knots. Ask your next question."

Dorma licked his lips and didn't look as if he relished the taste. "How does Sforza plan to overcome Venice's defenses?"

Aleri's corpse answered. "Fires. Many fires."

Dorma had more stomach for this than Marco did. "How?"

"Gunpowder. Laid charges. Lucifers in amulets in some of them. Spellcasters in the *Casa* Dandelo will begin to trigger them, when the fog comes. Agents will light the others."

"How do we stop it? What order must be given?" *A good question, milord! How the hell can we be everywhere at once?*

"Can't be stopped now. We made sure."

Petro sighed, then tightened his jaw, deciding, evidently, to focus on what he *could* do. "Where are the firebombs?"

And Aleri began listing place after place, scattered across the Rialto Islands

Petro frantically tried to write. "I'll never get them all. . . ."

"I will," said Marco, finally feeling that here was *something* he could do.

Petro nodded; that was the genius of the man, to know who and what he could trust and not worry about what he had handed off to others. He turned back to Aleri. "And who can Venice not trust? Who are your hirelings, your agents?"

Once again Aleri began listing. Marco found he recognized many of the names of Mama's sleepers that he'd written down so carefully for Caesare. And Count Badoero and the Tiepolos—the black lotos smugglers with their partisans, who would be coming across from the mainland. They were locals, they knew the lagoon and the city. And then . . . and then . . .

"*Caesa . . . aaaahhhhhh!*"

The scream was a horrible one; the more so since it came from the throat only. And it was echoed by Luciano.

The lamps went out, and so did the light from the ritual circle. The silence and the darkness were worse than the corpse-light. Kat's fingers tightened on his arm, and she whimpered a little, deep in her throat.

In the darkness Marco heard Luciano say, in a trembling voice: "The black one silenced him as soon as he tried to say that name. Chernobog has claimed his own."

Somebody kindled a light. A candle flame only, but it was still a beautiful sight, in Rafael's hand. That hand shook, and Marco couldn't blame him in the least. There were some things no one should have to witness.

Then, with the light, came the stench.

Marco backed up, gagging, dragged from what was left of the circle by Kat. Dorma staggered to the wall. Rafael covered his mouth with his hand and turned convulsively away.

Something had made sure that no one was going to reanimate Aleri's corpse again. There wasn't going to be enough of it left. It seethed with maggots. The stench of decay was enough to send them all fleeing, gagging, out the door that Rafael opened for them. Rafael had to help Luciano, as the man was barely able to stagger. He slammed the door on the horror in what had been his rooms, and they all leaned against the wall, Luciano included, with shaking legs that would not carry them further, at least for the moment.

First to recover, Petro turned to Marco. "I need you, now, to come and write down those lists." He took a deep breath. "And then we're going to have to decide how to deal with Caesare."

Marco nodded. His laced fingers released themselves from Kat's hand. "Yes. But Luciano looks like death warmed over. . . ."

Kat giggled, faintly—but in a tone that said in a moment she might go from giggling to screaming.

"Ah . . . er . . ."

"That—" Luciano somehow managed to wheeze "— was a poor choice of words."

Marco patted Kat's shoulder comfortingly. "Look, anyway—we ought to take him over to Zianetti's. It's just across the campo. I'll see you there in maybe twenty minutes."

Petro nodded. "If you see any Schiopettieri, send them here. I'd say we should all go there but I left word for Benito I would be here, and in that message that I sent to the Council, I asked that Schiopettieri be sent here."

Luciano nodded; Marco wondered where the old man found the strength. *Spiritual and physical.* "I'd like to get away from this place. But I must speak to you again, Dorma. The others of the Strega arm militant should be watching around here. I need to send them off to prepare defenses—and to eliminate two traitors. Lucrezia Brunelli was once a neophyte, who wanted to learn the Strega way. She was rejected at the rite of purification, but it seems that she'd found out enough to corrupt some of our people."

"Grand," Dorma said grimly. "Well, I'll leave that in your hands. Mine are over-full as it is."

Reluctantly, Kat parted with Marco. As they walked out of the lodging, one of Luciano's group emerged from the shadows. A hasty, whispered conversation followed and the nine watchers left at a run.

Slowly Luciano, Rafael, Maria, and Kat proceeded down the curving *calle*, between shuttered houses. They turned the corner. Two candles burned in a wall-sconce shrine to the Virgin, lighting the narrow alley.

They nearly walked smack into them, and there was certainly no avoiding Senor Lopez and his two companions. The Basque grabbed her shoulder. "This time you will not evade me, girl!" His dark line of eyebrow lowered heavily.

Kat reached into her reticule and produced the pistol, which she pressed against his stomach. "I have you, Lopez! You turn up like a bad penny every time there is evil about. You were there when that monk was murdered magically. You were there when Bishop Capuletti was killed. You're here now when Luciano has had this encounter with Chernobog."

"Name not that evil!" snapped Lopez. "And lower your weapon, girl!" His companions moved forward.

"Stop!" cried Maria. "I'll shoot at least one of you others!" The canaler was holding her own pistol two handed. She stood feet apart, weapon raised, looking like Nemesis.

The Basque priest seemed to be almost grinding his teeth. "Madness!" he hissed.

Chapter 85

"Thank God you've gotten back," snapped Erik. "We've been summoned to assemble in the courtyard. Every one of us, in full armor. Something is happening."

Manfred nodded. "We need to talk to Petro Dorma. I think it's time to shed pretenses."

"It's time to dress in full armor," said Erik, grimly. "I have a feeling we've left talking too late. But when this assembly is over we'll go and find Count Von Stemitz, and get him to authenticate you, and go and see Dorma. I tried to get out to fetch you earlier. This place is sealed tighter than water-damageable deck-cargo. They must have let you in, but Sachs's trusties are not letting anyone out. No one. Now move it."

Fifteen minutes later, they stood to attention in squads in the courtyard. The knight-proctors inspected them, reported back to the abbot, returned to their squads.

The abbot stood in front of serried rows of steel-clad men. He held up a wad of parchment. "These are a final and complete list of the Jews, Strega, Mussulmen and other ungodly ones in this pesthole," he announced in a triumphant voice. "I have addresses and maps. We will be arresting the ringleaders tonight, *Ritters*, just as soon as the tocsin bell in Saint Mark's square is rung. Tomorrow a full contingent of our Knights will be arriving from Trieste to help restore order in what will be the new southern frontier of the Holy Roman Empire."

Erik heard Manfred, standing next to him, draw a deep breath. He waited for the bull-like bellow. It didn't come.

Sachs had paused, as if he too had been waiting for something. Then he continued. "Knight-Proctors. Step forward and collect your orders. Squads are to remain together, at their assigned posts, until the tocsin bell rings. Then you will move out, with your assigned group of Servants of the Holy Trinity, to protect you from whatever magic these ungodly ones may attempt to unleash at you. Fear not! God and the holy Saint Paul are with us!"

Erik and Manfred found themselves assembled in a front salon along with some twenty knights, under the command of Knight-Proctors Von Welf and Von Stublau. Many of the other knights had been kept back in the courtyard.

He and Manfred walked up to the two knight-proctors.

"Who said you could break ranks?" snapped Von Welf.

Manfred took a deep breath. "We need to take you to see Count Von Stemitz, Von Welf. There is something he's got to tell you."

Von Welf smiled a particularly unpleasant smile. "We'll be seeing him soon enough. As soon as the bell in Saint Mark's Square begins to ring continuously. His name is on the top of our list."

There was a moment's silence. Erik heard footsteps shuffling behind him; quietly, as if heavily armored men were trying to move stealthily across a tile floor. Two or three of the knights in the salon were coming up behind him and Manfred.

He was quite certain of their purpose, and had to fight down a savage smile.

In the distance a bell began to ring. "That's early," said Von Stublau, quietly, almost conversationally. "But it's the signal. Such a pity that Petro Dorma ordered you killed. The evidence and report are on their way to the Brenner pass right now."

But Erik was moving before the Prussian had finished the last sentence. He knocked Manfred aside with a thrust of his right arm and spun to the left, dropping to one knee as he did so. The poignard in the hand of the knight assigned to stab him in the back passed overhead harmlessly. An instant later, the Algonquian hatchet sheared through the knee joint in the knight's armor.

The knight screamed and toppled forward. Erik rose up beneath him and added his own thrust to the topple, sending the armored man crashing into the two Prussian knight-proctors.

Erik glanced at Manfred. The prince had been expecting treachery also, of course. And if Manfred did not have Erik's lightning reflexes, he could move much faster than anyone would expect.

Erik's shove had sent him out of immediate danger, and by the time the knight assigned to murder Manfred had reached him . . .

The prince had his sword out. A sword he had learned to use extremely well over the past year. His assailant attempted a feint, which Manfred countered by the simple expedient of lopping his arm off. The knight went one way, the arm another. Blood poured over the tiles.

For a moment, Erik studied the remaining knights in the salon. They were still frozen in place, immobilized by the sudden and unexpected violence. Clearly enough, none of them except two had been directly involved in Von Stublau's plot.

Von Stublau and Von Welf were struggling back onto their feet— no easy task for heavily armored men sent sprawling to the ground. Von Stublau was on Erik's side, Von Welf nearer to Manfred.

Von Welf never made it up at all. Manfred's sword, in a backswing, shattered his helmet and the skull inside it. Von Welf sprawled back onto the floor and lay there motionless.

Erik disarmed Von Stublau with a quick hooking motion of the hatchet, a maneuver the Prussian neither expected nor had ever encountered before. He was still looking more puzzled than anything, when his attention was riveted by the razor edge of the hatchet—three inches in front of his eyes.

"Make any move and I'll take off your face," said Erik cheerfully. "That nose guard might as well be a lady's veil, as much good as it'll do you."

Von Stublau froze. The Icelander's thin smile was as friendly as a wolf's.

"You made two mistakes, Von Stublau. The first one is that bell. You see, that isn't the one from Saint Mark's Square. That's the Marangona, the bell they ring every morning at the Arsenal. It goes on for half an hour every morning, so you should know it. As this isn't morning, and as the Arsenal is working right now, I imagine someone has found out about your plot."

The knight-proctor looked startled. Then, began to pale.

"And the second one is that you shouldn't assume everyone is as stupid as you are."

He raised his voice. "Prince Manfred, Earl of Carnac, your uncle His Imperial Highness, Charles Fredrik, Holy Roman Emperor, has given me orders to kill any man who threatens your life." Erik grabbed the lower edge of Von Stublau's helmet and jerked him forward, kicking the knight-proctor's legs out from under him and driving him back down. The Prussian grunted with pain as his knees smashed into the floor.

"*Kneel, traitor.* May he be shriven first, My Lord Earl?"

Everything was moving too fast for the remaining knights to understand what was happening. Most of them were still slack-jawed with surprise. But at least two thirds of them, out of training if nothing else, had drawn their broadswords.

The doors at the back of the salon opened. The entry of soldiers or other knights might have simply made the situation explode into violence. Outnumbered sixteen to two, Erik and Manfred would have been hard-pressed to survive long enough for any kind of rescue.

Except . . . by an unarmed, haughty, imperially-dressed woman, accompanied by an elderly gentleman in court clothes. The woman looked like a princess. She certainly wore enough jewels.

Francesca smiled at them from under her tiara. The knights parted like the Red Sea before Moses, opening up to allow her and Count Von Stemitz to walk through.

She curtsied to Manfred. The count bowed low.

Manfred behaved as if he had, not a few moments back, been in a fight for his life, and didn't have a bloody sword in his hand. "Princess." His mind raced for a suitable address. Well. There were enough little principalities in the Empire. Let the Knots guess. "How may we assist?"

She smiled regally. "Your imperial uncle has asked me to deliver certain warrants to you." She handed him the sheaf of parchments he'd left with her not an hour before.

Manfred took them and leafed through them, as if he hadn't written them himself. "Count Von Stemitz," he said calmly, "Who am I? Please explain that to these assembled Knights."

Von Stemitz bowed again. "You are Prince Manfred, Earl of Carnac, Marquis of Rennes, Baron of Ravensburg. You are also Privy Emissary Plenipotentiary for his Imperial Highness Charles Fredrik of Mainz. He has invested you with the full and independent power to act for the imperial throne."

Manfred cleared his throat. "I have a message from Emperor Charles Fredrik to read to all of you. He says to remind the Knots that he holds their charter, the deeds to all their monasteries— *and* that they are perilously close to his displeasure. *And* that he has more than sufficient military forces to crush the entire order of the Knights of the Holy Trinity, should they persist in defying him. *And* to remind any confrere knights that he is their sovereign and their estates are his to dispose of."

The salon seemed to chill by many degrees of temperature. Charles Fredrik was known to be reluctant to use military force except when he felt it was necessary. He was also known to use it with utter ruthlessness when he did so.

The threat was particularly shaking, obviously enough, to the confrere knights who made up perhaps half of the force assembled in the salon. Not one of the confrere knights in the salon doubted for an instant that the old Emperor would make good his threat to kill all of them—and expropriate their families in the bargain. As surely as a farmer will butcher a hog for a feast.

Erik cast quick eyes around the salon. He could see at least four—no, five; then six—of the confrere knights start shifting their stance. Moving, now—and none too subtly—to be prepared to subdue the two regular knights who were most prone to religious fanaticism. And then saw the other regular knights sidling away from the two zealots. The sudden shift in the balance of forces was as palpable as a lead weight.

Count Von Stemitz coughed in the tense silence. "May I remind you further, *Ritters*, that standing in the presence of the Emperor's nephew and Privy Emissary Plenipotentiary with drawn weapons is—ah—dangerously close to treason."

Weapons were sheathed, hastily. With the naked blades absent, the tension began to ease.

Manfred, meanwhile, had been sorting through the bundle of parchments as if he had not a care in the world beyond scrupulous attention to the Emperor's correspondence.

"Here, Erik." He handed one to the Icelander, who still held the kneeling Von Stublau. "Show him that."

Erik held the parchment in front of the knight-proctor's eyes.

"See that seal, Von Stublau?" said Erik, coldly. "Your life, your lands, and your family's lands are forfeit. You and they are landless peasants. You are shortly going to be a dead landless peasant."

The big Prussian's eyes widened. He had been afraid of the axe. This—to the Prussian—was worse. "I . . . I didn't know . . ."

"You knew," said Manfred scathingly. He looked down on Von

Stublau. "You and Von Welf both knew. Now, you must pay the price of treason. Your lands are confiscate to the crown. I will, however, temper justice with mercy. I will not act against your family's holdings—*if* I am told the full details of your plot. Should it emerge, later, even twenty years hence, that you didn't tell us all you knew . . . then your kin can join the Polish peasants on your lands."

"The peasantry will kill them," whimpered Von Stublau. "They'll tear them apart."

"Maybe you should advise them to start some reforms immediately," said Von Stemitz dryly.

Erik gestured at the door. "Time for this later, Manfred. There are a lot of knights out there, and Sachs too."

Manfred nodded. "True. De Grinchy. Lutz. Take charge of this one. Bring him with us."

They marched out, with Manfred at the head of the column of knights. Erik, watching his back, reflected that power was a strange thing. Sachs, and the knight-proctors involved, would have chosen their adherents for this squad. Yet when Francesca had shifted their balance, the reins had ended up firmly in Manfred's hands. Even the two zealots—

Erik's lips twisted in a smile that was as bitter as it was wry. The worst of Sachs's camp followers would be the quickest to strike off any head from anyone who dared to dissent. And yet, really, in actual fact, they were still completely at the mercy of their former foes.

"How did you know to come now?" he whispered to Francesca. "And where did you get the jewelry?"

"I wouldn't like this jewelry examined in broad daylight or by a skilled jeweler," said Francesca quietly. "I've taken my task seriously, Erik. I've had my watchers keeping an eye on Manfred too, you know. He's a very valuable client, to say the least."

Erik's eyes narrowed. "Besides, you know Von Stemitz."

Francesca dimpled at him. "Indeed. You are too observant, Erik. Hendrik has been a regular, ah, friend. But I really don't think Manfred needs to know that petty detail."

Mutely, Erik shook his head.

Francesca's dimples were now quite dazzling. "Ah, what would you do without me?"

Mutely, Erik shook his head.

Chapter 86

Benito was a little edgy. For starters, the old man couldn't move very fast. For a second thing, the town felt like a powder keg. There was a tension in the air you could almost taste. He and Lord Montescue had gotten to the gondola landing to find several anxious-looking people with brass-bound staves waiting to take their vessel. There'd been someone running back across there. . . .

Then they'd entered the narrow winding calle which led to Marco's digs—and found a cluster of people in front of them, in the middle of what was obviously a tense confrontation.

And then he heard Maria shout: "I'll shoot at least one of you others!"

He left Lodovico and ran forward.

"Benito!" Maria nearly dropped the pistol. "You idiot! I almost shot you."

Lopez stared at Benito. "You!" Then, incongruously, he burst into laughter. "It needed only this!"

Benito noticed that Kat was pushing the muzzle of her own pistol into the Spaniard's belly. "Er. Kat. Why are you doing that?"

"He's maybe the one behind all the magical murders!" snapped Kat. "And he probably killed the bishop, too—that *you* nearly got executed for killing. He's certainly the driving force behind Venice's woes!" The lightning progression—*maybe; probably; certainly*—didn't seem to perturb Kat in the least. The youthful inquisitor, in full fury.

Benito took a deep breath. "He's also a Legate of the Grand Metropolitan in Rome. And—well, he's helped me."

Lopez bowed his head and smiled wryly. The fact that a cocked pistol was pressed into his midriff didn't seem to worry the man in the least.

"Here at the request of Metropolitan Michael to investigate the activities of the Servants of the Holy Trinity," he elaborated, in quite a calm tone of voice. "Particularly with reference to their persecution of magic-users. Since then I have been seconded to try to find out who was committing these magical murders, as well as how they were being achieved. And to determine—and thwart, it at all possible—the purpose behind them."

Luciano growled. "Well, look no further than your precious Servants of the Holy Trinity then. They're in league with Chernobog—be sure of it! And the woman you're looking for is that so-called 'nun' of theirs."

"Katerina," puffed Lodovico, who had just hustled himself forward. "What is happening *now*? And why are you threatening this gentleman with that pistol? Be careful, for the sake of God! You've got it cocked!"

Kat frowned, uncertainly. But her weapons training had been rigorous. She removed the weapon from Lopez's waistline; then, carefully and expertly, disengaged the lock. "I *hope* it may just be a misunderstanding, Grandpapa."

Benito heaved a little sigh of relief. Then pointed to Zianetti's, which was not twenty yards distant.

"That tavern's the place to settle this, not here on the street. Milord Dorma and Marco can join us there." He gave Lopez a polite little bow. "That's Marco Valdosta, I'm referring to."

Lopez nodded. "Valdosta, yes. There are portents attached to that name."

For the first time since Kat had ever seen the fierce-looking Basque, standing on Brunelli's balcony the year before, his intense face suddenly burst into an expression of pure good will. She was almost stunned by the sheer charisma the man seemed to exude.

"A tavern it is, then! Now, if you will allow me to introduce my companions—" He gestured to the two men standing behind him. "Father Pierre, from the Savoy; and Father Diego. Diego, like myself, is from Spain—although, poor soul, not blessed with being a Basque. On the other hand—also like me—he has the pleasure of being able to claim some Jewish ancestry."

The last statement was made in such an offhand manner that

the import of it did not register immediately on Kat. When it did, she relaxed still further. The Paulines, especially the more fanatical ones, tended toward religious intolerance. No Pauline zealot, for a certainty, would so casually announce that he had some Jewish blood running in his veins. Kat realized that Lopez had made the statement deliberately. The Basque, clearly enough, was a skilled diplomat, whatever might be the ferocity with which he seemed to act otherwise.

"Father Pierre, as you will see for yourself the moment he opens his mouth," continued Lopez cheerily, "is blessed with the usual Savoyard skill for mangling civilized tongues. But he is quite accomplished in other ways. The detection of black magic, for one."

"Welcome to Venice," said Benito, with a laugh. "Let us buy you a glass of wine at Zianetti's!"

Zianetti's tavern was relatively deserted. The Accademia was emptying fast, and they got a small private room.

"Time for straight talk," said Benito.

"Yes," said Lopez firmly. "The fate of Venice is at stake."

Benito shrugged uncomfortably. "I dunno about the destiny of Venice. But you kept me free and alive, true enough." Benito saw the puzzled looks around the table. "Look, never mind. It's a long story. I got into stupid trouble and he helped me out. He was very truthful—and very rude."

Father Diego laughed. "Ah, yes. The true Eneko! Don't feel bad. He's rude to everyone."

Lopez allowed himself a brief smile. "It has been on my conscience. But I have told you . . ."

The other priest, the Savoyard, said something. He pointed at Luciano.

Lopez looked carefully at him. "He says you are a mage. He says . . . there is a stink of blackness."

Luciano nodded, tiredly. "He's right. But the stink isn't coming from me, it's—like a man who's been in smoke and still smells of it. I have just been performing a rite, one which you Christians would term 'black.' On the other hand I did it—at the peril of my soul—to try to save this city and my co-religionists. I have been practicing necromancy on an agent of those who serve Chernobog."

There was a silence. And then Lopez said: "You are *Dottore*

Marina, of course. A Grimas, indeed. I don't really approve of necromancy, of course. But . . . there are worse things. What did you discover, *Dottore* Marina? And did you allow him to confess and be received back into the arms of God?"

Luciano shook his head warily. "Chernobog snatched him back from me. I was nearly drawn in myself. But we know now that this is his conspiracy, and that the nun who is with the Servants—"

"Sister Ursula," said Lopez. "Renowned to be one of the greatest practitioners of Christian magic in the Northeastern Frontier."

Luciano snorted. "She may once have been. But she's nothing more than a vessel for Chernobog now."

"But she is a nun!" protested Diego. "She bears the crucifix!"

Luciano pulled a wry face. "You will find that it is broken. Or bathed in the blood of unbaptized infants, or desecrated in some other terrible way. Or not even there at all. Chernobog's acolytes are masters of illusion. Masters of corruption."

Kat leaned forward. "What I want to know is why Lucrezia Brunelli should want Marco Valdosta dead. And why you, Lopez, stayed at the *Casa* Brunelli."

Lopez shrugged. "I stayed at the *Casa* Brunelli when I first arrived because the lodgings were offered to me, by a man well known in Venice and in good repute with the Grand Metropolitan. As for Lucrezia . . ."

Lopez seemed to shudder a bit, for just a moment, as if a sudden unpleasant memory had come to him. "I'm afraid I was perhaps oblivious to the woman's other vices, since I was so preoccupied with avoiding a particular one." He pursed his lips thoughtfully. "As to why she might want Marco Valdosta dead, I cannot think of a reason offhand. Except . . . She seems to have an insatiable appetite for men. Perhaps he turned her down too brusquely." His lips thinned. "The woman is, ah, quite taken by her own beauty."

"She's in this up to her elegant neck," said Kat savagely. "Deceive yourself if you like, Senor Lopez. I know for a fact she has ordered magical materials from the East. I've delivered them to her. But she's no Strega."

Lopez rubbed his face. "The worst I know of her is that she passed on a message from Capuletti that he would meet me at midnight at the San Trovaso Chapel, instead of in the morning. I had tracked this dealing in that vile black lotos to him, somewhat by accident, while dealing with a Signor Tassole. I confronted the bishop about it and the peril to his immortal soul. He denied it, but wrote to me later to say it was true and that my words had troubled him. He said he wanted to fast and pray for the night but had things on his conscience that he wished to confess. It was the letter of a deeply troubled man."

"I'll bet she was in that up to her neck, too," snarled Kat. "She probably dictated the second letter herself, and then killed him."

Marco and Petro Dorma came in looking for them. Petro seemed to accept Lopez and his companions as perfectly logical people to be there. "Still no sign of the Schiopettieri," said Petro, sitting down. "I've left a message over at Marco's old apartment for them to come here. Bribed several of the locals to wait for them. Still, if they're not here in ten minutes, I must go and rouse the Council of Ten myself. I wonder why they haven't arrived?"

Marco had been drowning in Kat's eyes, paying almost no attention to the conversation. It took a few moments for Petro's words to drum through.

"I wonder why they haven't arrived?"

That, and Aleri's last word—which he and Petro had agreed did sound as if Aleri might have been starting to say "Caesare"—finally registered. Marco's immediate reaction had been: *that can't be true.* But walking across the darkened campo the thought had come to him. . . . What allegiance did Caesare Aldanto owe to Venice? He was for sale to the highest bidder, after all. He'd always *seemed* good to Marco . . . but the way he had cheated Maria . . .

"Um . . . Would your Schiopettieri messenger have gone to Caesare Aldanto?"

Petro turned on him, pursing his lips. "It *was* his name! It *was* that name that the Chernobog destroyed Aleri rather than let us discover! Oh, Jesus. I've given the city defenses into the hands of a traitor."

"He's a traitor and a murderer all right," grated Lodovico.

Petro took a deep breath. "He could wreak more havoc than all the Montagnard firebombs put together. I can't take the chance, even if I've guessed wrong and he's innocent. What the hell am I going to do?"

Maria stood up. "What you should have done in the first place,

Dorma. Call out the Arsenalotti. They haven't joined your stupid militia because they are insulted by it. The defense of the Republic has always been their responsibility."

Dorma nodded. "Get me paper and sealing wax," he commanded Rafael. He turned back to Maria. "You obviously know the Arsenal, woman."

"My cousins are caulkers," said Maria stiffly. "My father was a caulker."

"Would they rally to the Republic, if you were to tell them that the defense of the Arsenal and the Doge's palace are in their hands, that they must deal with any rogue militia?"

Maria snorted. "You're so stuck up, Dorma, that you have no idea. Of course they would! And most of the boat-people too. Send Marco to rally them. They saw him with the Doge. And he has a reputation five times as good as yours. They trust him."

Petro stood up. "Good. Because I have work, tonight, for every one of you. You too, Lodovico Montescue."

"I am at the service of the Republic," said the old man stiffly. "But I hope that that work includes arresting Caesare Aldanto."

"That's dangerous work," said Petro mildly. "But I have another task for you. I want to know which of the Trieste-coasters is running messages to Trieste. You have the contacts. Get onto them. If need be, arrest them. I want to know to whom these messages are going. And I want to alter a message."

Kat and Lodovico gaped at Petro. "How—"

Petro smiled sardonically. "You can thank the Doge. I would have closed you down. He said the gray trade would exist anyway, and he would rather it was in the hands of someone we knew and who was loyal to Venice. Someone that we could use if need be. Besides, the Doge felt the Jews and the Strega did a great deal for Venice's wealth and well-being. He thought your trade supported them. Just because he has that childish devotion to clockwork devices doesn't make him a fool, you know."

Kat recovered her wits first. "Captain Della Tomasso. He is carrying messages for the Sots. And if anyone knows of any other secret messages being carried, it'll be him. His ship leaves on the full tide at about two o'clock this morning."

"I'll see to him," said Lodovico. "But who gets to arrest Aldanto? I can provide a charge."

"And I have evidence," said Benito, "in the shape of a bound and locked-up hired murderer lying in our apartment. Giovanni Matteoni."

Marco gaped at his younger brother.

Petro took a deep breath. "I will. My sister is going to be angry." He sighed. "And I must try to do something about Lucrezia, while my messengers rouse the Council."

"I've heard Ricardo Brunelli has sent Lucrezia away to safety," announced Lopez.

"Ah. Then, with you, Lopez, and the Doge's Swiss Guards, and what other force I can muster, we will go to the Imperial embassy and confront the Knights."

He turned on Luciano. "The attack is at least in part magical. The Strega must contest that. Can you damp fires?"

"Rafael will go to see that that is in hand. I must go to the Marciana library. There is a guardian . . . if I can arouse it, it will do more than any fire-damping."

"Very well. Marco. You will go with this lady," Petro pointed to Maria. "I will give you a signed order for Admiral Marchese. Ring the Marangona. Rouse the Arsenalotti. Send any men who can be spared to Piazza San Marco. And I want squads of men to proceed to as many of these addresses as they can. Take no chances. Douse any gunpowder they find, or toss it into the canal. And then proceed to rouse any of your canaler friends you can find. Send them to San Marco."

Marco looked alarmed. But nodded.

"Benito. Your task is the *Casa* Dandelo."

Benito smiled savagely. "Yes. Although I'll arrest Caesare first for you if you like."

Marco gaped at his brother again.

Petro looked calculatingly at him. "No. I'll do that. You deal with the *Casa* Dandelo. Neutralize it. Destroy it." He sighed. "I go beyond my authority here. To act against foreigners is easy, but a Venetian *Casa* . . . Even to order a search will take time and manpower I don't have."

"The place is like a fort," mused Benito, considering the problem. In that moment, he seemed much older than he was.

"I know. Do it."

Benito grinned. "*Si.* How much gold do you all have? I'm going to need a fair bit. And Maria—you going to come and help when you've finished talking to the Arsenalotti? I'll need a couple of your cousins. Good honest boatmen. I'll see you at Giaccomo's. We're going into the barrel delivery business. And the *Signori di Notte* and the Schiopettieri are turning a blind eye."

Maria nodded. "Come and choose them."

"*Si.* I'll need some gunpowder from the Arsenal anyway."

Petro looked rather warily at the imp he'd just set loose. But he dug into his pockets.

"I guess that leaves me," said Kat. "I'd better go with my grandfather to Della Tomasso."

Petro took a deep breath. "No. Lodovico Montescue is old enough not to need his hand held. You go with Marco. We may all be dead soon. You may as well—" He waved a little feebly. "Be together."

Lodovico looked at Marco Valdosta. Shrugged. "My house is in ruins anyway. Be happy at least, *cara mia.*"

Marco faced a crowd, a sea of faces. The torches made the planes of the faces stand out. Showed the lines of hard work and poor food, particularly in the clustered caulkers. Hard times and hard faces. Mouths set in a grim line. His stomach turned itself inside out. He looked at Maria. There was the same grimness, the same determination in that square jaw, as there was on the faces in the crowd. And Maria said that he, not she, must tell the Arsenalotti what Petro had said.

He looked at Kat. She reached out and squeezed his hand, and he realized just how right Petro had been. He still did need someone to hold his hand. "Introduce me," he said to Maria.

She stood up onto the marble step. "Arsenalotti!"

There were a few cheers. A number of smiles. A good many waves. Everyone here knew Maria Garavelli. Honest as the day was long, even if she had a temper on her that you could boil a kettle on. "What are you doing up there, Maria?"

"This is Marco Valdosta. He needs to talk to you. He's *Case Vecchie,* but he has doctored some of your kids. He's a good man and he's got a message for you from the Council of Ten."

Marco got up onto the step. "Thank you, Maria."

There were a few people clapping. He heard his name repeated. He cleared his throat and looked at Kat. She smiled.

"Who has always defended the Doge, the piazza? On whom has

the last defense of Venice *always* rested?" His voice cut through the silence.

No one answered. Then someone in the back of the crowd said "Not Petro Dorma's damned 'militia,' Valdosta!"

"Right," said Marco. "*Not* the militia. The Arsenalotti. That is the way it has always been. And that is the way it must *stay.*"

The crowd cheered.

Marco knew in his bones that he was doing the right thing. He had them. He held up a parchment. "Dorma made a mistake. He's man enough to admit that. I, Marco Valdosta, have his writ here. The Council calls the Arsenalotti to the Defense of the Republic." A strange power infused his voice. "In the name of the Winged Lion of Saint Mark, you are called to Arms! Will you answer?"

The assent itself was a roar. And to Marco's shock, he realized that they were chanting "VAL—DOS–TA! VAL—DOS–TA!"

He stilled them with a gesture. "This is my brother, Benito. He's the one who is good at organizing and plans. He'll tell you what the Council wants."

Benito, wide-eyed, was pushed to his feet to face the cheering crowd. "I'll get even with you for this, Marco," he said quietly.

"Face it, Benito," said Marco. "You tell people what to do far better than I do."

And Benito went on to prove him dead right.

Chapter 87

Erik stared at the desecrated Lady chapel. Grim. Silent. Pellmann had not run away after all, as his remains testified. But it was the bells that were the most offensive. Made from infant skulls, with a small thighbone for a clapper. The cross was broken. The walls were scrawled with strange and unpleasant symbols . . . scrawled in what could only be blood and excrement. Rusty stains marred the once white altar cloth. Pieces of clothing . . . A cotte. A knitted cap. A richly embroidered nightshirt . . . lay on the floor.

But of the Woden-casket, which had been placed there, there was no sign.

"I think I am going to throw up," said Manfred quietly. "Under our noses. Right under our very noses! Well, Sachs? What do you have to say to this?"

The abbot, defiant, furious, and threatening divine retribution until a bare minute ago, sank to his knees. "My God. My God! Forgive me."

"He may. But I won't," said Manfred, grimly. "Where is it and where is she, Sachs?"

The former abbot looked into Manfred's implacable eyes. Looked around at the desecrated chapel. "Sister Ursula, the casket, and an escort of knights left this late afternoon. There was a chance that the witches could . . ." He faltered. "That's what she said. She said they would try to liberate it. That it would be safer with our friends on the mainland. My God, my God, I have been weak, misled by the carnal desires of the flesh! My God, forgive me."

Erik hit him. "Enough time for self-pity and remorse later, you stinking swine. *Where have they gone?*"

Sachs whimpered. "I don't know. She said something about forts to Aldanto."

"The Polestine forts," said Francesca.

Erik turned to Manfred. "She's going to turn the Woden loose on the forts, presumably to clear the way for a fleet from Milan, which will be coming down the Po River."

Sachs nodded wretchedly. "Sforza is coming. But we didn't know . . . I thought—she said it was Christ's work. . . ."

Manfred pointed at the chapel. "Well, now you see whose work it really was. What is this about Trieste?"

"A thousand two hundred of our knights, the Chapters from Greifswald, Landsberg, and Schniedemühl, are ready to embark to restore order and seize the Arsenal. They wait for our message."

"So," said Manfred, sardonically. "You stripped the northeastern frontier for this adventure. The Grand Duke of Lithuania must be very pleased with you. What do you think, Erik? Shall we turn them loose to make a demonstration on the border against Emeric of Hungary? That'll keep him out of the mess, anyway, and them away from here."

"Yes." Erik nodded. "And we will need local guides. If we ride hard, we may get to the Woden-casket in time."

Manfred nodded. "Francesca and Count Von Stemitz—with an escort of Knights—can ride for the Brenner pass to reassure Uncle Charles Fredrik that I am still alive. Now we'd better go and look for Petro Dorma."

A knight ran in. "There is a huge party of Venetians disembarking outside. Looks like some mercenaries too. And cannon. Knight-Proctor Von Dusbad and Etten are readying defense." He stared at the horror in the chapel . . . "What is *this!*"

"Sister God-damned Ursula, is what it is. Hell's teeth! Let's see if we can stop this. You—" Manfred pointed to one of the knights. "You see to it that the Servants are marched in here to see this abomination." He pointed to the kneeling Sachs. "And take him and lock him away."

"Open up in the name of the Holy Church and the Republic of Venice!" demanded someone outside.

"Let us out the wicket door. You can prepare a charge in case there is a problem." Ducking, Manfred, Erik and several of the senior knights came out to face the Venetians.

Erik felt his heart lift to see Petro Dorma out there in the torchlight. Petro may have felt similar relief, but he didn't let that show on his face or stop the mercenaries lining up the small cannon. All he said was "Where is Abbot Sachs?"

"I sent him off to be locked up," said Manfred. "We don't want trouble, Dorma. In fact I need to talk to you . . ."

"*Ciao,* Petro," said Francesca, sweeping forward with her hands outstretched, as if greeting an old family friend.

Dorma's mouth fell open. His face seemed to flush a bit.

Francesca smiled at him. "You look like a catfish with your mouth open, Petro. Close it, dear. You really do need to talk to them. They've just foiled a plot against you—*and* the Holy Roman Empire. This large young man is the Emperor's nephew, as it happens. Who would have thought it? And, I believe, also his Emissary Plenipotentiary."

Having obeyed Francesca's first injunction to close his mouth, Petro Dorma then did an even better catfish imitation.

"You'd better come inside," said Erik. "We have found out who has been committing those murders."

"Do you have her prisoner?" asked a slight man with an aquiline nose and a solid single dark line of eyebrow. "I am Eneko Lopez, a Legate of the Grand Metropolitan of Rome. We demand to speak to 'Sister' Ursula."

Erik shook his head. "Too late. We've found her foul chapel. But she's gone. Come."

The doors were opened. Dorma and some of his party were escorted to the desecrated Lady chapel. One of the priests gagged immediately and clutched his nose. "Chernobog!" he gasped. "The stench is horrid! Fierce!" Even under the circumstances, the man's broad Savoyard accent was unmistakable.

Erik looked curiously at the fellow. He'd heard of witch-smellers, but had had no faith in them in times past. Now . . .

Erik sniffed experimentally himself. Yes. It *was* the same odor he'd smelled in Sachs's study that one day. He'd thought it was sister Ursula's perfume—and how odd it was for a nun to use perfume. It was . . . sort of sickly sweet. Confined in Sachs's room it had made him want to sneeze. Perhaps Sachs himself had been the victim of a powerful amount of magical manipulation.

Manfred was talking to Petro Dorma. "—three parties. Ten will remain here. The message to Trieste should stop the Knights. If not . . . well, those who remain here can pass on Charles Fredrik's orders. The rest are split into the party going to tell Emperor Charles Fredrik that I'm not dead yet, and the bulk of us are riding after Sister Ursula."

"Take us with you," said Lopez. "She is what we seek."

Manfred looked him over. "We want to leave as soon as we can get a boat to the mainland. Mounts may be a problem." He hesitated. "And it'll be a hard chase. Even for soldiers."

Lopez snorted. "I was a soldier once, lad—and longer than you've been, I venture to say. You think I got this limp from the stairs in the Vatican? Nor have I led what you'd call a soft life since."

Dorma interrupted. "I can solve one of your problems. We have remounts on the mainland at the landing at Chioggia. I'll send *Capi* D'Strozza with you. He's from Chioggia, and will see you through to the forts. And, as he says, Senor Lopez was once a knight. Despite the limp I think you can still ride, no?"

Lopez smiled. "Better than any *Ritter*, I suspect. We'll find out." The last sentence came out almost gleefully. Holy the man might be now—but, clearly enough, there was still that Basque truculence lurking somewhere within his soul.

Over on Saint Mark's Square a bell began to ring, frantically. Petro looked despondent. "The alarm tocsin! Now what?"

Erik smiled. "Part of this conspiracy that we have partially unraveled, I suspect. Give us your *Capi* and we'll be moving, and you can get back to Saint Marks." He peered into the darkness, at the hazy, haloed moon. "Looks like you're in for fog. I hope your *Capi* is a good navigator."

Petro smiled back. "The best. He was a smuggler before I recruited him. Fog was one of his favorite kinds of weather."

Down on the water, on the mainland side of Rialto, Benito could have told Erik the fog was thick enough to cut with a knife already. It smelt . . . odd. Marshy. Not the usual wet-wool and smoke smell of Venice fog. Benito wasn't going to let it worry him. Giaccomo was enough to worry about.

The heavy, balding man was not the type to be impressed by

Case Vecchie clothes or orders. Money would talk, however. Benito hoped he had enough. They'd picked up Valentina . . . Claudia was off somewhere. The way Valentina said "somewhere" meant: *Strega stuff, don't ask.*

"Your eyes almost seem to be glowing," said Maria, looking at him curiously.

Benito knew he could get killed doing this. So could Maria . . . So could other people. It didn't stop him loving it all. He was feeling brave, so he put a hand on her forearm. That was gambling with your hand, with Maria.

"It's in my blood. My grandfather . . . And my father."

She flicked the hand off. But almost gently. "Your grandfather I've heard about. Dell'este is a legend. But the Valdosta . . . I asked. They're like Marco."

Benito pulled a wry face. "We're half-brothers really, Maria. I think my father was Carlo Sforza."

She stared at him, wide-eyed. *Sforza. The Wolf of the North.* She shook her head. "So. Just what are we going to do to get into the *Casa* Dandelo? There are probably up to thirty Dandelos and their slave overseers. There are God alone knows how many Montagnards there too. We have thirty men and one thief."

"There must be three hundred slaves," said Benito. "And the way out is going to be through the *Casa.*"

Maria nodded. "True. And having been in there myself, killing a few slave-masters might be sweeter than freedom to a lot of them. Well, keep it simple. Clever plans go wrong."

"I'll do my best."

"You want *thirty* empty casks?" Giaccomo looked at Benito. Then at Maria. "What for?" He went on polishing glasses.

"And your small barge." Benito ignored the question, and began counting out gold coins onto the counter. He noticed that Giaccomo had stopped polishing glasses.

"You're with Dorma nowadays," said Giaccomo. "Quite the young *Case Vecchie* gentleman. With a brother who once tried to sell me fake relics. I want to know *why*, boy—or no deal. Not for twice as much."

"I'm not Marco," said Benito calmly. Giaccomo flustered Marco; Benito knew you just had to keep calm around him. "Have I ever done you wrong, Giaccomo? I brought coin for you once."

"Yeah. But I still want to know. And nobody else has barrels enough."

Benito shrugged. "Dorma wants me to blow up *Casa* Dandelo. Destroy the place. We had a dead certain tip-off"—he couldn't resist the pun—"that it's full of Montagnards. They're due to cause trouble when the invaders come." Benito smiled. "And we all know how Maria loves the Dandelos."

A small corner of a smile touched Giaccomo's face. "She ain't your tip-off?"

Benito knew that Giaccomo regarded even a whiff of magic as bad news. So he chose his phrasing carefully. "Party called Aleri. Heard of him?"

Giaccomo's eyes narrowed. He nodded. He didn't look friendly. "You can't trust him."

"Ah. Let's put it this way. He was answering certain questions for the *Signori di Notte* in an . . . involuntary fashion."

Giaccomo actually smiled. He pulled three of the stacks of coin towards himself. "I'd lend you some manpower . . ." He paused. "This has nothing to do with Aldanto, has it?"

Benito shook his head very firmly. Giaccomo pushed one of the stacks of coin back. Benito pushed it over again. "It's Dorma's money. And it's only right to tell you that if things go wrong you won't see your barge again."

"Aldanto's got money from Ferrara sitting here. Been coming in ever since you and that brother of yours showed up. You see him, you tell him there's two lots here." The expression on Giaccomo's face said: *and I don't mind if he doesn't fetch it.* "The barge is round the back. Jeppo will help you get the barrels loaded."

Fifteen minutes later, Giaccomo's barge was heading for the *Casa* Dandelo with a cargo of "wine." Benito hoped that Valentina had the gunpowder in position. When they'd cased the joint, picking up the guards on the roof, she'd said that it would be easy. He hoped she was right, because they'd need the distraction.

The cargo wouldn't get into the *Casa* proper, but there was an enclosed loading bay into the stores and slave quarters. He, Maria, and Maria's cousin Luigi poled the barge, little more than a floating flat-bed full of barrels, around to the front of the *Casa*. Benito went and pounded on the door.

"Who is it at this time of night?" demanded someone, far too quickly.

"Wine delivery. From Giaccomo's!" yelled Benito.

"Go away!" bellowed someone within. "We didn't order any wine."

Benito yelled back. "Party by the name of Aleri came in and paid for it, special delivery, tonight."

There was the sound of talk, as if a small argument were going on. But Benito was relaxed, confident. No one behind that door was going to turn down a cargo of wine. And the deliverers were not exactly a threat. A ragged fifteen-year-old boy, a seventeen-year-old girl, and an older bargee. Odds on, the "extra guests" had already worked their way through most of the Dandelos' wine stock—and with the war on, heaven knew when they'd see more.

The door cracked open. An eye appeared, examining Benito for a brief moment and then, for a much longer moment, the cargo on the barge. "All of that for us?"

Benito laughed. "You wish! Five casks. The rest are for Barducci's. The boss won't let us do 'one person' deliveries. And Barducci's is running dry. Gotta have it there inside the hour. Party there tonight, with everyone going off to war. You goin' to accept this load or do we take it away again?"

That dire threat brought the final decision. "Bring it round the side. Some of the men will come down and open up."

"Send someone to offload, too."

"Cheeky little sod. Does your master know you're so lazy?"

"Ah, come on—"

"On your way! The men will see you there."

On his way down the side canal, Benito whistled loudly, tunelessly. Out of the corner of his eye he had seen a glimpse of Valentina on the opposite roof, grappling hook ready. She wasn't going to swing across, herself. But the small barrel of black powder was going to pendulum across. Valentina reckoned it'd smash through those shutters like a knife through silk. It didn't matter whether it did or not, just so long as there was fire and trouble in the main residential part of the *Casa.* Still, Benito wished he could watch. He also hoped like hell Valentina *didn't* stay to watch.

The Dandelo men had already gotten the rusty portcullis they used to enclose their dock half up by the time they got there. When the barge was in, as Benito expected, the portcullis dropped again. That made good security sense.

What happened next was not, however, what Benito had expected at all. There were seven Dandelo men there. As soon as the portcullis dropped, the leader smiled at the barge crew and rubbed his hands. "Well! We got thirty barrels and three slaves for the price of five barrels. And it's on Aleri's coin! *Ha.* Take 'em, boys."

"Hey!" protested Benito. "You can't do that! Giaccomo knows where we are. And he'll send for the Schiopettieri. And you don't mess with Giaccomo's cargos!"

The slaver laughed. "By the time he knows you've gone, it'll be too late. Hear that Tocsin? You got in just before the bell, boy. Now we're shut up siege-tight until Sforza gets here. So come quietly or you're going to get hurt."

Benito was paralyzed for an instant, not knowing what to do. Then—dead on time—an explosion rocked the walls.

Bits of mortar fell. It was like a slap around the ears. Benito realized he still had a lot to learn about black powder. It certainly stunned the Dandelos, but Maria and her cousin Luigi were tipping barrels as if it hadn't happened. Arsenalotti were scrambling out from under, weapons in hand. Benito hadn't waited, either. He'd gotten between the doorway and the Dandelos. And the first fool didn't even try to avoid the rapier he'd snatched up from between the barrels.

He hadn't been prepared for the horror on that face. But he didn't have time to think. The blade was stuck right through the slaver, so he pulled his knife out. The next few moments gave him several reasons to write off part of Caesare Aldanto's crimes. Only the training he'd had at Aldanto's hand kept him alive.

Two minutes later, at the cost of one dead and three wounded men, the dock was theirs. And even from here they could hear the chaos that Valentina's black powder had generated.

They moved out, to the slave pens. Heavy hammers and cold chisels in the hands of two blacksmiths from the Arsenal began making short work of the locks. Two of the Arsenalotti stood by with a barrel full of cutlasses. In the meanwhile Maria and her ten escorts raced up the stairs, looking for the passage she'd found through to the *Casa* itself. The barrel of black powder they had with them should see that door blown open. Then it would be a case of shepherding freed, armed slaves up and in.

"Listen up, all of you!" shouted Benito. "We have to cut our way out of the *Casa*. Loot what you can, especially clothes. And don't kill anyone wearing these hats." He pointed at his red woolen cap. "They're our people. When you're out into Venice, toss the cutlasses into the canal. Scatter. Act like citizens, otherwise the Schiopettieri will put you away." *Not strictly true, but the last thing Petro Dorma wanted on top of his troubles was a rampaging mob of armed ex-slaves. Arsenal-issue cutlasses were cheap compared to that risk.*

There was a ragged chorus of cheers. Most of the slaves were still staring, unbelieving. They started to believe when big Gio smashed open the first lock with his cold chisel. Men and—from the next pen—women streamed out, taking the weapons as if they'd been handed the Holy Grail.

There was a small explosion from upstairs. A much more controlled-sounding one. At least Maria had an Arsenal gunner to manage *her* black powder.

"Up!" shouted Benito. "Up the stairs—and at the Dandelos!"

The cheer now was a wild deep-throated roar, like a tiger uncaged and seeking furious vengeance on its trapper.

Benito led them on up. Reflecting all the while on an old proverb he'd once heard about the risks of riding a tiger.

Maria had found being back inside this place a nightmare. It made her feel weak and scared. Not the fighting, or the danger. Just the horrible place itself. Still, they had a job to do. And *Casa* Dandelo would rue the day they had taken her prisoner. She heard the tumult of the slaves coming up the stairs, and saw Benito at the head of them.

There was a fierceness in his shining eyes. This wasn't the mischievous, laughing boy she knew—and had once made love to, a memory she found strangely haunting. This was the blood of the Wolf of the North. She didn't like it. She didn't like it at all. But when she thought about it, it had always been there, lurking under the surface. For all his charm, there was also something a little frightening about Benito.

She followed after the rush. Fifteen minutes later she and Benito were out on the Grand Canal in fog. The *Casa* Dandelo was burning behind them.

"Well. That's that," said Benito, rubbing his hands in satisfaction.

"I suppose you're proud of yourself?" said Maria quietly.

"Well," said Benito, swelling his chest a bit. "It was a good fight. We didn't expect them to have Milanese soldiers hidden in there. But those slaves didn't let arquebuses or even the magicians stop them. No finesse but lots of courage."

"They had lots of courage because they were desperate, Benito, and no way out. And you used them as cannon-fodder. And that 'distraction' of yours exploded in the family living quarters. You probably killed and maimed a whole lot of kids. So I hope you're not too proud of yourself, Benito Valdosta, because I'm not. We just did what we had to do, that's all."

Benito started to say something. Then he stopped himself. "So what should I have done, seeing as you are so clever?" he asked. But there was doubt as well as hurt in his voice.

Maria looked back at the burning building. "I don't know," she said quietly. "But that was the way the Wolf would do it. The Old Fox kills for family, not just for fun. He would have figured out a better way."

"Uh-huh. Well, I'll think about it when I haven't got a war to fight," said Benito. The adult male gruffness in his voice did a poor job of covering the hurt in the boy's. "We'd better get back to the piazza and find out what that tocsin was all about."

The bell was Lucrezia Brunelli's way of telling the city that its second most important citizen, Ricardo Brunelli, was dead. Murdered.

And not five hundred yards away, a building was burning.

A runner came up, panting. "*Arsenalotti!* Count Badoero has landed at the Sacca della Misericordia. *With many men!*"

Chapter 88

Nobody challenged sixty fully armored knights riding through the dark. They crossed the Brenta and the Piave bridges without opposition. Now, as the sky was turning gray with the dawn, they only had the last league or so to go.

"We might be ahead, you know," said Erik. "They landed at Mestre. We saved a fair distance by going around by sea to Chioggia."

"Hmm," said Manfred. "As long as they didn't meet up with Francesca."

"No point in worrying about that," said Erik. "More immediate is the problem of how to stop the forts from opening fire on us. Or what to do if we see Ursula and her escort."

Manfred snorted. "She has twenty-five Knights and a bunch of Servants of the Holy Trinity. We have sixty. We ride the bastards down."

Erik was tired and irritable. It had been a long night. "She'll have picked up an escort, probably from the Scaligers. Possibly arquebusiers. *Think*, Manfred. And this casket—how do you think she plans to use it?"

Lopez, who had been riding beside them as if he'd been born in the saddle—quite unlike his two companions—turned slightly and answered. "She and the Servants will probably abandon their escort, and head for the fort posing as distressed holy pilgrims. The fort will let them in, particularly when they see one is a woman and there are only five of them. Then I imagine they will release the Woden from the casket. They alone will be protected. When

750

everyone is dead—or flees, which most of them will—the troops will come up and turn the cannon in this fort on the other. And then the enemy will sail through to attack Venice."

Erik nodded. "That's what I'd do, I suppose, if that monster in the casket is so powerful. And what would you do about meeting the Knights and the escort?"

"It would depend on the terrain and the light," answered Lopez. "Arquebuses are inaccurate at the best of times and pretty useless at night." He eyed the large prince. "Or was the question aimed at you?"

Manfred sighed. "Erik's trying to get me to say a double feint or something, Senor Lopez. And then he'll say 'no, keep it simple, stupid. Always flank them.' He's a blasted teacher born."

There was a flash of teeth in the half-dark from the Basque. "A good one too, then. Simplicity is usually best—in war as in all things."

Their guide rode up. "There's a party of soldiers ahead. A barricade. Look like mercenary arquebusiers."

"Can we go around?"

The guide looked at the heavily armored Knights; shook his head. "Too swampy."

"They're not Venetians, are they?" asked Erik.

The guide shook his head again. "Scaliger colors." Erik was not surprised by the answer. The Scaligers were the ruling family of Verona; traditional allies of Milan and supporters of the Montagnard faction in Italian politics. Since they controlled the Adige route from Venice through the Brenner Pass into the Holy Roman Empire, they had been expected to intervene in the war in alliance with Milan.

"And how far are we from the fort?" asked Manfred.

The guide shrugged. "Half a league. Maybe less."

"I think we've got to move fast, *Ritters*," snapped Manfred. "I'll bet they've left their escort and are advancing on foot."

Erik shook his head. "Scout it quickly first. It shouldn't take ten minutes, it'll rest the horses, and it may spell the difference between success and failure. Ursula must plan to arrive when the fort's defenders can see them easily. That gives us a few minutes."

They halted. The guide slipped forward on foot. He returned to report that there were some hundred or so cavalrymen breakfasting on the edge of a field of peas.

"Right." Manfred took a deep breath. "We don't want to lose

the time fighting the troops and let Ursula get into that fort. If we defeat every one of them and she and her henchmen get in . . . we've failed. Remember that chapel. That is what we're dealing with, not some Italian mercenaries. Erik, you tell them how you want to run this. That way you can't complain if I get it wrong."

Erik nodded. Skirmish combat against wild tribes in Vinland was something he had three years of experience with. And more than that in the similar type of warfare which plagued clan-ridden Iceland.

"Knight-Proctor Von Oderberg, you are going to take care of the troops. Manfred, Von Gherens, Etten, and I will keep riding, with Lopez and his companions. Don't get your horses among the peas—you'll lose mobility. If you keep those Scaliger mercenaries dismounted and busy, Von Oderberg, that'll be fine. You don't have to do more than that. Try to tell our fellow Knights you have orders from Sachs to turn them back. But if need be, cut them down."

They caught sight of the little band bearing the casket not three hundred yards from the fortress's walls. By the sounds of it, Von Oderberg was butchering the escort. Or being butchered. Erik didn't turn around to look; he just bent low over his horse's neck.

One of the monks did turn, perhaps alerted by the sudden thunder of hooves. He shouted something.

The monks and sister Ursula stopped. Erik could see that Sister Ursula was scrawling something in the dust with a long staff. Wind, laden with grit and debris leapt at them. Horses reared and screamed. *Ritter* Etten and Father Diego fell. Erik struggled to stay on his horse. Hastily, almost falling himself, he managed to dismount. The horse fled.

Erik, Manfred, and Von Gherens, now dismounted, formed a phalanx of steel around Lopez and Father Pierre. As they began to advance, lightnings crackled off the steel. Behind them, Eric heard Lopez saying: "*Let that which cannot abide the name of Jesus, begone.*"

And somehow . . . the resistance eased. They continued plodding forward. Etten came up to join them. "Father Diego is too dazed from his fall," he muttered to Erik. "We won't have his help."

Erik saw that Sister Ursula was ordering the monks to lower the casket to the ground. As they drew closer, he could see that the casket no longer carried its heavy chains and securing locks. Nothing held the lid down beyond its own weight.

They were ten yards away, now. Ursula stood next to the casket at the center of the circle she had scrawled, her staff held upright in one hand, with the four monks standing like guardian statues at the cardinal points. The circle seemed to sparkle.

The nun's wimple had fallen and her hair was revealed: a great mane of it, in a dark corona around her white face. The face itself seemed to bear no expression at all. It might have been the face of a statue, if marble could blink its eyes and move its lips.

"You cannot prevail, Vessel of Chernobog!" said Lopez. "Repent and save your soul. I am Eneko Lopez, Legate of the Grand Metropolitan and master of Holy magic. You cannot prevail. Let your darkness begone! *Fiat lux!*"

Light leapt even from the stones . . . Except inside the circle.

Ursula laughed. The sound was mocking, but empty—as if an actress were feigning an emotion she had never understood, or had forgotten. "I might even be afraid, Lopez. Lucrezia told me that she failed to find the chink that most men have in their armor. Foolish woman. She thought she was as powerful as I. Impossible, when she refused to join herself fully with the Great Lord."

Erik's flesh crawled. Everything about the way the woman spoke was *empty*. The nun's habit fell aside. The body that was revealed wore clinging black silk. The half-transparent silk hid little; in fact, it seemed designed to tantalize rather than to conceal. But, again, the display was empty. There was no *woman* there to give the shapely flesh any real allure. Erik finally understood how completely Chernobog had consumed the creature.

She reached forward, and tapped the casket. "And I have my little friend here."

"Servants of the Holy Trinity, see what you have in your midst!" shouted Lopez.

The monks didn't move. They stood like statues, arms outstretched, warding.

"They are mine, body and soul," said Ursula. "Unlike Lucrezia I insist on total control."

"She stinks of ice and Chernobog," said Pierre.

It was true, thought Erik. That was what the smell reminded him of. Breaking sea ice, with a sickly sweetness over it. It was very strong now.

Suddenly, the Savoyard priest clutched at his crucifix and sat down, gasping. A moment later his eyes rolled back and he slumped on his side, unconscious.

Manfred ignored Pierre's collapse. He glanced at Erik and said lazily, "I heard she was fat as a sow when she joined the order. Sold her soul for a pair of tits."

Erik realized what Manfred was doing: Exactly what the Venetian swordmaster, Giuliano, had taught them. *Unbalance your enemy, make them angry.* It was a dangerous game. Erik was not prepared to leave him to play it alone. "She got cheated," he sneered. "She's still too ugly to get customers anywhere except the docks."

But the gibes seemed to have no effect on Ursula at all. Erik caught the tiny, tell-tale signs of Manfred tensing. When he lunged forward, so did Erik. So did Von Gherens and Etten.

Erik's sword struck the air above the circle. It was like hitting a wall. He caught a glimpse of Ursula swinging her staff. A huge and shadowy hand swung towards him. It didn't actually make contact, but fear and pain washed though Erik. He wanted to scream, to turn and run. Von Gherens stumbled and fell; Etten whimpered; Manfred grunted and tried to press forward—but was driven back.

Ursula shrieked words Erik did not recognize. Small biting, pinching imps leapt out of the air. They turned to ashes as they struck armor, but there were so many it impossible to see or move.

Then Lopez shouted: "Reverse your swords! Hold them like a crucifix! And ground the tips in the honest earth."

Erik and Manfred immediately obeyed. Staggering back onto his feet, so did Von Gherens. Etten tried, but the sword slipped out of his hands. Lopez began to chant in Latin. Immediately, the imps were immobilized in the air, then began to shrink, then vanish into wisps of smoke. The monk guardians began to crumple.

Ursula shrieked again. Another command of some sort. The four monks seemed to summon their fading strength and began scuffing the soil with their sandals. Within a moment, the circle which Ursula had scratched was broken at the four cardinal points. At the broken points, hot air seemed to eddy out of the circle and wash over Erik and Manfred and the others. The same hot air, swirling at the four compass points like miniature cyclones, sucked the monks dry in an instant; four skin-bags full of bones collapsed to the ground. The heated air seemed to glow and darken simultaneously, as if drawing power and form from its consumption of the monks.

"No closer!" warned Ursula. She laid a hand on the casket's lid. "No closer or I will release the Woden."

Lopez walked forward, coming to stand next to Erik. He held a very small crucifix in his hand. "This is a fragment of the true cross, witch. Evil cannot prevail against it."

Lopez's words seemed to have no effect. Ursula's lips curled in what Erik would have called a sneer, had it not been for the emptiness of the face which framed it. A woman can sneer; a vessel cannot.

"Besides, if you open that casket," said Manfred, "your plot is at naught."

At that moment, Ursula's face underwent a transformation. A horrid one. The face thickened, grew heavy; the shapely cheeks sagged into jowls; the fair brow swelled, looming now over sunken eye sockets. Inside the orbs, a woman's dark eyes became slits of pure black. And now, for the first time, *emotion* filled the face. Anger and cruelty, overlaid by triumph.

Erik understood that the vessel was now filled to the brim, and overflowing. This was not Ursula; this was Chernobog himself, lurking inside her flesh.

The horrible face—half-man; half-woman—bared white teeth turning yellow as Erik watched. "Do not presume to instruct your betters, stripling. There are plots and plots. If the Woden cannot accomplish one task, it can certainly succeed in another."

Erik's mind seemed to be working much faster than his body. He understood Chernobog's new purpose, and desperately tried to reach Manfred—to seize the prince and hurl him back, out of danger. But some magic was causing his flesh to move like soft lead. The same magic seemed to have frozen Manfred and Von Gherens completely. Etten was no longer standing at all. The knight had crumpled to his knees, his head lolling.

Chernobog/Ursula's voice rolled on. "Here, fool boy— uncontrolled and unwarded—the Woden will kill and kill and kill. You will be dead, and your precious Empire left with one heir the less."

Ursula's hand had remained female. Now, even more suddenly than her face, the hand changed. Grew, swelled, became first the hand of a large man and then the hand—the paw, rather—of something still larger. The claws plunged into the wood of the casket lid and began to raise it. Heat and darkness spilled out of the crack like a flood. A horrible stench came with it.

Lopez stepped forward and met the surge of darkness from the casket with the tiny cross. He shouted some words Erik did not understand. In Greek, he thought, not Latin. Neither the action nor the words seemed to have any effect on the swelling darkness, but Erik felt the paralysis which had kept him almost immobile suddenly lift.

He could see the Chernobog/Ursula face open its mouth. The thick lips began to twist, began to utter words of their own—words which, Erik had no doubt at all, would counter those of Lopez. The Basque priest was still shouting Greek phrases.

But the paralysis was completely gone, now. Erik moved faster than he ever had in his life. The Algonquian war hatchet sailed across the distance and buried itself up to the wirebound hilt in his/her skull. Blood gushed. The obsidian eyes seemed to flame black fire for an instant, before the body toppled back and fell to the ground. As it fell, all traces of Chernobog left the face and then, more slowly, the hand. But the talons remained longest of all—long enough to draw the lid of the casket open as Ursula fell.

The hot, stinking blackness poured out like lava from a volcano, sweeping over Erik and Manfred and all the others. Erik could hear the gleeful shriek of a monster somewhere.

That shriek was immediately overridden by another. Etten's voice, that was, howling in agony. Erik turned toward the sound, his eyes tearing from the heat and the stench. The Woden monster had seized upon Etten, he knew. Etten, the weakest of them, was being consumed by fire from within.

Suddenly, Lopez's voice rang out more loudly than Erik would have believed possible, coming from such a small man. In an instant, the darkness vanished and Erik could see clearly again.

Etten was writhing on the ground, his fingers clawing at the straps of his helmet. Smoke was pouring up through the visor. Von Gherens, nearest to him, leaned over and began to help. A flash of flame seemed to leap through the visor and smite the Prussian knight in the face.

Now it was Von Gherens' turn to writhe on the ground, screaming in agony.

"Quick!" shouted Lopez. "Use your swords!"

Moving together, Erik and Manfred grabbed their swords by the hilts and held them up like great crucifixes.

"One over each," panted Lopez. Manfred stooped over Von Gherens, Erik over Etten. After a moment, the smell of burning flesh seem to ebb.

Slightly. Not much. Erik glanced at Lopez. The Basque priest's face was drawn and haggard.

"It is too strong," he murmured. "Too strong—and too attached to Etten." Lopez's eyes seemed hollow under the solid eyebrows.

But whatever weakness the priest might be feeling, none of it was apparent in his next words.

"Kill Etten. Do it now, while there is still time."

Erik stared at him. The Basque shook his head. "He is dead anyway, Erik. The burning has already destroyed too much of his body. But we can still rescue his soul, if we release him from the Woden in time."

Still, Erik hesitated. He glanced at Von Gherens. The Prussian knight seemed unconscious. Erik could see enough of his face through the visor to see that there was still a face there. Whereas Etten—

He looked through the visor of the knight below him. Through that visor he could see nothing but . . . burnt flesh. Like a piece of meat charred in a fire.

Still, he hesitated. "And then what? Do the same for Von Gherens? And *then* what? Cut our own throats?"

Lopez shook his head wearily. "I cannot fight this monster in salamander form. If Pierre were still with us—or, better yet, *Dottore* Marina—"

Again, he shook his head. "I can hold it at bay, for a time, but not combat it directly. You will have to do it, Erik—you and Manfred."

Manfred had said nothing, but he had apparently been following the discussion. "Fat chance of that, Lopez! What Erik and I know about magic wouldn't fill half a manuscript page. And all of it would be gibberish."

Lopez's laugh was more of a crow's caw than anything else. "Have no fear of that! I cannot *fight* the thing, but I *can* transform it into something which you can fight. But I warn you—it will be monstrous."

Erik's hands tightened on the sword hilt. "Something flesh and blood, you mean?"

"Heh. In a manner of speaking, yes. A particularly horrid form of it, you understand."

"Flesh and blood is flesh and blood," growled Manfred. He hefted the sword higher. "And steel is steel. *Do it.*"

The last two words were spoken by a prince, and no one could mistake it. Erik hissed his own agreement, and Lopez bowed his head for a moment.

When the Basque's head came back up, however, there was not a trace of obeisance in his face. His was the face of a man born to command himself.

"Obey me, then. Erik, kill Etten. Manfred, stand back from Von Gherens."

Erik hesitated no longer. Using the hilt to drive the sword, he plunged the blade through the gaps in the armor into Etten's throat. Then, twisted it to open the wound before withdrawing the sword. Arterial blood fountained, for a moment. Not long. That wound would have killed an elephant.

He stepped back. Manfred had already done the same. Von Gherens began to writhe again as smoke, again, began to rise through his visor.

Lopez shouted something—again, in that odd language which Erik had thought was Greek but now suspected was something else entirely—and held the crucifix high. What seemed like a clap of thunder struck the world all around. Erik flinched; so did Manfred.

Von Gherens screamed and arched his back. A stream of black *something* spewed out of his gaping mouth and spilled onto the ground several yards away.

Another clap of thunder; a wave of darkness.

Then, for the first time since the battle had begun, Erik felt all traces of magic vanish. The sunlight was clean again, with no obscuring darkness. He felt enormous relief pouring through him and took a deep breath.

And . . . deeply regretted it. The stench was worse than ever.

But at least now the source of the stench was clear and obvious. On the spot where the black *something* had spilled, a monster rose on its haunches.

It was huge; half again Manfred's size. Somewhere in its misshapen and hideous form Erik could detect the remnants of something which had once been human—or close to it. Mostly in the upper face, which still had a recognizable aspect. The one eye possessed by the monster—the other was scarred over, as if the eye had been torn out sometime long ago—was quite human in appearance. Bright blue; piercingly blue. The eyebrows were as blond as Erik's own.

The rest . . .

The lower face protruded in apelike jaws; though they bore a closer resemblance to those of an eel than those of an ape when the monster bared its teeth and roared its fury. A thick tongue writhed purple behind teeth that were not even remotely mammalian. They reminded Erik of shark's teeth more than anything else.

Everything about the monster had that bizarre, horrible half-and-half quality. The hind legs were those of a land animal of some kind. A giant wolf's, perhaps—except the skin was naked, almost scaly. The arched heavy spine was also that of a mammal, with a straggly mane that resembled human hair more than animal fur. But the heavy tail was purely reptilian.

The front limbs were perhaps the worst of all. Heavy, powerful arms—almost human, except for their size—ended in a demon's taloned paws. Except no demon Erik had ever heard of possessed suckers on its palms and forearms. As if an octopus were part of its ancestry.

Again, the monster roared. There was a peculiar glee to the sound. As if the creature had been forced into silence for so long that the mere act of making noise was a joy in its own right.

"Any advice, Lopez?" asked Manfred cheerfully. The big prince was holding his sword by the hilt, now, ready to fight.

Erik glanced at the Basque priest. But Lopez, he saw immediately, would be of no more further assistance. The man was clearly exhausted. Lopez simply shook his head and whispered, "This is your affair now, Prince of the Realm. I can do no more. God and the Right."

Erik felt a moment's dismay at the last words. He knew that Manfred would—

Sure enough. "*Dia a coir!*" bellowed the prince, striding forward two steps and bringing his heavy sword down on the monster with a great two-handed swing.

Reckless idiot! Erik lunged forward.

The monster squalled—half in fury, half in glee—and evaded the blow deftly. The sword sank into the soil. An instant later, spinning, the Woden's tail lashed around and knocked Manfred's legs out from under him. The prince landed on his back, his sword flying out of his hands. Fortunately, Erik's training in wrestling enabled Manfred to break the fall by slapping down his arms.

But, for that moment, he was helpless. The Woden charged forward like a crocodile, great jaws gaping. A taloned and suckered hand raised for the death blow.

This time, it was the monster's turn to misgauge. Erik moved far faster than the Woden expected. His sword met the downstrike and removed the hand at the wrist as neatly as a carrot top removed by a knife. The hideous thing went sailing through the air and plopped into some nearby bushes.

The Woden shrieked in agony, black blood pumping from its severed wrist. The jaws lunging at Manfred's throat veered aside and snapped at Erik.

Another mistake. Again, the monster was caught by surprise. No human it had ever faced moved as quickly as the Icelander. Erik sidestepped the snapping jaws; then, as they gaped wide again, his sword slid through the teeth, mangling the great tongue.

The Woden squalled in pain and fury and twisted aside, blood gushing from its maw. The tail lashed around, striking at Erik's legs. But the blow was blocked. First, by Erik driving his sword into the soil; then, by Manfred lunging forward and grappling the monster's hindquarters. The prince gathered his legs under him, ignoring the claws scrabbling at his armor. Then, with a grunt, heaved the monster completely off the ground and slammed it into a nearby tree. The tree—a sapling, really—broke under the impact. So did the Woden's ribs.

Erik was astonished. He'd always known that Manfred was far stronger than the average man. But he realized now that he'd never really seen Manfred exert his entire strength. This was—almost superhuman. The monster must have weighed at least four hundred pounds.

Again, the Woden lashed its tail; and, again, knocked Manfred down. This time, however, the prince had been expecting the blow. So he was simply staggered to his knees rather than upended.

Desperately, Erik raced forward. As badly injured as the Woden was, the horror was still alive and still quite capable of wreaking havoc. And Manfred—his charge and responsibility—was facing another attack. Unarmed, and on his knees.

The Woden sprang at the prince, using its hind legs to drive and its remaining forelimb for balance. The jaws opened like a shark's—and if the tongue was a ruin, the teeth were not.

To Erik, everything seemed to move as slowly as ice. The jaws were approaching Manfred faster than his sword could intervene. Jaws now gaping wide enough to close on Manfred's entire head, helmet and all—and Erik didn't doubt for a moment that those jaws were quite capable of crushing the helmet like a snail.

Manfred broke its jaw. One punch, with an armored fist, skewed the Woden's bite into a harmless snap. The monster coughed blood, half-stunned. But its forward momentum knocked Manfred on his back again, this time with the Woden sprawled across him.

Erik hesitated, unsure where to strike with the sword that wouldn't risk hitting Manfred.

Then—

"*Gah! What a stink!*"

The monster's head and back suddenly lurched up. Manfred, lying beneath the creature, was holding it up with his big hands clamped firmly around its gullet. Holding it up—and steady.

"Do me the favor, would you?" hissed the prince. Erik's sword drove into the glaring blue eye and deep into the Woden's brain. The monster twitched and shuddered. And kept twitching and shuddering, after Erik jerked the sword loose from the skull.

With another great heave, Manfred tossed the thing off. Soaked with blood, he rose to his feet and stalked over to the place where his sword had been sent sailing. Then, stalked back. The Woden was lying on its side, still twitching and shuddering.

Manfred spent the next considerable period of time hacking it into small chunks. He didn't stop until each single piece of the monster was lying motionless and the blade of his sword was as dull as a table knife.

Erik tried to restrain him, early on, so that he could examine the prince for injuries. But Manfred would have none of it. "*Dia a coir!*" was repeated perhaps two dozen times, intermingled with other expressions which were vulgar and profane beyond belief.

Eventually, Erik gave up and went to help Lopez, who had begun tending to Von Gherens. The Prussian knight was alive, though still unconscious. But now that the Basque priest had removed the man's helmet, Erik was relieved to see that the burn marks on Von Gherens's face were not as bad as he had feared.

"He'll be all right, with a little rest," murmured Lopez. "The facial scars will be bad, but—at least he's a Prussian. They treasure the things, so there should be no really adverse consequences."

He glanced at Manfred, still furiously dismembering the already-dismembered carcass of the Woden, and smiled slyly. "Unlike your friend, who—I daresay—is adding years in purgatory with every oath that comes out of his mouth."

Erik wasn't quite sure how to respond. Lopez shook his head. "Not your problem, my fine young Icelandic friend. You are *not* responsible for protecting the Hohenstauffens from God, after all."

Erik couldn't help grinning. "True enough." Seeing that Lopez needed no further help with Von Gherens for the moment, Erik went over to retrieve his hatchet from the corpse of Sister Ursula.

But . . . there was no corpse; just a burned piece of grass.

And there was no hatchet, either. Only the wirebound shaft remained.

After a time, Erik fell silent. Lopez clucked his tongue. "And I daresay you've just added as many years. Where *did* you learn to curse like that, anyway?"

Stolidly, Erik stared at the priest. Then, pointed at Manfred, who had finally left off with his hacking.

"Oh, sure," grumbled the prince. "Blame everything on me!"

Chapter 89

Erik and Manfred stood in one of the bastions of the northern-most of the Polestine forts, watching the Venetian cannons fin-ish pounding the last of the Milanese galleasses into rubble. It seemed a somewhat pointless exercise, since the galleass had ceased being a water-capable means of transport quite some time ago. But a quick glance through the gunports in either of the bastion's retired flanks was enough to see the reason. The ditch in front of the curtain wall was a charnel house, with nothing more to fire at beyond a relative handful of wounded and maimed soldiers in Visconti colors.

Nothing alive, at least. The ditch was mounded with shattered bodies, all that was left of the Milanese mercenaries who had stormed the fortress thinking a quick rush would be enough to overwhelm the few surviving defenders. The rising sun cast a pale reddish glow over a landscape which seemed red-soaked already.

The mercenaries trapped at the curtain wall had tried to surren-der, soon enough. But the Venetians were in no mood for terms. On this day, at least, the normal conditions of Italian condottieri warfare had been suspended. Milan had tried to destroy Venice; the city of the winged lion was returning the compliment. The gunners in the bastions had kept firing on the men piled up along the curtain wall until they had been turned into so much ground meat. Then, still raging, turned their fire onto the grounded and crippled galleasses. There too, clearly enough, they would not be satisfied until the ships had been turned into so much kindling.

Manfred squinted into the distance, where the retreating Milanese army could be seen frantically trying to build fieldworks. Their galleasses destroyed and the assault on the forts having been driven off with heavy losses, Sforza had led the Visconti forces into a retreat along the river. Had tried to, rather. Now, finding that Enrico Dell'este had cut off his retreat with a far larger army than anyone believed Ferrara could possibly put into the field, Sforza was doing what he could to prepare a hasty defense.

"No 'Old Fox' out there today," mused Manfred. "He's looking for Sforza's blood, or I miss my guess."

Erik did not argue the matter. That was his assessment also. He thought the Duke of Ferrara was behaving foolishly, but given what he knew of the personal history between Dell'este and Sforza he was hardly surprised. The Old Fox had waited for years to obtain revenge on Milan, and now that the day had come he clearly intended to show Carlo Sforza who was *really* "the Wolf of the North."

They heard footsteps behind them, clambering up the stone stairs to the bastion with an oddly arrhythmic pace. Before they even turned their heads, they knew it was Lopez. The Basque priest had been tending to his two companions in the fort's infirmary below. Diego and Pierre had both survived the encounter with Ursula and the Woden monster, but they had been badly shaken.

Lopez limped over to stand next to them. He spent no more than a moment or two studying the distant scene, with eyes which had clearly seen more than one battlefield in times past.

"Stupid," he pronounced. "We have no idea what is transpiring in Venice itself. While Ferrara obtains his revenge here, the city may still be lost."

That neatly summed up Erik's assessment. Manfred's also, judging from his nod.

"Come," commanded Lopez. "If we can reach Dell'este in time, we may still be able to convince him to forego his pleasure." He turned and began limping off.

"What can we—" began Manfred, but Lopez's impatient wave of the hand stifled the rest.

"You are the Emperor's nephew, young dolt! And I have a certain talisman which may help. Now come!"

"I'm not entirely sure I care for that man," said Manfred sourly, as he and Erik followed the Basque toward the fort's stables.

Erik smiled. "And I, on the other hand, am *entirely* sure that Father Eneko Lopez doesn't care in the least what you think of him."

"He should," grumbled Manfred. "I'm the Emperor's nephew, dammit!"

By the time they reached the Ferrarese lines and were able to negotiate their way through to the duke's presence, the battle was well underway.

Not that it was much of a "battle" yet. Clearly enough, from what they had seen as they approached, the Old Fox hadn't lost any of his tactical acumen. Since he had Sforza trapped, he intended to bleed him with gunfire as long as possible before ordering any direct assaults. Dell'este's own soldiers were mercenaries, for the most part. Professional soldiers—highly experienced Italian ones, especially— had little use for commanders who wasted their lives in premature assaults.

The duke's field headquarters consisted of nothing more elaborate than a simple open-air pavilion erected on a small hill overlooking the battleground. They found Dell'este standing just under the overhang, studying Sforza's lines with a telescope. Like all the optical devices of the day, the telescope was a heavy boxlike affair mounted on a stand. The old duke was slightly stooped, peering through the eyepiece.

Hearing their footsteps, he stood erect and turned to face them. He gave each of them a quick study in turn. Perhaps oddly, he spent most of his time studying Erik and Manfred, the two men he had never met before.

"Knights of the Holy Trinity?" he asked, his lips quirked into a wry smile. "Not wearing full armor? I think you might be excommunicated, if you're not careful."

Manfred frowned; Erik chuckled. "I'm from Iceland, Your Grace. Spent time in Vinland also. Full armor, in today's world, is just stupid."

The duke's eyes fixed on Manfred. "And you, large one? Do you agree?"

Manfred was clearly struggling not to glare outright. So all he managed in reply was a muffled grunt which could be taken as a form of agreement.

"I declare you honorary Italians," pronounced the Old Fox.

Then he faced Lopez, his smile disappearing. "There's no point in discussing the matter, Father. I know perfectly well why you came. Venice is Venice, Ferrara is Ferrara. I've done enough for Venice this morning. The rest of the day—and tomorrow, and the day after, if that's what it takes—belongs to me and mine."

He turned his head, his fierce old eyes glaring at the distant Milanese lines. "I will have Sforza's head. And spend the rest of my days planning to reap Visconti's."

"Me and mine?" demanded Lopez. The priest reached into his cassock and drew forth a small object. When he presented it to the duke, Erik could see that it was a miniature portrait. He had wondered what the object had been that he'd seen Lopez tucking into his saddlebag when they left the fort.

"Do you remember what you said to me when you gave me this, so-called 'Old Fox'? 'Old Boar,' more like. Dumb as a nearsighted pig."

Erik was surprised to see that Dell'este did not bridle under the sarcasm. Indeed, for a moment his lips even twitched, as if he were trying to control a smile.

"Lamb of Christ, is it?" murmured the duke. "'Lynx of Christ,' more like. Feral as a starving cat."

Lopez ignored the riposte. He simply held the portrait up in front of Dell'este's face.

After a moment, the old man looked away. "Most of all, you must remember the mother."

Eneko lowered the portrait. "Exactly so." He pointed toward the Milanese. "It was not *Sforza* who murdered your daughter. Other crimes can be laid at his feet, I've no doubt. But not that one."

"Had he not abandoned her," hissed the duke, "Visconti would never have dared to strike at her."

"The same could be said of *you*," retorted Lopez instantly.

Dell'este's face turned white as a sheet. His hand—old and veined, but still muscular—clenched the hilt of the sword buckled to his waist. The eyes he turned on Lopez were hot with fury.

Erik held his breath. Next to him, he could feel Manfred tensing.

Eneko—

Never flinched. The little Basque priest returned the Duke of Ferrara's glare with one of his own. Which, in its own way, seemed just as hot.

Indeed, he rubbed salt into the wounds.

"The father condemns the lover?" he demanded. "For the same deed which he committed himself?"

Lopez pointed a stiff finger at the unseen figure of Carlo Sforza. "What that man *did* was give you a grandson. A grandson who is—today; now; this minute—fighting for his life in the streets of Venice."

The Basque dropped his arm contemptuously. "Like father, like grandfather. No doubt you will abandon the grandson as you did the mother. Nothing may be allowed to interfere with a petty lord's overweening pride. A sin which he will try to mask by giving it the name of 'honor.'"

Erik's eyes were on the duke's hand, clutching the sword hilt. The knuckles were ivory white, and the sword was now drawn an inch out of the scabbard. So he couldn't see the expression on Dell'este's face or that of Lopez. But he couldn't mistake the sneer in the Basque's voice.

"'*Old Fox.*' Was ever a man more badly misnamed? To give up his chance for vengeance on Visconti—who *did* murder his daughter—in order to salvage his pitiful dignity on the body of a lover?"

Erik glanced up quickly, seeing the twitch in the hand holding the sword. The fury in Dell'este's eyes seemed . . . adulterated, now. Filling with cunning—surmise, at least—instead of sheer rage.

The duke's teeth were clenched. His next words were more hissed than spoken.

"Explain."

Lopez, once again, demonstrated what Erik was beginning to believe was an almost infinite capacity for surprise. The priest's face suddenly burst into an exuberant grin.

"Finally! The Italian asks the Basque's advice on a matter of vendetta! About time."

He rubbed his hands, almost gleefully. Then, crossed himself. "I cannot speak to the point concretely, you understand. I'm sworn to the work of Christ. But, at a glance, it seems to me that the son is better suited to settle accounts with the father than you are. At the appropriate time. And—given some sage advice and counsel from his grandfather, in the months and years to come—is certainly the best choice to settle accounts with the mother's murderer."

Again, he crossed himself. "God willing, of course. But, on this matter, I suspect the Lord will smile kindly." Again, he crossed himself. "Provided, of course, that the son is alive tomorrow. And provided"—again, he crossed himself—"that he manages to avoid falling into the pit of sinfulness the day after."

More sedately: "Um. To be precise, manages to clamber out of the pit. Being, as I suspect he is, already halfway into it."

The sound of the sword hilt slapping back into the scabbard jolted Erik a bit. The duke's harsh chuckle even more so.

"I'd ask you to become his counselor," said Dell'este, "but I suspect that would fall into the category of putting the fox in charge of the henhouse."

Lopez managed to look aggrieved. Not much.

"How soon do you need me in Venice?" asked the duke.

The priest shrugged. "The sooner the better. But—" He glanced out at the Ferrarese forces constructing their own fieldworks. The quick assessment was that of a man who had once been a veteran soldier himself. "Under the best of circumstances, you cannot manage the task sooner than the day after tomorrow. That should be good enough. Even if the enemy wins the battle in Venice today, they will not be able to fortify their position in less than a week. Not in Venice, not without Sforza."

The duke nodded. "Very well. I'll start today. But I intend to bleed Sforza—and Visconti—of everything I can before leaving."

"Goes without saying," agreed Lopez, nodding sagely. "Drain every lira from his pay chest. Leave his mercenaries moaning their lost money but savoring their salvaged lives. They won't be able to do anything about it anyway, since you will naturally demand their guns and their pikes." He pursed his lips, considering the problem. "Probably best to leave the officers their swords. Except Sforza's, of course. You'll want to break that over your knee in front of him."

The Duke of Ferrara was smiling thinly, now. "Fierce, you are! Father Lopez, the days when I could break a sword over my knee— a good Ferrara blade, anyway, and be sure that's what Sforza possesses—are long gone."

"Allow me the privilege, then," said Manfred forcefully. He extended his huge hands. "I won't even need a knee."

"Oh!" exclaimed Lopez. "How rude of me. I forgot to make the introductions. Enrico Dell'este, Duke of Ferrara, meet Manfred of Brittany. He's the Emperor's nephew, by the way, and has some incredible list of titles. I can't remember them all. Earl of something, Marquis of whatever. Baron of this and that."

Dell'este's eyes may have widened a bit, but not much. Mostly, he seemed interested in Manfred's hands. "You'll need a pair of iron gauntlets," he mused.

"Damn things have to be good for *something*," growled Erik.

Manfred snapped Sforza's sword like a twig. The commander of the Milanese forces, Italy's most famous condottiere, did not so much as flinch at the sound. Whatever else he was, Carlo Sforza was no coward.

"You look just like your son," commented Manfred mildly, as he handed Sforza the point end of the broken blade. "Except Benito's not reached his full growth yet, and he isn't as mean-looking."

Sforza's round, hard, muscular face registered surprise. As much at the return of the blade, perhaps, as the mention of his son. "You've met him?"

"Yup." Manfred held his right hand above the ground, about an inch lower than the top of Sforza's curly hair. "So tall; don't think he'll get any taller." He gave Sforza's stocky form a quick once-over. "But I think he's going to wind up even thicker than you. The kid's already got the forearms of a small bear."

For a moment, a shadow seemed to cross the condottiere's face. That was the first expression other than stoic resignation Erik had seen Sforza exhibit since the surrender ceremony began in mid-afternoon. And it was now well into sunset.

"I haven't seen him in years." The great captain's words were almost whispered.

"You will," predicted Manfred. He held up the hilt end of the broken sword in his left hand. There was more than a foot of the blade left. "I'll be giving this to him, when I see him next." He nodded toward the Duke of Ferrara, standing stiffly some distance away. "As his grandfather commanded. Some day—don't ever doubt it, Sforza—he'll be coming to get the rest of it."

"And when that day comes," said Erik between tight jaws, "I strongly urge you to have found another employer. Or your guts will be the carpet he uses to get to Visconti's throat."

Sforza's dark eyes swiveled toward him. Erik's grin was quite savage. "Believe me, Carlo Sforza. I'm an Icelander, and I know a feud when I see one. I've met Benito also."

"I'll consider your words." The dark eyes got even harder. "I *told* Filippo Visconti this was a fool's errand. Damn all dukes and their complicated schemes. But . . . he pays well. Very well."

Manfred snorted. "Idiot. Benito'll spill your purse before he spills the rest of you."

"That's my boy," murmured the Wolf of the North. "Others doubted. But I never did."

Chapter 90

The grayness swirled thick, carrying the sounds of combat and dying. Despite everything they'd done, some of Aleri's agents had survived. Fire bloodied the fog to the south, and the smell of it was thick in the air.

Marco turned to Kat, a heaviness in his chest, and the edge of despair in his voice. "We're losing. In spite of everything, we're losing. Count Badoero must have brought at least a thousand men. Caesare has made sure the damned militia are ineffectual. The Arsenalotti and the boat-people fight well. But this fog—it confuses everything. There's something wrong with this fog. It's like it's fighting for *them*."

"It feels heavy. Not natural," said Kat. She'd acquired a cut on one cheek and two ash smudges on the other. With or without them, Marco still thought she was the most beautiful, wonderful person he'd ever met. She lightened the fog around her, and in the face of her hope and determination, he lost some of his despair. If Kat believed in him, in their cause, maybe—

She patted his arm. "You're a good general, Marco. People rally to you."

He pulled a face; he didn't *want* to be a general, and it wasn't what he was good at. If only there was something he could do to make a bigger difference than merely whacking at people he'd rather be meeting over a glass of wine at a *taverna*! "Benito is twice the organizer. And I hate this killing."

Someone came running out of the fog. It was Rafael, gasping for breath. "Luciano says . . . needs you . . . the Marciana . . ."

They headed across at a run. They weren't that far from San Marco anyway.

Rafael led them upstairs to a room, and they burst through the door. Sigils and arcane symbols were chalked on the floor and all three of them came to an abrupt halt before they so much as touched a toe to one of those sigils. A complex triple circle with squares at the cardinal points and an internal octagon occupied the center of the room—*that* wasn't chalked, it was inlaid onto the floor of the room.

This is a—a working chamber, Marco realized. *A place for magic, and nothing else.* Christian magic? Jewish? Strega? All three, perhaps? There was some overlap—more than just s*ome* if Brother Mascoli was to be believed. Emeralds twinkled from the cardinal square nearest them—sapphires from the one across the room—topaz to the left and rubies to the right. The lines of the diagrams were laid out in—*gold and silver*? Well, for some Strega magic, the magic with the purest intentions that called only great spirits, silver and gold were a good thing, not something to be avoided. *Silver for Diana, and gold for Dianus. Or silver for the Moon and gold for the Stars. Or silver for Earth and gold for Heaven.* The jewels glittered, and the whole of the diagrams seemed to scintillate. The boundaries weren't fully up yet, but the energies that would create the walls between the realms weren't white, they were opalescent, rainbowed. The air was thick with incense.

Luciano, clad in a long white robe, loomed out of the scented smoke. He looked old and tired—older than Marco had ever seen him before. And frail. His skin seemed translucent, as if the motral part of him was wearing thin and his soul shining through it. "Are we winning?"

Marco sighed, and shook his head, despair once again pressing down on him. "No. We have more men, but Badoero and Caesare are just too damned good. And they have the certainty of more men coming. Kat's grandfather got the message off to Trieste—if that works, at least we won't have to deal with the rest of the Knots. Manfred and Erik and Lopez rode off to try to save the Polestine forts from that nun. We won't know for some time whether Sforza is on his way here with the Milanese. In the meantime, we're fighting fires—and each other, often enough— in this damned fog."

Luciano's lips thinned with anger. "It is indeed a 'damned fog.'

It is caused by Chernobog, working through someone here in Venice. Lucrezia Brunelli, I would think, is the only one powerful enough to do it alone. But she's supposed to have left the city, so perhaps it is several mages working together. The only good thing about it is that it's taking nearly all of their energy. Weather magic is hard, expensive magic."

"They've obviously got gold to burn," said Marco bitterly.

"The expense I refer to is of magical energy," said Luciano tiredly. "And what I have been doing is also—expensive. I had hoped to avoid this, but it seems we have little choice . . . I will perform a summoning. If it works, it will save us. Save *Venice*. But it calls, of all things, for one of the *Case Vecchie* blood. One of the *longi*. And only four families are listed. Two are no more. The other two are Valdosta and Montescue."

"What do I have to do?" asked Marco, a bit doubtfully. A summoning? Just what was Luciano going to summon? *Not necromancy, dear Jesu!*

"Be within the circle of invocation. Give some of your blood." It seemed simple enough. Some of his blood—that couldn't hurt. Not here. It was a token sacrifice, not an actual one; something, perhaps, to remind a greater spirit of a promise from long ago. *Blood to blood.*

"I'll do it," said Kat decisively. "It says Montescue, doesn't it?"

Luciano shook his head. "The script is faint, but it clearly says 'a son.' This—this is a Christianized attempt at a far more ancient ceremony, but it is all that I have. Hence—" he waved an ancient bronze knife vaguely at the rest of the room "—all this. According to this it should be the Metropolitan who is doing this, but—"

He didn't finish the sentence.

"What will this do?" Marco asked, feeling oddly detached and strangely calm.

Luciano shrugged. "The spell has only been used twice before. Yet this is a very ancient copy of an even more ancient spell. It is called the Lion's Crown and it invokes the spirit of the lion of the marshes. One of the oldest of the great neutral spirits. The Guardian of the lagoon, the marshes, the islands. And, yes— the Lion is still here, and strong. It influences much, still. But mostly it slumbers, waiting for Venice's hour of need. It is what Chernobog has feared most all along, and why he maneuvered so stealthily. If the Lion awakes—awakes fully, as only you can do—not even Chernobog can stand against it. Not here, not in Venice."

The memory of a brushing of wings passed through Marco's mind, but was gone before he could snatch at it.

Luciano looked directly into Marco's eyes, as if weighing the heart behind them. "I think this is that hour of need. And not only do you bear the blood, you carry the mark of that Lion. Scrying glasses turn to you. I've long known you would wear the Mantle after I'm gone, but you can also wear the Crown—and do it *now*. Are you willing?"

The mark of the Lion? Mantle? Crown? But this was no time for questions, not now. Questions could wait until after, when this was over. If they all survived. This might be the only way for them all *to* survive. Certainly the enemies of Venice, whether they were evil spirits or came with fire and the sword, would not leave any of them standing. Marco nodded. "It's my city. And they are my people."

"I am your person too," said Kat quietly. "And I'm scared for you, Marco. I don't understand any of this—and—and—it sounds like a sacrifice!"

He leaned forward and—for the first time—kissed her cheek, gently. "It'll be all right. And . . . if we don't do something it won't matter. The city is burning. Caesare and Count Badoero's men are winning."

Somehow, she composed her face, stilled her trembling, drew herself up, and stood like the daughter of Montescue that she was. "I love you, Marco Valdosta."

His heart swelled with pride for her. "And I love you too, Katerina Montescue."

Luciano stamped his foot impatiently. "Come on! There are auspicious times for doing these things. And one of them is dawn. It's hard to tell in this fog, but that must be soon. Step inside the circle and let me close it behind you. This is a great spell and it will tax me to my utmost."

Kat was left standing, head bowed, disconsolate, his kiss still warm on her cheek, to watch as the ward-fires flared. A tear trickled down her nose. This was dangerous, horribly dangerous. She felt it in her bones, no matter that Marco didn't seem to think anything of it. A Strega mage practicing a Christian version of a pagan spell? It was crazy—how much could go wrong, or *had* gone wrong in the transliteration? Luciano was taking on more than he should ever have dared and he had dragged Marco in after him. Or was she just getting overprotective about Marco? She fumbled out her talisman and took comfort from the fact that at least the medal was cool.

The door opened, and Kat whirled, one hand on her Saint Hypatia medal, the other on her dagger. The medal flared with heat.

Lucrezia Brunelli stood there, smiling in triumph. "Crying for your lover, little Montescue?" she asked smirking cruelly. "It's a waste of time and tears."

Kat gasped. "You're supposed to have left!" Then, as the words themselves penetrated: "And damn you! I'm crying for a good man."

Lucrezia laughed, throwing her handsome head back. "There's no such thing, girl. Believe me—I've tried them all, from Capuletti to my brother Ricardo."

Kat gaped, for a long moment, as Lucrezia waited for the sense of that to penetrate, unable to believe what she had actually heard. "Your *b—your brother!?*"

Lucrezia smiled lazily, but the smile had a nasty edge. "Cleopatra slept with hers. He did crawl into my bed when he thought I was too young to understand, but in the end, he was just a man. And I did have my revenge, after all. I've had him killed for it."

The words, so cool, so unemotional, chilled Kat to the bone.

"And now," Lucrezia continued, "I need to kill these two while I still have the strength. Weather magic is wearisome."

"B–b–but—" Kat was trying to ask why, but the words wouldn't come. By now the Hypatia medal was almost burning her hand. But was that caused by what Luciano was doing, or was it Lucrezia's presence? Or both?

Lucrezia obviously understood what she meant to ask. "Oh, for many reasons—but among others, it's enough that they are two of the three who ever turned me down. Strange. Those potions you brought me from Ascalon were very effective, you know, and to have them fail so significantly on two occasions, your sweet little boy and that upright priest . . ."

Priest? "*Dottore* Marina isn't—"

"I wasn't talking about him. Unfortunately, Luciano disappeared before I had access to those philters. If I'd had them—" she licked her lips, as if she tasted something bitter "—perhaps we wouldn't be having this discussion now."

Rafael, who had been standing ignored on the other side of the room, chose this moment to try to deal with her in a rush. He stopped as if he had hit a wall, paralyzed. Kat's medal enveloped her in warmth.

At Lucrezia's gesture, Rafael dropped the knife and folded, to sprawl before her feet.

Lucrezia shook her head. "I am far too powerful for little Strega with their little knives. Lie there, little Strega, and watch as your friends die—for I believe that I will allow you to die last of all."

She turned back to Kat. "I learned a great deal from the Grand Duke of Lithuania's emissary, you know—in no small part, what *not* to do. She allowed Chernobog to possess her, in exchange for her beauty and power. I have not made that error."

"You—" Kat tried to speak.

Lucrezia smiled viciously. "And oh, my dear little *virgin* Montescue! Luciano made a most incalculable mistake in allowing *you* here, for you will make the perfect sacrifice to break the circle of power."

Inside the circle, Marco was unaware of all of this. Luciano's words were like the droning of bees as he walked the sevenfold circle. *Why seven? Why not three or five or nine?* He tried to remember what Brother Mascoli had been teaching him. Seven wasn't a Strega number, though it was pagan. It went back a lot farther than that, to the Romans, or the Etruscans. It felt right, though; each time Luciano completed a circuit, the rest of the room receded a little, the sound from outside faded, and the less important what was outside seemed. He noticed vaguely that someone had come into the room, but—

Well, it just didn't matter.

Marco found himself transported with the words of power; they carried him somewhere else, or perhaps it was that the interior of the circle *became* somewhere else. The air was not full of incense. Instead it was a smell he knew far better that: the smell of driftwood fires. Of the marsh-reed pollen. Of the delicate scent of water lilies, of marsh-mallow, of sweet-flag blossom. The air glowed with the thick, amber light of the sun cutting through the mist.

Luciano beat on a drum; or was it a drum? It was more like his own heartbeat, but slow, slow, and full of heat. The air thickened until it was as sweet and heavy as honey, and Luciano's voice wasn't chanting words anymore, it was the bees that were droning the chant.

Then came a rumble that built up slowly, and from a distance in the thick air. Thunder?

No—not thunder. A *roar*. Marco heard a roaring echoing across the marsh, the last great refuge of lions in Europe. But no lion had ever roared like this, no lion *he* had ever heard of! This roar was thunder in the sky, from a throat like the mouth of a volcano!

He glanced at Luciano for reassurance.

But—Luciano didn't look right. He was pale and sweating, the hand that held the little drum shaking, and his breathing coming hard.

"Chiano?" he asked—but Luciano didn't respond. The steady drumbeat faltered.

The beater fell from Luciano's hand; a hand that clutched at the front of his own white robe, looking remarkably like a claw.

"Chiano!" Marco shouted, panic in his voice.

Slowly, Luciano's knees gave out and he sank to the ground. Slowly, the drum, too, fell from his hand, rolled across the floor, and overset a bowl of some dark liquid that had been laid aside when Luciano had completed the circles. And Luciano Marina toppled over onto his side and did not stir.

And then Luciano was silent. The mists and brightness around him cleared and Marco understood why.

Luciano Marina would not be summoning anything again. Whatever this was . . . it had been too much for him. His eyes were glazed, staring—and empty.

The yellowed old book was still on the pedestal where Luciano had been standing. A long-bladed bronze knife was lying atop the open pages.

Marco took up the book. It was only a book—but what was in it had killed Luciano.

The circles of power still held, but the magic within them faded with every passing moment.

I have to do something—

But what? He was no magician. Besides, looking at what was

said at the top of the page, this called for a willingness to make the greatest of sacrifices. What had Luciano said? "Only been done twice before. And two of the families listed are no more."

Perhaps . . . perhaps it had been no token sacrifice. Valdosta . . . and Montescue were left. *I am Valdosta. . . .*

A faint sound penetrated the thinning circles of power, and Marco looked up. As if through a mist, or through frost-covered glass, he saw Lucrezia. Saw Rafael fall. He tried to push through the barrier that Luciano had raised. It was like steel. He beat at it. He might as well have pounded on a rock with his fists.

They were watching him now—Kat, with one hand at her throat and the other clutching her medallion; and Lucrezia. Lucrezia had a cruel smile on her face and a long steel and silver dagger in her hand. The handle like a dragon, or a winged serpent, with eyechips of ruby. Marco's arms fell to his sides; he felt frozen with fear and indecision. They all seemed frozen in time, insects caught in amber.

Something cold touched his foot, and he jerked out of his paralysis. He looked down. The puddle of spilled liquid oozed across the patterned marble and touched his foot, mingled with a thin trickle of blood coming from Luciano's outstretched wrist. And a mist passed over it for a moment, and Marco saw, as if from above, Venice burning. Children screaming, dying. And the body of Kat sprawled, abused. And then a sequence of people he knew, and loved. Gutted. Raped. Burned. And the face of Lucrezia . . .

Laughing, with a great darkness behind her. He knew it for a true scrying vision of the future. A future which Luciano—his friend and in many ways, more truly a father to him than his own blood had been—had been prepared to sacrifice himself to prevent. Perhaps, when he failed, Luciano had dared use his last lifeblood, the *last* of his own magical power, not to save himself, but for this vision. So that Marco would know the consequences of failure, and act.

Marco took up the bronze knife, put it against his chest and began to read the words from the ancient book. From outside the enchanted circle Lucrezia gaped. If he read her lips aright before the brightness and mist engulfed him, she was saying "No!"

"No! Caesare!" Benito looked down from the barricade he'd just climbed.

Caesare Aldanto looked up from Maria. He had an arm around

her neck, and a knife against her breast. "I nearly killed her when she came through the gap," he said, conversationally. "Quite a reunion, this. Where's that brother of yours? Also around?"

"Why?" demanded Benito. "Do you want to make a clean sweep of the Valdostas?"

Benito tried to figure out what do next. He had an arquebus in his hands. But the weapon was far too inaccurate—even in the hands of someone expert in its use—to risk a shot at Caesare. As inexperienced as Benito was with firearms, he'd more likely kill Maria. But Benito made himself a promise that if anything happened to Maria . . . he'd blow Caesare's mocking, smiling face apart. At this range, not even Benito would miss.

"Now, why would I do that, Benito?" said Caesare. "I've always looked after you."

Benito scrambled down. Other Arsenalotti faces appeared. But there were several of Caesare's men too, all with arquebuses.

"You got money from Ferrara, for looking after us," said Benito coldly. "It's sitting at Giaccomo's. You never really did anything for any reason except for money, did you?"

Caesare snorted. "What other reason is there?"

Benito smiled. "Tell you what, Caesare. I'll show you another reason. You let her go and I'll fight you."

It took Caesare a moment for the implication to sink in. "Maria?" he said, incredulously. "You love this—peasant?"

"I dunno about 'love,'" said Benito carefully. "But I care a whole damn lot about her. Use the word 'love' if you want. So I'll fight you for her freedom."

Aldanto laughed. "Cocky little brat, aren't you? At your age you think you're immortal and you expect to win."

"No," said Benito calmly. "I don't. But you'll have to let Maria go."

"*NO!*" yelled Lucrezia, gazing in horror at Marco and the knife. She looked around wildly.

"I must stop him. Kill him! Come here, girl! I need you."

For an instant, Kat felt the sheer power and compulsion of that voice. Then, a further warmth, a heat, a *fire* spread from the Saint Hypatia medal that she held, and with a shake like a spaniel pulled from the dirty water of a canal, she shook off the compulsion.

Instead of answering Lucrezia's beckoning hand, she pulled her pistol from her reticule. She'd reloaded five times in the fighting. The last time she'd had to take powder from a dead arquebusier. But the balls he'd carried had been too big. So she'd filled the barrel of the pistol with some metal junk from a ruined shop. Thrust it down and hoped it would work.

Lucrezia laughed. "Your little toy won't do me any harm, you stupid child! Do you think I haven't taken the simplest of precautions? I command the spirits of air and water and darkness! The powder won't fire, the balls will miss!" As Kat hesitated—*can that be true? Can she really do that?*

Lucrezia sneered at her. "Besides. You don't know how to use that silly thing, anyway."

Doubt assailed her and once again, Lucrezia was using all her powers. Kat wanted to drop the weapon. Run closer.

Warmth rushed over her again, and—

—a glowing, delicate hand, insubstantial as a kiss and warm as life, closed over the hand that held the pistol.

She squeezed the trigger instead.

The metal junk cut into Lucrezia, who had half-turned, ready to throw her knife. It knocked Lucrezia to the floor.

Lucrezia screamed; and of all the screaming Kat had heard that day, this was, by far, the most horrible sound she had ever heard in her life. It went on, and on, and on, as Lucrezia writhed on the floor, thrashing spinelessly, her thrashing as horrible as the scream.

And then, the woman's body began to change. Metamorphose.

The point of the knife broke the skin, and a single drop of blood formed on the blade. Strangely, there was no pain.

Before he could press harder and end the ritual with his own death, something—took him.

The light, the mists, thickened again in an instant, golden, sweet, the honey of the Jesolo, and held him so that he could not move.

Light blinded him, and light *permeated* him. It became him, and he felt himself change . . . felt a roaring in his ears that came from his own throat, felt great golden wings spring from his back and begin to grow and grow.

"It's been a long time," said the great voice that was within him, but was not him. Huge muscles flexed and stretched. His golden hide twitched. He was no longer indoors. Instead, from the column-top, he looked out over fog-shrouded Piazza San Marco.

"So. A Valdosta again, is it?" said the great voice. "Last time it was a Montescue. They're more bloody minded." Marco felt his wings extend, though *he* was not the one to flex his muscles, stretch his claws, spread his wings.

"Who . . . who are you?" he asked timidly.

There was a roar of laughter, warm and full. "I am you. And you are me. You have taken up the Crown as well as the Mantle— the first to do so in many centuries. And *we* are the Lion . . . the Lion of Venice, now. The Lion of Etruria that was."

The back and shoulder muscles tensed, enormous wings beat down in a great surge of power, and the lion bounded up through the cloud and out into endless blue of the sky.

"The Lion of Saint Mark?" Marco looked down as the Lion looked down. Fog was streaming away from the downbeat of the great wings. Below he could already see the piazza, clear of all but the last wisps of it.

Again the Lion laugh-roared. "Saint Mark! I nearly ate him. He wasn't even the Mark of your Four Books, you know. You little children, you've confused him with one of my Romans! A secret Christian, that Roman, a Christian who hid his fellows in the Jesolo—*Marcus Fidelus*—that was what they called him, Mark the Faithful, and you people managed to get him confused with the other! '*Hic requiscet corpus tuum*— On this spot your body shall rest.' It was meant as a threat, not a prophecy."

The Lion roared with laughter, and Marco had to admit it *was* rather funny.

"But that Marcus was pious enough, and holy enough, and had the magic—the magic—even if up until that moment he didn't know it. *I* knew it. And you four little swamp thieves—Terrio, Montescue, Lacosto, and Valdosta—you that had set out to rob him and instead became his converts, begged for his life. You were *my* people, and he won you! Won you fairly! But you were *my* people, and when you begged—what was I to do? I let him live, and gave him leave of my domain. Ha. Not only did he make free of my marshes, he also took *seizin* of me, to come and go and look and know. He became one of *mine,* save only that he was first and always the child of Christ. And in exchange that we be of one heart, and would I still hold sovereignty here and not be driven from the place by later mages of Christ, that my people be free to make their own choices in who they serve—he laid this form on me, this binding with the blood of the four families. I think it a good bargain. I steer my families and look after my lagoon, my marshes, and my islands. And sometimes, when the need is dire, they take the Crown and they steer me." The great, laughing roar shook the body again. "So. Steer me, Valdosta. What do we need to do?"

Some grasp of the great strength that was his to command dawned on Marco. "First, let's get rid of all of this fog. It's not *right.*"

The Lion spiraled upward into the dawn sky, above the cloud. "Yes. It is a magical one, a sending from a great and evil power. But this is *my* place. *My* lagoon, *my* marshes, and *my* islands. My power is stronger here."

The great wings beat down. The wind beneath those wings was more than just air. It was bright with strength and the wild primal magic that was the Lion. Marco felt not only the beating of the wings but the rushing of blood to those great wing-muscles. He knew that the very arteries and veins of the Lion were somehow channels that nourished the reedbeds, the canals that carried the trade. And they all moved to the heartbeat of the sea. The Lion was Marco. It was also the soul of the lagoon. It was rich with the love of the generations of Venetians. Of many, many people, not just some few wealthy lordlings, but all of its people.

And, like them, the Lion treasured its liberty and independence.

The fog . . . the fog was no mere cloud. It was a thing of strangling darkness. Of hatred and domination, issuing from the bleak northeast. But although it might overwhelm cities and kings, it was feeble against that independence of spirit, of the love Venetians had given this place, this special place over the centuries. The Lion was a repository of all of that. Chernobog was great. But it was also a great distance away—and was now trying to extend its power to a foreign land. Foreign to Chernobog, not to the Lion. The Lion who was also Marco drew its strength from the land, the water and from many many small sources. Generations of them—brought together in the unity which was the Lion. Individually they were mere drops of water against stone that was Chernobog. Together, they were like the raging torrent . . . and Chernobog a mere loose cobblestone, flung willy-nilly before the fury.

Magical power surged like the sea with each great wingbeat, and below them the fog scattered and tattered. The last spell-shreds of Chernobog's power here tore. Venice and the lagoon appeared, the sun striking the red roofs and dancing brightly off the clear water.

"And now?" asked the Lion.

"Let us break up the fighting. Put fear into the hearts of those who want to destroy Venice." Somehow Marco knew that was the right thing to say.

The Lion rose higher, toward the rising sun. "Let them see my shadow. In the minds of our enemies, the shadow of the Lion is more terrifying than the Lion itself. It releases their fears. To those who love Venice, my shadow is a shield."

In a slow spiral the Lion turned above the canals of Venice. Marco's keen Lion-eyes picked out the knots of fighting men, picked out his brother on the barricade. Picked out Maria. Picked out Caesare Aldanto, and saw into the core of him, saw him for what he was. He roared. The air blurred and shivered with the sound.

The roaring was like that of a thousand trumpets. But it was a glad, bright noise. To Maria it was like an infusion of strength. That little fool Benito was going to get killed!

It must have had the opposite effect on Caesare, because suddenly she was able to pull free. She spun around and, with all her strength, kicked him in the testicles.

Caesare folded up nicely. Maria scrambled up the barricade. She heard the roar of an arquebus, but if it was fired at her the bullet went wild. And then the fresh sea-scented wind hit her in the face.

"What the hell—" Benito pulled her flat; arquebus fire boomed. Fog streamed in the sudden gale, a gale so strong that it flung masonry fragments from the barricade. The dawn sun came striking at the walls. . . . Bright and warm.

And then there came a huge winged shadow—

Maria suddenly realized that Caesare's Schiopettieri were running away, as if in a panic. And so was Caesare. Running as if the very devil was on his heels.

And somewhere between Venice and the rising sun a huge winged being flew, caressing the city, its lagoon and marshes with the shadow of its great wings.

❀   ❀   ❀

Kat stared at the devilish thing that had been Lucrezia. It was red-eyed, silver bodied, snaky like Lucrezia's dagger handle had been—and it was wounded in a dozen places. Maybe she hadn't quite killed it but she'd certainly stopped it. It was leaking black ichor from the wounds.

And from the moment Marco had fallen, it had no interest in her. Instead, it was struggling to fly on torn, batlike wings. It was heading for the windows as if drawn by an invisible wire.

Half the town seemed to be fleeing for their lives. The other half appeared to be chasing them.

Benito would have sworn he was the only one who looked up as they pursued Caesare's party across the Piazza San Marco. It might have been the brightness of the morning sun, but he'd swear that he saw the winged lion settle back onto its column.

"Is there anything more?" the Lion asked.

Marco looked around, and couldn't see anything. There was—something—far off—

"It is of no consequence," the Lion said dismissively. "The Christ-mage, the one who limps; he and his knights have conquered it, and its vessel. And there is another, but believe me—" He laughed, this time a deep rumbling in his chest. "Your young mate and *her* Power have *that* well taken care of. Now—shortly, you must become yourself again. But, Marco Valdosta, you not only bear the Winged Mantle *now*, but you have also taken up the Crown. As long as you live, only *you* may be the one to call me. No mage may do it for you. You must take care, Marco Valdosta! You must have a care for yourself, and most especially, when you think it might be good to leave my lagoons and my islands. Should Venice need me in your absence, it will not have me, for only you can call me!"

"Yes, Lion," Marco replied obediently, feeling the burden of responsibility settle on shoulders that stiffened to meet it. "I will remember. If I leave—it will be because there is no other choice, not only for me, but for Venice."

The Lion seemed satisfied. "You do not complain. Good. It does not seem a great sacrifice to me. I do not know why you humans are so itchy-footed. Now—time to put an end to this, before you—or I—come to like it all too much!"

❀   ❀   ❀

The monster crawled towards the window, and Kat felt fear mixed with rage. It—she—was going to get away! Lucrezia had unleashed war in the streets, had killed men with her own hands or her own orders, had hurt Rafael and she was going to get away!

Not this time, little sister.

The golden, glowing hands over hers made her drop the pistol—made her reach to the side, and take a book from a shelf there—a very, very, *heavy* book, which must have weighed several pounds, encased in a silver-chased cover.

A *Bible*?

—and throw it.

It landed squarely on the monster.

There was a flash of light that was somehow *black,* a scream that cut through Kat's skull so that she clapped both empty hands over her ears in a futile attempt to block it out.

Then there was nothing.

Nothing but a silver-chased Bible in the floor, and a snaky black smudge on the marble.

Hmm. What's appropriate, I wonder? "A little knowledge is a dangerous thing?" "The Word is mightier than the blade?" Ah, I know! "Let Evil beware the Weight of the Word of God!"

There was—a golden *laugh* that washed through her, erasing the pain that the scream had left behind, and the feeling of *uncleanliness.* Then the presence was gone.

Kat shivered convulsively. Then . . . saw the candles in the magic circle suddenly snuff out, saw the air suddenly clear, and the glittering circles of power fade to nothing more than the silver and gold inlaid on the floor.

"Oh God—*Marco!*" She pushed forward past Luciano's body. Marco lay still and cold, with the blade still pressed into his breast. Katerina had the impression of a misty and insubstantial gold crown on his head. But the image faded almost instantly, and she had no time to think about it. She tugged at the hateful, fateful dagger. It fell and snapped as if it had been made of the finest Venetian glass. She stared. There was no blood. She ripped at his shirt, scattering buttons.

Marco's chest had a tiny, V-shaped cut on it—not a fingernail deep. Kat seized his wrists. She was shaking too badly to feel for a pulse. She pressed her ear to his chest. After a terrible instant of fear—silence!—then she heard his heart beating. Beating steadily.

Suddenly, Marco breathed deeply and put his arms around her. She clung to him like a drowning woman.

"I can never leave here, you know," he said softly. "*He* said so. I have to stay, or he can't protect Venice."

She burrowed against his chest, not giving a damn who *he* was. "I will never leave here then, either."

It was Benito who found them, nearly an hour later. He walked in and stared at the two of them.

"Thank God Claudia knew where this place was. Otherwise you two lovebirds might still have been here tomorrow. Tore the shirt off him, eh, Kat?" He was grinning broadly. "I must get Maria to have a little talk with you, girl. Tearing the breeches off him is much more satisfying for everyone."

"Benito!" roared Marco.

It was a real roar. The windows rattled.

Benito started at the sound, but the grin stayed on his face even if it became a little less broad.

But as he looked around, studying the room, the grin faded away. The bodies. The paraphernalia.

"So I *didn't* imagine the Lion," he said quietly. "I think you two had better get out of here, before someone else finds you. I've got news for the two of you; besides that, Dorma and Montescue are both searching frantically for you."

They got up. "Tell, Benito," said Kat. "What's happened?"

Benito managed another grin. "Well, lots of stuff. The Doge has stopped slipping into a coma, but he's really weak. He's offered his resignation, as he says the city needs a strong Doge in these times. I reckon Petro will be chosen, even as young as he is. A boat's just come in from Chioggia. Grandfather Dell'este and the Knights of the Holy Trinity and the boys in the Polestine forts made my father and his army head back to Milan." His good cheer faded. "But it looks as if Caesare Aldanto managed to escape."

"What?!" They both exclaimed simultaneously. "Damn him," added Kat, snarling.

Benito walked toward the nearest window, still covered with heavy drapes. "Let's get some light in here, what say?" He shrugged. "Nothing's ever perfect. Aldanto had a galley ready—in case things went wrong, I guess. That'd be just like him. When the fog cleared and the Lion's Shadow spooked them, he took advantage of it. Just in time, too. Petro Dorma is spitting mad about it. And he's looking for you pair of lovebirds." He looked quizzically at them. "So what are you going to do now?"

Marco took Kat's hands. "Kat. You realize that this doesn't change anything? I made my promises. I'm still married to Angelina."

Kat smiled. "Marco. I'll be your mistress if you want me. I'll be your friend if you don't. But I *won't* leave you again."

Epilogue

VILNA

The shaman raced frantically through the water, trailing blood from several gashes. Behind him, their jaws leaving their own red trace, came the vengeful undines.

Insofar as the shaman could think at all in his state of panic, he was sure he could elude his pursuers. He was well into the open waters of the gulf now, beyond the lagoon, and he was a better swimmer than the undines.

The thought was not especially comforting. Undines were not the only menace he faced. The shadow of the Lion, sweeping across the lagoon, had not only cast terror into the minds and hearts of Venice's enemies. It had also emboldened Venice—and its friends.

Among those friends, often enough, the tritons of the gulf and the open sea could be counted. And those, more fishlike than the undines, he could *not* outswim.

For that matter, the blood he was trailing might draw sharks as well. And if the sharks were no friends of Venice, they were no friends of his either.

Again and again, he cried out in his mind for the master to rescue him. *Open the passageway! Open the passageway!*

There was no answer. No passageway.

When he sensed the disturbance in the water, quite some distance away, the shaman veered aside. That was the sound of a ship breaking up and men spilling into the water. No threat to him, in itself—but it might draw tritons. Occasionally—not often—the sea creatures rescued drowning sailors.

But his master's voice, finally appearing, commanded otherwise.

Find the ship and its sailors. Seize the strongest one and bring him to me.

The shaman did not even think to protest the order. Partly, because he was too glad to finally hear his master's voice. Mostly, because he had never heard that voice groan with such a terrible agony. As if the master himself were trailing his own spoor of blood.

The shaman was indifferent to the master's pain. But not to the rage that pain had so obviously brought with it.

When the shaman found the sundering vessel, he had no difficulty selecting the strongest man of its crew. He was the only one who had not drowned yet; and was already sinking below the surface himself, gasping with exhaustion. Fortunately, his golden hair made him easy to find.

The shaman seized the collar of his tunic in his sharp teeth. He hoped the master would open the passageway soon. The drowning man was larger than the shaman in his fishform. He did not think he could tow him any great distance—certainly not while keeping the man's mouth above water. The shaman was nearing exhaustion himself.

But the master was apparently alert. A moment later the passageway formed. Gratefully, the shaman plunged into it, bringing his golden-haired burden with him.

Dripping water, but no blood now that the shape-change had closed his wounds, the shaman lay sprawled on the floor of the grand duke's private chamber. Gasping for breath and feeling as if he could not move at all. Next to him, the golden-haired sailor gasped also. His eyes fluttered for a moment, blue gleaming through the lids, as the man began to return to consciousness.

The shaman sensed the huge form of his master looming over them. When he looked up, half-dazed, he was paralyzed still further by the sight. The grand duke's forehead gaped open; his face was coated with blood. The shaman could see his master's brains through the terrible wound.

The shaman had long since understood that his master was not really human any longer. Had he any doubts, that wound would have resolved them. No human being could have possibly survived such an injury, much less have been able to move and talk.

"I must have food," hissed the grand duke, in a voice almost hoarse from screaming. "*Now.*"

Glancing toward the great stove against the wall of his master's private room, the shaman could see that the fire was already burning in its belly. Drops of blood spilled from his master's head wound were sizzling on the side of the huge fry pan. The cleavers and flensing knives were ready on the butcher's table nearby.

The grand duke seized the half-drowned sailor by his golden hair and lifted him up, as easily as he might an infant. But then, seeing the man's face for the first time, he paused.

"Him," he muttered. Despite his fear and exhaustion, the shaman was fascinated to see the way the grand duke's forehead wound was beginning to close up. Much more slowly than one of his own wounds would heal during a shape-change, of course. And the shaman could only imagine the agony the grand duke was suffering. No wonder that the master craved his . . . special food. It would speed the healing immensely, and alleviate the pain.

The shaman was so fascinated by the sight that he didn't pay attention to his master's odd hesitation. It wasn't until the grand duke lowered the golden-haired head back to the floor that the shaman tore his gaze from the wound and looked at the eyes below.

He wished he hadn't. Even before he heard his master's next words.

"I may have use for this one. I can get another shaman."

The grand duke's giant hand seized the shaman by his long hair and dragged him toward the butcher table. The shaman fought in a frenzy along the way, but he might as well have been a toddler for all the good it did. Once on the table, a blow from the grand duke's fist ended his struggles.

Which was perhaps just as well. The shaman was too stunned to really feel the blade which began flaying him. His screams didn't start again until much of the skin was already gone. But, by then, the master was ready to prepare the blood sauce. A quick slice of the knife ended the screams.

When Caesare Aldanto finally returned to full consciousness, he discovered himself sitting at a table. A man he didn't recognize was working at a stove nearby. Huge man, he was—inches taller than Aldanto himself, and perhaps twice as broad. Adding in the walrus fat so obvious under the heavy robes, he probably weighed three times what Aldanto did.

When the man turned around and approached, Aldanto hissed. Partly because of the wound on the forehead, the likes of which he had never seen except on the body of a corpse. Mostly, because of the black and inhuman eyes under the heavy brow.

The man—the monster?—shoveled something out of the fry pan

directly onto the table. "Eat now," he commanded. "There is no time for platters."

Caesare stared at him, then down at the food before him. When he recognized what it was—the tattoos alone made it obvious—he hissed again and began to draw back. A savage blow to the head half-dazed him. Then, a hand with the strength of an ogre seized him by the hair and shoved his face into the food.

"Eat it like a dog, slave. I have no use for fancy table manners. Neither do you, from this time forth."

THE PIAVE RIVER

"I think it would be best if I were escorted into Venice by your troops instead of my own, Enrico." The Emperor scanned the countryside along the Piave, the muscles working in his heavy jaws. "Bad enough I've brought them this far. But so long as Venice itself doesn't get its back up, I'm not too concerned about the reaction of the rest of Italy. Not at the moment, at least, when the bastards are cowed."

The Duke of Ferrara nodded. "I agree, Your Majesty." He hesitated a moment; then: "But I urge you not to be *too* cautious, either. The Scaligers of Verona have managed to infuriate just about everyone by now. Venice, Ferrara, and Rome by their actions; Milan and the rest by their failure."

Charles Fredrik's lips parted in what a shark might call a smile. "You think the time is ripe to take them down a peg or two?"

"Break them in half, rather," growled the Old Fox.

"Well said," snapped Baron Trolliger, riding to the Emperor's left. Unlike the Emperor, Trolliger was wearing armor. He seemed as annoyed by the martial equipment as he was with the state of the world in general. Trolliger was a courtier, not a soldier. Or perhaps it was simply that he detested travel.

"See to it, Hans," murmured Charles Fredrik. "Use Wilhelm Gneiss and his Bavarians. You can leave the military details to him. But make sure the Scaligers are bloodied. You needn't besiege Verona, I don't imagine—but tell Wilhelm not to hesitate if necessary. I want the territory under the control of the Scaligers shrunk—in half, as the Duke of Ferrara says. Spread the pieces around as seems best to you during the negotiations." He glanced at the Old Fox. "Make sure Ferrara gets the biggest slice."

"I've always been partial to Legnano," said Dell'este, almost idly. "Pretty town."

After Trolliger trotted off, riding his horse about as awkwardly as a man can and still stay in the saddle, the Emperor glanced behind him at a figure who was riding her own saddle with considerably greater ease and skill.

"Would you allow us a moment in private, Enrico?"

"Certainly, Your Majesty." The Duke of Ferrara trotted his horse away with the same superb skill that the old man handled a sword or a hammer. The Emperor waved Francesca forward.

When she drew alongside him, Charles Fredrik glanced at her manner of riding and made a face. "How do you manage that, anyway?"

Francesca smiled. "It's the fashion in the Aquitaine for ladies, Your Majesty. I learned to ride sidesaddle when I was barely old enough to walk." She plucked the dusky folds of silken lace-trimmed twill covering her thighs. "I could hardly wear something like this straddling the horse."

"It's quite a costume," agreed the Emperor. His tone was . . . meaningful.

Francesca gave him a sidelong glance. "I did not think Your Majesty would appreciate it much, if I were seen in my usual costume. Discretion and modesty seemed . . . well advised."

"Smart woman. Not—" The old man gave her a sidelong glance of his own. For a moment, his eyes seemed those of a much younger man. "—that I wouldn't have appreciated the other, I'm quite sure."

Francesca said nothing. Her smile was almost that of a Madonna.

Charles Fredrik cleared his throat. "And why *didn't* I see that other costume, Marie-Françoise de Guemadeuc? Since your arrival at Innsbruck, you've both dressed and behaved as a most modest and chaste demoiselle. In my experience—which is considerable—most courtesans would have cheerfully pitched over a prince for the sake of snaring an emperor."

Francesca hesitated, a little play of subtle emotions running over her face. Before she could speak, the Emperor continued.

"Three possibilities come to mind. The first is that you have a rigid sense of honor, which would preclude that course of action on the grounds that it skirts incest. But since you are Aquitainian, I think we can dismiss that possibility out of hand."

"We *do* have a reputation." Francesca's accompanying chuckle was soft and throaty. "Indeed, I agree. We may dismiss it out of hand."

"The second possibility, then. You have formed an attachment with my nephew which transcends the obvious bond between a courtesan and a young nobleman." He stopped abruptly, cocking an eye at her.

"Um. I *am* fond of Manfred, Your Majesty. Genuinely so, in fact. But—"

Charles Fredrik heaved a sigh of relief. "Thank God. I'm not dealing with a madwoman."

Francesca's chuckle, now, was neither soft nor throaty. Indeed, it was almost an open laugh. "Please. Manfred is charming, vigorous, good-humored—often genuinely witty—and far more intelligent than he likes to pretend. His company, more often than not, is quite delightful. Far more so than that of most of my clients. But anything more serious . . ." She shook her head firmly. "There's nothing in it, neither for Manfred nor myself. Although I'm good for him now, Your Majesty. That I do believe."

The Emperor nodded. "I also. I have no objection to a continuation of your liaison. Actually, I'm in favor of it." He cleared his throat. "You do understand, of course . . ."

"Yes, yes—certainly. Now that Manfred's identity is in the open, he can hardly remain simply one of my clients. A rich young knight can share a courtesan. A prince requires an exclusive mistress."

It was her turn to clear her throat.

Before she could speak, Charles Fredrik snorted. "Yes, yes—certainly. I know it'll cost me." He examined her briefly, spending more time on the modest but expensive clothing than on her well-covered but intrinsically immodest figure. "Plenty."

The way in which Francesca smoothed the fabric of her dress was demure propriety itself. "Perhaps—"

"Which brings us to the third possibility," said the Emperor loudly. The gaze he now bestowed on Francesca was almost angry. "Every now and then—not often—a whore becomes *truly* ambitious. And— if she's smart enough—realizes that the ultimate coin in this sinful world is trust."

Francesca meet the fierce eyes with calm ones of her own. "Trust which would be quite shattered if I abandoned the prince for the emperor. For the one as much as the other."

The Emperor nodded. "Good. Now—it is time to speak honestly. I will allow you two lies. No more. What do you *want*, Marie-Françoise de Guemadeuc? Tell me all of it."

She grimaced. "First of all, I don't want that name. Francesca is now—"

"That's the first lie. Be careful, woman."

For the first time since he'd met the courtesan, her aplomb was shaken. Francesca almost jerked in the saddle.

"It is *not* a lie," she hissed. "I am simply—" She broke off, staring at the countryside with eyes which clearly saw a different one. "My God," she whispered, "it is a lie."

"Of course it is," snapped Charles Fredrik. "The mistake your mother made, Marie-Françoise, was settling for *revenge*. She should have bided her time, and waited until she could triumph."

They rode on in silence for a bit. Then Francesca shook her head, as if to clear it. "Yes and no, Your Majesty. Oddly enough, I find that I like Francesca de Chevreuse rather more than I did the girl she was. So I believe I'll stick with the name—within, as well as without." Again, that soft throaty chuckle. "But . . . yes. I will keep an eye out for the possibility of triumph."

"Good. What else?" He waved a thick hand. "Wealth, ease, comfort, all that. Naturally. But what *else*?"

Francesca seemed to be groping for words. The Emperor clucked his tongue. "Well, it's time you *did* start thinking about it. Clearly, for a change." He twisted a bit in the saddle, until he was facing her almost squarely. "Let an old man provide you with some assistance. The 'what else,' I'm quite sure, is power and influence. Your *own* power and influence, not that which you derive from befuddling a man's wits with your—no doubt magnificent—legs and bosom."

Francesca hesitated. Then, nodded abruptly.

"Good. That ambition an emperor can trust. For the simple reason that it cannot be achieved *without* trust." His smile was almost that of a cherub. "And I must say you're doing quite well, for such a young and innocent girl."

Francesca began that soft throaty chuckle again; but this time she choked it off almost before it began. "Good God! You're *serious*. Um—Your Majesty."

"Of course I'm serious." The cherub smile was replaced by something infinitely grimmer. "Take it from an emperor, child. What you know about *sin* is pitiful; what you know about wickedness . . . almost nothing."

Again, they rode on in silence. After a time, the Emperor spoke again. "I'll be sending Manfred off, soon enough. It's time for the next stage of his education—as well as the education of the Grand Duke of Lithuania."

Francesca's eyes widened. "No, girl," said the Emperor softly, "I am *not* sending him off to war. Not directly, at least. The time isn't right for a war with Jagiellon. Not with Emeric on the throne in Hungary, still unbloodied, and now this rot in my own—"

He broke off. Then, cleared his throat. "Never mind that. But I do think a demonstration is called for. Since that Lithuanian bastard chose to use a demon from the Svear, against the Svear it shall be."

Francesca seemed to wince. The Emperor grinned. "Oh please, demoiselle! I do not expect you to traipse around with Manfred and Erik in the marshes and forests of Småland! But I *will* expect you to accompany them as far as Mainz. And then, possibly, to Copenhagen."

The Emperor's grin widened, seeing the eager light in the young woman's eyes. "Yes, yes—intrigue with the Danes against the Sots, all that. You'll have a splendid time of it. But there's something else, more important, we need to discuss."

"I am all ears, Your Majesty."

"Thought you would be. Have you ever given much thought to *finance*, Francesca de Chevreuse?" After a short pause: "Didn't think so. Time you did. More than anything else, girl, wars are fought with money. Don't let any one ever tell you different, especially generals. And—take it from an old emperor—organizing the finances of a major war is even more complex and difficult than organizing the supply train. Takes even longer to do it right, and it's far more treacherous. To begin with—"

On they went. Across the Piave, now, heading west toward the city of the winged lion. The Emperor never stopped talking—

"—great financiers, especially with war looming, are always old men, you see. It occurs to me that a gorgeous young woman—especially one with a disreputable past and a flavor of scandal about her—especially a smart and witty one—"

—and Francesca was all ears.

VENICE

It was easier, Kat was learning, to triumph over evil than to explain it.

She and Marco, holding—no, clutching—hands openly, were spared having to repeat what had transpired in the magic chamber over and over again, only by the intercession of Petro Dorma. With an efficiency that was almost terrifying, he'd sent them straight to the Doge's palace, where they'd been fed and allowed to rest—*rest,* not sleep, although both of them were swaying with exhaustion.

They hadn't gotten much past the first few mouthfuls when Marco's Strega friend Rafael joined them. He didn't look any better than Marco. Both of them had huge, bruised-looking circles around their eyes, and both of them must have been existing on nervous energy alone. Heaven only knew *she* was, and she must look much the same. Here they were, three tattered and stained vagabonds in a room that usually entertained the most prominent folk in Venice—and often, in the world. The murals on the walls alone were stunning works of art worthy of the Grand Metropolitan's palace in Rome, and the amount of gold leaf on the carved woodwork didn't bear thinking about.

It could serve to repair Casa *Montescue five times over.*

"What are they going to do with us?" Rafael asked dully.

The answer came from an unexpected source; Petro Dorma himself, who entered the sumptuous dining room behind a servant bearing a gold pitcher.

"Ah, my weary young heroes," Petro said, quite as if *he* was not as weary as any of them. "I want you to eat and drink while my messengers round up everyone who has any interest in what went on in that chamber where *Dottore* Marina's body was found. Then I want you to tell your stories, answer questions for a reasonable length of time—which will probably be quite a bit shorter than usual, given that we are all rather the worse for wear. By that time, you won't be able to walk three paces without staggering, so you will all be escorted to comfortable bedchambers here in the palace, where, I suspect, you will probably sleep until this time tomorrow."

Unbelievably, terrifyingly, efficient. If Petro became the new Doge, which was the rumor Kat had been hearing, he was going to be something to be reckoned with.

Petro joined them, thus making a tableau of four tiny figures who were dwarfed by the chamber and humbled by the crimson-and-gold trappings. Mostly gold, Katerina couldn't help but notice. She thought *Casa* Montescue's desperate financial situation had probably been somewhat alleviated by the recent events. *Surely the money-lenders won't harass us for a few weeks.* But, maybe not . . .

They ate slowly. Katerina concentrated on every bite, not least because the food was delicious—out of all expectations, considering the conditions of the last day and night. *When did I eat last?* she wondered. It seemed a year ago or more. Whenever it had been, she was as hungry as she was weary. But hunger, at least, could be easily remedied. They were only just finished and nibbling in a desultory manner at sweets, when a servant in Dorma livery arrived and Dorma rose.

"We seem to have collected everyone we're going to find," he said. "Come along; the sooner this is over, the sooner we can all sleep." The three of them got slowly to their feet—Kat, at least, was aching in every limb—and Dorma escorted them all out.

Both grandfathers were there, Montescue and Dell'este—sitting side by side, for a wonder. Nine men who, Dorma had whispered briefly as they entered, represented the Senate—but Kat suspected were really, along with Dorma himself, the entire Council of Ten. And Metropolitan Michael, of course.

All these Kat had expected—but not the cluster of priests surrounding Michael, nor the horde of secretaries seated at tables running the length of the room behind the notables. She felt uneasily like she was falling into the hands of inquisitors.

"Gentlemen," Dorma nodded to all of them. "These young people are the first we will hear, beginning with Marco Valdosta, continuing with Katerina Montescue, with—" He shook his head, clearly going blank when it came to Rafael's name. "Ah—their friend, who also witnessed what happened, as the last of the three. Hold your questions until they are finished, and try to keep them brief."

Marco began, omitting nothing, and although Kat found herself blinking in stunned disbelief when he got to the part where he apparently collapsed in the magic circle, and described what had happened. But neither the Metropolitan nor the priests with him seemed at all surprised.

A spirit? A pagan spirit, but also the Protector of Venice? The very Lion that met Saint Mark?

"So—now I'm bound to the Lion," he finished wearily; then, out of nowhere, managed a brilliant smile. "And my Pauline relatives will surely disown me now for such blasphemy!"

His grandfather, the Old Dell'este Fox, snorted, and *her* grandfather choked on his drink—with suppressed laughter, she realized a moment later.

"Those of your Pauline relatives who are stupid enough to be fretted about blasphemy after all this—none of whom are on *my* side of the family, I might mention—can go hang themselves," the Old Fox growled. "I'll lend them the rope."

"Nonsense!" barked Lodovico Montescue. "*Sell* it to them. I'll go in with you in a *Colleganza.*"

The room erupted in a roar of laughter—and there was an end to *that* topic.

The priests added a few questions, mostly about the Lion, what it and Marco had done, and the awakening spell. But very soon the Metropolitan himself called a halt. "Anything more we can learn from the book, and it will be more certain than this young man's memory," he said. "I will confer with Father Lopez when he returns, but I am satisfied that there is not so much as a whisper of evil about this creature—to whom, and this young mage, we can only be grateful."

And then it was her turn.

Everyone listened in silence until she got to the part where Lucrezia Brunelli appeared. "*Ha!*" exclaimed one of the priests, smacking the table and making her jump. "Father Pierre was right! I thought he was."

"Don't interrupt her," commanded Michael sternly; then, unexpectedly, smiled at her.

She continued, wanting to close her eyes to better recall Lucrezia's exact words—but knowing that she didn't dare to, because if she did, she'd fall asleep. She managed well enough until she got to the part about the warmth that filled her, coming from her Hypatia medal; the pure, sweet voice in her head, and the glowing golden hands that overlaid hers. Then she saw something that she would never, ever have imagined.

She saw Metropolitan Michael's eyes widen and his jaw sag. Actually, at that point, there were many jaws dropping, especially among the priests. The only one who didn't seem surprised was Marco, who squeezed her hand encouragingly. No one interrupted her, though, and she continued doggedly, through the point of Lucrezia's transformation, the seizing of the Bible, and the aftermath.

"And then the voice said, *Let Evil beware the weight of the Word of God,* and then—I suppose it was gone, because the warmth went away," she concluded. She prudently omitted the other outrageous puns that the voice had made, as well as the remarks that had prefaced and followed the aphorism she'd been told to use.

Heads nodded wisely all over the room—

—except for Metropolitan Michael's. He appeared to be choking for a moment, but quickly composed himself.

Did he get the joke? A moment later, a glance from his dancing eyes confirmed her suspicion that he had.

Oh, dearest Dottore *Marina, now I understand what you meant about history becoming somewhat cleaned up and simplified.* Who, except perhaps for this single cleric, would ever understand the full version? Who would ever appreciate it for what it *meant*? Yes, there was terrible evil in the world, and yes, they must fight grimly to defeat it—but there was also peace, love, and joy . . . and to forget that, would be to forget there was a God.

"I have no questions, but I would like to examine the young lady's medal," Michael said gravely. She pulled the chain over her head and handed it to the page who came for it, feeling uncomfortable and naked without it. Michael and his group of priests each examined the Saint Hypatia medal closely, and they put their heads together and muttered for a moment.

Then the Metropolitan handed it back to the page, who brought it back to her. She put it back on, with relief.

"I would like to place into the record of these proceedings that we have found the original protections placed upon this talisman by the Order of Hypatia. As well as a very recent reinforcing spell, placed on it within the last three months or so, by some other magician. Whom I believe to have been *Dottore* Marina." He paused significantly. "*All of which* bear the completely unmistakable aura of sanctity. This medal has been used within the last day as a vehicle for one of God's own spirits. We are not prepared to state *which* spirit, but I believe we can assume it was, at the least, one of the angelic order of the cherubim." Michael raised one eyebrow. "Possibly higher. Possibly the saint herself. But without having a Christian mage as a witness, we cannot state that this was a *bona fide* Hypatian miracle, and therefore we will confine ourselves to pronouncing it a genuine case of divine intercession."

Well, that caused as much of a buzz as Marco's revelations, and Rafael got off with doing no more than providing confirmation for her story and Marco's with no questioning. And very shortly after that, they were all three dismissed and followed their page—stumbling, as Dorma had predicted—to their rooms.

Kat found attentive maids waiting, who stripped her with the same terrible efficiency as shown by Petro Dorma, popped a nightdress over her head, and eased her into a bed she didn't even see. After that—she didn't even dream.

But the next day . . .

All of the peace of mind which had come to her came crashing down the moment she stepped out into the public corridors. Two pages were waiting for her, and whisked her off to join Marco, chattering at her the entire time.

She and Marco, it seemed, were the Saviors of Venice. Father Lopez, still covered with dust from his hurried return to the city, explained it all to them.

Never mind Petro Dorma, or the Arsenalotti. Forget the brilliant tactics of Dell'este. Ignore the subtle intervention of the Emperor. Completely discount the actions of the Knights under confrere Manfred and his friend Eric Hakkonsen. Pretend that Father Lopez never battled Sachs and Ursula and the horrible thing they had brought in on behest of the dread Grand Duke of Lithuania. *She and Marco* were the Saviors of Venice.

Dorma was with Marco, and Senor Lopez joined them a moment later. "You must make an appearance," Dorma told them firmly, before they could make any objections. Lopez nodded, even more firmly. Kat discovered that, when sandwiched between two such forceful personalities, *no* becomes a word that does not effectively exist.

Dorma and Lopez took them both to the very, very public *Scala di Giganti,* where the new Doges were always inaugurated, and as they all stepped out onto the top step, a roar went up from the

Piazza San Marco. As she stood there, once again clutching at Marco's hand, half-blinded by the sun and deafened by the noise, she realized to her horror that the piazza was packed solid.

"Smile," Dorma shouted into her ear. "Wave."

She did; the crowd roared again.

"Now come this way." Dorma took her arm and steered her along the second-floor balcony to the side that faced the lagoon as Lopez did the same for Marco. The piazza was too densely packed for anyone to follow, but that hardly mattered, since the wave of sound propagated along as they passed. And when they got to the seaward side of the balcony, it seemed that *every floating object in Venice* began parading past.

At least here, facing the Doge's palace and the lagoon, where not so many people could crowd up against the building, it was easier to hear.

"Keep smiling and waving," Lopez said gravely, doing the same. Then he and Dorma explained to them how and why it was that *they* were suddenly the Saviors.

"Dell'este is not *one of us,*" Dorma said, bowing as one of the House racing-boats passed with every scion of nobility the House possessed manning an oar. "The Knights—well, so far as the average Venetian is concerned, they have only *just* redeemed themselves for the actions of Sachs and the Sots. And, besides, they aren't *our people* either."

"Nor are we, the foreign clerics, and never mind who sent us here," Lopez agreed wryly. "And Petro Dorma—" His lips twisted in an attempt to suppress a smile. "Petro Dorma is a fine example of the best of the *Casa Vecchie,* and he will surely make a great Doge. But he is balding, middle-aged, and has an undistinguished nose. Not the fine figure of which legends are made."

Dorma chuckled. "True enough. Not"—here, a bit smugly—"that my humble nose is going to stop any of the single ladies of the *Casa Vecchie* from seeking out my company with an eye to matrimony. But, yes, I will be the first to admit that I do not make an appropriate figure for the future statues which will commemorate this triumph."

He gazed at Marco and Kat. "*You,* on the other hand—you are both handsome, young, and—well. That problem still has to be dealt with, but the rumor of your little romance is already sweeping the city. Not so little, actually. You have ended a feud between your families to rival that of the Capuletti and Montague in Verona. You have served as the vessels for the oldest of Venice's magical protectors, and of a *bona fide* angelic power. So, I can hardly blame the people for deciding that we old men only sat and twiddled our fingers while you two saved the city. Smile," he added, as Kat began to object. "And wave. This is what is meant by *noblesse oblige*, as our Aquitaine friends would say."

The two youngsters did as they were instructed. But Kat had the sinking realization—sinking like a stone anchor at sea—that the "rumor sweeping Venice" was going to make her life a lot more complicated than it already was. The ugly term *adulteress* crept into her mind, making her wince. She wasn't sure if she should keep holding Marco's hand. But—

His grip was far too firm to resist anyway. Even if she'd really wanted to.

CASA DORMA

"You have used the children quite enough. Go any further and you imperil your souls."

Eneko Lopez's words were spoken softly; but, to Enrico Dell'este, they seem to ring through the luxurious salon in *Casa* Dorma like hammer blows on the anvil in his workshop. As always, the concept of *uncertainty* seemed utterly foreign to the Basque priest.

The Old Fox's lips twisted in a wry smile. "If the Grand Metropolitan of Rome refuses your request to found a new order, Father, you might consider taking up prophecy as your new vocation. I'm quite sure you could learn to carve stone tablets, with a bit of practice."

A nervous little laugh rippled through the salon. Lopez, showing that easy humor which—oddly enough—always lurked beneath his implacable surface, flashed the Duke of Ferrara a quick grin. Then nodded, acknowledging the hit.

The acknowledgement, of course, did not sway him for a moment. "The fact remains, milord, that you cannot manipulate everything for political purposes. Not without risking eternal damnation."

Petro Dorma coughed, drawing attention his way. "There's no

need to argue the theology involved, Father Lopez. As it happens—for political as well as personal reasons—I agree with you."

Dorma had not spoken so far, since the discussion over the fate of Marco's marriage to Angelina had first begun. Everyone had expected him to be one pole of the debate—and quite the opposite one—so his statement brought instant silence.

"A *Case Vecchie* who is wise instead of shrewd," murmured Eneko. "Truly we have entered a new age of miracles."

Again, laughter rippled through the room—less nervously, this time; almost with relief.

Dorma shrugged. "I have done my best for my sister. But the fact remains that Angelina is . . . unstable. And Venice cannot afford to have Marco Valdosta in an unstable marriage. Nor, for that matter, can it afford to have Katerina Montescue develop the reputation of an adulteress."

He gestured with his head toward the great window overlooking the Grand Canal. Even though the window was closed, and the Piazza San Marco was some distance away from the Dorma palace, the roar of the huge crowd filling the streets and piazza in triumphal celebration was loud enough to be heard easily. Now in its second day, there seemed no sign yet that the festivities were abating.

"Some of that applause is for the Emperor, of course. Charles Fredrik is the first Holy Roman Emperor to visit Venice in two centuries, and since his visit—unlike the last one—is seen as a show of support for Venice, the crowd is casting its republican sentiments aside."

"For the moment," growled Lodovico Montescue. "If the Emperor isn't smart enough not to leave within a few days, you watch how fast that'll change. And good it is!"

"Oh, stop being a grouch," drawled Dell'este. "Look on the bright side. The Montagnards have been dreaming for years of the day when the Emperor would enter Venice—and now that it's finally happened, they're all hiding in their cellars."

He and Lodovico exchanged cold smiles.

Petro Dorma sighed. "Montescue, your house is still in dire financial circumstances. So you can't afford assassins anyway."

"I can," interjected Dell'este immediately. "And Lodovico can find them for me." He turned his head and smiled gently at Antimo Bartelozzi, seated in a chair behind him. "No offense, Antimo. But I always feel it's wise to consult the local experts."

Antimo nodded solemnly. "Quite so, milord."

"Enough!" snapped Petro. He glared at the Old Fox. "Ferrara is *not* in charge of Venice. Insofar as anyone is, at the moment, I am. I'm certainly in charge of the Lords of the Nightwatch." Discreet as ever, he did not add: *the Council of Ten, also.* "So if I discover either of you—or both together—have been conspiring to assassinate Montagnards, I'll take measures. Don't think I won't. I've had enough—so has Venice—of these damned factional wars."

The Old Fox was tempted to rise to the challenge—*and just how will you take measures against Ferrara, Venetian?*—but he resisted the temptation easily enough. He had nothing to gain, and everything to lose, from entering a pissing match with Petro Dorma. Besides—

"I give you my word, Lord Dorma," he said, almost insouciantly. "But it won't stop the crowd from doing it. Word is the Arsenalotti have organized their own assassins. And the canalers are guiding them to the Montagnard hideouts."

Petro made a face; then, shrugged. "What the Venetian commons do at the moment, to settle their scores, does not concern me. They'll crush the snake and be done with it. *Casa Vecchie* vendettas take on an insane life of their own."

Lodovico Montescue had the grace to flush and look away. A bit to his surprise, Enrico Dell'este found himself doing the same.

"My word," Dell'este repeated. This time, with no insouciance at all. After a moment, with a tone of aggrieved resignation that brought another little ripple of laughter, Lodovico added his own vow.

"Good enough," said Petro. Again, he gestured at the window. "What I was about to say, however, is that *most* of that applause is not for the Emperor. It is—as everyone here knows—addressed at Marco and Katerina." He rubbed a hand over his bald pate, smiling ruefully. "About whom the wildest rumors are sweeping the city."

"What's wild about them?" snorted Lopez. "Marco Valdosta *does* carry the Mantle of the Lion. And wears the Crown also, it seems." Seeing the uncertainty in the faces of the hard-headed Venetian grandees in the salon, the Basque chuckled harshly. "Oh, yes—have no doubt about it. Metropolitan Michael tells me he was able to study enough of what *Dottore* Marina left behind to understand what happened, even if he could not duplicate the thing himself. I'm not sure anyone could, except a Grimas."

From the back of the room, where he had been sitting uneasily in a chair—he was not accustomed to such society—Father Mascoli spoke up for the first time. His words were soft, but firm for all that. "There were many witnesses, milords, who saw the lion leave and return to the pillar. I have spoken to several of them."

Petro swiveled in his chair and examined the priest. It was at his insistence that Father Mascoli had come. "You have spoken to Sister Evangelina?"

Mascoli nodded. "Yes, Lord Dorma. And she has agreed—provided Angelina is not coerced in any way."

Petro nodded and turned back. "I have not coerced her. In fact, it was Angelina who first made the suggestion herself."

His round face took on an expression which was partly one of chagrin, partly one of fondness. "My sister's moods swing back and forth, rather unpredictably. At her best—" He straightened in his chair. "Her marriage to Marco was a fiction, as all here are well aware. Angelina, in her way, has grown very fond of Marco. And seems now to have become determined not to be an impediment to his happiness."

He raised a fist to his mouth and coughed into it. "She proposed, in fact, a simple annulment on the grounds that the marriage was never consummated. Which, as it happens, is quite true in this case. But—"

He broke off, his expression clearly showing his unease.

Enrico immediately understood the quandary, and slid into it with all the grace of an expert swordsman in a fencing match.

"Petro. Naturally you would like to avoid the public embarrassment of admitting that the child is not Marco's." Dell'este saw no reason to add the obvious: *even if no one in Venice except halfwits believes it anyway—and even the halfwits don't believe it once they see the bastard's hair.* As always, for *Case Vecchie,* formalities and appearance were as important as the reality.

"I see no problem, Petro," he continued easily. He glanced at Father Mascoli. "If Angelina has agreed to take Holy Orders, that gives another ground for annulling the marriage. One which is much less awkward, for all concerned."

"What about the baby?" asked Lodovico. "Angelina can't very

well take her with her to a nunnery. And if you give her up, you undermine the whole purpose of the subterfuge."

Dorma smiled; again, the expression conveyed that odd mix of fondness and chagrin. "I've spoken to Marco. He immediately offered to raise the child as his own. Truth to tell, he already spends more time with the girl than does my sister."

Dorma hesitated. Then, his innate honesty forced him to keep speaking. Dell'este was quite delighted. Venice would need an honest Doge, in the time to come.

"I must point out the possible problem," said Petro. "An annulment due to my sister joining a religious order will take quite some time. The Grand Metropolitan will agree to the annulment readily enough, I'm quite sure. But he will insist on following the established procedures." Dorma half-turned his head, looking back toward Mascoli. "The Hypatian Order requires a one year novitiate, before the final vows can be taken. Until that time passes, the annulment will not be final. In the meantime . . ."

His words trailed off into silence. Most of the people in the room shifted uneasily in their chairs. *A year* . . . And it took no great perceptiveness—certainly not for anyone who had seen Marco and Kat in each other's company over the past few days—to realize that the two youngsters were hardly likely to wait . . .

"Can't afford another scandal," gruffed Lodovico. "Certainly not," echoed Dell'este. "We'll have to insist that they see each other rarely, and then only with a proper chaperone in—"

"Oh, for the love of God!" snapped Petro Dorma's mother Rosanna. Since the discussion began, the old woman had been sitting against the wall tending to her point-vice embroidery. "Men! Katerina is a sensible *Case Vecchie* girl. She'll understand the precautions needed—and where to find them."

The faces of all the men in the room grew pinched. Except that of Eneko.

"Hah!" barked the Basque priest. "Of course she'll know where to find them. She's been *trafficking* them, I don't doubt." The faces of the other men grew *very* pinched. Lodovico's expression was downright vinegary.

"And what little she doesn't know from lack of personal experience," Lopez continued blithely, "she'll have no difficulty at all learning from her close friend Francesca de Chevreuse."

Rosanna Dorma almost cackled. "For that matter, I could—never mind."

She and Lopez exchanged smiles. The Basque shrugged. "I see the moment of wisdom has passed, replaced by that detestable *shrewdness.*" He made a motion with his hand which might have been that of a prophet, carving stone. "Be done with it, o ye wise men of Venice. Allow them their love in peace, in whatever manner they choose, until they sanctify it in marriage. There will be no harm done, and you have used the children quite enough. Look to your own souls."

The Venetian grandees stared at him, their jaws a bit loose. The church had never formally condemned such practices, true; but they were much frowned upon by clerics. Not to mention fornication and adultery.

Lopez returned their stares with his own; and his jaw was not even a bit loose. "Chernobog has seized the throne of Lithuania," he said, almost snarling. "If anything, Emeric of Hungary delves into even blacker arts. The church rots from the inside or takes on the coloration of its enemies. The rumors from Egypt—"

He rose to his feet abruptly and began limping toward the door. "Enough! Worry yourselves sick over matters of petty shrewdness if you will, grandees of Venice. I return to the wisdom of the crowd, saluting its young champions."

After he was gone, Dell'este looked at Dorma and Lodovico. Then shrugged and rose himself.

"And why not? The worst that can happen is another bastard. Won't be the first in our families; and certainly not the last."

THE PIAZZA SAN MARCO

A few days had done a great deal to change the city and the political landscape, thought Benito, looking at the celebrating crowd.

Horsemen had come in to report that the Scaligers were scrambling out of Fruili, with the whole countryside rising against them and imperial troops hot on their heels. A sharp merchant had brought the first pirogue-load full of fresh vegetables down the Po, past the sunken remains of the Milanese invading fleet. Venice's foes had put the bulk of their forces into that fleet, and now they were in dire trouble.

Benito wasn't sure he wasn't in dire trouble, too. Maria hadn't given him the hero's welcome he'd rather thought he was going to get. Instead she'd said: "I fell in love with a wolf once. I'm not giving my throat to another one, Benito. And I'm not sure if what you are is fox or wolf. You're still young. It's hard to tell. But I've had enough of wishing to be something I can't be." And she'd turned on her heel and left him standing there.

After a while, he'd shrugged. He'd try later. In the meanwhile half of the girls in Venice seemed very pleased to see him. *They* thought he was hero, at least.

Later in the afternoon, someone took Benito by the arm and drew him away from a young female admirer. Oddly enough, he didn't feel any urge to resist even before he saw that it was Petro Dorma.

"I've got news I felt you should hear right away. A crew that arrived this morning came upon a shipwreck in the gulf the day of the fighting. I just got the word. Caesare Aldanto's galley, it was."

"Are they sure?"

Dorma nodded somberly. "They say there were big seas that afternoon. Probably stirred up by the gale that blew the fog away. They saw a galley in bad trouble and were heading for a rescue when a double wave came through. The galley snapped in two and broke up. By the time they got there—the waves were very severe . . . it was all over. No survivors.

"After the sea calmed, they recovered some of the bodies. Caesare's was not among them, and they say it was much too far from land for anyone to have a hope of swimming ashore."

Dorma took a deep breath. "There's more. Part of the wreck was still floating. The captain had a look and they've hauled that section out and brought it back. Someone had hollowed out a great chamber in the keel. When it hit the waves, it snapped. We think this must be how the other galleys were lost. We'll be checking them all now."

Benito closed his eyes briefly. The smuggling scheme . . . now he wondered if it had really been a smuggling scheme, and not just Caesare's way of sabotaging Venice's commerce. Whichever it had been: *Caesare's own mischief had come back to sink him.*

❀   ❀   ❀

After Dorma left, Benito wandered through the huge throng aimlessly. He was trying to decide how he felt about Aldanto's death. On the one hand, he'd planned to kill him anyway, if he could. On the other . . .

He sighed, remembering all the little ways in which Caesare Aldanto had helped him. For his own purposes, to be sure. But . . . not always, perhaps. And even if it *had* all been done for nothing but mercenary reasons, the help itself remained.

Benito had long known that life couldn't be separated into neat blacks and whites. Now, he was discovering that gray is also a much more confusing color than it looks at first glance.

Out of that welter of confusion, one thought came clearly. *I want to see Maria.*

The piazza was redolent with the smells of feasting. Not a few of the Arsenalotti had already been dipping deep in the casks of good Veneto red that Petro Dorma had caused to be set among the tables. Benito found laughter, smiles, and winks from pretty girls and even snatches of song amid the laden trestles. What he didn't find was Maria Garavelli. It worried him. He'd been looking for her for quite a while.

The afternoon was rich and golden. Everybody was full of happiness. Everybody except Benito Valdosta, it seemed. And Maria, maybe. He thought there'd been a tear in her eye when she left him earlier. Or maybe . . . he just hoped so.

Only, where the hell had she got to? Ah. A familiar face. "Hey Tonio. You seen Maria?"

The bargee nodded. "Yeah. Saw her heading for the moorings down by the side of the Marciana."

"Thanks!" Benito quickened his pace and walked off towards the moorings beside the library.

She was sitting on a bollard, staring out across the gently bobbing rows of gondolas and the forests of masts in Bacino San Marco. A lonely figure—sheltered from the noise and laughter of the piazza. Here only the occasional gull shrieked and squabbled overhead.

"So what's wrong now?" He knelt down next to her and put an arm over her shoulder. She shrugged it off.

"I just want to be alone," she snapped. "You wouldn't understand."

"Try me."

She lifted that square jaw. "It's not a *Casa Vecchie* problem. Now go away."

"What's this *Casa Vecchie* stuff? I'm Benito!" He stood up and backed away a pace, raising his hands in protest.

She looked him up and down. Benito was acutely aware of his velvet and lace. "It's a poncy outfit," he muttered. "But Dorma insisted."

Maria stood up and turned to face him, hands on her hips, her dark eyes fulminating. "Oh. The next Doge insisted. You poor thing."

Benito flushed, acutely aware that she was slightly taller than he was. "So?"

"I am a *canaler*, Benito. You, on the other hand. You're behaving like an absolute copy of Caesare, strutting about."

Benito felt that was unfair. All right, so he'd been enjoying the victory. Enjoying the waves and . . . yeah, enjoying the kisses some of the girls had given him. Maybe that was it. "What's wrong with you? Why are you biting my head off?"

"I'm not. I just asked you to leave me alone . . . seeing as you only seem to want to see me when it suits you."

Benito felt his mouth drop open. "Give me a break! I've had to spend time with Marco and my grandfather and Dorma. And there just hasn't been much time. And I've been to see you . . . twice. And you were with Kat. Or out."

"Twice!" said Maria. "Oh, I am sorry. I should have stayed in just in case you came to call. I'm a canaler, Benito Valdosta. I have to work, you know."

Benito took a deep breath. "Well. That's sort of what I wanted to talk to you about. I thought—"

What *was* he thinking, anyway? He'd been wandering around with a vague notion in his head of "making it all work out with Maria."

The thought finally came into clear focus. He was too surprised to keep from blurting out the words.

"Well, then, you and me should get married. Maybe," he added hastily, seeing the storm signals.

There was a long silence.

"I mean . . . you wouldn't have to work or . . . and Dorma and my grandfather said they'd set me up. Um . . . Get some experience in trade. One of the colonies . . ." he trickled off into uncertainty.

"You're proposing to me," she said flatly. "To get me off the canals."

"Well, yes." Benito said awkwardly, flushing. "I thought it would be best."

"I don't."

"But . . . but you'd be rich and comfortable and . . ."

"And a canaler in the *Casa Vecchie*. No thank you. I won't marry for that reason."

Benito was bright red. "We could go to Corfu. Or Negroponte . . ."

"Oh, excuse me. Where Venice can't see me?" Maria's voice would have cut steel.

"I thought you would want to marry me. You don't *have* to," said Benito, beginning to get angry himself now.

His anger was nothing to her white-hot sarcasm. "Oh! What a favor the next Doge's brother-in-law's younger brother is doing me! A poor little canal-drab like me should be so delighted at his attentions. Well listen to me, Benito Valdosta . . . *Va'funcula*." And she turned and walked off to her gondola, leaving Benito still gawping at the obscenity. A few moments later she set off, a lone vessel heading up the Grand Canal into a virtually deserted Venice.

Benito wandered back. There didn't seem much point in staying here. He was not concentrating on his footsteps—or where he was going. It took severely disturbed concentration to walk into someone the size of Manfred. Benito managed it.

Manfred looked more amused than anything else. "Ah. My crazy young friend from our visit to the Dandelos, and a little assault in court-house! Dressed like a princeling, today, not an urchin, or a Dorma servant. What are you doing walking around with a face like your girlfriend just gave you some really bad news. What's wrong?"

Benito shrugged. "Women," he said trying to sound casual about it.

Manfred laughed. "I know what you mean. My uncle seems too fascinated by Francesca for her to have any time for me either. Can't figure it out. He's not even staring at her cleavage." His shrug was a massive copy of Benito's. "Women, just as you say. Let's go and find some wine. Wine always has time for us. And wine doesn't mind if you have another goblet of wine either."

THE GRAND CANAL

It came to Maria that someone had been whistling to her for some time. She looked up. Valentina. And Claudia. With a very suspicious-looking bag.

"Maria Garavelli, I wish the Schioppies were as dreamy as you," said Claudia from the *fondamenta*. "Give us a lift, will you?"

She pulled up. They slung the bag in. It clinked. "A good time to be shopping," said Valentina cheerfully. "Everyone is at the celebration."

Claudia looked curiously at Maria. "Why aren't you?"

"I didn't want to stay," said Maria, curtly.

"I would have thought Benito would want your company?"

"There is nothing between me and . . ." Her lip quivered. "Benito. He doesn't love me. And I don't need him. Anyway, I'm going to marry my cousin Umberto. I just made up my mind. My family's been pestering me about it for weeks. They've got it all set up."

There was a startled silence from the two thieves. "Oh. That's very sudden," said Claudia. "We thought . . ."

"It's not exactly something that can wait," said Maria bluntly.

Valentina and Claudia exchanged glances. "How long . . ."

"At least two months," said Maria, shortly. "And, no—I don't know who the father is. Probably Caesare. Um. Maybe not. I always took precautions with him, after the first few days. The other thing happened too quickly—"

She broke off, squaring her shoulders. "What difference does it make? It's either Caesare or one other, and either way if I don't get married it's a bastard."

She shook her head. "Never mind. My cousin Mario is a sweet man—I've known him since I was a kid—and he says he doesn't mind. It'll work out. I won't marry for security and I won't marry for position and I definitely won't marry someone who still doesn't know if he's a fox or a wolf."

She looked at Claudia and Valentina. They were staring at her.

I'm babbling, she realized. *And why am I telling this to a couple of thieves?* "So. Enough of that. Where can I put you off?"

"Er. Here will do fine," said Valentina. She sounded as uncertain as Maria sounded to herself.

THE ROAD TO ROME

When Father Eneko Lopez and his two companions recognized the three horsemen who overtook them on the road to Rome, their jaws fell. Even the Basque priest, for a moment, lost his composure.

"*Your Majesty?*" croaked Diego. He glanced at Lopez, seeking confirmation. Lopez had spent time with the Emperor in private discussion; Diego hadn't.

Eneko's jaw snapped shut, almost audibly. "This is *most* unwise, Your Majesty. The Holy Roman Emperor should not be traveling the roads of Italy escorted only by two bodyguards." His eyes squinted at the costume Charles Fredrik was wearing. "Especially not disguised as a prosperous merchant."

Charles Fredrik's scowled. "Nattering at me like Trolliger! And here I'd been looking forward to your company, too."

He plucked at the rich fabric. "As for this, it's far more comfortable than my imperial robes—much less armor. And it's necessary, anyway, to keep my identity a secret. It is essential that I be able to meet with the Grand Metropolitan in person." Breezily: "I'll not forget to put in a good word in favor of founding your order, Eneko, be sure of it." Less breezily: "And—ah—I felt the secrecy was needed, not for only for its own sake, but because—ah—"

Pierre barked a laugh. The Emperor's face darkened a little.

"Well, yes," admitted the most powerful man in Europe. "The last time a Holy Roman Emperor visited Rome he may have left some residue of ill will. Seeing as how he sacked the city. So I felt a certain modesty and discretion would make for better diplomatic results. I have *got* to bring this damn Petrine-Pauline feud under control. Down to a simmer, at least." He brought hard eyes to bear on the three priests who hoped to found a new brotherhood of struggle against a rising Satan. "As I'm *sure* you will agree, under the circumstances."

Eneko nodded. "As to that—certainly. But . . . Your Majesty, it's simply *dangerous*."

The Emperor's laugh sounded like a lion's roar. "Oh, nonsense!" He slapped a meaty hand on the even meatier shoulder of the man riding to his right. "Here I have my nephew, who quite recently"— the ferocious old man couldn't keep the pride out of his voice— "broke the back of a Svear demon. You saw it yourself, Father! And to my left—"

Another meaty hand slapped a shoulder which, though sinewy rather than massive, sounded more like iron than flesh. "The finest scion of Clann Harald!"

Eneko smiled grimly. "Who, on the same day—unless I'm badly mistaken—gave Chernobog himself the worst headache of his life." He raised his hands in a little gesture of surrender. "I suppose you're right, Emperor. With such an escort, you probably don't have much to fear from highwaymen."

"I'd say not," murmured Diego. "In fact . . . I'd feel a little better myself, having them accompany us."

"Done, then!" pronounced the Emperor. "You will provide us with still more in the way of disguise—pilgrims going to Rome— along with your own convivial conversation, of course. And we will keep the odd ruffian from pestering you."

Pierre nodded solemnly, in the sage manner of peasants everywhere. "Well said. Ask any Savoyard. It's always best to have a second string for your bow."

THE PIAZZA SAN MARCO

Venice slept. The last celebrants had gone home. Dawn would be here in a few hours, but for now the great winged lion looked out over a sleeping town. Well, nearly.

Kat and Marco stood in each other's arms at the base of the Lion's column, looking out at the moonlight on the dark water of the lagoon.

The moonlight cast a great winged shadow over them, and the piazza that is Venice's heart. Like a shield.

Characters

Principal Characters

Aldanto, Caesare: Sellsword, spy, Milanese of aristocratic family, formerly a Montagnard agent.

Bespi, Fortunato (Harrow): Formerly Montagnard assassin.

Dorma, Petro: Head of the commercially powerful House Dorma, head of the centrist faction, member of the Council of Ten, one of the Lords of the Nightwatch.

Dorma, Angelina: Petro Dorma's younger sister.

Lopez, Eneko: A Basque cleric and magician.

De Chevreuse, Francesca: Courtesan, formerly of Orleans.

Dell'este, Enrico, Duke of Ferrara: The Old Fox. One of Italy's leading tacticians. Grandfather of Marco and Benito.

Garavelli, Maria: Boat-girl, part of one of the Arsenalotti clans.

Marina, Luciano (Chiano): Strega Master Mage.

Montescue, Lodovico: Head of the formerly powerful House Montescue. Sworn enemy of the Valdosta.

Montescue, Katerina (Kat): Lodovico's granddaughter.

Montescue, Alessandra: Lodovico's widowed granddaughter-in-law.

Valdosta, Benito (Benito Oro): Grandson of the Duke of Ferrara, illegitimate son of Carlo Sforza.

Valdosta, Marco (Marco Felluci): Grandson of the Duke of Ferrara.

Manfred, Prince, Earl of Carnac, Marquis of Rennes, Baron of Ravensburg: Nephew to the Holy Roman Emperor.

Hakkonsen, Erik: An Icelander, and bodyguard and mentor to Manfred.

Minor characters

Aleri, Francesco: The head of the Milanese trade delegation, also the spymaster-in-chief of the Montagnard faction.

Badoero, Count: A pro-Montagnard noble.

Bartelozzi, Antimo: Agent and adviser to Enrico Dell'este.

Belgio, Father: Cleric and healer.

Boldoni, Ugo: Pastor of a poor parish in Venice.

Brunelli, Lucrezia: "The most beautiful and courted woman in Venice," sister to Ricardo.

Brunelli, Ricardo: Head of the pro-Rome faction.

Calenti, Lord: One of the Lords of the Nightwatch, one of Lucrezia's admirers.

Capuletti, Bishop: A pro-Pauline bishop.

Chernobog: A Slavic demon.

Destre, Giuliano (Jewel): Minor thug, Dandelo bullyboy.

Evangelina, Sister: A Hypatian Sibling.

Foscari, Doge Giorgio: Doge of Venice. Elderly.

Frescata, Aldo: Venice's condottiere.

Von Gherens, *Ritter*: A Prussian knight.

Giaccomo: Owner of a tavern, connected with smuggling.

Gianni: One of the "loco" in the Jesolo marshes.

Guiseppe: Trusted elderly servant at the *Casa* Montescue.

Jagiellon: Grand Duke of Lithuania and Poland, possessed by a demon (see Chernobog).

Laivetti, Mercutio: A flashy young thief.

Valdosta, Lorendana: Deceased. Mother of Benito and Marco, daughter of Enrico Dell'este. Headstrong, loyal Montagnard.

Madelena: Trusted servant and former nursemaid at the *Casa* Montescue.

Maggiore, Father: Head of Servants of the Holy Trinity in Venice

Matteoni, Alberto, Stephano, Luciano, Giovanni: Enforcers, debt collectors and rent-a-beating boys.

Pellmann: Erik's batman.

Hohenstauffen, Charles Fredrik: Holy Roman Emperor.

Sforza, Carlo: The Wolf of the North, Milan's chief condottiere. A military legend.

Sophia: The partner of Chiano, a Jesolo marsh healer.

Von Stublau: Knight-Proctor.

De Tomaso, Raphael: Artist and friend of Marco Valdosta. A Strega initiate.

Della Tomasso, Captain: Master of a smuggling coaster.

Trolliger, Baron Hans: One of the Holy Roman Emperor's courtiers and advisers.

Uriel, Brother: Straight-laced monk, one of the Servants of the Holy Trinity.

Valentina & Claudia: Thieves, musicians, Strega.

Ventuccio: Commercial House which gives shelter to Marco and Benito.

Visconti, Filippo, Maria: Duke of Milan.

Sachs, Abbot Hans: Head of the Servants of the Holy Trinity mission to Venice, in charge of the Knights of the Holy Trinity there, too.

Sister Ursula: A nun and one of the leading experts in Christian magic, accompanying the Servants and Knights.

GLOSSARY

Adige: River to the west of the Venetian lagoon, barge-route to Verona, and thence the Brenner Pass.

Aquitaine: An independent kingdom, encompassing parts of what in our universe would be France and England.

Armagh, The League of: A loose alliance of Celtic/Nordic states.

Arsenalotti: The workers at the Arsenal, Venice's state shipyard.

Ascalon: A port in Palestine.

Aqua alta: Winter high-water.

Auslander: Foreigner—a term of derision

Bacino: Harbor basin.

Barducci's: A tavern well known for music.

Botega: An artistic studio. A group of artists gathered together for commercial production of art, usually under a master artist.

Brenta: River just to the west of the lagoon.

Bretagne: Brittany. An independent Duchy, part of the league of Armagh.

Basse taille: An enamelling technique.

Capi di contrada: Officer of control.

Carnac: Capital of Celtic Brittany.

Case Vecchie: Great houses.

Chioggia: Settlement on the West of the lagoon.

Chrysostom, John: Charismatic preacher associated with St. Hypatia, at the breakpoint between this universe and ours, born 349 A.D.

Colleganza: A collective trading venture.

Collegio: Senators of the Venetian Republic.

Curti: Lit. short—the *Case Vecchie* who had not been ennobled for many years.

Caique: Eastern Mediterranean sailing vessel.

Cassone: A carved chest.

Cotte: A surplice-like garment—the predecessor of coat.

Dalmatia: The Western Adriatic coastline. Once the source of much of Venice's timber.

Emeric: King of Hungary.

Ferrara: City-state in the Po valley in Northern Italy, known for steelworking, particularly swordsmiths.

Fruili: Region to the northeast of Venice.

Fjells: Peaks (Norse).

Godar: Priest-chieftain.

Guidecca: Long island across a wide canal from the Rialto Islands.

Galliot: Small galley.

Hohenstauffen: The ruling house of the Holy Roman Empire.

Hypatia, St. Of Alexandria: Patron Saint of the Hypatian order. Neoplatonist philosopher and librarian of the great library at Alexandria. Her saving of the Library from the mob instigated by Cyril the Patriarch of Alexandria is, along with Hypatia's conversion to Christianity and alliance with John Chrysostom, the breakpoint between this universe and ours.

Ilkhan Mongol: A Mongol khanate, ruling Egypt and much of the Near East.

Istria: Peninsula to the south of Trieste. A Venetian possession.

Jesolo: The marshes to the east of Venice in the Venetian lagoon.

Koboldwerk: Cunningly wrought mail made by dwarves.

Longi: Lit. long—a *Casa Vecchie* which has been ennobled for many years from before the creation of the Doge.

Marangona: The bell which rang for half an hour from dawn, to summons the Arsenalotti to work.

Marciana: The library and art gallery across the Piazza San Marco from the Doge's Palace.

Mestre: Mainland port of Venice.

Murano: Island in the Venetian lagoon reknowned for glassworks.

Marquetry: Inlaid work in wood or ivory.

Popli minuta: Lit. small people. Workers, commoners.

Misericord: Thin dagger intended to penetrate joints in armor.

Narenta: Large river on the Dalmatian coast.

Negroponte: Venetian trading outpost on the east coast of Greece.

Outremer: orig. *Outre mer*—Beyond the Sea; i.e., The East—on the far side of the Mediterranean.

Paulines: The faction of Christianity taking its lead from the writings of St. Paul. In this universe the dominant religious faction in the north of Europe. More heirarchical and militaristic than the Petrine faction.

Petrine: The "gentler," more tolerant southern faction of the Church.

Piave: River flowing into the Venetian lagoon on the east.

Polestine Forts: Venetian defences on the river Po against invasion from the North.

Pells: Heavy wooden posts used for sword practice.

Poignard: Dagger.

Ritters: Teutonic knights.

Racasse: Scorpion fish, with highly toxic spines.

Rebec: Stringed musical instrument.

Scaliger: The ruling house of Verona.

Schiopettieri: Mercenary soldiers under the control of the Lords of the Nightwatch (*Signori di Notte*)—roughly equivalent to police.

Scuolo: Guilds.

Signoria: The Doge, Ducal councillors, heads of the forty, de facto the government.

Småland: Part of Sweden, near Lake Vattern.

Spleto: Lit split—a port in Dalmatia

Squalos: Trans: sharks. A Jesolo marsh gang of particularly unsavory reputation.

Swabian: From Swabia—southwestern Germany.

Seizin: The act of taking possession, and what is so held.

Surcoat: Loose sleeveless garment with insignia normally worn over armor.

Tintoretto: Artist.

Trompe l'oeil: A still life painting designed to give the illusion of reality.

Veneto: The region of northern Italy, which includes Venice.

Veneze: People of Venice.

Vinland: North America.

Visconti: The ruling House of Milan.

Water-door: In a city of canals: a door straight into the water.

Zianetti's: Student tavern.

HERBS & DRUGS

Agaric (Fly Agaric): Powerful hallucinogenic and psychotropic.

Artemisia: Source of artisminin, a treatment for malaria.

Belladona: Deadly nightshade. Psychotropic, also containing atropine, used as a cosmetic or part of a cosmetic to dilate the pupils of women's eyes.

Colt's Foot: Leaves as wound dressings—anti-inflammatory.

Corn-poppy: Sedative.

Red and White Clover: Cough remedy.

Dead-Nettle: As a tea—a treatment for earache.

Lotos: Blue and black, hallucinogenics. A drug originally from North Africa, the black is much stronger and enormously addictive.

Lance-leaf Plantain: Leaves used for poultices and dressings.

Opium: Commonly available from Turkey and Greece, as a painkiller and soporific, especially mixed with alcohol (laudanum).

ITALIAN TERMS

Barene: Marshy areas with sparse vegetation.

Ciao: Greeting—hi (also used for parting—good-bye).

Calle: Street.

Camerata: Salon.

Canale: Larger canals.

Ponto: Bridge.

Fondamenta: Levee.

Finocchio: Fennel.

Pasticceria: Pastry-cooks.

Rio: Lit. river (narrow canals).

Sotoportego: A built-over alley.

Velme: Vast muddy areas.

FOOD

Asiago: Semi-hard cheese.

Boccalao: Salted dried fillets of cod.

Bruschetta: Crispy toasted white bread, rubbed with garlic and sprinkled with olive oil. It is sometimes served with a topping.

Ciabbata: Loose-textured country bread.

Castagnaccio: Chestnut-flour cake.

Coppo ham: Marinated air-dried neck of pork, rolled.

Cotechino: Highly spiced pork sausage.

Fagioli stufata: Stewed beans.

Frittata: Italian omelette.

Marchpane: Marzipan.

Pancetta: Air-dried ham.

Risi e bisi: A thick soup of rice and young peas.

Sarde: Sardines.

Taleggio: Hard cheese.

Toresani: Pigeon squabs.

Zuppa di fagioli: Bean soup.